16 x 8/10 √ '/11
17 x 2/M √ 11/14

PB

D0042244

Pain Killers

ALSO BY JERRY STAHL

Fiction

I, Fatty

Perv—A Love Story

Plainclothes Naked

Love Without (short stories)

Nonfiction

Permanent Midnight

Pain Killers

JERRY STAHL

wm

WILLIAM MORROW
An Imprint of HarperCollins*Publishers*

HarperCollins books may be purchased for educational, business, or sales promotional use. For information please write: Special Markets Department, HarperCollins Publishers, 10 East 53rd Street, New York, NY 10022.

FIRST EDITION

Designed by Lisa Stokes

Library of Congress Cataloging-in-Publication Data
Stahl, Jerry.
    Pain killers / Jerry Stahl. — 1st ed.
        p. cm.
ISBN: 978-0-06-050665-0
    I. Title.
    PS3569.T3125P35 2009
    813'.54—dc22   2008037339

09 10 11 12 13   OV/RRD   10 9 8 7 6 5 4 3 2 1

For Monah Li

I spend most of my time not dying.

—Frederick Seidel

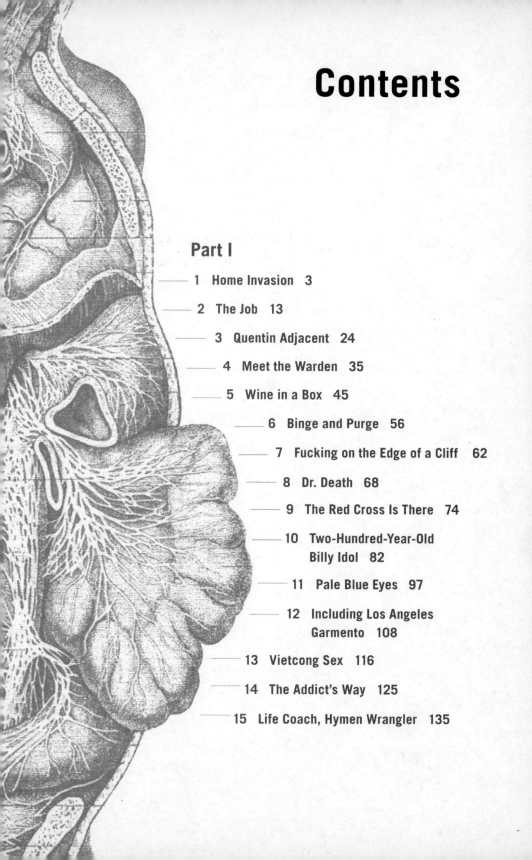

Contents

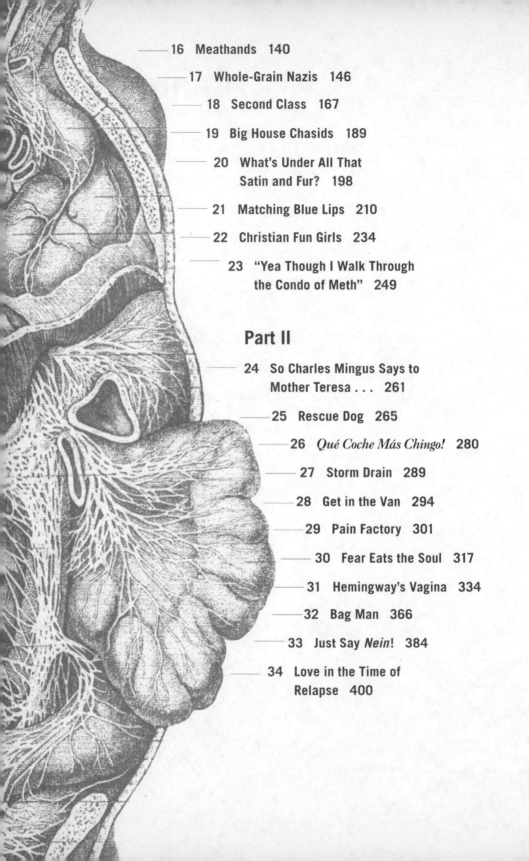

Part I

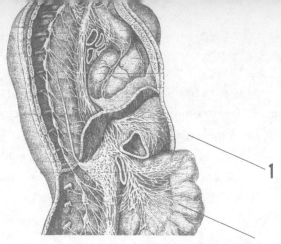

Home Invasion

Sun Myung Moon looked great in a bikini.

The sight did not inspire me to schedule gender reassignment, but it was undeniably engaging. As my eyes strayed to the other eight-by-ten glossies on the bedroom dresser, I found myself wondering if the arrangement was random or if there was some coded message in the way things had been laid out.

The buxom Sun Myung, sandwiched between a muu-muu'd Pope Benedict and a severely hog-tied Clarence Thomas, floated directly over Jerry Falwell, who appeared to be reading the Bible while spanking a hefty, ball-gagged blonde with CHOOSE LIFE branded across her coccyx. Of the four, Falwell was the only one who looked like he was enjoying himself. Maybe that was the message the home invader meant to convey: *Party like Falwell!* Or maybe, in the manner of burglars who relieve themselves on the carpet after stealing your silverware, the message was the fact that they were able to leave anything at all. The message was: *Hey, asshole, look what we can do!*

There was, certainly, a lesson in Justice Thomas's comportment.

Despite the obvious pain and degradation, his expression was one of infinite patience. Gentle understanding. I had never been a fan, but • his stoic bearing won me over. The man had nobility.

I basked in that thought for a moment, then reality clawed me again. My home invader might still be in my home. I cried out, feeling like an idiot, *"I'm a cop!"* That's when I noticed a black and white photo, smaller than the others, wedged behind a dresser leg.

This one showed a smiling, gap-toothed fellow in a uniform. He might have been Jack Lemmon's cousin, if Jack Lemmon's cousin had a trim mustache and served in the SS. The twin lightning bolts on the lapels were a dead giveaway. The officer in the photo was in a laboratory, a forbidding nurse at his side. He clamped calipers in both hands, simultaneously measuring the budding breasts of naked, pubescent twin girls on his left and right. Stamped under the shot, in block letters, was BEIDHÄNDIG. Below that, in a looping scrawl, someone had penned the translation: *ambidextrous.*

The ex-cop in me knew I should stop staring and deal with the situation—however it is you deal with strangers planting celebrity perv pics in your bedroom. But the image of that smiling SS man and his calipers was so disturbing, my eyes retreated to the puckish Moon. Why shouldn't the Korean messiah enjoy some dress-up? Think what early Christians would have done if Jesus had been resurrected with cleavage!

All speculation was shattered by a gravelly voice behind me. "They're not real!" Before I could react, something cracked the back of my head. I don't remember going down. I only remember coming to, blinking away twirling stars, in a forced crouch. Trapped in a tiny aluminum jail.

"Christ!" I cried.

"Him, I got no photos."

I blinked some more and realized I wasn't in jail. I was cramped within the four legs of a walker. A heavily jowled old man waited for me to raise my eyes, then spat an inch from my knee.

"Putz!"

I considered punching the senior intruder in the testicles. They were, in my Guantánamo crouch, at eye level, drooping prominently behind the shiny weave of his poly-blend Sansabelt trousers.

"What kind of schmohawk gets mugged by a seventy-two-year-old with a walker?"

"Happens all the time." I yanked myself up by a walker leg so that my new friend and I were jammed face-to-face, like two guys squeezed into a telephone booth. "Just last week an old lady brained me with her orthopedic cane, and the day before that some prick with Alzheimer's kicked me down a flight of stairs, then forgot he did it and kicked me down another flight."

"Oh, a funny guy."

"That's me," I said. "May I?"

I lifted one of his hands off the grip and eased by him. The old man's breath stank of sardines and horseradish. When he picked something fleshy off his tongue and flicked it at me, I slapped him.

"That's disgusting."

My attacker rubbed his face, his mouth forming a smile that looked like it was made of other people's lips. "How 'bout that, the kid's not a complete pussy."

I kicked the walker away and caught him when he fell forward. I was that tough.

"How about you shut the fuck up so I can decide whether to strangle you or not? It'd be legal—you broke in!"

This seemed to make the jowly old man even happier. "So what's stopping you?"

"I'm curious. You make a habit of hobbling around, planting bad tabloid shots in people's houses? There money in that?"

The old guy spat out another fleck and I backhanded him.

"I live here, Pops. Stop hocking on my carpet."

He spat again. This time when I tried to slap him, he caught my hand. His grip was a shock, but no more than his reflexes. He kept grinning until he let my hand drop. "Bad habit," he said.

I winced, which I knew he'd enjoy. Then I righted the fallen walker and handed it back it to him. "You still haven't told me about the pictures."

"I got a job for you."

"So that's why you Walker Texas Rangered me?"

"I wanted to get your attention. The pics are fakes. Photoshop."

"Fuck the pictures. What are you doing here?"

He shrugged. "You break into a man's home, you want to give him a show. Ha!"

The old man feinted left with a jab and cackled when I ducked. Enough strange things had happened in my life that the bar for "strange" was fairly high. But this was getting up there.

"Okay, I lied," the old man blurted. "They're not all fakes."

He tapped the gap-toothed SS man in my hand.

"This one is real. He's the only one I'm interested in."

"The Nazi. Uh-huh. You know where he lives?"

His meaty lips crumpled in a kind of private giggle. "San Quentin. Ever been there?"

"No."

"It's prime real estate. Right near the ocean."

"I've got a lot of questions, but I'm going to start with 'Why me?'"

"Look at this place. Your life is for shit."

"That makes me special?"

"It makes you a guy who might think San Quentin's an improvement."

"You trying to hire me or put me away?"

"Hire you."

"To go to prison? Wasn't that a bad Steven Seagal movie?"

"As opposed to the many fine ones. You're not listening. You won't be *in* prison. You'll be *at* prison."

"Right. So when I'm gang-raped in my cell, all that D-block dick will be *at* my ass, it won't be *in* it."

"For God's sake!" The old man slapped the photo of the SS man in my hand. "All you have to do is check him out."

I studied the photograph. "If he's even alive, he's gotta be a hundred-something."

"Ninety-seven. Twenty-four years older than me."

"It sounds like you know him."

"We've met."

I waited for more. Nothing. "Who is he?"

A shadow passed over the old man's face. His bluster was suddenly gone.

"Josef Mengele."

Just saying the name somehow drained him. I had to help him into a chair. For the first time it occurred to me that maybe my uninvited guest had wandered out of a rest home. Maybe his worried loved ones were scouring the streets.

"Mengele died in 'seventy-nine," I said as gently as possible. "I saw it on the Biography Channel. Chances are he's probably still dead."

The old man regarded me with clear eyes. "He might be. Or he might be in San Quentin. All you have to do is talk to him. You'll know."

"Why me? There must be a dozen Simon Wiesenthal guys trying to find him."

"Ten dozen. But nobody's asking you to find him. He's been found. All you need to do is identify him. See if it's really him."

"How do I do that?"

"By helping him."

"Helping him?" Now *I* wanted to sit down. "What are you, a fucking Nazi?"

"Far from it. This is part of a plan. And it's all set up. Do you have anything to drink?"

I grabbed a bottle of water from beside the bed and gave it to him. He gulped heartily and handed the bottle back with a steady hand. His voice was strong again. "You pose as a drug counselor. Teach a class. There'll be a few of you in the group, and one of them will be Mengele—or won't be. You'll all be sharing your stories."

"You think Mengele, you think sharing."

"Go ahead and mock. Are you familiar with the term 'recovery'?"

"I've read about it," I said.

"Well, that's what you'll be doing. You'll be teaching a drug awareness class."

"And I live up there?"

"Just for a few days. You do the job, and maybe when you come back, you still have a home."

He reached in his jacket and pulled out one of the flyers the Realtor had stuffed into the buyer's box she'd spiked into the lawn. NOTICE TO FORECLOSE. She kept sticking them in the box, I kept ripping the box out.

"It makes you feel like an American," I said, "when you have the same problems as other Americans. . . . But it's hard to keep up."

"Like I say, don't think San Quentin. Think Marin County. Prime real estate. You'll be right on the water."

He could see the hesitation in my face. I've never been good at just saying no.

"What happens if it is him? A bunch of Jews have him killed?"

"Which Jews?"

"What do you mean 'Which Jews?'"

"The ones inside or out? Jews in the penitentiary are different than Jews on the outside."

"I'm guessing, inside or out, there's a bunch who'd like to skip a trial and go directly to revenge."

"Some might want to take him out for revenge. Others to hide complicity. I'm talking about Jews, but not necessarily Jew-Jews."

"What?"

He stared at me with something like pity, then lifted his heavy old man's body out of the wing chair.

"Some might want to take him out for revenge. Others to hide complicity. I'm talking about Jews, but not necessarily Jewy Jews."

"What?"

"As I was trying to tell you, there is a difference between Jews who are incarcerated and those who aren't. See, inside, white trumps Semite. Plenty of Jews are ALS."

"They have Lou Gehrig's Disease?"

"Shmuck! Say that too loud, you're going to break out in flesh wounds. ALS stands for Aryan Land Sharks. They're about White Power. The baddest of the bad. They don't take too kindly to being confused with a charity disease." He put his hand on my shoulder in an avuncular fashion and shrugged. "It's a different world. Name's Harry Zell, by the way."

What could I say but "Nice to meet you, Harry"?

Zell looked at his watch. His shirtsleeves covered his wrists. I couldn't see if there was a faded number. But there were many other things to mull over—beginning with the proverbial elephant in the room, swinging its trunk between the double bed and dented portable TV.

"So, Josef Mengele is alive, huh?"

Zell kept his response nonverbal: rubbing his fleshy nose and making an *accch* noise.

"I mean, if it's true, this is a pretty huge event."

This time Zell drummed his fingers on the walker.

"Hey! It's not like you can walk into a man's place, smack him on the head and ask him to find somebody. Well," I corrected myself, "you *can*. I'm just saying . . . *Mengele*? I can't believe he's just sitting there. Waiting to be found. If he's telling people who he is, what makes you think he'll even be there when I show up? Or that I'll be able to get past the CNN trucks?"

Zell repeated the *accch*ing and finger drumming, then pursed his meaty lips, sucked in his breath and blew it out in one long sardine-scented sigh, as if a lifetime of disappointment and resignation had prepared him for this one big one.

"He is saying who he is, right?"

"Sure," said Zell. "There's another old freak who says he's Mickey Mantle, three more screaming they're Jesus, and let's not talk about Elvis. If you were an *alta kocker* in a jail cell, wouldn't you want to be somebody else?"

"Maybe. But not a genocidal maniac with a price on his head. Even if it's him—he got away with it this long, why would he come out of hiding now?"

"Because he wants credit."

"For what?"

"Exactly! All you know about him is the genocidal maniac stuff— what about the good things?"

"Are you insane?"

"Me, no. But I'm depending on you to tell me if *he* is. His psych eval describes him as borderline schizophrenic. I checked. Who's gonna believe a schizo in jail? But he doesn't act out. They don't have him on file as a gasser or anything."

"So they don't know what he did to his patients when he was done with them?"

"Not that kind of gasser. Don't you watch *Lockdown*? Gassing is when a prisoner throws urine or feces at a guard. Sometimes they make a soup. The thing I do know is he's vain. So never take him seriously. As in, do not show him respect. Do not react. No matter what he says, no matter how horrible. If it's him, that will drive him crazy. A vain man at the end of his life. That's as close as we're going to get to DNA. I'll give you ten grand."

"Ten grand's not much, considering."

"I'll get your house back for you."

I did not want to argue. I'd been living on fumes for a while. Continuing to live that way seemed suddenly unbearable. But still . . .

"It's just too fucking unlikely," I said.

"Unlikely?" he repeated, brightening for the first time. "Exactly! Looking at your life, I said to myself, 'Here, Harry, is a man who has never had a problem with the unlikely.'" His voice began to rise, and I kept an eye on his walker in case he tried to swing it again. "I said, 'Here is a man whose own past history, if you had to stick it in a box and put a title on it, that box would say UN-FUCKING-LIKELY. Here is a man who married a woman he met when she murdered her husband with drain cleaner and broken lightbulbs in a bowl of Lucky Charms.'"

"No need to flatter," I said. "Cops meet all kinds of interesting people. Sometimes they even marry them. I'm glad you did your homework—but what does my checkered past have to do with anything?"

"Isn't it obvious? I need somebody I can trust. Who's also desperate," he added, meeting my eyes. "If you weren't desperate, you wouldn't take the job. But if I couldn't trust you, I wouldn't want to give it to you. It's not an easy combination."

"You still haven't told me why you want Mengele."

"The man has his reasons for saying who he is. I have my reasons for finding out the truth."

I started to say something else, and he held up his hand. "Enough. The warden knows everything. You'll meet him first."

I followed him out to the living room, where he stopped to take in the photo of my wife and daughter on the wall.

"Your family?"

His tone was somewhere between inquiry and concern. I gazed at the picture, surprised by the sudden flood of emotion at the sight of my sullen, long-lashed sixteen-year-old daughter and my beautiful, high-cheek-boned newly-ex wife.

"My family, yes. Good to know they're out there," I heard myself croak.

When I opened the front door, he stopped and delivered his final instructions.

"Remember, with Mengele, you can be polite, but show no respect. Don't take him seriously. For him, any disrespect is—"

He didn't finish. He just grabbed the walker and smashed it into a mirror.

"Do you understand?"

"I get it," I said, picking glass out of my eyebrow.

"Good. Then we understand each other. You'll get an envelope with details and cash."

Zell kicked the walker out of his way and strode with crunching, great man strides out to a waiting limousine.

I shook a few more mirror shards out of my hair, then watched him open the limo door himself and get in. I wasn't mad about the mirror—why would I want to look at me? Business being what it was, I was not even that upset at Zell's perverted and violent mode of job recruitment.

No.

What bothered me, more than anything, was that I knew I was going to take the job.

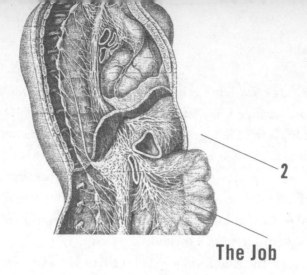

2

The Job

Burbank to San Francisco was a one-hour flight. United only had two rows of first class. It was weirdly satisfying to be sitting in one of them, feeling the eyes of lesser-ticketed humans as they passed by after I'd been boarded and seated. The resentment in their glances was almost tangible: *Why is that shabby bastard sitting in first?*

The tickets had been hand-delivered in a gray envelope with the cash, along with a copy of the smiling SS Zell had left on my dresser and a time-projection etching of ninetysomething Mengele. It was odd to see the same technology used for missing-children flyers applied to a nonagenarian Nazi. Instead of baby Nancy at three and thirteen it was Dr. Mengele in his Jack Lemmon–circa–*The Apartment* prime and in his current dotage.

A smaller envelope within contained a passport, driver's license and Social Security card. It would have been cool, in a *Mission: Impossible* way, if I'd been given a new identity. That scene in every movie where the spy is told, "From now on, you will be Laszlo Toth. You were a furrier in Madrid." Sadly, this being real life, I was given my own identity. My own SS number, my face on my driver's license. It was like finding out there's reincarnation, then coming back as your-self. I had not realized my wallet had been emptied of ID until the walker bandit, Harry Zell, gave it back to me with the tickets. Mostly I used cash, when I had it, so I didn't pull out my wallet a lot. The credit cards were pretty much there if I had to break into a locked door. Which A) I did not often have to do, and B) never really worked except on TV. In real life, if you don't have a locksmith and burglar skills, you were pretty much fucked.

Ever thoughtful, Zell had included the San Quentin visitors' dress code in the envelope. "No blue denim! No orange jumpsuits!" (Be-cause, really, why *wouldn't* you drop into a state prison dressed like a state prisoner?) But my favorite deal-breaker was "No see-through tops!" Who knew? Zell—or whoever packed his packages—had also thrown in a paperback of *Chicken Soup for the Prisoner's Soul.* I left it in the sick-bag slot.

The only fraudulent part of the paperwork was my state certifi-cate, proof of my status as licensed drug and alcohol counselor. I had a diploma from somewhere called Steinhelm Life-Skills Institute. It looked as legitimate as I did.

————————

From the road, San Quentin might have been a vast, oceanside nine-teenth-century resort. The sprawl of brick and stone blended into the upward roll of land over the Pacific. Think Hilton Head, but institu-tional, with a death house.

I gave my name at a gate that looked like an overgrown toll booth. A steely blond woman took my driver's license and picked a green receiver from a wall phone. While I waited I took in a ruined gazebo halfway up a curving driveway to the right: a tiny haven, ringed by stone nymphs, where a robber baron might have thrown a birthday party for his daughter in 1911. W. C. Fields might have lumbered out of it with a croquet mallet and a flask.

"Officer Rincin will be down to meet you in a few minutes."

There was nowhere to wait. The sun was merciless. I watched an older prisoner in denim and a blue shirt push a wheelbarrow over to a bed of flaming red flowers by the entry road. He kneeled down and touched the first one, gave it a moment, tamped the ground around it a little, then moved on to the next flower and did the same thing. On one level, this scenario stood out as a profound statement about man's ability to transcend his surroundings and experience beauty even in the direst circumstance. On another, it was a guy kneeling in dirt, blowing his bad breath on a flower, a guy who'd grow old and die sleeping four feet from a toilet.

A screen door slammed. I saw a pair of middle-aged ladies in straw hats and vacation wear step from a small building I hadn't noticed. The San Quentin gift shop. I checked the pathway down from the brick administration building, saw no one hurrying my way, and headed over for some souvenirs. Sometimes you just have to pamper yourself.

Inside, the ladies giggled over a wooden paddle with a droopy convict in stripes painted on it, over the caption BETTER BE GOOD.

"Is this not the cutest?"

"Ed can put this up right over the bar!"

Lucky Ed. They were still tittering when I stepped inside. The shop occupied a small white room with four glass cases and walls hung with prisoner art and handiwork. A handwritten sign over the old-fashioned cash register said GO AHEAD, SHOPLIFT! Behind the register was a closed door.

I wandered to the first counter. Leather goods. Wallets, belts with eagle-clutching-the-flag buckles the size of hubcaps, and some snazzy handcuff holders. Next to that, management had arranged a paddle display—from spatula-sized on up to small snow shovel. Each smacker was decorated with the same droopy, hand-painted convict as the one the ladies were holding. Beetle Bailey in stripes.

What really impressed were the paintings. An array of pastel-tinged sunsets, azure waves over rocky shores—nature scenes—filled every inch of wall space behind the counters. Whoever painted them had spent a lot more time in motel rooms, staring at the pictures over the chained-down TV, than in actual nature. No doubt, after enough seventy-nine-hour blinds-closed binges, smoking meth under the bed, those pink skies and shiny seascapes *were* nature.

"See something you like?"

A small, perfectly proportioned blond man in a blue prison shirt eyed me nervously from behind the counter. I hadn't seen him come through the door, and he made sure to keep that burp gun–era register between us. His face was an unlined fifty. A faded patchwork of tattoos blued his chest where his collar opened.

"All the paintings you see here are done by inmates," he recited. "You'll notice there are no signatures, only their prisoner number."

The counter in front of him contained a dozen key chains: dominoes on one side, a drawing of the prison and gun tower and SQ on the other. He backed up a little when I approached. Startled. I found myself speaking slowly.

"How much are the key chains?"

"Four fifty."

I pulled out a twenty. "I'll take four."

As he reached in the case to grab them, I saw that he was missing his middle fingers. Before I could decide whether to ask about them, he whispered, "Got a lighter?"

"Don't smoke anymore."

In fact, I did have a lighter. You never know when you'll need to fake some charm or camaraderie by lighting somebody's Camel. But I didn't tell him.

"We're not supposed to either." He kept his voice low, eyes aimed at the counter. "That's why a pack goes for thirty dollars."

"Thirty, huh? Next time I'll bring a carton."

His eight fingers fluttered with excitement. But they stopped when I didn't say anything else. What I wanted to ask was how much he got for snitching out visitors. You didn't get to be gift shop trustee by slipping the hacks free cup holders. He started to make change from the cash drawer, then stopped. He stared at the money in his hand as though he had no idea how it got there.

"Keep the change," I said.

Tension came off him like steam. "There's change?"

When he handed me the bag, he looked me in the eye for the first time.

"Enjoy your life," he said. "I can't."

"*There* you are!"

My contact, Officer Rincin, sauntered toward me from the ID window. He was a stocky, red-faced grinner of sixty or so. One of those skinny guys with a belly—what beer drunks call a "party ball"—pushing apart the buttons of his tan correction officer's shirt as though it were still inflating. Gray hair wisped out of his brown baseball cap. He might have been top floor man in the Sears appliance section, except for the mild menace of his wire-rim reflector shades and the cuffs on his belt.

"What'dja get?" he inquired, indicating the paper bag in my hand.

"Key chains."

I opened the bag so he could see in. To show him I wasn't smuggling anything.

"Great stocking stuffers," he said. "I understand you're law enforcement yourself."

"Was. Young man's game."

I said it like I'd simply aged out of the profession, as opposed to crawling out with a bag of dirty money and a wife with "perp" after her name. *Memories!*

"Didn't want to end up dead or behind a desk," I blathered on. "Not that there's a hell of a lot of difference."

"I hear ya," my new friend sighed, still grinning. The grin was disconcerting, until I realized it never stopped. Which was more disconcerting. It was like rictus, with jowls and cop 'stache. "You didn't give Twitchy a lighter, did you?"

"No, why would I?"

"Because he asked."

"Well, they always want to get over one way or the other, don't they? My experience, dogs bark, cows moo and convicts con. It's their nature."

"You're all right," he said. "Course, if you'd have given him that lighter, we'd be marchin' you to intake for a bun-spread yourself. They take the contraband thing here real serious."

"But you didn't really have to sweat me, you have it on video, right?"

"Aren't you a sharpie!" Rincin grinned some more, then pointed to my gym bag. "Travel light, huh?"

"Yeah, I left the cologne and tuxedo at home."

"Aces. We'll just sign your butt in, get you a badge. They can use the photo off your DL. They're puttin' you in the Can Patch. Little trailer park on the ass end of the property. Lot of guards live there when they're startin' out."

"Great," I said.

Rincin just grinned. Of course. We walked toward the gray and stately administration building, where I was surprised to see more inmates in denim walking by, single or paired up.

"A lot of your lifers are pretty mellow," he said when they ambled by. "It's the transitionals are the knuckleheads, punks just comin' in who got something to prove. They're the ones in orange jumpsuits."

We stepped inside, into the smell of furniture polish and dust. A bored middle-aged woman, chewing gum behind a grille on the left, buzzed us through, toward another pair of Goliath-sized glass and wood doors.

"Hey, Lil," Rincin said to the buzzer woman. He pointed at me. "Temp staff, here's his DL." She snatched my license while we waited in between the doors that locked behind us and the ones still locked in front of us. A pair of mustached young men with gym memberships and dark suits were buzzed out. They eyed me as they passed. My own outfit—black T-shirt, gray Dickies pants, scuffed boots and black leather jacket that made as much sense as ear muffs in the heat— earned a professional size-up from the exiting suits. The taller one waved to Lil and she winked back as she slid a form through the slot. Office romance.

"Have him fill this out," she said to Rincin, who replied, "Will do, pretty lady," and handed it to me like I was invisible to everybody but him.

I wrote down the address of my storage space, where most of my possessions used to live. For an extra five a month, the owner accepted mail. The one thing you couldn't do, Omar the U-Stor-It man informed me when I signed on, was party in the storage space. "Gypsies," he'd explained, without elaborating. "They ruin the fun for everybody."

At the line requesting Social Security, I didn't hesitate. Anyone stealing my identity would be blessed with much more debt than credit. I was happy to share.

"Done," I said, as if I'd passed some mighty test. Rincin snatched my paperwork and slid it back to Lil. She buzzed us through the second set of doors, past the warden's office. The whole place was high-ceilinged and airy. The floor shined like it got polished hourly.

Nobody seemed concerned about their proximity to killers, thugs and sex maniacs. The air had a testosterone and Endust tang.

I followed Rincin to a courtyard facing another beautiful stone building, 1852 on a keystone over its entrance. A half-dozen contractors banged away just under the roof. Or maybe they weren't contractors. They all had muscles and back ink. Swinging sledgehammers on a scaffold two flights up struck me as misguided, but maybe OSHA regulations didn't apply to prison labor.

"That there's the original prison site," Rincin tour-guided. "They're finally tearing her down. Lots of folks wanted to come in and photograph the dungeon, but the warden isn't having it. What's the upside of letting the *Chronicle* come in and take pictures of the rack, or all the chains still hanging from the wall rings?"

"Well, it's history," I offered.

"That's my point," he said.

Rincin yanked off his hat, gave his bald spot a scratch, and slapped it back on without explaining himself further. He pointed to another edifice, from which a large Latino guard escorted a moon-faced white inmate in hand and ankle cuffs. The hefty guard waved across the courtyard to my host.

Rincin waved back. "*Hola*, Pedro!" It was one big happy campus.

"This here's the AC, the Adjustment Center," Rincin said. "For guys too violent for gen pop. You work in there, you pretty much have to eat and shit in riot gear. They keep 'em down twenty-three hours. Roll 'em out for an hour exercise in a cage. Then back in the hole."

It was another second before I realized he was leading me over there. I swallowed and tried to smother my fear in the crib.

"So, uh, Officer Rincin, you're not putting me in . . . ?"

I pointed at the adjustment center in what I hoped was a casual fashion. Rincin's grin got a little bigger.

"What? No! Should I?" Then he got sly. "Had you worried, huh?"

"Little bit."

"The environment takes some getting used to. But like I say, you'll be stayin' in a trailer. It's comin' up. Just around the other end of the lower yard. We'll pop in my car."

We rounded a corner and that's when I saw it: the yard. As featured in every prison entertainment from *Twenty-Thousand Years in Sing-Sing* to *Oz*. The inmates really did walk the track in slow circles, clusters of like-skinned fellows strolling together discussing the fine points of the Council of Nicaea, the falling dollar or other subjects of interest. Blacks owned the hoops. Cannonball-bicepped white guys spotted each other on weight benches. A row of ripped skinheads curled plastic gallon jugs of water. Despite the blast furnace heat, nobody seemed to be slathering on sunblock. Maybe that was the real reason they tattooed their arms to sleeves. It wasn't that they wanted to blanket their epidermis in flaming tits and swastikas, they just wanted to block out the killer UV rays.

"I know what you're thinking."

Rincin nudged me as we headed past a fat hack checking names on a clipboard marked YARD LOG, out onto the track.

"You're thinking, *What do the Mexican guys do for exercise?*"

"How did you know?"

"Folks always do. See, for one thing this isn't the only yard. For another—and this'll surprise you—your Mexicans hold down the tennis courts."

"Mexican prison tennis," I repeated dumbly. I didn't know if he was fucking with me, but since he didn't march out Samoan badminton I let it go.

"There's a lot of things that would surprise you," he said cryptically.

"No doubt."

Nobody in the yard showed overt interest, but I felt the eyes. Once or twice I thought I heard somebody whistle. Not the kind of thing you want to turn around and check. I didn't tell Rincin what really surprised me—beyond the fact that someone was possibly hard-up enough to find forty-year-old white meat worth whistling at. What spooked me even more was how *normal* the residents looked.

Watch enough of the nonstop *Lockdown* and *Lockup* on basic cable, and you'd think the guys inside were all malevolent freaks. Much more chilling, it was just the opposite: the majority wandered the track staring blankly, pasty faces stamped with nothing more menacing than resignation and fatigue. More than half had committed their crimes while intoxicated. Half of these sobered up in the delousing shower. Or just came out of their blackouts in state clothes.

Rincin nudged me. "Check out Hiawatha."

I looked where I thought he was looking. On our right, in the patchy grass, sat a trio of broad-shouldered, ponytailed young men styling plucked eyebrows and shaved stomachs, one with pubescent starter breasts showing through his shirt.

"Regulations let 'em unbutton to the solar plexus," Rincin said to fill me in. "What they do is roll and knot the tails right here, for maximum midriff." He tapped the top of his hard, round stomach, just under his man cleavage. "Turns a prison shirt into a bikini top."

He watched me watching. "As you can see, they like to show off their titty beans." Rincin banged me hard on the arm. "Now check this out."

In a fenced-off square of earth just off the yard, a shirtless, overweight man with white hair down his back ducked into the mouth of a low hut and disappeared. "Warden lets 'em have their own sweat lodge."

A young Native American, hair in braided pigtails down his back, squatted on a wooden bench, hands on his knees, staring back at me with no expression.

"Say one thing for the red man," said Rincin, "there ain't a lot of white boys I'd want to strip down to my skivvies and sit in the dark with."

"You ever go in there, look for contraband?"

I imagined the pigtailed man had somehow read my lips and felt his accusing eyes on me. Was there such a thing as too paranoid in prison?

Rincin shook his head. "You've seen too many of them jailhouse shows. 'Round here we call 'em 'prison porn.'"

"What does that make you guys? Fluffers?"

For a second Rincin didn't reply. Even though his grin remained intact, I could see him thinking: *If an inmate doesn't do it, I'm going to shank this asshole myself.*

Then, even before the buzzer, everybody in the yard dropped to the ground. I started to hit the dirt and Rincin grabbed me. Yanked me back up by the shoulder. He wasn't gentle. "Dumbest fucking thing you can do is get on the ground. You stay on your feet, standing up, the tower shooter knows you're one of us."

Eager to move on, I pointed across the field, in front of the bleachers, where a team of paramedics was trying to pluck a thrashing orange jumpsuit off the ground onto a gurney. "What happened to him?"

Rincin grabbed my hand and pulled it down. "Don't ever point in prison."

"Sorry," I said.

"No biggie." Rincin looked back at the paramedics, now carrying the stricken inmate off on a stretcher. "Guy's probably a flopper. In this sun, some boys just keel over and have seizures." He turned back to me, gripped my shoulder and wagged a finger at me. "Crank and sun don't mix! Tell your kids!"

"Words to live by," I said.

"Better believe it. . . . The car's right over here."

I followed Rincin down a steep row of wooden stairs to a dusty parking lot. He held out his key and beeped it at a black Impala. "Sorry if I was a little rough back there."

"No, *I'm* sorry. I'm the green one."

"That would be true," he said.

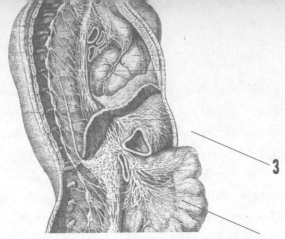

3

Quentin Adjacent

Rincin drove with his elbow out the window, expounding on the sights. "What you're looking at is a small city. Four hundred and seventy-three acres. We are now going by North Block. The death house, built in nineteen twenty-four," he announced, with the canned enthusiasm of a tour bus operator touting Grauman's Chinese Theatre. "Somebody here may tell you that Scott Peterson can see the spot where they fished his pregnant wife out of the water by the bridge. They may be telling the truth."

"Wow."

I felt him staring at me.

"No, I mean that. Wow!"

"Right. Over there you got your infirmary. Behind that, your South Block. Behind that, your dining hall and water cannons." With this he reached into the backseat into a cooler. Pulled out two cans of Coke. He popped both pop-tops at once and handed me one. That must have taken practice. We both sucked fizz from the lids and wiped our mouths.

"Coca-Cola," he said. "Calms my nerves."

"You still get . . . not calm?"

"I've stroked out twice." He stared away from the ocean, toward the water tower. "You know, I been here twenty-eight years." His smile, unchanged, now seemed poignant. "You know what's different now? I'm *old*!" Suddenly he snapped his fingers as if he'd remembered something important. "I bet this might interest you—I was here for the Kosher Mosher reclassification fight. In 'eighty-eight."

I told him I hadn't heard of that.

"Really? I figured you for a Jew."

"Uh-huh."

Rincin knocked back the last of his Coke and belched. "Well," he said, crushing the can in his hand and grabbing another one. "That's the tragedy, isn't it? When your own people forget."

A blue and white sailboat floated out in the bay, in some shimmering world that had nothing to do with this one. The outs. I wondered if the sailboat people knew that they were half a mile from the Hillside Strangler and 317 other killers with nicknames, professional and recreational.

It would probably be scorching later, but right now the temperature was perfect. The CO handed me another preopened can of Coke. Somehow knowing I'd finished my first.

"So who *was* Mosher?" I asked, since it seemed expected.

"An Orthodox Jew, an actual rabbi, in for domestic. What happened is, he got stuck in a cell with a shot-caller for the ALS. A real peckerwood. Zeke Mosher. Whole thing was somebody's idea of a joke. But the rabbi, he's so tortured by his celly, he keeps tryin' to get himself reclassified as a nonwhite man. Claims he's the victim of race baiting."

He took a breath, guzzling between sentences. "They keep races together when they assign cells. Shouldn't be that way, but TLIP—that's life in prison. Anyway, the whole thing was like some kinda joke to the staff and the fellas on the tier. But it was no joke for the

Jew! He's got the whatchamacallem, the shylocks, growing outta his temple. He ties little boxes to his head with leather straps, the whole shmear."

Rincin looked proud to have gotten the "shmear" thing in.

"Did the administration go for it?" I asked.

"Go for what?

"The reclassification. Did Kosher get to move out of the cell with Mosher?"

"Let me tell the story. What happened is, one day the peckerwood crossed the line. He ripped the prophylactic right off the rabbi's arm while he was praying with it."

"You mean the phylactery."

Rincin snapped, still keeping his grin on, "Did I say I was an expert? The peckerwood, he cooks up a shot in a contraband spoon and says, 'Know what I'm shootin' up? I'm shootin' up *pork juice*!' Then he takes *his* phylaka-dakkies, this leather strap with wooden boxes attached, he ties off and fixes with it!"

"What happened?"

"You mean after? *Right* after? The rabbi had a little heart attack. The case went to the penal board, who heard experts talking about how Jews were a race, or they weren't a race, they were a religion. One expert, from Alabama, said they were a cult. On the other hand, skin is skin. Nobody made a federal case when black Muslims shared cells with Baptists."

"That makes sense."

"Not to the rabbi's representatives. All that mattered to them was that Nazi thought Jews were a virus. Ask any hard-core Aryan, he'll tell you straight up. 'They look white, that's how they sneak into the mainstream and start polluting the race.'

"All this came up, but in the end the board decided white's white, even with the dangly shylocks."

"*Payots,*" I said.

"Pay us for what?"

"*Payots.* That's what that hair tuft is called, the sidelocks, on the Orthodox guys."

"I'll take your word on that, sir. But the board decided to put him back in the cell. Said it was a bad precedent. And, I gotta tell you, you'd walk by the cell, day or night, it was like watching a buffed-up Aryan cat and a little squeaky Jew mouse. Every day it was something, but the Aryan won't come out and kill the rabbi. He's having too much fun. I'm telling you, this was nothing nice. Poor Hebe was in hell—or whatever you people call it."

"*Dos Gehenem.*"

"That some Jew word?"

"Yiddish for eternal jury duty."

"I'll take your word. I'm just saying, these guys were stuck with each other day in, day out. That's when I realized it was perfect."

"Perfect for what?"

"Sitcom."

"That could work," I said, just to say something.

"You're telling me," said Rincin. "Problem was I never met any Jews. I mean, if you're gonna write, you gotta know your subject. So what happens, I finally get to know a Hebrew, and who is it? Bobby Bernstein."

"I know the name, I just can't . . . Wait, was that Son of Sam?"

"That was David Berkowitz." He looked disappointed. "I'm surprised at you. Bobby Bernstein happens to be one of the baddest, meanest, toughest sonuvabitches in the ALS. And he happens to be a Semite."

"Isn't that like a black guy joining the Klan?"

"Apples and oranges," he said. "You look at Bernstein. Shaved head. Ripped. Full carpet of white power ink."

He made a fist, straightened his arms. Tapped his left wrist—"Star of David over here." Then he tapped his right—"Swastika over *here*. Now, I don't meet too many sons of Abraham in my line of work, but am I goin' out on a limb if I say Bernstein isn't typical?"

"No, he's definitely not typical."

We were halfway up the dirt road to my trailer. My stomach lurched and he elbowed me. Rincin was turning out to be an elbower. "So what are you sayin'? About my idea, I mean."

"I'm saying, you want a sitcom, give it a twist. Forget the peckerwood. Put the Orthodox Jew in with the Jew who's the Nazi. Mosher and Bernstein. Better yet, make them brothers."

"You mean black guys?"

"What? No, no, I mean *real* brothers—so on visiting day their mother can come. A Jewish mother visiting her boys in jail—one's a practicing Orthodox, one's a big man in the ALS."

I could sense him squinting at me under his reflector shades. Suspicious. "I write the thing you just said, it becomes *Two and a Half Jews*—it's your word against mine."

I clapped him on the back. "My gift to you. If it takes off and you want to give me a point, I wouldn't say no."

"Are you in show business?"

"Very peripherally."

"Well, what you want to do is establish yourself as consultant. That's what guys do. I give you a consultant credit, that's money in the bank. Who knows, you might go full Bruckheimer."

"A guy can dream," I said. "So, you think the doctor's the real thing?" I realized my blunder before it was out of my mouth. I'd been here five minutes and possibly blown my cover.

"The real thing? The doctor? He the real old German guy?"

He took a last swig of Coke, flattened the can and tossed it in the backseat with the others. We drove in silence across the main road where the ATM and the gift shop were. "Up here are the employee residences. Those are some nice little houses. You won't be living in those."

He swung the Chevy up a bumpy dirt road that curved around the nice houses, toward a gravel lot onto which a dozen double-wides had been dragged and dropped. We parked at the far end beside a fresh-scrubbed trailer, water still plinking from the roof.

Officer Rincin got out and tugged a ring of keys out from a pull string on his belt, then began flipping through them. He eyed me as he tried the first one on the door. As it turns out I wasn't moving into the just-washed baby-blue double-wide. My new home was the wagon behind it. An old-time snailback, like something Lucy and Ricky would attach to the back of their sedan on a fishing trip.

"Who lived here before me, a hunchback?"

"Actually, the term is 'scoliosis.' My daughter is afflicted." While I tried to swallow my tongue, he patted the trailer's flank, waking a cloud of gnats. "I raised eleven children in this rust bucket."

"Are you serious?"

He unlocked the door and let the key ring zip back to his belt, then gave me the elbow and burst out laughing. "Gotcha!"

Before this I didn't know what fun was.

"Prison humor," Rincin said, wiping his eyes. "Boy, you wanna make it in here, you gotta work on your bullshit filter. I thought you was edgy-cated."

"Edgy-cated, that's good."

I chuckled along, big enough to have a little laugh at my own expense. I wasn't thrilled about establishing my moron credentials so soon, but it was worth it if it meant he'd forget about the Mengele blunder.

Rincin kicked the door open hard and jumped back, as if expecting gunfire from within. It seemed as ludicrous as waving a hat on a stick. But then, this was his job.

Before we stepped inside he turned to me. "What did you mean before, about the doctor being the real thing?"

"I mean," I said, making it up as I went along, "I heard the doctor might still be using. See, I really want to work with people who are serious."

"You're the serious type, is that it?"

When I'd taken this job, I'd figured the big problem would be not spooking Mengele: trying to ID the old man without getting him nervous and without getting anybody who might be after him nervous. What I did not anticipate was having to bivouac in a tin-can petri dish barely bigger than a handicapped stall.

On the plus side, I didn't have a cell mate. And the ceiling was high enough so that I only had to lean slightly sideways to keep from scraping my scalp. The real challenge would be breathing. That smell. This wasn't just a trailer, it was a biosphere. The site of what appeared to be an extended experiment on the interplay of mold and mammal discharge, with shag carpet, fold-down bed and kitchenette.

I knew certain spores could alter brain function.

"Excuse me," said Officer Rincin, and squeezed past me close enough for his Taser to brush my genitals. It was an odd sensation. Odder when he reached toward me, arms extended. I was about to tell him I was a virgin when I realized he wasn't going for a man clench but reaching for the two exposed screws above my head.

"Beg pardon. Handles are missing. Bed folds out like so."

He pulled the single bunk down to eye level, then yanked down the built-in particleboard ladder. They say particleboard gives off peroxide, but they don't say when. We both admired the efficient design. On impulse, I reached up and touched the sagging foam mattress. It was damp. Before this, I'd never even thought the word "soilage." But there was something else. Teeth marks.

"Hang on," I blurted. "The guy before me was a biter?"

"Good eyes." Rincin nodded, lapsing back to canned tour guide delivery. "Now, if a citizen sees this, his first thought is, *What made a man sink his teeth into rotting foam?* But a CO? First thing *he's* thinking is, *Nobody just bites. Not to judge a fellow officer, what* else *did this perv do on Nibble Nights?*"

"Whatever it was, I can't say I like the idea of sleeping in it."

But smiling Corrections Officer Rincin was ready for that.

"Rubber sheets. Right now there's a foam shortage. Good news is, we wrap her in rubber, you'll be fine," he said. "And we'll get these handles fixed for you ASAP."

I was impressed. He seemed unfazed by the eye-burning stench.

"Guy before you, name of Turk. Big fella. He drank a little. . . . His wife left him after he started as a guard. That happens. Administration got him this snailback. Then he drank a little more. Big Boy kept keeling over, grabbing the handles. Ripped 'em right out of the wood every time he fell. The investigators said that's how it happened."

"How what happened?"

I focused on keeping the fingers that had touched foam away from my face. That's how you get staph infections.

"The accident." Rincin kneeled and yanked up a chocolate-colored splotch of carpet, revealing a bloodstain beneath. "They cleaned 'er up pretty good."

I didn't ask any questions. The splotch, the bite marks, they pretty much explained it. The stench didn't come from simple fungus. Or out of a cat. It was desperation. Left to ferment. Man fungus.

Rincin checked his watch. "What say you take fifteen to get squared away. Then we'll meet the warden. I'll be right outside."

After he left, I thought I heard muffled heaving, but I wasn't sure. The smell was so bad it affected my hearing.

I'd moved into a lot of places. It's weird. The first thing I always do is open the drawers. Looking for clues. Not that any were necessary. It's not like it's hard to figure out the kind of person who would end up in this kind of place. Once you hit the ground, does it matter how many floors you fell?

I put down my bag, shoved the port-a-bed back into its slot and got to work.

The silverware drawer came out with a yank. Empty. A cabinet over the sink window hung by one hinge. For a second, I took in the view. A high fence separated my row of trailers from a trio of much nicer double-wides. My tin can was plopped on soiled dirt; grass grew between the trailers on the other side and a gravel pathway led from the road to each front door. Up the path to the first, a white guard walked behind a black couple—following as stately as the flower girl in a wedding. The convict was rail thin in prison denims, the woman in large sunglasses, tasseled red leather vest and Capri pants that clung to the dimpled pillars of her calves. They'd already started to split in the back.

They disappeared around a corner. I eased open the overhead cabinet, releasing an avalanche of magazines. Fat glossies bounced off the throbbing egg on my head, a souvenir of Zell's walker. I glanced down at a picture of a doe-eyed Asian girl in traction. She pouted from her hospital bed, in a neck brace, one arm and both legs in traction, a sliver of white bush-shmushing panties peeping out between them. I closed the magazine, but there she was again—the Japanese victim-girl—beaming and damaged, legs drilled with metal pins, one eye black, an arm in a sling, from the glossy, waterlogged cover of June 2004's *Broken Dolls*.

I didn't hear Rincin open the door. He tilted his head, glanced at the cover of the magazine, then straightened up and looked back at me. "Glad to see you've made yourself at home."

I waited for him to say "Gotcha!"

When he didn't I scooped a couple of magazines from the sink: back issues of *Moppets* and a well-thumbed *Clown Sex* catalogue. Rincin saw the things and raised his eyebrows. "Hey," I said, "I didn't bring these from home."

By way of reply he grabbed a copy of *Pony Girls* featuring a big-thighed brunette pulling a bald man in a two-wheeled carriage on the cover. *"Yippy-ki-yay!"* he said with no enthusiasm.

"Moppets, clown whores and pony girls? No wonder the guy drank," I said.

"Naw." Rincin started scooping up the porno. "He didn't drink 'cause he was a perv, he drank 'cause he was a perv who liked the taste of Schlitz. Besides which, he was probably selling these inside." He opened an *Ebony She-Male* and eyed the glossy contents appraisingly. "You could get five bucks a page for this out on the yard. Six if they're cherry."

I didn't ask what he planned to do with them. Maybe we each had something on each other. Maybe not.

"By the way," said the sergeant, indicating the splendor around us, "this is just temporary. They're hooking up the power on a new box, just for you."

"Really? 'Cause I'll miss this place." I ran a hand over the mildewed counter. "Kidding! That sounds good."

"I don't know about good, but it's better than this pud hut. Meanwhile the warden wants to see you."

"Right now?" I don't know why I was panicked.

"Not till after I bleed my lizard," he said, squeezing past me again. "'Scuse me, the little boys' is this a-way."

I didn't want to stand there, so I stepped outside. His stream was so high-impact the snailback's two good wheels vibrated. Then I looked up and realized it was a helicopter coming in for a landing. Rincin saw me watching the chopper when he stepped out behind me, plopping his hat back on. "Don't worry, Dr. Drew, it's probably a medevac. They're not coming for you."

"Funny. But I'm not really Dr. Drew."

"I know that. But you do what he does, right?"

"Oh, sure. Except I'm not a doctor. I don't have my own TV and radio show. And he probably has a lot more money."

My chaperone got back in the car. "Well you don't have to brag about it," he called back. "Time to say hello to the big dog."

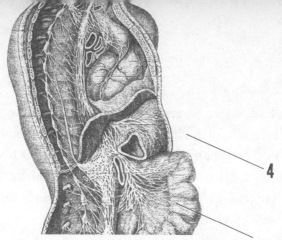

4

Meet the Warden

The warden, a ramrod-spined ex–navy boxer, was working a Bernie Kerik: shaved head and brush-cut law enforcement mustache. He was five foot four but blessed with a square and enormous jaw. That jaw looked like it could handle itself. I could imagine it pushing ahead of him, clearing a path through a world of massive bad guys twice his size. He eyed me across the desk, tenting his fingers between the little U.S. flag and the flag of California. I stared back, a little over his head, at a framed photo of him gazing up at Arnold Schwarzenegger. I wondered if the warden had to resist the urge to brag—he may have been a foot shorter, but his chin looked like it could bench-press ten times more than the governor's.

"So," he began, "as part of your undercover work, you'll be running a drug rehabilitation workshop."

"That's the idea."

"You've had some experience with drugs?"

"I've done some research, sir. I just didn't know it was research at the time."

"That a joke?"

"More or less," I said, instantly regretting it. The man stared down serial killers every day. He didn't need me to amuse him.

"Cute," he said, then picked up a document and studied it. I read "Department of Corrections" on top, upside-down. The warden skimmed a few more papers attached by paper clip, then raised his eyes. "I'm surprised you never visited us before."

"Is that a joke?"

"Prison humor," he continued when it was clear I wasn't going to laugh. "You'll get used to it. There's some funny stuff that goes on. But," he said flatly, "we do have Nazis."

My own voice came out tinny. "Right, of course. I knew that. . . ."

"Mr. Rupert?"

"Yes!"

"You'll be dealing with six addicts."

My ears were ringing.

"Sex addicts?" I shifted in my chair. "They didn't mention . . . I mean, not to judge, I'm just saying . . . who hasn't—I mean, I'm not sure in terms of sobriety, if, you know, sobriety is even the right word—"

"Mr. Rupert?"

"Yes, sir?"

The warden tapped his pencil on the desk and stared at me. He'd put on reading glasses, the kind with round little lenses that made whoever wore them look somehow critical, disapproving. His magnified eyeballs seemed appalled. And I didn't blame them.

"Not sex addicts," he said, after I'd repolished the chair by squirming in it for a minute. "Six addicts."

"Six addicts?"

"That's what I said."

"There have to be more than six addicts in San Quentin," I said.

He took off his glasses and picked up a miniature ball-and-chain made from papier-mâché. The one-ball made me think of Hitler. They sold them in the gift shop.

"There are six addicts," he continued, "who I think can really benefit from your kind of program."

"And what kind of program would that be?"

"The kind that can really benefit them."

"Well," I said—where were we going with this?—"it would be great if I could help out in that way."

"Don't worry," he replied drily, "I know the reason you're here. I also know your history. A cop and a drug addict. Interesting combo."

"Ex," I said, trying not to sound too touchy on the subject.

There was an awkward silence. Suddenly I saw myself as he saw me. Battered black leather and soul patch. Your basic faux badass. A tattooed, middle-aged white law enforcement loser who thought shooting dope for a decade gave him some kind of street cred. In other words, from where he was standing, the worst kind of civilian—the kind who thought he knew what time it was.

I bit my lip to keep from defending myself. I wanted to share my theory: all of us, at some point in life, choose our cliché. But I held my mud. Or tried to.

I had, I should explain, a bad habit of thinking I knew what people were thinking while I was talking to them. Sometimes I actually replied. Which was never good. Even if you were right about what was going on in another man's head, there was no upside to responding if he hadn't actually said anything.

"Some powerful people," the warden went on, "obviously think you're the right man for the job. Of course, it's a little unorthodox."

"Of course."

"Well, I'm a little unorthodox, too. Right, Colfax?"

"So I've read, sir."

I'd felt someone looming, and when Colfax spoke I felt free to turn around. Colfax was six-six, no wider than a Volvo, three hundred pounds of order-maintaining muscle, packed in a snug deputy's uniform and topped with a shaved head, acne-pocked skin and the requisite handlebar mustache. He must have come in after we'd sat down. *Even big men learn to walk like cats in the big house,* I thought. (And wondered why I was suddenly channeling promo lines from the Turner Classic Movies channel.)

"Look at me!" The warden snapped his fingers and I jerked my head in his direction. Everything in prison is a test, but it hadn't occurred to me the warden would be testing, too. It should have. But just when I thought he was going to go all "this is my house" territorial, he went somewhere else.

"Let me put this on the table," he said. "Just because you're here undercover, that doesn't mean you can't do some kind of good with these fellows. Drug addiction is a scourge. I realize you're not actually here for that purpose, but there's no reason, as a kind of side benefit, you can't show these fellows something. We've had UC inside before, for all kinds of things. We had a fed undercover in D Block for six months, trying to flush out a baby raper named Mooney."

"Flush out?"

"We had him on a parole violation. But we knew he'd had relations with his girlfriend's daughter. Problem was, girlfriend clammed up after she reported it. That happens when your boyfriend sticks your face in a pot of grits. Of course, missy wouldn't report that either. So that's where the UC came in. To get Mooney to say what we already knew."

"Of course," I echoed, as if I myself had been around the track with facial grits situations. "So, how'd that work out?"

The warden leaned sideways, talking past me. "Colfax, how'd that work out?"

"Not well, sir."

Just then a trustee who might have doubled for Uncle Ben—before he was updated—limped in with a tray. The warden rubbed his hands. "Ah, chamomile. Like some?"

"I'm good," I said.

"Suit yourself."

The tea man poured and backed away. The warden took the cup and blew delicately. He sipped, somehow making even that look macho.

"Not well," he repeated with a satisfied sigh. "That pretty much sums it up. To get close to Mooney the UC had the idea that he should act like a kiddie diddler. So Mooney would trust him. Trouble is, he was a little too convincing. They became best friends."

"What happened? He get into a fight?"

"Not exactly a fight. A young Zulu out to make his bones heard Mooney and the UC swapping cookie recipes, or whatever the hell pedophiles talk about, and stuck a spork in his aorta. Our man just kind of bled out. Convicts hate pee-pee bandits. They're fair game."

"How do they feel about drug counselors?"

"Fine, as long as you don't get any of their customers clean. That's messing with their money." His Gibraltar jaw lent gravitas to every pronouncement. "Long as you don't take money out of their pocket, you can all hold hands at meetings."

"So then—there's nobody from gangs in the class?"

"Oh no. Everybody's in a gang in a prison. If you have a race, you have a gang. Fact of life."

"So then everybody in the class is already clean?"

"Bingo. All clean." The warden took another sip of chamomile and smacked his lips. "Unless they're not. We do random UAs."

"Piss tests?"

"Piss tests. Right."

I felt a tingle of panic. A tiny quarter smile rode over the warden's cowcatcher jaw. "That's not going to be a problem, is it, Mr. Rupert?"

"What, the piss test? No. God no. Of course not. No problem at all."

I let my voice trail off. Or maybe it just wandered off on its own, wanting to get as far away from me as possible. The warden let me sputter out.

"Just so we're both clear," I started up again, "I'm here because they want me to find out about the old man, the German. Everything else—helping guys get clean, teaching them life skills—that's great. It's fantastic. But, at the end of the day, it's gravy."

"Gravy. Uh-huh." The warden sat back and tented his fingers again. "You, sir, are an interesting fella."

The way he said it—like he had footage of me touching myself at bus stops—made me cringe all the way to my toenails.

The warden stood and extended a dainty hand. For a dizzy second, I didn't know whether to shake it or kiss it. "Well," he continued, "I guess you'll just have to decide your own level of commitment. Colfax?"

The big CO stepped forward with a cup sealed in a plastic bag. He produced it from behind his back, like a dog treat. The warden smiled again. This was fun.

"You know the drill, right? Print your name right on the cup and seal 'er up tight."

Now it was my chance to smile. "You need this now?"

The warden clapped me on the back. "Of course not. Bring it tomorrow. Now how about we get to your group? Like I say, I've selected some fellas I think can benefit from a week of recovery know-how. Here's the team," he said, and slid a stack of folders in my direction.

I stared at them, certain I should say something—but what? "You know, I'm not really here to—"

"Oh, come on," he interrupted, mistaking my reticence as some kind of prissiness in the face of raw crime. "You being ex-police and all, you're not going to be shocked at what some of these fellows have done."

"I'll read it sitting down," I said, "just in case."

"Read it sitting down. That's a good'n. Hear that, Colfax?"

"Long as he pees standing up," said the corn-fed guard. More prison yuks.

There was a long, odd silence, then the warden snapped his fingers again.

"Rupert!"

The warden crooked his finger, then leaned forward himself, thrusting his Greyhound bus of a jaw over the table in my direction. What would life be like with a cudgel like that under your lower lip?

"You know, Rupert, there's one thing you learn in my line of work."

The warden clicked his tongue and grinned, plainly on fire to tell me what it was. I didn't bite. (Life, for a neurotic, so often boiled down to a battle of wills in which only one side realized there was a battle going on.) The warden brushed imaginary dandruff off his lapels and re-tented his hands, steepled forefingers meeting at the tips and pointing my way. The gesture could not have been more menacing if he'd been aiming a Luger.

"You get pretty good at reading a man."

"Really?" This time I decided to go along. Why antagonize? "How do you do that, Warden?"

"You're asking me *how*?"

"Unless it's a trade secret. Something you take a blood oath to keep under your hat at warden school."

The warden recoiled visibly.

This always happened. Ninety-nine percent of the time, I was cool. But in the presence of those whose favor and approval I most needed, I regressed. Succumbed to some residual antiauthority reflex, as unseemly in a man my age as a Rolling Stones lapping-tongue tattoo on your grandmother's breast. Substance-abuse professionals said you stopped maturing at the age you started getting loaded. Forever fifteen. The warden leaned toward me. "You want to know how I read guys? It's simple. I don't listen."

"You don't listen?"

"Nope." His voice dropped an octave by way of transmitting some bit of arcane and dangerous wisdom. "I watch the hands."

"The hands?"

I raised my own palms in front of my eyes and stared at them. Who were these dangerous strangers? Then we both leaned forward again. Had either of us gone further we'd have bumped foreheads.

"So," I said, "say somebody's across the table pointing their fingers at your solar plexus like a .357; how would you read it?"

"That's easy. My read would be they're letting me know they're armed. In every sense of the word. I'd say they were saying, 'Don't try anything, fella, 'cause I've got your number before you even start counting.'"

I put my hands up and sat back in my chair. "Point taken. Don't shoot."

The warden checked his watch, snapped his fingers and pointed to the door. Which was apparently Officer Colfax's signal to step behind me again. Colfax took a car-crusher grip on my shoulder, holding me down. Was the warden afraid I was going to attack him? Or did his bodyguard just like me? In prison, everything was something else. Which was true on the outside, too. Just not as vividly.

The warden moved smoothly to the door, where he stopped and faced me. "Might want to study those files. See who you're dealing with. They're all very excited."

"And the German?"

"You'll meet him. Then you can tell me. He's supposed to be *whosis* again?"

"A doctor," I said.

Zell had implied the warden was in on it. But here he was playing ignorant. Which meant either Zell was lying or the warden was testing me again. Retesting. To see if I'd be on the level with him.

"Dr. Josef Mengele," I said.

"Right right right!"

The warden snapped his fingers again, causing Colfax to tighten his pincer grip on my trapezoids. I resolved not to cry out. I was an easy crier as a boy.

"The Doctor of Death," he continued, heading for the door. "I saw a thing, on the History Channel."

It was obvious he wanted to leave. I didn't take it personally. There were important chow hall trazor incidents to adjudicate. Funding to nudge out of Sacramento. But I couldn't just let him go without asking—even if it made me look desperate.

"Do *you* think it's him?"

He stopped in the doorway, eyes narrowing as he made a snap decision to give up real information. "He's a ninety-seven-year-old man who talks German to himself. You ever listen to German? It sounds like when you get glass in your garbage disposal. Even when he talks American, the old guy's accent is so thick it sounds like he's farting out of his mouth."

"Nice. He say anything you remember?"

For one bad second I was sure he was going to order Colfax to go supermax on me. Leave me sobbing on the curb with a bus ticket in my mouth and a broken collarbone.

"Wernher von Braun. That's the only thing comes to mind."

"Wernher von Braun?"

"Do I have to repeat that for you? I have a penitentiary to run."

He started out again, and before I could consider the consequences I heard myself plead, *"Wait!"* It came out more shrieky than I'd have liked.

The warden thrust his jaw back through the door. Even if he was under control, I was pretty sure his jaw wanted to kill me. "Did you have abandonment issues, son?"

"I just wanted to know, what is he in for?"

"Who?"

"The old man—I guess we don't really know if he's a doctor."

"I'd say he was a man of science."

"Why? What did he do?"

"Hit-and-run."

"Hit-and-run? How's that make him a scientist?"

"When they picked him up, he had his own little lab going. They don't know what he was making, but he was making something. Any more questions, I suggest you ask Officer Rincin, and he'll refer you to the proper individual."

This time he didn't say good-bye. Before he followed, Colfax unclenched my tendon and gave me a little hair-tussle. I wanted to believe the hair-muss was some traditional CO "Now you're one of us" maneuver—like when mafiosi gang-kissed a newly made man or Skull and Bones lay naked in coffins while John Kerry urinated on them. But I suspected it meant I was a bitch.

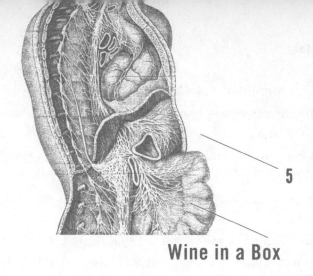

5

Wine in a Box

Back in my snailback, I slapped the stack of intake files on the kitchen table—yellow for violent crimes, red for non, though it seemed like it should be the other way around. That's how *I'd* have done it.

A lady police therapist once told me that control issues were really just fear of lack of control disguised as power. She interviewed me when I asked for a stress-related early pension, about a thousand years ago. She was very sincere. I asked if what she meant was that all strong people were weak. Was all power just fear of powerlessness in disguise?

Something I said must have moved her. Or else she was just lonely. Suddenly, she tiptoed around her desk, dropped to her knees and performed frantic, bristly fellatio while I studied the adorable kitten-tangled-in-yarn painting over her desk. In retrospect, I wondered if it was painted by a convict. *If I were a child molester,* I remember thinking when she put me in her mouth, *I'd paint kittens.* With that unwanted insight, my prospects shriveled, I showed the impulsive mental health professional the love and respect I felt for her by shrinking in her mouth. Sometimes women are as romantic as men. Beside the kitten, I noticed a black and white picture of Fabio. Signed. I couldn't make out the inscription, but it looked meaningful. If the kittens hadn't killed my erection, the sight of Fabio stomped on it with man sandals.

At the end of the session, the police therapist informed me that I had problems.

Two weeks later, I got the dread POP letter, the Police Officer Pension Board. They voted to deny. Citing, as a key factor, the therapist's assessment that I was trying to "use the system." All this happened before I actually quit the force—after I met Tina, nearly became a congressman, fucked things up and began my stellar career as an independent investigation professional on the West Coast.

Now I sat hunched in the sticky kitchenette, facing inmate files and breathing mold spores. I couldn't tell what made the furniture sweat, if the moisture came from within, oozing out, or vice versa. Wherever I sat there was a sodden *thwop* and squish, like the sound a shoe makes stepping on a snail in a puddle.

The first file I needed to see was Mengele's. If it *was* Mengele. I reached for the stack—then stopped myself.

Until now, I had focused on everything but the simple reality of sitting across from a real-life Josef Mengele. I suddenly realized my naïveté. You couldn't just pull up a chair and start chatting with an evil legend.

You had to prepare.

But how *could* you prepare?

I pushed the files away. Then pulled them back toward me again.

I have never done a brave thing in my life when I had time to think about it first. And this moment was no exception. I didn't know if I was more scared that the Butcher of Auschwitz would be here or that he wouldn't. So, instead of bold action, I decided to kick back and give in to the ball sweat, palpitations and shortness of breath of a well-earned panic attack.

I had put my trust in an old man who broke into my home, berated me, showed me some two-bit celebrity candids and beat me with his handicap appliance before offering me a job.

But why obsess on past idiocies with the good times to come? What if I met Mengele and just lost it? Started to cry? Or what if all this was a front and I was actually being *delivered* to him? Like a lab animal. How did I know he still wasn't doing experiments? Maybe my own shoe-leather liver—the third of three transplants, thanks for asking—would be used for some infernal, Mengele-esque purpose. They kept putting them in, and they kept going bad. If the doctor were still in the camps, he could transplant the severely hep C–infected organ into the body of a twelve-year-old Gypsy. Just to see if it made the young Romany scream at his family, then short out and spiral into a hate-nap.

Which is where I was headed. Until, with three brain cells still awake, I landed on a way to actually do the job I was so scared of.

I wouldn't run away from my quarry—but I wouldn't run toward him either. Instead of riffling through the prisoner files, scoping out a ninety-seven-year-old's mug shot and yelling "Bingo" when I found it, I'd pluck files out of the pile at random. Leave it to the penal gods.

Surprise required less preparation.

I started with a yellow file. Holding my breath—I was ready—I opened to a photocopied mug shot of Prisoner C-099419. A delicate, sleepy-eyed young felon with long hair and a face as flat and expressionless as a Mayan king's. Definitely not Mengele material.

ERNESTO NEGRANTE, 24, AKA CRANKY H [Hispanic] Four counts of assault with a deadly weapon. 18th Street gang member, L.A.

The file rambled. As if somebody had sat down and read a bunch of other files and scribbled up highlights—or left out some details.

CO NOTES: Inmate jumped into La Eme 11/06.
ARRESTING OFFICER HECTOR DELGADO: Perp in vehicle with his
brother TITO NEGRANTE AKA JOKER KGA [known gang associate]
when Tito was shot. Perp claimed brother picked him up on the way home
from school. QUOTE: How'm I supposed to know Joker was so dusted he'd
start shootin' outside the cop shop? UNQUOTE

I skipped ahead. . . . Cranky was a one-eight. Eighteenth Street. He
was seventeen. His mug shot showed the face of a frail youngster. Seventeen going on twelve. Sentenced as an adult to ten years in Quentin.
Now he was a soldier in the Mexican mafia. Which explained why
he'd signed up for drug class. I'd read, in the L.A. *Times* "California
Section" crime page, that La Eme had issued an edict that members
inside get off meth. Or face the consequences.

I gave Cranky an approving tap. *At least you'll be motivated.*
Next, a red file. Why not?

MOVERN DINKLE, 39. African-American. Eleven months, parole viola-
tion. ARP [alcohol related parole violation].
Subject released 1.27.08 at approximately 1100. Returned to facility 1.27.08
1700.

Free for six hours? My fucking hero! Something about luck that bad
gives a man hope. I couldn't explain it, but I already liked him.

Subj. prev. served 97 months of 144 mo. sentence. Five counts, involuntary
manslaughter . . .

Five? A large coffee stain blotted the rest of that page, up to:

. . . completed alcohol education program.

Paper-clipped to the file was a small scissored-out newspaper article: "Under the influence, Mr. Dinkle had a head-on collision with a van full of Cub Scouts. Four scouts were killed on impact. The scoutmaster, a high school track star, Iraq vet, Sunday school teacher and dad-to-be, was left a quadriplegic before succumbing to viral pneumonia. . . ."

ARRESTING OFFICER: At approximately 1300 perp cited for urinating in muffin case at Starbucks.

"Starbucks? Movern, listen!" I leaned down close so Movern's mug shot could hear me better. "Nobody drinks at Starbucks. What do they teach you in alcohol education, anyway?"

No doubt, with my help and expertise in the field, the next time Movern got sprung, he might make it twenty-four hours before getting sloppy drunk and exposing himself again.

The next file was written by hand on carbon paper. Quaint.

INMATE D-7664C2 ROSCOE BENTON, 55. African-American.

Beside Roscoe's prints and mug shot was a more recent photo, from the *Bay Guardian*. "Inmate Doing Life Helps Others Live." The young Roscoe glared like Miles Davis and the old one, down thirty-six years, stared back like Buddha, if Buddha'd been a lanky, locked-down brother with a soul patch, a beanie and eyes that did not take the same things seriously that you did. I stared into those eyes for a minute and felt mysteriously better before reading how Benton got life for killing a plainclothes cop while holding up a dry cleaner. The officer, in fact, was there *to pick up his uniform.*

What are the odds?

It didn't seem fair. How was Roscoe supposed to know the man was police if his blues were on a hanger?

Roscoe, I learned, founded the Black Guerilla Fighters prison gang—the BGF—at San Quentin in 1971 with George Jackson, his fellow Panther. The late George Jackson. Then something happened. In his forties, Roscoe'd earned a GED, BA and masters in comparative religion. Now he ran inmate meditation classes and the "Living with Hep C and HIV Inside" support group. I placed my hand on the file like it had the power to heal. I squeezed my eyes shut and tried not to hear my own tiny whisper.

"I need some fucking help, Roscoe!"

I myself had dodged AIDS, back in my needle jockey days, but not that hepatitis C. My liver had gone New Media, fully viral, and not even nine months of rage-inducing interferon shots in my belly fat had been able to cure it. The stuff powered the viral load to under twenty million, down from a bloated seventy mil but still high enough for my liver to function as efficiently as a paperweight.

Hep C was like having an old-fashioned anarchist's bomb implanted in your liver, waiting for the fuse to burn down and blow you into full-blown cirrhosis, then over the finish line to cancer. You just never knew how long the fuse was. But nothing, as any hepatotoxicologist could tell you, got it burning faster than alcohol. This made for some regret over my decision to start drinking again. Then again, I was getting tired of organ number three. Time for fresh meat!

I'd found the box of wine under the sink when I looked for something to poison the roaches. If they even were roaches. From the sound they made skittering in the cabinets they might have been small farm animals.

I hadn't planned on drinking the stuff. I'd just wanted to see how it tasted. Wine in a box! Gallo Sparkling Rosé. It tickled the palate like melted-down hospital gloves and Splenda. The stuff probably would have killed the roaches, or at least disoriented them, but I didn't want to share. There weren't any glasses, so I drank straight from the box, out of a plastic pop-up nozzle that scratched the inside of my mouth.

I had, I confess, a checkered history of oral hygiene. I fell out of the habit of dental visits when I had a habit of heroin. After Tina left, I developed a burning urge for root canal, generally followed by a prescription or two for Percocet. (Or one of its loving cousins.)

Now my gums bled when I said hello. Which meant easy access for any strain of hell canker that the last social climber who slurped out of the nozzle had left there. Along with fatigue and brain fog, the hypotenuse of the hep C triangle was a compromised immune system. "Compromised" meant that if someone had a fever in Cleveland, I caught the flu. But I wouldn't die from it. And even if I did, I'd probably be too confused and logy to notice.

I tamped the blood off my lip with the back of my wrist. Took another sip, careful not to spill any on the files, which I had sworn to give back to the warden. I couldn't tell if I had a buzz or a migraine and stared out the window of my trailer, trying to decide.

I rarely drank, even before the five years I stopped taking anything that affected me "from the neck up." And now I remembered why. Alcohol never made me happy—it just made unhappiness embarrassing and sloppy. For a professional drug addict, alcohol was what you got when you couldn't get what you needed. And you always needed something.

Now I remembered.

By the time I mustered the inner strength to stop reminiscing and go back to the files, it had gotten dark. My lower back was killing me, and my thighs itched where they had been in contact with whatever was soaking out of the seat cushions. I didn't know where the light switches were. My lighter, for the cigarettes I no longer didn't smoke, was in the pocket of a jacket I couldn't see. It was amazing how fast things went to shit when you started drinking, after not drinking. An hour and a half after I'd begun to slurp from the wine carton, I was already reeling in the dark, cracking my knuckles and scratching myself, gripped by cellular torment and trembling at the notion of trying to make it through the next five minutes. What I really wanted to do was pour the sparkling rosé up my nose to kill the stench.

Instead, I began to sneeze. I tried to believe this was from trailer spores, but I knew it was the Windexy Gallo.

Just retasting the stuff resulted in testicle pain. I clamped a hand over my mouth and nostrils, but I could not escape the smell. I tried to imagine the man who'd occupied the trailer before me. I unclamped my nostrils and shut my eyes. Breathing in, I visualized a molting pile of sweat socks and frayed underpants. In the middle of that sat a naked fat man eating rotten meat out of a greasy paper bag, jerking off over the August '99 *Shaved Amputeens*. I could almost hear his sock-swaddled meat slapping off the face of the one-armed cover girl. *I know what you want, you little stump slut!*

No doubt the snailback's previous occupant had pleasured himself precisely where I was sitting. As if to back up my wine-box vision, the banquette gave a phantom squish.

One can only do so much damage in an alcoholic stupor (assuming one is not behind the wheel, like Movern). But, as hard as I tried, I never made it to unconscious. I bolted out of the breakfast nook, swiping the air in front of my face like it was trying to bite me. It took a while to find the door. I fumbled with the locks, convinced a cockroach had flown into my mouth.

Spitting and gasping, I forced the lock and hurled myself in the dirt beside the trailer, where I threw up with quiet dignity.

I remained in the dark, wondering if my performance had been recorded by the video cameras mounted on the prison walls. Perhaps they could run it for my drug awareness class, a sterling example of the kind of life they too could enjoy. The possibilities were endless.

The lights were on in the double-wide opposite the fence. This was what Rincin had called the "love shack." A conjugal visit in progress.

I stood up and saw a face in the double-wide's porthole window and dropped to the ground again.

It couldn't be.

When I raised my head again, the face was gone.

It . . . could . . . not . . . be. . . .

But it was.

The door opened and I saw Tina, naked. She stepped out of the trailer and lit a cigarette. Even if I couldn't completely make out her face, her naked sway gave her away. Tina liked to light up naked outside at night. And she swayed when she smoked. The tip of what I knew by the waft of stale menthol was one of her bought-by-the-carton Newports glowed brighter orange. The sight was so familiar, I forgot I was watching and not remembering. Somebody else lurched out the door. In the moonlight I saw the shaved head, steroid bulk and full-body ink of a man who doesn't work for Prudential Life Insurance. When the bullet-headed freak lunged for my ex-wife, I stood back up. Like I could do anything. Like I had to. If anybody could take care of herself it was Tina.

Tina turned, almost casually, and the moon went behind a cloud. In the darkness I could see the orange chaser of her lit cigarette moving fast. Then sparks. Then nothing. Just a muffled *"FUCK"* as the man staggered backward, clutching his arm, and stepped back into the open trailer. Tina stopped just long enough in the doorway to light another Newport and show me her body in silhouette.

We'd been married a year before I could finally decipher her body. Her left shoulder angled slightly higher than her right, due to a drunken stepfather's penchant for swinging her around by her right arm when she was a baby. She claimed her earliest memory was flying sideways through the air, the centrifugal force so huge the stepfather got nosebleeds and her little-girl shoulder lurched permanently out of its socket. This lent her, from the front, the aspect of someone permanently shrugging off the world. It was subtle. But in profile, her skewed shoulders created the unsettling impression that whichever breast was further away was bigger. She once explained that this had to do with her tit lacuna and cited some law of Newton's. Whatever the physics involved, Tina knew how to dress and assemble herself so as to look even. But naked, splashed with moonlight, the dipping collarbone and slightly off-kilter tits were on spectacular display. Even in the dark her nipples looked ironic. She couldn't be anybody else. As though I'd been spun around myself, I rolled onto my back on the whirling earth and stared up at the impossibility of everything.

The first night we spent together, Tina had sworn that she would quit smoking when she could hold a cigarette under her breasts. Ten years later, she was still smoking. The gift was genetic, she said. Her grandmother grew up on a tobacco farm. *"Nobody ever talks about white sharecroppers."* Her natal mother, who also picked the leaf as a child, was the model for the "Mud Flap Girl," the kneeling, long-haired, buxom female silhouette made popular by long-haul truckers in the seventies. As far as I knew, she never collected royalties. I doubted it was true, but then, what was?

I lifted my head, considered some kind of rescue—at least a call for help—then let myself fall back in the dirt. What did I owe some muscle-bound con? He married her. If she maimed him with a lit cigarette, it was his fault. I hoped she didn't blind him.

Now I was glad I was drunk—or at least sweating and nauseated, a close second. Without the antifreeze, the import of what I'd just seen would have had me chewing mud. But Gallo in cardboard could only do so much. The stars loomed like threats. The stone walls hummed. Why had I agreed to go to prison and pass myself off as sober and capable? Was it to forget that Tina had left me? That maybe I'd made her leave?

I didn't know how love worked. But I was an expert on how it didn't. Once the worst thing I could imagine happening happened, the only thing that could take my mind off it was something worse. Sometimes I had to really work to find it. But now I was lucky.

I obsessed about what she and the wide white felon were doing on their conjugal visit. I had a peep-show booth lodged in my brain, and I could not stop feeding it quarters. What were the odds my newly ex wife would marry an incarcerated muscle-head and have trailer sex in a San Quentin love hut—the very night I arrived in San Quentin?

One thing about Tina, she always had good stories.

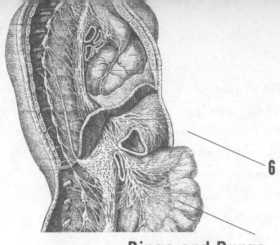

6

Binge and Purge

The night before she left, after nine years of marriage, Tina told me she was four months abstinent.

My first thought was, *If you're abstinent, then who have I been having sex with?*

I'd just rolled off her, pleased with myself. The memory inspired a retro-cringe.

She said it wasn't that kind of abstinence. She meant abstinent— as in not binging, not purging. She confessed that she'd been making herself throw up since she was nine. I didn't have to ask why. Her father was still doing time. I was all set to say something supportive when she announced that, working her Overeaters Anonymous program, she'd realized that I was the reason she'd been throwing up. My moods made me hard to tolerate; she had to get numb. I wasn't doing well in the private investigation business. Worse, I took my work home with me. "How can I be the reason," I asked, more defensive than I'd intended, "if you started when you were nine?"

"You're the reason I'm doing it now. You're so angry."

I had hurt a man in traffic that same evening. I ran him off the road, yanked him out of his car and threw him against the side of his baby-blue Honda Civic. He'd given me the finger trying to get on the 110 South. I hadn't expected anybody so large to be in a Civic. Hadn't expected him to come out swinging. I'm not a great fighter, but I know enough to jab somebody in the neck before they get a punch off. Lucky for me he crumbled. That happens if you crunch a windpipe. Which I did, with a smile on my face, so quickly that I was able to get down on my knees and act like I'd stopped to help a man having a heart attack. Before taking his license I whispered that I'd find out where he lived and eat his heart if he tried to do anything. Then I got back in the Lincoln, where Tina waited with a face like a death mask, and we drove home in silence.

"So what am I supposed to do?" I asked when she made her announcement.

"Deal with your anger. Or don't. What I have to do is leave."

"Why?"

"I just told you. If I don't stop I'm going to burn out my esophagus and die. The stomach acid has already eaten half my teeth. I don't want our child doing it."

"What child?"

"If we ever have one. Just thinking about it makes me want to die. That I could do damage . . ."

I was shaken at my cluelessness. How could I have been living and sleeping with her and not known? It was like finding out you were a collaborator—when you didn't know there was a war going on. Tina had had a lifetime of pain and weirdness before our paths crossed, before she hooked up with me—but the thought that I caused this was too much. I wanted to rip my own heart out with a claw hammer.

I'd held her while she cried. It was windy outside, and I stared out the window of our bedroom at a walnut tree that seemed to be wagging its finger at me. Tina recovered fast, as if she'd never even cried. She eyed me almost sympathetically.

"So you're bulimic," I said, hearing the words come out wrong before I even uttered them, "and that's my fault?"

"Until you can get rid of the buttons, you have to get rid of the button pushers."

"Is that why you got rid of Marvin?"

When she gets angry, Tina's cheekbones sharpen up like Faye Dunaway's, but more feral. I watched her transformation from grief to rage, in awe of her peculiar beauty. Even with cleavage so unapologetically asymmetric, she *had* something. I breathed in and out, determined not to react, to just listen.

"Collateral damage. You want to know how many obese women roll over on their babies every year? It's a disease, honey. Like alcoholism. Just as fatal to the people around it as to the people who have it."

"I guess I'm lucky to be alive," I said, attempting to inject some humor into the dialogue. "I like it when you roll on top of me."

She placed her hand on my cheek. "Why couldn't you have been this sweet before now?"

"You know me," I said, "the sweet gene's recessive."

"That's okay," she said. "Marvin was sweet. And he was also a repellent idiot."

"Well, you showed him!"

Marvin, for the record, was her husband. The one I found dead after she'd Dranoed his Lucky Charms. I was the homicide detective. We were in a small town outside Pittsburgh. I threw the tainted cereal in the garbage disposal before the evidence techs showed up. They called it an accident. It was not what Hollywood would call a "meet cute."

I knew she was guilty. But I fell in love on the spot. Insane as it sounds, the situation made me feel protective and safe at the same time. But now she had reached the point where she had to puke herself numb just to tolerate my company. Being born a Jew, guilt stuck to me like lint to Velcro. On top of which, it now looked like the real reason we split was so she could free herself up for a studly convict. An Aryan brother she could bone in a prison pump-wagon . . . Love!

I'm leaving out some details. I had a sixteen-year-old daughter from an earlier marriage. Lola wrote occasionally to ask for money in her mother's handwriting. She lived with my ex-wife, Donna, who did public relations for pharmaceutical firms. I was in love with her samples. Donna caught me riffling her bags for painkillers on our honeymoon. That was before I cleaned up. I talked my way out of it by saying I needed a Kleenex. Then she caught me again, stealing sample packs she was supposed to distribute to doctors. After that she changed the locks, had the marriage annulled and still refers to me as "He who shall not be mentioned." I'd made my peace with that. Though it was hard knowing I didn't see my child as often as I wanted to. Her thinking was, "Just because you love her doesn't mean it's good for her to have you around." Needless to say, things didn't get better once Tina came on the scene.

Until our divorce—my second—Tina and I lived together in a small house in Los Angeles. I'd made a semi-decent living dividing my time between being a private investigation professional and a consultant on television shows and movies that wanted to sound "authentic." There was, like Rincin said, a whole industry of ex–law enforcement, ex-criminal, ex-gangbanger, ex-anybody-who'd-lived-on-either-side-of-"crime" types who were able to capitalize on the entertainment industry's appetite. A studio executive would pay money just to sit in a room with somebody who once sat in a room with somebody real. I was a double threat, an erstwhile cop and erstwhile dope fiend. It happens. Not to brag.

To my surprise, there was an investigation into the handling of

Marvin's death. They decided that I had tainted the crime scene. I confessed, pleading narcotic inebriation. I was "self-medicating." I was remanded to a twenty-eight-day spin-dry: hospital withdrawal followed by rehabilitation. The real problem was that I fell in love with the perp.

Why forget the good times?

I was still in touch with the doctor. He was an "addictionologist."

While in rehab, I caught him fixing in the handicap restroom. Which, at four in the morning, he'd forgotten to lock. Afterward, it was our little secret. I didn't extort much: painkiller scripts whenever I wanted them, sleeping pills as needed for Tina and progesterone for her cat, who had feline osteoporosis. I later found out the hormones were for her. After hoarking the calcium out of her system for thirty years, Tina had the bone density of an eighty-year-old. But she was still hot.

My future ex-wife murdered her husband, but me bitch-slapping a Sunday driver was too much. She told me that she'd learned to vomit soundlessly, without even needing a finger. *Look, Ma, no hands!* She could have given bulimia lessons. But she thought I had the problem. We used to fight about my negativity. My catastrophizing. Tina would tell me what her father used to say: "Worrying is just praying for what you don't want." I'd dread things so much I actually made them happen. And all this time, she had a secret.

Eating disorders are brutal. But let me confess: beyond knowing how much pain she'd caused herself, what hurt was knowing how much she had concealed from me all those years. Any cop could tell you—if a perp was hiding one thing, they were usually hiding something else. Or maybe it was just my ego. When things got bad she gave me an Al-Anon schedule. "Codependent" sounded like something you wore with an adult diaper.

As Tina was leaving, I grabbed her arm at the door and spun her around. Tried to pull her close, feeling weirdly like John Huston cuddling his daughter-slash-granddaughter after shooting her sister-slash-mother at the end of *Chinatown*.

I pleaded with her. "Just tell me, before you go."

"Tell you what?"

"If I made you come," I blurted, serving up a slice of my secure and romantic inner life.

"Buckets," she replied, "and now you're making me go."

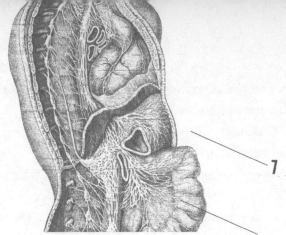

Fucking on the Edge of a Cliff

Once you saw how your wife killed her husband, you lived with a certain back-of-the-head hum. You knew what could happen. You'd seen the evidence. But still . . . You didn't think about it. Not all the time. Just on special occasions.

Had anyone asked, I'd have explained it like this: If you were fucking a beautiful woman on the edge of a cliff, would you look down the whole time? Or would you look at her? By definition, if a woman is beautiful enough for you to fuck on a cliff, she's beautiful enough to make you forget to look down. Except when she wants to remind you how close you are to the edge. What would happen if you rolled off. Or she pushed you. The problem was, the beverage I'd found under the snailback sink had skewed my perception. Not one part of me believed Tina could have feelings for the inked-up skeek I'd glimpsed out the trailer window. Wedding an ALS brother seemed like a long way around just to make a point. But maybe there was something else going on. What did I know? The box wine left me pining for something more full-bodied, like Listerine.

I did not even realize I had passed out until I picked the leech off my eye. It turned out to be a waterlogged Band-Aid. I tried to sit up and banged my head off the bottom of the trailer. Facedown, if the variety of floor-flora stuck to my mouth was any indication. I'd thrown my jacket on and found the lighter. I flicked it, illuminating a pit of moldering magazines, old-fashioned brogans and dental molds, metal cabinet drawers stuffed with carbon and typewritten files. A flaky *Time*, wedged under a brick, showed J. Edgar Hoover on the cover, staring down Commies. Underneath the *Time*, a rusted Red Cross lockbox jutted from the ranks of other antiquated but seemingly freshly dumped items.

I didn't care about the garbage. I remembered the first time I arrested a junkie Dumpster-diving behind a hospital. He had four bottles of expired resperidine, an antipsychotic favored by families who needed to shut up senile screamers, and a gross of tongue depressors jammed in his army jacket. Hospitals could be gold mines. (The only better pickings, drugwise, were the trans cans outside airport customs. Many an international traveler with pills in their pockets lost their nerve and dumped them. But the airport janitorial staff had the trash can action sewn up.)

Grabbing two Red Cross boxes, I headed back inside and scraped the side of my face on something that turned out to be the missing light switch. Thus illuminated, I pulled down the bed. I spread a *San Francisco Chronicle* on top and dumped the boxes on it. Then I re-hit the files. I needed to distract myself from rerunning the Tina highlight reel in my head. Thankfully, the love-hut lights had gone off. If I focused, I could pretend I'd hallucinated everything and go back to work.

DAVID "DAVEY" ZELOVSKY
Caucasian, 21 months for parole violation. Weapons possession.

This one was bad. This one was *wrong*.

The face just stopped above a nubby bottom lip, which barely covered his gums and left his teeth exposed, giving him the look of some feral hillbilly insect.

Five years, domestic abuse.

In a blackout, Davey jammed his wife's hand in a waffle iron in front of his twin son and daughter. Under occupation, he had put "catalogue model." He had also had a small part in a soap opera. He was that kind of handsome.

Reading details of his "weapons possession," I marveled at the immense variety of fate. Davey's crime: he botched a suicide attempt and got violated for having a gun. Hard luck. But the law's the law. That's what's wrong with it.

A sketchy psych eval shed no light but added details.

Perp's wife had taken their twins with instructions to relatives not to tell him where she went. He visited her father to plead. Father-in-law rejected him.

I studied his sideshow grill. The drama of the nongifted criminal. Can't stalk her if you can't find her, huh, buddy? Who hasn't been *there*?

Perp purchased gun from Mex. (unknown) gardener who kept the .45 in a case of hose nozzles. Seepage may have warped the barrel.

"Andre Duquesne" was handwritten on the next file. Possibly the classiest name I had ever heard. But the file was empty.

BERNARD ROOKS, 21, African-American, possession with intent to distribute 100 grams of crack cocaine, 15 years.

As opposed to the one and a half he'd have gotten if it had been powder. The photo showed a burly, sad-faced youngster. There was a CDC memo paper-clipped to the file cover. Now that the U.S. Sentencing Commission had issued retroactive sentence reductions to balance the crack versus powder disparity, offenders could appeal to the original judge who sentenced them. Nothing said willingness to a sentencing board more than completion of a drug program. Someone else with real motivation.

And finally, his file yellow—"Fritz Ullman, 97, Caucasian" stared up from his mug shot with the same mocking, outraged eyes, trim mustache, and Jack Lemmon–esque features I'd seen the day I stumbled onto Sun Myung, Clarence Thomas, and Jerry Falwell on my bedroom dresser. The face had another five decades on it. The hair was white. Gone was the smart SS uniform.

The original file was almost completely blacked out, leaving only a few "of"s and "the"s. Along with this information-free document, someone had inserted a single folded sheet of legal paper. I unfolded it and read, in pencil:

> *Arrested for attempted vehicular manslaughter, perp convicted of hit-and-run and fleeing the scene of an accident. Three years.*

. . . More intriguing, a search turned up evidence of "lab equipment—probably drug-related—in his van, which belonged to the Department of Animal Control. A public defender got the van search thrown out, so "Fritz" did not have narcotic charges added to his vehicular manslaughter. . . . A supplemental psych eval revealed:

> *Inmate C-899923 exhibited delusional behavior, possibly methamphetamine psychosis. (The court noted defendant's "angry affect" and "explosive outbursts.") Inmate claims to be "Dr. Josef Mingola" (sic) a "high-ranking SS man and 'race scientist,'" and demanded to speak with the head of the FDA.*

. . . Asked if he heard voices, perp responded in affirmative—"but none
of them speak German." Believed to be highly intelligent. Prescribed
Depakote for bipolar disorder, Effexor for depression, a senior multivitamin
supplement, and a weekly enema.

Maybe he was enjoying himself.

I sat back to ponder my quarry.

He seemed, on the face of it, an unremarkable old man. Who was possibly a mass murderer. He wanted the world to know. Which was either a strong indication he was lying or evidence of his veracity. Assuming he wasn't simply schizophrenic, possessed of a peculiar sense of humor or paid to impersonate Josef Mengele . . . My guess was poor Number Four: senility.

Zell wanted my opinion. I needed the work. I didn't tell him the dirty little secret: the least-effective method of finding out if someone over eighty is telling the truth is by talking to them. Everybody told stories. But, unlike younger liars, sometimes our senior prevaricators did not know they were telling them.

I'd known Alzheimer's victims who took on the identity of TV characters and historical figures. They forgot details of their own past but superimposed, like senior idiot savants, facts and details from the lives of others. Back in Upper Marilyn, the small town where I cut my cop teeth, I'd rounded up two wandering octogenarian men who thought they were famous, one Lincoln and one Lee Marvin, and a great-grandmother who claimed to be Lady Bird Johnson and kept taking her clothes off in mall fountains. If you were old enough, nobody called you a liar. They didn't even call you lewd. They'd say you had dementia and blame the behavior on declining faculties.

I heard a talk show doctor say they'd found an Alzheimer's gene. If Mengele had it, he was hanging tough. Or maybe he'd spotted the senility gene in full bloom in his own ninety-seven-year-old DNA and somehow deleted it, breeding it off the Master Race roster altogether.

To me it was pretty clear: Mengele was demented. But he didn't have dementia.

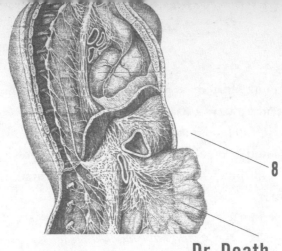

8

Dr. Death

In a perfect world, I would have gone back to the crime scene. (The hit-and-run in L.A., not the death camp in Poland.) Interviewed witnesses. Unearthed the facts about the woman he ran down, seen if perpetrator and perpetrated had a connection; found out where Ullman/Mengele lived and who he'd spoken to after the bumper party.

Any crackpot with TiVo, Google skills or a library card could dig enough death-camp trivia to pass himself off as an OG from Auschwitz.

I dove into the rest of Zell's Mengele info pack. A dozen smudged carbon copies detailed the doctor's varied and disturbing intended-to-save-the-race procedures. At Auschwitz-Birkenau he had sewn twins together. He reasoned that if they were fused, the resulting megatwin could do twice the work for half the feed. He experimented with hydrochloric acid douches and scrotal radiation by way of low-cost sterilization.

Zell had unearthed a handful of Mengele diary pages. The random sample I picked reeked with stilted self-regard. Mengele wrote like a man giving himself medals. *"There are two ways to save the race: by eliminating lesser races, and enhancing the superior one. This is the duty of a scientist of the Reich—a duty that I, Mengele, fulfilled!"*

Searching for ways to build a better Aryan, he got big into eyeball transplants: replacing lowly brown eyes with blue ones. Unable to connect optic nerves, the doctor left his victims bleeding and blind.

Of his eye transplant techniques: *"Had the wretches been able to see, for but one moment, they would have thanked me for the glorious cerulean blue gracing their faces."* He tried dyes after that, but the end result was that they remained brown and blind.

These notes went on and on. His biggest passion was twins. Twins held the secrets of fertility and genetic control. His next loves, after *die Zwillinge*, were the deformed, and then dwarves. In his capacity as Selektor, he procured specimens from the trains. Had the Nazis won, this was the Mengele who would appear on his own stamp: the dapper *Hauptsturmführer* standing on the ramp, deciding who lives and who dies. Tallies varied. Mengele ordered the death of either a hundred thousand or half a million. The horror, for the Jews, was that it was Jews who were being exterminated. The rest of the world—including America—was more or less okay with it. Until the very end. In 1939, the United States turned away the SS *Louisa*, full of Jewish refugees. President Roosevelt was concerned about the political fallout from helping Jews. (*"New Deal—not Jew Deal!"*) The ship returned to Hamburg, where passengers were promptly dispatched to the camps. The State Department set up a Jewish settlement in Sosua, in the Dominican Republic. The DR's president, Trujillo, believed his countrymen were too black. He wanted some whites to move in and improve the racial ratio. I wouldn't say I was a history buff, but I was an insomniac, and Nazis were a perennial fave on the late-night Discovery, History, Biography and Military Channel menu. Arcane details just lodge in the mind.

The possible presence of the man himself infused the facts (selections, experiments, perfumed scarves) with new juice. I kept reading.

His twin prose degenerated from grandiose to floral: "With what luster doth the womb of a single woman bloom forth with two, three, four identical flowers?" Other times he sounded like a transcribed infomercial: "My goal was to increase the good, eliminate the bad. Say yes to Nordic Splendor. Say no to cripples, Jews, Gypsies, harelips and the rest of the germs that pollute the gene pool!"

Much of Mengele's "fertility research" work involved genital dissection. He claimed more accurate results when the girls were alive. His ongoing, secondary experiment was the study of how much pain a human could endure. Lessons learned on vermin could extend the life of the Master Race. Why experiment on mice?

I needed air. I stuck my head out of the reeking trailer door. Pretended it wasn't to scope out my ex-wife—frolicking in the night with her incarcerated hubby—or find out if I'd hallucinated her in the first place. What did that make me—succumbing to personal torments, evidence of the violation of an entire people spread out before me like tarot cards?

I stood outside for a vacant minute. It must have been three-something A.M. There were no signs of life in the conjugal unit. Tower-mounted vapor lights softened the forbidding architecture beyond. Their glow lent the retro buildings an insect-buzzy, Edward Hopper feel. I couldn't tell if the buzzing came from insects or the electric fence. (I remembered how, when the camps were being liberated, some inmates were so delirious with happiness they ran for the fences. Their first act of freedom was electrocuting themselves.)

You hear a lot about prison rape on cable, but I didn't hear any screams. Just the ones inside my own head.

I urinated—on my shoe, as it turned out—and thought how Mengele had spent his glory years in proximity to high-voltage fences, guards in uniforms, gun towers and inmates. And here he was again. One big difference from his Auschwitz time was that the Nazis kept their prisoners weak. In concentration camps, it was the powerful against the dying. In American prisons, the prisoners were bodybuilders. So it was, more often, the powerful against the buff.

As I zipped and went back inside, I still felt a little ashamed that I'd been too weak to just dive into the files and dig straight for the doctor. It was a shame I was used to. I had wanted, very badly, to find out from the file that this was a hoax, in which case I could be in and out of state supervision in record time. I had not wanted to admit the reality of what I'd signed on for. Whoever and whatever my quarry was, I was going to have to deal with it. And I didn't *like* dealing with things. Which, oddly enough, was a good quality for a cop. But otherwise it made for a life based on avoidance. Every plan I'd ever had was shaped by whatever I wanted to avoid. *The Fear-Driven Life.* I did not have much in common with Pastor Rick Warren. Paranoia, for me, was not so much evidence of mental illness as a side effect of heightened consciousness.

Running a game on criminals is a bad idea under any circumstances. But doing it here made me so nervous I couldn't make myself read about Mengele. I'd had to wait until his file showed up in my hands.

I stress-yawned and turned around. Now all possibility of avoidance was over. Back inside, I sat down at the sticky table and started making big X's next to passages I thought I could use. In one interview, Mengele's son announced that his father felt cheated out of the honor his work deserved. Dad believed this was because he didn't use anesthesia. Small minds could not understand that this was science, not sadism. They did not know the miracles he'd discovered, the results he longed to give to the world. But the world, comprised as it was of very, very small minds, would rather suffer and die of deadly diseases than admit that Mengele had found the cure. Rolf, who grew up to be a political moderate, claimed to be horrified at his father's deeds.

According to Mengele the younger, his father had lugged three boxes of lab notes from country to country. Dad's last letter to his son, one sentence long, captures his loathsome tone-perfect note of self-pity and narcissism: "History has chosen me to judge, so as not to have to judge itself."

There was more: Mengele suffered from a rare medical condition. Rare for a human, at least. Because of his lifelong habit of chewing his mustache, hair had settled in his intestines and created a growth called a bezoar. He underwent an operation in 1957, in Caracas, to remove what was, when you stripped away the niceties, a hairball.

Where did Zell get this stuff?

I felt unnamable emotions, staring at pictures of naked Gypsy twins: teenage girls whose hands had been amputated and resewn onto each other's arms, holding lollipops. Shock and pain had blasted all expression off their faces. Then I realized what I was really staring at: their two thick bushes. I nearly passed out hating myself. Who was Herr Doktor kidding? Why were they naked?

Zell's notes said that Mengele (with the help of IG Farben) had used the skin of actual women to create the seductive and easy-to-clean coating for his "field hygienic love partner." A love doll. The specs were included. "Borghilda is flexible, elastic, anthropomorphic and capable of doing everything your special girl or devoted *mutti* waiting at home can do." She bore the same full pubic forest as the unlucky Gypsies. But blond.

"We Germans wanted mature women. Real women. We did not want them to shave their nether hair. We did not infantilize. Unlike American men, who want their women with outsized breasts and hairless vaginas, so they can have Mommy on top and a little girl on the bottom. I made my Rhinemaiden, Borghilda, as nature intended." I read on: He submerged babies in freezing water. He played Schubert's *Serenade* on the violin.

He found a Hungarian pianist to accompany him and trained a guard dog to attack her when she hit a wrong note.

The music room was in Building Ten, beside the lab. What was harder to believe: that he transplanted hands? That he actually thought transplanted hands would be able to play the violin? Or that he had all the hands he wanted?

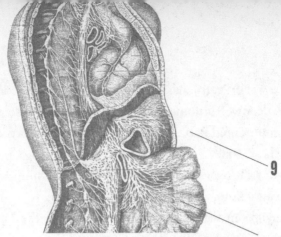

9

The Red Cross Is There

Feh! Huuu-ACCCHHH!

I lurched awake, soggy, gripped by some kind of death sneeze. Mengele's documents lay scattered all around me. Somehow, during the night, a team of surgeons had entered the trailer and relocated a badly diseased, radioactive hog rectum in the cranial pouch where my brain used to be. From the coating on my tongue, it was clear they'd gone in through my mouth, shoved the thing north through my sinuses, then wedged it behind my own nonblue eyeballs. I could feel it, propped atop my cerebral cortex like roadkill on a stick. I wanted to stick my tongue out as far as it would go and bite it off. *Mengele dreams.*

I needed to hit something. I slapped myself in the head, then banged the top of an antique Red Cross box. To my surprise the top popped open, revealing a pristine batch of metal syringes and sealed vials inside. I grabbed a vial and made out the logo—BAYER, 1919. Back then heroin was legal. Aspirin was the newfangled, not-to-be-trusted devil drug. More Discovery Channel fallout.

I squinted for a better view of the label, and there it was, in curlicued Calvin Coolidge–era lettering: MORPHINE SULPHATE.

I was surprised by the jolt this gave me. Just seeing the words. Until that moment I had not been thinking about drugs. But as soon as I saw them, *I needed them*. And not just because of the hangover. I'd had hangovers before. But nothing, nothing like the throbbing pork butt of death left in my head by the boxed wine and mildew party. I visualized my brain spooned from the skull, floating in a jar, bloodied with fresh tattoos of the woman I once thought was going to save me, naked. Every time I moved, my lungs were punctured by the flattened soup can of grief.

But this is the point: the pain was endurable until I saw the pain-killer. That's called being an addict. The craving began on sight. Out of nowhere, an option no normal person would have entertained suddenly made sense. (Normal people don't look at abandoned, half-drunk cocktails in airport bars and think about knocking them back when no one's watching, either. But ask an alkie if he's ever had the urge. (If he answers no, he's not an alkie.) If the feelings were bad enough, and there was a way to obliterate them, it was obliterate first and deal with the consequences later. If you're a junkie, obliteration is your job. You have a hole to fill. Not to mention self-pity and ball-clenching fear to try to relieve.

I heard the distant crunch of tires on gravel. Then I watched my hands assemble the screw-in syringe like they'd gone to nursing school in 1910. Just holding the paraphernalia had my bowels churning. My fingers left grimy prints on the glass tube. I slid it into the metal holder like a shell into a cannon, worked the needle into the slot at the business end. And stared, amazed, at the rig in my hands.

The gravel crunch was getting closer.

I hadn't shot up in years, but my veins were still tough as bark. Breathing slowly, I coaxed a blood register into the old-timey works. Still not sure I was going to do it. And then *BANG-BANG-BANG!*

"Anybody home?"

Without thinking, I pressed the plunger. *Shit!*

"Just getting up!" I croaked.

It took a few seconds for the century-old morphine to detonate. The rush came on with fluid warmth. Like my heart had wet itself.

By reflex, I broke down the rig and stashed the Red Cross box under the sink, where it looked like it belonged.

Rincin knocked again. "C'mon, bub, what are you doing in there?"

My voice came from far away.

"Gimme a minute there, Officer."

"Sure thing. Mind if I pop in?"

"Wait!"

I forgot that to law enforcement, "Wait!" means *"Come on in!"* I watched the knob turn with dim fascination. Had I also forgotten to lock up after last night's festivities? Did Rincin have a key? Panic flared and subsided. The drug was working. But I knew that the pain it killed would be resurrected later. Then that thought disappeared with a hiss and the door banged open. Rincin walked in and winked. Maybe I was just feeling the effects of the preservatives.

"I'm early," said my new friend. "Gotta use the head. Two sips of joe and I gotta whiz so bad I could cry." He paddled past me, jumped into the telephone booth toilet and grunted. "Hey, buddy? You forget?"

Something bounced off my chest. I groped for it and felt the crinkly plastic wrapping. The piss-test cup. My stomach plummeted.

I turned on the kitchen tap. Unleashed a dribble of fluid that tasted flammable. A drop got in my eye and stung, but I kept gulping. Rincin talked from the bathroom. The CO hadn't bothered to close the door. His stream banked loudly off the metal bowl and he groaned like the lead in a bad porno, "Oh yeah, oh God . . . Fuck that is good. That is so fucking go-o-o-d."

I tried not to think what the Model T morphine might do to my liver. I'd shot up shoe polish once and survived. What was one more toxic drop in Love Canal?

Rincin sighed loudly from the bathroom. "Man, oh Manische-witz!" His high-impact relief ebbed to a mere torrent. He stepped out of the toilet, hitching his balls in his khaki uniform. "You dressed, new fish? 'Cause we got to drop your UA off and get you to class."

"How long does it take?"

"How long does what take?"

"The piss test."

"Why, you worried?"

"Not unless they made beer illegal!"

This seemed like a Regular Guy thing to say. Rincin just stared.

"You got the Parkinson's?" he asked, zipping up. "You got kind of a palsy thing going on."

"Shaky night."

"I used to get those. Boy howdy! Then I cut out the bug juice."

I lurched by him to the bathroom. The black spore that grew on the mirror gave me a face full of blackheads. It was like being four-teen again, except for a haunted yellow tinge in the eye and the deep grooves that time and clean living had carved in both cheeks like initials in a tree. My daughter referred to the parentheses around my mouth as "puppet lines."

At her age, I had no idea that one day I'd be sweating over clean pee. Getting busted at Quentin, on day one as drug counselor, there were bound to be repercussions.

"Idiot," I hissed at my smeary image.

"Talkin' to me, Rupert?" Rincin's voice came through more baf-fled than indignant.

"Singing," I replied, before picking up the pee cup and peeling off the plastic.

Shaking off a century of dust, the post-rush opiate buzz kicked in.

I was ready to give up, but in a moment of devil-may-care ingenuity, I spotted the little urine lakes Rincin left on the floor. Happily, the linoleum had deep divots, deep enough to scoop up a sample cup's worth of pee.

"Okay, let's do this," I said, trying to smile as I came out of the bathroom

"Do what?" Rincin eyed my sample with something less than ardor. "Less you're planning on goin' Gandhi and drinkin' that, I'd put a lid on."

"Gandhi drank his pee?"

"Secret of successful nonviolence," Rincin called over his shoulder. "Make sure you got piss breath when you negotiate, and sit close."

He stepped out of the trailer while I weaved behind him.

"Did you just make that up?" I asked.

"History major. Humboldt Junior College. Speaking of which, you don't think the Holocaust happened, do you?"

"Jury's out." I shrugged with no hesitation whatsoever. "What makes you ask?"

"Oh, I don't know." Rincin unlocked the driver's side of a Crown Vic with CDC on the door. "I work with a guy, I like to know where he stands."

"Who doesn't?" I said inanely.

I wasn't sure if our little exchange was cause for alarm. Or not. Just a couple of regular guys talking Holocaust. By now, the opiate blast had passed. Paranoia was back. Now cut with disorientation and dry mouth. I wondered vaguely if impaired judgment could be carried by bacteria.

"Get in." Rincin slammed his door shut and patted the passenger seat. "You're riding bitch."

A trio of prisoners with rakes on their shoulders stepped by and peered in the car. Rincin shooed them away and squawked into his walkie-talkie. "The package is on the way. Ten-four."

"The package?" The sensation of being set up damped the last embers of euphoria.

Rincin winked. "You gotta package, don'tcha? I bet you're a regular Johnny Hog-leg."

I didn't take the bait. If that's what it was. Instead, I looked at orange jumpsuits circling the yard in clumps of two or three. Half the convicts looked like they'd gotten off at the wrong bus stop. The other half looked like they'd kill the bus driver for a dime bag of anything. A few of them—pink cheeked and well scrubbed—gave off the impression that maybe they'd eaten their mothers.

"Apologies for the hog-leg remark." Rincin lowered his head, genuinely contrite. "The quality of people around here, it lowers the real estate, conversationally speaking."

He pulled into a dirt lot and sat with his hands clamped around the steering wheel. He stared straight ahead, at the back of North Block, the condemned unit.

"Around here the Devil wins more than he loses, you know what I mean?"

"Not exactly."

"Let me rephrase, Your Honor. Think there's such a thing as a good prisoner?"

"You'd know better than me. Do *you* think people can change?"

"Oh, they can change all right. I've seen 'em. The problem is, they keep changing into the same thing." This came with a full frontal of the CO's perma-grin. "Have there been some famous convicts beloved by the outside? Sure. Hell, they're the ones they make movies about. But the guards always know."

"My favorite's *Birdman of Alcatraz*."

"You have got to be kidding!"

For the first time since we'd met Rincin slid off his shades, revealing pale green eyes of such startling luminosity I wondered if he wore the reflectors to keep from showing them to the lifers. "No knock on

Burt Lancaster," he went on. "The character's real name was Robert Stroud. Stroud was at Leavenworth when my great-uncle was a hack. Forget the birds. All he did was write letters to kids, describin' stuff he wanted to do to 'em."

"The Birdman of Alcatraz was a pedophile?"

"That part didn't make it into the movie."

"Thanks for clearing that up," I said. "I was going to try and find a guy serving life to babysit my child, but not now. I owe you."

Shades back on, Rincin shook his grin. "You're a funny guy. All I'm sayin' is, you walk out that class today, you might think you met some of the greatest guys in the world. Just remember, they didn't get here for skipping jury duty."

"Point taken," I said, eyeing the low building just off the yard where a group of cons had already gathered. "You know why I'm here?"

"Do-gooder, I guess." He made sure I saw him spit. "Looks like your students are waiting. Maybe one of 'em brought you an apple."

He came around the passenger side and grabbed my arm as I got out. "I'm pulling your leg about the apple. They bring you any kind of foodstuff, I was you, I'd check it for feces and ground glass."

"Will do," I said, freaked by the mention of ground glass. Was Rincin letting me know he knew how my second wife did her first husband? That he knew everything about me? Did everybody know everything? Was anything accidental?

Fuck.

"We're in the old furniture factory. We got a li'l conference room in the corner."

That's when it hit me: I had made no preparations for class. I'd become so obsessed with Mengele, I had no idea what I was going to say.

Mister Addiction Specialist.

We passed the open garage of the fire department. A tiny muscleman in big black boots stood on the front bumper of a midsixties

Mack fire truck. He leaned over the hood, one hand inside a chamois mitten. He polished slowly, in tight, soft circles, as if stroking an ass he couldn't get enough of.

"Showtime!" Rincin hissed. "Bring snacks!"

I turned, but Rincin wasn't talking to me. He was talking to the fireman. The mini-Schwarzenegger saw me looking and grinned, giving the air in front of him a few mocking little mitten-spanks.

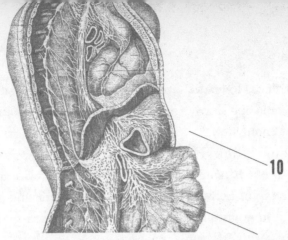

10

Two-Hundred-Year-Old Billy Idol

Except for Davey, the guy with the half face, I didn't recognize any of my students. Mengele wasn't there. I hadn't considered that possibility. With him absent, I'd have to fake competence for no other reason than to keep anybody from finding out I was incompetent. If I had to pick a place to get drug sloppy, where better than state prison, after showing up to teach the inmates how they, too, could live the dream of being clean and sober?

I was two seconds from full spinout. A door across the room banged open. A wheelchair rolled in, bearing a slender, slightly hunched old man with glowing skin, perfectly parted peroxide-blond hair, matching brows and mustache. He looked like a two-hundred-year-old Billy Idol. I couldn't take my eyes off him. But it didn't seem smart to show it. Pushing him was Movern Dinkle. The free-for-six-hours guy.

Movern's plump baby cheeks rested on top of a string-bean neck and shoulders, as if his face needed to go on a diet and his body needed nutrition shakes. I nodded at him and he nodded back. Not friendly, not unfriendly. A professional.

The chairs were arranged in a circle. I grabbed the one up front, next to Davey, whose remaining face appeared strangely chipper. He'd shaved his head.

"Hey, I'm Manny," I said, extending a hand. "You must be Davey."

"How'd you know? My good looks?"

Despite the fact that the bottom of his face was blown off, enough of Davey's mouth had been put back to let him talk normally, if a little Tom Brokaw–ishly He must have been a handsome kid. Above the catastrophe of scars and skin grafts, where his chin would have been, he owned all-American features. Reconstructive surgery had not re-constructed him so much as rounded him off. Up close, I spotted fresh scarring. The last surgeon to have a go at him had tried to fix his lower lip so it covered his gums. But the graft had not quite adhered, and the skin of his lip on one side flapped a little, like peeling wallpaper. He was basically lipless.

I let go of his hand and turned to the other side, where a wiry African-American, middle-aged with old-school processed hair, slunk in his chair, arms crossed over his chest. "Do not even," he said. "I hear you a cop."

My surprise must have shown.

"Ain't no secrets up in this bitch. First thing you be learnin' is how to spot a UC. Right after how to keep your tush cherry and get your womens in here to visit."

This was going well! A paunchy white Rasta in wire-rims dropped in the chair opposite. "No disrespect, but ease the fuck up, Andre."

My neighbor was instantly upright. "Motherfucker, I tol' you, I don't go by Andre. I go by Reverend D."

So Rev. D was the mysterious empty file, Andre Duquesne. The skull of the white kid ragging him sprouted broccoli dreads. A few of them stuck straight up at least half a foot. I didn't recognize him from the files. One more way the warden was letting me know he cared.

The white Rasta covered his mouth with his hand and giggled. "I'm Jimmy. I didn't have dreads in my mug shot. You're a friendly policeman, huh?"

"Was."

"You ever shoot anybody?"

People always ask that. I always answer, "I don't remember."

This bought me a few more seconds to study my new friends. I recognized Roscoe, the Panther turned philosopher. Older by far than everybody else, Roscoe's salt-and-pepper goatee graced a lean, serene and unsmiling face. He might have been a black yogi. A solid *ése* to my left sat tapping his fingers on the desk, chewing his lip. If it was Cranky, the Mexican trying to kick crank, he'd obviously been lifting weights. Maybe that's what Mexican speed freaks did up here. His blue shirt was open over a wife beater, revealing the top half of the Virgin of Guadalupe.

"I was gonna go around the room, talk a bit about who I am, all that crap, but what the hell, let's start with the shooting thing. It's an honest question, and I wanna give you an honest answer."

I glanced at Mengele again. I couldn't resist. Underneath the Rutger Hauer–circa–*Blade Runner* hair, his anthracite eyes were piercing and suspicious, the taut skin over his face weirdly smooth. But what really creeped me was the globe of muscle in his bicep. Not large so much as tight. I thought of the switch-handed twins and wondered, *Can a surgeon transplant his own arms?* Obviously not both on the same day. No way to check for a scar unless he wore a sleeveless T-shirt. But from his ironed, buttoned-to-the-top shirt and buffed fingernails, he didn't seem like the sleeveless type.

Our eyes met and I thought I could see what was in Mengele's head: *Dance, little Jew-monkey, dance.* The race scientist had written his PhD thesis on how to tell Jews from the folds in their ears. Ten seconds with the calipers over a lobe, no need to check for foreskin. He must have been the life of the party.

Tearing my gaze away, I met all the eyes in the room, then went into full blurt: "Toward the end, it was no big deal to come to with blood on my shirt or a clump of hair stuck to my dashboard. Little things . . ."

"If thass what the man call little, Movern gonna shit his drawers he hear what's *big*." Movern laughed at his own joke, but no one else did.

"Movern, mouth," Rincin said from his post in the corner. He jingled change in his pocket and popped his gum. I realized that I was no longer high. I also realized that I'd stopped talking. But I was a professional: I knew how to make a flake-out look like a pause.

"One time I came to with a couple of clips missing from my nine. This time there was a puddle of blood in the backseat. But I never got that knock on the door."

I looked at each of them individually, wrinkling my forehead to signify depth.

"You know the knock I'm talking about. Like when you drive home in a blackout and next day your bumper's bashed in, and there's a flattened high heel trailing panty-hose stuck to the front tire. You're scared and hungover, so what do you do? What do you think you do? You stick the hoopty in the garage or steal some license plates from a Denny's parking lot to switch up. Hit-and-run's a total loser crime," I said, looking at Mengele, who was in there for it. "Scum of the earth. But some people have no self-control."

What was I doing, trying to flush out a mass murderer with vehicular manslaughter insults? I rubbed a hand over my stubble and winced at the eau de trailer on my fingers. I didn't need a shower as much as I needed steam-cleaned.

Roscoe, who thus far had said nothing, regarded me mildly. Nonjudgmental. Which only made me feel more judged.

"Why am I standing here telling you the demented shit I did?"

" 'Cause you demented?" offered Andre, AKA Reverend D.

Half-faced Davey glared. I noticed that his eyelashes were thick as Bambi's, as if in compensation for the tragedy underneath.

"Guys," I soldiered on, "demented is five flights up from where I was. Sometimes it still is, but that's a different story. . . ."

Silence. Neurosis didn't play well in the penitentiary.

Cranky piped up. "C'mon, homes, you a cop." Every few words he had to stop to grind his teeth and chew his lips. "Cops are your gang." *Chew. Grind.* "They ain't gonna snitch you off." *Grind, grind.* "And it ain't like you gonna kick the door down and cuff your own white ass." *Grind, grind. Chew chew grind chew.*

"You sound kinda pissed, Cranky. So, you ever had a problem with drugs?"

"My name is Ernesto, mang. I'm Cranky with my family."

"Me too," I said, "and the Lexapro didn't help. I still hated them. Shit's supposed to be an antidepressant. But how can you not be depressed when the shit turns your dick into a doorbell?"

Shut the fuck up! I screamed at myself in my head, then wondered if I'd been talking out loud.

It didn't matter, at least not to Cranky. He'd twisted around to make sure Rincin was listening, giving me the chance to admire the fresh "XIII" inked on the back of his head. For the thirteenth letter of the alphabet. M. *La eMe.* Which had just made doing meth a beat-down offense.

"Here's the deal," I said, my voice low so it would sound serious, if not entirely coherent. "You want to stop using, you have to find out why you started. You got to look at all the shit you got high 'cause you couldn't face. . . ."

Then the white Rasta threw down a challenge. "This is just me, Jimmy, talkin'. But I didn't get high for none of that, man. I got high 'cause I liked fuckin' two hos all night with that chronic and cocaine. And some Hennessy for when the sun come up."

"That's what I'm talkin' about," echoed Reverend D. " 'Cept you should lose the alcohol, son. Womens you can enjoy till you eighty, but you gots to lose the booze. Man, I had this little Chinese girl once—"

"Hold that thought, Rev." I knew I had to chime back in or lose the semblance of control. "What I wanna know, Jimmy, is how you felt when you *couldn't* get the hos or the drugs." This sounded school-marmy, even to me. I was so ill prepared I was defaulting to Nancy Reagan. I had spent all my time on Mengele. But if anybody asked about real-skin Nazi sex dolls, I'd be all over it.

Jimmy threw his arms out and mugged for the class. "Look at this face. Dude, I always got the hos and the drugs. And when I'm on the outs, I intend to get 'em again."

"Then why are you here?"

"Why you think? Addiction education's gonna look real sweet to the parole board."

"When's your hearing?"

"Twenty twenty-nine."

"Well, don't rush into anything. . . ."

Somebody let out a loud, whistling fart, after which Mengele stirred in his wheelchair and declared, "That's the first intelligent thing I've heard all day."

This got some chuckles.

"A fart joke, thank you." I pretended to be offended. Superior. Try-ing for a tone I imagined a vain man might find infuriating to his van-ity. "What took you down, Mr. Burgermeister? Bratwurst and beer?"

Mengele stiffened. "It's doctor."

"Of course it is," I said. "And does the doctor have anything in his past that makes him want to blank himself out when he remembers it?"

Mengele met my gaze steadily. "I have done nothing regrettable. I have had regrettable things done to me."

"Such as?"

It was just him and me now. The room disappeared. I hadn't ex-pected to get this lovey-dovey until later on.

"I have been denied recognition for my achievements! I have made extreme sacrifices."

"That sounds like resentment to me. You got a lot of resentments? No need to be ashamed. We all do. Problem is, resentment is like taking poison and hoping somebody else dies."

"You do not know what you are talking about." He slammed a hand down on the arm of his wheelchair, startling Movern, who'd begun to doze.

Rincin eased away from the door. One hand on his billy club. "Easy now, Doc."

Mengele regarded him with a raised peroxide eyebrow, upper lip curled in a sneer of infinite weariness. His accent was comprehensible—once I stopped trying to pick metal shards out of my ear. "No one in this country has a concept of how to run a prison. Do you know the resources you are wasting? The benefits being squandered?"

"Hey, I get full dental," Rincin chimed in. "Even paid for my daughters' braces."

Mengele tensed. "Not those kind of benefits."

"See that," Movern said, shaking his head. "Rincin always playing them head games."

Mengele ignored this and kept going, his voice a guttural mixture of pleading and contempt. He did not so much *speak* words as stab them and push them elegantly off of a balcony. "Your people can still be saved."

"See that? The doc know. He talkin' about the Rapture."

Mengele laughed, a hacking half note followed by a cough. "The Rapture is nothing but a terrorist plot, run by Christ instead of bin Laden. And who is Jesus Christ? The illegitimate son of a Jewish bitch."

"Hey now," said Reverend D, trying to get a word in.

Cranky clamped his hands on his head like he was trying to keep his thoughts from flying out. "Wait wait wait! You ever see that

Twilight Zone episode, where the aliens come down with their special book, *To Serve Man*, and all the earthlings are, like, scrambling their asses to get on that spaceship, except for this one dude, who comes running up behind them, and he's screaming, 'Turn around, fools! It's a cookbook! *To Serve Man*!' It's like the messiah was a cannibal. Oh, shit! Maybe people think they've being Raptured up, and it turns out they're just, like, *ingredients. . . .*"

Movern shook his wide head back and forth, jiggling his Gary Coleman jowls. "Ho no! Ho *no*! Ho *no no no no no*!" He crossed his arms over his pigeon chest. "That is the second time my Lord been slandered in this room."

"Ha! I've read about your Lord in Revelation." Mengele chewed his mustache and scoffed gleefully. "When the warrior Jesus returns, he will invite the righteous to heaven. He will hurl nonbelievers into *a lake of fire.*"

"Tell it!" said the reverend, slapping skin with Roscoe, the professorial ex-Panther, who smiled mildly under his wire-rims. "Old man throwin' down theory now. He goin' all Christopher Hitchens."

Mengele basked in the attention, his mustache gleaming from his own spittle. "What is the Rapture but divine genocide? The only difference between Jesus and Hitler is that Hitler showed up. And instead of a fiery lake we had the ovens."

"Dude," Jimmy the white Rasta interrupted, "no disrespect, but Jesus had way better hair."

Mengele angled a glance at Jimmy. The white Rasta blanched. He didn't need to know who the old man was to be scared. The old war criminal's eyes radiated something they did not have words for. You could only feel it. And *yet . . .*

Beholding Mengele, I was struck less by the banality of evil than its chattiness. Mengele had thoughts he thought were important. He talked like he was standing behind a podium—or at a train siding, lecturing a captive audience.

"The Third Reich is a story the new Germans don't want to dwell on. Because it happened. The Rapture is a story the evangelicals do nothing but dwell on. Because they *want* it to happen. It's not the Final Solution, it's the grand finale. How will six million compare to that holocaust in Revelations? *'Those who reject him will be cast into a lake of fire.' Mein Gott!* Every man, woman and baby on earth who has not accepted the Good News—hurled into boiling flames. Buddhist monks, adorable unbaptized babies, Jew, Muslim, Hindu, Baha'i . . . All of them." Mengele's eyes bored into me. "You call it End Times. I call it waiting for Jesus to turn on the ovens. Hitler read the Bible, too."

"Uh-uh. No!" Movern wagged his finger. "Now you see that? That right there? *That* is over the motherfuckin' line."

Roscoe shrugged. "The so-called righteous always think they know who deserves to die."

"Wrong," said Mengele. "It was *science*. For the select to prevail, millions must be delivered into flames."

"Been there, done that, huh?" I said. I thought maybe an attaboy would get me on his good side.

"Pops just hurtin' 'cause he ain't at the control," said Reverend D.

Mengele seethed. "I am not your pops."

"Come on now," said the reverend. He flashed a smile that showed off his gold dental work. "You sure you never tapped no *schwarze* ass, a sophisticate like you?"

Cranky snapped his fingers, sucking blood out of his chapped lips. "Oh shit, Rev's punkin' an old man."

Even Rincin stopped jingling his keys to watch.

Mengele, if he was Mengele, sat perfectly still, eyes closed to vicious slits. The way he didn't move made you think he was dangerous in some unspeakable old-man way.

Prison was full-up with gangsters and hit men. But these were all small-timers. The real mass practitioners were the ones who ran the country. I had a feeling the old German was thinking the same thing.

Mengele allowed himself a sour smirk—just enough to show he knew he didn't belong.

"Let's stick to the topic," I said. "We're supposed to be talking about addiction. So let's break it down. In the beginning, a man takes a drug; in the end, the drug takes the man. . . ."

I'd sat through enough twelve-step meetings—either as participant or on the job—to march out my share of lifesaving clichés. For a cop with a quota, church basements full of recovering junkies and drunks were great places to fish for parole violators. A lot of substance abusers washed onto the shores of sobriety with outstanding warrants. Though it was an article of faith in law enforcement that AA and NA members didn't snitch on each other. (SLA—Sex and Love Anonymous—was apparently a different story. My experience with them was limited.)

"One's too many, a thousand's not enough," I said, marching out a sobriety chestnut. Somehow it was deeply gratifying when Movern and the reverend nodded.

I followed that up with another slogan. "We're only as sick as our secrets. What we need to do now is start talking about the stuff that we got loaded to keep from thinking about." I pointed to the man who might be Mengele. "Does that make any sense, Mr.—I'm sorry, what was your name again? Mr. Mongol?"

He seethed. "It is actually *doctor.* Dr. Mengele!"

"Dr. Mendel?"

"*Mengele!* Are you mentally ill?"

"Excuse me. Doctor, what did drugs do for you? What did they do *to* you? You were a . . . what again?"

He glared and I smiled innocently.

A part of me screamed, *Turn him in! Call the authorities!* Another part wanted to fuck with him. Not for personal pleasure. For *my race.* But taunting was candy-ass, considering the crime. Left to my own devices, I lacked the moral clarity to do anything more enlightened than rub his face in the dirt, make him scream *"I'm a filthy little Nazi!"* six million times.

Mengele nibbled his lip hair. I could see his conflict: driven to sell himself, but knowing he was casting his master race pearls before San Quentin swine. He stared in a middle distance, as if watching a movie of himself played by Tom Cruise. "Many many years ago, I was an important man. Doing important research. In some very unpleasant conditions. There were times when it was up to me whether this one lived or that one died."

"So you were in the service industry?" I asked him.

"Sound like he a shot caller," the reverend said.

"I was a *scientist.*"

"Where did you work?"

"At the end, a little town in Poland."

I waited, eyes wide with polite interest.

"Auschwitz."

Hearing the word in real life, in real time, as opposed to in some documentary, set my nerves quivering. La Eme maintained KOS rules for members of the ALS. Kill on sight. What standing orders did Jews have for encounters with Nazi death camp doctors?

"I made the selections. I was the only one who could do my job sober. Others fell apart. They drank. Took morphine and cocaine and engaged in the most debauched sexual practices with prisoners. They had no discipline. The SS demands discipline."

"You were in the SS?" I asked the way you might ask a neighbor if he'd ever been to Cleveland. I lifted my arm, tapped under my armpit. "Did you get the tattoo?"

I broke it down for the others. "When you get into the SS, they put your blood type under your arm."

Jimmy giggled into his hand. "Dude, you know a little too much about this Nazi shit."

"I'm a bit of a buff," I admitted.

"Don't take no *buff*," Cranky snorted. "Gang ink is gang ink."

"And look," said Mengele, "what happened to you for having your affiliation on your neck. No, I did not get the tattoo."

Davey pounded his fist on the desk. "Stop interrupting my doctor!"

"Stop interrupting *your* doctor?"

Mengele beamed. "Thank you, David." The failed suicide lowered his eyes and batted his Bambi lashes.

"You should have seen David when I met him, right, David?"

Davey managed a no-lip smile. "Ah yooshed to tawk lak ish."

"You must be very proud of your progress," I said with no sincerity whatsoever. "But wait . . . you did surgery inside?"

Mengele was happy to accept my awe.

"Doc," said Rincin from his corner, tapping the side of his nose again, "remember there's rats in the rafters."

Mengele sat back in his chair, imperious. Pleased with himself. "Mengele is not afraid of rats."

He eyed Davey critically, extending a hand in front of him as though already carving and replacing. "I am going to make him Nordic."

I gulped. "Plastic surgery?"

"Transplant," Mengele replied almost dreamily, talking more to himself than me. "The things you can do, when you have a *supply.* . . ."

"Right on, Kaiser!" Rasta Jimmy pumped his arm. "My man was a soldier. Hey, we all do shit we wanna forget. Without the drugs and alcohol, there ain't nothin' to hold the memories down. Shit backs up like a clogged toilet. Same with them old 'nam dogs, sleepin' under bridges. Dudes back from Iraq and that there Afghanee-stan."

"Look at you two," I said. "From different worlds, but connecting."

Cranky craned his speed-kinked neck sideways and up, like he was trying to bite the ceiling. "Don't be goin' all after-school special, homes. Next thing you'll be tellin' us *addiction is color-blind* and all that bullshit."

"You sound like you've heard it all before."

"Prison ministry come in here, talkin' about how if we pray, Jesus gonna take the craving away."

"Uh-*huh*!" Reverend D nodded his head. "That is *exactly* what he can do. I know, 'cause he help me. Prison ministries is a growth industry, too."

Cranky wiped sweat off his face. "Jesus wanted to help, he coulda come down from heaven and got me an eight ball when I was hurtin'."

Movern, who'd been resting a plump cheek on his reedy arms, suddenly revived. "I done stuff I cain't admit to my own self. On the real. There's thoughts in my head I ain't even *let* my ass think."

Mengele reentered the conversation. "None of you understand. You *can*not understand!" His smirk was superior but mirthless.

"Hey, guten Tag there, buddy!" Jimmy the Rasta tried to high-five Mengele, who ignored him. "Like, I don't know what kinda gnarly shit you were involved in—but, dude, we've all pulled some skeevy shit, be-fucking-lieve me. But, like, there's nothin' you can't unload, man. You won't have to work so hard to forget once you give it up."

Mengele gripped his peroxide, sunken-templed head. "I do not want to forget anything. I want to *remember*. But I feel memories slipping away." The words came out burnished, as if he'd said them thousands of times, millions. In front of mirrors when there were mirrors; in his head when there was nothing but a bed and a chair. "I have records, notebooks. Experiments down to the last decimal. In sixty-seven years, I have never let my data out of my sight. Now I want the world to know. I have found a way to end congenital diseases, to vaccinate against speech defects, so many things." His face tensed, neck tendons taut as watch springs. I braced myself for his shouting. Instead, his voice dropped to a whisper, a faint lament. "I have a contribution to make to the world. To the *children* . . ."

"Children!" I repeated. *"Awww!"*

This time his sneer was perfunctory. But his eyes looked like they could squirt battery acid. "They called me a monster, but my experiments can save generations of youngsters! There was a *reason* I removed their organs."

What made the performance more arresting was that it didn't *look* like a performance. He might have been standing in a Santiago slum, shilling for the Christian Children's Fund with Sally Struthers, in bloated but sincere post–*All in the Family* feed-the-hungry mode. He spoke like he believed.

"Holly-cost never happened," Jimmy stated flatly. "It's like the moon shot. Fake. 'Cept, for the Holly-cost, somebody staged them pictures of bodies and smokestacks. Then voi-fuckin'-la, Jews get their own country and more aid than we give to all other countries combined. Read your David Black. Maybe a few thousand died. Tops. And guess what? They probably killed themselves. Just like a Gypsy twisting a baby's arm so it'll get more money from saps."

I snuck a glance at Rincin. He gazed approvingly at the dreadlocked David Duke.

"People," I said, "let's stick to addiction. Not history."

"One and the same, youngster." Roscoe again. He spoke without rancor. "See, the white man made addiction part of the black man's history. Part of his own, too. Addiction to genocide, addiction to destroying the planet. Addiction to fear. Addiction—"

"We get it, Roscoe, that's—"

"Oh, he just warming up," Movern let me know.

"No thing," Roscoe continued. "I just read, in *Harper's Magazine*, where they laid the blueprint of a slave ship on the middle passage on top of one for the supermax at Pelican Bay. It's almost a match! What's that tell us? Break it down, addiction ain't nothing but slavery—and this country was founded by slavery. That's why I say this country is addicted to addiction."

Movern did his faux call-and-response again. "Tell it, Roscoe. Country strung out on bein' strung out."

"Shut the fuck up," said Cranky.

"Or what, bitch?"

Movern smiled. This was just casual chat to them.

"Fellas." I banged the table. "You can listen to your own bullshit anytime—right now you listen to me!"

The room went quiet. Even Rincin stiffened. If I'd gone too far, there was nothing for it now but to keep going. "Definition of a junkie," I blurted, "guy who steals your wallet, then spends an hour helping you find it . . ."

I felt their eyes on me. Realized I was sweating profusely. I wiped my face on my sleeve. Sensed my mouth going in one direction and my brain in another. The fluorescents hissed like they knew something. Somewhere far away a metal door clanked shut. Suddenly it was hard to breathe as though someone were pressed against me, preventing my lungs from expanding. Like a hundred naked strangers were crammed in a room made for twenty-five. It was a panic attack—except what had me panicked had happened already, and not to me. When vapor wafted from the floor vents, it drifted so slowly that there was time to watch. The mist carpeted the room, floated lazily upward. People tried to climb on top of one another, to escape the rising poison. That's why bodies were found in a pile.

I blinked into the faces before me, realizing that Mengele had probably made the drug, and made it psychoactive or psychedelic. The last thing I remember saying was, "Who's got a success story?"

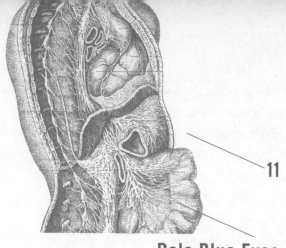

11

Pale Blue Eyes

When I came around my lips were moving and I was still standing in front of the Quentin drug class. I seemed to have had some kind of out-of-body experience—or else I'd blacked out and just kept talking. As mentioned, the lush high from my first aid kit had died before I made it from the trailer to Rincin's Crown Vic. But I kept getting residual mini-rushes. Random pleasure shudders. Who knew what kind of residual opiate drift was still in store? Stuff happens when you're your own guinea pig. While I would never experiment on another human, I had a history of injecting bad science projects in my arm.

"Here's the thing," I heard myself announcing. "They want you to be loaded!"

Cranky rolled his eyes. "Who the fuck are they?"

"That's the question, isn't it!"

My insight was met with the blank stares it deserved. Rincin slowly inflated and deflated his purple bubble gum. Who was I kidding?

I badly needed to take a stress pee, but Rincin managed not to catch my plaintive gaze. He blew a bubble gum bubble the size of a baby's head. Suddenly the door flew open and the bubble burst in his face. A white bodybuilder, flashing ALS ink from neck to leg irons, shouldered into the room as though facing a strong wind. Two guards in full riot gear trailed him, which accounted for the into-the-wind illusion. The guards had flipped down their protective masks, hiding their faces with SRP. Shit-resistant Plexiglas. No one breathed.

"Bernstein," Movern whispered.

"That's Bernstein?"

The white-power Jew was a ferociously cut five-nine, with a taut, owlish face framed by black-rimmed state eyeglasses and a perfectly maintained goatee. He might have been pale five years ago. Now even the skin on top of his shaved head shone a translucent, creamy gray. (One benefit of not seeing the sun for years at a stretch was all the UV rays a prisoner avoided—though the baby-smooth faces of aging serial killers could be disconcerting.)

Bernstein turned immediately in my direction, and Movern muttered behind his hand, "Kill you later, son."

The white guard shot me a concerned expression but the black one scowled. Both tightened their grip on his belly chain. The black steel ran through a metal ring over Bernstein's beef-slab stomach and dangled between his legs, locking to his leg-irons.

Gritting his teeth, Bernstein strained into every step. If you squinted, it was almost like he was pulling the guards in an invisible chariot. Like Charlton Heston in *Ben-Hur,* if Heston had played a horse.

Here was someone I did not want to piss off: a chained Semite so savage he had managed to maul his way to the top of a gang that existed to exterminate him—along with all his relatives. To my relief, Bernstein began to scan the room. He stopped when he saw Mengele and offered a heartfelt *"Sieg Heil!"* Then, dragging the helmeted guards behind like vassals, he clanked closer. It was like watching some kind of medieval pageant.

"Doctor, it's an honor. I have come a long way to shake your hand." Bernstein spoke with formal solemnity. "All Aryan honors!"

That voice! I knew it! I'd heard that voice the night before, barking at my naked ex outside the conjugal visit trailer. So this was the white power fireplug Tina'd shacked up with? I still couldn't swallow the idea. Tina was not one of those women who liked bad boys, let alone violent bad boys. She had, on more than one occasion, explained her thinking on the subject: only good girls found so-called bad boys interesting, and then only because they were getting back at Daddy. In her opinion, the worst fucks in the world were bikers. All the beer. So why would she wed the white power shot-caller now hijacking my bogus drug class?

Bernstein lowered his shaved head and proffered his twin sleeves of white power tattoos to Mengele. He might have been like a diplomat showing his credentials: runic SS symbols; lightning bolts; the 88 (8 for "H," the eighth letter of the alphabet, as in *H*eil *H*itler); the Nordic warrior with his fair-haired woman, in his and hers horned Viking helmets . . . A Moon Pie–sized swastika graced the top of his right forearm; a matching Star of David showed proudly in the same spot on the left.

Chaos makes sense in chaos.

Mengele pressed his thin lips together. Silent. Bernstein raised his eyes and, gulping back emotion, paid almost cringe-worthy respect. "You, my liege, are the last living link." He pointed two fingers upward, squeezing his eyebrows together to highlight the Gothic number "14" inked on his forehead. "The fourteen words," he intoned, and proceeded to recite the pledge. "We must secure the existence of our people and a future for white children."

I might have appreciated the theater of it, if not for the fact that my ex-wife had been late-night intermission. I tried to see what Tina saw in the guy. Sure, Bernstein was a level-four white supremacist overlord whose "KOS" status brought Crips and Bloods together in rare unity. But a Jew was a Jew. Somewhere, between the sword-wielding Valkyrie riding his chest and the flaming 666 stamped on his back, his heart pumped blood that flowed all the way back to the shtetl. I knew Tina had a taste for the sons of Moses, but I still couldn't picture her with Chaim McSwastika.

Mengele studied his acolyte for a minute. Finally he spoke. "The first thing we did to vermin in the camps was shave their heads. The next was give them a tattoo. We branded them. And do you know why? No? Well let me tell you. *Because they were slaves.* And yet, you brand yourself *voluntarily.*" The old man's chest rose and fell with mounting indignation. "And you dare to call yourself a Nazi? You dare to wear the swastika of the Reich?"

Bernstein's expression was a pressure cooker of rage and cool.

Rincin had filled me in on the white power Jew. Four years ago, somebody'd slipped him a trazor and handcuff key on the way to the shower. He poked a hole in one correction officer's aorta and skewered another one's Adam's apple. Since then he'd spent twenty-three hours a day locked down in the adjustment center. The *Hole.* Even if he was never going to get out, he had major juice, enough to buy a walk from isolation to the furniture factory classroom.

Whatever it cost Bernstein, he hadn't shelled it out to be disrespected. Not by a bottle-blond ninety-seven-year-old. He canted his head toward a guard, who reached over and slid Bernstein's black glasses up his nose for him. He shifted his neutral gaze at Mengele, breathing slowly. Then he suddenly lunged forward in his chains, yanking the guard on the left to his knees. "You're in my house, old man!"

Mengele's tongue darted over his lip hair. In the flesh he was less Jack Lemmon than James Mason with a fetid taste in his mouth. He observed the Nazi Jew the way he might have observed an albino dwarf. In genetic work, anomaly was always valuable. "My life's work," declared Mengele, "is to preserve the race!"

"I *am* the race now, motherfucker!" Bernstein shouted as the guards lifted him off the floor. "You're just a has-been with a scalpel!"

Two more guards grabbed Bernstein's Popeye arms. Rincin ambled over and, almost affectionately, Tasered him. Enduring the voltage, Bernstein kept his jaw clamped, fists clenched, so it looked like Rincin was not so much shocking as *recharging* him. Then he cracked Bernstein across the shin, bringing him to one knee.

I was watching a generational struggle. The far-flung fallout of history. Aryan Jew Godzilla versus King Kong Master Race Doctor. It should have been on pay-per-view.

"I smell dead sauerkraut," Bernstein hissed, spitting the words out like razor blades. *"I run this prison!"*

For the first time Mengele smiled, revealing the gapped teeth I'd seen in the photo on my dresser. "You run it? Good! Then get me a key." He nibbled his mustache, delighted, as Bernstein, now horizontal, thrashed like a fresh-caught marlin. Mengele swept his arm at the hooting inmates. His smile did not so much light up the room as make you want to back out of it slowly. "Get us all keys! The purpose of the race is to multiply. If you have found a way to propagate with the hind end of your brothers, please show me. As a scientist, I would like to study baby-making sodomy."

"Probably like to watch too," Cranky said.

Rincin buckled a muzzle over Bernstein's mouth like you would a rabid pit bull. He emitted snarled curses as a paramedic in tinted shades rushed in to jam a syringe in his neck. By the time they got the living legend out the door, he was slack faced, unconscious. I was almost jealous.

Rincin rattled into his walkie-talkie and a young, jug-eared guard ran in. He spun Mengele's wheelchair around.

Mengele chose this moment to zero in. "Enjoying yourself, Mr. Rupert?"

"I'm gonna need an incident statement," Rincin sighed to the ancient but surprisingly wiry and vigorous German. "You know I have to write this up."

"You want a statement? Fine." Mengele did everything but click his heels. Face forward, shoulders back, he recited, "I am a eugenics scientist. I believed in improvement of the species, preserved and strengthened by applied biology."

Roscoe raised his hand and waved the CO quiet. "Applied biology?" His calm demeanor belied the intensity of his words. "I look that up in a German dictionary, am I gonna see 'genocide'?"

Mengele's gaze went feral. "If a man finds vermin in his family home and poisons them, does that makes him a mass murderer—or a man who takes care of his family?"

"There it is," said Roscoe. "Definition of political power—who gets to decide who the vermin is—"

"Oh no!" the reverend interrupted. "Huh-uh!" He shook his head vigorously. "Now you gettin' into what they call a real slippery slope. And I ain't talkin' 'bout no lubed-up Chinese ho. I'm talkin' 'bout this here. 'Cause this here is some sick-cookie *bullshit*!"

Mengele shrugged. "Maybe so, but the Nazis didn't bake it."

"Fuck that s'posed to mean?" Now it was Cranky's turn to be agitated. "I thought we were supposed to be talkin' how to not get high."

Mengele dismissed him. "You wouldn't have to get high if you weren't ignorant. Your whole country is ignorant."

"We back to the cookie thing?" The reverend was not impressed. "You kinda jumpin' around. I'm thinkin' maybe you got a little bit o' that Altzheiny, Doc. You know what I'm sayin'? Maybe you're sick. What I hear, Hitler was a one-balled lunatic."

Before I could jump in and play peacemaker, Mengele slammed

his hand on his armrest. "I will ignore the uniball remark. But lunatic? No. I want you to listen to something."

Mengele closed his eyes and raised his arm like an orchestra conductor waving an invisible baton. "'It is better for all the world, if instead of waiting to execute degenerate offspring for crime, society can prevent those who are manifestly unfit from continuing their kind.'" He dropped the invisible baton and opened his eyes, cupping his hand over his heart to convey his deep emotion.

"No disrespect," said the reverend, "but that shit is sick."

"That shit," hissed Mengele, "is from an opinion by your Supreme Court justice Oliver Wendell Holmes in nineteen twenty-seven. *Bell versus Buck*. The issue was forced sterilization. Should I keep going?"

"Oh, please do," I said.

"'The principle that sustains compulsory vaccination is broad enough to cover cutting the fallopian tubes.' Is this not poetry?"

"Don't rhyme," said Jimmy.

Mengele ignored him. "Where do you think Hitler got the idea that subhumans—drunks, syphilitics, Jews—were a disease, to be wiped out?"

Mengele raised himself up. Decades of perceived wrong infused his words with self-righteous fury, almost enough to hide the self-pity underneath. "You inspired us! America inspired us. Don't you see! I *wanted* to go to Auschwitz. To conduct research, and preserve the race, in a new way. At Auschwitz, we were able to destroy more than a million germs!"

Mengele's face colored with passion. "Eugenics was the future." He tried to smile. "It was the—how do you say?—like your Silicon Valley in the nineties . . ."

Jimmy the white Rasta covered his mouth and giggled. "Right on. Eugenics was the go-go industry."

"Go-go? Like go-go boots." Reverend D rubbed himself through his pants. "Chicks in go-go boots! The reverend get his bone on just *sayin'* that. No lie!"

"Okay," I said. "We're getting a little far afield. We're here to talk about why we use drugs and alcohol. What do they do for you? What did they do to you? We all need to get used to talking about stuff that a lot of us got loaded to keep from thinking about. One way to do that is to see everybody's secrets are the same. . . ."

"Shit be shit," said Movern sleepily.

"That's deep," said Reverend D.

I couldn't tell if they were mocking or on board. Or killing time until somebody flashed the "throw the junkie Jew over a chair and ride him like Amtrak" sign. I was swimming in quicksand here. I had to sound like I had a game plan.

Mengele squeezed his hands into fists. With what looked like enormous effort, he willed himself calm and, to my surprise, apologized to his detractors. "I am sorry," he said. "I have waited a long time for the chance to give my testimony. Please . . ."

He sounded wistful. Almost human. I could think of no more unsavory notion: a human Mengele.

"If you want the world to know who you are," I asked him, "why didn't you just announce it?"

"Ah," he said with a rueful smile. "I was going to, until the police, as you say, delivered that knock on my door. But perhaps . . ." His voice trailed off, then regained steam, like a train chugging uphill, cresting, then picking up speed on the way down. "Perhaps it is better this way. If I can persuade the staff here, I can persuade the world."

"I don't think you'd have to persuade them," I said. "They'd be more than happy to believe they found you alive, so they could execute you."

"At my age, execution is redundant. Why shoot a plane out of the sky when it's already in a nosedive?"

The reverend nodded. "I'll say it again. *Deep.*"

"You want deep?" Mengele seemed hungry to be understood, to share his passion. "I did not quote you the last line of the Chief Justice Holmes opinion. 'Three generations of idiots is enough.' Do you understand what this meant? We, in the Fatherland, needed a scientific way to remove the unfit. And here, in the enlightened USA, twenty-nine states passed laws to sterilize the feeble. You showed us the way! America handed Germany the matches, and Hitler started the fire."

"Give me a .357, I'll start a fucking fire," Cranky bragged, missing the import of Mengele's pitch.

"I'm sick of all y'all's bullshit," Movern complained, to audible assent.

"There you are," said Mengele, disgusted. "America is sick of it. Meanwhile, America's enemy, al-Qaeda, sends Down Syndrome victims into the market with remote-controlled bombs on their back. This is *genius*! Why kill the unfit when you could use them as weapons! *That* is true ecology."

"Yo," said Movern, "what's German for 'shut the fuck up'?"

"Let him finish," I said.

I knew I was taking an insane amount of time with one old man. That was the trouble with undercover. . . . When you were closest to success was the very moment you were at risk of appearing the most obvious. My front was shaky to begin with.

"The camps!" Mengele shouted. "At the camps hundreds of thousands, and more, could be cleansed. At Auschwitz, we were able to destroy more than a million germs. This was my chance to contribute. To learn. To achieve greatness."

He actually raised his face as he said this, in profile, as though posing for a coin. Then he went back to chewing his mustache, sucking the wet hair with bitter satisfaction. "Five decades I have eluded capture. And now, when I want to be found . . . *Accchh!*"

This was my portal.

"Why do you want to be found now?"

"Why? To claim the honor that is rightly mine!" Spume flew from his mouth. "Wernher von Braun, that whore, ran slave camps and came here because JFK, that priapic, Addison's-diseased fraud, was more interested in vanity moon shots than the life-and-death struggle to save his own race!

"Because, and this is nature's cruelest joke, the unworthy populate like maggots. Today, whites have their fertility clinics! Well, *Mengele invented fertility clinics.* Auschwitz was the first! My science as a eugenicist was always striving to increase the good—and eliminate the bad: the dwarves, the androgynes, the deformed, the sickly. Now you have genetic testing. You find the sickly gene—and you eliminate it!"

"Hell yeah!" Cranky nodded and clapped at Mengele's spiel. I was not sure how thrilled he was to be so enamored of the old-time race killer's style. "Just like La Eme, man. Hit comes down, they tell you 'No humans involved.' That means fuck it, kill everybody, ain't nobody from the hood, ain't none of our people. NHI."

"What is life?" asked Mengele. "Killing the weak to save the strong. If it takes a trial to reveal my accomplishment—get the honor I deserve as a man of science—then so be it! Try me! Try me now!"

There it was. The man did not just want to be caught. He wanted to be lauded. To be—I felt the bulbous visage of Dr. Phil peeping over my shoulder—to be *loved.* Or be Heryet, worshipped.

Mengele's voice grew higher. "This is America. I deserve a speedy trial! You are violating my rights!"

Rincin signaled the jug-eared younger guard, nodding to the spewing Mengele. "Get him out of here. And find out if he's takin' his meds. . . ."

And that was that. As mysteriously as Mengele had rolled in, Movern steered his wheelchair back out again.

For a beat or two nobody said anything, then Cranky wondered out loud. "Who that old freak say he is again?"

Reverend D answered. "He say he was an SS man at Auschwitz."

"SS? Like in Super Sport? They make Chevies in Germany?"

"Cranky," said the reverend, "ain't nobody that ignorant."

"Ignorant, huh? I know one thing, homes, you don't fuck with Bernstein."

I'd always wondered what it would be like to teach. Now I really wanted to rush home and get my credentials. Davey, who'd had his head down for a large part of the proceedings, suddenly roused himself. *"I can't take this violence."*

"I know," I said, "I don't like it either. Violence is a trigger for a lot of people."

I had no idea if this was true but needed to say something to reel things back to within shouting distance of a drug education class. I was two seconds from asking everybody to say what animal they thought they were—a rehab staple—when the door opened again and Rincin came back in, grim faced, and crooked his finger at me.

School was out.

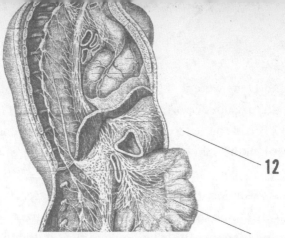

12

Including Los Angeles Garmento

The warden was contemplating his steepled hands when I walked in. He saw me and flipped his fingers forward, aiming the steeple at me.

"Still pointing that thing, huh?"

I could, in my undercover days, pass as drug dealer, seller, hit man, porn purveyor, every breed of sleazebag, including Los Angeles garmento, but the one thing I could not pull off was regular guy. I should have known better than to try.

"Sit," said the warden. Everything in here was code and signal. He was communicating that he knew something about me I didn't know he knew. He lifted a cup of tea from a saucer and blew daintily. "Chamomile. Soothes the nerves. Pour you a cup?"

"My nerves are fine, thanks. I can't even feel them."

"Ahhhh."

The warden slurped pleasantly. "I understand you had quite an exciting first day."

"I didn't know Bernstein was going to show up. You didn't give me his file."

"Uh-huh. I confess, I've always been fascinated by UC work. How a man can live a lie. Posing as one thing, doing something else."

"I guess it's something you get used to."

"Is that right? Anything you'd like to tell me, Manuel Rupert?"

I shook my head. But he didn't move. "This Mengele business, it's extraordinary," he said. "It's like something out of *Reader's Digest*."

"I'm just trying to do my job," I said. "What's your take?"

"My take? If they really suspected it was him, they'd arrest him. If they're wrong, let him sue. He's ninety-seven. But I don't make the decisions. There's something else going on."

"Zell tell you what it was?"

"Zell? I'm not sure—"

I cut him off. "He told me you knew when he hired me. He said you were the only other person in on it. Maybe you can tell me what else you're in on?"

"I'm not the one with a secret, Rupert." He picked up a sheet of paper and waggled it. "Don't forget, we have the results of your UA. We don't just test for narcotics. You must know that. Anything out of the ordinary triggers a flag. Sure there's nothing you want to discuss?"

"Could we discuss my living situation? I'm no health nut, but the mold in the trailer sink actually moves."

"Cute," said the warden, pressing a button on the desk like an executive in a fifties movie. "Annabel, send Officer Colfax in here. With Officer Rincin."

The warden savored another sip of herbal tea. "Any problems with your escort?"

"Problems, no. He seems like a great guy."

The warden regarded me with curiosity. "You know, I walk among deviants and killers all day long. I like to think I'm a reader of men."

"Oh really?" This was plainly my cue to ask what he read when he read me. Before I had the chance not to, he offered another Deep Thought. "The more a man has to hide, the more it shows."

"I suppose so," I said. "Assuming anybody's paying attention."

Colfax strode in and stopped before the warden's desk. "Ah, Colfax," said the warden. They exchanged sharp salutes, which was unsettling. "And where is Officer Rincin?"

"Present and accounted for," said Rincin. He walked in dunking the butt of a cruller in a mug that said SAN QUENTIN—WORLD'S GREATEST PANCAKES! He popped the soggy pastry in his mouth, then took his post to the left of Colfax and saluted with his mouth full. The warden sniffed the caffeinated air. "Still drinking coffee, eh, Rincin? Why not just give your prostate an acid bath?"

Rincin made a show of taking another big gulp and smacking his lips.

The warden squirmed in his chair. "Two hundred toxic oils in one bean. Might as well pluck your man gland out with tweezers and rub it with a cheese grater."

Colfax cleared his throat and the warden dropped the subject. The acned rookie seemed to function as his boss's manners consultant. "Never mind," said the warden. "It's your body. I happen to like my prostate, but that's me. I have sex. I love my wife."

Rincin flushed, his smile never wavering. "Well, sir, mine ran off with the plumber. I wanted to put one of those chips in her neck, like vets do for when your dog gets picked up, so you know where it is. Even found a Korean breeder in Mendocino who said he'd do it. But the bitch left before I could make the arrangements." Colfax ran his finger across his throat and Rincin flushed. "Sorry! Caffeine makes me a Chatty Cathy. Close that door behind you."

The warden turned to me, and I felt the same panic I used to get in the principal's office in high school, back when it was still okay to paddle. The warden was like a principal with armed guards and an electric chair.

"Okay, Rupert. Let's get right to it," said the warden. "We did your tox screen."

Rincin smothered a belch unsuccessfully, and the warden glowered. In spite of myself I glanced at Rincin. It was striking how much he resembled your basic D-movie, belly-over-the-belt-buckle prison guard. I had judged him for that central casting brush mustache, those designed-for-menace reflector shades. But now I was jealous. In situations like this, you appreciate the wisdom of fitting in.

"You know," the warden continued, "San Quentin was one of the first institutions to recognize transgender inmates. Once they have the surgery, they're moved to a woman's prison. Until then, we keep them in segregation."

"That's why you see some of the inmates with trainer titties," Rincin added helpfully. "You know, CWDs." He planted his hands on his chest and waggled his pinkies. "Chicks with dicks. We call 'em 'mone-o's.'"

"What's a mone-o?" I asked, if only to savor my last moments as an equal in the conversation, before they charged me with something.

"Slang for 'hormones,' and in my opinion a pretty disgusting term," said the warden. He leveled a withering glance at the CO. "It's not obscene, but it's nasty."

"I've heard worse," I said, "but I thought you were talking about my UA. Why are you telling me about transgenders?"

At this, Colfax cleared his throat, looking away. Rincin licked his lips and touched a finger to a fresh-bloomed boil on his neck.

"About that UA . . ." The warden sniffed his chamomile and read his own palms for a while before continuing. "It's all right, Rupert, we know."

"Know what?"

"We found the estrogen, son. We found the Dilantin and the Prozac. And we found the naltrexone."

"Opiate blocker," Rincin added helpfully. "You're doing something about the problem, that's what counts."

Before I could process that, Colfax chipped in. "Had an uncle took Dilantin. He kept getting fits behind the wheel of his semi. Stuff really helped."

Rincin grinned a little bigger. "Hey, I got a touch of epilepsy myself. You, me and Julius Caesar, buddy."

"And, uh, about the other . . . ," said the warden.

I felt my neck flush. "The other?"

"Female hormones," the warden whispered discreetly. He put his hand on my wrist and screwed an expression of concern on his face. "It's okay, Rupert. We understand."

Had I actually *been* a budding transsexual, I would have been touched. As it was, his compassion was mortifying.

"Busted," I sighed. "I'm an epileptic pre-op trying to stay off the hard stuff. And I'm depressed."

"Attaboy," said the warden. "Always better to be honest."

I was dying to tell them they were discussing CO Rincin's bloodwork. But I couldn't. I had to play it out.

"Tell you what I'm *not* depressed about," I chuckled bravely, "I'm not using the same surgeon who went to work on Davey's face. I mean, no disrespect, but I can only imagine what he'd do with a sex change. Or do you outsource surgery?"

"They don't show everything on those prison shows," Rincin said cryptically.

I waited for elaboration. But the CO decided to chug the rest of his prostate burner. A moment of quiet, then the warden snapped his fingers in my face. Without thinking, I grabbed his hand. "Stop doing that!"

I didn't realize I was clutching his wrist until I saw him staring at it. When I let go, the warden tipped his chair back against the wall and parked his snakeskin boots on the desk. He licked a drop of chamomile from the side of his mouth and beamed. "Whatever you got going on between your legs, you got balls. I'll give you that much."

"Not for long," Rincin snickered.

"Okay," I said, "joke's over. For your information, I'm taking the stuff to prevent baldness."

This was a gamble, but what wasn't? I plowed on, pulling at a lock of my mouse-colored head fur.

"How do you think I got this crop right here? I was starting to find tufts on my pillow, so I tried, whatchamacallit . . . jeez, I'm blanking on the name of the stuff. . . ."

"Great Day?"

"No, that's a *dye*." Was he trying to trick me? "I'm talking about the stuff that makes your hair grow back. See, the reason guys lose their hair is because of excess testosterone. So, you know, to counter the extra male hormones you take some female."

"And get some nice fun bags," Rincin chimed in, then saw the warden's scowl and retracted it. "Sorry, boss!"

I kept my eyes on Rincin. I couldn't tell if he was avoiding my eyes. Then I began to wonder. Was it me, or were his hips wider? Did that happen?

Rubbing his wrist where I'd grabbed him, the warden broke into my Rincin hip reverie. "The state makes every corrections officer take sensitivity training. Speaking personally, I don't judge a man by what he is, I judge by what he does. We've all got demons. Hell, I used to drink myself silly. My concern is that you do your job and you don't interfere with us doing ours."

"Thank you," I said, trying not to squirm too visibly.

Colfax gave me a supportive thumbs-up. Then Rincin turned his pocked face to mine. "One day at a time, right? I'm in OA myself. Chronic overeater."

"That cruller count as a relapse?" the warden joked.

"I'm laughing on the outside," said Rincin, locking his gaze on mine. Had he figured out I'd stolen his urine? Or did he think he'd met another future vagina owner?

The warden chose that moment to stand up. Colfax took my left hand and Rincin grabbed my right. His palm was soft as a newborn's head. We completed the circle.

"Manny, would you like to kick off the serenity prayer?"

"Me? Uh, sure . . . God," I began feebly, and then a klaxon blasted. Something was happening somewhere, but we kept praying. An attractive Latina with faintly black-haired legs and a juicy birthmark rushed in, then backed out as quickly as she'd entered.

The warden smiled. "It's okay, Dulce's seen me pray before. Bring it home, Officer Rincin."

". . . courage to change the things I can," Rincin intoned, sneaking a meaningful glance in my direction. Who was I to doubt the power of prayer?

Until now, I had never contemplated the courage it must take to have your penis removed. Talk about faith! While we a-mened, I wrapped my mind around the fact that these three believed I was a woman trapped in a man's body. I have to say, they were sterling about it. Not even a hint of behind-my-back smirks.

"I tried Jenny Craig," Rincin confided when we dropped hands. "But I was still stuffing my feelings. I *needed* the program." Maybe the hormones were making him emotional.

The klaxon sounded again and the warden clapped me on the back. "Looks like we have a situation," he said. He headed for the door, then stopped. "Forgot to ask, Rupert, have you thought about a name?"

"A name? For what?"

"For the new you, when you make your transition to he-she, or guy-gal, or whatever you all call yourselves nowadays."

"I believe the term is 'transgendered,'" Rincin corrected him.

"*Oops!*" said the warden pleasantly. "Just funnin'. Guess somebody needs to bone up on his sensitivity training. So what *are* you thinking, name-wise?"

"Mindy," I lied, out of nowhere.

"Mindy's cute." He tapped a finger thoughtfully off his mega-jaw. "But since you started off as Manuel, why not think about Manaloa? It means 'beautiful.'"

"In what language?"

"Honolulu," he said, smiling big.

"Wow. That's nice."

"My gift to you," he said.

"Thanks!"

The warden gave a little wave, and I caught a flicker in his eyes. Despite all this PC chitchat, I suspected he was deeply creeped—no doubt fearing I might break into a cancan or start stroking my nipples at any second. It was hugely embarrassing, and it took everything I had not to defuse the whole charade with a little honesty: "For Christ's sake, guys, I have enough trouble living *with* a woman, let alone living *in* one!" But I'd gone too far down the road to turn back now. What mattered was my mission, not my image. If the head of San Quentin thought I was popping hormones and heading off for a lop job, I'd just have to live with it.

"Okey-doke," said the warden, waving again. "Duty calls."

No sooner had his boss gone than Rincin sidled up and planted a hand on my back. "It's good that we had this talk," he said, slipping a card in my shirt pocket. "You need help, call me. Twenty-four seven."

"Do I look like I need help?"

"You know anybody who doesn't?"

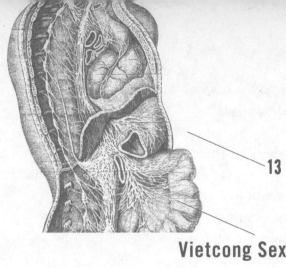

13

Vietcong Sex

I heard her voice before I got in the trailer. "What happened, they couldn't find you anything in D Block?"

"*Tina!*"

My ex-wife was kneeling on the kitchenette counter in black fishnets and CDC jersey, backside protruding as she cleaned the windows over the sink. If her ass could talk it would have shouted "Run!"

Before it did, Tina squirmed around and faced me on the counter, idly spreading her legs. She tugged the fishnets tight over her crotch, hooked in a finger and ripped them, then eyed the damage. "Oh, gosh, look at that *nasty* hole!"

Thrilling as this was, it was hard to enjoy the show, on account of the mold fumes. I reached over her head and tried to jimmy the window. At first it wouldn't budge, then the Plexiglas jerked free and flew out of the trailer. I didn't care. I gulped in deep breaths of sea air as if saved from drowning. Tina grabbed my face and burst out laughing. "Can you quit the home repair and listen? You're going to fucking *love* this!"

"If it's about you and Bernstein, I doubt it."

Tina boasted a fairly demented personal history. Which made for great stories. But until now, her true-life tales of tragic debauchery had involved people I didn't know—unless you counted Leonard Cohen (when she was sixteen), whom I only knew *of*, and a Belgian performance artist named Zik who used to wear rubber and flog her. These days he managed a juice bar in West Hollywood. We ran into him once when we popped in for a smoothie. Back in the car, Tina told me about the floggings, his rubber suit and the chain he made her wear around her ankle so she couldn't leave his loft. "It paid for the drugs, and he let me have friends over," she'd explained, as if I were a pinhead for asking why she did it. "But the main thing," she'd told me, sucking the last drops through her straw before crushing the cup, "he tipped big and he was kind of famous. That means something when you're seventeen." Somehow, now that he looked like a swollen Barry Manilow, whatever Zik made Tina do all those years ago didn't matter. Which brought us back to Bernstein.

"Trust me, nothing happened," she assured me. "The closest we got to sex, he showed me this photo of Golda Meir in seamed stockings. He kept it in a mahogany box, with a certificate of authenticity that looked forged. He wanted me to *look* at the photo with him."

"Should I even ask if she was naked?"

"God no," she replied, as if I was somehow sick for even asking. "But you could see a lot of leg."

"I feel nauseous."

I leaned on a cabinet for a second, then the wood gave and I cracked my knee on a corner of wall trying to break my fall.

"Oh shit!" Tina burst out laughing and covered her mouth. She had a huge heart that did not stop her from loving YouTube clips of drunks falling off camels or stumbling into traffic with their clothes off. "I'm sorry," she managed as her giggles subsided, "are you okay? You should put some ice on it. Let me get some."

"Tina, *NO!*"

Before I could stop her, she opened the fridge and choked. I kicked it shut.

"Not plugged in," I gagged. "That's where the stench comes from." I grabbed a rusty corkscrew off the counter. "Open it up again and I'll get it." She reopened the fridge and, holding my breath, I stabbed what looked like a maggot football with the corkscrew and tossed the whole mess out the missing window.

"Fuck me," I said. "I don't even want to know what that was."

When I turned around, the dead freezer was still open. Tina was staring in at the Technicolor fridge mold, reciting, "'We are all conceived in close prison; in our mothers' wombs, we are close prisoners all; when we are born, we are . . . prisoners still, though within larger walls.'"

Tina slammed the freezer door and said, "John Donne." Then she plopped back on the counter, pulled her knees up and hugged them, facing me, so I couldn't miss that pantyhose hole, the sliver of puffed-out cunt like a furry earlobe.

This is who we are, I thought. *This is what we do.*

"Hey, stress monster! What's wrong with you?"

"Nothing's wrong. Take a sniff. Things are perfect. I'm in a San Quentin snailback that smells like gangrene with an ex-wife I'm in love with. And by the way, thanks for the show last night."

"Manny, would you try to listen?"

But I kept going, like a dog hunting the pain. "You must have known I could see from here. You're not a coincidence person. I mean, what the fuck?"

"Are you done?"

"No. Give me a year and a half to punch myself in the forehead."

"There's melodrama and there's Manny-drama."

Tina plunged a hand in her purse and pulled out a dark prescription bottle of Hycodan, hydrocodone cough syrup, and guzzled. Just what I needed.

"What are you, a Houston rapper?" I asked. "Hitting the purple drank now?"

"Okay, so I've crossed over," she said, tipping one back. "How about you?"

"Clean and loving it," I lied.

"Of course," said Tina, "I start to enjoy myself, and you go all gym teacher."

"Did you fuck him? The Jew Gestapo-wannabe?"

"I already told you. I didn't."

I touched the top of my head. It still hurt. Twice as much since I had passed out under the rotting trailer.

"I can't believe I'm having this conversation," I said.

She screwed the lid back on the bottle. "You really want to hear this?"

"Absolutely not. So don't leave anything out."

Tina shrugged. "He said his daddy told him about Vietcong B girls who kept razor blades up their snatches. GI sticks his dick in. *Chop-chop.* I said, 'Vietcong? Your daddy told you not to have sex 'cause of something that happened to guys in Vietnam? That was a long time ago, honey.' I mean, the guy worked so hard for that badass front, but I could see what was under it." She stopped, took another guzzle of syrup, and kept going. "Guys like that, you just have to stick it to them. I was like, 'What else did Daddy warn you about? Panty 'fros? Not that *you'd* know anything about panty 'fros.' 'Oh, I know,' he said. 'I know.' So I said, 'Son, have you been race mixing?' As soon as you call one of these hard cases 'son,' you're their mother. Even if you're younger than they are. So he got all serious, like, 'Ma'am, I would *never*! I seen pictures. That's how I know.' I'm like, 'Know what?' And Bernstein—he's like a little boy—Bernstein says, 'No, *I can't*!'"

Tina stopped again, pulled out her Newports, grabbed one and ripped off the filter and lit up. Just remembering, she burst out laughing through a gust of Newport smoke. Though it might have been the cough medicine. "So Bernstein . . . Ah, my God, Manny, you'd have loved it. So Bernstein . . ." She tried to continue but broke herself up again. Finally, waving her hand, she managed to finish the story. "So Bernstein says, 'That's how I know you got some Negroid in *you*! 'Cause I know you're part Negroid.' Can you believe that? 'Part *Negroid*'!"

"But you *are* a quarter black. He was right."

"I didn't say I wasn't, you asshole." She punched the Newport out on the counter and threw it out the window. I half expected an explosion. "I know what I am," she said, her mirth turning to annoyance. "I'm just saying, nobody ever called me *Negroid*. It sounds like a gland."

She reached in her purse for another cigarette and muttered, "See, this is what I forget when I think I miss you. What's happening *right now*. The *bickering*."

"I'm just saying," I said.

She threw the cigarette at me. "You should stop *just saying* shit and fucking *say* it."

"Tina . . ."

She shook me off. Then she reached between her legs. "You ever think about how we met?"

"What do you think?"

I watched her touch herself and thought about praying mantises. Name the thing that makes male mantises fiend for females; they must know what's going to happen, but they still do it. There had to be rumors. *Hey, man, did you hear about that guy, got his head bit off while he was fucking?* They knew. But they climbed on anyway. That's what it means to fiend for something. . . . You need it more than you care that it's going to kill you. . . .

Tina idly stroked herself. "I haven't done *anything,* baby. Even though I *could,* since we're not together. I hate to disappoint you, but nothing happened." I didn't say anything, which always drove her crazy. "For Christ's sake, Manny, what are you thinking? You know you're the best lay in the world. You fuck like you want to kill death."

"Ferlinghetti? Oh, come on. . . ."

"No, me." She pouted for a second, then snapped back. "Don't tell me you're thinking about praying mantises."

Being known was an uncomfortable aphrodisiac. "For a second," I admitted, "yeah. I was thinking about mantis sex. But before that I was thinking about those GIs in Saigon. How many of *them* do you think planned on saying 'Nothing happened'? Until they ended up with chipped ham in their pants. It's hard to lie with a bloody package."

"Oh, you think I'm lying?" Her tone was part amusement, part malice. "What are you gonna do about it?" she taunted. "You gonna clamp your fingers around my neck? You gonna slap me across the face?"

She paused long enough to fish yet another Newport out, rip the filter off and light it. "Fuck! *Put your uniform on!*"

"I didn't bring a uniform. I'm undercover. At least I *was.* . . ." Then I got struck sentimental. "The first time we fucked, you said, 'Try to make me happy but don't leave marks.' I didn't know it was from a movie."

"*I'll Kiss You When I'm Dead.* A cult classic. Could you please shut up and hurt me?"

"Is *that* you, or is that from another movie?"

Sometimes when I had sex with Tina, I thought of that scene in *The Godfather* where the senator from Nevada cowers in a whorehouse in his underwear, trying to explain the dead hooker beside him to Robert Duvall. "*We've done it a thousand times before. . . . She* liked *it.*"

Just like old times. Until Tina threw a curve and whispered, "Call me Satan's little whore."

She slid her hands down the wall, stuck her behind out and shrieked dramatically. "Unless a woman be pure of womb, she may not know the Lord. But the Devil has a portal! Make me a whore of Satan!"

"*What* did you just say?"

She kept her voice low, barely audible. "Do me up the ass."

"*Up your ass?*"

"You used to love it."

"I didn't say I didn't love it." Now *I* was whispering. "The last time we committed sodomy as God intended, I got that bacterial thing. Fourteen weeks on Flagyl."

"Oooh, Daddy!" she shrieked, startling me even more. "Keep me pure! Slap my booty! *Make me your virgin cum-bucket!*"

I saw her check over my shoulder. That's when I spotted the lens poking out of the unlatched bed overhead.

"What the fuck!" I stood up for a closer look. "A hidden camera? Are you going to blackmail me? Is that why you're acting like you're on crack?"

Tina looked offended. "This is *not* how I act on crack! And it's not a *blackmail* thing. I was going to tell you."

"Tell me what?"

"Don't get mad, but there's this website. Bible Sluts. I know it's ridiculous. But it's a paycheck. All you do is quote Corinthians or something while you, you know . . . put on a show. Why are you looking at me that way?"

"You have any other Bible buddies?"

She acted insulted. "Come on, I wouldn't do it with anyone but you."

"Were you planning to tell me I was starring in Christian entertainment?"

"I thought it would be fun. I really wanted to fuck you."

"You left *me*, remember?"

"I had a disease that required my full attention. Can we talk about something else?"

"Fine. You still haven't said why you're here."

"The reverend pulled some strings."

"*Reverend D?*" I backed away—as far away as you can back in a shoebox. "Where'd you meet a walking rap sheet like him?"

"NA. We were both court ordered." Tina bit her thumb. "You know, things haven't been great since we split. . . . I needed to make some money. He had some work."

"*Work?*"

She read my expression and said, "Look, there wasn't any sex. I mean, not *real* sex. That's how I've been paying for treatment. It's not what you think. I thought it would be fun to do something with you."

"Tina, for Christ's sake!" I didn't mean to shout, but it was impossible not to. "I saw you out there, remember? With Bernstein. *Naked.*"

"If I knew you were in the audience, I'd have waved."

"How the fuck did you know I was here?"

"A girl has ways. I told you, I took the job to surprise you."

"I'm surprised. In fact, I'm more than surprised. I'm fucking tormented! Who hired you to spend the night with the kosher Nazi?"

"Didn't I tell you already? The old guy."

She slid her fishnet-pantyhosed calves into knee-high boots, doing it slow, like a cam-girl. That kind of nasty. Then, out of nowhere, I made the connection, blurting, "Golda Meir!"

Tina stopped her show and looked at me. "Not the reaction I was going for, baby."

"No," I said, "I mean Golda Meir's stockings, in Bernstein's fetish photo."

"That was pretty twisted."

"Exactly. Dead icon perv. Fits right in with the faux candids Zell laid out on my dresser. Sun Myung in his two-piece and the rest of the team."

Tina curled a finger under the elastic of her pantyhose. "Does that tell you something, baby?" She pulled the fishnets away from her belly, showing me the deep diamond impressions left on the flesh underneath, mashing her pubic hair so that it looked like she'd been pressing herself against a screen door. What kind of early damage made that necessary?

"It tells *me* that the same freak who gave you Golda broke into my bedroom and planted a photo of Sun Myung Moon in a bikini."

Tina let go and the elastic snapped back with a smack.

"Ow!" she cried, touching the fresh red mark on her skin. "Do that again!"

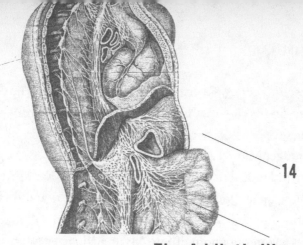

The Addict's Way

An hour later, I leaned back with my head against a folded newspaper—protection from the trailer ooze—and watched Tina dress.

My ex-wife had a way of putting on clothes that was dirtier than taking them off. She was covering up, but you knew what was underneath. When she finished dressing, she applied makeup from a compact at the fetid kitchenette.

"So tell me again," I said.

"Tell you what?"

"Why you had to meet Bernstein."

She snapped the compact shut. "I told you, the old guy, Zell, wanted me to give him a message and a package."

"What kind of package?"

"Cash."

"I still don't get it. Why you?"

"I know the reverend. The reverend and Harry do business."

"Now it's *Harry*?"

Tina rolled her eyes.

"The old guy's in financing. Distribution. He's got a piece of the reverend's escort agency, Christian Fun Girls. The same ones who do outcall appear in his movies. They've got stuff on the Web—"

"Born-again porn?"

"Don't judge, Manny. You've done worse for less."

"I'm not judging. I'm asking. I want to know. For Christ's sake, Tina. You show up at Quentin. You do . . . whatever you did. Then you break into this dump. Just tell me what the deal is."

"Do you have a memory disorder? I had a message for Bernstein."

"What was it?"

" 'The eagle has landed.' "

"You're fucking kidding me!"

"So it's not original. Look, Zell told me I wouldn't have to screw the Nazi."

"And you believed him?"

"Hey, I'm a big girl. And he wasn't lying. I told you, Bernstein and I just hung for a while. He's really only interested in one thing. No, two things—his right and left bicep."

"What did you get out of it?"

"Besides money?" She ran her hand from the throbbing bump on my head, down over my mouth, across my lips. "Well, Zell told me you were going to be up here. So . . . I figured I could see you. I thought it would be hot. Wait!" She straightened up. "Is it the Alterna.com stuff? Is *that* why you're so paranoid?"

"If I knew what that was, I probably would be."

"You haven't seen that site? Nothing but extreme fetish and depravity. It's like dirty anthropology. These women post pictures with these demented thumbnails. Then, when a guy sends photos of himself in Boris and Natasha drag or a nice note about strap-ons, they get his address and blackmail him. The reverend told me about that."

"Wow. We've been split six months and you're already making a splash. Couldn't you have taken a waitress gig?"

"Are you kidding? I just spent six weeks in an eating disorder clinic. I needed something I could do in my spare time to pay for treatment. It's not like I have health insurance. I didn't ask for a dime, if you'll recall."

"I wish you would have. So was somebody hacking the server or what? How did you get their addresses?"

"Off their driver's licenses. When they finally meet for a face-to-face, the first thing you do is check their license. Second thing is leave."

"Wait! You actually meet? Do you go to bed with them?"

"Where these types go does not always involve bed. The concept doesn't apply. Anyway, the Alterna.com scam's a side gig. I love you being jealous, but basically, I'm a dispatcher."

"For an escort agency."

"Yeah, but not regular prostitutes. It's a Christian outcall service. All the girls are saving themselves for Jesus." She pulled out another Newport, ripped the filter off but stopped before she flicked the lighter. "I light a flame in this trailer, is it going to blow? I'm not sure how methane smells."

"You've already smoked about ninety," I said, "but the next one could trigger Armageddon." I snatched her cigarette and threw it in the sink. "Better safe than sorry."

Tina shot me a look that could cure cancer. She knew fifteen different ways to get on her knees.

"Think of all the guys who'd pay to do all the shit I want you to do to me."

"I thought you didn't do sex."

"I don't. I said think of all the guys who'd pay me if I did. Now tell me what's going on with you."

She aimed her eyes up at me. Eased my zipper down. I pulled it back up.

"Baby, please. I just need you to listen. . . ."

I filled her in on the rest of the saga: from Sun Myung to the warden, my upcoming accidental sex change and the drugs I found under the trailer, up to the subject of my investigation. . . . When I mentioned his name, Tina blanched and slowly slid down the wall.

"*Josef Mengele?* That's just . . . That's just *sick*!"

Tina stood back up and made her way blindly to the damp mattress and sat down. Her eyes darkened. "I went through a Holocaust phase in junior high. I read about everything. It really got to me. I was a troubled teen."

"That was your job."

"Yeah, but I was also anorexic." She took a puff of Newport, blew the smoke out fast, then raised her fist to her mouth and bit it. "So all those photos of emaciated bodies really got to me. It was like torture porn. *Look how skinny a human being can get and still be alive.* I was so obsessed with the starvation I didn't know about the other stuff until they showed us a movie at school. They talked about Mengele. The experiments. After that, I was in the library all the time. Do you know what that sick fuck did?"

"Besides shooting typhus into three-year-olds and wearing perfumed scarves to the ramps every morning to decide who got the Zyklon B? I have an idea."

Tina went even more ashen. "But the other stuff . . ." She pushed out her lower lip and twisted it, as though causing herself pain to counter the pain she was describing. "Like his twin genital fetish. How he'd force twin sisters to have sex with other twins. If the twins were a boy and girl, he mated them. To see which would reproduce twins. He'd start dissecting them while they were alive. . . . It always came back to carving up their matching little things. He'd surgically remove their wombs and preserve them in jars."

"Twin reproductive research. Mengele would say he was trying to save his race."

"And I could cut your heart out and say I was researching razor blades."

Tina began to shiver and I put my arm around her. Her voice had shrunk. "Can we just go to bed? I feel diseased. . . ."

Suddenly I noticed how hollow-eyed she was. "Baby," I said, as unaccusingly as I could, "have you been taking care of yourself? How's the food thing going?"

"How do you think?" She threw a cigarette on the floor, looking disappointed the place didn't go up in flames. "At least being a junkie has cachet. Shooting up in gas station bathrooms is classy compared to throwing up in them. You don't get to feel like some junkie outlaw. You feel like a pathetic freak. There's nothing lower than eating a Sara Lee pound cake in your car. Unthawed. Then going to Arby's for three milkshakes and a place to puke it all. I had nearly nine months, then yesterday I relapsed."

I know I've said it before, but for most of our marriage, I lived in total ignorance of my wife's secret eating. It was as if she occupied a parallel universe. When I found out, I felt chumped off. *As if she'd done it all to me.* No doubt this is why narcissists make bad ambulance attendants.

Tina's darkened eyes held on mine. "I ate five microwave Zone meals and a box of cake mix."

"Quit bragging," I said.

It was an all-purpose response. But it made her laugh. Until her sobs bubbled up underneath. She threw herself against me and wept into my chest.

Somehow, in all this pain and squalor, I never loved her more. Never felt more alone. I wondered how it was that I had attracted a person in that kind of turmoil. Maybe it was that I never had to explain. With Tina I could relax.

Then an odd thought lodged in my brain.

Tina grabbed my hand. "What?"

"Nothing."

"*What?*"

"Okay, if you want to know, I was thinking how people like us don't even need Mengele. We're our own medical experiments: you emptying your body, me filling mine up with cut chemicals and Mexican smack. Then I thought about my old man. . . ."

"Your father? You never talk about him."

"He left the motor running in the garage, did himself in with carbon monoxide. I mean, what the fuck? His family saves him from the Nazis when he's ten, and what happens? Three decades later he gasses himself." I rubbed my hand over my face. "Does that make him some kind of retro-collaborator? You know, like the Jewish capos in the camps?" I stared off, saw my father's face—forever wry, sweetly sad—and suddenly the pang of loss tore so deep a knife in the heart would have tickled by comparison.

Her slap brought me back.

"Baby," she said, "you're a million miles away. I need you here. What the fuck are you on?"

"Me? Are you serious? We were talking about you!" Nothing fired up my indignation like accusations of drug use. Especially when I was on drugs. "So why do you think you relapsed?"

"Why do you think? I had eight months, twenty-seven days of abstinence. I did everything right—and where did it get me? Stuck in a San Quentin love nest with some cranked-out Kosher super-Nazi, trying to keep my skin from crawling off my body. So yeah, pretty me was off everything. Drugs, alcohol, food—*whoo-hoo!*—and I have this to show for it! I mean, look at *this*." She swept her arm to indicate the stink box we were sitting in. Then she sighed. "Oh well."

"Oh well what?"

"Oh well, in fourth grade, I was the girl who drew unicorns on her notebook with condoms on."

"You drew unicorn dick?"

Tina recoiled. "What? No! Are you *sick*? The rubbers went on their horns. Magnums. Same brand as Daddy."

As usual, I felt responsible for her difficulties—even the ones I had nothing to do with, including the crime blotter of a childhood that continued to warp her behavior in ways that broke my heart. We hadn't even talked in six months, and our first nonmarried fight followed the exact curve of all the fights we had when married. "You just love me 'cause I'm damaged," Tina said. "It saves you having to do it."

"Okay, I'm sorry your childhood sucked. I'm sorry this isn't the Ritz. I'm sorry I'm on a case. I'm sorry I have to work for a fucking living. You think I like doing this shit?"

"Oooh, *drama*!" Now Tina was chipper. She thrived on fights. "Hey, at least you *had* a career to dump in the toilet. It's like I do these things—the fetish con, the Christian sluts, this trip to Quentin—and I keep thinking, *Why can't I do something better with my life?*"

"I don't know," I said. "Self-esteem issues?"

"Hey, fuck you!"

"Fuck *you*! Welcome to the world. You're an artist, trying to survive."

Tina brightened. "You really think so?"

"Sure. Who knows what fantastic thing is in your future—but you couldn't go there if you didn't go here."

Tina smiled with genuine surprise. "Sometimes you can be so supportive."

"Hey, I love you," I said. "There's no accounting for taste." I didn't mean for my voice to rise. "But what the fuck possessed you to agree to fake-marry a Bernstein?"

"I needed a job that didn't require a résumé."

"So where'd you hide the cash you brought up?"

"Where you do you think? Between my legs."

"Really? I'm thinking even in hundreds, ten grand is a wad."

"I fit *you* in, didn't I?"

"Cute." I was tired of talking, and there was only one question left. "Did Zell give you your share?"

Tina smacked her forehead, like the shills in V8 commercials. "That's what I meant to ask you. Did you check him out?"

Now it was my turn to squirm. "I dug around," I said vaguely. I *had* taken a stab at the DMV—illegal, but possible, if you had a loose C-note and a state employee willing to tickle a few keys on their computer and slip you a printout. Then it was on to CLC, the commercial license lists; L.A. County tax rolls; AARP; gas and electric; NCIC— he didn't have a record—up the ladder to property tax rolls, military, DBA . . . I hit half a dozen boilerplate skip-trace sites, half-assedly trying to nail down the identity of the man who was paying me.

"You dug around?" Tina repeated. "Great. What'd you find?"

"Nothing."

"Nothing?"

"Doesn't matter. I've always trusted my gut."

"Yeah, and how's that been working out?"

This stung. "*You* seemed to think it was okay to take a job from the guy."

"Exactly! Only people like him hire people like us. Didn't you think you should at least find out what Zell wants to do when you nail down the Angel of Death?"

"I will."

"When? Manny, I'm serious. If there's even a possibility it's actually Mengele, you have to kill him. *Now.* Hit him with a wrench and call 911. Make him pay."

"I'm sure that's what Zell intends to do. He just wants to be sure."

"Really? So he hires *you*?"

"Okay, okay!" Bad as the Doughboy-era dope had made me feel, I already missed it. "Maybe some of the pieces don't fit. . . ."

Tina plucked out her cigarette to make room for her thumb. She bit on *that*, then stuck the cigarette back in. Busy woman. She lifted her eyes with a plaintive *What the fuck do you expect me to do?* gaze. Her bites made little kittling sounds. I'd rarely seen her in this condition. She was usually the strong one. Now that she was nonpukaholic, all the unstuffed feelings splashed everywhere.

One of life's sorrier truisms: when you think you're functional with an addiction, it's because the addiction allows you to function. Someday I'm going to write a book. *The Addict's Way.* Get a nice suit and go on Charlie Rose. Ask him where he buys his hair. What *he's* on. (Nobody's going to tell me the man's not at least drunk.) Really *engage.*

I yanked my brain back from visions of self-help millions and stealing kisses from Marianne Williamson backstage at Total Empowerment Seminars. Tina stared at me like she was trying to set ants on fire.

"Baby, what's going through your mind?" I asked her guiltily.

"*Mengele.*" She pronounced the name like it tasted oily. "To be even peripherally involved with someone like that and not destroy him . . . That's unforgivable."

"I said I'd take care of it."

"And I asked you when."

"What is this? I feel like we're married again. There's another class tomorrow, okay? By the way, are you planning on sleeping here?"

"No."

I tried not to man-pout. "Why not? You meeting another Third Reich Bar Mitzvah boy? You know, the last one didn't get along so well with Dr. Mengele, if it *is* Mengele. Did I tell you that? Guards had to drag him off. Bernstein would have killed the old fuck if he weren't in chains."

"That doesn't make sense."

"Trust me, the chains made sense."

"I'm not talking about chains. I'm talking about Bernstein trying to kill Mengele. He raved about him like he was a rock star."

"How long have you known Bernstein?"

"One night. But one night's a long time if all a guy does is yammer. Trust me, if that skeek had any more meth inside him he would have talked backward. He idolizes the SS."

"That's the trouble with meeting your heroes. They disappoint."

She didn't answer. Just took another swig of cough medicine and stared out the missing window. "Look at that moon," she said finally, licking a few drops off her fingers. "It's the same one that hung over the death camps."

It's the same one that hung over the death camps."

"And what the fuck did it do about them? Nothing! Look at it. It's like a blob of white shit stuck to the sky."

"You shit white when you have liver disease," I said.

Tina nodded. "Well that's what you are when you have the chance to clean somebody like Mengele off the planet and you don't. You're a white blob of shit."

"Can we stop with lunar stool metaphors? Why the fuck aren't you going to sleep with me?"

"I didn't say I wasn't." She peeled herself carefully off the trailer foam. "Just not in here. The smell would make a dead fish sick."

"I still don't know what that was in the fridge," I said. "It might have been a hand in a mitten."

"Let's go to my place."

"You have a place?"

"A girl has to stay somewhere."

"So where are you?"

"Two spaces over. The minivan. Don't ask."

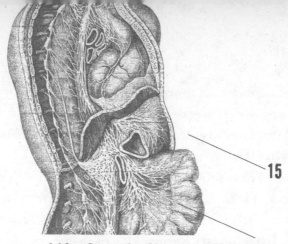

15

Life Coach, Hymen Wrangler

Bathed in tainted moonlight, I made out the cross on the minivan's door. As we crunched closer over the gravel, I aimed a penlight. Tina's ride sported more than just a cross. Depicted, in airbrushed pastel, was the crucifixion. Three buxom, kneeling Mary Magdalenes—black, Asian and blond—clasped their hands in supplication before a very buff Jesus. The Son of God appeared to be peeking down their tank tops. Above the tableau ran Reverend D's flamboyant, curling signature. Below it, in Gothic letters: CHASTITY IS NOT A VIRTUE . . . IT IS A REWARD!

"Provocative," I said.

"And then some." Tina aimed the beeper and the minivan's doors unlocked with a satisfying *crunk*. "If you look close, Jesus is wearing a crown of thongs."

Still holding the key-beeper in front of her, she turned back to me. "One of the girls did an outcall to Mengele. You should talk to her. Her name's Cathy."

"Are you serious? When did she see him?"

"I don't know. Maybe a month ago." She looked away as if seeing something she didn't want to see. Unlike me, Tina did not get happier on opiates. So of course she did more of them.

"God, Manny, I was clean when I was binging and purging. I mean, I was burning my uvula down to a stump, but I was clean and sober. . . . Now I'm abstinent and look at me."

"Transitional relapse. You're stressed out, you're taking the edge off. It's not like you're holding a gallon jug of morphine and pouring it on waffles at IHOP."

"Can we talk about something else besides food?"

"Sorry. You're right. Insensitive. So, how did you—never mind."

I found the handle and yanked the panel door sideways. My paranoia genes were riled up. Standing in the open talking, even off campus, invited attention, if not outright surveillance. I tried to nudge her into the minivan, but she wouldn't budge. Instead she punched me in the chest.

"How did I what?"

"Nothing."

"Ask it, Manny."

"Okay, but get inside. We probably shouldn't be out here."

She finally relented and got in. I ducked in after her and slid the door shut behind me. It was dead black.

"Tina?"

"Ask!" she said.

"All right." I couldn't see her, which made it easier to talk. "Tell me the truth. The Christian escort thing, the Alterna.com scam . . . Are you, you know, back in it?"

"*It?* No! I told you."

"Thanks, baby."

I reached for her, got an armful of air and leaned sideways to reach for her again. Nothing. *She was gone.* I heard her clump into the backseat. Or the second to back seat. I didn't even know how many rows there were.

"God, it's darker in here than outside."

"Smoked glass. People see big tits and Jesus, they're going to want to peep in. Hang on." She unsnapped her purse. Cupped the flash of a lighter, followed by orange Newport glow. "To answer your question, Reverend D kept me on to work with the girls."

"What kind of work?"

The glow deepened; I could hear her staccato puffs. Blowing smoke rings in the dark. "The reverend sold virgins."

"What? Like nine-year-olds from the Ukraine? He pimped out cherry girls? Fuck! He didn't strike me as *that* evil. What the fuck were you doing working with him?"

"No, no! I told you. They were evangelicals. And they were all over eighteen. They just wouldn't let a man put his organ in their vessel of procreation. They were technical virgins."

"*Technical* virgins?"

"I didn't say they were innocent. I said they hadn't been deflowered."

An odd conversation in the dark.

"So they didn't fuck."

I felt her finger scratch lazily across the back of my neck.

"Not vaginally. But they *would* do naked prayer sessions. Along with Greek, Russian, bareback oral or facials."

"And still leave a customer feeling virtuous."

"You can't put a price tag on pure."

"So . . . your job again?"

I was glad for the dark. It cushioned all this new reality.

"I showed them how to keep their female organs penis free. The reverend liked to say, 'Takes a man to show a little girl how to make love, but it takes a woman to show her how not to.'"

"Barry White meets Dr. Laura. Nice. So what was your title?"

"Life coach. Hymen wrangler."

"There money in that?"

By now she was kissing my ear. From behind.

"Don't laugh. I did consultation work in seven states. The reverend knows how to get the Family Research Council and government abstinence-ed money. He had a little rap for visiting suits, the faith-based financial gatekeepers." She did a strikingly lifelike imitation of the rev, throwing in a smidge of Isaac Hayes. " 'Virgins in the ghetto. Jesus himself could not work a bigger miracle.' " Evangelicious!

"Let me guess. Then he'd get them blow jobs, right? " I realized how that sounded and corrected myself. "Not Jesus. The reverend . . . The girls would have told him about an old Nazi perv, right?"

"They wouldn't have had to. Rev D took all the calls. He would have booked him."

I felt the impact as she crawled back over the seat beside me.

"Wait. Back up. . . . So Zell finds out there's a war criminal living in Reseda. What does he do?"

"Depends."

God, I loved what her fingers did with my neck. She pressed her hands over my ears. Now there was no light and no sound.

"That's so good," I said, moaning as I answered my own question. "Either he has him arrested or . . . Maybe he wants to do something with him. Whatever it is, he wants to be sure. So he gets Mengele somewhere he can be observed. . . ."

Tina didn't say anything, just squeezed tighter on my ears till I heard the ocean. Her body pressed mine from behind.

". . . Then he sends *me* to observe him. Which still makes no sense. If you even suspect, you fucking arrest him. Unless . . . Zell's pro-Nazi. But if he wanted to help the bastard, he'd sneak him back to Brazil. Before some state-trained Israeli shows up and goes Judah Maccabee on his ass. I keep going over and over this. . . ."

Soft fingers caressed my cheek. I thought I smelled . . . lavender. *"Mmmmmm . . ."*

The fingers on my face were like a child's. And so dainty. In spite of myself, I imagined the grave faces of the Viennese girls after Dr. M removed their arms. The horror of *that*. They looked, on the screen of memory, like little twin Tinas. I thought *hand transplant* and bolted forward with a strangled gasp. *"Tina!"*

I wheeled around, flailing. A forearm jammed across my windpipe. *Hairy,* I thought stupidly, so I knew it wasn't Tina. First suspect is always next of kin.

I tried to kick and banged my toe on what felt like a lead pipe, wearing a shoe and wedged against the seat in front for leverage.

I started to scream again. "Ti—"

I heard the top of my head crack before I felt it. Thought *peanut brittle*. My eyes blinked into scalding white. Runny faces floated over me, features contorted, as if enduring savage g-forces. One face loomed close. I flashed on a mustache made of worms. Swinging blind, I connected with a crunch. Blood-spray wet my cheek, so I couldn't see what I'd hit. Maybe a tomato with bones.

Then I *was* the tomato. Squeezed in a can. Everything dark, cramped. The ringing stopped. Say what you will about vegetables, they're calm.

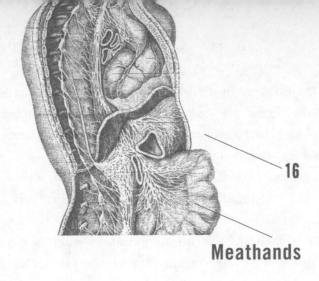

16

Meathands

I came to, my face wedged under a sink, hands cuffed behind me, in a room too small for me to extend my legs. I tried to move and my mouth scraped cold rust. A slit of light leaked over the top of a door. The ringing in my ears made thinking painful. I focused on the last things I remembered: that white, diseased-liver moon . . . the mini-van . . . talking in the dark with Tina. But this dark was different. Only the fetid smell placed me. And the slime on my arms. Trailer scum. I was home! *Yeccch*. When I wriggled, it felt like I'd been dipped in rotten Vaseline. Almost accidentally, my left wrist slipped out of the old-school handcuff. It took more effort to liberate my right. Either they'd clamped it tighter, or I had a case of fat arm. I had to claw off a layer of wall ooze, smear it around the metal, then twist it back and forth. And the bracelet still scraped a layer of knuckle skin coming off.

Free at last, I rolled over and spotted a ball of light through a hole in the floor. I pressed my back to the wall in case the light strayed upward. But somehow my shirt had gotten shoved up to my shoulders, and where my skin hit the slimy wall it puckered, making a sound like someone smacking their lips.

I froze. Then something banged against the trailer floor, bouncing my head off the metal toilet. The blow left me facedown on the marinated linoleum. The stench was hallucinogenic. I came to seeing rotten yellow stars and hearing voices.

"Why'd they stick the shit in old Red Cross boxes?"

" 'Cause they were already here, dumbfuck . . ."

The second man spoke in a crusty whisper I knew I should identify. Only I could not focus. Between the screaming fire alarm in my skull and the struggle not to gag, I had to fight the urge to just break off a table leg and beat myself in the face for the sheer relief of keeling over. I wanted to pray—but for what? My earlier nausea was like a happy memory. Until this moment, I'd never really known what people meant when they said their "gorge" was rising. But now my gorge— whatever it was—was accelerating north, swelling with every breath to some kind of acrid-tasting tsunami of bile and fear. I felt a bird's nest of ganglia pulsing at my left temple, terrified that the strain of trying to gulp back the rising tide would amplify the throb until my head simply exploded like an overpumped tire from cerebral pressure.

The man with the crusty whisper kept talking, but the words went in and out. "During World War One, convicts"—*wah, wah, wah*—"made these Red Cross boxes. . . . War ended"—*wah-wah*—"Contractors"— *wah-wah-wah-wah*—"storeroom next to dungeon."

I bit my lip until I tasted blood, but the fire alarm only stopped temporarily.

"Or maybe," another voice chimed in, this one older sounding, *"the poor fucks in the dungeon required a lot of first aid."*

Suddenly I had to sneeze—and I was a loud sneezer. I pinched my nose to stifle the volume. And, still pinching, sneezed again, even harder, the pressure searing my eardrums. By the fifth sneeze, I thought my eyeballs were going to pop out of their sockets like bloody comets. After the eleventh, they stopped. But I kept the squeeze on my nostrils, sucking small blasts of air into my mouth, to mitigate the

tang of piss and mildew and sixteen breeds of decay moldering beneath me. When I was upright, I'd just had to inhale the stench. Now,
on the trailer floor, I was basted with it, like some kind of hell-glazed
ham. Worse, I realized when I looked through the rust hole in the floor
that there was no tank under the toilet. It emptied straight onto the
ground. And stayed there. One more ingredient in the potpourri that
made the snailback such a festival of stank.

"Listen," Crusty Whisper Man declared, "the wrecking ball swings
tomorrow on the original lockup, and they threw this stuff out with
everything else. On the off chance somebody finds it, they're gonna
think it just looks like a bunch of old medicine. I hear the Kraut
antiqued the dope. Anybody bothers to run it through the lab, the
shit'll test out a hundred years old."

I heard that, and my first thought was *I've been shooting up good
drugs!* My second was, *Why the fuck didn't I grab more?* That's what happens when your junkie muscle goes slack. You lose vigilance. Though
I knew, from years of research, that it didn't take much to morph back
to full-blown junkiedom. I also knew that after the first shot or three,
all the time you'd spent on the straight and narrow might as well never
have happened. One day you've got it all together, the next you're in a
stinking bathroom, living the dream.

"What I hear, shit's somethin' special," said the first guy I'd heard,
who I suspected was the youngest. "What I hear, the old fuck makes
some kinda Nazi skag that's stronger than street shit."

I heard a smack and then that familiar but still unplaceable crusty
whisper. "What I hear, you fuck, is I catch you tryin' to pinch off a
taste, you're gonna end up with a rig full of battery acid in your neck
so you don't do it again."

That was it. I nosed a flap of dank linoleum to the side and peeked
through the rust hole. I needed to see who was talking. But I needed
to use my nose, because my hands were still useless from the cuffs.
Numb, but not tingly numb. *Meat* numb—hanging like skinned ani-

mals from my wrists. I'd have to make do until feeling came back. But maybe feeling was overrated.

All I could see was a set of white hands, some work boots. The men grunted, venting muffled curses when the footlocker banged against the rotting trailer bottom. With each bump I shuddered. My big fear was that a corner would catch on my fist-sized peephole, peeling the rusted-out metal I was sprawled on like the lid of an upside-down sardine can, sending me face-first into the outhouse gumbo below. I flexed every muscle, trying to levitate. But they dragged the locker way out with no undue damage.

I leaned closer to the hole in the floor. Not just to sneak a peek—I suspected, for some reason, that the men were guards—but to take in a breath. I'd just maneuvered close enough to breathe when one of them said, "Fuck it, dawg!" and dumped a shovel-full of muck back in the hole. Something awful splashed up onto my lip, and I jerked backward.

"Fuck it, dawg. This place stinks worse than a crack ho's panties."

"You oughta know, you did your mother's laundry!"

After this bon mot, they bailed. I heard the crunching gravel as they walked off, trying to wipe whatever'd splashed on my lip. A second later a car started, rolling slowly, almost soundlessly off. I waited a minute, quickly uncurled myself, maneuvered my way upright and tried to work the door handle with my meathands. By now I could kind of flutter my fingers. But it didn't help much, so I kicked the door open. Peeked outside to see if anyone was waiting to brain me again, then tumbled and gulped the air like it was nectar.

Freed from trailer fumes, my head cleared halfway up, enabling me to panic rationally. As I started to breathe normally again, I wondered, *Where is Tina? How is Mengele involved? What else did they stash beside drugs?* And, just out of morbid curiosity, *Who was in that minivan? And why the fuck did they windpipe me and cuff me to the sink?*

More or less refreshed, I staggered back inside to consider my situation. Weaving over the kitchenette sink, I turned on the tap and splashed water onto my face. I squeezed my eyes shut, feeling the not unpleasant burn of industrial solvents and PCBs tightening my pores as they ate through them.

Feeling my body sag, I remembered something Roscoe'd said in class: *"When shit gets bad, you gotta find one thing to be grateful for. One thing. Otherwise you go minimal. . . ."*

I wasn't sure what going minimal was, but I had a feeling it was already happening. When life shrank to nonstop calculation about how to make it through the next five minutes, that had to be minimal. Normally I steer clear of affirmations. But this one came from a convicted cop killer with no hope of parole and more serenity than Buddha on Xanax.

Absent immediate danger, the adrenaline drained off and the effect of all the abuse my body and nervous system had taken since signing for Mengele duty began to make itself known. Thankfully, the one mirror on the premises had been shattered before I showed up. So I could only feel the damage, as opposed to having to look at myself.

I touched a finger to the top of my head, expecting bloody peanut brittle. Instead, there was only a minor-league knob. No blood. Right there—something to be grateful for. My bruised windpipe made swallowing painful. So of course I could not stop swallowing. My left temple still throbbed. Here and there my skin burned, courtesy of the chemical gelatin coating my trailer's innards. Something else hurt, farther down, under my right rib cage. My liver. But that didn't worry me. The pain was like an old friend that wanted to kill me.

Without meaning to, I sat down at the dinette and passed out. When my watch alarm went off at noon, I was still sitting up. Drug class kicked off at one fifteen.

I had about ten minutes to try to clean up. Sniffing myself, I nearly keeled over. But I found some Clinton-era Right Guard under the sink and sprayed it under the arms of my shirt, the front and back of my pants and up and down my legs. My first choice, needless to say, would have been dry cleaning and a hot shower. But in this life you work with what you have.

I scanned my attire for visible stains and contemplated my next move. I could of course have just sneaked off and gotten as far away from this weirdness as I could. But, having run away too much early on, my tendency in my wobbly thirties was to stay too long. So, as originally intended, I decided to hit the classroom.

It took a few minutes to find my briefcase and copies of the inmate files. When I grabbed them, a scrunched up, slightly soiled napkin floated out of the pile. On it, by sheer chance, was the writing assignment I'd thought up and promptly forgotten: "HAVE YOU EVER MADE A BAD DECISION UNDER THE INFLUENCE OF DRUGS? DESCRIBE."

Who has the time?

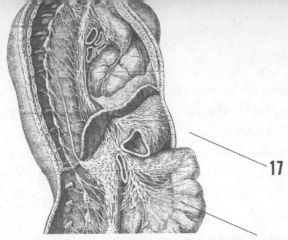

17

Whole-Grain Nazis

Through the twin sets of admitting doors, I stepped toward the lower yard with a new wariness. I didn't know if going back to drug class was the best move after getting knocked out and abducted by someone with doll hands in a minivan. It was, if nothing else, definitely the least likely. Which is sometimes better. People were always trying to be smart. Sometimes stupid got you more.

I held the door open for a long-lashed young guardette with a beehive while she signed in triplicate. The process took her longer than I'd expected. I didn't know whether to just let the door go, which felt rude, or stay there and wait, which felt uncomfortable—would she think I was trying to pick her up?—and could take hours.

I began to wonder if I was drawing attention to myself. Though I realized my perceptions were skewed. Whatever narco-treat had been in my Red Cross box, it had launched me into short-lived euphoria, directly on to mild disorientation, semidepression and itchy nose. Then again . . .

On one level, since checking into Quentin, I'd managed to roll into my fetid guest trailer and reenact my own low-end, mini–Joe Campbell hero-goes-to-hell-and-claws-his-way-back-again routine. On another, I had already fucked up so badly I'd be lucky if I didn't end up getting mail here for the next ten years.

All I really wanted to do was stare at that Ronettes do. Was it a retro thing or had time stopped at San Quentin, fashion-wise, in 1967? I had seen plenty of sixty- and seventy-year-old James Dean–era juvenile delinquents. They strolled the yard, working pompadours, butch-waxed crew cuts and Chicago boxcars—brushed high on the sides, flat down the middle to a perfect spit curl. My guess was the bouffant behind me read "rockabilly" more than "female peckerwood."

I was so enthralled by the big hair that I committed one of the cardinal sins in a penitentiary—I collided with another convict. In this case, a Pacific Islander, in a baseball hat and a cut-off sweatshirt that exposed his side-of-ham arms from the shoulder down. The right one was festooned with swaying palm trees on an island. Above which were letters that swayed just like the tattooed palms: 100 TONGAN.

"Jesus, sorry," I mumbled, hyperalert for the glint of a shiv. But the mountain of Tonga did not even look at me. He just moved on.

I didn't notice the note in my hand till I checked my skull egg, a few steps later, to make sure it still hurt. The paper had been folded several times, down to postage stamp size. Opened, it revealed four words: "VISITING ROOM" and "BRING CANTEEN."

The note seemed written in two different hands. I studied it while pretending to retie my tie—a last-minute wardrobe addition. The right accessory can cancel out the effects of chemical depravity. (I'd have to write that down and put it in *The Addict's Way*. In the chapter on clothes. *"As an addict, your life depends on continual evasion—so dress accordingly!"*)

I had no idea how to get to the visiting room. And in a place like this, you didn't want to get lost. By chance, I happened to look behind me and saw the Samoan. He nodded faintly. And, keeping his hands down at his waist, he pointed both forefingers east. Toward the condemned unit? Back to administration? He did it again, then took off when he saw that I'd reversed course.

There was a line at the visiting room window. I was eleventh, which left ample time to admire the humanity in the orange plastic chairs. Mothers and girlfriends nursed babies, checked makeup, chatted with the other ladies who'd made the trek. Their beauty seemed extreme, maybe because their devotion was so naked. *Here I am, taking a nine-hour bus ride up to see you, baby.* The children colored in coloring books. The men on hand seemed oddly washed out. You didn't see a lot of gangsters. Mostly sad-eyed little boys and proud old men.

One thirteen-year-old black kid, already inching toward six foot, held court for younger newcomers in front of the inmate-painted mural, pointing out details of trees, mountains, deer and other bucolic wonders. It was all browns and greens, like a geography book illustration, but achingly lush in contrast to the plastic and penitentiary lighting. One elderly African-American woman, in a pillbox hat and white knit shawl over a patchy fur coat, read a large black book I assumed to be the New Testament. It turned out to be *Blackwater*, by Jeremy Scahill. Under different circumstances, I would have loved to ask if it drove her mad knowing that guys who got high and killed people walked if they worked for right-wing, politically connected security firms. And that men who didn't, most likely including her son or husband or brother or fiancé, were not walking anywhere but to chow.

A starchy, heavily made-up white woman breathed chili fries when I made it to the window. Her nametag read SERGEANT DARNELL. Her plump cheeks, Big Beautiful Woman scarlet lips and painted-on eyebrows registered permanent surprise. "Visiting condemned today? They're in the adjustment center."

Did I look like a condemned visitor? "I'm visiting a, uh . . . a non-condemned. My name is Manuel Rupert."

"I do not see your name in our files."

"Try Manuel."

"Thank you for helping me do my job, sir. Are you sure you submitted your application?" I couldn't tell if she was being sarcastic or reading from a card taped to her computer screen. I only knew it took under a minute to make her despise me.

"There is a six-to-eight-week processing time for visiting forms, sir. If you have not heard from us, that does not mean you have not been approved—that means we have not yet gotten to your file."

"Right, right," I stammered. "It's kind of an impulsive visit. See, I'm teaching here, a drug prevention class? Then I remembered . . . I have a cousin here, so I thought—"

What was I thinking? How could I waltz into the visiting room without knowing who I was supposed to visit? You can make dumb mistakes at a Taco Bell takeout window. But not in San Quentin. It was an adjustment I thought I'd made but clearly hadn't. "As I said, sir, there is a six-to-eight-week processing time for visiting forms. All visits must be approved in advance. No same-day."

"No same-day! You sound like a Chinese laundry!"

Officer Colfax shouldered his way over and interrupted my losing plea. "How goes it?"

"Well," I said, "to tell you the truth—"

"Roger that, big man." He clamped a hand on my arm, squeezing just enough, I suspected, to let me know it might be a good idea to shut the fuck up. Done squeezing, Colfax squatted so that his face was level with Sergeant Darnell's. "Looky here, Darlene."

He opened his wallet and showed her something I couldn't see. It could have been a fifty-dollar bill or a monkey paw. "Don't go by looks," I heard him whisper, "Manny's a friendly."

"Really?" she said, giving me a once-over that made me check to see if I had pants on. "I thought he was from San Francisco."

It was clear that this meant something to Colfax and his friend behind the reinforced glass window. And what it meant was something less than flattering. Insanely, I came close to protesting—*Hey, I'm not from San Francisco!*—before I realized there was no percentage trying to persuade prison guards you were cool. As she could see directly into my mind, Sergeant Darnell plucked a few fallen strands off her forehead and tamped them back up into her teased pineapple of red hair. "Mr. Rupert, this is San Quentin," she said, giving me her most withering Sarah Palin–ish smirk. "It's not high school with lethal injections."

"That's a great line," I said. "How many times a day do you get to use it?"

For a moment we held each other's eyes, me trying to exude impassive blandness in the face of her snark, her making sure I knew this was her world, and don't be fooled by the big boobs and bouffant—she had bigger balls than I did.

"Darlene's a pistol, isn't she?" Colfax chuckled.

At first I thought he was helping me out—smoothing out an awkward prison moment—but when I saw the glaze that had formed over the big, acne-scarred guard's cow-brown eyes, I knew it was something else altogether.

When Sergeant Darnell shifted her gaze from me to Colfax, her plump face softened into discreet affection. Unconsciously or not, she put her thumb over her wedding ring. Just because their office happened to include killers, random violence, incarceration and lockdowns, that didn't mean an office romance couldn't bloom. Colfax did everything but float a foot off the floor and bat his eyelashes at his ample amour. I wondered if his ardor was rewarded or more in the realm of chivalric poetry, where the whole point was devotion and unfulfilled desire—as opposed to consummation in a stolen hour of conjugal bunk time. All I knew for certain is that if we kept standing there, little red cartoon hearts would probably start fluttering from the burly guard's chest. And the line of tired, excited, understandably upset prison visitors behind us might get violent.

"Driver's license," said Sergeant Darnell. I slipped it under the bulletproof glass. She slid it back with one plastic-gloved pinkie and told me where to sign.

When I put down the pen she said, "Inmate nine-six-five-seven-six is sitting down right now in front of the microwave."

"The one with the sign that says 'Out of Order,'" Colfax added, snapping his fingers and pointing a finger gun at his special girl. I saw him touch her fingers as she slid my visitor pass out her slot. "Darlene," Colfax declared, looking around to make sure nobody who mattered was listening, "I am going to pick up the phone and call the governor. You are fan-forklift-tastic."

"Thanks, hon," said Darlene, already smiling past him at the elderly prisoner mom and dad behind us. "How are you two today?" she asked them sweetly. "How are those precious little granddaughters?"

If his sweetheart's sudden about-face affected Colfax one way or the other, it didn't show. He led me from the window without a word and pointed to Jimmy. The white Rasta was waving from the back, arms spread over a couple of chairs, in front of a microwave with the door open and a handmade OUT OF ORDER sign taped to the window.

"I guess Jimbo wants some extra counseling," said Colfax.

"And some extra room," I said. "I have a hunch he put that sign there himself."

"The guys call him WBM. For White Bob Marley. You have to give 'em nicknames."

"And White Bob can just schedule a visit?"

"Hey, I just work here," he said.

I expected Colfax to head straight for Rasta Jim. Instead he cut left and I nearly ran into him. We were going for the vending machines.

"Sandwich, fruit, soda, chips, candy, popcorn," Colfax called over his shoulder. "You wanna load up on snacks before you sit down. That's the way they do it. Got dollar bills?"

I fished in my pocket, pulled out a soggy twenty with some kind of white rind hanging off it. I shook the bill, and the rind flew off, then tried to wipe my fingers on my pants without being obvious about it. It's like I was becoming my trailer. For all I knew I smelled like the snailback and had grown so inured to the odor I didn't notice. On patrol we called it "homeless nose."

My hand was halfway to my other pocket when Colfax pressed a thin stack of bills into it. "Thirty singles," he said, keeping an eye over the heads of the other guests. "They don't make change. Your best bet is nachos, but put the peppers in before you microwave."

"Microwave looks broken."

"They're not bad cold, either."

Colfax gave my shoulder a manly squeeze and marched off, no doubt for more dalliance with Darlene. For all I knew prison guards led secret double lives as swingers and cheaters. Who could blame them, after eight hours a day trying not to get hit with piss bags, or worse. The big CO's exit left me to fend for myself at the vending machines. They all worked—one thing that prison life had to recommend it. I had to walk carefully to keep from toppling my junk food mountain of M&M's, Mallo Cups, caramel corn, jumbo pretzels and barbecued potato chips. I threw in a mushy apple for nutritional purposes, though it looked more unhealthy than any of the snacks.

Rasta Jim was less than appreciative. "You think I eat this crap? And what were you doing with Dudley Do-Right?" He lowered his voice and leaned forward. "I'm FBI, asshole."

"If I had your hair, I wouldn't be calling anybody asshole," I said. "And you're not FBI, unless they canceled their dental plan."

"Prosthetics. You think this is my real hair? I have to take this off at night and walk it."

"I'm still not buying."

Playing the role, he let his head fall sideways and gazed up at the fluorescent lights like they were telling him to eat brains. I was afraid he was going to drool. "202-44-EAGLE. Tell him Agent Carol said to call. He's my top."

He saw that I didn't believe him. So, when no one was looking, he slid the dreads on his forehead back, showing cheesecloth underneath.

"Nice work," I said, "but unless the toupee says 'Property of U.S. Government,' that doesn't tell me much. And you know I can't call now. No cell phones."

"Rupert, goddamn it, do you know how many ways the federal government can fuck you?" He held his head askew, still pretending to be tripping on fluorescent mysteries. "We can audit. We can tap your phone, we can read your e-mail, we can send you kiddie porn and then arrest you for owning it."

I unwrapped a Mallo Cup and took a bite. "You had me at 'audit.'"

"Asshole." He spat on my candy. "Now tell me about Zell."

"You know why he hired me," I said, fishing to see what my tax dollars were paying for. "What's that tell you?"

"Don't play games, okay?"

"I'm not the one playing games." I plunked a napkin in his hand. "And wipe your mouth. You've got white cream on your lip. This is *prison*, dude. Who you really after?"

"A war criminal. You know who?"

"That was easy. You think he's the real deal?"

Jimmy slipped out of his Rasta bonghead mode long enough to glare at me before going back to character.

Half of me wanted to tell him Tina was missing and get him to find her; the other half did not want to give him anything he could leverage later. I didn't know how exactly he could fuck me, but he was federal law enforcement. He could do a lot more to me than I could to him. Even for a chronic catastrophizer, the sudden plethora of awful possibilities was alarming. I switched tracks from emotional to moral consequence—what if, due to some fuck-up of mine, Josef Mengele escaped? *Again.* I started to reach for his collar.

"If you think it's him . . ."

Agent Carol–slash–White Bob Marley sat up fast. I willed my hands back to the table. Recalibrated my voice from hiss to whisper.

"If there's even a fucking *chance,* how can you not take him? *Now.*"

In Rasta wack mode, he tilted his head sideways and gave me a fed's rendition of a ganja giggle before bringing in the heavy artillery. "Ever heard of a threat assessment? Like what are the odds I could give a signal right now and an inmate bites off your finger? The Mossad had him in Buenos Aires in 1960 and let him go so they wouldn't blow the Eichmann snatch. Israelis made an assessment, decided a bird in hand is worth two in the bush."

Before I could ask why they didn't napalm the bushes, he went back to business. "We've pinned flags on fifty serious Jews who would pay for the privilege of killing Mengele. Word gets out, they're gonna descend. Ever think of that? The security involved? These are professional Nazi hunters. Plus all the weekend Wiesenthals. Before I could take him, I'd have to do a full alert. IFS-DOUBLE-C. International, federal, state, city, county. We're talking about Lee Harvey Genocide here. If it means a little wait to stave off some wannabe Jack Ruby— real name Rubenstein—so be it. What kind of hardware you bringing to the party?"

"What are you talking about?"

Nearby, a Sureño—one weeping eyeball and a blood-red "13" turning the back of his shaved head into a criminal billboard—happily scooped up Cheez Doodles for his family. I started to offer him my bounty and Rasta clamped a hand on my wrist. "Don't."

"Why?"

"Not done. So tell me."

"Tell you what?"

"Isn't that why you came up here? Zell doesn't seem to know who you are. So if you're using him as an excuse, then you're freelancing, and the only money in that is if you bag the target."

"That's right. I'm here to shoot him. Dead. But I have to do it one handed, on account of I need to hold my camera steady with the other. I use an Elph. Put it right on the iMac."

"All right, all right," he said, rasping back to his weed-creepy blond Bob Marley routine. "Riddle me this: Who's better off with Mengele alive in prison? Who's better with him dead? And why hasn't he already been caught, exposed and shoved on camera as the last living Holocaust perp walk? Unless he knows something. Or has something."

"Something—I'm just spitballing here—like a photograph of the doctor and some notables taking the air at Auschwitz? Wait—is it Prescott Bush eating a Jewish baby?"

"People know that some of our finest families believed they had a friend in Hitler. There are others things—other individuals—no historian knows about. We don't know the extent. But corroborating material exists."

"What *do* you know?"

He fixed me in his G-Man stare, burning right out from under the Rasta wig. But when he spoke, he sounded like a pilot on Southwest announcing delays over Phoenix. "Let's just say it wouldn't be good for America."

"So," I said, "are you gonna keep me on the hook or tell me what we're talking about ?" I hate other people's secrets.

"If I told you," he said, "I'd be bound by law to take myself out on sight. Nobody touches him till I get the word."

"So what are you saying? He gets a pass? Maybe I don't want to be a collaborator."

"Keep it down, Manuel."

"Who all knows that Jo—"

He put his finger to his lips. "I'm not going to ask you again."

We did the manly eye-lock thing, then conversation proceeded. "Who all knows?" I continued, my voice reasonably low.

"Theoretically, just you, me, the warden and Mr. Zell. But as you may have noticed, the Man Who Would Be Mengele is dead set on spreading the news. You know what they say, no secrets in prison." He waggled a finger at my chest. "So, the cross-dressing. I don't get it."

"You mean my transgender hormone regimen? Give me a break. Do I look like a guy who wants tits?"

"That's not a subject I'm comfortable with, Rupert. I hope you can understand that. Whatever sewer world you live in, I respect you for signing on, but I don't need to know about your personal life."

"If you were FBI, you would know you're not the only one working undercover."

"I did your urinalysis, buddy."

"That a hobby, or they teach that at Quantico?"

"You have a degenerate nature. That's not your fault. It's genetics."

"Too late to sterilize my mother," I said. "She had a hysterectomy. Plus she's dead."

It wasn't that I didn't want to tell him I stole someone else's urine. I just didn't want to out Rincin. I didn't know my compulsively grinning chaperone very well. And I wasn't sure I liked him. But I still didn't want to rat him out as a tranny if I didn't have to.

Jimmy lost interest in my fertile urine and changed the subject.

"Look at this!" He sifted through the canteen food on the table. Sniffed the mushy apple up and wrinkled his nose. "God knows what this is preserved with. One thing Nazis never get credit for is health food. Hitler tried to get everybody off meat and dairy. I've seen pictures of his dinner. Looks just like what we used to get back home."

"Where's that? The Ruhr Valley?"

"Bountiful, Utah."

"FBI, right. You're Mormon."

"And say what you will about Mormons, we eat fresh. We eat organic. You look like you could stand a little health food yourself."

"Show me where I can get organic lard, and I'm in."

"Very funny. I'm not saying I like anything else about them. But they did practically discover whole grains. Soybeans, too. They used to call them 'Nazi beans.' Hitler knew his protein."

"White Bob, or Jimmy, or whatever your name is, I'm not sure where you're going with this. But Josef Mengele wasn't Gregor Mendel. He didn't torture beans."

"My point exactly. Don't tar the good people. The horticulturalists. The whole grains advocates. That's all I'm saying. America does plenty of things in our name you probably don't like."

"Pretty risqué opinion. You sure you're FBI?"

"Affirmative. And as such I like to know what kind of American I'm talking to. I happen to love my country. That does not change the fact that the Nazis outlawed lead in toothpaste tubes fifty years before America. I'm not saying ignore the bad, I'm saying look at the good. World War Two, American housewives were busy dyeing margarine yellow. Meanwhile, Reich scientists discovered butter-yellow coloring was carcinogenic. IG Farben was the number-one manufacturer of food dyes—and they agreed to stop producing. They put purity before profit."

"Why not? They probably got back what they lost in dye jobs with what they saved using slave labor."

Jimmy flinched like I'd slapped him—and he wanted to slap me back. Good. I was beyond fatigued. I reeked. If my liver'd had a mouth and telephone access it would have called a lawyer already.

"You're just a fed with a sinsemilla haircut," I said.

If he wanted to throw down, maybe I could hit him with a chair. If not, at least it would be over fast. I tensed, letting him know I was ready.

Naturally, I'd misread the situation.

"What are you, crazy?" His whisper was high pitched. "You think I'm gonna start anything in the visiting room? You need to calm down, man. I'm not saying the Nazis weren't monsters. I'm saying the fact that they were monsters doesn't cancel the fact that they were early vegetarians. Bad food and chemicals were outlawed. Hitler was obsessed with cancer. He even forbade coffee. He thought caffeine was poison."

"He didn't need it. His doctor shot him up with amphetamines. Stuck a needle in his ass every morning."

"You're missing the point. Nobody's perfect. Hitler was all about getting rid of the toxins. That's what the camps were for, too! The man even outlawed Coca-Cola."

"No wonder we went to war. America could live with death camps. But Hitler should have known, you don't fuck with Coca-Cola."

"He didn't."

"You just said—"

"What? You don't think corporations can hide? The Third Reich served Fanta. Orange. Fanta was a subsidiary of Coca-Cola. But it was hush-hush. The stuff's still popular in Europe and Brazil."

"Why are we talking," I said, "when you should be arresting a mass mutilator? Is this some kind of test? I need to make some notes for class."

I started to get up. He hooked his leg in my chair so it wouldn't budge. "What now?" I asked him.

"Nothing's black and white," he said, ignoring my question. "You heard of Operation Paperclip? We accepted Nazi scientists if they had something we wanted. Why do you think you never hear about the Japanese Mengeles? Because there weren't any? Guess again. Look up Colonel Ishi—but not on a full stomach. MacArthur signed away the pursuit of all charges in return for American scientists getting his research. Nice and quiet. No Nuremberg."

"Why not?"

"We punished the people we couldn't use."

"And now you think Mengele's useful?"

"I'm not saying he doesn't deserve to hang. But without his early work on caloric intake we might not have your low-carb diets today."

"We're back to death camp diet tips? Are you *insane*?"

"Okay, forget carbohydrates. Hitler outlawed tobacco in the thirties. Are you saying that makes not smoking a bad idea? Read your George Bernard Shaw. 'Ideas aren't responsible for the people who embrace them.'"

"They teach that at BYU?"

"I don't know, I went to Yale. Mormons can get educated, you know."

"You and Mitt Romney."

"The man on the gay wedding cake. Just 'cause he's one of ours doesn't mean we like him. Speaking of Yale, that's where I met your ex."

"You know Tina?"

"Knew. Not a lot of Yalies make it to where *she* ended up, huh?"

"She doesn't talk about that part of her life."

"Marvin was this guy who used to sell ex in New Haven. I couldn't believe she married him. She beats all the odds. Gets a scholarship from Nowheresville and what does she do?"

"She never told me any of this."

"Right. I guess when you met her she was pretty far down the road."

"Not a conversation I want to have right now. Can we," I suggested, "restrict the conversation to you not nailing Mengele when you had the chance?"

Jimmy the Rasta ignored the question and pushed the small mountain of canteen snacks my way. "Have some Cheez Doodles or something. It looks weird if we don't eat."

I'd been waiting for the right moment. I shoved a handful of popcorn in my mouth and talked around it. "I still don't believe you're undercover."

"I don't give a shit what you believe. All I want is for you to tell me how you came to have a relationship with Harry Zell."

The table beside us filled up with an extended Latino family. Four scrubbed-up boys stood in line to show their report cards to Dad. "I don't have a relationship," I said, "I have an arrangement. He hired me, with minor coercion, to do a job."

"So you're working for him?"

"Boy, you don't miss anything."

"Please, Mr. Rupert. Do you know what Zell does? I know you did your private-eye-school skip trace."

"I could have done more."

"It wouldn't have mattered. Zell got a scrub. And I mean the best you can get. Government documents, Google, any kind of paper—all scrubbed. That takes juice and money."

"I don't even know what you're talking about. You can pay to have yourself un-look-up-able? Why not just a fake name?"

" 'Cause then people could look up your fake name?"

He had me there. But I still wasn't buying it. "I don't know, man. That scrub thing . . . It sounds like an urban legend."

"That's what they want you to think, friend." It was hard to place the expression on my snack partner's face. "All you really need to know is this: Harry Zell saw the train coming. The man's a visionary."

"What'd he do?"

"What did he do? The man invented prison reality shows. He knew prison was the new porn. He got rights to go in before he even sold the idea for *Lockup* to MSNBC, or *Inside* on the NGC."

"What's that?"

"National Geographic Channel. You know, they're not stuffy any-more. No more bare tribal breasts in the African village. Now they show prison gang docs. That's way more NGC. And every inch of footage is shot, syndicated, supplied and owned by Zell. Zell knew. He was like Bob Hope buying up the San Fernando Valley when all people could see were orange groves. Well, before Zell, all people saw when they looked at prison was . . . prison. Not Zell. He looked, and he saw the future. He was buying up prime real estate in ten B.C."

"Ten B.C.?"

"Ten years before cable."

"So it sounds like he did great. I still don't get why he had to go full scrub, or whatever you called it. Not that I don't think you're com-pletely bullshitting me to begin with. What was his beef with Men-gele?"

"Mengele wanted to go public, supposedly. The old man wanted the honor due him before he croaked."

"Thinks he got a raw deal?"

"Victim of circumstance. He's got this Wernher von Braun fixa-tion."

"So I gathered."

"Mind you," said the undercover agent, "I can't say as I blame him. Von Braun builds V-2s in slave camps. Ends up palling around with Jack Kennedy like a couple of playboy kings. JFK was more concerned with getting to the moon than breeding pure-blooded Aryans. So what if Wernher developed the V-2 and aimed them at London? Ever hear that Ray Charles song from the fifties? 'Shoulda been me—with that real fine chick. Shoulda been me—eatin' ice cream and cake.' That's Mengele. He was ahead of his time."

"I didn't have you pegged as an R&B fan."

"What can I tell you? I had you pegged as a guy with no pegs. But I'm trusting you with this. Now give *me* something."

"Give you what? I still don't get how Zell loses if Mengele's brought in. It's fucking surreal that you even have to *think* about nailing a mass murderer. Lots of guys pretend to be Vietnam vets. Desert Stormers. They want part of the glory. The German doctor's too old for those. So he comes here to play out his senior years as a big shot. Hey, he could do worse than Dr. Mengele."

"You can't be serious."

"Why not? Maybe he wanted a Nazi marquee name. Or not."

"The point is, assuming, for the moment, that Mengele is Mengele, Zell's going to lose money if he gets arrested now."

"Why? No, don't tell me—he's doing a reality show with Mengele?"

"Not exactly. Zell wants exclusive rights to the capture."

"Why does law enforcement care what Zell wants? Why do *you* care?"

Rasta Jim did not honor that with a response. His very nonanswer declared the obvious: Mengele was a death celebrity not even countless A&E *Biography* reruns could diminish. Figure it out.

The guy I still thought of as White Bob Marley sighed and tore open a box of Cracker Jacks. "You know, they take the prizes out ahead of time. No prizes in the joint."

"Why? 'Cause they think felons don't deserve prizes?"

"There's that. Lot of them are plastic is the main thing. Cons can melt 'em, sharpen them on the concrete floor. Pretty soon your little blue X-Man's melted down to a two-inch aorta poker."

"Fuck the Cracker Jacks. Answer the question. So the government doesn't want to arrest Mengele? Is that what you're saying? We're back to what Zell has on them?"

"Somebody went to night school."

"You gonna tell me what it is? Or are we going to sit here until I OD on hydrogenated fats and prove the Nazis were right about whole foods?"

"I'll give you a hint. San Quentin gets a lot of money from Big Pharma."

"They perform experiments on prisoners?"

He gave in, unwrapped a pack of peanut butter crackers and tucked one in his mouth. "I'm just sayin'. And who knows more about human experiments?" He twisted his topmost dread, the one that stuck straight up like the top of a Christmas tree, minus the star. "From what I hear it's been going on since, like, World War One. But of course that's just a rumor. Completely unsubstantiated. Wink-wink snicker-snicker."

"I've heard stuff like that," I said. "I read this book, *Acres of Skin*, about the perfume tests doctors did on inmates at Holmesberg State Prison, in Pennsylvania. They used to put chemicals under their skin. They showed pictures. After a while the poor bastards had backs like checkerboards. Went on for years."

"You read a book, huh? You're not half-dumb for a small-town cop with questionable taste in women and substance abuse issues."

"Should I even bother to ask why you know so much?"

"You should be asking how. The small-town stuff's in your file. The substance abuse, I'm looking at your pupils. You ever think of wearing shades?"

"I was hoping Mengele could dye my eyes."

"Yeah, green really shows the load," he said. "It's all in the pupils. And buddy, I gotta say, you're more pinned than a Baby Doc voodoo doll."

"In that case, you know where I have to go."

"Rehab?"

"Close. I have to go teach a drug class, remember? Where I believe I'll be seeing you. Maybe together, we can lick this thing."

My unlikely FBI reverted to form.

"Listen to me, Rupert. If Mengele doesn't get his shot at the von Braun treatment, he says he's going to spill. They read his outgoing mail. He's already tried. Certain people are not happy about this. Prison Experiments—if there, you know, *were* such things—would be a state run growth industry. Let's face it, in this economy there aren't many of those. Look at Abu Ghraib. Think the scandal was Lindsey England, the leashes and hoods? No, that was micro. Macro would be the *New York Times* publishes a story that a certain big-ass pharmaceutical company arranged the whole damn mess to test new mood stabilizers. Same thing at Guantánamo. But that's not happening, right? No proof. So hey, its all just crazy talk. No evidence whatsoever. Forget I ever said anything."

"When your whole life feels like the stress position, you need . . . Guantanamax!"

"You done bein' an ass? If Mengele spills, it's gonna be too big to pin on a few bad apples. I'm not saying they couldn't frame somebody. More likely they'd just kill the old prick before it came to that. Too big a deal, you know, with the roots running under a lot of respectable graves."

"That's a lot of information, man."

"What's a lot of information?" He stared at me like I was insane. "Did you hear me say anything? You must be experiencing aural hallucinations. Stress does that. UC work can be hell on the nerves."

"I know," I said, "I could use a mood stabilizer right now."

We got up at the same time. Jim reverted to his UC character, Anglo Rasta man, doing a little jim-jim dance as he scooped up his canteen treats.

When we shook hands he held mine an extra few seconds and looked me in the eyes. "I know what it's like undercover. The trick isn't going under, brother, it's coming back up without getting the bends."

"Thanks for the advice—and the information," I said. "You don't pick that platinum blond old fuck up by tomorrow, I'm going to make a fortune off the *Enquirer*. I don't care who goes down with him."

Jim the Rasta stopped. For the first time I imagined how he would look without the clown hair—beneath that twenty-first-century-hippie façade lurked the chiseled features of a daytime soap star. He let loose a trippy giggle for the benefit of onlookers and spoke the rest low. "Let me give you some advice, drug addict: never show your hand—until you're sure it's still attached to your arm."

"Good advice."

The man was no joke. I was glad I hadn't mentioned that I got knocked out and woke up tied to a toilet, or that my ex-wife had disappeared. He might have worried about me.

The UC fed said his good-byes under his breath. "Thanks for the snacks. See you in class, Mindy."

I stopped. "Who snitched me out? Or did you bug the warden's office?"

White Bob Marley smiled. "If you do anything to impede, denigrate or in any way, shape or form dingle-butt my case, I promise you, I will make sure everybody knows about the estrogen."

I shrugged. "Do what you gotta do. Might open up a whole new client base. Trannies have problems too."

Before returning his hand, I turned it over. The knuckles were thick, sprouting wiry ginger hair.

"What are you doing?"

"Checking for tiny doll hands," I said.

"Dude, if you're on psych meds, I suggest you change them. If you're not, I strongly suggest you consider them."

"What worked for you?" I asked him.

Our repartee was interrupted by a scream. A beautiful young Filipina had leaped up and hurled hot coffee on her boyfriend's face. He screamed and tumbled off the chair. She kneeled down and yanked his T-shirt over his head, raked her nails across his exposed back, directly over a phrase tattooed across it in swirling letters: SA MAARI BUHAY AY SAY MAPOOT.

Jim read it and translated: *To Be Alive Is to Hate.*

"You speak Filipino?"

"Gang detail. I saw a lot of Flips. Watch her left hand."

"Ya-*bang*!" the Filipina shrieked. "Ya-*bang*!"

"That means 'pride,'" Jim whispered under the chaos.

With her right hand, the girl slapped and back-slapped her poor boyfriend's face. He didn't flinch, but tears came anyway. Then, with a last slap before the guard arrived, she jammed her left hand up to the elbow in her boyfriend's pants, then slipped it out so fast I wasn't sure I'd even seen it.

By now the whole place was hooting. "See that," Jim cried under their shouts, "she keistered him! Everybody thinks he's a bitch, meanwhile the Flip probably made a grand."

I turned to see two COs carrying the shirtless Filipino life-hater off horizontally. Another CO, the ever-present Colfax, led the angry girlfriend off with a firm hand on her back. I could hear him chiding her. "Now just what the heck were you thinking, missy?"

When I turned back to Jim, he was gone. For a second I stood there, wondering what kind of narcotics the Filipina shoved up her old man. But I had bigger problems. I still had no idea what happened to Tina. Almost as scary, in fifteen minutes I had to walk into a room full of convicted felons, some of whom might actually be law enforcement, and share my wisdom on the subject of addiction and recovery. If I was lucky, I wouldn't keel over from a delayed reaction to the Red Cross medicine. I could handle being dead, but I'd hate to set a bad example.

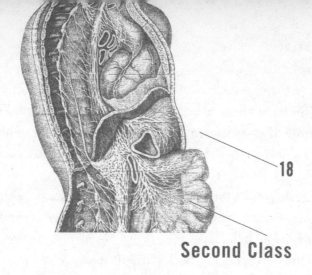

18

Second Class

Regret clawed at my brainpan like a cat scratching a couch. The confab with Rasta Jim was too weird to contemplate. But it did little to mitigate my twin terrors: the fact that Tina remained MIA and that I'd had the chance to grab Mengele by his peroxide hair and drag him off. But I hadn't. And I had to ask myself why. How exactly can you distinguish fear from caution? Was this how Roosevelt felt deciding whether or not to bomb the camps?

With Mengele walking the earth, the blue sky was an affront.

I stepped past a cluster of men with briefcases. We sized each other up. Would they have been standing around if they knew Mengele was there? Avoiding their eyes, I thought of the old race doctor's irises: black and light-sucking. Six hundred thousand he killed. Personally. I imagined the compressed energy of his victims' fear like a swarm of bees. But who did the honey nourish? The dead or the living?

Approaching the classroom, I stopped and took a breath. The FBI Rasta was behind me. He clutched a cup of coffee in one hand and a bag full of visiting room snacks in the other. He put the bag in his teeth so he could clap me on the back. Then he took it out so he could talk.

"You all right, bud? You look a little peaked."

"I'm great, Jim." I returned the backslap and bent toward his ear. "So, is there, like, a special department? An undersecretary for not catching genocidal maniacs?"

Rasta Jim returned my back-pat and gave me a man-hug. "Just stick to what you know. Like drugs and hormones. Comin' in?"

"In a minute. This is when I like to smoke and collect my thoughts."

"You can't smoke."

"That's one reason I'm nervous."

I took a last breath, looked around at the yard and the houses scattered on the hill beyond. What fun, having a state prison at your feet. I wondered if residents sat on their back porches, feet up in their chaise lounges, binoculars perched on their noses, nursing a cold one and checking out the shank and riot action. No different than watching NASCAR, waiting for flaming wrecks.

I had not expected to be so happy to see the guys: Roscoe, Davey, Cranky, Movern, Jim the Rasta-fed, even Tina's AA Christian porno pal, Reverend D. Although the rev and I now shared some awkward personal business. Awkward enough to send me ambling over as I greeted the rest of the fellas, trying to make it look casual when I leaned down and hissed in his face, *"So where the hell is Tina?"* He smiled wide enough to show off the gold trove in his teeth. The Nazis made millions gleaning precious metal from the mouths of death camp residents. They would have loved Rev. D.

"No hello?" the reverend said. "No 'how are you doing in the struggle to stay clean and sober in an unclean and insane environment'?"

I did my best to freeze an easy grin on my face. "Cut the bullshit, Rev. I need to know what you know."

"Sex and checks," he sighed. "Nine times out of ten, it's sex and checks what drive a man back to the gettin' high side of town."

Roscoe approached and stared in my eyes like he was reading the paper.

"Thought you was gonna shine us on," Rasta Jim haw-hawed from across the room. Back in character. "We was gonna have a riot or some-thin'."

Reverend D backed him up. "That's right. You best be mindful, bein' in a room alone with felons and all. You like Siegfried and Roy up in here, without no Siegfried."

"White tiger chewed Roy's ass up!" Movern cried, surprisingly passionate. "Can't tame a white tiger. Big cat do what a big cat do."

"Dude!" White Rasta waved away the entire notion. "It wasn't the fucking tiger. It was Siegfried. He gave the secret attack signal."

Movern slapped the table. "Why the fuck would he do that? You over there all amped up like you dialed into some secret-ass informa-tion. Like your stoned cracker ass know shit about shit. You always say this dumb-ass shit that make no fucking sense."

"Don't have to make sense. It's a fag fight," said Rasta Jim. "You ask any cop. He'll tell you. Gay dude knifes another gay dude, he never do it just once. He sticks him, like, ninety times, then bitch-slaps him when he's bleedin'. You're talking about the body of a man and the emotions of a woman."

"Sound like you." Movern pushed back his chair so hard it fell over when he stood up. He pointed at Rasta Jim. "Yeah, I said it. Whatchu gonna do, bitch?"

"Things heatin' up," said the reverend. "And here you are, in the same cage as the animals. You lookin' at worse odds than Roy, son."

"At least I'm not wearing sequined pants."

But I saw what the rev meant: *no Rincin* . . . If one of the violent offenders on hand took issue with my classroom manner—and packed a shank—I'd be hard-pressed to fend him off. The thought started my heart banging on my ribs, like a prisoner hitting his cell bars with a spoon. We both wanted out of there.

"Still a few minutes before class," I said to no one in particular. I pretended to study some scribble in my notebook. If I ran out now I'd look weak. But if I stayed I might end up ventilated.

Reverend D leaned in close enough to whisper before I took my seat. "Tina told me to tell you she's okay."

The reverend was a master of casual menace. But freighted as the conversation was, it was better than sitting there wondering if I could stave off mayhem with a ball-point and a three-ring binder.

"Why did she leave?" My voice had a catch in it.

"That's nothin' I know," said the reverend, eying me sideways. "But here's somethin' I do know. Cathy, that shorty who did the doctor? She tol' me he liked to have her take her clothes off, then walk whichever way he pointed and do stuff."

"What kinda stuff?"

"Don't matter what kinda stuff. Ain't about what she did—s'about makin' her do it. The old man wanted to remember what power felt like."

"So it wasn't about sex?"

The reverend cocked his head at an angle and looked at me. "You playin' with me, dawg? *Everything* about sex."

"Sometimes a crack pipe is just a crack pipe," I said.

"You smoke crack," Cranky cut in, "you suckin' a glass dick."

"No! You suckin' on *Satan*." Movern was as worked up as I'd seen him. "The Devil put crack in the ghetto to turn our women into hos."

I waited for Movern to finish expressing himself before quietly responding to the reverend. "Whatever you wanna call what she did, if little Cathy did it with Mengele, I need to talk to her. But I need Tina first."

"Every man has needs," said the reverend. "All *you* need is some faith!"

"No doubt. Thanks."

I didn't want to get into a debate about my needs. I had too many to think about at once. I needed to figure out what I was going to say to the class. I needed to figure out if I was hatching a plan or a parasite had entered the bruise on my head and laid eggs. I needed to know more about Zell. I needed to talk to Mengele's Christian escort, Cathy. Find out about his hit-and-run. I needed to learn more about Bernstein, too. What I didn't need was the persistent paranoia I'd felt since sharing with J. Edgar Rasta Man. That I was somehow sticking my face into some elaborate interagency web, spun by Jim's DC handlers, engineered by the feds and Interpol, Scotland Yard, the CIA, MI 5, Mossad and a team of security guards at the Addis Ababa McDonald's. Who knew who else? I made up my mind. I'd have to find a way to get to L.A. and back by class tomorrow. Assuming I lived through this one. Under and over everything, behind and beside, there was the treacherous mystery of Tina.

The reverend barged into my deliberations, his wink nastier than the magazines that nearly decapitated me. "You like Christian pussy?"

"Never thought about it."

"Well," said the reverend, "here's your chance to remedy the situation."

If he saw Cranky's gesture he didn't acknowledge it. Coming on more pimp than informant, he gave me details about the girl who'd serviced the doctor.

"This one's nasty, but she clean, too. She keep her pussy pure for Jesus. She still a virgin. But she ain't afraid to use the Devil's portal, you know what I'm sayin'? Front door's locked, but the back door's open. That girl do love the Lord."

"I'm not looking for a date. I need to know what she knows."

"Well whatever you want to call it, she's down in L.A. In the Valley. You want to fly down, I can set up a meeting. Tina knows her. She tell you she was helpin' school the girls?"

"She mentioned it." I had to clamp my jaw to keep from screaming at him. "If you know something about what happened to her, then fucking tell me."

The reverend smiled.

"Let me tell you about a miracle," he said. "I was in the chow line at Folsom, waiting for oatmeal, when the Lord came to me and said, 'Young buck, you need to minister to them fallen women.' Someday, Manny Rupert, the Lord gonna tap you on the shoulder."

"You think?"

Maybe He was tapping me now! For a few heady seconds, I imagined sharing my recent experience, as a cautionary tale. *Take it from me, you may be years from your last shot—but you're two seconds from your next one.* . . . It could be cathartic.

"Addictive behavior," I kicked off, clapping my hands. "Anybody have any problems?"

Three hands shot up: Half-faced Davey—who'd come in late—Cranky and Rasta Jim from the FBI. Cranky waggled his hand back and forth over his head like a second grader who needed to pee.

I gave him the nod. "Bring it, Cranky."

"Okay, I got a fuckin' problem, homes! When I was in Chino, I's supposed to be learning how to dry-clean, right? I'm thinkin' I'm gonna sign up and learn some kinda trade. Meanwhile, them fools in there was soaking lint in dry-cleaning fluid and callin' it PCP." He smacked his chair for emphasis. "I'm serious. They be rollin' that shit up and passin' it off in the yard as sherm. Lemme tell you, mang, sherm was fuckin' pasteurized milk compared to this bunk. But guess what? I knew what the shit was, *and I still smoked it*!"

This got an appreciative chuckle from the clean-livers on hand.

"There it is," said Roscoe, doling out a Buddha-like smile. "What people don't know: Addiction is not a substance. Addiction is a *be-hav-ior*." He gave it three syllables. "Until we understand the nature of the problem, it doesn't matter what we do. We are never going to solve it."

"Uh-huh," said Cranky. "I don't got a drug problem. I got a *me* problem."

Just then Mengele entered, led by Rincin and Colfax. The wheelchair'd been scrapped. Maybe he found a pair of legs to transplant. By way of not obsessing, I waved to Rincin. "Glad you could join us, Officer. As I recall, whatever we talk about here stays here, right?"

"I am a corrections officer," Rincin said. "When a CO makes a report it's not the same as snitching."

Roscoe smiled his sage smile. "See how they do? Staff always has to mess with a man's head."

Cranky, gripped by sudden panic, clutched his head with both hands. "Hey, man, you ain't gonna write me up, are you? Does dry-cleaning fluid count as a drug?"

"Poor man's PCP," said Rincin. "To tell you the truth, I just got here."

Cranky lowered his head. "So, you gonna charge me?"

Rincin's grin made him threatening and pleasant at the same time. "Depends how my uniform looks when I pick it up. I find soilage, I'm gonna blame you for hogging the chemicals."

"Better watch your ass," the reverend snapped. "Pretty soon you gonna be Martinizing."

"People," I interrupted. "Remember it's not about what you do. It's about why you do it. It's about that hole you're trying to fill."

"You want to talk about *hole*?" It was Davey again. Half a face but a thousand-watt intensity. "With me it ain't even drugs."

"Don't have to be a drug to be a drug," Roscoe intoned, speaking so softly we had to strain to hear him.

"That's what I'm sayin'!" Davey's voice quivered. He teared up. "I ain't talkin' 'bout no dope or pruno. . . . It's like I can't stop—you know . . . another thing."

"Say it," I said. "Once you name it, it loses power."

Davey screwed up what was left of his face. He put his hand to his lipless mouth as though ripping the words. "I'm addicted to porn."

"Good for you," said the reverend. "Own it and bone it."

"Reverend, please," I said.

"I'm not talkin' about regular shit. I'm talkin' about sick stuff. On the Internet. With me it's porn, mang!"

"Beelzebub cast a web, and man called it the Internet," said the reverend.

"Whatchu mean, like JailBabes.com?" Jim giggled, back in character. "Them bitches is tore up!"

"Naw, man, JailBabes is like Little Miss Muffett compared to these sites. I'm talking about them personals websites. On that one, Alterna. com, jeezy-fuckin'-peezy, I saw a video of some blonde wrapping rope around her tits. She made these Japanese knots so tight her mama-bags swol' up blue like they was going to burst. It was horrible, man, but, like, at the same time it was *hot*. It was like I had a demon."

I stopped listening. If I found out Dave was jerking off over my ex-wife, then what? I went over the films in my head from our time in the trailer, but I didn't remember any rope burns on her breasts. If you look hard enough, there's always something to be grateful for.

Davey rushed on, dabbing at his lipless mouth and shifting on his chair, mega-agitated. "It's that one with the personals, with ladies who want to put clothespins on their titties and all like that? Man, it's like sick hot, 'cause, you know, it's not posed, it ain't porno porn. It's like, this is what they're into. . . . And it ain't even that the stuff they do turns me on so much, you know. . . . *It's that they wanna do it!* I'm sitting here, trimming my toenails, and there's some lady in Kentucky who looks like my mom on the webcam, squeezin' an avocado out of her ass. In her profile she says, 'All holes are the property of Master Don from Hollywood, Florida.' I guess he's the guy who got to put the avocado in. And right at the end, it says, 'Will do doghouse.' I don't even know what that means, but I know it's super-fucking-nasty. And it's like, these are regular folks. They ain't models. Spankhappy72 wants to meet a dude for kennel training." Davey looked genuinely scared. "I'm serious, man, this stuff is all real. I thought my head was gonna explode!"

"Your head already exploded," said Cranky.

"Cranky," I said, "come on, okay?"

But Davey was too deep in it to hear anyway. "Naw, man, I'm serious." Sweat coated his face, somehow rendering the cosmetically enhanced patches more waxen. "It's so wrong-like, but at the same time, it gives me some weird kind of hope. Like, Jesus gumdrops, there's chicks out there who wanna drink mailman pee, get tea-bagged by fat guys. Maybe there's a girl out there for me."

Reverend D let out a sigh. "A romantic. Ain't that the shit?"

Things got quiet, except for Jimmy giggling behind his hand. Davey whimpered. "It's killin' me, man. I'm on the computer, supposed to be preppin' for my GED. . . ."

"So," I said, "should I even ask how you get the computers?"

Rincin shook his head. I said, "Forget I asked."

"I can tell," Davey sniffed. "I get three hours a day, on accounta my educational status."

"And they're not monitored?"

"I think maybe the guy who's supposed to be monitorin' gets off on that sick-ass shit as much as I do."

"See that?" said Roscoe. "And you want to stand there and ask *this* black man how he knows there is an all-powerful, all-knowing Creator—bless him by any of his thousand names. Don't even! 'Cause depravity is a virus that comes in every color."

Davey stared straight ahead, his jaw sliver working furiously. He worked a bony fist in his eye, dislodging some unspeakable image of online personals degradation. *"Caramel cutie craves party-fist. . . ."*

Now everybody was talking. Except Mengele. He had his eyes closed. But that was okay. Tribes who didn't easily interact were interacting. Maybe that was the ticket to world peace: the universal language of nasty ass and pussy.

Finally Davey got down to the real problem. "I got a chafe like I been rubbing my johnson on a screen door."

"Son," said the reverend, "how long you been down? Ain't you heard of lotion?"

"Can't use lotion, stupid. That shit gunks up the keyboard."

Taking pity, Jim slipped Davey a Twinkie from his canteen stash. But the half-faced porn dog was so wound up he squeezed it in his hands, crushing the cream out. "Look at that, he even chokin' his Twinkie."

Davey wiped his hands on his pants, too desperate to take offense. "You don't know, man. Fiendin' for crack ain't nothin' compared to this, 'cause it's endless, man. . . . You get on and you start lookin' at freaky shit, then that links to some other freaky shit, and that links to some other freaky shit. . . . It's like the broom in 'The Sorcerer's Apprentice,' you know, in that Disney movie."

"Fantasia," said Rasta Jim.

"Yeah, yeah. Fanazia. And before you know what happened, you're goin' bug-eyed over some big-ass ho from Hueto, North Dakota, tit-clamped to a shower nozzle with a ham sandwich hanging out of her kitty. . . . It's like, it ain't even sex no more."

Now Cranky pulled up his shirt and slapped his stomach. "Man, I'd love me a ham sandwich. Meat in this place taste like it come from raccoons or somethin'. They say it's ham but only thing hammy about it is it's bein' served by pigs." He turned in his chair. "Just kiddin', Officer."

"Well, see if I am," the CO said cryptically.

"I'm still sharing," Davey whined.

Reverend D jumped out of his chair. "Give somebody else a chance. Fuck's wrong with you?"

"Ain't nothin' wrong with me. You the one jumpin' out your chair."

Roscoe interrupted. "Son, how old were you when you come into the joint?"

"Seventeen."

"How many women you have?"

Davey looked over, fighting back tears. I quickly stood and clapped my hands. "I think what Davey did here was pretty brave."

"The fuck he do but whine and get pervy?"

"He made the link between addiction and behavior," I said, feeling *Welcome Back, Kotter*–ish. "He got that addiction isn't a substance, it's an action."

"You said that last time, hoss." Movern opened up a magazine stuffed in his notebook. It looked like a *Modern Bride*.

"I'm addicted to saying it," I said. "An addiction is any action we take, compulsively, over and over, even though we don't want to, and even though we know it's gonna make us feel horrible, we are powerless to stop. Might be drugs, might be sex, might be lookin' at sex, might be anything—as long as we don't wanna do it and we don't stop."

Cranky cackled. "Hey, mang, that mean my grandma's an addict? She's always fiendin' for churros, you know? She's this skinny old lady, but she's, like, scarfing down churros from morning to night."

"Sounds to me like she has an eating disorder."

"Nothing funny about that," said Reverend D. "I know plenty of girls, size minus-three, they look in the mirror they see Queen fucking Latifah. I blame the media."

Suddenly Mengele, who until now I'd been successfully blocking out, aimed his gaze at me and slapped the desk, infuriated. "What I don't get is the Nazi stuff."

What an opening. "You mean like *Ilse, She-Wolf of the SS?*"

"Yes! You have seen that?"

"I have. As a matter of fact, it was shot on the set of *Hogan's Heroes*, on weekends."

He ignored this bit of trivia, clucking his tongue. How was Josef Mengele supposed to know about *Hogan's Heroes*?

"Ilse was nothing like that . . . that character. This is what I'm saying. The American ignorance of my work. The continuing insult." He sputtered as if the sheer quantity of wrongs done him were too vast to mention. "You always get it wrong. Something as simple as Waffen-SS insignia . . . The uniform. Always the lightning bolts, the women in leather boots . . . *Accch!*"

"I ain't got nothing against women in black leather boots," said Movern.

Mengele winced. "I cured influenza. What you call the flu. Your so-called flu vaccines? You might as well hang flypaper to catch machine gun bullets!"

"Sound like somebody gonna be winnin' that whatchamacallit prize," Roscoe teased.

"What prize?" Mengele wanted to know, hungry for anything.

"You know, the one that don't ring—the No Bell!" Roscoe scoffed out a laugh that sounded like *kick kick kick*. "The No Bell Prize."

But Mengele was sincere. "I don't want the Nobel Prize. I want to help. . . . I want my notes to be read! I want my work to be recognized."

Fourteen words kept blaring through my brain: *Get out of your chair, walk three steps, stick a pen through his heart*. Why not? I already had friends in prison.

Mengele's frustration came out like a whimper. "I want to do good!"

"Gimme fifty dollars," said the reverend. "That'd be real good."

Jim giggled behind his hand. Movern clucked his tongue. Davey hugged himself.

I vacillated: seeing the ninetysomething bottle blond with a chewed-on mustache, then imagining his younger self, the dapper scalpel-wielding monster whose legendary cruelty was the reason I was there.

History had just shown up. I couldn't focus. I had a head full of Heil Hitler ringtones and spinning iPhone screens, each projecting random Mengelalia: the castrated dwarves, twin vagina surgeries, the selections. The deliberate wounds. The dissected babies, their intestines. The murder murder murder murder murder murder murder der murder murder murder murder murder murder murder murder murder murder. *He who has done that is here.* But what was I supposed to do?

I could have texted the papers, alerted CNN, posted something on Huffington. Surrounded by San Quentin convicts. I thought about the other prisoners, the ones he dispatched straight from the trains to the ovens.

Rincin, I noticed, had his hand on his mace. I managed a mild glance at Mengele.

"So, uh, what's bothering you again?" *Never respect him.*

"Besides the fact that degenerates have perverted the noblest idea of the twentieth century and turned it into masturbatory fodder? Reduced it to the whip-wielding dominatrix with stylized SS wear? What bothers me is when they show so-called soldiers. SS men."

"What bothers you about that?" I'd have to meet the Christian hooker to find out if he was who he said he was. In the meantime, it was dizzying trying to reel him in.

I thought he would say "disrespect," then rant on about Jews running Hollywood. Instead he said, "They get it wrong. The outfits, the insignia. They mix up death's head and lightning bolts like it's meaningless. But if you know the Wehrmacht, or the SS, that's like sewing a Doberman's head on a goat."

That analogy alone told me he was the man. But I needed more.

"Have you tried that?" I asked. "The goat and Dobie?"

"Is that a joke?"

His rage was only terrifying because I knew history. History was terrifying. Especially when it was still happening.

The ball of shame lodged in my gullet: Was I a collaborator at heart? What would I do to save myself? What I would do to save Tina? If you were a Hungarian Jew in 1943, was it better to get on that train knowing where you were headed? Or was it better not to know what would become of you?

"There are thirty kinds of lightning bolts!" Mengele barked. He raised his hands for emphasis. His palms glowed the same translucent blue as his temples, wafer thin. He combed his long pianist's fingers through his hair. Not the kind of fingers attached to doll hands. "These people could not tell the difference between the Waffen-SS hat badge and the Iron Cross First Class that Hitler gave to Henry Ford. In your insidious war movies, one moment the SS man will show up in the gold pin of the Norwegian railway fighters. In the next, he's wearing the death's-head insignia of the Totenkopf!"

"That like an English muffin?" Movern wanted to know.

"For your information, the Totenkopf were the SS who guarded the camps. This was not, sadly, a prestige position."

"Does it really matter?" I wondered what Mengele would look like if he blew a gasket.

"Does it matter what's tattooed on the rump of some performing whore in a Gestapo hat? Yes, it does! This is America! Nazi S&M films may be the only history lesson they ever get. For this reason, it pains me to see the inaccuracy. I saw a piece of pornographic trash where, just before the strapping Gestapo lad favored a hausfrau with his essence, the camera moved in on a close-up of the Himmler Leb-ensraum Mutter brooch on the soldier's lapel. *A Mutter brooch!* Be-stowed upon racially pure Rhinemaidens for coupling with SS men and giving birth to heroes! It signifies the wearer has borne babies of highest racial purity. *'Every mother of good blood is a sacred asset of our existence.'* This is a travesty!"

He may have been right. But it didn't help me any. The only way I was going to confirm his identity was to talk to the born-again hooker. But I needed to keep him on the hook until I could sneak off.

"Did you ever think," Roscoe asked politely, "back in the day?"

"Did I ever think what?"

I expected Mengele to treat African-Americans like talking dogs. But he was no more contemptuous and sneering than he was to anyone else.

"Did you ever think," Roscoe asked pleasantly, "that the entire ideology of the Reich was going to be reduced to a bin in porno stores? How does that feel, having your most cherished symbols end up as white trash prison tats? Ol' Adolf thought the whole world was his bitch. Now who's wearin' the red dress?"

Rasta Jim bit the back of his wrist, bobbing up and down. "Oh, shit!"

"Cold," said Movern.

I wasn't sure if Mengele would respond. He had a way of making himself still. Learned, I suspected, from years spent staring at lizards in São Paulo, running a coffee plantation. I kept trying to fix him in my mind. To reconcile the well-preserved blond with the Puccini-whistling lady killer who could make a Jewess swoon on her way to the gas.

"No," he said. "I foresaw defeat, but not degradation."

Along with the baby-smooth skin and punkish dye job, I noticed that his neck didn't sag. Maybe he'd lifted his own face. But his left hand rocked from side to side with subtle palsy. Just like Bunker-era Hitler. And occasionally his lips smacked together, seemingly of their own volition, as if they were fed separately.

"Okay, let's cut the bullshit, Doc. What were you addicted to? That's all we deal with in here. So what was it?"

"What do you think? A stimulant. Germans invented amphetamines. The very first was called Pervalit."

Movern shivered. "Y'all Pervy about everything."

"Would you forget the Germans? The forties are over. Let's get specific. Where did drugs take you that you never thought you'd go? What was your bottom?"

Mengele raised his chin. He took a sneering chew on his mustache to show the esteem in which he held me and everybody else in the drug class.

"This is it," he said. "Talking to you. This is worse than the Paraguayan shit shovelers I had to live with in Ascunción. I stayed in some pile of sticks near New Germany, this hellhole founded by Nietzsche's sister Elisabeth and her husband, Bernhard Förster. They thought being Aryan and hating Jews was enough to keep them alive in the jungle. The whole colony starved trying to raise llamas and grow yerba maté. South America is not a place for Aryans! Only impure races can tolerate that kind of sun."

"Albinos must be gods," I said.

"Hah! No one recognizes greatness!" He stammered, "You—your whole country—would rather die of the diseases I could cure than admit they were wrong in not letting me cure them! I offer myself, now, with all the risks such an action involves. And look! Look—look where they have me! With this," he sputtered, indicating the class. "With this and this and this and this!" Voice rising, he pointed to Roscoe, who seemed bemused, then, one by one, to half-faced Davey, Movern, Cranky, Reverend D, Rasta Jim and Rincin and back to me.

Done raving, Mengele checked his watch, pulled out a tiny container and removed a brown pill and a large red capsule. "Ha!" he cackled. "What I have in this pill could save a generation from heart disease and diabetes. I have arteries like a fetus. But because of ignorance, you suffer, and I breathe the flatulence of subhumans!" He ate the pill with a flourish. Delusional or not, his performance was riveting. No wonder Zell thought he could make a fortune on the old genocider. His preening self-regard made it impossible not to watch.

"Subhuman flatulence," I repeated, with nothing in particular to add.

"Look like a motherfucking cold capsule to me. Time-release Contac," the reverend sneered.

Since the talk with Tina, I was only half-worried whether it was him anymore. But I needed the hooker to make sure. I was more worried about what Zell wanted with him. And why I'd been selected as go-between. I was shy on specifics. But a scenario in which the smart move, all around, was to dispense with him would not have been implausible. God knows, it would have been easy to arrange. Half the men under the San Quentin roof were professional dispensers. Tina was right. I'd jumped in too fast.

There was only one way to find out who was protecting who. I got out of my chair and moved toward Mengele, reaching my hand in my pants like I was pulling a shank out. Before I made two steps Jimbo was on his feet, Cranky had launched himself out of his chair, Rincin had whipped out a blackjack and three members of the extraction team burst in armed with stun shields. They were usually brought in to pry ab seg prisoners out of their cells when they refused to leave for a shower. "Everybody down!" one of them shouted.

The rest of the room dropped. I managed to spin around to the extractors, flashing the pack of gum in my hand, so all six Mengele defenders could see.

"The fuck," said Rincin, putting his weapon away, then moving in to put six words in my ear. "Nothing happens to the old guy."

"Sorry," I said to the room in general.

The extractors raised the front windows on their helmets, uniformly pissed.

"My bad," I said. "I just wanted to offer the doctor a piece of gum."

Jim didn't look too happy either. Rincin seemed to seethe under his grin. I wasn't surprised about smoking those two out, but Cranky, the La Eme speedster, I didn't see coming. For all I knew, everybody in the room was UC something. Except for Mengele. And he might have been a fake . . .

"Okay, excitement's over," I said, waiting for the extraction team to clank out. "Let's get back to work. I want to start with an exercise. Everybody think about what kind of movie their lives would be. A lot of what fuels our drugging and drinking is a need to project a certain image. So, if there was a movie of your life, what would it be?"

"Patch Adams," Mengele said at once.

"Patch Adams? Really."

"I love the children, like Patch," said Mengele. "I have also heard that your Jerry Lewis made a movie based on me." He sniffed. "'Der Tag der Clown Weinte.' *The Day the Clown Cried.*" He ran his tongue along his mustache as though tickling himself. "I have done research. Jerry Lewis's real name was Jerome Levitch. Like me, he is obsessed with childhood disease. Muscular dystrophy. Every year he raises millions. I have research I believe he would find very very hopeful. I imagine he would pay for it."

Without changing expression, he mimed playing the violin for a moment, then explained himself.

"Sometimes, with *der kinder,* if I knew an experiment was going to be painful, I would play the violin for them. A waltz could be so soothing. I did not use anesthetics. On special days, I dressed like a clown to perform the surgery. A Jew clown from a circus in Budapest showed me how to apply the makeup. Moishe Moishe. He was kind enough to leave it to me when he expired. Of the influenza."

Suddenly his face went dark. "Thanks to Moishe—and his generous lungs—I found the cure."

"You a great man!" said Rasta Jim, the white Bob Marley.

Mengele accepted the compliment with a grimace.

"It was not just influenza. I had the cure for cancer too. A vaccine." He pointed a manicured, slightly palsied finger at me. "When any American dies of cancer, he should blame you for not allowing me to present my cure in this country. They call me evil? What about the people who prevent me from sharing cures—the millions they condemn to die? They are the killers now—who knows how many millions?"

"I'd call my congressman," I said, "but he doesn't even believe in abortion."

"You joke!" he snarled. "You joke!"

Mengele's smile was thinner than onion skin. He stood up and placed his hands on my shoulders, letting one finger stray to my throat. It felt bony, fleshless, but made of steel and—this is what made me cringe—*warm*. That Mengele gave off human warmth made being human feel revolting.

He seemed eager to see my horror, so I tried to look bored. Squelched a yawn. Up close, his shirt gave off the scent of lavender. His breath was minty. I could see the white roots showing under his Billy Idol hair.

I shook off his hand and he raised it to my face. "You Americans love to judge. But let me give you a little lollipop called the truth."

He pretended to hold out a sucker. I role-played, eying his hand with disdain.

"A lollipop? Do I look like a three-year-old who hasn't eaten in a week? You think conning traumatized pre-pubes makes you powerful? Why don't you put on a clown nose, see if anybody in here lets you cut their balls out and transplant ape testicles."

"I operated on plenty of grown men. I am a doctor of medicine."

"Is it called medicine when you don't care if they die? Okay, let's get back to drugs."

I could have done more to reel the discussion back to recovery. But how often do you get to insult one of the vilest characters on the planet? It was addictive, which felt fairly vile to admit. Reverend D whispered behind his hand to Jim. Once again, natural enemies suspending their enmity to share. Be still my heart.

"Okay," I said, "who wants to talk about the bad decisions they made on drugs?"

Mengele glared. "You are a rude young man."

"Feeling slighted, that's another addict trait. Thank God you're here, Doctor, you're better than a textbook."

Movern had some wisdom he wanted to add. "Soon's I sniff me some of that 'caine, I used to think people was talkin' about me. Soon as I sniff me a bit more, I start to feel like they sayin' bad things."

"Turd at the center of the universe," said Davey. "It's, like, a syndrome."

Movern sniffed. "Who you callin' a turd, white boy?"

Rincin ran his finger across his throat. My heart skidded, then I realized he didn't mean my throat was going to be cut—he meant *time's up*. At least I hoped so.

"Gentlemen," I said, "I hope you're cured and ready to spread your healing insights to others. If not, I'm back here tomorrow."

Roscoe stood up first. "It's been real," he said. I waited for him, or anybody, to say a few words before leaving. As though I'd actually offered some kind of solution for anything. But nobody seemed inclined to share one-on-one. "Okay, guys," said Rincin, "Officer Colfax will meet you outside."

I had to get to San Francisco, catch a flight south. But first I needed to speak with Reverend D. During class, I'd managed to keep the lid on my Tina fear. Now it was simmering. "Reverend," I said brightly, for the benefit of anybody listening in. "I wondered if I could talk to you for a second, about that thing you said."

"What thing is that?" The reverend wasn't going to make it easy.

"You know what thing," I said, turning my back to keep it from Davey, who was lamely pretending to tie his shoe. "What happened to Tina?"

The reverend regarded me with something like curiosity. "If she's your woman, she's your business."

"She was working with you."

"Yeah, and when she was working, she was my business, but it was strictly business, understand?"

"Look, Reverend, somebody knocked me out, and when I came to, she was gone."

"Turn your back on a woman," said the reverend, "the fuck you expect?"

Rincin stood by the door, watching. His smile never wavered.

"Are you saying Tina knocked me out?"

"I'm sayin' be a man. Ask her your own damn self. If she wanna be found," he said, not unsympathetically, "you gonna find her."

"Okay," I said, "here's what you do . . ." The idea dropped out of the sky. Like most junkies, whether or not they still used junk, I fought best on my back. Ass on the griddle. When every day is a zero-sum struggle against bone-shearing pain, creativity becomes an adrenal function. The good old days.

"Tina gets in touch," I said to the reverend, "tell her I'll be in L.A. Tell her I'm going to take care of a thing, then go to Zell's place. Tell her to meet me there."

The reverend did not look thrilled. But he didn't blow me off. "Where's that at, playah?"

"I don't know," I said, my heart sinking as I heard my plan out loud. "I'm going to find it when I get down there."

"Look at you go," said the reverend.

I hadn't realized until now how badly my stomach was churning. I was glad to finally get out of there. I hadn't gone five steps when Rincin fell in step. "A fascinating day in the marketplace of ideas," he said.

"Officer Rincin, I really have to use the men's room."

"You don't mind urinating outside, you can go in the trough right by the yard."

"Unfortunately," I said, "there's a little more involved."

Rincin sighed. "This is something civilians don't understand. On this job, you train yourself. Your body can't pinch a loaf whenever it feels like it."

The way he said it, I wanted to take my body aside and slap it around a little for being so undisciplined. But I was on a schedule. I had to get to Burbank, interview a Christian hooker and find out if Harry Zell had offered me a job or a suicide mission. If there was time left, and I didn't get killed, I planned to pick up some clown feet and a big red nose for Josef Mengele. But my real mission, much as it pained me, was to find Tina.

Now that she was my ex-wife, and M.I.A., all I could remember were the good things.

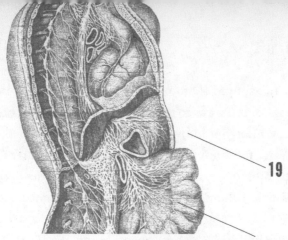

19

Big House Chasids

A gaggle of prison employees clustered at the east gate under a glassed-in tower box. A crusty old guard, who might have been there when Governor Reagan visited, walked into the road and stood there with a handwritten sign: GUN TRANSFER. I wasn't sure what that meant, but to the naked eye no one was transferring anything, unless you counted the jumbo takeout Taco Bell bags two young COs were hauling. While I waited, heads rotated fast. I followed in time to see the warden leading a delegation of cameras and suits, one of them huge, into H Unit. Doubtless to show off the wall-to-wall beds that gave the place the rehabilitation-friendly warehouse feeling. Rincin told me the warden didn't mind fund-raising, he just wished he didn't have to give so many tours. After *Oz* and all the prison docs, civilians wanted to experience the magic. "What folks never count on," Rincin'd chuckled, "are the fumes. Cram in a few hundred guys, you're talkin' about a lot of ass and feet. It's stinky enough down there without marching in the pols from Sacramento." From the oohs and aahs, I wondered if the huge man was Schwarzenegger. (Did he know Mengele? Did his Nazi father?)

I was a pawn. But I didn't know what the game was. I only knew what it wasn't: a simple ID job. Not anymore, at least. Tina once told me that when her back was to the wall, she'd try RT. Reverse thinking. Assume everything you know is wrong, and start from there. Maybe the point wasn't me finding big M. Maybe the point was letting him get his hands on me. That felt suitably paranoid. Was it Zell I should have been worried about all along? One more delightful reason to get my ass down to L.A. and do some digging.

There was an old-fashioned phone booth beside the gift shop. I called the number on Rincin's card. Left a message about my mother's heart attack, which I'd just found out about. I said I would be back in time for class tomorrow. Then I stood at the bus stop and tried to decipher bus schedules. A group of schoolgirls was already there, in identical blue uniforms. The one white girl, a pigtailed redhead holding a Bible and a *People* magazine, blew a bubble out at me and yelled, "Fag!"

There was no reason to risk anything to save face with a homophobic twelve-year-old. So I didn't pick up a shovel and hit her in the face. Instead, I ducked into the gift shop to wait. According to the schedule taped to the door, the next bus was in fifteen minutes. Twitchy the clerk peered up from his Word Find, over his state bifocals, not all that happy about having a customer. I stared at a painting of a red barn and he went back to finding "of" and "ten" in "often."

Keeping up the Tina reverse mode, I rolled out every fact I had and tried to peek behind them. As in: maybe Zell's documentary stuff was a front. Why else would he make himself so untraceable? Huge as his prison doc franchise was, maybe it covered something bigger. The documentaries got him in and out of penal institutions all over the country. Maybe he was shooting Mengele's prison experiments. Cable gold!

Before I could go further down that road, Twitchy stepped from around the corner.

"You the drug guy?"

Before I could congratulate him on his intel, he pushed up his ironed denim sleeves. "See that? Clean as a daisy."

"Congratulations, how long's it been?"

"What time is it now?" His laugh morphed into a hacking cough that had me ducking out of spume range. "I did the RD last week. With the sauerkraut."

"You lost me," I said, peering out the window to see a Chasidic man, clutching a briefcase to his chest, fumble with the keys to a black Mercedes.

"Rapid detox," he said. "They bring in the old German guy. The doctor. Strap you down, knock you out, and ding-dong-ding, you wake up desmacked. Unstrung. Not so much as a craving."

"The old German did that? Really old, with blond hair?"

"Straight-up Nazi from Nazi-town," said Twitch. "Got the accent to prove it. That's why I trusted him."

Rapid detox. One more piece of the warped-around-the-edges Mengele puzzle. I considered telling him the doctor made his bones injecting malaria in babies, among other things, before Twitch was a twinkle in his mother's eye. But I decided to keep it upbeat. "And you feel good, huh?"

"Never better! Scuse me."

He whipped around and puked into a small bucket behind the counter. When he was done he tamped his mouth with a Kleenex Junior and smiled beatifically.

"Still gettin' my sea legs."

"What I hear, they grow back, buddy. You take care of yourself."

Somebody was letting Mengele practice in a state facility—if knocking some poor bastard out, pumping him full of Narcan and squeezing the dope out of his cells even counted as practice. That same somebody had to be giving him a room and instruments.

"Keep it up!" I said, and backed out the door with one eye on the Chasid now struggling with the trunk of his Benz. "One bucket at a time!"

Twitchy grabbed my wrist before I could get away. "Thing is," he said. "I got a funny feeling he left something inside. Here, look."

He grabbed my hand and pressed it to a postage-stamp-sized square on the back of his neck. It felt hard and metallic.

"Could be a locator chip," I said. "You try and escape, they can track you by satellite."

Twitchy nodded, taking that in. "I bet the president has one of those."

I didn't like where this was going. I waved good-bye, stepped out of the shop and jogged down the small hill, startling the Chasid as he was saying a prayer over his rental car.

"Scuse me," I said, trying not to sound like an escapee. "You going to Auschwitz?"

"What?" The young Chasid twisted his payots nervously.

"Airport. I mean the airport." What was wrong with me? "The *airport*," I stammered, and pointed to my throat, as if that would explain my behavior. "Holocaust Tourette's."

"The heartbreak," he said. His eyes swelled behind his glasses.

"So you are going to the airport, right?"

"I am. Yes. But . . ."

Clearly the prospect of bringing me along thrilled him more than pork chops.

As we spoke he kept trying to get his trunk open. He aimed his key-beeper from different angles, squatting, then standing up, then reaching over his head. He reminded me of a bullfighter.

"It's not a geometry problem." I stepped over and snatched the key chain out of his hand. "Battery's dead," I said.

"That can't be. The radio works."

"Not that battery. This one." I bent down to insert the actual key in the trunk and open it.

My new Orthodox friend may have been dressed for shtetl success, but I was the pushy Jew. "So, when's your flight?"

He threw his briefcase in the back, closed the trunk. Back on the driver's side, he gripped the handle without opening. He plainly wanted me to leave but had too much conscience to say so. Guilt was such a useful emotion.

"I really appreciate this," I said. "I've got a family emergency, in Los Angeles."

He didn't ask, which was just as well. As giddy as I felt making my escape from San Quentin, I wasn't exactly headed for a fun getaway. I had less than twenty-four hours to locate and grill a born-again hooker, try to unravel Harry Zell's reality TV–Holocaust connection, and, most embarrassingly, find out the real reason I'd been offered the job of verifying the identity of the Nazi doctor. That, of course, and find the woman I wished I hadn't divorced.

"So," I said as we floated over the Golden Gate Bridge, "where do you guys get your suits?"

"This?" He pulled up the flap of his long black jacket. "It's a *rekel*."

"It's not that bad," I said.

"No, it's called a *rekel*. This one's got the concealed button, in the Bobover tradition."

"You don't mind my asking, how do they treat you at Quentin, you walk in like this?"

"The one lady, in visiting, a Latina—"

"Officer Darlene?"

"You know her?" he said, crestfallen, as if the girl of his dreams had been exposed as a bag of herpes.

"Know her? Naw. I just remember her face. She's got the *cholita* brows? Right? Painted on? She's very attractive."

"I think so, too. She's exotic, you know? Not like the Lubavitcher girls. She always wants to touch my tzitzit."

He saw my look and waggled the little fringes at his waistcoat. "The knots in the waistcoat. This blue thread, from an animal called the chilazon, you cannot even find anymore."

By the time we exited the freeway, I'd gotten a course on Chasid fashion.

"Not a lot of guys can pull off the fur hat. But you're one of them."

I already regretted the plan forming in my head. But there was no other way.

"Hey, there's a gas station," I said. "Let me fill it up."

"Really?"

He seemed a little surprised when I went around to his window with the gas nozzle.

"Tank's on the other side," he said. Then he saw the lighter and put it together. His reaction was less surprise than resignation.

"Roll down the window," I said.

He shook his head. I didn't want to shout our conversation, so I put my face close to the window, squishing my lips on the glass.

"I want you to know, my friend, this is not a hate crime." I didn't want him to think I didn't like him, even though I was about to fuck his world up very badly. "I just need some clothes. I don't *want* to squirt gasoline on you and set you on fire. That's not *me*."

"You want my clothes? Why don't you just ask?" He seemed mystified. "What are clothes?"

"Really?"

"I am happy to help a fellow Jew."

I ran around to the passenger side and jumped in. The Chasid had a .22 out and pointed at my stomach before the door slammed.

I tugged his gun hand into my stomach. "Pull the trigger," I said, keeping up a friendly smile. "Go ahead. I've got a vest on. That peashooter won't make a dent."

I'm not sure what movie I stole that from. But I believe the line was uttered by Elisha Cook, in black and white. It was not enough to make him lower his gun. But I saw his eyes go wide and punched him in the face before he could regroup.

"Park behind the air pump. Give me everything."

"Owww . . . okay! I'm sorry about the gun."

"Don't be," I said. "I don't like punching people I like. The piece made it easier."

A family of tourists pulled up beside us, and I realized how it would look stripping an Orthodox Jew in a gas station. "Change in plan, Rebbe. Pull behind the bathroom."

Now that I had the gun, things were a lot less complicated.

Still, when he was down to his tallith, I started to feel bad. He held up the tasseled fringe and smiled sadly.

"This was my grandfather's, from Lithuania."

"All right, all right," I said. "You know where I can buy one? In L.A.?" He pulled out a business card and scribbled an address on the back. "Tell Solly I sent you." Then he looked up. "But why am I writing it down? I could show you. Give me my clothes back, I'll take you myself. Get you a deal."

"Cagey," I said, "but I'm sorry, I can't drive around with a guy in his underwear."

"You can in San Francisco."

"Funny," I said.

"You think? I'm an attorney, but I also do some stand-up. You know, a chomedian. *Chomedian*, get it?"

"I get it. You're the new Seinfeld. Now listen. There are things I have to do, things you'd probably approve of but I can't talk about. What were you doing at Quentin anyway?"

"I represent Larry Boiget. He's a Jewish fellow, wants to eat kosher."

"Fighting the good fight," I said. "In the tradition of an Orthodox prisoner named Mosher."

"You know about that?"

"Indeed I do. So I can just get a tallith off the rack?"

"Yes, yes, but what about—"

He stared down at the spindly legs extending from his boxers, as if just discovering what his body looked like, and slunk further down in the seat. I realized I should have done all this in the men's room. But this was the first time I'd ever stolen a man's clothes.

"You're going to leave me here? Like this?"

"You shouldn't have worn all those blue Massengills."

"They are called *chilazon*."

"Chilazon. That's what I meant." I pointed his own peashooter at him. "Out."

A minute later, he was out of the car, crouched between Super and Supreme. I could see the disbelief stamped on his face, as if nothing in life had prepared him for a Jew lying to his face.

"I know, it's a drag, being shoved out of a car in your boxers. But maybe this'll make you think next time before you wipe some species off the planet 'cause you need some tallith dye. Extermination is extermination."

"Are you kidding me?" he said. "What do you know from extermination?"

"Just give me the hat," I said.

"No hat."

A couple of bikers had roared up. One had a fat girl riding behind him, her tramp stamp visible where her jeans rode low over her butt crack. She spotted the Chasid and squealed as if she'd found a unicorn.

"Hey, Ernie, look! It's one of *them*!"

While my new friend was weighing his options, I grabbed the *spodik* off his head. To my surprise, the sidelocks came with it, attached by safety pins inside the hat. Without them, the crew cut lent him massive insignificance.

"You really are a comedian," I said.

"It's a long story," he replied.

"I hope so. But I don't feel as bad now leaving you in your underwear. What about the beard?"

"I can't just yank it off."

I reached up to grab it—a fraud, in my mind, was fair game—but he quickly rubbed his hands together, worked up some kind of friction and ripped the beard off in one piece, like a slice of hair rind.

"That's not sanitary, sticking it right on yours," he said.

"I'll spritz with Bactine later." A small crowd was starting to gather. I grabbed the thing, which felt uncomfortably warm. "Maybe you can work it into a routine," I said before jumping in the Mercedes.

Two blocks away, I parked and adjusted the rearview. I planted the *spodik* and Chasid hair on my head. It was magic. I was transformed. From unshaved fortyish seedy guy to grown-up Yeshiva boy. I wanted to pinch myself on the cheek and give myself a macaroon.

———————

At the airport, I checked myself out in the men's room. The Chasid who stared back from the mirror was as interchangeable as all the others I'd seen strolling Beverly Boulevard in satin overcoats on ninety-degree Saturdays. I was suddenly invisible. Perfect!

As a bonus, I'd picked up the faux-Chasid's wallet. Myron Goldman. The best crimes are the ones you don't mean to commit. *Improv.* The Second City approach to lawbreaking.

Presenting Goldman's ID and ticket to security, I was struck by the barely muted hatred aimed in my direction. Full-on Orthodox, I looked like the Jews Julius Streicher caricatured in Nazi propaganda cartoons.

A freckled little towhead saw me in line and pointed. "Look, Mommy, a *devil*!"

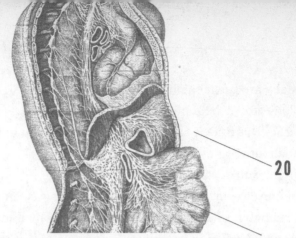

20

What's Under All That Satin and Fur?

I felt the eyes of the passengers with open seats, the expressions of naked dread and loathing as I passed, a walking bundle of hot-day satin, fur and frills. *Please don't sit here. . . . Please don't sit here. . . . Please don't sit here. . . .* But a big creamy blonde, I guessed a not-so-long-ago cheerleader, licked her lips when I parked my shtetl-stud self beside her in 9A. She put down her copy of *Exodus*, by way of broadcasting her Semitic leanings. Her teeth were health-book perfect, her blue eyes blasting troubled smarts.

What's under all that satin and fur? my seatmate's eyes seemed to be asking. No sooner had I opened my free *USA Today* than she canted sideways and whispered, "Is it true?"

"Beg your pardon?" My head itched but I was afraid to scratch for fear my locks would fall off.

"You know," she continued, "is it true about the sheet? That you only do it through a hole in the sheet, once a week? Is your God kinky or what?" I watched her twist her wedding ring, trying either to keep it on or yank it off.

"You have no idea," I said.

It turned out she'd already had a little gin party in the airport lounge. Three Beefeaters later, on a fifty-minute flight, she'd told me her name was Dinah, after Dinah Shore, which was her first inkling that her mom was gay. Gay Dinah-Mom dumped Dad and moved in with the mail woman, Denise, who had three older daughters, Daisy, Dot and Deborah, who all hated her. People's lives. Dinah also let me know that she was forty-two and formerly married to a "beefneck" named Ned who worked in her father's sportswear emporium, and she really really wanted to try some "sheet-holin'." A term with which I was unfamiliar. "You know," Dinah giggled, tamping spilled gin off her beige pantsuit, "Jew sex. Gettin' my Orthodox on. Doin' it kosher style."

"Is kosher style the same as kosher?"

"Better be." She dipped her finger in a gin puddle on her tummy, raised it to her lips and licked. I was enchanted. This was what Davey'd been ranting about—why he went spewy over the Alterna.com fetish Betties. It wasn't what they *did* that made them hot—it was that they *wanted* to do it.

"Do you stick it through the hole and then lay down, or do you cover me with the sheet, then move the hole till it's right over my cookie?"

Mistaking my silence for shock, she grabbed my arm. Concern flashed from her Aryan blue irises. "I am a big, big supporter of the Israeli people."

"Thank you."

What else could I say? Was there a wave of blonde-on-bagel sex I had no idea about?

She reached for my *shmidok*. "Can I try it on?"

"No!" I said, seizing her hand.

"What are you doing?"

"It's a man hat. Only men can touch it."

"Wow . . ."

We both stared at my paw wrapped around hers. Then she withdrew and parked her hand on her chest, as if to express her virtue. *"Wow!"* she repeated.

"Yes, it's in the Bible," I lied. "Only men!"

I shuddered to imagine what would have happened had she lifted my locks off, found out I was in Bobover drag.

Her thigh pressed mine. "I know a hotel near the airport. I can't stop thinking about that *sheet*. Egyptian cotton—or is that too . . . Muslim? I bet they have percale." She clasped my shoulder with new urgency. "Do you cut the hole yourself, or do they have kosher party stores?"

It didn't matter whether Dinah was "my type." The fact that she had this thing that got her hot—the specificity of her freakdom—would have flicked my switch, in some *Wild Kingdom* kind of way.

While I passed up a date, I did take the opportunity to peek in the port-o-pharmacy, disguised as a Marc Jacobs purse, that Dinah left on the seat when she went "to tinkle." Depakote, lithium, Lexapro, Boniva, Valium. I thought about filching her Valium. But the way she'd spilled her drink, it felt criminal to deny the woman her relief. I had to live with myself. I still had the piggish reflex to steal drugs, even if I didn't intend to use them. My first year off of everything, I continued to raid medicine cabinets on general principle. I wasn't proud of it. I was so miserable, I did not even *want* the drugs. I just didn't want anybody else to have them. *Drug Grinch*. I knew, if I wanted to survive with any kind of serenity, I had to unclench the fist that was my ex-dope-fiend heart, just so I could live in a world where other human beings got high and I didn't.

Dinah staggered back and passed out on contact with her seat cushion. She drooled prettily until we landed.

Eating at Quentin had been problematic. I'd purchased a small suit-case in the SF airport and dropped a minor fortune on fruit salad, stale Starbucks sandwiches and a few bags of cashews packaged when I was in grade school. I stuffed all my provisions in the case and zipped it up. The thing had wheels, but I carried it by the handle. I'd had one in Cincinnati that got stuck in the up position. I couldn't get it in the overhead on a puddle-jumper to Akron and had to leave the plane and go by bus. So now I just carried. I assumed they were all broken.

The first thing I did at Burbank airport was find a pay phone and call the five numbers I had for Tina. (I'd given up on cell phones, which ended up like sunglasses, lost, smashed or left somewhere within seventy-two hours of purchase.) The first three had greetings in other people's voices—two female, one male. I left the same message at all three. *Tina, pick up.* Then I said I was "in town to meet our friend." The fourth number picked up, said nothing and beeped, which seemed like Tina's style. And the last one just rang. Also her style.

I put the phone back in the cradle. I didn't expect to find her that way. But the important thing was faith. (If you didn't have anything else.) And right now I was manufacturing the belief that if I could track down Zell and find out what made his clock tick, the cosmos would reward me with Tina. If I could sniff out Zell, she could, too. What I could not do was stay still.

Without knowing where I was headed, I stepped out of the Bur-bank airport and a fellow Chasid, somewhat older than me, tried to grab the suitcase out of my hands. He stood back when I resisted. He stared at me in horror, while passengers swirled around us, as though I'd sprouted horns and a tail. "What?" I said, playing the indignation card. "Aren't you my driver?"

"My name is Jack," he began, in a Russian accent so thick I could smell the borscht. "I was told to meet—*wait!* Where's your tallith?"

He clamped his hand over his mouth, horrified.

"My tallith?"

I looked down. No fringe. *See what happens?* I thought to myself. If I hadn't gone all Good Samari-Jew with Myron, I'd be fully tallithed and in a car by now. I didn't know where I'd be going, but it would be somewhere. Nineteen hours isn't very long, and that's all I had before I had to turn around. I hadn't worked out my ports of call. No matter. Now I was in the airport, lying to a man I'd known two minutes. I had not foreseen the consequences of going fringe-free.

"Stolen," I said, "long story."

I fought the urge to yank out a picture of Tina and start shoving it in the faces of arriving passengers.

"Stolen?" The driver stared at me.

"It's no big deal," I said, picking up the bag and nudging him on.

A crowd of passengers I recognized from my flight passed by. Jack and I were dressed identically, standing face-to-face. "Two Jews arguing over a nickel," I heard a red-faced exec in a Burberry raincoat say into his cell phone. His eyes met mine. He knew I heard. But he didn't flinch. Jews are not known for bouts of sudden and impulsive violence. I assumed the man had never seen Bernstein in action. I did nothing about the insult and he kept walking.

"What kind of man," asked the driver, "takes another man's clothes?" And then, as if from a well of bitter personal experience, he answered his own question. "A schmuck, *that's* what kind of man. A *schmuck*."

The way he kept scrutinizing me, I wondered if he could tell my *shmidok* was hot. It was arrogant to think I could fake my way through a world I didn't know. But it still made sense to try. If anybody saw me, they'd see an Orthodox Jew. That's what *I'd* see. I was going to show up places where I had no business showing up. Places with receptionists and housekeepers and security guards. If things went south, let them remember *Fiddler on the Roof.* It's not like anybody's heard of a Chasidic burglar.

"A schmuck," the driver declared again when we got in the car, cementing my intention to make good on my earlier *rekel* theft. I remembered the card Myron Goldman had given me and pulled it out.

"Mendel and Mendel," I read, before he could ask me anything about who I was supposed to be, "serving the Fairfax district for thirty-seven years."

"Solly Mendel? You getting married?"

"Why?" I opened the stolen wallet and saw a wad of hundreds and closed it fast.

"Solly does wedding suits. Groom. Best man. His father must have kept sewing till he was a hundred and twenty. Eyes like a kosher hawk."

"No wedding," I said as we headed for short-term parking, "just a suit."

Nearly two hours later—half of that in single-file on the 10 East, slowed by looky-loos shooting cell-phone pix of a jackknifed beer truck—Solly Mendel was stroking his four chins and frowning. He was a round man whose own shiny black *rekash* fit him as snugly as sealskin fits a seal.

"That's not you," he said, reaching for the *shmidok*. Why was everybody interested in taking my hat off?

"It's me enough," I said, holding the brim with both hands. "I want the same thing, but new."

He frowned down at my sleeves, which stopped just below my elbows, Johnny Knoxville style.

"And this time, it should fit?"

"A man can dream."

Tina, where the fuck are you?

"Uh-huh," Mendel grunted. "Tallith?"

"That too. I'm surprising my great-aunt," I said, as if that explained everything. "I just want it to look right."

"Maybe you'd like a yarmulke too. We do the best yarmulkes in the city."

"All the big Jews!" an old lady warbled from somewhere.

I spotted her in a folding chair, behind the counter, between racks of pants.

"Mama, please," Solly pleaded. "The man doesn't care. I'm trying to do business."

He Zero Mostelled his shoulders up to his ears, a parody of a shrug. "My mother. What are you gonna do? I want you to take a look at something."

Solly extended his arm and bowed his head, as if introducing a dignitary. "Maybe something like this." He stooped and eased a hatbox out from a shelf underneath the cash register. "Open it," he said. I did, and saw a lush satin skullcap, wine colored, set on an upside-down golden bowl. "Better than all the Beverly Boulevard *alta kocker*s."

I tried to imagine appearing in public with something like that on my head.

"Not every day," he said, reading my mind as easily as if I'd texted him. "High Holy Days. Now flip it," he said, making a motion with his hands. I turned the hat over and saw what he was talking about: inside, tucked discreetly to one side, in Hebraically stitched English letters: NEVER AGAIN.

"You wear it so it's right on your temple," he said.

Our eyes met in the mirror, his sad for two thousand years, mine yellow and blurred.

"Do you need that to remember?" I asked.

"Not to remember. To honor."

Just hearing the word "honor" made me wince.

"We do all the big Jews!" the old lady yelled again.

Mendel snatched the yarmulke back, slapped the lid on the box and the box back behind the counter. He rolled his eyes to show what he had to put up with and yelled back at her.

"They were big twenty years ago, Mama."

I smiled at her, just to do something with my face. What I was thinking was, *If I were Tina, where would I go?* It all depended on whether she thought she was being chased.

My Chasidization was painless. When he found a coat, Solly held it up, extended his arm and bowed his head. Same with the pants and tzitzit. Miraculously, everything fit.

Solly wrapped the clothes I'd worn into the store with brown paper from a roll overhead, like a butcher. He tied the paper with string and checked on his mother, who was still muttering. "She doesn't get it. Today, if you're not making a jockstrap for Stephen Spielberg's godson, you're nothing." He smiled sourly. "They don't want to buy suits from Mendel and Mendel. Fine. But you know what they *do* buy? Hugo Boss. You know Hugo Boss?"

"Above my pay grade."

"Good. Hugo Boss designed the SS uniforms. Famous for their slim fit. And guess who did the sewing? That's right. In the morning, a Gypsy or a Jew might sew the epaulettes on the shoulders. That night, the Gestapo pig who drags him out in the snow and kicks him to death might be wearing it. Hugo Boss. I went to the *Shoah* premiere. Half the *macher*s in the theater had their *tuchis*es in Nazi suits."

When he handed me the bundle, his face had an appraising expression. I wondered, for a nervous second, if he was actually undercover himself. Maybe the Russian mob was moving in on Chasidic haberdasheries. Maybe it was a front, like the medical supply stores in West Hollywood, with their windows full of dusty prosthetic limbs. When the vodka dons took over, suddenly you could buy a fake leg on every corner.

Solly pulled the stub of a pencil from his shirt pocket and made some calculations on the back of a paper bag. He talked without looking up. "Mister, I don't know what kinda trouble you're in. But from the way you're *schvitz*in' over there, it's nothing good. Tell you what I'll do," he said, "I'll give you the Full Jew—the coat, hat, pants, yarmulke, tallith—for eighteen hundred dollars."

"Fourteen hundred."

"Fifteen," he said, "and I'll throw in *payot*s. You need some sidelocks."

His mother got up off her chair, the same height standing as sitting, and waddled back through the store. She disappeared through a door from which floated the scent of brisket. Sense memory! My own grandmother secretly made bacon at three in the morning and ate it alone.

I pulled twelve hundred-dollar bills out of my wallet, followed by a fistful of fives and ones that I slowly unfolded on the counter.

"Thirteen eighty-five," I said. "Unless you want to follow me and check for quarters under my cushions."

I'd stashed the rest of Myron's wad in my socks in the changing room, so it looked like my wallet was empty. But Solly was sharp. He indicated the limo outside. "In that thing maybe it's worth it."

"You think I'm paying for the limo? Chasid, *please*!"

Thieving was not, in general, my MO. But the wallet came with the coat.

Solly scooped up the bills fast. "Mazel tov. Wear it in good health!"

Transaction done, I put the string-tied bundle back on the counter. "Do me a favor," I asked on impulse, fishing Goldman's card out of my sock. "Send this stuff back to the address on here."

"You want to explain?"

"Not really. Except it's the right thing to do."

"The right thing? In that case I'll do it," he said, "just for the novelty."

I found two more hundreds in my pocket. "This is for FedEx. Keep what's left."

"Next-day morning or next-day afternoon?" Mendel stepped away from the counter and pulled a battered metal lockbox from a shelf of yarmulke boxes.

"Afternoon's fine."

I figured it would take Goldman—or whatever his real name was—a little while to get home.

"Big Jews," Mendel mumbled, locking the money in the box. Anybody that lax about stashing cash had to be connected. "All day *mit* the big Jews. Twenty years ago, maybe, they were big Jews. Now, not so much."

The way he said this reminded me of Zell. *There's* a Jew who must have been big twenty years ago. From his brown-bag arithmetic shtick, I had a hunch Solly Mendel did not input names and addresses in a BlackBerry. Sure enough, I reached behind the counter while his back was turned and pulled out a black and white speckled composition book marked CUSTOMERS. Even with my limited technical expertise, I knew they had not yet found a way to scrub names out of people's address books from afar. In that way, if no other, pencil and paper were still superior to the Internet. I quickly flipped to the back. Found the Z page. Coughed to cover the sound of ripping it out and slipped the book back under the counter.

Solly slammed the metal box back on the shelf and made his way toward me, unsmiling. Maybe he had secret cameras. But then— wouldn't he have been holding something? Like a phone? Or a gun?

When Mendel son of Mendel was a foot away, I braced myself.

Only he didn't hit me or shoot me. He opened his arms and gave me a brisket-smelling hug. "To quote the rabbi of Lunt, 'It is a good thing to help a man in trouble, a bad thing to have him move in.'"

"Did he really say that?"

"Those old Talmud jockeys were blunt."

I caught my reflection in the mirror and felt a prickle of sweat. Who was I kidding? Solly's eyes met mine as he stepped around the counter and held the shop door open.

"'The first shekel I give is to make you feel welcome, the last is so you never come back.'"

"The rabbi of Lunt?" I asked.

"No, that's me," he said, and shut the door in my face.

———

The driver listened when I gave him Zell's address, then hit the ignition and jerked the limo onto Fairfax in front of a bus with a giant Bruce Willis painted on the side, cuddling a monster rocket launcher that seemed to sprout from between his legs against a background of red, white and blue. Sometimes it seemed too bad that America wasn't born with a bigger penis, so it wouldn't have to keep waggling the junk it had all over the planet.

"You see Solly?" Jack the driver asked.

"I did," I said. "Why didn't you come in?"

Jack made a clicking sound with his tongue to convey his disgust and resignation. "Solly makes a good yarmulke, but he's a schmuck."

After this unbidden assessment, he began to bite his nails feverishly. At the first red light, he twisted around in the driver's seat like a bearded owl.

"I just started with the company. You *are* Goldman, right?"

"Right. That's me," I said, and then blurted, "I'm looking for my wife. My ex-wife."

The driver met my eyes and held them for a second. Now he understood. What man didn't? He untwisted his owl neck and faced forward again, meeting my gaze in the rearview. "Is complicated. Life."

"So I've heard," I said, meeting his soulful Russian gaze until the light changed and the car behind him hit the horn.

We didn't say another word until he dropped me off in Brentwood, on Carmelita Drive. I closed my eyes and tried to send out psychic SOSs the entire ride. *Tina, pick up.*

I gave him $500 cash to park and wait.

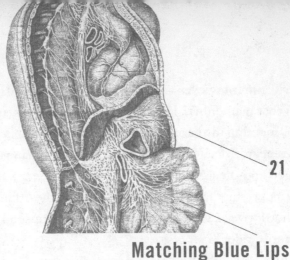

21

Matching Blue Lips

Zell's housekeeper buzzed me in after no more than five minutes of crackly back-and-forth on the intercom. I said I had an appointment. She said he was running late. I said he told me to. She said she wasn't sure I should. I made sure to smile into the security camera, and finally she opened the gate.

I thought I heard giggling as I walked up the drive. A car cruised by behind me. A Crown Vic. Universally recognizable undercover cop car. Maybe this wasn't even the right house. The housekeeper opened the front door. I was surprised that she was white. Maybe Russian. Kind of drifty on her feet. She paddled off with a vague gesture toward a corridor off to the right.

I hiked through the living room, which was vast enough to make me feel lonely and featured a white fur, sunken conversation pit that might have been airlifted intact from 1970 and not used since.

The housekeeper's giggling echoed from somewhere in the house.

Either the acoustics were skewed or I was. The living room opened onto a gently sloping hallway flanked by glass walls and a view of the tropical splendor on both sides. Zell had hired topiary wizards to trim his hedges into Hebrew letters and naked nymphs, as though he planned on throwing a party for swinging Kabbalah scholars or rabbis who liked the ladies.

I didn't know what I was looking for—or where I was going to eat my next meal. What I did know was that the man who hired me collected bent celebrity pix, had a foot in born-again porn, and harbored the dream of starting an all-prison reality network. Premiering—if the showbiz, law enforcement and penitentiary stars aligned—with the official on-screen arrest of Josef Mengele. But something in my gut told me there was more. And whatever secret was buried in the bowels of San Quentin had drawn me here, to the Brentwood McMansion of Harry Zell, I hoped against hope that Tina would show up. She had a history of surprise appearances—but nothing to surpass her sudden, naked, near-stroke-inducing presence in the Quentin love nest the night before.

The glass hall fed into a hushed bedroom, done floor-to-ceiling in an almost disturbingly soothing powder blue. Powder-blue carpet, powder-blue walls and powder-blue ceiling combined to create the illusion of stepping into a waterless ocean. I was already feeling seasick when I saw something move on the powder-blue bed. I tiptoed closer and threw back the blanket. There was Dinah. My flightmate from seat 9-B. She hadn't mentioned that, after her beef-head husband, she'd traded up for Harry Zell. She'd also traded in the beige pantsuit for— what else?—a powder-blue silk robe with some kind of fur collar dyed the same shade. Her blue eyes were open but by now they were just decoration. There was no blood. But her tongue protruded alarmingly.

It looked like some viscous, tide-pool amphibian had crawled halfway into her mouth and given up. Below that, things got less attractive. Strangling generally crushed the hyoid, but this went beyond strangling. What had been Dinah's throat was now wide as a thigh, purpling over her massively shattered hyoid bone and ruptured esophagus. Strangling was puppy love compared to the damage I was staring at.

I urged the blanket further south and gagged. Mrs. Zell's head had been twisted the wrong way round. She faced the same direction as her own buttocks, staring up at me over the top of her intact scapula and spine. She might have been a doll some very strong, very sadistic child who'd seen *The Exorcist* had decided to play with, then gotten bored with and mutilated.

I heard a flush in the bathroom and jumped. The door opened. Out walked Tina, like we'd been married twenty years and she'd just put down a magazine to go pee. "Hi, hon," she said, as if we'd planned a picnic.

"*Tina!*" My voice couldn't find a register.

Not for the first time in our relationship, I had to combat the impulse to simultaneously slap her face and plaster it with kisses. My joy was so deep, I cupped my mouth with both hands in the manner of speechless game show winners. All I could say was, "Tina, Tina, Tina," until some semblance of cognitive function returned and I could patch together a sentence. "Baby, what are you . . . I mean, I can't believe . . . you're *here!*"

She stepped into my arms and kissed me, then touched my rank beard and lifted my hat off. "Love the look. But you picked a strange time to go fundamentalist."

"I thought it might be a good disguise. But look at you. . . ."

For the occasion, she was dressed in a pinstriped business suit, with plastic baggies on both feet. Nobody else could make foot-baggies so alluring.

"*Tina Tina Tina . . . ,*" I began to babble again. Her name was *me*.

Amazing how desire could roil up at the most inappropriate moments. *Especially* at inappropriate moments. I'd almost forgotten the screaming cranial pain, my constant companion since the last time Tina and I had crossed paths. I had to will myself to do more than gawk and babble, to salvage enough rubble from my crumbling psyche to assemble a question, something beyond "How?" or "Why?"

My words, when I was able to form them, came out like butchered haiku translated from some dyslexic Croatian subdialect. "I wanted . . . Last thing . . . That white-shit moon . . . Doll hands . . . What happened in the minivan?"

"Baby, this is the wrong time to lose your shit," Tina said. She slapped me across the face and I slapped her back. After that we were both more relaxed.

"My shit has been found," I told her. "So, did you talk to the rev?"

"What are you talking about?"

We both glanced at Mrs. Zell, then back at each other.

"I'm talking about telling the rev, right before I left, that if he talked to you, to let you know I was going to try and check out Zell's place."

Tina rolled her eyes. "I didn't need to talk to the reverend. After you told me the shit Zell pulled to get you to work, I figured the prick might not pay. So then I figured if I put in a visit to his place, he'd get that I wasn't the don't-have-to-pay type."

"The what?"

By now the blue room had begun to spin. Choppy seas. My vision clouded and I felt such sudden, quivery affection for my ex-wife I wondered if I was having a stroke. I grabbed her and kissed her again, unable to resist the taste of her. I breathed in the scent that gathered in the damp in the back of her neck. . . . I could have eaten her skin.

Tina sighed like she wanted this but needed that, then pushed me off. "For God's sake, Manny, have some respect for the fucking dead."

She was right, of course. I turned back to Dinah, whose blue lips matched the walls and bedspread. Why shouldn't death be color-coordinated?

I knew it was pointless, but I could not stop wondering what would have happened if I'd taken her up on the sheet-hole offer. The whole notion was a myth—like Jews burying their dead standing up or drinking the Christian baby blood. (Well, maybe on Passover . . .) But for Dinah, a.k.a. Mrs. Zell, the facts didn't matter anymore. Tina watched me watching and stepped away.

"You knew her, didn't you." She didn't even say it as a question.

"Yes. No. I just met her," I said, surprised by the choke in my voice, "on the plane from San Francisco."

"Well what the hell did you say to her?"

"What do you mean?"

"She swallowed a pharmacy." Tina snatched me by the wrist and led me along the perimeter of the sea room to the open door of the bathroom. The toilet seat and the floor around it were splotched with vomit, whole pills still visible in the chunk and bile. Even the pills were blue. Those Valiums. The same prescription bottles I'd scoped in her purse flying down were dumped in a small trash can inlaid with some kind of ancient gold coins. From where I was squinting, the profile on them might have been Zell's. But I had to close my eyes to remember the pharmaceutical highlights in her purse. I recited them like a conductor announcing stops. "Depakote . . . lithium . . . Lexapro . . . Boniva . . . Valium." I was jokey because the tears in my eyes freaked me out.

Seeing them, understandably, made Tina even more suspicious. "How close were you?" Her left eye closed to a slit the way it did when she was mad, as if she were aiming down the sight of an invisible gun. "Manny, tell me now. Are they going to find your DNA in her throat?"

"That's not even funny."

"No, what's funny is you dressed like Joey the Dreidel Boy. What's funny"—her voice edged toward the border between edgy and hysteria—"is you knowing what pharmaceuticals a dead woman, who happened to be living with Harry Zell, stuffed in her purse before she killed herself."

"I wanted a disguise." I touched my tender scalp and stole another eyeful of the victim. "Does that look like suicide to you?"

"She could have convulsed. I've seen people break their own backs." I knew how my cunning and beautiful ex-wife skewed the universe. She was unwilling to lavish any sympathy on the departed now that the dead woman had been identified as competition. Tina rattled the empty prescription bottles in the clamshell trash can to make a point. "The lady of the house wasn't trying to get rid of a headache. She wanted out. Which maybe makes sense, if you're married to Harry Zell."

"I keep going back and forth on Zell," I said.

"It's black and white," said Tina. "Whatever his ends, if his means involve working with Mengele, he's the enemy. I'm guessing Dinah knew. She was probably pulling a Clara Haber."

"Clara who?"

"Clara Haber. She was married to Fritz Haber. He invented Zyklon B."

"Death camp gas. I hope she was proud."

"Not exactly. Fritz was Jewish. And his wife was so mortified at what her husband did she took his service revolver and shot herself in their front garden. After that Fritz renounced his Hebraic roots and tried to join the Nazis. They wouldn't have him. He lived long enough to see his relatives die from the chemical he invented, then suffered a massive heart attack fleeing the country."

"Jesus. That's kind of the gold standard for self-hating Jew. How do you even know that?"

"I told you, I was a morbid child. I wanted to be Jewish."

"So you read this when you were a kid?"

"Okay, I lied. Sort of. I was fascinated with that stuff growing up. But after you mentioned Mengele, I went on the Web. It's like, there are the horror stories you expect—the big stuff, like the camps, like genocide—and then there are all the twisted sideshows. Like Fritz fucking Haber. When I saw Mrs. Zell, I flashed on Clara Haber. What woman wants to be married to a collaborator—even fifty years after the war?"

"You think Dinah knew?"

"She could have."

As we talked, Tina handed me two plastic bags and pointed to my shoes. "It's too late," I said. "I've already walked around."

"Just put these on. It'll hide your prints. Give the forensics team one more thing to think about. *'How did the guy disappear from the middle of the room?'*"

"You really think that'll work?" I held on to Tina's shoulder and still nearly lost my balance putting the bags on.

"It's science," she said, handing me two pink rubber bands to keep the baggies from falling off.

"Oh well, never mind," I said, sealing my pants around the ankles. "But I don't buy the convulsion theory. Unless she strangled herself, it doesn't hold up."

"So maybe somebody interrupted her suicide and killed her. Like in *Magnolia,* when the guy jumps out a window and gets shot on the way down. Which still doesn't explain how you know what's in her purse, sweetheart."

"For Christ's sake, I told you. We met on the plane. She was some kind of Chasid groupie."

"Hole-in-the-sheet, right?"

"Is that something women fantasize about?"

"There's nothing somebody doesn't fantasize about." Suddenly her face lit up. "Wait, it's perfect!"

I knew that look, and I wasn't thrilled about it. "*What's* perfect?" I asked.

By way of reply, she hooked one baggied toe on a corner of the blanket and tugged, dragging the baby-blue bedding onto the baby-blue floor. Then she worked her foot into the sheet and pulled it back onto the bed and over the body. Sure enough, a tennis-ball-sized circle of skin was visible over Mrs. Zell's wrong-way ribs.

"You know," I said, trying to ignore the body beneath and focus on that perfectly scissored hole, "this isn't actually the way the Orthodox do it."

"Her bed," said Tina, "her fantasy."

"It's really Mrs. Zell?"

"Third of three. You should have checked her driver's license when you were scoping her drugs. Her pictures are all over Zell's study."

"So you really think she killed herself?"

"Well, you do have an effect on women."

A thought elbowed its way into my brain: Tina somehow gets wind of me and Dinah on the plane. Tina gets wrong idea. Tina heads over and kills Mrs. Zell in horrible fashion and, now that I'm here, has the chance to take it a step further—to either frame me for Mrs. Z's homicide or go "full Marvin," i.e., murder me the way she'd murdered her first husband, the ill-fated Marvin.

"Baby," I said, "you didn't . . . you know?"

What's the sensitive way of asking your ex-wife if she savagely mutilated and killed a dead woman you're both staring at?

"Do this? No." Tina pointed to my feet. "Honey, your baggie's slipping."

Her tone was matter-of-fact. I might have asked if she ate the last slice of pie.

I felt a strange kind of admiration as I watched Tina pluck a few Kleenex out of a box by the bed and start to wipe things down: the nightstand, the headboard, the light switch. Then the bathroom, where she attacked the sink and toilet.

"Under the seat," she said, lifting and lowering, "the one place bad guys always forget. I saw it on *CSI*."

"How would people fight crime without prime-time television?"

"I don't know," she said, "but one wrong move and I'm going to be on Court TV explaining why I'm in Harry Zell's house. With you as my character witness."

"Is my character that bad?"

"I think it's sterling. But on paper you're a little sketchy."

"Forget I asked. What are you really doing here?"

"I told you, I *really* wanted to find out about the man who hired us—make sure he pays."

"No, I mean now. What are you doing? Why are you fucking around with the body?"

"Why are you asking me so many questions?"

"You don't think it's questionable?" Whatever calm I had was beginning to curl at the edges. "And speaking of questionable, I still don't know what happened to you in the minivan."

"What happened to *me*? You're the one who disappeared."

"I disappeared? Is that what you call getting hit on the head, dragged out of the Christian ho van and locked to my trailer toilet?"

Dinah's still-open eyes held me fast. There's nothing quite like the feeling of being judged by a corpse. I stepped over to close her eyes, but the lids wouldn't stay down. They kept flying back open like tenement blinds. Finally I closed them again and pressed down on her lids, but not too hard. It felt a little like pressing on a chocolate-covered cherry. I imagined the lifetime of horror in store if I accidentally caused postmortem eyeball burst. But I couldn't take her unblinking stare. I eased my fingers off the lids and they stayed shut for a few seconds. Then the left one opened up halfway and stayed there, so it looked, despite her fatal mutilation, like she was only pretending to be dead and was trying to keep an eye on things.

I heard myself gulp and tore my gaze away from the peeking dead woman, back to Tina. "This is the wrong place for a fight," I said. "We need to think."

Tina stopped what she was doing and nodded. "I agree."

"Okay, good. So what do we have? Basically, the guy has a dead wife with a kosher sex fetish."

"That's not all we have."

Tina opened her purse and pulled out a framed photo. Twin brothers. Pimply thirteen-year-olds. Teenagers. One buff, one slender, in matching talliths and yarmulkes. They flanked their father and his new bride, the late Mrs. Zell, in an elaborate powder-blue dress. The buff brother held a Torah in his arms, resting the scrolls against his shoulder like he was burping a baby.

"Look familiar?"

I squinted. "I'm not sure. I think that's Temple Beth El. The one where you have to know Barbra Streisand to get seats for the High Holidays. I've seen it in the paper."

"I'm not talking about the temple, you idiot. I mean the boys. Remind you of anyone? Check the one on the left."

"Bernstein! Jesus Christ . . . I'm surprised you recognized him with his clothes on."

"Manny, let it go," she said. "It was part of the job. Anyway, that's not what makes him hard to recognize. He's got hair. And no glasses."

"Not to mention no neck ink."

"I think they save the neck ink till after the Bar Mitzvah. Or maybe Reform's different. It *is* his Bar Mitzvah, right?"

"I don't know. Maybe it's their dad's wedding." I searched the photo for clues. The rabbi wore a *shmidok* just like mine, a fellow

tribesman. "That's a pretty fancy dress. Maybe it was a Bar Mitzvah/
wedding combo. 'Today I am a man—and my father just married a
sheet-hole-crazy shiksa.'"

"Imagine what that must do to a boy."

"Well, in Bernstein's case, it set him on the happy road to San
Quentin and the ALS. But the other one." I tapped my finger on the
second brother's face. Something about the tilt of the head, the cast of
the eyes, how he peered up at his brother . . . the perpetually unher-
alded second son.

Then it clicked.

"*Wait!*" I took the photo and studied it closer, angling it to catch
the light. "That's Davey! He's in my class—or what's left of him. He
tried to blow himself away but only got the bottom of his face. He's a
medical miracle. Mengele operated on him."

"Mengele does surgery in prison?"

Tina had just finished wiping the place down. I observed her,
fighting powder-blue seasickness. "We really should leave," I said.

Tina took a last swipe at the bathroom doorknob. "We are
leaving. Answer the question. Do they let that genocidal freak do
surgery?"

"Yeah, I think he gets to operate. There's a whole other world in
there."

I grabbed a Kleenex from the "designer" box by the bed. It showed
a Currier and Ives–inspired winter scene: a covered bridge in New
England, a wagon with Mom, Dad and two towheaded children on the
way to Grandmother's house. NO JEWS HERE might as well have been
inscribed under the sheet count.

"Did you say something?"

"Mumbling." I covered the sliding lock on the garden door with
a designer Kleenex and unlocked it. Then I remembered. "He's also
doing RDP."

"Rapid detox? He's curing junkies up there?"

"He got one of them off junk. I don't know if that's the same as curing. Nobody I know ever stayed clean without kicking. Anyway, we need to leave. Someone's bound to wander back here."

"Who? The maid's high as a Ping-Pong ball, and the boys are in San Quentin."

"What about Zell?"

"He's up there, too," she said. "I saw a receipt for a plane ticket."

"Man, how much more of that place is there to film?"

"Maybe he's not shooting prisoners."

"Then what is he doing?"

"Mengele," we both said at once.

Tina eagle-eyed a piece of white lint on the carpet—anything not powder blue stood out boldly—and crouched to pick it up.

"You're really wearing the full Jew, aren't you? I'd kind of like to fuck you in it. This is the closest you've ever looked to innocent."

I stared over Tina's head back at Dinah—still sprawled on her blue bed, body down and face up. I was conflicted, to say the least. Then the phone rang. Tina pulled away. I shook my head *"No!"*

Tina ignored me and answered.

"Zell residence," she said, sounding Russian. She put a finger to her lips. "Mmm-hmm. Mmmm-hmm. All right, I tell him."

She hung up and shrugged. "Somebody named Mendel. Zell's yarmulke is ready."

"Nice accent. You're so good at this."

"First thing they tell you in acting class. Pretend the situation is real."

"What's that like?" I said, cracking the garden door a little wider. A stone path led through the beits and alephs and zaftig topiary ladies. I wondered what the gardeners thought.

"Anybody home?"

I recognized the halting Russian accent of my driver, Jack. Tina grabbed the clamshell trash can over her head and rushed behind the bedroom door. He walked in and she slammed the can down on his skull. Jack blinked at me, perplexed. As he crumbled, Tina pushed him. He landed on the bed, on top of the late Mrs. Zell's middle.

"Why did you do that? He's my *driver*." Tina ignored me and went to work on Jack's black wingtips. "What the fuck are you doing?"

"What's it look like I'm doing? Untying his shoes, then I'm going to take his pants off."

She unbuckled his belt and popped the buttons on his pants.

"You could help, you know."

"Wait! I *like* the guy."

"That's nice. When this blows over, you can go bowling together."

"Tina, what the fuck are you doing?"

"You have to ask?"

"I don't know what to ask first."

Why am I even here? That was the thing about being attracted to a borderline personality. I found myself doing things normal people didn't do, and going along, because *I* was a borderline personality.

This was the woman I loved. We pulled the driver's pants down in tandem, our heads nearly above him. I wanted to get out of there, but Tina was Tina.

"I'm sure there's a good reason you're messing with a crime scene."

"What do you think?" She wiped a bead of sweat off her arm. "Maybe Zell hired somebody to kill her. She might have flipped out and told him what she thought about him teaming up with Mengele. Or maybe she was so upset, she wanted to check herself out."

I gave up and left the driver's pants at his knees. "Or somebody killed her to get back at Zell."

"Please. You think one wife more or less makes a difference? The man's been married five times."

"Three. You always embellish."

Tina aimed a gaze of pure uranium.

"Harry Zell deserves to hang for doing *any* kind of business with

Mengele. And believe me, when word gets out his wife died in the saddle, riding kosher, he's going to squirm."

"You're doing this to make Zell feel worse? It's not bad enough his wife's dead—he has to hear she went out riding Chasid?"

"Believe me, it will hurt him more than her fling with the club tennis pro."

"How do you know she did that?"

"They all do."

I leaned down to my pal Jack. He was still breathing. Unconscious, but among the living. Thank God.

"You know," I said, "if Zell's behind this, what's he going to think when he hears his wife had an affair after he killed her?"

"What would you think?"

"I don't know, but it would make me nervous. I'd think somebody knew something."

"Well then. Let's do this and get out of here."

Tina's cheekbones shone with the effort of moving two full-grown humans around. Her concentration was fearsome.

"This doesn't freak you out, Tina?"

"The world freaks me out. All I'm trying to do is control a little bit of the freakdom."

"Yeah, well," I said, "Jack here may have a different opinion."

"Hey, he's in it, too." Tina flashed me her *man up* look. "The good news is he's never seen your face when you weren't Orthodox."

"Tina, for fuck's sake, I'm not talking about him ID'ing me. I'm talking about him waking up naked next to a dead woman. He doesn't deserve this."

"And we do?" Tina threw up her hands. "C'mon, Manny, like this is your first time at the dance?"

"What the fuck does that mean?"

"It means we need a smoke screen. Or would you rather be the prime suspect?" A sleep bubble of saliva appeared between Jack's lips, and she reached down to pop it. "Do you *want* an APB out on your ass? 'Cause I guarantee, if we'd let your boy just walk in and find a dead lady, the first thought in his head would be that you did it."

"I told you, he thinks I'm somebody else."

She glared. "So do I—'cause you didn't used to be this dense. What are you, on crack? How hard do you think it would be to trace you back to the airport? How many Chasids do you think flew in today? They'll track you all the way back to SF—or wherever the hell you got the bright idea of dressing up like the Baal Shem fucking Tov. You ever think of finding a disguise that blended in?"

"They didn't sell wigs in the Quentin gift shop. I had to improvise."

"Oh, baby." Tina sighed and touched my nose, the one part of my face that didn't have hair sprouting out of it. "I can't believe we're bickering. Open his mouth."

"What for?"

"For these."

Tina opened her fist on a handful of white pills. "Rufies."

"Why are you walking around with Rufies?"

"I'm not. They're Zell's. Or hers. I guess they liked to party. You think you're the only one who raids medicine cabinets?"

"I don't do that anymore."

"You're a credit to your race. I just thought they might come in handy. And see that, they have! C'mon, hold his mouth open. We shove a couple of these down his gullet, it's gonna look like date rape."

"Right." I didn't move. "Why don't we slaughter a chicken and write 'Kill the Pigs' in blood on the wall, too? Just to throw 'em off. Make it look like some kosher Santeria Manson thing."

"You're missing the point."

"The point doesn't matter. If we try to stick them down his throat while he's out, he might choke to death."

"And?"

Now I was doing the glaring, and Tina backed off. "And any third-rate coroner would find the things undissolved in his thoracic tube and know they were shoved in postmortem. I can't believe I'm even *having* this conversation."

Tina closed her fingers back around the pills and crossed her arms. "Okay, Rabbi, then what?"

"Then nothing. Let's just finish this and get out of here."

"Man of action," she said. "That's why I love you."

It took us another minute to reposition poor Jack on top of the hole-y sheet and the late Mrs. Zell naked underneath.

"I'm surprised her pubes aren't baby blue," Tina said. "Do you want to put him through the hole?"

"Are you kidding me?"

Tina started to reach for the driver's crotch but I pushed her hand away. The only thing more revolting than grabbing his johnson myself would be watching Tina do it. I knew that she'd banked on my reaction. She knew it, too, and smiled.

"Look at you, manning up!"

"Tina, please. Not now."

Holding my breath, I tried to grab Jack's organ. But somehow it had gotten wedged between his balls and his thigh, and when I tried to move his scrotum, the spongy dampness gave me a shock. "*Yec-chhh!*" Either Jack suffered copious testicle sweats, or he'd urinated when Tina knocked him out.

"What's the matter?"

"Sweaty," I managed to say without gagging, and jammed my hand back down for a second try. This time I got a grip on his organ—and thought I felt it stir. I wasn't sure, but as I tried to extract the thing it began to swell. "Oh, Jesus!" I said, and let it go.

"Now what?" Tina snapped.

"I don't know," I said. "Can the comatose get hand jobs?"

"For Christ's sake," Tina replied, "I know you liked the guy, but this is ridiculous."

"Fuck you," I said. Biting down on my lip, I guided the now rubbery organ, which felt like a dog toy, through the opening in the fabric, in the general proximity of Mrs. Zell's landing strip, then rushed to the bathroom.

"I have to wash my hands."

"Not there, I cleaned." With her baggied hand, Tina eased open a bed-stand drawer. "You'd get more germs on a doorknob. Now where do you think they keep the handcuffs?"

"No!" I ass-bumped the drawer shut and grabbed my ex by the arm. "Baby, *enough*. We're leaving."

The first stab of sun was startling after the aquarium light of the bedroom. As we darted from sculptured nymph shrub to six-foot aleph, I kept wiping my hands compulsively on my pants and complaining. "I still don't see what posing the driver accomplishes."

"Could you stop whining for one second?" Tina hissed.

I stopped and faced her. "I am not whining. I'm just saying, now that we've done it, making a crime scene look like Jewish fetish sex gone wrong might not even help us that much. It'll take a good criminalist three minutes to figure the scene was staged."

"Maybe, maybe not. But if you're Harry Zell, and you already know your wife's proclivities, you probably don't want the rest of the world to find out about them."

"That," I said, "or he comes back with a crew to get it on film. Mostly I just feel bad about the driver."

"Enough with the goddamn driver!" Tina stopped beside a buxom sprite hacked from a juniper tree. "Did you even know him? This jim-jim picks you up, lets you think he believes you're someone else, and just drives you around? Really? How do you know he wasn't biding his time, waiting for orders?"

"From who? Diva Limousines? I'm just glad I tipped him big."

"Don't be. That just makes you more suspicious."

Tina stopped and looked around. Dust motes circled in the shafts of light that made it through the overgrown shrubs and trees. "I keep expecting a fucking unicorn to come trotting out."

"Jew-nicorn," I whispered back as we started moving again.

Tina punched me in the stomach.

"*Owfff . . .* What was that for?"

"Fuck, Manny, if we're going to be together, I need to feel like you can protect me."

I contemplated a ten-foot bush carved into Hebrew letters: בראשית (in the beginning). The first line of Genesis. I recognized it from my Bar Mitzvah, where I'd had to sing it right out of the Torah. I had no idea, at the time, I'd be cashing in my Israeli gift bonds for drugs.

"First of all," I said, willing myself back to the present as we started moving again, "I didn't know *we* were together. You left, remember?"

We hadn't gone ten feet when we faced a black metal gate. Tina reached for the handle and I grabbed her, spinning her back toward me. "Second," I said, holding her by her shoulders, "knocking somebody out with a trash can is not the same as protecting. Shit like that creates more problems than it solves. And you don't want to leave prints on the gate."

"Yeah," she said, her voice suddenly sultry, "tell me what to do, Daddy."

She stood on her toes to kiss me but I pushed her away. "Not here."

"Why not?"

"This is Brentwood. We probably triggered ten kinds of motion detectors and a silent alarm crossing the yard."

I ripped a fern leaf big enough to cover my hand and unlatched the door.

"You know what I wish?" she said, before stepping through. "I wish we could just talk about normal stuff. Like normal people."

"Such as?"

"I don't know, that's the problem. We're in the black Prius."

"What happened to the Virgin pussy wagon?"

"I got tired of that giant-ass carbon footprint. A girlfriend loaned me her Prius." By "loaned," I suspected, she meant "left the keys in." But this wasn't the time to press.

Sure enough, the black Prius waited like a cute puppy on the other side of the Hebrew jungle. But before Tina and I tiptoed out of the copse, she pulled me back. "I'm with you now, Manny. But where the fuck are you?"

"Meaning what?" I was getting sick of dramatic pronouncements.

"Meaning, I love you, but you shouldn't do drugs. They're not your friends."

"And you think they're yours?"

"Hey, I'm not the one in a beaver hat and a Bobover makeover. I'm functioning."

I had nothing to say to that. The limo I'd arrived in was still parked kitty-corner on the lush street. Some men in suits milled behind it, conferring with their backs to us. We ducked silently out of the shadows to her Prius. Tina started the soundless engine. She U-turned out of the mega-upscale Brentwood lane and aimed us back down to Sunset.

For a minute and a half I steamed with indignation, but that passed by the time we made it to the first stop sign. "Shit, Tina. You're right. I am fucking up. I got into some strange powder I found up there under my trailer."

"Under your trailer?"

"Don't ask. It came in a Red Cross box. But I was fucking up before that. I should have gotten more on Zell in the first place. Scoped out his home and office. That's the reason I came back to L.A. But I didn't expect to find his wife dead and you in his bathroom. I'm just"—I knew I had to dial back the emotion, but I'd been numb for a while—"I'm just really happy to see you."

Tina took her eyes off the road and scrutinized me while she steered. "Look at us, huh? Maybe we had to pull a Burton and Taylor. Split up just so we could reconnect."

Somehow the prospect sounded as tiring as it did exciting. I said, "I don't know, baby." But when I stared at her, I did know.

Today, from a certain angle, she looked Björkish. Critical cheekbones and straight bangs over her eyes. The sirens closing in made the moment movie dramatic. Maybe the ditzy housekeeper finally checked on the lady of the house. Or maybe the driver came to.

"Zell's got an at-home office. His den," Tina said quietly. I groaned, realizing I'd forgotten to check. Tina read my mind. "That's all right. *I* remembered. But he's one of those guys who keeps everything in his head." Then, not bothering with a transition—mutual ADD made transitions unnecessary—she added, "You need to lose these."

She snatched my fur brim and forelocks and flipped them into the backseat.

"There, Detective, you look better already."

"Detective. What lifetime was that?" I said, tugging my tallith off. "But I like you in a Prius. You make it look dangerous."

"I'm all about saving energy, sir. But the smart money's in solar vibrators. You want to talk about where we go next?"

"I was just thinking about that," I lied. "I was hired to get information on the doctor, but so far I've found out more about the guy who hired me."

"Hey, somebody hires you to identify Josef Mengele, you want to know all about your employer."

"A life tip I only wish I'd have heard earlier. I get impulsive."

"It's funny, him having twins in Quentin. Especially with the king of twin dissection in the house. Maybe it's coincidence, but it's still weird."

"Not as weird as him having a big Jew son who's a shot-caller in the ALS."

"Which reminds me." Tina fished in her open purse between her legs on the seat, then gave up, muttering to herself. "Fuck it, I can live without a cigarette. . . . I think. But I forgot to mention. His second wife's maiden name was Bernstein."

"Good work."

"Not really. I found his canceled checks."

Just then we heard peals of laughter. A car full of white teenagers whooped it up at a red light beside us. The driver wore his L.A. Kings cap sideways. He worked a gangster lean and gunned the engine.

"BMW M6, convertible," Tina said. "A hundred and thirty-nine thousand dollars."

When the driver saw Tina staring, he flipped her off.

"Oh yeah, baby," Tina moaned, "my daddy runs a studio and I'm all pimped up and I take biology at Crossroads with Dustin Hoffman's nephew."

I glanced past her. The acned Romeo behind the wheel started smooching a cheerleader, holding his extended middle finger behind her head. The hip-hop consumers in the backseat hooted appreciatively. A whiff of weed drifted up at us.

Tina looked over at me. "I bet if he had some kind of little accident, he wouldn't file a police report. Even if the kush was medicinal."

When the light changed, Tina sharked the car forward a length and cut left. The Beemer swerved to avoid her and jumped the curb, clipping a trash bin and a mailbox before screeching to a bumper-dragging stop a few feet from a bus bench.

Tina continued at the speed limit, composed as a soccer mom on Xanax.

"Was that necessary?" I said.

"I'm helping the economy," she replied. "The front end alone is going to give a body shop work for a week. So what were you saying?"

"You might want to get on the freeway. I doubt Ferris Bueller and his pals got your license number. But it might be a good idea to put some distance between you and your moving violation. For fuck's sake, Tina!"

She rolled her eyes. "Could we just go back to what we're talking about?"

"Fine. I was saying I still need to do what I said I was going to do. Find out more about Mengele."

"Have you Googled him?" Tina shuddered. "The fan sites are really creepy."

"How's his Facebook page. That's what I need to know about. The new Mengele. The one who's up there bragging in Quentin—and the people colluding with him, for whatever un-fucking-godly reason. We have him picked up, we might never know what his deal is—and who he's got deals with. It might be Zell, the warden . . . who the hell knows?"

"It's pretty easy to discredit a ninety-seven-year-old war criminal who's been taking meth."

"If it is meth. As opposed to, say, crystallized Gypsy adrenaline."

"Nice."

"I'm not making it up. But why discredit the prick when you can just kill him? Anybody with something to hide gets wind Dr. Death is on the hook, all they gotta do is blow on him and he'd keel over. I only have till tomorrow morning. I wanted to see you; now we need to meet with what's-her-name, the born-again hooker who did Mengele."

"Cathy," she said. "Only . . . there may be a problem."

Tina chewed her lip and clamped the wheel a little harder.

"I know you, baby. When you say 'little problem,' grown men duck. You have a previous engagement or what?"

"Not me, but Cathy, the girl . . ."

"All I want to do is meet her. Ten, fifteen minutes."

"You can meet her," she said, "she just might not be there, if you know what I mean. . . . After her date with Mengele, she started hitting the crank pretty hard. Oh!"

As was her manner, Tina changed the subject on a dime. She unclamped her purse, digging through God knows what, and held up a black T-shirt.

"You like?"

"Please tell me that isn't Zell's."

"Of course not. It's James Perse. Come on, take the coat off. And lose the face beaver."

"What, you don't think I look biblical?"

"You look," she said, "like what would happen if Lincoln had unprotected sex with Bette Midler."

This seemed like a good time to try chewing my mustache, just to see what Mengele got out of the practice. But I stopped as soon as I started. The lip fur got wet right away, and after that it was like nibbling a damp sweater. Tina saw me chomping and made a face. "That is really disgusting."

"I'm just trying to see why *he* does it. What's so disgusting about it?"

We swung into the freeway on-ramp and got in line behind a Hummer. Tina took a sidelong glance and considered. "You know how hypnotists in movies are always telling volunteers to act like chickens? You look like some hypnotist told you to eat pussy."

"Only you," I said, and fingered the tainted fur away from my mouth. "Maybe it's different when it's your own hair."

As the Prius idled behind the tank-sized Hummer Tina gunned the engine, an eager puppy snapping at a bear. When it was our turn to go, she reached over and ripped off the beard, then floored it and shot onto the 405. For a few seconds it hurt so much I went blind. Then I saw pain stars on the inside of my eyelids. I had to wipe tears off with my sleeve.

"You enjoyed that," I said when I could see again.

Tina cackled. She changed lanes with abandon and recited like a schoolgirl, "'Bliss like thine is bought by years / Dark with torment and with tears.'"

"Now you're busting out Def Leppard lyrics?"

"Close. Emily Brontë." She ran her fingers down my cheek and I winced. My face felt like it had been dragged over a cheese grater, then steam ironed and doused with hot sauce. . . . When I could speak again, I remembered the shirt I was twisting in my hands and held it up. "So who's James Perse—and why do you have his shirt?"

"It's not his shirt, you idiot. He's the designer. They sell him at Barney's. I found an old credit card and got myself a gift certificate. Then I bought something for you."

"Thanks," I said, gingerly touching my cheek to see if I was bleeding. "Sometimes I forget how thoughtful you are."

Tina leaned over and kissed me, right where it burned. "You're welcome, baby. Now relax. They can't arrest you for wearing something that costs over twenty dollars."

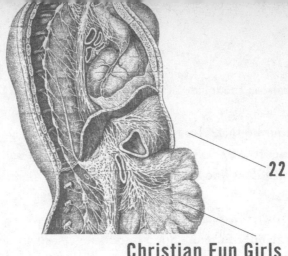

22

Christian Fun Girls

Reverend D's Reseda crib was a two-story slats-falling-off-the-roof semi-dump next to a 7-Eleven in Van Nuys. The rev financed it with joint grants from ex-president Bush's Abstinence First Foundation, the Family Research Council, and State of California Prop. 486, which allocated funds for halfway houses and prison work-fare programs.

"Four girls bunk upstairs, four down. Two to a room," Tina said, giving me the tour. "Then there's the reverend's office-slash-bedroom."

"Sounds very Hugh Hefner."

"Yeah," said Tina, "it's just like the mansion, except skanky and in the Valley. With no grotto."

Stepping over a teddy bear with a cross on his chest—"Watch out for Jesus Bear!"—we entered the reverend's spiritual headquarters. I AM CHASTE! was painted on the cottage cheese ceiling, directly over a water bed with a giant Ten Commandments scroll propped behind it. Two cameras on tripods rested against a backdrop of Golgotha on the wall opposite.

On a battered metal desk I found a stack of Christian Fun Girls video offerings, old-time VHSs. On the first box, a buxom Latina in a toga stared off the cover, her collagened lips parted suggestively as she stole a sloe-eyed glance over her shoulder at a manly Roman soldier. I saw the title and held it up for Tina. "*Spermin' on the Mount*? Are you fucking kidding me? This is a genre?"

"Hey, I'm not saying it's on par with *Rapture Babes*, okay?" She indicated the boxed set underneath. *Rapture Babes* I through IV featured a bevy of wholesome, panty-clad Midwestern girls who would have been carded had they tried to buy cigarettes. And the director's comments. The corn-fed talent gazed heavenward, arms over their heads and clothes in a heap at their feet, as though ready to ascend and back that thing up for the Lord. The back of the box showed one doe-eyed blond believer, on her knees in front of the Son of God, who resembled Steve Railsback playing Manson in a TV movie. "Tina, listen to this. 'What girl wouldn't want to give a lap dance to Jesus? Well, Tammi Nelson is about to get her chance.'"

"I've seen that one," she said. "Jesus tipped big."

I tossed the videos back on the desk, beside a motel Bible. "How much money does he pull in turning out young churchgoing girls?"

"He doesn't exactly turn them out. He'd tell you he was putting the shield of Christ between their legs."

"'*Ladies—why settle for regular old panty shields when you can get . . . the Shield of Christ!*' Actually, that sounds pretty good. *I'd* buy it, if I had a Christian vagina. I didn't even know He had a shield."

"You haven't read the New Testament. Anyway, he makes most of his money from downloads. I mean the reverend, not Jesus."

"Either way. Religion's kind of like the ultimate free download."

Tina gave me her patented eye-roll. "Heavy. We supply content for a dozen different Christian sex sites, including a bunch we run out of here. Studio's upstairs."

I unfolded a glossy brochure featuring thumbnails and titles. "So if I'd sodomized you in the snailback, I'd have ended up in one of these?"

"'The loins, the place of the Last Judgment.' William Blake," she intoned. "There are a lot of ways to be saved."

"I'm getting that. You didn't answer the question."

"Okay, then. No. You would not have ended up on video."

I was ready for some righteous indignation; now I felt shunned. "Why not?"

She hesitated, then closed the file drawer with a bang. "Because the lens cap was still on. I was so excited to see you, I got sloppy."

I didn't say anything. Sometimes it was enough just to watch her. Tina raised her chin, flicking her bangs out of her eyes, something she did when she wanted to make a point. Especially when the point was *Fuck you*. Tina stood on her toes and plunged her arm in the top drawer of a filing cabinet, up to the shoulder. She retrieved a few catalogues and tossed them over her shoulders. Finally, finding what she wanted, she yanked her arm and yelped, "It's a girl!" before throwing a vividly veined, fur-clefted dog toy in my direction.

I caught the thing, which was as nauseatingly moist to the touch as my San Quentin trailer mattress.

"Porta-pussy," Tina explained helpfully while I held the squishy device away from my face.

"Tell me it's not damp because it's been used," I pleaded.

"Not in a while, anyway," she replied reassuringly.

I studied the tawny, disembodied fur slit, trying to figure out which side was upside-down—if there *was* an upside-down. "This must be the ultimate dream date for guys who really want to fuck rubber chickens with hair."

"Don't knock it till you try it," Tina said.

"Who's knocking it? I'm surprised he's not selling them for fifty a pop on the yard at Quentin."

"The Doc Johnson people made a fortune on them in the eighties. But the reverend was first into Christian sex toys."

"Born-again dildos. Who knew? The man's a trailblazer."

"Baby," Tina huffed, "that stuff's just for Christian freaks. Once he got the idea of pimping sanctified live vaginas, he forgot about the rubber ones."

"The only Christian freak I'm really curious about is the reverend. I've met him, remember? And now you're living under his roof."

"Just while he's gone. I'm getting five grand a week to play den mother."

"And doing a hell of a job. Come on, what else? He let you direct?"

"I was going to. We were actually working on a script. A feature. He got financing for race porn. Basically triple-X with an Aryan message."

"An Aryan message? Look at you, Leni Riefenshtup!"

"Fuck you, Manny. It's not like they're really Nazis. I mean, the producer's a black man, and they're written and directed by an ex-addict and prostitute with some Canuck in her blood."

"And let me guess, featuring the ever popular stock character *der Geile Jude*."

"What's that?"

"The Libidinous Jew. One of the only things I remember from my brief stint in a college."

"Come on, we wouldn't shoot you from the waist up. Where's your sense of humor? Porn is more mainstream than the Special Olympics. I figured I could do something subversive. We could bill you as 'the Lion of Zion.'"

"I prefer 'Hebrew National.'"

"I don't care if you call yourself Shecky Mazeltov. I just think we could do something subversive."

"I'm sure that would really impress the cineastes on D Block. Let me give *you* a quote, baby. 'Self-delusion is the key to happiness.' Voltaire. It's the only one I know."

"Then how come you're not happy?"

I must have looked stricken. She burst out laughing.

"Just kidding. You're right. It's a stupid idea. *Mein Cunt.* Anyway, it's not going to happen. Not with me. The rev's shot a lot of white power porn, but usually just sex scenes strung together. He finds film school geeks to work on them."

"The world's full of sleazy gigs. They're the only ones left." I went back to riffling the reverend's drawers so I wouldn't be looking at her when I asked what I was about to ask. I couldn't help myself. "Tina," I said, "just tell me you weren't turning tricks."

"Honey," she replied wearily, "do you know how many times you've asked me that? I'm strictly in administration."

"Administration? You make it sound like it's the gas company."

"Come on, Manny! I did the hands-on stuff when I was a teenager, okay? You never had a job that made you hate yourself?" She saw the look on my face. "Dumb question."

"Forget it," I said. "You know me, I don't acknowledge my feelings. I just fall off the wagon, then wake up in Cleveland with a bag full of toupees and blood on my pants."

"So what feelings are eating you up now?"

"Besides what happens in my chest when I look at you? It's Mengele. Dinah Zell. The whole thing."

"Gotta learn to compartmentalize, baby."

"Is that what it's called?"

I dumped out an envelope of smudgy receipts for "love offerings" made out to Foundation for Christian Love Ministries, another of the reverend's DBA names.

I stole a glance at Tina. The Björk resemblance disappeared. Pissed off, her face shape-shifted. Took on that that Susan Tyrell/Faye Dunaway kind of scary beauty. Cheekbones of death. Savage in repose.

"I like the water-bed-next-to-the-desk arrangement," I said, scooping up a batch of canceled checks and pre-stamped U-Serve money orders. "But the bookkeeping's a little shaky."

The top drawer, when I tugged it open, spilled a small library of Thai takeout flyers. The drawer beneath was stuffed with sanctioned twelve-step booklets, mixed with homemade pamphlets containing the reverend's inspirational thoughts and sermons. The pamphlets were hand-assembled, folded-over pages copied on a Xerox machine that needed toner and hand-stapled on the crease. The first pamphlet I grabbed featured a sketch of a long-haired girl with one hand propped on the wall over a toilet, one hand shoved in her mouth. Over the picture was a line of Gothic script that I read to Tina: 'The Second Word in Heaven Is Heave.' "

Tina stiffened. "That one's about bulimia. Most of the girls have eating disorders. There's some wing of OA in the Valley that donates bed and board for Christian overeaters."

"Whatever helps."

Tina slammed the bottom drawer shut. "This is pointless. We need his computer for addresses."

"So the rev cranks out white power porn and born-again jerk-off fodder. I still don't get exactly what business Zell did with him."

"I'm pretty sure it had to do with distribution."

"Of course. Zell's a big Jew."

Tina gave me a funny look.

"It's an expression," I said. "I heard it from Mama Mendel, mother of Solly Mendel, the yarmulke king. . . . Long story."

"You do look good in kosher," she said, smiling.

"Enough, okay? Let me think. We already found out Harry Zell's son is a card-carrying star of ALS. It's no stretch to imagine Daddy bankrolling white supremacist sex-ertainment. Maybe he sells it to the Aryans exclusive."

"What if Bernstein's just in with the Aryans to do family business?"

"In that case I hope those swastikas on his neck wash off."

"He can wear a tallith."

"How do you know about talliths?"

"Client wanted a girl to dress up."

"Like a rabbi?"

"Cantor. He wanted her to sing. One of the girls knew 'Hava Nagila' from interfaith camp."

"You know, I'm dying to find out more about your thing with Reverend D. But I'm dying even more to know about your friend Bernstein. He did everything but kiss Mengele's ring when he met him. And Mengele shined him on. That's what doesn't figure. You look at the old fuck for two minutes, it's obvious he's this craven, narcissistic, dried-up praise sponge."

Tina shrugged. "Did you forget? Bernstein is Jewish."

"I didn't forget, but in prison Jews are white and whites stick together."

"Maybe in prison, but not in concentration camps. Think about it," Tina said. "Mengele came from eugenics. Caucasian or not, at Auschwitz, Jews weren't even considered human."

"I love that you know this stuff," I told her, and meant it. "I'm crazy about your looks, and your body, too. But I really fucking love you for your brains."

"You better," she said, but I could tell she liked hearing it.

I dug into the pile and plucked out another pamphlet. In this one centurions whipped Jesus while he held up a Holy Bible. A thought balloon over his head said, "The Jew calls this a dirty book!" Historical Jew-hate, disturbing as it was, was at least history. The sight of anti-Semitic literature as modern as *Gossip Girl* triggered a much more visceral fear. Not because it could happen here, but because it was happening.

An involuntary shudder made my lip twitch. "Business or no business, it's one thing for a Jewish dad to have a son in San Quentin, it's another to have him join a white prison gang and drink the Third Reich Kool-Aid."

"Otherwise known as Powdered Hitler," said Tina, "but Zell has *two* sons." She kicked me in the shin. "What about brother Davey? Zell could be paying Mengele to give the poor kid a jaw. I hate to say it, but you probably do get mad scalpel skills when you practice on living flesh instead of cadavers."

"That would mean Mengele takes money from a Jew."

"Oh, please," said Tina, "money's green, no matter who touches it."

"Color me naïve," I sighed, and settled back to watch Tina pick a nurse's uniform off a rolling rack full of them. NANCY was stitched over the left breast.

"Don't tell me, he's running a home health care service, too?"

"That's one way to describe it. Nurses are the number-one fantasy."

A shoe rack, like you'd find in a bowling alley, took up most of the wall behind the uniforms. Half the rack was full of nursing shoes. I stepped over and picked a pair at random. The size was shocking. Eighteen, triple E.

"Who's this for, Nurse Shaq?"

"Some of the T-girls run big. You'd be surprised at the special requests."

"I doubt it." Then something occurred to me. "I wonder why Davey didn't honk on being Bernstein's brother. Having a bro who's a wheel in the Aryans could make life easy."

Tina stopped. "Maybe Davey is the modest type."

"Or maybe Davey and his dad weren't so sure Mengele didn't care who touched his money. Nazi doctors viewed Gypsies and Jews as two-legged tumors. So maybe they figured Mengele might accidentally forget to sterilize his instruments if he knew he was transplanting a jaw into a Jewish face. That's a pretty big reason to conceal Bernstein and Davey's fraternal bond. I'm gonna be looking over my shoulder till we figure out if Mengele and Zell are partners or enemies."

"Don't drive yourself crazy; plenty of people are both."

Tina hung the nurse wear back up and plucked a gingham dress off the rack. The collar was high and lacy and it buttoned up to the chin, in the pervy-wholesome fashion favored by schoolmarms in Westerns. "So how's your daughter, by the way?"

"What makes you ask about Lola? The schoolmarm dress?" It was a look I never got. "She's over her granny phase. Which I kind of miss. I had lunch with her a month ago and she showed up in a body stocking and hoodie. One of her friends saw us. Later she asked Lola what it was like dating a cool old nerd."

"That's sweet."

"Don't," I said. "I don't even like talking about her in a place like this. We should go."

"Fine. We can leave now if you want." Tina rehung the gingham and selected a white leather coat with a fur collar. Then she put that back and grabbed a tight gray coat that buttoned from the ankles up. It fit like it was happy to be there. "The thing is, we're fucked without the computer. We're gonna have to depend on Cathy to remember where Mengele lived. Come on."

"Where to?"

"Well," she said, "Reverend D calls it the guest bedroom, but that's kind of a stretch."

Upstairs, I saw what Tina meant about the bedroom. We walked in on three female residents. The trio were all in ratty panties, smoking crystal from a glass-bulbed pipe and sprawled on a stained shag carpet. It was hard to say what the original color might have been. The air had a chemical tinge. From the doorway, the girls seemed to be marooned on an island of Romilar DM bottles, empty forty-ounce Cobras, spilled-over ashtrays, odd bits of circuitry and shiny metal parts and cereal bowls brimming with yellow-gold liquid.

"Tell me that's apple juice," I said.

"You pee, you lose your turn," Tina explained. "The good news, on crank you don't pee much. You forget."

"It's the little things," I said.

Sheets had been tacked over the windows and a "Viva Viagra" commercial played on the unwatched fifty-inch flat-screen propped against a wall with the sound off. A few mattresses, minus sheets, were shoved in a corner. Beside the leaning TV stood a wooden podium with CHRISTIAN LOVE hand-stenciled on the front and a red Bible on it. None of the tweakerettes so much as noticed when we entered. Two of the young ladies, one Latina and one black, fought lethargically over the glass stem. "Pipe is mines, bitch." "Bullshit. I will kick your funky black ass right now." You had the feeling they'd been arguing for five years.

A few crumbs spilled from a baggy on a cracked dinner plate between them. But neither appeared energetic enough to do more than bicker. The Latina, who might have been under thirty if she lied on her driver's license, owned a pair of impossibly firm torpedo breasts. They stuck straight out, titanium solid and far too large for the popsicle stick Darfur rib cage saddled with the task of supporting them. It occurred to me that maybe she couldn't stand up. She'd just have to loll on the ground, victim of crank and gravity, until somebody hauled her off or she smoked herself down to nothing, leaving only those twin towers and a pair of cracked lips to show she ever existed. The black crank fanatic trying to snatch the pipe was just as sucked up, but a foot taller, with deep-set eyes and a big crucifix dangling between her much daintier bosoms. The way Jesus dangled in her cleavage, it looked like He was dying to stretch out his arms on the cross and squeeze her nipples. She kept crying, *"Mine mine mine, mine mine mine,"* as if she'd forgotten what the word meant or how to stop repeating it.

"Fucking perfect," Tina said after we took in the tableau. That's when the third girl, the white one, noticed us, and Tina pointed. "That's her."

Cathy was rocking on her side, carpet fetal, but sat up fast. Still rocking, she gazed at us with the slack-jawed, cracked-glass stare of an alien abductee.

"Psychotic?" I wondered out loud.

"On a good day," Tina said. "Crank does that."

Tina turned on the light, and all three girls skittered in place like roaches on glue. In the one-hundred-watt glare, I could make out the red tide of tiny bumps up and down Cathy's arms and legs. I stepped back instinctively, fearing contact. "Are those fleabites?"

"Not even," Tina replied. "Crank does that, too. You get enough of that shit in your system, it finds a way to get back out."

The piles of clothes and makeup scattered around the room made me think of a plane crash. But it was hard to say if there were any survivors.

Cathy stuck her thumb in her mouth and scooted backward. I noticed something shiny, electronic and broken on the carpet behind her. Something with its innards plucked out and arranged according to a system that probably made sense if you'd been up for three days, really concentrating. Gink work. The idea, generally sparked when all circuits were firing, was to take something apart, figure out how it works and put it back together—which no one since the invention of going without sleep had ever done. Cops trawling for tweakers pull over and put their vests on when they spot a driveway full of engine parts.

Tina kneeled and picked up the silver tray. "Well, now we're fucked," she said. Somehow, in her hands, the thing more resembled what it was: the gutted husk of a laptop, piled with colorful bits of circuit and wire that once made it possible to Google "methedrine + psychosis." "The rev had all his addresses in his PowerBook."

"And there's no backup?"

Tina rattled a few of the larger pieces around, retrieving a black box the size of a pack of Camel straights. A scissored USB cord dangled from it, still plugged in. Tina sighed. "External hard drive." She held the box to the light to show me the holes where it had been pierced clean through. They formed a perfect cross.

"It was Satan!" Cathy screamed. Her eyes jittered wildly in their sockets.

"He must have used power tools," Tina said.

"He was in the computer! I saw his face. His eyes were words. The screen was *bleeding*!"

Suddenly she leaped to her feet, flailing, like somebody trying to climb air. Then she dropped, both hands scratching frantically at the red letters spelling SAVIN' IT FOR JC over the crotch of her formerly white panties. The panties rode low, tragic and saggy beneath the protruding plates of her pelvis. Somehow—maybe it was the bagged-out JC undies—her body gave the impression of having been recently plump.

"The screen was *bleeding*! *Tell them!*" Cathy screamed to the pair on the carpet, who were still feuding in desultory fashion over the next hit. "Roxie, *tell* her. . . La-*tee*-sha! *Help me!*"

"Huh?"

Roxie, the one with breasts that made me think of armor-piercing depleted uranium shells, amassed the energy to turn her head. When she did, Lateesha snatched the pipe out of her hands. She fished a questionable chunk out of her own thong, jammed it in the business end of her stem and tried to light it. Before Lateesha could catch a flame, Tina leaped up again and kicked the pipe out of her mouth. It hit the wall and cracked, scattering speed crumbs. Lateesha let out a high-pitched *reee-owwww*, like a feral cat with a nail in its eye, and all three girls dove for the drugs at once.

Tina broke into the scrum and grabbed Cathy by the hair, leaving the other two to salvage what high they could from the shattered glass.

I helped Tina get our target out of the room. In the hall, she propped her against a wall and slapped her. "Cathy, stop being such a tweaker!" Tina had a way of saying this kind of thing with genuine tenderness. She wanted to strangle the girl but she'd also *been* her. And she remembered. Her own life made her kindness genuine. Not for the first time, it occurred to me how lucky I was. Lots of guys wanted nice girls. I had a woman who'd been as far down the chemical bad behavior ladder as I'd been. Farther, in Tina's case, since I'd never murdered a spouse or added a side-dish of eating disorder. I didn't judge her, she didn't judge me. She wasn't nice, but she was knowing. Which made me much more comfortable. I didn't do well with nice. I never knew what to do with it.

Cathy rested her head on Tina's shoulder. Love was a demented negotiation. Or maybe we just find people demented the same way we are—so as not to feel . . . demented. Or—*Shut the fuck up!* Clearly, I'd breathed in some eau de methedrine. But it only made me think *more*, not better, the way speed always did.

Cathy began to vibrate. I watched Tina stroke the shaking girl's face. She rocked her and murmured, "It's okay," over and over, whispering to the black roots of fried blond rat's nest. Cathy might have been sixteen or forty-six, depending. But when Tina held her she was five.

"Cathy, honey, when's the last time you went to sleep?"

"I don't know. Is it today?"

"Help me get her out of here," Tina said.

I danced with the stars through the obstacle course of shit and piss bowls and knocked-over bottles. "Maybe we should come back in hazmat suits."

"Too late," Tina said, "I've already breathed the fumes."

"Me too. The sick part is I like it." I took one of the girl's arms, and Tina took the other. "That's the beauty of drugs," I said. "Who needs Mengele when you can turn your own body into a biohazard?"

It did not cheer me up that Cathy was our best hope.

Suddenly we heard a scream, and Tina left me holding Cathy to hopscotch across the room and open a closet door. Inside was a Chinese girl with a bowl haircut, naked, chewing her lips and smoking speed.

Seeing her, Cathy came to life, eyes wide with jangled reverence. "Lee-Lee! We thought you were in heaven!"

Lee-Lee clamped her hands over her ears, then waved them in front of her, batting away the flying things we'd let in with the light. She was frantic to explain but could only string words together with difficulty. The corners of her mouth were caked in white paste. When she managed to speak, tiny speed feathers puffed out of her mouth. "Bitch! . . . My feet are like . . . *the Devil!* . . . You stole my candy cane!"

"Cathy, make sense or shut up," Tina said, offering her hand to the Chinese girl. "Lee-Lee, come on."

The naked girl hid the pipe behind her back like a five-year-old. I watched Tina gently unclench her fingers and remove it. She threw the pipe to me and I nearly dropped the thing. It was still hot.

"That's my candy cane!" Cathy shrieked, blowing out more whites. "God is like . . . *You better* . . ."

"That's okay, sweetie. Manny will hold your candy cane," Tina said. "He'll make sure nobody takes it."

I grabbed a pink halter from a pile in the closet and wrapped it around the scorching glass. Lee-Lee stared like she was waiting for the commercial to be over. Tina excavated a pair of moderately stained Juicy sweats. Tina helped Cathy put them on over her three-day panties, talking softly as she tugged them up. "Lee-Lee, how long have you been in here?"

"*In where, Mami?*"

She spoke like she was on TV in her head. Tina shot me a glance that said *You can't save them all.* I tossed her a dingy wife beater. She maneuvered Cathy into it while I dug up a pair of flip-flops and a shiny blue jacket with CHRISTIAN FUN GIRLS fake-graffiti'd across the Jesus-in-a-crown-of-thongs logo across the back. Marked with a little TM in a circle.

"So the reverend has his own clothing line?"

"Everybody has a clothing line," Tina said. "Why not a religious pimp?"

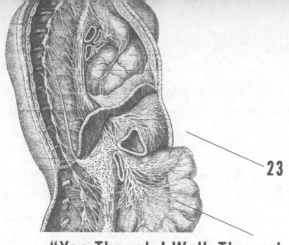

23

"Yea Though I Walk Through the Condo of Meth"

Tina sat sideways in her Prius, holding hands with Cathy, who vibrated in the backseat. I drove aimlessly down Van Nuys Boulevard while my ex tried her patented tactic of compassion and slaps to try to get the girl talking. She was still trying after half an hour.

"Remember the German doctor, honey?" *Slap.* *"Cathy!"* *Slap.* "Sweetheart, you really need to pay attention."

"Fuck!" I interrupted. "It's already six o'clock."

"Manny, please. Just drive."

"Yeah, *Manny-pants.* Just *drive.*" Finally inspired to speak, Cathy lapsed into a bad Marilyn. "The hair doctor," she giggled.

Tina laughed along with her. "You mean he asked you to call him 'Herr Doctor'?"

"Unh-huh. He's the *hair* doctor."

"What color was his hair?"

"I dyed it blond."

"He lived close, right?"

"Reseda."

"You remember the address?"

"On Seaview. I remember. Seaview Apartments."

Time was passing. "I'm sure there's only a few hundred of those."

"She'll remember," Tina snapped. "Just go."

"Maybe we should give her a Valium," I suggested. Now I wished I *had* stolen Dinah's Valiums. I kept seeing her wrong-way face in the windshield instead of the traffic of Van Nuys Boulevard. The last flashback, I had to hit the brakes to keep from rear-ending a Hummer. Then something thumped on the back of my seat. I whipped around and saw Cathy banging her face off the upholstery.

Tina tried to grab her. "Cathy! Sweetie, stop that!"

The light changed and I had to watch the road again. Suddenly Cathy screamed, her voice charged with passion. *"My vagina is a gift from Jesus!"*

I nearly swerved into a bus.

"One of the reverend's slogans," Tina said.

Cathy had begun to sway in the backseat like a human metronome. The swaying got faster and faster, until Tina reached under the seat and pulled out a short dog of Old Mr. Boston. Cherry brandy. "I keep it for colds," she said before taking Cathy's face in her capable hands. "Come on, honey."

Cathy sank backward after a blast of brandy. She coughed some up and gagged. Then she swallowed and let out a long sigh, like she'd remembered how to breathe again.

"Yum," she mumbled, just south of a slur. "I took the virginity pledge four years ago, after Laura Bush came to our high school and opened her white first lady Bible to First Thessalonians four:three to four. 'God wants you to be holy, so he shall keep thy female chalice free of sin and foulness.' That's why I remember the hair doctor's address. 'Cause it was four-three-four-four."

It made sense to her. Which is all that mattered.

The rest of the drive, Tina slapped and cherry-brandied Cathy.

She cooed her down off the methedrine ledge, dialed her crank-fed psychosis back to simple mania. Cathy relaxed. She got chatty and let us in on Christian escort tips. I wanted to know if her clients were born again or disciples of Satan. "What kind of man wants to defile a nice Christian girl?"

"*Defile?* That's what you would do," Tina said, though she didn't sound mad about it.

The day got dark. Dusk showed up and left. Traffic crawled. The night was a slow drive through drying concrete. We watched a blue-haired matron in a white Eldorado apply depilatory to her lip while her husband, whose eyebrows barely topped the steering wheel, snuck hateful glances at her.

"Marriage," snorted Tina. "And yet, I look at them and I'm jealous."

This set Cathy off again. "Marriage is why I save my maidenhood," she recited. "'Believing that true love waits, I make a commitment to God, myself, my family, my friends, my future mate and my future children to a lifetime of purity. I promise sexual abstinence from this day until the day I enter into biblical matrimony.'" She took another taste of Old Mr. Boston and snorted. "Like, that *sounds* nice, okay? But, like, all the girls at Reverend D's talk about is Jesus and sex. Sometimes—I shouldn't even say this—we talk about sex *with* Jesus. Well, think about it! We *are* saving ourselves for capital-H Him, right? We say it's for our future husband—*Oh goodie, a beefy UPS man with butt acne!*—but we hold on to the secret desire. Like, sometimes at night, I think about Jesus, in a tank top, with bulging muscles. He has long golden hair like in the Bible pictures. Fabio hair."

Cathy's story didn't add up, but I didn't press her. Lots of stories don't add up. Or else they add up but the math is wrong. Especially when there's a lot of bathtub stimulant sprinkled in.

We passed a minivan that reopened my San Quentin minivan

wounds. I caught Cathy's eye in the rearview. "I don't mean to be crude. But about the chastity thing? Is it true? You do everything with tricks except—"

"I don't call them tricks. I call them love partners."

"That's what I meant," I lied. "So you do everything with your love partners including . . ."

"Anal?" She tossed her hair sideways and hugged her knees. "Why don't you just come out and say it, doofus?" She suddenly rolled the window down and stuck her head out of it. "Anal!" she screamed at the top of her lungs. *"Anal anal anal anal!"* Until Tina grabbed her by the arm and slapped her.

Cathy sat back and began talking normally again, as if the smack and "anal" hollering were just what she needed to relax. "You think born-again guys don't like the back door? Well let me tell you, most of them are mouches—half-man, half-couch. Like, anal makes them feel all *gangster*."

Talking about it got her metronomey again. Her vibrating made me dizzy. Tina pulled her close and held her. When she stroked her hair, Cathy regressed instantly. "I need to sleep or do more, Mommy."

"Then you go to sleep, honey. Just lie down and let it happen." Tina spelled words on her forehead with her finger. "You're going to be f-i-n-e."

Cathy pouted, then tipped sideways, apparently unconscious, mouth agape and snoring gently.

"Nice work," I said to Tina.

"I used to have to say that to myself," she said.

A second later Cathy bolted upright, ripped open the door and tried to fling herself out at a crosswalk.

"Anal!" This time she wasn't screaming so much as wailing. "Anal, anal, anal!"

Tina managed to reel her in quickly. Either nobody'd heard the outburst or nobody thought it was that odd.

I kept my hands on the wheel, staring straight ahead. "For Christ's sake, Tina, either flag down a cop and ask him to arrest us, or put a lid on her."

"Hey, be glad I put her in a seat belt. Besides, nobody cares."

Tina sat back and closed her eyes. She was more tired than I was, and I'd been too tired to notice. "It's YouTube," she said wearily. "People are hard to shock because so much that's supposed to be shocking is staged. And the really shocking stuff nobody looks at."

She rolled her head sideways on the headrest and sighed. "I'm sorry I blabbed. I have to tell you something. The reverend did come on to me."

I pounded the steering wheel. "I knew it!"

"No, listen," she said. "I told him there was nothing he had that you didn't have bigger and better. After that, I never had a problem. I just do the work. The reverend's not a bad guy for a pimp. It's okay till I find a less fucked-up gig."

"You went to Yale," I said.

"I know, baby. I also went to my dealer's house. And then I married him."

"The ghost of Marvin rears its ugly head."

"I'm just saying." Tina gave Cathy's hair an idle stroke. "I know I'm not great at making a living. I'm not the only person in the world with that problem. You take these gigs to survive and be an artist, then the gigs get big and the art gets small."

"And here we are," I said, "four-three-four-four."

A chain slung between two posts held up the graffitied announcement: RENTING NOW—BACHELORS AVAILABLE!!!

"It's all about those three exclamation points," I said as Tina eased

Cathy sideways on the seat. "They really convey the excitement that any bachelor would feel about moving in."

The place was identical to thousands all over the Valley: two stories of painted-over cinder block, sky-blue washed to rancid mayonnaise by sunlight and acid rain, swimming pool visible through glass double doors in front.

High on the faded wall, in a carefree 1970s come-on-in-and-live-the-dream California swirl, was the name the original owners had seen fit to give the building. Sea View Apartments. The Pacific was seventeen miles away, which was still a lot closer than it was to Buffalo.

"Smart place to hide," said Tina, locking the door on Cathy after we stepped out of the car. We hadn't gone two steps when the reverend's voice blared behind us. *"Man washes a bitch's feet, that's a man ain't afraid to act like somethin' LESS'n a man. . . ."*

I ran back and banged on the passenger window. Tina beeped the doors unlocked but Cathy, holding one of the reverend's CD boxes, hunched over the CD player as if trying to drink the words. *". . . Jesus act like a foot-washing little puss, 'cause he know, he SO MUCH A MAN ain't nobody gonna call his ass out. Jesus was bad enough to be a BITCH!"*

"You babysit her," I said. "I don't have time for this shit."

———————

I walked into the grubby lobby, if you could call it that, and studied the names on the directory. It was the old-fashioned kind in a glass case, with plastic white letters pressed onto a black plush background. "What name . . . What name?" I glanced back at Tina. She appeared to be speaking into the window and banging the roof, I guessed for emphasis. I was glad I could keep an eye on her, thanks to the parking space I was lucky enough to grab by a fire hydrant.

Reading down the directory, I spotted *Ullman—5A*. And pressed his buzzer. I pressed again and heard a squall of babies over which a thick Latino accent tried to communicate. *"Quien es?"*

"Is Dr. Ullman there?"

"Nadie en casa!"

Nobody home. Perfect. He might have said something else, but the babies drowned him out. I could imagine no circumstance in which Josef Mengele would let Latino babies crawl on his floor. Sweeping a pile of Thai takeout menus off the windowsill, I saw a dozen letters scattered about unclaimed. Not many people would use this entrance. Anybody visiting or living there would park underneath, take the elevator up. In most parts of the Valley, walking was suspicious. I leafed through the abandoned mail.

Near the bottom of the pile, there were three letters rolled in a rubber band. Addressed to Fritz Ullman. The name was visible in a transparent window, across which someone—maybe someone busy with an apartment full of screaming children—had scrawled MUVED. All three letters were mailed from L.A. Small Animal Rescue Shelter. I memorized the address before I put the envelopes in my back pocket, in case someone stole my pants.

I ran back to the car in time to grab Cathy, who'd managed to jump out. She was weaving on the sidewalk, reciting in violent singsong, "Yea though I walk through the condo of meth."

Seconds before I snatched her, Cathy danced into the street and hiked up her T-shirt, flashing her rashy, malnourished tits and screaming at passing cars, *"Who wants Christmas?"* I had to hold my hand up like a traffic cop and snatch her, then pin her to the passenger door until traffic thinned enough to open it. Misreading the gesture, Cathy screamed, "Rape!" and started whipping her head from side to side, making a scene. Tina banged on the window. *Open the door!* But I couldn't—cars were shooting by so close behind me the door handles grazed my jacket.

Until traffic thinned, opening the door would be suicide. Between four and six in the Valley nobody cared what they hit. Finally I saw a lull. But just as I opened the door, a VW Beetle changed lanes. The driver braked hard. I saw the Rottweiler in back stick its head out the window a second before it hit me in the face. The next I thing remember is a terrified yelp and the sloshy *thwop* of dog tongue. The impact stunned me, until Cathy, who had no idea I'd just been Rottweilered, stopped screaming rape and started grinding her skeletal buttocks at me. Her horrible Marilyn morphed into horrible black Marilyn. "Want me to wiggle, Mister Man? You know you wanna tap that ay-uss!"

After that I didn't even look. I just grabbed her, ripped open the passenger door, pushed her in and slammed it. Brakes squealed behind me. I managed to jump behind the wheel and get the key in the ignition before anything else hit me. But I was too mad to drive.

"How did that happen?" I yelled at Tina, gripped by retroactive panic.

She barely shrugged. "How does anything happen? Her parents fucked at a truck stop; twenty years later their baby girl is flashing her rack for strangers."

Tina's tone was as lackadaisical as mine was agitated. "Tina, that's not all that happened! I was nearly decapitated by an Escalade door handle. . . . I almost bit off a dog's tongue. . . . Little Miss Jesus was out there screaming rape."

"Uh-huh. Poor thing's going to crash hard." Tina stroked Cathy's head in her lap, gently brushing hair out of her eyes. "You find anything inside?"

It was always like this. The kind of calamity and chaos she'd survived left her inoculated; I could never get Tina to share my panic. The preceding near-death-in-rush-hour-Reseda experience might as well have never happened. I gave up and got back to business.

"Yeah. I found something," I said. "But I want to talk to her first, I want to know what he asked her to do."

"I'll ask. She doesn't like you." Tina ran a gentle finger over

Cathy's fluttering eyelids. "Honey, tell me again, what did your old German do?"

Traffic had picked up. A Benz whizzed by, leaving a trail of NPR. I had an odd awareness of strangers listening to news of atrocities that didn't happen to them.

Cathy talked like her voice belonged to somebody else. "Like, first he had me strip and walk whichever way he pointed. Then he, like, wanted to examine my hymen? I told him how Reverend D says after Jesus prayed, he didn't say 'amen,' he said 'hymen.' But he had, like . . . *instruments*. He told me in his country they had baby factories, where perfect women went to be pregnant after they were impregnated by perfect men. He really wanted to talk. A lot of guys do. But they don't talk about this stuff. He said he had a very important job. Half of it was keeping the impure races from multiplying, half was trying to help the pure races multiply *more*. It's like he wanted to save the world or something. I told him, 'Hey, Daddy, don't worry. Jesus is coming!'" Her gaze was solemn as a nine-year-old's. "That's what global warming is. It's Jesus, getting closer. Giving off His holy heat."

She trembled and scratched a scab on her neck.

"Reverend D said after the Rapture the world's going to have to fill up again. Girls are going to have to breed. And who is Jesus going to want?"

"Let me guess," I said, "virgins?"

"Yes! The Bible is so *hot*! When the old man saw my coochie, he said it looked like a hairless chihuahua. I shave it, but that was kind of gross. When I told him my vagina belongs to the Man Upstairs, he got really confused. 'The man upstairs? Mr. Wong?'" She erupted in a giggle, then stopped just as suddenly. "He told me if I ever lost my hymen not to worry, he could get me another one. 'Not even the Lord would know the difference.' Like, is that *creepy*!"

Cathy's words came faster and faster. Her scratching got more feverish. She raked her nails over her scab-dotted wrists.

"So I said to him, kind of teasing like, 'What do you have, a box of hymens under your bed?' And then, the old German guy, he was really *old*, he says—*HICK!*"

She stopped, covered her mouth with a scabby hand and hiccupped again. *"HICK HICK!"* The hiccup turned to a spasm and the spasm brought a shock of clear vomit, which she wiped away as she sputtered. "He says, 'Not anymore. I had to get rid of them.'"

That was enough. She was on her stomach, flopping in the backseat. I twisted out of my jacket, still driving, and threw it over her. "God, look at her. . . ."

"You had to start!" Tina said. She pulled my jacket up to Cathy's chin. Blue TV light shined out of condo windows.

Tina put her thumb in her mouth and bit into it. "So what did you find out?"

"Somebody's already moved into his place. But I found out where he worked."

I tossed the banded envelopes in her lap and hit the blinker.

"L.A. Small Animal Rescue Shelter?"

"The pound," I said, pulling out. "He's still gassing undesirables."

Part II

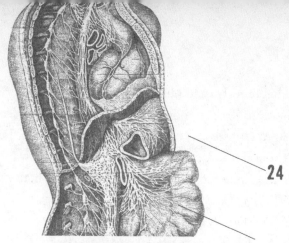

24

So Charles Mingus Says to Mother Teresa . . .

Tina dropped me off at my house so I could grab my old Lincoln. I found it parked in the street, under a layer of dirt, bird shit, swap meet flyers and eleven parking tickets, ten of which turned out to belong to somebody else. Somebody who owned a Kia. What kind of scam was that? Did they think I'd pay? The whole notion made me unaccountably happy. It was refreshing to think about old-fashioned, everyday malfeasance, as opposed to sick, mind-cracking, destroy-your-faith-in-mankind-on-the-off-chance-you-had-any derangement.

After allowing myself that little pleasure, I returned to the real world. *My* real world. The one in which I could not stop thinking about how much I wanted my wife back. Or what I'd do for the rest of my life if she wasn't in it. Did the possibility of being alone hurt as much as the Holocaust? That in itself was painful to think about. But pain only hurt if you could feel it. Maybe the problems of two people did amount to a hill of beans. Inside of a much bigger hill.

What I had meant to do was MapQuest the address of the pound. I let myself in, MapQuested, found the right freeway and, instead of taking a piss, which I was dying to do, stayed at the computer and

Googled Mengele. It turned out that was one of his experiments, too: denying urination. Testing how long Jehovah's Witnesses could hold it, as opposed to Gypsies, as opposed to Jews Jews Jews Jews Jews.

But fuck that. I knew enough about what he did. I wanted to know what he *was*. . . . I needed a portal to get inside the man.

EDUCATION. *Don't care.*

MILITARY SERVICE. *No.*

SOUTH AMERICAN EXILE. *Not that either.*

I figured I'd know it when I saw it. But by the time I did I was sweating and tapping my leg and taking short, choked breaths. I had made not-urinating a holy test, as if God commanded it.

To squirt one drop meant that thousands might die.

I began to vibrate. The pain came in sheets. Waves of sudden perspiration. Don't let a man urinate. It was that easy. You'd think we were designed for torture. Maybe mankind, in the end—and in the beginning—is just a prolonged experiment on man. It made sense that God was more like Mengele than Gandhi. If God were like Gandhi, we wouldn't need Gandhi.

The pain was making my brain sweat.

I kept Googling.

RELIGION. *No.*

My eyes watered. I chewed through my bottom lip.

I needed to relieve myself so badly my feet were swelling. I thought I could hear them squish when I crossed my legs. Then it felt like I *was* peeing. But I was dry.

I linked to a Mengele quotation on the same page as quotations from Charles Mingus and Mother Teresa. *The Wit and Wisdom of* . . . Josef Mengele: *"The more we do to you, the less you seem to believe we are doing it."* Charles Mingus: *"White man? No such thing as a white man. He pink."* Mother Teresa: *"God's love touches the lowest first."*

I belched and swallowed back what I hoped was bile. Could I have somehow pissed my mouth? Can that happen? Without thinking, my fingers typed in "Mengele + Mother." Then I saw her: Walburga. Mengele's mom, in black and white. A hard-faced, obese woman with eyes that could hate through steel. Squeaks escaped my throat. I saw another name: Wilma. Mengele's Jewish mistress . . . Every racist liked a little verboten on the side. Look at Strom Thurmond. Wilma was too obvious. But Moms Mengele really grabbed me.

I stood up, still reading. I was going to squirt. I read, "Mrs. Mengele brought his father's lunch to the family tractor factory every day, and often chided the men who worked for her husband for their slovenly manners at table."

You looked at her and you knew: every day Daddy got the big shame strudel. His employees must have thought he was married to a tank. Maybe some were jealous. But Mommy doted on Joe. "Walburga's pet name for her little Josef was Beppo."

Beppo.

I knocked the chair over scrambling to the bathroom. When I got there, I couldn't go. I put the seat down and sat. Turned on the tap and stuck my hand under the hot water. Finally—*Thank you, Jesus!*—a trickle, the relief almost worse than the pain. Sitting there, peeing, I had to lean forward and hold on to the hamper. I rested my head on the wicker lid and remembered the pills I'd stashed. I was always stashing shit so I could surprise myself someday when I was in bad shape. Although since Tina left, the surprise would have been a day when I wasn't.

I reached down and dug through a week or three's worth of laundry. Felt something hard. Dug up a bar towel I didn't recognize— who'd name their joint the Tsetse Fly?—and unwrapped a prescription bottle. Percocet. I counted twenty-two. Surprising myself, I stood up and dumped the pills in the toilet. Flushed. Then I dropped to the floor so fast my kneecaps cracked and stuck my arm in the bowl. My hand scrabbled over the porcelain bottom like a crab, trying to rescue some pills before they dissolved. *What the fuck?*

I stood back up, pants at my ankles, and stared at myself in the mirror as I washed my hands. *Look at you, champ!* I knew people who did affirmations. But that's what came out.

Minutes later I realized I was still washing my hands. And stopped. Still staring at myself, lips moving.

Mengelosis . . . Mengeloid.

I felt some kind of curdled twitch in my mouth and my own smile scared me.

I grabbed my jacket and keys and ran out the door, forgetting all about MapQuest. But I knew I'd get there.

Mengelomaniac.

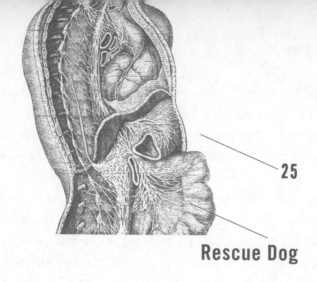

25

Rescue Dog

Karala was no more than an alley running alongside the Metro Rail tracks between Avenue Fifty-one and Avenue Fifty, a half a block up from Figueroa in Highland Park. Turning off Fig onto Fifty, I made a quick left into the lot behind Chico's, a yellow concrete box of a restaurant with a mural of a red chili in a poncho riding a burro out front. Multilayered graffiti graced the back wall, some fresh, some freshly crossed out. RESPECT YOUR HOOD was black-lettered over the door.

I hadn't eaten in so long I'd forgotten you were supposed to. The overpriced airport grub was long gone.

A waitress watching a *telenovela* popped out of a booth when I entered.

"*Hola.*"

"*Hola.*"

My Spanish consisted of twenty words, and *hola* was five of them.

The waitress had straight black hair and a flat face that might have gazed off a frieze on a temple to Quetzalcoatl. She didn't bother to ask if anybody would be joining me, and I could tell she didn't think I was half as beautiful as I thought she was. But she was kind enough to recommend the enchiladas *verdes.*

A blue and red plastic parrot hung in a cage over a mural of a man fishing and a woman pounding maize beside an ocean that continued over two walls. The only other customers were a toothless *viejo* who mad-dogged me over his soup and a table of laughing women in green scrubs and hospital tags enjoying beer with their guacamole.

It was twenty to eight. I wondered if the beer was to help the hospital ladies get over their shifts or get through them. Of course, people who don't have substance issues don't obsess about what other people do with their substances. Some people preferred to bird-watch. I figured I'd give that a try and focused on the plastic parrot. Maybe it would suggest a plan, since I didn't have one. What I did have was a burglar's all-access pass, a pair of bolt cutters, under the spare tire in my trunk. And a loaded .38 in an oily rag underneath that. This was not a neighborhood where anybody wanted to be caught breaking and entering. I was a white man snapping the locks off an animal shelter. If I got caught, I'd just say I was on the trail of a war criminal. *Hola!*

The parrot held his mud. But the enchiladas *verdes* were good enough to renew my faith in humanity. I got two more to go, just in case, and asked if they had anything for my dog. The waitress came back with a paper bag inside a plastic bag, brimming with bones. She pointed. *"Pollo . . . Puerco . . .* Goat . . . Beef. Is okay?"

I said, *"Muchas gracias,"* and gave her two twenties for the enchiladas and dog treats. Told her to buy a couple more rounds of Corona for the Kaiser Permanente health care professionals. What the hell, I used to have health insurance. I hoped they were brain surgeons.

Thanks to perpetually failing tire pressure and blown-out shocks, the black Lincoln rode low, which in this neighborhood was a plus.

In my trunk, along with those bolt cutters, I carried a crowbar, cuffs, Ex-lax, Sominex, a switchblade and two-hundred-watt police "blind 'em" lights. It wasn't that I was prepared, I just never took anything out of my trunk once I put it in. I also had a suitcase with a change of clothes, empty water bottles, a blanket, towels and an air mattress. In the tire well I hid a high-powered telescope and paper bags full of crumpled-up sweats, work boots, tennis shoes and Tiger's Milk bars.

On my last job (as a needle wrangler for a Lifetime pilot about a junkie ballerina who secretly didn't know how to read, and her love for an Iraqi talk show host), the studio guard who checked my trunk said he didn't know Lincoln made trash compactors.

Unless I wanted to go full ghetto and wear a down jacket on a ninety-degree day—hiding the bolt cutters underneath like a sawed-off—I needed something to put them in. I owned a briefcase that looked fairly professional. But the last thing I needed to look in a Highland Park alley was professional. I settled on a burlap bag.

I was eyeballed when I walked out of Chico's. The lookout squatted in front of an open door, peering through the wrought iron that ran along the top-floor walkway on the three-story apartment fronting the parking lot. He was a skinny shaved-head kid in a white T that fit like a muumuu. In black shorts so baggy they hung around his stick legs like lampshades that stopped at the tops of his white socks. It's not like gangbangers wanted to hide their occupation. They were as easy to spot as FedEx.

I got in the Lincoln, made a right on Avenue Fifty, a left on Figueroa, then cut back up Avenue Fifty-one from the other direction. One stoop had some occupants whose heads all turned at once. But nothing more eventful.

The pound was a low cinder-block building with a half-dozen slanted spaces out front. I parked in the handicap spot, close to the entrance, marked only by a small sign on the door with HOURS OF OPERATION and a faded sticker: IN CASE OF EMERGENCY, DIAL 911.

A retaining wall ran across the alley to the dead-looking house.

The homeowner had ceded in the war against graffiti. As a result, the wall was nearly solid with stylized letters and numbers whose import was as arcane as Kabbalah—except for the odd 187. Police code for murder. As any wannabe who'd listened to more than three tracks of a rap CD since 1987 would know.

I tried to look purposeful, keeping the bolt cutters close to my leg. Made my way past the front entrance and up the small broken-glass path that ran between the shelter and the back of a quiet house. This was pit bull territory. Once a dog lost a fight, the fellas liked to toss it out of a moving car. I imagined the ones that survived the bounce ended up in the shelter, and they probably weren't happy about it. Just in case, I'd mixed up a knockout paste in the car, in the lid of a Kiwi shoeshine can, and smeared it on Chico's dog treats. My old partner Razetti had taught me how to make the stuff. He called it Somi-lax, after its two main ingredients, ample helpings of Sominex and Ex-lax. It worked on humans, so I assumed it would do the job on dogs.

I reached a fence in the back but heard no snarling. Nary a bark or whimper. Odd. Streetlights weren't a problem, either. They'd all been dismantled for copper. All I had to do was climb the six-foot cyclone fence without dropping anything. Somewhere inside was a bigger clue to Mengele than anything Google could produce. I just didn't know I was going to have to wash it and feed it.

I clawed my way to the top of the fence, tried to shimmy sideways so I'd land on a pile of tires on the other side. Before I made my move, my Chico's bag tipped over. Bones and meat chunks landed with a splat, followed by a fevered *"Pendejo!"* I was so startled, I slipped. The right pocket of my leather jacket ripped on the fence and I dropped on top of a truck tire. The tire moved, then morphed into a jumpy older version of the kid I'd seen doing lookout behind Chico's.

"The fuck you doing, mang?"

He stood up and wiped a blob of chicken parts off his grimy face. I didn't see the knife until he waved it at me. "He sends a gringo to kill me? My ass is green-lighted, right?"

I smacked the blade out of his hand. He scrambled for it, ranting.

"I didn't even rat him out. I said he hit the bitch. Thass it, I swear. I didn't say what really happened. They had my *ass,* mang. You know what I'm saying? I got two strikes."

He stood up again, knife in hand. This time I grabbed it. He didn't resist. "I didn't know they was gonna arrest him, okay? Somebody saw the shelter's name on the side of the van. I ain't no snitch. I didn't say nothin' 'bout the shit we did."

"What shit?"

He didn't answer. Just kept talking.

"It's my ass, too. He thinks I'm gonna rat my *own* ass out? I ditched the van, too. I told the lady who runs the shelter somebody stole it, at gunpoint, like, she doesn't even ask me to make no police report or nothing, just fires me on the spot!"

"Hey, slow down," I said. But he just talked faster. Was there anybody who wasn't enhanced with bathtub crank?

"That's the thing. Once you're in a gang, nobody ever believe shit you say. I don't care who the fuck he say he was, I ain't goin' down for that shit. It was his idea, mang!"

"Shut the fuck up!"

I needed to straighten him out, so I backhanded him. But not in a mean way. He staggered a few steps and sat down hard on the ground.

"Listen, compadre, nobody sent me to do anything. And who are you talking about . . . with the van?"

Even though I knew already, I needed him to tell me. But my new friend was more interested in those chicken and goat bones. He was the same height as me, six feet even, but if I'm two hundred he had to be pushing one forty-five. I knew, because I used to be that skinny, when I was young and strung. Homeboy was sucked up and grimy.

The haunted whites of his eyes contrasted with the black film covering his face and hands. He snatched up a half-eaten chicken leg and ripped into it. "This shit is good."

I knocked the Somi-laxed fryer out of his hand before he ate any more. "That shit's for dogs," I said.

"Think I care? I am so fucking hungry. But I can't show myself. I seen what he can do. I know his skinny ass is in Quentin, but—"

"Who is he?" I repeated. "Maybe we're looking for the same guy."

"I'm not lookin' for nobody, he's lookin' for me."

"Goddamn it, who?"

"The old German. The freak."

The back of my neck tingled, the way it does when I'm *close*. Even if I didn't know what it is I was close to—or how close it was.

"What kind of freak we talkin' about? He some kind of *chomo*? A diaper viper?"

"Naw, dawg. He's no diaper viper. He—naw. Never mind. I don't even want to talk about it."

"Can you get us inside?" I put my hands on his shoulders, talked to him like he wasn't as crazy as he looked. "Let me get you something to eat."

"*Food* . . ." He lit up at the idea, then dimmed, sagging, as though eating was an exotic dream, like talking about what you were going to do with the cash when you won the lotto.

"Is this the key?" I asked, slipping the ring out of his pocket while he hallucinated chorizos. He nodded, then grabbed my arm. "They come in at six. Is it nearly morning?"

"Relax. It's gonna be night for a while. What's your name, hombre?"

"Fuck you wanna know?"

"So should I call you 'Fuck' or 'Fuck you'?"

"Carlos," he said.

"There an alarm system, Carlos? Some kind of code?"

"Keypad's on the wall. Four two one oh five."

"Hitler's birthday," I said. "Your boy ain't hidin' his tracks."

"Whatever. I need to eat."

I found the keyhole in the dark. I didn't know what was behind the door. Inside it was pitch-black, except for a blinking green light. I pressed the Führer's digits. The light beeped and went out.

"Good lookin' out."

He reached for the switch and I stopped him. A pair of lights swept the window. "You heard of B&E, Carlos? That's what we're doing. Right now. You and me."

"Hey, I got two strikes!"

"You don't keep it down, this is your last night on the outs."

The headlights blasted the room and we ducked. They wobbled and swept the other way. Whoever was driving was turning around, not parking. The lights swept back through the shelter reception, reflecting off the chest-high metal counter that cut the room in half. Red footsteps painted on the floor led to one end of the counter, over which a sign said ADOPTION HOURS. The light moved before I could read them, briefly illuminating green footsteps to the other end. DROP-OFFS MUST FILL OUT FORM. NO EXCEPTIONS.

"Enchiladas *verdes*, Carlos. I've got two, from Chico's."

"That place is good."

"They're still hot. Wash up."

"You a faggot?"

"You lonely?"

He muttered something and dropped to a crouch like he was threatening to wrestle.

"Why you want me to wash?"

"'Cause the enchiladas are in my car and we're gonna get them together. And you look black. You walk around lookin' that black in this hood, one of your boys will put you in the ground."

His eyes went wide. He hoisted himself over the counter and pushed through the black double doors behind it. The stench broke like a wave of cat piss and industrial-strength cleaner fumes. I hit the flashlight and saw the cages, some wolf size, some cat or beagle compatible, lined up along one side of the room. The creatures curled three or four to a cage. I couldn't tell what they were. Nothing moved. It was beyond disturbing.

Carlos doubled over from the exertion of walking eleven steps. I talked while he panted.

"That's what you gangsters do, right, to keep the neighborhood clean? Kill blacks?"

"You know?"

"Come on, Carlos. It's been on the news."

"It has?" His voice cracked high with panic. "When?"

"I don't know, a year ago."

"A year? Oh, ha! Fuck, you're talkin' about—ha, that's good."

"What did he say he was going to do to you?"

"Who, the German? He didn't say shit. But he was always talkin' about his connections. I'm like, you got connections, why the fuck you gassin' dogs with a ninth grade dropout? Man, he got so mad. He was always fuckin' with the machines, you know? 'Makin' improvements.' That's what he said. So, after I disrespect him on his connections he says, 'Come on, I want to show you somethin' I'm workin' on.'"

"What was that?"

Carlos stared in abstract confusion at the dials and hoses. "I been givin' flea baths to dogs and cats for two and a half years, now I'm blankin' on how to work the sink."

"Carlos, what was he working on?"

I pulled the hose down and twisted the blue faucet. A stream of water thick as a fist hit him in the face. He staggered backward with his hands up. I sprayed his arms.

"Come on, Carlos."

"I can't. . . ."

"What was it, Carlos? Is it here?"

I hosed him again. He spun around and I shot the tire grime off the back of his skull. I took no pleasure in this. Anybody who'd been deloused at County knew the ball-numbing misery of it.

Carlos straightened up. I handed him another towel. His dried off from tattoo to tattoo, watching each materialize from under the grime: a full-lipped, doe-eyed chola; a low-rider in wraparound shades, bandana and droopy mustache at the wheel of a '68 Chevy; and on his chest, in the position of honor, a skull wearing a fedora with a bullet hole in it—insignia of L'Avenida, the Avenues.

"Carlos? Talk to me."

He held his hands up and squealed until he realized I'd stopped spraying. When he was done washing, the towel was black. Now he looked like a clean young banger—the "18" on the back of his neck as crisp as the number on the side of a plane.

"It was the van. The dog-catchin' van."

"What about it? What'd he do?"

"I can't. . . ."

"Carlos!" Now I stepped closer, letting the nozzle dangle, loosely swinging a foot of rubber hose. Letting him know I wasn't asking anymore.

My flashlight caught a tear, squeezed from the corner of his eye. His chin quivered, but he was trying to stay macho. "Gas."

"What?"

"We—no, *he* rigged it up. . . . Then, the first day, he showed me. We picked up some strays in Mount Washington. Except they weren't straying anywhere. He straight-up dog-napped these motherfuckers. Till we had seven. Then he says, 'Don't worry, it's ecological.' I'm like, 'What's ecological?' He says instead of goin' into the atmosphere, the exhaust goes back in the truck, and we can use it. Me, I'm sayin', 'What?'"

"So you gassed animals in the van? As you were driving?"

I found the Big Dog water-absorber towels under the first sink and threw one to Carlos. He caught it and stood there, grime dripping down his face like runny mascara. He opened his mouth to explain but nothing came out. I helped him along.

"Yo, Carlos, why are all the dogs sleeping?" I leaned close to a cute little Pomeranian. He scratched himself.

"They're not all sleeping, homes. Some of them are dead."

"*Dead?* Why are they in a cage?"

I stepped back quickly and bumped into a ceiling-high cabinet. Beside that was the cleanest appliance in the place. It looked like a medieval washer-dryer. The dull metal door and steering wheel handle had been polished to a sheen. On impulse I turned the heavy steel O. The thick door swung open without a squeak. I don't know what I'd expected or what I was after. But Mengele had worked there, and this was an oven.

I stuck my head into the sparkly clean interior. Twisting my neck, I could see the pipes above and below the door, each with eight rows of sixteen holes. White bits of what looked like popcorn stuck to the top and sides.

I banged the top of my head popping out, the same spot where I'd been whacked in Tina's minivan at Quentin, and by Harry Zell before that.

I reeled backward, wiping grime off my hands.

"Know what I used to trip on?" Carlos asked.

"Can't say I do." I checked the top of my head for blood. What *I* was tripping on were fascinating facts I recalled from the Discovery Channel. It took twenty minutes for a human body to burn in the oven at Auschwitz.

"What tripped me out," Carlos said, "was thinkin', like, *Why can't we use the microwave?* I always wondered, you know? But, check it out, when I mentioned it to the old German, you know what he said?"

Carlos's lips were so cracked they bled when he laughed. "He said, 'Microwaves cause cancer.' You believe that shit? I'm like, 'How they gonna get cancer, they're dead?' But this dude, I'm tellin' you, he got this look on his face, make you feel like shit, you know? He starts chewin' on that raggedy-ass mustache and smiles, clownin' me off. 'I'm not talkin' about who's *in* the oven, Herr Carlos, I'm talkin' about who's *runnin'* it.'"

On the way out, I stumbled over something—an Adidas tennis shoe. Odd. But, in the grand scheme of things, not worth noting. Not then.

Back out front, I hopped over the counter first, accidentally switching my light on when I landed. The beam caught a tacked-up flyer for Reconcile, a canine antianxiety drug. In the photo a golden retriever gazed sadly by a picture window. *Reconcile—because pets have stress, too!*

"He said *man* in the oven?"

Carlos averted his eyes. "Yeah."

My nerves were on red alert. I craved a little Reconcile myself. I swept the flashlight over the wall of caged, unmoving animals, then forced my attention back to Carlos. One nightmare at a time. "All dead," I said. "It's unbelievable. Why does he kill all the dogs?"

"Not all. Some are drugged. He gives them another injection in the morning and they're usually okay. Unless they're crippled up. Or dead."

"So they're knocked out at night? Cranked up in the morning? If they're not . . ."

"Dead or so fucked up you know they wished they were."

"You think animals get suicidal?"

"When the doctor gets through with them? Fuck yeah. I seen this one kitten, nothing but a head on a pink tube . . ."

I wondered if Carlos was completely out of his mind, maybe hallucinating the whole thing. I drifted to the nearest cage, reached in and poked at a reclining mutt. Cold dog belly. It felt like a cement bag with teats.

Carlos was getting squirrelly.

I tried to keep it casual, as casual as you can be when you're discussing rolling pet genocide.

"Did the old Hun say why he wanted to kill the strays before bringing them back to the shelter?"

"Hell yeah." Carlos bent to adjust his socks. "He wouldn't shut up about it. He was runnin' his mouth 'bout Darwin. Like, the dogs that got caught deserved to get caught or some shit. And what's the other fuckin' word he always sayin'? Oh yeah, 'ecology.'" Carlos did his best Mexican-tinged version of a German accent: "'This is ecological.' Fuck, the dude was freakalogical. Freak-tagious. Freak-tagious," he repeated, pleased with himself. "Damn, I should write that down. I rap, you know? Kinda like Lil' Cuete or Kemo the Blaxican."

"Kemo, yeah," I nodded, like I knew what the fuck he was talking about. "How 'bout you gimme your CD later, okay? Finish what you were saying."

"About what?"

"Jesus, Carlos! About the German."

"Yeah, yeah. Right. He said it saved energy. He's a weird dude. Can we get some food now?"

A few cages were stored by the door, on top of a minifridge. An overweight basset hound lay on its side, one plaintive eye open, following us. I had a feeling the hush puppy knew something I didn't. Right before the double doors I stopped. There was something else that bothered me even more. One specific thing. I was about to say something when Carlos spotted me grabbing a mint from a bowl between the employee log and plasti-glove dispenser. "Oh shit," he cried, pointing at my hand. "They're for dog breath."

"In that case it's probably not strong enough." I tossed the mint back in the bowl. "But there's one thing I still don't understand. Why do they let him do this? The pound people."

Carlos grabbed a handful of candy and tossed it into the cages. "Something they can take to heaven," he said, which made me like him.

"That's nice, man, but the people who run the pound, who are they?"

"It's a lady. But she don't know. Nobody knows. Old dude's last out, first in, you know? Plus I think she likes the old fucker. He's dapper, you know. Mrs. Gutierrez is forty or somethin', but I think he's fuckin' her. He's, like, a hundred and seventy-five or some shit and he still fucks."

"Guess he takes his vitamins."

"He calls them 'formulas.' He says he can extend life. But what he mostly do is bitch. And brag. Whatever it is, he can do it better. Like when we transition, you know, when we bring the dogs from the van into the pound? He's always bitching. Like, why do we go to all the trouble of getting them out of the van and inside the cages? Transition's the most dangerous time, 'cause you just took an animal used to roamin' free, then cooped his ass up in a broiling tin can with a bunch of other animals. Think about it. After a couple hours, you don't know what you gonna get when you open the doors. I seen chihuahuas lunge out the van straight for a motherfucker's juggler."

"Bad way to go," I said. "Killed by a chihuahua. Nobody'd be able to keep a straight face at the funeral."

"Ha-ha-ha. Laugh laugh. You ain't seen what I seen. He retooled the dogcatcher vans. So when you get back all the dogs and cats are already *muerto*."

Carlos stared absently at his now-clean hands.

"Used to be you hear their claws and shit, scrapin' the floor, slidin' around when we took a curve. I used to imagine, you know, what if

I was the animal? I'd think about skidding across the van floor in the dark. Every time the driver makes a turn or stops your little paws just slide. You and the other cats and dogs are all slammed into the wire mesh. . . . They'd be barking like crazy, whimpering, meowing, howling like you wouldn't believe. Then he rigged the van. Had me solder all the cracks, made it airtight. Now we don't gotta worry 'bout getting bit or clawed. We just empty 'em out."

The vision was grim. For a moment neither of us spoke. Then Carlos yawned and grabbed his stomach and muttered, "Fuck." I heard volcanic rumbling. Maybe he'd dipped back into the Chico's party bag. Maybe I'd used too much lax in the Somi-lax. There was an audible *blurp* from Carlos's pants. He gritted his teeth. "You ain't a cop, right?"

"No."

"And you can help me get this old dude off my back?"

"Yeah."

"The first time, after he rigged the hose? After ten minutes, all we hear is bodies clunkin' in the back. No barks, no meows. Nothin'. So quiet, it scared me, homes."

I checked my watch. Carlos saw me and said, "What?"

"We need to go. Don't worry, I have clean clothes."

"I don't know, man," Carlos mumbled as I followed him back through the swinging double doors to the reception area.

At the front door, I spotted that keypad again and thought of baby Hitler. Born 4/21/05.

"Gotta reset the security code," Carlos warned. "Let me do it."

"Be my guest."

The street was dead. I waited until Carlos pressed the last number. He said, "Okay." I opened the door. Five different kinds of floodlights blasted on. The alarm was so loud it hurt my hair.

Carlos froze. "Guess I fucked up."

"You think?"

The Lincoln was backed to the shelter door. I popped the trunk, moved some crap around, found a pair of U Miss sweats and threw them at him. They'd come with the car. Then I grabbed the enchiladas. Once Carlos had them in his hands, they were gone in under a minute. While he scarfed, I slid the .38 in my waistband. Then I slammed the trunk and unlocked the car.

"Shit, man. Where we goin'?"

"I don't know. Why don't we stand here and talk about it until the cops show and you get that third strike you been dreamin' about?"

"Don't fuck with me, homes."

I rolled us down the street with the lights off, giving it enough gas to slink onto Avenue Fifty just as the blaring cherry-tops nosed off Avenue Fifty-one into the alley. I cut ahead of a line of cars, made a left onto Figueroa and swung right again, onto Avenue Fifty-two, down the ramp feeding the 110. The avenues were numbered like that up to sixty. I slipped south to the on-ramp and steered my mushy tires onto the freeway.

"You shouldn't make fun of me," said Carlos, fighting off a yawn.

"I'm not. I'm trying to save your ass," I said as he tugged on the sweatshirt. "Jesus, Carlos, are you that sensitive when you're doin' drive-bys? Now where's the van?"

A trio of black-and-whites raced past us in the other direction. "I never did that shit. That's been all blown up by the media. Avenues got a bad rap."

"Whatever you say. Just tell me where the van is."

"You're going the wrong way. Go back and get off at Avenue Forty-five. The Southwest Museum, where they keep all that Indian shit."

I checked the rearview. Nothing. The good thing about driving a thirty-year-old car was that it looked like it belonged to somebody in the hood. It would have been a problem in Beverly Hills.

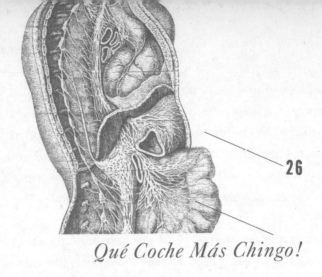

26

Qué Coche Más Chingo!

We crossed the tracks at the top of Avenue Forty-five, then made a hard right beside a big art deco building flying a U.S. flag—the Southwest Museum.

A row of sawhorses and NO ENTRY and CONSTRUCTION VEHICLES ONLY signs blocked the entrance. The winding driveway curved behind the museum, up the steep hill beyond.

"Van's up there."

"Then get out and move the fucking signs."

Carlos jumped out and did what he was told. As he moved the last NO ENTRY out of the way I imagined what would have happened if the cops had caught us in the pound. With enough dead dogs to make Michael Vick look like Saint Francis of Assisi. I could almost picture the public defender's face when I gave her my alibi. *Josef Mengele did it.*

I always get nervous *after* things go down, when the adrenaline curdles to strychnine retro-panic. I kept the motor running. Carlos stopped to admire the Kennedy-era Lincoln.

"Qué coche más chingo!"

"Say what?"

"Cool ride. I love them suicide doors."

I slapped the Lincoln into drive. "But we're not talking about suicide, are we, Carlos? We're talking about homicide?"

Carlos gulped audibly and clutched his stomach. He licked his cracked lips as we crept up the closed-off road. He pointed when we came to a weedy dogleg. Beside the husk of an old truck, under a ramshackle lean-to, was the animal protection vehicle. I killed off the ignition, waiting for Carlos to speak.

"S-s-s-so," he stammered after a little while. "You know?"

"I know everything," I lied, and held out my hand. "Keys to the van?"

"Under a rock, *hijo*. . . ."

Carlos bent forward as he walked, clutching his stomach. It had startled to drizzle again.

"S'matter, Carlos, you scared 'cause you gave him up?"

He stopped so suddenly I slipped on the wet mud trying not to bump into him. Carlos caught me before I fell.

"You don't know shit, do you? You know if I'm a stereotype to you, you're a stereotype to me, fool!"

"What the fuck's that supposed to mean?"

"It means you don't know shit!"

He could have let me go down, kicked me in the head and stolen my car keys. Instead he held me up and laughed in my face. "I'm scared cause I *didn't* give him up, *whetto*! I told the cops about the hit-and-run. I didn't say nothin' 'bout the other stuff."

"So now you can tell me about it."

We huddled behind the van, under a big leafless tree that dropped some breed of itchy fluff down the collar of my shirt. The shelter van looked normal enough, a battered gray box roughly the size of four porta johns stacked two on two, a single door in back and no windows.

Carlos kneeled down and groped under a clump of leaves and branches. He scooped up a key and got back on his feet.

"Tell me about the other stuff, Carlos."

This time, by way of reply, he just pointed down, under the bumper. The hose, painted the same drab gray as the van, snaked from the exhaust pipe up under the back bumper and into the container like a wily boa. "You know, homes . . . The gas."

Carlos doubled up. Maybe from the bad dog paste, maybe from the memory of what he and his shelter buddy had done together, in this vehicle. A Santa Ana blew scratchy fuzz down from the tree overhead and I thought, inanely, *If they give the wind a name, why not smog?* Something to make airborne particulates—the local brew that turned L.A. babies into adorable asthmatics—sound really exotic. On very rare occasions, the Santa Anas actually brought rain. And this was a very rare occasion. "I think I gotta shit," Carlos groaned. He fought back serial yawns.

"Unlock the van first."

"I only have the key for the front." Talking was a strain. "Can't hold it, mang."

For his sake, I hoped Carlos passed out before he soiled himself. I took the .38 out and jammed it in his back.

"Unlock it, now."

"Damn, mister!"

Sweat beaded on Carlos's shaved skull, so it looked like the eyeball on the back of his head was crying. He lurched forward, arms coiling his waist in pain. "Why you pointing that thing at me? For serious, I can't hold it, mang."

"You're gonna have to, *mang.*"

"Yeah?" Fighting cramps, Carlos straightened up and hissed at me. "You don't know who you're fucking with. I could green-light you, too, you know."

But there wasn't much heart in it. He grunted and squirmed sideways, squirming between the van and the tin wall of the lean-to. I aimed the flashlight at the door. He jerked the key back and forth, then yanked it out, wiped both sides on his pants and tried again. This time it opened.

"You ride bitch," I said, grabbing the key and muzzle-shoving him. I waited until he got in before hoisting myself behind the wheel.

I didn't need to hold a gun on him. Carlos jerked forward and grabbed the dashboard, grunting. I yanked him back in the seat by the collar. "I'm sorry," he squealed, "I can't—"

The wave passed. I needed him to relax.

"It's okay, Carlos. The *pistola*'s for insurance. Just tell me what you two did in the van."

"It wasn't my idea, I swear. . . ."

"So what happened? He hear how your homeboys like to do their own racial cleansing?"

"You better watch it, *cabron*."

"What's your crew?"

"Avenue Forty-three, Tiny Locos."

"No shit? I remember when your homeboys made the headlines: 'Street Gang Race Murder.' Blowing your African-American neighbors away in broad daylight. Keeping Highland Park brown and down."

"Street cleaning."

Race murder—what the hell else were an SS doctor and a Mexican-American gangbanger going to talk about?

"Must be tough," I said. "Feds put a gang injunction on the Avenues in 'ninety-nine, right?"

"Gang injunction is bullshit," Carlos said. "I bump into my cousins at a birthday party, they take us in 'cause we're not allowed to meet in groups. You think they ever pull that shit on white people?"

"White people weren't your problem, Carlos. You were trying to keep blacks away. Mengele help out with that?"

Carlos hung his head.

"How many?" I asked him.

"I'm sick."

"I know, I got a nose. How many?"

Carlos groaned. "Three."

He opened the door and slid off the seat again. I held him up by one ear and rolled down my own window.

"How many?"

"Four . . . Five," Carlos squeaked. "I'm the one who told him."

"Told him what? Talk normal."

"About killing the *mayates*. The blacks. The old man said he knew a better way. He said we wouldn't have to worry about them tracin' the bullets, finding the knife. And no bodies. He told me about the war. Them concentrated camps—"

Carlos strained to stay awake and stave off the projectile diarrhea.

"Old man said, before they opened the big joint, Ouchwiz, they drove around in vans, pickin' up retards and Jews. He got real scientific. Hemoglobin and shit. How the fumes fuck up your oxygen, so—"

"Forget the science. How could you stand it, hearing somebody suffocate five inches behind you? Didn't they scream? How many did you kill again?"

"Six, all right? Seven. *Seven!* I don't know, I was high!" he shouted, and clutched his guts. "I had to be high, man. They fucking screamed." His voice grew quiet. "But that wasn't the worst."

I stuck my hands between my knees to keep them from hurting him. "What was the worst?"

"The worst was their lips." Carlos's eyelids drooped. His voice went dreamy. I spotted the nail, pinched between his thumb and forefinger, slowly slicing his arm from the top of the elbow down the wrist. "I'm tellin' you, mang. When we opened the van, their mouths were open, like this"—he pushed his own cracked lips into an exaggerated kiss—"and they were super-red, like they had lipstick on. That hemoglobin thing. It was like, these two niggers didn't just die—they died and went gay. We did a gringo after that. I guess it was a contract, I don't know, but it was even worse. We put him in, he's some regular jim; we take him out, his face is the color of a chili pepper and he got a mouth like a tranny. Like them dead motherfuckers put lipstick on."

"But," I croaked, building a wall between that visual and the rest of my brain, "you did it again."

"One time, I had to—*Oooooofff . . .*"

Carlos clawed his stomach and angled sideways, seizing up. His face mashed on my shoulder as he farted helplessly.

"You had to what?" I shoved him back to his own side, trying to speak without breathing. "What did you have to do, Carlos?"

Carlos jerked back the plaid shirt collar, exposing a tattooed "13" I hadn't spotted at the pound. He saw me eyeing it.

"You know what that is?"

"Thirteenth letter of the alphabet. M."

"We gotta keep going over this, motherfucker? La Eme runs the Avenues. Just like they run forty-seven other gangs." His voice sounded like it was squeezed out of a small animal. "FL thirteen? Florence and Normandy? They're the ones took out a buncha Crips in 'ninety-nine. It's all prison gang bullshit. The order came down from Pelican Bay. KBOS."

"Kills blacks on sight."

"That's what I said, fool. Straight-up NHI. No humans involved."

"I bet the old guy really loved that concept."

"Matter of fact, he smiled." Carlos broke it down—sitting in his own shit, explaining gravity. "Mexican Mafia same as the ALS same as the Black Warriors. Don't matter if I think it's penetentiary bullshit. I'm just a soldier. They wanna put that race bullshit in the hood, to make a point inside, you gotta show scalps or get scalped."

I was still thinking of those red lips.

"Your pal, his real name's Mengele. I met him up at Quentin."

"You were inside."

"I was there. And believe me, the color brown is scum to him, but you know that, right?"

"Whatever. He like the color green. Shot callers want all the *negroes*"—he pronounced it "nay-gross"—"out of the hood. But see, that's a hate crime. That's federal. The German, he knew all this shit. He's like, 'Why shoot the schvartzes'—he always called 'em that—'in front of witnesses?' We put them in the van, we can gas them while we're going through a McDonald's drive-through, buyin' Quarter Pounders. We did, too, man. Every time, we'd go get food. He even took care of the bodies. So what the fuck you gonna do, shoot me?"

I was easing the .38 into his neck. *Never pull a gun out unless you don't plan to use it.* I just wanted to scare him. When he kicked the door open, trying to jump, I dove across the seat and grabbed his collar. But he wasn't trying to run. He was ripping his pants off, bowels spray-painting his thighs. I plucked out a wad of Taco Bell, McDonald's, and KFC napkins jammed between the seats and threw them at him.

"I guess you're not lying about the fast food. What aren't you telling me?"

"You think I'm leaving shit out?"

I let the barrel nuzzle his ear like a friendly pony.

"Okay, there was some drugs."

"What kind?"

"He say it was crank. But I don't know . . . it ain't like normal *bombita*. One hit and you start running like your fucking heart is pulling you down the street. I remember once, this *hyna* was suckin' my dick. . . . My homegirl, you know? And right in the middle, she's like, 'What's up with that?' So I check out my cojones and they're all, like, boom-*BOOMP*, boom-*BOOMP*. Like I had a fucking alarm clock in my sack."

"What was it?"

"It was my *balls*, man, they were like big ol' jumping beans."

"I meant what was the drug?"

"He called it, like, 'dreen' or some shit."

"But not methedrine?"

"No, man, I know methedrine."

"Of course you do. What about . . . Adrenaline? That sound familiar?"

"Adrenaline?" Carlos tried to clean himself, then splattered the ground again. "Oh, Mama . . . Yeah, that's it! He said it was all natural. But I don't . . . It's like the crank was on crank, you know what I'm sayin'? And the shit made you hungry. We go down to IHOP and put away two, three plates of them Belgian waffles, with whipped cream and all that shit."

"You on it now, Carlos?"

"Ask my PO, motherfucker. I fill a cup whenever my number comes up."

I figured he had to be on *something*. Either way, how could you not respect a man who could still give attitude half-asleep and blowing his insides out of his sphincter?

"Just curious," I said. "Let's get to work. How do you unlock the back of the van?"

"Below the blinkers. Orange toggle switch."

I flipped a switch and an ominous clacking filled the cab, as if the van had backed into an MRI machine. The soles of my shoes vibrated.

"Not that!" Carlos darted a hand under the steering wheel to flip it off. "That's the floor sealer. It's sheet metal."

"Floor sealer?"

"Keeps the fumes in, man."

He bit his lip, reached back under the wheel and hit another switch. This time there was a simple click.

"Just unlock the fucking back door."

"Gimme a second," Carlos said in a choked voice. He unbuckled his pants and shoved them down to his ankles. Then he opened the passenger door and clung to the armrest, covering his package with his hand and making his own little mountain. I stepped out of the van, facing the other way when I talked to him.

"You're going to be fine," I said with no conviction whatsoever. "Walk it off. Come on, open up the back."

I helped Carlos to his feet. He doubled up and farted, groaning as though passing chunks of his own flesh. He was in bad shape. But I couldn't pop down to the twenty-four-hour Sav-on for Kaopectate and man-Pampers.

I helped Carlos to the back of the van, zigzagging the shrubs and blue-tarped construction site with the flashlight. I didn't see anything, but I knew. The way you know somebody's watching, when the bad dog tongue of intuition laps the back of your neck.

Carlos bunched the sweatshirt over his flat belly in pain, trailing liquid panic. By now I was used to acrid odors. They followed me like dolphins behind yachts.

Then that dog on the back of my neck threw open its jaws and bit. The thought almost made me bleed: if all the animals in the pound were dead for the night, that meant somebody had to have dosed them. And, according to Carlos, nobody did the dosing but Mengele.

"Open it," I said, willing my voice calm.

Carlos dug a hand into his stomach and muttered. "I ain't your bitch, bitch."

I let it pass. If this was a setup, I did not want to be the one standing in front of that van door. Backpedaling as Carlos stepped forward, I felt a tingling in my head wound. Maybe I'd suffered a cerebral hematoma. Or maybe I'd become clairvoyant.

A second before he grabbed the handle I turned and dove.

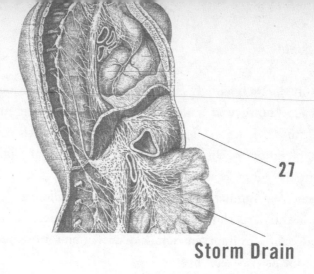

27

Storm Drain

My face crashed into branches. The van door swung open and somebody fired a gun. The bullet ripped Carlos's ear from his skull. It clung to my pants like a feral scallop. Carlos froze. He touched the spot where his ear had been with an expression of vague confusion, as if he'd misplaced his cell phone. Then he screamed, whipping his head back and forth, giving the clump of dying grass beneath his feet red highlights. "Fucking *cabron*! I knew you were a pig!"

I'd barely made it to a gully five feet from where Carlos was screaming. I wanted to scream back at him: *"It wasn't me!"* If I did we'd both be dead. If I didn't, whoever shot him would figure out who he was screaming at.

Another blast spun him around. It looked like a dance move. Dead man's salsa. A black car roared around the curving drive, lights sweeping the trees. It parked hard, twenty feet away, aiming its lights at us. Carlos stumbled a few steps into the high beams, in my direction, one arm coiled over his shoulder as if trying to scratch his back. Then he uncoiled. He studied his bloody fingers like he'd never seen them wet and fought his way out of his sweatshirt.

Shirt off, lit by headlights, Carlos was so skinny he looked two-dimensional. The second bullet had punched a smoking nipple over his ribs. Exiting, it blew out a ragged pancake of back. Carlos was liver-shot, bleeding brown. It looked like he was hemorrhaging A1.

Two more shots tore through the meat of his right and left palms, leaving matching stigmata. The bullets were a smaller caliber. A .22. I wondered if the palm shots were a fluke or the shooter was a dead-eye who hated hands. All speculation, however inane, was preferable to focusing on what was right in front of me.

Carlos dropped to his knees. He laid down on the side of his torso that had not been ventilated, one bleeding finger uncurled and pointing to my right. I couldn't leave him there. His eyes were rolled back in his head. Somebody killed the headlights and I grabbed his arm and dragged him out of harm's way. I figured whoever opened up on Carlos would want to know what happened to him. When they came looking, I could double back and get to the van.

This wasn't much of a plan. It needed fleshing out. But before I could start fleshing I scrabbled backward, then tumbled down a gully into a muddy storm drain, slick as a toboggan chute. Carlos and I slid downhill for what felt like half a mile but may have been fifteen feet. We stopped when we hit a giant metal screen, the kind they put in to keep small dogs from washing down the storm drain out to the ocean. The impact stunned us both. We came around at the same time, blinking into the floodlight drenching us from a nearby house. The lights went out in thirty seconds, which was long enough to take in Carlos's drooly grin. "That was just like the Matterhorn!"

"Just like it," I whispered, amazed he was still alive and chatting. But glad he was happy. Maybe I'd misdiagnosed the severity of his wounds. I couldn't tell if he was still bleeding. We were submerged in a puddle of wet leaves. Carlos grabbed my shoulder and squeezed, proving the palm shot had missed his tendons. I expected the shooter to come screaming down the chute, guns blazing. But Carlos had this thing he needed to tell me. How do you tell a corpse to shut up?

"My best friend, Lazy, he tol' me dyin' was just like Disneyland." Fighting for breath, Carlos giggled and blew a taffy apple blood bubble. Red and sticky. It burst and he squeezed my shoulder. "He got it in the neck two blocks from school. Drive-by. We were nine, man. Lazy, he was lying on my foot. I was afraid to move, so I just stood there. I asked him what it was like, and he said, 'It's just like the Matterhorn, Carlito. Just like at Disneyland.' I thought he was bullshittin'." He grinned through bloody teeth. "I guess he wasn't."

Now I felt like the nine-year-old Carlito, with Lazy on his foot. I didn't want to move but I couldn't stand still. As gently as I could, I eased him off my legs and out of the wet onto a bed of plastic bags and beer cans, site of some long-ago party.

"Carlos," I whispered, just to see if he was live meat or dead.

"*Sí, señor,*" he said, mugging feebly up at me. Dead man mocking.

I didn't know what else to do. Carlos was humming. Until now, I'd managed to compartmentalize the fact that the Boy Scout beside me had helped to run a mobile ethnic-cleansing operation. I'd even managed to put Tina's behavior on a shelf. But you couldn't compartmentalize bullets—or playing human luge in an L.A. storm drain, pursued by the famous, mysteriously undead Holocaust doctor.

Carlos stared up at the smog-tinged stars.

"How you feelin'?" I asked.

"Oh, mang, I am beautiful."

I picked a twig off his face. Dying seemed to agree with him. "What I don't get," I said, "if you had this successful gas thing going, why would you run over an old woman? It doesn't make sense."

"She dissed him." Carlos pulled himself up by my shoulder. He spoke with mild surprise. "S'funny, mang, in the movies, guys who get shot always say 'I can't feel my legs.' My legs feel fucking fine, man. So I can't die, right?"

"Right," I agreed, feeling a pang of guilt that maybe I should have called an ambulance. I thought he would be dead by now. If he lived, I'd apologize. "Carlos, maybe I should—"

"Fuck that," he said, "ain't nothin' you can do now." He sneezed blood and continued. "We were in the Superior Market on Avenue Forty-five. It's this cheap-ass discount supermarket. You know the kind, big as a football field, where you gotta bag your own groceries? Hombre Viejo, he don't know this. He standing there, holdin' up the line, waitin' for some bagger to bag him up. So the checker, this middle-aged white lady, a real *gordita*, she say to him, like, 'This is a megastore, sir, we keep prices low. You have to bag yourself,' the lady says, real slow, like he's retarded. 'Is there someone outside to drive you home? Did you come in a senior van?'" He laughed more blood spray, then passed out, coughing.

I crouched there, cradling him. . . . Cough. Blood. Barking. Mengele in a Hispanic discount market. I raised my eyes, hoping to see something that would make sense. The sky looked like it was painted with lead.

"Wait," I said suddenly, "*gordita*. What is that?"

"Fat. Big, white and fat. That's the thing."

Visions of Walburga swam before me.

"Two minutes later, we're at the train crossing. Waiting for the Metro Rail to pass. The gate was down. This fat Mexican lady, I don't know if she's homeless or what, she pushes this shopping cart in front of us. He starts wigging, spitting all this crazy shit. 'I'm sorry, you blubber bag. You cow! But I have to kill you.' I'm like, 'What?'

"Then the old man hits the gas. Knocks her down, and the whole time he's screaming, you know? Really goin' off. '*You fat cow . . . You stinking sofa!*' Stuff in German, I don't know what the fuck. I couldn't believe it, then he backs up, watches her struggling to get all her shit back in the cart. And when she gets back up, he starts screaming, 'See, see! She's a parasite. Look how she won't stay down!' And as soon as she pulls herself up he hits her again, mang. Before this, I never seen this side of the dude, you know?"

Carlos coughed, blood staining his hand. "Then—this really freaked me—the old man looks over and goes, 'Do you believe I can roll over her head without putting a scratch on her body?' And I'm like, 'Chill, Doc, there ain't no hit out on the bag lady.'"

"What did he do?"

"What do you think? He slams it in reverse, knocks her down again and guns it—so you can feel this *wa-BOMP*, like the opposite of when you drive into a pothole. I felt sick, man." Carlos coughed and channeled Mengele. "'This is a skill I developed at Auschwitz. If I needed a jaw, I could back a Mercedes up over a forehead, not even scrape the probiscum bones.' That's what he say, mang, *'probiscum.'*"

"You've got a great ear," I said to him. "You could do dialect in voice-overs. . . ."

"'You could do dialect,'" he mimicked, talking white before going East L.A. again. "Next thing, we hear the sirens. All I'm thinking is if cops check the van for DNA, that's it. . . . Game over. I'm gonna be playing handball with Richard Ramirez. So I say, 'C'mon, Doc, she's still alive, let's throw her in the back and take off.' But the old man, he's like, 'We'll have to drive halfway to Vegas to gas her fat ass. . . .'"

Carlos burped exploding cherries and barked out a bloody last laugh. That was it.

I had heard that a man's spirit flies out when he dies. If this was true, Carlos's flew into a storm drain. And he died laughing.

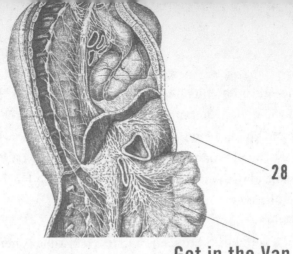

28

Get in the Van

I couldn't cut through yards. Dogs would bark. Lights would go on. The sidewalk was out of the question. No one stole the copper out of the streetlights in Mount Washington, so they worked. I hugged the storm drain, moving low, following the concrete gully back up the hill to the rear of the museum.

At the top, under a streetlight, was a distinctive silhouette. You don't see many profiles missing half their profiles. It was Zell's other twin boychick, Davey.

Either no one had told him about Dinah or he was taking his mind off his loss doing muscle work for Mengele. I wondered what he and bro Bernstein would do when they found out that Tina and I had rearranged their stepmom's corpse to make it look like she died having Sabbath sex with a Chasid. If I were a praying man, I'd pray that my driver woke up and got out of her bedroom before he was arrested for strangling her. I didn't expect God to do much for me, but what had the driver ever done?

The family Zell had enough juice inside San Quentin to arrange conjugal visits, plastic surgery, L.A. getaways. God knew what they'd do to my driver if he got sent up for doing Dinah Zell. Assuming he lived long enough to get sent anywhere. If anything happened to Russian Jack, it would be on me.

Davey leaned on a utility pole tagged top to bottom. He scratched his head with the muzzle of a Beretta. *For Christ's sake!* I wanted to shout at him. *Didn't you learn the last time you put a gun to your head? Accidents happen!*

I found a rock the size of Davey's missing jaw and thought about braining him. I'm not a tough guy, but I watched a lot of violence on TV as a child.

I knew men on the force who spent years learning martial arts, each with its own particular philosophy of Tao or Chi or harnessing the flow of the universe against your opponent so that he ultimately defeats himself. My approach was more basic: sneak up from behind. You could do anything to a man if he didn't see you coming.

A gun butt to the head would have done nicely. But my gun—a sturdy and inelegant .38—had popped out of my hand in the storm-drain slalom. It wasn't registered to me, but still, we went back a long time. This being America, the gun would no doubt wash up next to a grade school where a twelve-year-old would pick it up at recess and shoot his cousin. Then again, things never fuck up the way you think.

I had a dozen attack-from-the-back moves, all variations on "sneak and strike." One involved the guitar string garrote in my sock. But garroting could be tricky. Once, in Manhattan, I'd tried to wrap a wire around the throat of a crackhead who had half a foot on me. He must have been six-six. Instead of killing him, I got my finger caught under the wire at his throat and I rode him from Eighty-sixth and Broadway to Eighty-third, where he knocked me off trying to get on the number five bus. I'm still missing the tip of my right middle finger, forever ending my chances at becoming a Mason—they only take "whole men"—and denying me the chance to give anyone the two-handed finger.

I couldn't decide whether to move in on Davey or sneak around to see who else was behind the museum. I just hoped they didn't have night vision. I crouch-walked a few feet left, trying not to break any branches. From this angle, I could make out the car: a 2002 Cadillac DeVille. Room for six. The perfect vehicle if my whole drug class decided to take a school trip to L.A. to kill me—and wanted to travel in style.

Then Davey made things easy. He ducked toward me into the bushes, glanced over his shoulder and opened a prescription bottle. He tipped his head back, tapped a few pills into his lipless mouth, and started to gobble them dry. No doubt it hurt being him.

I waited until the first pill hit his gullet. Then I jumped up, palm raised, as though planning to spike a volleyball, and popped the plastic bottle down his throat. A prescription bottle cap had been enough to take out Tennessee Williams, so I pulled my spike. I didn't want to kill anybody, just put him out of commission. That's why I only shoved the bottle midway down Davey's esophagus.

Davey reeled backward, choking louder than I'd expected. Now I'd have to do something else to shut him up. I snatched the gun out of his hand and swung it off his temple. He crumbled. We were already in the bushes, so I didn't have to hide him. But I didn't feel good about any of it. I pulled a thin wallet out of Davey's pocket. It was still stiff and shiny. The kind somebody's grandparents would give a ten-year-old before he needed a wallet. Touching. Until I opened it up and saw the twin lightning bolts embossed on the pocket. Maybe it was a gift from his brother.

"Must have been exciting," I said to him, "getting to use your wallet and all." For the moment, he wasn't responsive.

The only card, a driver's license, said "David Zellkoff." How many names did these people need? His twin brother was Bernstein, he was Zellkoff and his daddy was Zell. On his license, Davey stared at the floor like he couldn't meet the camera's eyes. I looked down at him. Even out cold, he radiated pain. "It's hard, huh? Some days you wake up and say 'Why fucking bother?' Believe me, I've been there."

Nobody listens better than the unconscious. Except for the dead.

I pocketed the license and slid the wallet back in his pocket.

Walk a mile in another man's chin . . .

Locking the safety on Davey's nine, I took off at a low trot around the perimeter. Somebody lit a cigarette in the cab of the van. They must have gotten out of the car and hopped in. I stayed in the shadows, angling toward the van from the right. I was holding the Beretta with both hands. Before taking off again, I checked myself for red dots. Halfway there, I had to stop and check again. One of my biggest fears was spotting the infrared dot from a sniper's sight on my torso. I'd only seen them in movies, but that didn't make my fear less real. What could you do if you *did* spot the dot on your crotch? The instinct was to strike a defensive posture—cover the spot—thereby explaining the high percentage of sniper victims who die with bloody paws. My plan was to keep low to the ground until I was directly behind the van, where I wouldn't show up in either side mirror. I didn't want to end up in dead man's Disneyland with Carlos.

When I saw the van's back door was slightly ajar, I eased the barrel of Davey's Beretta inside. Slowly pulled it back. Nothing. Darkness. I didn't realize my flashlight was gone until I reached for it. "You fucking idiot," I said, louder than I meant to.

"Who you calling an idiot?"

I recognized the reverend's Isaac Hayes drawl, then his hand snatched the gun out of my hand and the door flew open. Perfect.

"Reverend! What the fuck? I was talking to myself."

A gun barrel gently introduced itself to my forehead. "Nice piece," he continued pleasantly. "Bad day, huh? We all have 'em."

That was the definition of a hustler—stick a gun in your face and still sound like the best friend you ever had.

"Man named Jesus Christ had a bad day," the reverend continued. "He ended up on a cross. You look like shit, my man."

"Spare me the fucking sermon," I said. "I go all to hell when people shoot at me."

"You wet yourself?"

"No, why? You want to get that on film? You branching out? You could put a robe on me and call it Paul pissing his pants on the way to Damascus."

"I was shooting at you, you'd be shot. How about you get your drug-counseling, talk-it-like-he-walk-it white-boy ass in the van?"

"Who *were* you shooting at?"

The reverend laughed and showed off his gold grill. "Whoever got hit."

As soon as we stepped in the van, the interior light went on. The van's walls glistened like shiny tin, with burnished whorls of blue and green like you'd see in a puddle of gasoline: beautiful enough to be what gassed souls left behind. I was sure if I stared long enough I'd see faces in the whorls.

Sitting stiffly, in the exact middle of a bench that ran along the back wall, was Mengele. He was in full SS wear, from the insignia on his SS-*Hauptsturmführer* cap to the shiny black boots. His skin looked remarkable. There was none of that Dick Clark Naugahyde vampire bloat you see on old men who've had "work done." (I saw the real Dick Clark once in an elevator at Sony, and his skin had the sheen of a hydrated car seat.) Mengele's face actually glowed, which only made his rheumy eyes more unsettling. His mustache grew in a doggy pewter, contrasting strangely with his Billy Idol hair. The fresh air outside of prison seemed to agree with him.

The reverend nudged me with the gun and pointed at him. "Check it out. Looks like an aging leather queen, don't he?"

But my attention was drawn to the figure beside him. It was propped against the wall, wrapped head-to-toe in a blue blanket. I had a feeling about who was under it. I could have drawn Tina's silhouette from memory: hair, shoulders, waist, hips, off-kilter breasts. Or maybe it was some extra sense that lets a man know when his wife is under a blanket. He can't see her, but he knows.

Mengele raised one hand, as if he'd rehearsed, and slowly peeled the blanket down from the top. Just far enough to reveal Tina's face. I willed myself still. Studying her there-and-not-there gaze.

I thought, *Don't show him you want to kill him. Wait.* Mengele smiled like a celebrity backstage, a man used to having the right props at the right time. "Former policeman Rupert. Good to see you again."

"So what is it?" I said, peeling my eyes off of Tina. "If you had a drug problem, you could have called a hotline."

"You Americans. Always tough. Germans are not tough. Germans are strong."

He tilted his head toward Tina. "An attractive woman. Experienced." I vowed again not to show him what the sight of her in this condition did to me. Power to generate fear was all he had. Zell had mentioned how much he wanted respect. But the doctor, apparently, did not just want it for his scientific prowess.

"You can touch her if you like," he sneered.

"You mean if *you* like, don't you?"

Reverend D muzzle-tapped a warning on my back, but I kept going. Disrespect was the only weapon I had. At the moment.

"Pretend it's an experiment so you can watch us fuck. That's your thing, right? Like when you'd mate brother and sister twins. Or make starving Gypsies copulate in a freezing room to measure how much heat they could generate before their hearts gave out?"

"Results of my hypothermia studies have saved many lives—including those of your Navy SEALs."

"Maybe I don't want to be part of your experiments."

"Too late. You already are. The antique heroin you pilfered? It's a serum designed to grow ovarian tumors. I mixed it with a compound of dolphinex—the most addictive opiate ever invented."

"Dolphinex? Never heard of it."

"You wouldn't have. Though you may be familiar with its cousin, Dolophine. Both names derived from Adolf. Dolophine is better known in your country as methadone."

"We've met."

"I assumed as much. Dolphinex was never distributed commercially. It was too effective. One shot and the user literally wants to die if they cannot have more. A result I was particularly pleased with. But then, you know that feeling."

"You're talking about the crap in the Red Cross boxes? It wasn't that great."

"For a tough number like you, of course not. But addicted prostitutes, whom the state would like to prevent from breeding, will willingly inject it. When they do, they die. Childless. And young. I can hardly wait to see what effect it has on you. In a week or two, I suggest you check for breasts."

That's when the floor decided to hit me in the face.

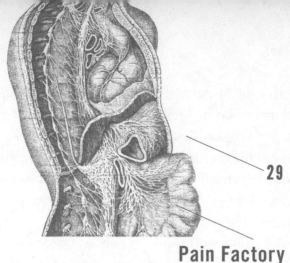

29

Pain Factory

Sweat prickled down my back. I breathed as slowly as I could to counter the blood sloshing around my head. If Mengele had pumped
Tina full of cancer juice, I'd take a bullet just to die with my hands
squeezing his throat. And I'd die happy.

But the reverend was a step ahead of me. Before I could lunge, he
caught my collar and hoisted me up off my feet as if for the doctor's
inspection. Tina's glazed stare registered nothing.

"So she's going to have tumors now? In her ovaries?"

"You have no need to worry," said Mengele. "I gave the Fräulein
something else. Also one of my discoveries. It's very clean. I am proud
to say the advances we made at the camps are still bearing fruit today."
Mengele beamed. "My goodness! I've gotten so wrapped up I forgot
to set us on our way. That's what happens when men of science begin
to talk."

"*You're* talking," I said. "I'm just trying not to puke or laugh in
your face."

"Easy," Reverend D whispered in my ear. Mengele banged on the roof of the van and I heard the engine turn over. That meant a third person driving. Maybe a fourth riding bitch.

The van lurched downhill.

Rage singed the edge of my vision. I saw Mengele through a tunnel of smoke. He gave off a faint odor. The kind that made dogs bark. "What did you give her?"

"Adrenaline. The finest quality. I use it myself."

"Adrenaline? The stuff you were selling to gangbangers?"

"Ah, our little detective has been working. Well, let me educate you, Herr Detective."

"You do that, Hair Doctor."

"With pleasure. Let us go back sixty years."

"Dr. Mengele and the Wayback Machine."

"Excuse me? To get the highest quality, I needed glandular discharge generated in extremis. The more terrified the victims, the more potent the adrenal broth I tapped with my little friend *der Shunt*."

"A shunt?"

"*Ja.*"

Mengele tapped his own Adam's apple. I thought, *What if I bit him? Left his throat exposed the way someone left Dinah Zell's? Would the rev shoot before I got to chew his larynx?*

"I inserted it just so, in the throat," said Mengele, pride lighting him up like a letter from home.

"Aw, look at *you*!" I cooed. "If there's anything more pathetic than an old man kvelling about who he used to be, it's an old Nazi man. Newsflash: you *lost*, Doc. Not your country. *You*. All these other scientific geniuses landed on their feet. Von Braun brought his whole team to New Mexico. Even Erich Traub—Himmler's mad virologist—got set up on Plum Island. Just him, a forest full of infectable mammals and a lab full of global bacteria. Think they didn't ferry in a few Fräuleins when the old germ warrior hit them with Lyme disease?"

I had a hunch he wouldn't hurt me till I stopped. Something you learn when you're a cop: criminals are narcissists. And Mengele had the narcissist's hunger to be talked about. Praise was gravy. I wasn't usually this chatty, but the prospect of imminent death will do that. You want to get it out while you can.

"Then there's *you!*" I got snarky because I was mad. But not at Mengele. At myself. The man deserved to die, and I was throwing him a one-man roast. "Golden boy Beppo—goin' all gooey over glandular shunts! How's it feel to be one of those guys, when you die, people say 'Gee, I didn't even know he was still alive.' I mean, is that really the best memory you have—freaking out slow Gypsies and milking their fear?" I turned to the reverend and shrugged. "You believe Dr. Party-shunt here?"

"Hey, *fuck* shunts!" The reverend gave a little shiver and rubbed his face. "Man, an hour ago, I didn't even know what a shunt was. Now I'm ready to stick one of the motherfuckers in my own damn jugular. Bleed out fast, not have to listen to this."

"Come on, Rev," I said, "I know you and the old shunt-meister do some business together. I'm sure you're used to the Master Race routine by now."

The reverend raised his eyebrows, more amused than defensive. There had to be more in it for him to take orders than to blow a payday and save me. But I guessed I'd find out. "Hey," said the reverend, "I was you I'd—"

"*Stop!*" Mengele shouted, pounding his leg with his fist like a five-year-old. He looked ready to drop to the floor and start kicking it. He might as well have screamed *Respect me! Respect me! Respect me!* "I am telling you something important. If you weren't so ignorant, you would consider yourselves lucky you get to hear this!"

"'Lucky' ain't the word that comes to mind," the reverend said, but Mengele was too entranced by his own fantasies of medical mastery to notice.

"I said quiet!" he yelled, and started up again. "Rather than collect the fluid in a tub I hung a small container on the end of the shunt."

The reverend groaned. "Oh, here we go."

"Enough! This I did in honor of my new country, of its Vermont, where I have seen calendar photos of natives tapping a tree and collecting buckets of syrup."

"If you tell me you put it on pancakes," I said, "I'm going to throw up."

Mengele glared at me and nibbled his mustache, now so frayed it might have been assembled from schnauzer hair. He made no secret of his enthusiasm for his subject, but at the same time his attitude was detached. "When you revive a man into a situation of complete terror, the spike in his adrenal output is astronomical. That initial spurt is the purest. Unlike semen, where premonitory squirts may be nothing but fluid, adrenaline starts off strong. Zero to a hundred, as you Americans say."

"We don't say that about glandular fluid," I said.

Mengele ignored this, caught up in his own drama. "Let me tell you something else I think will amuse you. Carlos knew I was using the van to kill his race enemies. What he didn't know was that his enemies were not killed right away. No. I would bring them back to the shelter. Terrorize them. Which I did, in the back room, at night. The walls were already soundproofed. The specimens were intact and easily revivable. Do you want to know what I did to them?"

"What I want to know—and don't take this the wrong way," I said. "Back then, was everybody like you?"

The question caught Mengele off guard. "Like me how?"

"You know," I said, "the other SS guys, the other doctors—did they all wake up every day and click their heels 'cause they were so happy to be working in a death camp?"

"Proceed with caution," said Mengele. "For me, Auschwitz was a living laboratory. In which, among many other achievements, I developed efficient methods of adrenal harvesting. Synthetic equivalents, for reasons mysterious as God, never possessed the same force. Each adrenaline-generating device—"

"Otherwise known as victims, right?" I interrupted.

"Each adrenaline-generating device," he repeated, "had to be kept in a state of highest terror."

"Whoa, hold up," said the rev, who more and more seemed to be feeling his oats. "I'm with Manny on this. Them poor folks you be scarin' to death—you callin' them 'devices.'"

"They owned human organs," the doctor replied drily. "But scientifically applied terror can weaken a human with such ferocity the system simply collapses. You would be surprised how few ways there really are to generate fear! Oh, I could tell you stories."

"Nobody wants to hear them!" I shouted. This was a lie. Which might explain why my knee kept pumping up and down on its own until I had to lean on it, like *The Thinker*. Hateful Knee Syndrome. Rage made me want to slam him face-first into the van wall. Some terrible fascination made me want to listen even more. This was the guilty truth, and Mengele seemed to count on it. He waited calmly for further interruption, sneered when there wasn't any and paraded more stories.

"There was this feisty young Jew from Hungary."

I had to dig my nails in my palms to keep my hands occupied. The tension seemed to feed him. He needed to make people uncomfortable.

"One day, after he'd heard I had operated on his brother, he saw me. He was on a work detail, cleaning the ramps. No more than a boy of fifteen. He saw me and he spit in my face. The guard grabbed him and I showed him my scalpel. Again, he spit in my face. I cut off his tongue, and even then, before passing out he spit blood at me."

"Boy had heart. He woulda done well at Q," the reverend said, to no one in particular. "Say whatchu want, there's Jews got big *huevos*."

"For as long as we let them have them." Mengele smiled, making his little joke. "But this one had a soldier's will, I admit." The memory gave rise to a chuckle. "He was fast enough to pick his tongue out of the dirt and throw *that* in my face before the guard could stop him. For that, the capos were furious and showed no kindness as they dragged him, at my request, to my laboratory in Building Ten. But I needed to know: what is the source of this will? I suspected amphetamines. But when I performed the autopsy—for reliable results, of course, the subject must still be alive—his system was clean. Not just of drugs. I mean devoid of calories or stimulants. This made the chemical composition of the work camp resident easy to quantify. He was a churning pain factory. And pure pain made for pure adrenaline. It was almost as if his fear nourished him. So of course, I nourished the fear. It was the least I could do."

I was starting to feel dizzy. The closeness of the van, the unnatural light, just standing on my feet for so long . . .

"What's more powerful, hate or pain?" I heard myself ask. Availing myself of a killer's opinion was not condoning it. It seemed all right to ask him a few things if I knew I was going to kill him later.

"Pain or hate. The eternal question," Mengele replied with something like approval. "A question no one who wants to understand the human race can afford not to ask."

"See that," said the reverend, "the man's game better than yours. He makin' it look like you 'n' him be about the same shit."

"Peas in a pod, is that not the expression?" Mengele took out a hand mirror and checked his hair. "Science does not care who calls it science," he said as he slicked down a patch up front. "You may ask, did I give the spitting Jew an anesthetic? Well, does nature? *No!* And yes. Suffering was essential. The threat of it. But then, what fear and pain produce, in any man, is a way to handle fear and pain."

"Oh, that's deep," I said.

"Perhaps," said Mengele, "you will appreciate the concept when you experience it. The adrenal glands are like jet engines. When they have fuel, they can choose their course. When they're out of fuel, gravity chooses for them. They have no choice. For truly broken men, just the chance to lie down—even if it comes with knives attached—is a tremendous blessing."

"I'd like to lie down," I said. "Does listening to you count as torture?"

I actually tried to kneel, hoping to just tip sideways, but at a nod from Mengele the reverend grabbed me again and hoisted me up.

"Mr. Rupert, I have not finished with the Hungarian." Mengele sounded a little hurt.

"I can't fucking believe this," I said.

"Nor could I," Mengele continued, "but that was the pleasure of camp work—the sweep of cases you encounter."

"Pleasure?" I said.

"Let the man talk," the reverend snapped. I decided he was playing it smart—backing Mengele one minute, me the next. Covering the angles. As Mengele slid his mirror back in his pocket, the reverend winked.

"You will appreciate this," said the doctor, aiming his comment pointedly in my direction. "In the middle of surgery, I saw this Jew look down at his own exposed liver, and the sight of it made him weep with joy. Later, as he sputtered prayers on his deathbed, I removed the liver and held it over him, and I understood: to his pain-maddened eyes, the organ was a newborn baby in my hands. His tears were tears of bliss that he had given birth. *'Mein kindela!'*"

The reverend groaned again. "You never hear of a brother pullin' this kinda ill shit."

"You like giving people pain, doctor? Just between us girls."

"What I was giving him was a chance for *glory*!" Mengele straightened in what I imagined he considered a display of his full and imposing power. "Even a parasite can have his moment of honor."

"Finally," I said, "I know what to put on my headstone."

"Mockery is understandable." Mengele smiled, no doubt knowing the last thing I wanted was his understanding. "The Jew's hallucination moved me so much that, in the end, I *did* administer morphine. To myself. It was a treat I allowed myself on special occasions. Did I mention he spit in my face—again!—before he expired? He died honorably."

"With you holding his liver."

"As I would a beautiful baby."

"Wait," I said, knowing before I asked, "now I get it. You have this on film."

Mengele jerked sideways as if struck. He stopped talking.

"You do, don't you? How much did Zell offer?"

Again, silence. The sound of our collective breathing. And the muffled *womp-womp-womp* of the van's overworked valves.

I pushed. "What's the problem? You don't want to sell? Or Zell won't pay what you want? Or wait. *Fuck!* This is perfect! He won't pay anything at all? Let me guess. He threatened to expose you if you wouldn't give the film to him?"

"Damn," said Reverend D. "Man's gettin' his PI on."

Mengele just stared, calculating. "A Jew is a Jew. He saw a bargain."

I thought I saw Tina blink. But I wasn't sure. Everything was too close and too far away at the same time. The van seemed to be swaying.

Mengele tightened his thin lips. "This is science, not commerce."

"You know what they say—one man's science project is another man's torture porn."

Mengele bristled. "You—you are truly a Jew. You smell like a Jew. You think like a Jew. Yes, the prisoner suffered and died from my ministrations. But this wasn't torture. It was humanitarian research.

Thanks to his secretions, I discovered the means to generate and harvest something that could help the Fatherland win the war."

"Yeah?" The reverend suddenly punched the wall. "How'd that work out?"

Mengele faced him, unfazed. "Mercenaries do not get to have opinions," he said calmly. "Now listen, because we are coming to the sixty-four-thousand-shekel question. If our own bodies generate a substance, is it technically a drug? If it isn't, does it become one when we remove it and give it to someone else?

"Today," he said, head held high, "the human body is the future of drug manufacturing. It's like God was waiting for man to discover this final glory. We needed the freedom of the camps to see it."

"I'm not thinking about God's glory," I said. "I'm thinking how much you could get for your hormone formulas. And how much Zell wanted to get them from you."

"You think that is what this is about?" He raised his eyes to whatever swastika'd demigod resided in the ceiling of the gas van, then stood and weaved his way toward me. "Let me put it in language you can understand. Fear turns on the epinephrine faucet. Fear is a biological delivery system. Try the spinal fluid of a man reduced to jelly by flashing lights and Wagner." His mustache nearly scratched my eyes. "Adrenaline has a sweetish taste."

"Swedish?" the reverend asked. "Like Swedish meatballs?"

"*Dummkopf!* I said it is sweet."

Tina lolled slightly sideways. I thought she was waking. Mengele smiled at my concern. "Speaking of sweet," he said, no doubt seeing himself in a movie as the epitome of old-world charm.

The idea of Mengele and my ex-wife . . . There were so many things in this new world I had to focus on not thinking about.

"You gonna tell him about the horse?" Reverend D asked.

"Horse? Like in heroin?"

"Ah, the horse," said Mengele, moving his tongue in his mouth, as if the memory were delicious. "You see, the horse is what gave me the idea," said Mengele.

"For what?" I asked.

"For the whole process."

"Yeah, yeah," said the reverend. "I had to listen. Now you gonna have to."

"If you're through bickering," said Mengele, chastising the reverend and me. "One of the few intelligent characters I met in São Paulo was a Mexican horse butcher. He'd committed some *indiscretions* in his home country. He, too, was an exile, so—"

"Wait," I interrupted, "a horse butcher? Is that code for something?"

"It is not code. Europe, if you would let me explain, has retained its taste for horse. But America has outlawed horse butchering, so the animals are sent south of the border. Where—this I learned from Rudolpho—master butchers practice the art of pithing. A skilled operator slips the knife above the withers, in the spinal column, precisely at the base of the neck. Properly done, the procedure leaves the animal able to move its head and nothing else."

"So what?" I said.

"So this minimizes the risk of injury to the knife artist when he butchers the animal alive."

"You want to tell me why I'm listening to you drool over horse torture?"

"Ignorant!" Mengele shouted. "If you would stop with your stupid interjections, you would know. Why do devotees prefer to slice the meat off a conscious horse? Because—you see, there is a connection—the adrenaline generated by its terror sweetens the meat."

The reverend elbowed me. "Nasty, right?"

"You're the one working for him," I said.

He snarled. "Reverend D don't work for nobody but Reverend D."

"Gentlemen!" Mengele curled and uncurled his tongue, showing what he no doubt thought was his playful side as he sat back down. "I told Carlos and his friends that I turned men into dogs and showed them the cages. They thought I was a *brujo*."

The old narcissist sat back and crossed his arms. As if allowing me suitable room to be wowed by his story. I yawned in his face.

"Let me ask you something, Doc. Have you found the gland that makes you delusional? The one that excretes hormones that make people think they're interesting?"

Mengele glared. "Where are you, and where am I? Who is the delusional one?"

I didn't reply.

"I thought so," he said. "We have a ride ahead of us. So why don't I tell you what happened when I tried grafting additional adrenal glands into the glands of healthy males."

"Oh, Jesus," I said. "Can I just request the gas?"

"That ain't even a joke you want to make," the reverend warned.

"On this, I would agree," said Mengele. "I will choose to ignore it. As I was saying—"

"Just answer the question."

"I will, but not that one. You see, I had far fewer resources at the pound than I did at Auschwitz. But as the degenerate composer Stravinsky once remarked, 'The more limitations I have, the more creative I can be.' So . . . I managed. I got rid of the gang's enemies—and I used them for what I could before destroying them." He stopped to aim his rheumy eyes in my direction. "And I know what you are thinking."

"If you knew what I was thinking, you would have killed me already."

"Oh, please," said Mengele, "if you would stop trying to be so heroic, you might actually learn something."

"From you? I doubt it." My mouth had gone dry, but I worked up just enough saliva to spit. "I don't plan on starting a human hormone farm any time soon."

"I am talking about ecology," he said. "Nazis were green! We wasted nothing! Unbeknownst to them, the gang members were like pygmy headhunters, eating their enemies' hearts."

The reverend fought back a gag. "Bullshit. No way them bangers gonna eat nigger heart."

"What the fuck, Rev?" I couldn't believe what I'd just heard.

To my horror, Mengele shared my revulsion. "A disgusting locution," he said, looking genuinely disgusted. "You are talking about your own people."

I snorted. "You're going to lecture us about disgusting?"

"Ain't no us, motherfucker!" The reverend glared. "There's just you, me—and the German."

Mengele cleared his throat. "Forgive me. I assumed you both grasped the concept of metaphor. The gang was not, of course, consuming the hearts of what you call 'African-Americans.' They were consuming their glandular discharge. This is a nice symmetry, no?"

"Nice?"

I kept thinking of that Adidas tennis shoe on the floor of the pound. What its owner must have endured. But now was not the time to dwell on past horrors, with the one in front of me.

"Tina!" I hollered, cupping my hands as if she were across a far abyss. "Tina, can you hear me?" Her mannequin gaze gave back nothing.

"Adrenaline?" I screamed at Mengele. "That's bullshit. She looks like she drank shellac."

"Ah!" The remark seemed to please him. "I was hoping you'd notice. People forget adrenaline is not just the fight-or-flight hormone. But when the fight is over, the animal surrenders. Endorphins flood the system, the balm before the claw."

"Tina!" I yelled again.

Nothing. Her eyes looked like they were placed in their sockets by taxidermists. I stared at my ex-wife and imagined the things I'd say if I ever had the chance. The anger I would promise not to display. The love and kindness I would never again take for granted. I was losing my grip.

"Where are we going?" I yelled.

Mengele slumped. "Where do you think? We're going to hell," he said sullenly, "with the rest of your ignorant nation."

The reverend took offense. "Who you callin' ignorant, Doc?"

Not for the first time, I wondered if maybe Rev D was on my side. He'd stopped jamming the gun at me twenty minutes ago. I considered shoving him into the old man, then grabbing Tina and leaping out of the moving van. But if the door was locked, I'd be fucked. Even if the reverend *did* seem sympathetic, it didn't mean he wouldn't shoot me for the right money.

"You want to know what I never imagined?" Now all pretense of calm was gone. Mengele was steaming. He was roaring. "After holding my breath for decades in shitholes a goat would be ashamed to be seen in, I never imagined I would move to the United States and find more Spanish. Then I arrive, and what do I see? More brown people. I see they are allowed to live, uneducated, ill housed, in order for your country to maintain a supply of restaurant workers and hotel toilet cleaners. A different solution, but just as final."

Mengele blasted something from a spritzer up his nose and perked up. "But life is imperfect! I love America!" he exclaimed. "Hitler himself understood that without America, there would have been no Reich."

"You blaming us?" I asked.

"Blaming? I am thanking. Listen to me! My earliest hero was J. Marion Sims. In eighteen seventy-five, he did experiments on African-American slave women in Alabama to find a cure for vaginal fistulas. *With no anesthetic!* And this man is considered the father of gynecology. Oh yes! Americans showed the Germans how to apply eugenics. How to use the inferior man to serve the superior. Would you like another example?"

"No," said the reverend and I at the same time.

Mengele ignored us, swept up in his own saga. "Let's discuss the environment. German scientists practiced recycling before America even had such a word."

"What are you talking about," I asked him, "making lampshades out of skin?"

"I am talking about this van!" Mengele declared. "What truer example of recycling—a self-contained germ elimination vehicle, designed to keep the race pure and the air clean at the same time. Nazi genius."

For an instant, after he said that, the reverend and I both fought back nausea. It was not so much that death was all around us. It was that we were *inside* of death. Mengele reached behind him and tapped a fine-meshed metal vent. I spotted a single long black hair in the grate and thought my knees would buckle.

The reverend spoke deliberately. "This where you pump the shit in?"

"The *shit*, as you call it, is carbon monoxide. Which would be pumped out there if we did not pump it in here. Instead of harming the lungs of innocent citizens, it goes into the lungs of scum. And it does not even require a chemical engineer to do the job. Even Carlos was able to do it."

"No need for the past tense," I said. "Carlos is still alive." I tried to sound matter-of-fact, or as matter-of-fact as I could locked in a van with a mass murderer. "Carlos is probably back on Avenue Fifty-five by now, rounding up homies. You didn't know he's a shot caller?"

"Shot caller?" Mengele smiled his hideous smile again. "Is that like *capo de tutti capi*?"

I smiled back at him. "Keep laughing, Doc. You have no idea of the shitstorm comin' your way."

"You see," said Mengele, not without a hint of admiration. "The Jew is a natural liar."

He was right. Carlos was probably dead. But why not make the old prick sweat if I had a chance?

"Carlos is hard-core, Doc. You disrespect him, he's gonna come after you. There's probably a dozen low-riders right now, full of twelve-
year-olds with shotguns lookin' to make their bones. All lookin' for
this van. Soon as they spot this van, they're gonna start blastin'."

Mengele didn't even pretend to listen. He waited for the words to
stop, studying the reverend and me with eyes that absorbed the light
like black sponges. "Do you know why I wanted to go to San Quentin?" He blurted the answer immediately. "Testicular transplants."

"Don't want to know about it," said the reverend.

Mengele tongued his lip fur with delight. "This makes you
squeamish? Relax. This was a while ago! In nineteen nineteen,
military surgeons were experimenting with new solutions for genital trauma. And so they came to San Quentin and inserted testicles
of recently executed inmates and goats into the scrotums of living
prisoners."

"That is wrong," said the reverend.

"What is wrong," Mengele sputtered, suddenly erupting, "is that
every time some so-called medical atrocity is uncovered, there are the
inevitable comparisons to Dr. Mengele. Well, I have news. Prisoners
have always been like two-legged petri dishes. You think I invented
the idea of using incarcerated subjects? True scientists have always
known their value."

"Doctor, excuse me," I said, "but if you're going to keep talking,
I'm going to need some adrenaline. . . ."

"You do not fool me," he said. "You're fascinated."

I didn't reply. If he was right, I was not going to admit it. So
Mengele just kept going. "Merck pharmaceutical infected four hundred prison inmates in Chicago with malaria. Did anybody take Mr.
Merck's company away? No. As a matter of fact, your *Life* magazine, in
June 1945, detailed medical experiments conducted on state prisoners
by the American Office of Scientific Research and Development in
their effort to develop a vaccine for malaria. A noble effort. And yet,

after the Allies emerged victorious, three Nazi doctors who did death camp malaria studies were hung. Why?"

The reverend shook his head in disgust. " 'Cause they were fucking Nazis—and the Nazis lost. Why the fuck you think?"

But Mengele was not to be stopped.

"Where America led, Germany followed," he rhapsodized. "How to comprehend a country so crude, yet so advanced! Ninety years ago, California adopted 'pure race' laws. Public health officials were trained to be on the lookout for oversexed women of lesser races. The signs: extra-large labia and meaty clitori in the inferior races."

"Maybe I'm just an ex-pimp," said the reverend, "but all that science sound like an excuse to do nasty shit to me. The whole damn thing stink like perv sex."

"I shall not even dignify that," said Mengele, "and if I were you, I would consider my attitude very carefully, Reverend."

"You let him bitch you out like that?" I said, causing the reverend to shift his wrath to me.

"I ain't the kind of preacher you get to call a bitch, son."

While the rev and I bickered, Mengele went from menacing to sentimental. "Hitler wrote something deeply meaningful in *Mein Kampf*." With that, he closed his eyes and recited, " 'There is today one nation which was the model for the Reich—the United States.' Today, perhaps, I believe the Führer would have liked to retire to America. Don't you see? The entire purpose of Nazi science was to keep the unworthy from polluting our pure Nordic blood. Then, lo and behold, a week ago I go to a Whole Foods market, and what do I see? An entire aisle stocked with *blood purifiers*. If only the Führer could see how his work is being carried on. I have no doubt he would have liked to retire to Los Angeles and take up yoga. He swore by homeopathics!"

"Who needs Zyklon B," I said, "when you can bore people to death?"

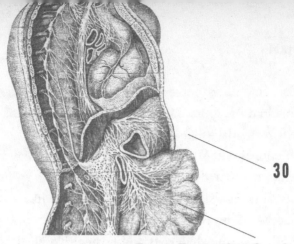

30

Fear Eats the Soul

focused on not losing my nerve. Fronting. I couldn't tell if I was carsick, paranoid, starving, crackling with fear of what my captor would do to Tina or fear that, whatever he did, I'd have to watch. Helpless. Impotent as a shtetl Torah scholar watching a Cossack rape his wife.

When had I not been in this van?

I didn't know if Tina was coming back from wherever Mengele had chemically launched her. Her once-in-a-while-blinking eyes met mine with no more affect than a statue. *Where was she?*

The van banged up and down. The driver must have been taking potholes at sixty. Something dragging from the chassis scraped the asphalt. The racket filled the metal box, then stopped. I made out a thought in this chaos, like a far-off light in the fog: *Maybe fumes have been seeping in all along.* There were smoky fringes in the corner of my vision, as if film were being fed through a projector straight into flames.

I wasn't scared. I was working my way up to fear. What I felt was a kind of inchoate vagueness. Maybe Mengele had transformed his own body odor into an anesthetic.

The road smoothed out and the van hummed as it picked up speed. Mengele droned on. The guy at the party you had to listen to because he had the drugs. Or the gun.

"By the end, World War Two wasn't even a war. It was a custody battle. Operation Paperclip. America competed for scientists with the Communists. The Russians and Americans were like pedophiles in an orphanage, stabbing each other in the back to get to the camp scientists and all their knowledge. It makes me sick, all these years the Jews and everyone else decrying the Holocaust." He imitated what I supposed he thought to be a lisping Jew. "'Oi oi oi! How could it happen? How could it happen?' When the Jew knows the truth more than anyone: it is all business."

"I can't imagine why they wouldn't want your ass," said the reverend with equal parts sincerity and sarcasm.

"Yeah, why didn't they want you?"

"The Jews made me a symbol; why do you think? IBM did more to kill the Jews than I ever did! They invented the computer to keep track of death camp inmates. But does that keep anybody from buying their products? Look!"

He reached in his pocket and carefully slid out a plastic-covered card the size of a credit card slip. He read it out loud.

"Prisoner code eight was 'Jew.' Code eleven was 'Gypsy camp.' Code zero-zero-one was 'Auschwitz.' Code five was 'execution by order.' Code six was 'gas.' And who made the gas? IG Farben. Parent company of Bayer pharmaceuticals."

"Can I see that?"

I reached, but he quickly pulled the artifact back, close to his chest. "Are you brain damaged? Do you have any idea what this could get on eBay?"

The reverend shot his cuffs. "I believe I could help you with that."

"Not now! The point I'm making is, *nothing has changed*. Bayer and Rockefeller paid me to inject typhus into babies; why? Was it torture?

No, fever relieves certain conditions. When his temperature exceeds one oh six, a Mongoloid can read the Bible."

"So what's the deal, man-to-man? Do you just, like, make shit up and believe it?"

"This was world-changing science, believe me. After the war, I can tell you, I found out what was what. There are no countries, there are no wars—there are wardens who run the world and inmates who live in it. One nation runs all nations: Business-land."

"And all these years, you still can't get your passport stamped."

"Enough!" Mengele shouted, producing a peculiar old pistol.

"Jesus, is that a Luger?"

"It is." He put the gun away and sniffed. It was getting very close in the van. "If I wanted a new gun I could get one. Now listen to me: there are Jews who will tell you of the good things Mengele did. But do you hear about them? No!"

"I'll bite," I said. "Tell me something good."

My plan now was to wait till he fell into some swoon of heroic memory, then stomp on his foot and knee him in the face when he fell forward. I'd just have to take my chances with the reverend. You had to die of something.

"I developed something sweet," Mengele declared. "Exitotoxin, so that the Jews would eat their gruel. You know it as aspartame."

"You invented aspartame?"

"As more than a sweetener, I'm afraid."

"What's that mean?" Tina lived on Diet Cokes. Now I had to worry about sugar-free Nazi pop?

"What it means," the doctor explained, "is that once consumed, it breaks down into amino acids and methanol, degrades to formalde-hyde, morphs the brain of whoever consumes it into a neurodegenera-tive stew of multiple sclerosis, Parkinson's, or Alzheimer's. Sometimes all three. But did I get a patent? Do I get residuals? What do *you* think? In nineteen sixty-seven, IG Farben and Monsanto started a joint ven-

ture to put aspartame in drinks—using my formula. Your Donald
Rumsfeld pushed it through the FDA for his friends at IG Farbenfab-
riken—whose own palate was sweetened with General Motors money
during the war. The fruits of the Holocaust!"

"You sure you're not taking more credit than you deserve? Just a
teensy bit?"

"What?" Mengele went red-faced. "You don't understand. For
America and Germany, eugenics was our arms race. A race to save
the race! Grateful Americans sent me a gold-plated bust of an Aryan
youth for my work with irradiated benches. I found a way to sterilize fifty inferior males at once. Sit them down on my irradiated
metal, pretend they were there to fill out a dental chart, and before
you could say Richard Wagner their sperm would be as useless as
toothpaste."

He closed his eyes, his voice now weaker. He fumbled in the
pocket of his waistcoat and pulled out the bullet-shaped canister. He
sprayed it up his nose. And sat up again, re-revived. "Why do I mention the radioactive gonads? Because one of my counts, at Nuremberg,
centered on this very breakthrough. Which I had planned on coming
to the States to market. But never mind. I was the evil radiator. Meanwhile—this is the injustice!—since the twenties, in America, children
had been slipping their feet into shoe-fitting fluoroscopes. Every shoe
store had to have one. *Scientific shoe-fitting.* What fun to see your foot
bone there in the radioscope! Do I need to tell you that a decade
later there was an epidemic of deadly cancers and genital deformities?
But did anybody prosecute shoe salesmen? Was the inventor of the
foot fluoroscope forced to abandon his family and migrate south of the
border? Quaker Oats paid Harvard to feed retarded children oatmeal
spiked with radioactive tracers. The object was to see how preservatives move through the body. Were any Quakers hung? Was anyone
from Harvard charged?"

Reverend D responded without smiling. "Remember, Doc, anger is a luxury we can't afford. Right, Manny? You're the recovery guy; *tell 'im*!"

"Reverend's right," I said, unearthing another nugget of recovery: "You're angry 'cause you're afraid. And what is fear? False Evidence Appearing Real!"

The classes in San Quentin might as well have happened in another galaxy. There was Mengele and pre-Mengele. And right now there was Maximum Mengele. I waited desperately for Tina to blink again, to give some sign that she was alive. I'd seen her like this once before, attractively embalmed and propped up, when she'd scored us some ketamine, then done it all herself when she got tired of waiting for me to come home. I walked in to find her in a total K-hole, flat on her back on the kitchen floor. Her eyes were open but her body was stiff, as though plucked prematurely from the pod where she'd been deanimated until arrival on Saturn. I tuned back to Mengele's ranting.

"Was I angry when von Braun, who ran slave camps and developed the V-2, was flown to Hyannis Port?"

"Rocket man again? You must be mad," I said. "You won't shut up about it."

Jimmy the Rasta had been right. The von Braun thing killed him. It was almost worth the unpleasantness just to listen to his torment.

"While I was being condescended to by brown-skinned cretins, kissing President Stroessner's cankered ass to stay in Paraguay, Wernher von Braun was rubbing thighs with Jackie Kennedy, listening to Pablo Casals at White House dinners. So he used Jewish prisoners as slave labor to build V-2 missiles. What did JFK care? Dead Jews don't matter when you need to go to the moon. One small step for man, one giant step for Nazi science! The president painted von Braun's swastika red, white and blue and made him a hero. Americans are so self-righteous because they do not even know their own history."

"Somebody be sittin' on the pity pot," said the reverend. "You had your run, *Swasti-cuz*! Have a little dignity. Don't be dyein' your hair an' shit. Makes you look like some bathhouse toad ain't heard the eighties is over."

I still didn't know the deal the two had worked out. But mutual respect was plainly not part of the contract.

"Am I kidnapped," I asked to annoy him, "or do you just need to lock people in vans to get them to listen to your life story?" Mengele stiffened. Still unaccustomed to mockery from subhumans. "I guess Auschwitz was the high point, huh? And I don't mean 'cause it looks good on a résumé. I mean 'cause of all the research opportunities! The *freedom*! Spot a fresh set of mixed-sex teen twins? March them back to the lab for your famous climate study. Plunge Ugo and Uta naked in a vat of freezing water. Then march them outside, dripping wet, in the Polish winter, so they have to do things to each other to keep from dying of hypothermia. If you take notes, it's science."

How often does anyone have the chance to chat with a living nightmare? There was so much to ask.

"Did you follow," I heard myself ask, "in 'eighty-five, when your victims had a reunion in Jerusalem? They tried you in absentia. The saddest was the man who only appeared behind a curtain, because you had removed his penis when he was a boy. He was still ashamed."

"They were not victims. They were subjects. No one expects a layman to understand science."

"Really? How fat was your mother to make you need to do that?"

"My mother?"

Reverend D reached over and slapped the back of my head. "Boy, like my toothless grandma used to say, 'If I was you, I would put my *mouf* in the *mouf* garage and shut the motherfucking garage door.'"

I let that go. Some other time I could parse the reverend's loyalties. For now, my mouth was all I had to hurt Mengele. "Was Walburga proud you followed in her footsteps?"

Mengele stiffened, as close to confusion as I'd seen him. "My mother? What are you talking about?"

"You both made cripples."

"Oh, snap!" laughed the reverend, earning a Mengelic glower.

"So," I continued, "there's no mandatory retirement age for mass murderers? You just switch to pets? How could you even be who you say you are? You were declared dead by drowning years ago."

"Please. The São Paulo coroner was bribed. It is not hard to persuade an international committee that wants to be persuaded."

"And so you survived to go peroxide and put down schnauzers."

"That," he said, "is unfortunate."

"Yeah, especially for the schnauzers, huh, Beppo?"

This alone seemed to sting him. But it wasn't the Mama's-boy nickname that wound him up. It was accusing him of hurting animals.

"I love all God's creatures," he protested. "Which does not include the vermin—the Jews, the Gypsies, the Slavs, the homosexuals. We were doing what needed to be done to save humanity. We were willing to be beasts in the eyes of the world. To save what was finest in us. But animals. Oh no! With them we have a sacred bond. In Germany, you know, we passed the Tierschutzgesetz."

"Sounds like it hurt," the reverend chuckled, in no way cowed by the old bottle-blond's glare.

"For your information, that means the Animal Rights Act. Germany," Mengele proudly declared, "was the first country in the world that defined rights for animals. Tierschutzgesetz declared that they, too, have souls."

"Then how can you stand there in Highland Park and kill them?"

"Quite easily. The Tierschutzgesetz applied to German dogs. Let me explain to you one of my greatest discoveries, Mengele's Law. By definition, every species contains within it the best strain of itself. Think of it as the species equivalent of the master race. My triumph is the development of Mengelatin, a substance so powerful it can only be described as 'the elixir of life.' This contribution—and its race-saving applications—would be salvation enough to make up for the so-called six million. Fellow scientists would reward me for the formulaic elegance as for my patent and the sweep of its applications. I am not without compassion," he pronounced grandly. "Even those breeds below master race could benefit."

"So what does it do?"

I hated to admit it, but I was curious.

Mengele chewed a few wet mustache hairs before he answered. "Why should I tell you? What I will say is that every race, from subhuman to superior, produces its own best of breed. Its valuable essence. A by-product of adrenaline, which can be generated and gathered."

"You honkin' on that shunt again?" The reverend was getting less ambivalent about his affections.

"The science is complicated," said Mengele, pleased to have been asked. Then he turned to me, his sudden friendliness more disturbing than imperious repulsion. "I lied," he said to me. "I didn't just give her adrenaline. I shouldn't have teased you."

"What?"

For the second time, I was ready to lunge, but the reverend caught me.

Mengele, meanwhile, had gone weirdly mellow. "No, you'll like this," he said. "It's a *good* thing."

When the insane sound reasonable, the ground always gets shakier.

"A couple of months ago," he said, a little wearily, "there was a headline in the *New York Times*: 'Scientists Develop Love Serum Oxytocin?'"_

"Oxycontin? The Rush Limbaugh drug?" Now I was the one so nervous I sounded like a chatterbox. "Man, I gotta tell you, anybody don't believe in evolution, take a look at the American dope fiend. From Charlie Parker to Rush Limbaugh. That fat fuck should get an award for makin' dope uncool."

"Maybe that's why he does it," the rev said. "For the kids. Who wants to be a junkie when the poster boy is a pasty Republican fat-ass looks like he skated on a MSNBC *To Catch a Predator* bust?"

Mengele took another hit off his pocket vial. The blast left his voice slightly warbly. "Not oxycontin, *oxytocin*. It's a hormone, mostly found in vaginal secretions when a woman climaxes. It induces bonding by decreasing cuddle inhibitors."

"So I guess you can see how I might be able to help out with that," said the reverend, surprising me again with his shifting alliances.

"Not really," I said, putting no finesse in it. "Can girls even get moist when they're that tweaked?"

Reverend D flashed the gold in his grill. "When I'm on the case, there's a smile at both ends."

Mengele harrumphed. He wanted the attention back. "Johns Hopkins found that oxytocin injected into cerebrospinal fluid causes spontaneous erections and weeping. Your CIA thinks it might be useful to spray at political rallies. To sway opinion. And your Pentagon wants it for chemical warfare. One spritz and Moishe puts down the rocket launcher and kisses Mohammed."

"Wow. I wonder what an OD would look like," I said.

Mengele looked pleased. "That's a very important question. That's what we're here to find out!"

Apparently this was the reverend's cue to open a locker on the back wall. He pulled out a hazmat suit and green rubber booties that Velcro'd over the ankle. When he handed one to Mengele my mouth went dry. The reverend and Mengele stepped into the gear like they dodged toxins together all the time.

So there it was. No matter how you divided "they need gas masks" by "I don't get any," the result was not good. Mengele cracked an ampoule and filled a narrow-gauge syringe. The reverend tightened and retightened his Velcro bootie.

I could think of no compelling reason to let myself and the woman

I loved, whatever condition she was in, be fumigated in a van in front of masked men. I would never call myself brave, but given the choice between a protracted death and a fast one, it hardly seemed heroic to go for slow.

"It's been fascinating, but we're gone," I said.

I launched myself off the bench and screamed in Tina's face. "Get up!"

Nothing registered.

I shouted again. *"Tina!"*

Still no response. I slapped her face and pulled her off the bench. Nobody stopped me. Both men, now in masks, watched with mild insect-interest. I tried the door handle. I kicked and punched at it. "You think I'm gonna stand here and get exterminated? Open the fucking door!

"Whose side are you on?" I asked the reverend. He pointed to himself. Big surprise.

Then Mengele yelled through his mask, so that it sounded like he was talking on a cell phone, "Nobody's exterminating you. On the contrary, I'm going to make your life worth living." For one weird moment, he sounded like a televangelist. Jimmy Swaggart with a Colonel Klink accent. "I am going to infuse your existence with emotions few people ever get to experience. The feelings of love oxytocin generates—"

"You're not doing shit," I said with all the bravado a thimble could hold.

I felt the reverend's steel grip on my shoulders as Mengele approached with a syringe.

"You're going to thank me," he said, going for "soothing" despite the grinding, fork-in-the-garbage-disposal unpleasantness of his voice. "It makes women want to cuddle. In men, feelings of love are magnified. Introduced into the cerebrospinal fluid of rats, it causes spontaneous erection."

"Sounds like MDMA," I said, babbling to hide my panic. "I tried that once in the nineties and French-kissed my mailman."

"MDMA and Ecstasy are pale imitations of a hormone we produce naturally during orgasm. What I've done, as I did with adrenals, is harvest it."

"You're the Mr. Green Jeans of glands. Do they make a lab coat that comes with bib overalls?"

Mengele was too busy to listen. He began to whistle, some grating mash-up of "Raindrops Keep Falling on My Head" and Wagner. Then, biting the orange cap off the syringe, he tapped three times on Tina's throat, like it was a secret code, and plunged the point in her neck. I wanted to pounce, but not when he had a needle in my soon-to-be-ex ex-wife's neck.

He got a blood register, then thumbed the plunger back down while the reverend held me in place by the shoulders. "Somebody," he said, "is going to have a very wonderful evening."

I tried to stomp the reverend's shoe but he moved his foot.

"So you shoot up her up with O juice, and she goes mad?"

"Actually, I just injected her with superadrenaline. Oxytocin is delivered nasally, in a mist. You'll both be getting the love."

Mengele nodded and took his seat on the bench beside the reverend, who kept a pincer grip on my shoulder. He banged a few times on the front of our rolling party pad, to whoever was in the cab. Then he pulled a video camera from the compartment where the hazmat suits had hung. He fiddled with the lens, then pointed the thing my way. I wasn't thrilled about it, but at the moment, acting without a SAG card was the least of my worries.

The floor began to rattle and hum, building up to a brain-rattling epic MRI. *Clack . . . Clack . . . Clack.* I wanted to eat my arms. But Tina showed no reaction. Mengele—and again, I tried to remind myself, it might not be Mengele—refastened his mask. Then the clacking stopped. Replaced by a hiss. Mist rose from a grate in the bottom of the van.

Time went sideways. Adrenally fired up, Tina's eyes focused. She took in the pair in gas masks and slowly rising fog at her ankles and screamed at me.

"They're gassing us, and you're standing there?"

"You were out of it. It's not that kind of gas. It's oxytocin. The bonding hormone. It—"

"I know what oxytocin is!" she shouted over the rising fog. "I read it in *Jane*. I just can't believe you believed him!"

She stepped around the rising vapor, seething, and punched me in the face. I thought the veins in her eyes were going to bleed. She swung again, connecting with my neck. Then she tried to slap my face. I grabbed her by the wrists and she tried to head-butt me.

I tried to dodge her, more pissed at the reverend for filming the assault than at Tina for launching it.

"Well, I guess—ouch, ow, *hey*!—I guess the adrenaline's working."

She dropped her arms to her sides, literally snarling. "Josef Mengele puts on a gas mask and tells you he's pumping love gas? *And you believe him?* Are you on drugs?"

"The wrong ones. But the oxytocin's on the way."

Tina kicked me in the knee. "So why do they have gas masks on? They don't want the love?"

The fumes rose in slow, expanding circles.

I let in a staggered breath of almond-flavored vapor, expecting the worst. Instead, I crumpled against the wall, in the sudden grip of a wrenching, up-from-the-toes swoon. Suddenly I wanted to lick the color out of Tina's eyes. Longing was almost like a drug—and borderline unbearable enough to make me need one.

Tina glared. So I got the love and she got the hate. That would be an experiment. I pressed my hand over my chest like I was pledging allegiance but was testing to make sure I could still breathe.

"There's a second oxytocin receptor in the heart," I heard Mengele say.

I needed to kiss her so badly I didn't care if we were going to die. The need dragged me toward her, like a dog tugging on a leash. I stared at her mouth, recalling how Carlos described the mouths of men who died from carbon monoxide: like they were wearing cherry-red lipstick. The stuff didn't just kill you, it turned your corpse gay. I didn't care. I didn't care about anything. The love coursing through my veins crowded everything else out. Because there was no everything else. Or everything was love.

I know how this sounds. *Today.* But in that whirling moment, I had no thoughts at all. Some Big Bang had happened. I had been blasted apart and reassembled with delicious new ingredients. Gripped by the delirious, inchoate sensation that some obvious, beautiful, terrifyingly perfect thing had been missing all my life. And now it had been revealed. If I could just remember what it was . . .

The universe vibrated with happiness. All I had to do was let it. But buried under the cosmic bliss was the dim sensation that my past had been amputated. Fear was like a phantom limb that was just beginning to itch. Somehow, I knew that if I scratched, I would make it real.

Then I opened my eyes, and Tina's face was better than never dying.

We charged toward each other. *Yes!* I opened my aching arms. *Oh, God, thank you, yes!* Tina moved in to meet me. She raised her eyes. I parted my lips. She opened her mouth. "Oh, baby," I groaned. Tina clutched my face. Her fingers shot knee-wobbling pleasure rays straight to my heart.

She stared in my eyes. *"What the fuck is wrong with you?"*

I backed off, shattered. "What do you mean what's wrong? You don't feel it?" My voice degenerated to a desperate rasp. "The love?"

"The *what?*" Tina slapped at my tears like they were flies. "You fucking asshole!"

By now the cloud was floating up to our faces. We inhaled, as if by mutual consent, and breathed into each other's mouths. I wanted to sew myself to her back, like one of Mengele's demented twin experiments.

Then I began to choke. I could not tell dying from love.

Tina's words made puffs of vapor: "Son of a bitch!"

Her teeth ripped at my lips. My lungs needed her lungs. We kissed like people trying to kill each other with mouth-to-mouth resuscitation.

Suddenly—I had forgotten we were even *traveling*—the van swerved. The reverend slid sideways on the bench, slamming into Mengele as Tina and I crashed into a whorled metal wall.

I couldn't tell if the wailing siren came from inside my head or leaked in through the airtight gas van. Tina kept tearing at me. I tried to pin her arms. She fought by kissing harder. Then we swerved the other way. And—

BOOM!

Something hit us. Metal crunched but the walls held. The van was spinning. My head slammed the floor inside the almond gush of mist. A fire extinguisher fell out of its wall brace and clanked on the floor. I thought, *What was that for?* And crawled on top of my never-more-beautiful ex-wife.

For a long time, maybe years, Tina and I clung to each other. The van spun like a plate on a stick. I ended up underneath her. Tina, to my dizzy surprise, positioned herself with legs apart, producing her own batch of oxytocin. I felt her slide down onto me. *Grinding.* Then the van tipped over and floor became ceiling. The fire extinguisher sailed past my head, then clanged by me, bouncing the other direction and crashing into the whorled metal wall.

Stillness. The silence that only comes after a crash. Eyes closed, I waited for my cosmic bliss to reintroduce itself. I tried to stay positive, to be grateful I'd had the gift of knowing such a feeling existed. But I knew the truth: now I had the curse of knowing it was gone. Joy had become the phantom. As ever. And fear was real.

I slowly opened my eyes. Before me, the reverend lay still, face-down. Mengele, crawling slowly and muttering in German, was reaching for his mask. Then someone banged on the van door and he froze.

I heard voices. Gunshots, or a car backfiring. Or somebody firing back at a car. I rolled on top of Tina, done moving but still inside her. Carlos had not said if Mengele had bulletproofed the van when he customized it.

I was in the mood to take artillery for a woman I loved. Mengele pulled a gun from inside his hazmat suit. His hand shook, but a gun's a gun. Before I could go for it, Tina kicked it out of his hand without taking her lips off mine. She always had scary reflexes. *"Growing up,"* I suddenly remembered her saying, *"the family motto was 'Nobody moves, nobody gets hurt.' "* Somehow, in the crash, my amputated past had become reattached. Now I remembered everything.

The van door swung open, sucking out a whoosh of love mist. My vision was blurry. But my ears had stopped ringing for the first time since Zell brained me with his walker. I heard a cackle I recognized. White Bob Marley's. I blinked until I could see the head full of exploding-squid dreads. Rasta Jim, with a blue windbreaker with an FBI shield dangling on a chain around his neck. He took a whiff and backed off, keeping his eyes on Tina as she held on to my shoulder with one hand, tugged clothes on with the other. "Some people can party anywhere," he said, coughing into his hand.

"I wouldn't call it a party," I said, feeling weirdly compelled to defend my wife—or ex-wife's—honor. "More a command performance."

"Thank you, honey," said Tina.

Rasta Jim put his hands up, conciliatory. "Don't explain. I've been following you since the museum."

He opened the door wider. A Mexican vendor rolled up in his corn-on-the-cob cart and peeked in. A small crowd of curious faces pressed behind him, some munching carne asada, others eating pineapple on a stick. I recognized the cart. Jesus . . .

I'd thought we'd driven a hundred miles. But we were only on Avenue Sixty, about ten blocks from the pound, maybe a mile or two from the Southwest Museum, where I'd left my car a few thousand years ago.

"Baby," Tina whispered. I moved into her kiss, cells still humming with hormone-triggered empathy. I was astonished—and maybe ashamed—that I'd managed to forget myself in front of an audience. Let alone one that included a digital camera and Josef Mengele.

Mengele!

I swung back in time to hear the shot and see the bullet explode from the White Rasta's throat. In the back of his neck and out his Adam's apple. A through-and-through.

But I couldn't see the Angel of Death. Instead, expressionless as ever under his state-framed black eyeglasses, Bernstein stepped sideways into view, where Rasta Jim had just been shot. He worked his jaw at the sight of Tina. For a moment, affection for the neo-Nazi bloomed inside me. Despite the fact that he'd just killed a man I liked. Despite the fact that he had been with Tina two nights before. Clearly, not all of the oxytocin mist had left my system. I had to restrain myself from grabbing the Aryan killer in a bear hug. That oxytocin delivered the love.

"You didn't have to do that!" I cried.

"Do what?" Bernstein spoke quietly. "Do's over. We talkin' 'bout *done*. This is goin' down how it's gonna go down."

I spotted Mengele pinning himself to the side wall of the van, trying to hide by the door. No one would see him until they stepped onboard. His palsy had progressed to a steady fluttering. He was either pointing his gun at Tina or trying to swat flies.

I figured I could block him long enough to shove her out to safety. But before I did anything, another voice boomed into the van.

"Boychick, what did you do?" Harry Zell shambled up to Bernstein, grabbed his face by the cheeks and kissed him on the forehead. When he noticed me, he pointed and roared. "You! Did you think you could double-fuck Harry Zell?"

"What are you talking about? You wanted me to find out if this freak is Mengele? Like you didn't know? There's been a whole other movie running since you hired me, hasn't there, motherfucker?"

"You should know," said Zell. "You're starring in it."

"Enough!" Tina banged on the van wall. Whirling red and blue lights swept in and out of the open door. "You jerks want to stop measuring dicks? Somebody just put a fed in the ground, and his friends are here."

Zell hoisted his heavy bulk into the van, followed by a shirtless Bernstein. The Nazi-inked Jew started to close the door, but somebody pushed it open again. That's when I spotted the smaller figure, in mask and protective suit that hid his face, sitting very still on the bench. The reverend was slumped against it, bleeding from his middle.

Hazmat man said nothing. He remained still when an arm curled around my throat from behind and plunged in a syringe. It was oddly painless. I remember thinking, as soft black smoke began to fill my skull, *What is that, my thyroid? Mengele always goes for the glands.* I was almost grateful to go unconscious again. At least he didn't hit me on the head again. That wound was almost beginning to heal. And I still felt a lot of oxy-love.

The last thing I saw was a pair of little hands making a church and steeple.

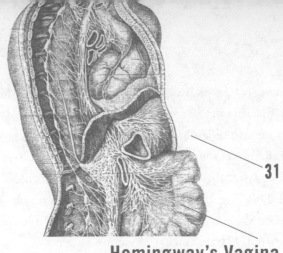

31

Hemingway's Vagina

In the baby dream, I stand on the platform, quirt slapping smartly off the tops of one polished boot. Steam billows from the guts of the train as it slows. The stench arrives before the cargo itself. An acrid air-bath of urine, rank sweat and feces infuses the clean wind from the forest with something secretly sweet. My eyes tear, not from that stink of confinement, nor from that pink-black nonstop meat smoke belching from the towers. From sheer joy.

I touch a manicured finger to the high starched collar of my uniform. Breathe. Feel the tingling in my groin. The sky looks ready to drip lead. My boots shine. I sniff the lavender water sprinkled on my collar.

Now the labored hissing slows. A final gasping blast escapes from the train's brakes. Nothing else will escape. I could kiss every battered slat in the freight car.

"Soldaten! Die Tore!"[1]

I clap once. Twice. The officers nearest, bull-necked blond boys, hop to. One snaps the lock off the sliding doors. The second wrestles with the handle, frozen in place. It gives with a violent *clack*.

---

1. "Guards! Doors!"

Before they slide the giant doors open, I can see, through the myriad ragged holes—metal clawed apart or chewed—shining eyes in the dark. Each car a rolling constellation of fear, full of germs with faces.

I raise my chin, legs apart, boots planted firmly on Reich-occupied earth. Ready to select. My favorite moment.

Except—is the God that does not exist taunting me?—except instead of men, women and children, the usual clutching families, there is nothing inside the train but babies. Babies. Their faces the faces of old men. Pain-suckled, wizened; giant, hollow eyes accusing. A mountain of babies topples and spills over the siding, onto the tracks, out to the platform itself. As each hideous infant hits the earth it begins to crawl toward me. Together, they form a single mewling, vicious mass. And yet—

The guards shout, as if nothing were out of order. *"Beeilt euch! Komm Schon!"*[2] As if this infant militia were the norm. The guards scream what they always scream. *"Bewegt eure dreckigen jüdische arsche!"*[3]

I step backward, appalled. Unable to take my eyes off those awful, obscene features. Old men's heads on naked infants whose genitalia, too, are fully grown. Organs the size of plucked chickens drag through dirty snow as they crawl in my direction.

I back away, swinging my quirt, to no avail. I kick, and the crunch of boot through skull stops nothing. I stomp and I stomp. There are so many, I cannot step. They are a moving carpet. I try but cannot wipe the smear of baby-face from under my sole, nor knock off the clumping brain and eye that clogs my boot heel. They surround me now. A tiny ragged fist grabs my pant leg. A second pinches.

"Hör auf!"

I unsnap my holster. Remove my Mauser. Point it at the crawling army.

---

2. "Move it! Come on, get out!"
3. "Move your filthy Jewish asses!"

"I'll shoot! I'll shoot! You think I won't!"

But babies are not men.

I fire. The first swollen head explodes. But what does death mean to a newborn? They are not afraid to die. It is useless. They are braver than men. The baby beside him does not shudder. Does not slow.

"Zuruck! Zuruck, ihr dreckigen giftzwerg!" [4]

My starched collar wilts. The sun leaks blood. Why do they hate me? You want to know the biggest serial killer in the world? It is life! The second we are born, life starts sharpening its claws. Life is there laughing.

"Americans!"

Suddenly I hear him.

"The Norse gods lived for eternity. But Americans don't care about racial purity—they want thinner thighs."

That wheedling voice penetrates my skull. The doctor is not in my dream—he is *here*.

———

I wake up annoyed—actually just *dreaming* I'm awake—and discover I am not the Seletor. I am a baby. And I am crying because something happened to me. A pain like teeth in my scrotum. A rat? Another feral tot?

"NO!"

I bolt upright. Or try to. I rise up half an inch, then stop, restrained by the fat leather strap across my chest and arms. I am flat on my back. On a gurney. Or no. *Worse.* An operating table. But—scarier than the pain—now there is no pain. There is no feeling at all.

I blink upward. The water stains and fluorescent lights are familiar. In drug class, I stared at the ceiling when I had nothing to say. It was

———

4. "Get back! Get back, you filthy poison dwarves!"

an old cop trick —it made you look thoughtful while a perp squirmed. Now *I* was the squirming party. Mengele's respect-craving old-man voice leaked into my ear like mercury. "If America wanted to keep from being overrun by immigrants, they'd sterilize them at the border. How? I have the solution. Radioactive benches. In the camp, we could do fifty at a time. I know; I invented the benches. Give the folks a form to fill out, a few bowls of chips, and by the time they list all their relatives and their favorite dinner, their ability to reproduce—to make what you call 'anchor babies'—has been zapped. Ten minutes, with no immediate side effects. In the beginning, true, there was some burning. Yes, *flames*. But I, Mengele, smoothed out the kinks!"

Jesus. I'd been dreaming I was *him*, dreaming that *he* was a baby—a baby *he* killed. Somehow it made sense when I was dreaming it. . . . Maybe I had some kind of oxytocin fallout.

I strained to see down the length of my body—and made out only white. My knees, apparently, were bent and spread and—this wasn't good!—I was in stirrups. Like a woman visiting her gynecologist. Tina used to say she never understood women who felt violated at their gynecologist. *"If that's being violated, I don't know what you call my daddy's moves. . . ."* But to feel violated you had to feel. And I felt nothing.

The worm of panic swelled to an electric eel in my chest. My toes tented the sheet high over my middle. I couldn't see under and I could barely see around. On either side of the Linen Curtain, I made out faces. I sensed, though their features blurred, that they were staring raptly, maybe with horror, at what I couldn't see. But why was everything a blur? I fought back waves of fear. A tsunami of worst-case scenarios. Beyond the mystery between my thighs, my eyes. I knew too much about Mengele. Now I wished I didn't. Wished I had thrown the mad old man out of my house when he blindsided me, ripped his phony pictures up and thrown them in his face. But it was too late. Because I knew: those on whom Mengele bestowed blue eyes he also left half-blind.

I rolled my head back, opened my mouth to scream. A hand clamped my mouth before I could. I recognized the texture. The scent. This missing divot under her thumb. Tina. But how? Why? Thankfully—or not—the more I blinked, the more my vision unblurred. The world looked more waxen than I remembered. More disturbing was the breeze that tickled my wishboned and elevated thighs. *Was someone touching me?* I tried to wriggle and reencountered my restraints. I still did not see Mengele. I heard him, on the other side of the sheet tent, but the flicker of the overhead fluorescents distracted me. Somehow I was confusing sound and light. Maybe my brain had been tampered with. Then I heard a pair of words and that made me forget my brain. At least I thought I heard them—and tried to scream them back against the palm on my mouth.

"Sex change!" The palm pressed hard, then softened.

Had it happened? Was it about to happen? Would I be out of surgery if I'd had a lop job?

I wondered if I had a vagina and thought of Hemingway. Not Papa, Gregory. *Gig.* His youngest son. Who had a sex change in Florida, when he was sixty, then got drunk by himself to celebrate and ended up dead in the Biscayne County women's jail. Ask not for whom the bell tolls. . . . Ask who surgically removed your bell.

"Turn on the TV, the first thing you see is a doctor selling a pill designed to make men bigger between their legs. Between their legs!"

Mengele's forced jocularity only made him sound more Teutonic and hectoring.

"You Americans and your size fixation. With your Extenze and your MaxiDerm. Let me tell you about *my* breakthrough, gentlemen. What I am about to tell you will revolutionize the penile implant industry."

He paused, and I could almost hear the noxious slurp of his tongue on the rogue hairs of his mustache. "Let me put it in terms you Americans will understand. It is not the length of the baseball bat—it is the size of the baseball balls!"

Whoever he was talking to was silent. I groaned. It wasn't bad enough I was strapped down with my legs up and my ass and package on view to an audience in San Quentin. The Angel of Death was *tummling*. Trying to make a joke. And he was tanking. His spiel sounded stiff and memorized, a parody, if it's possible—or even morally advisable—to parody a genocidal murderer.

"The size of baseballs!" Dr. Mengele repeated, doing his own little callback. "This is true!"

"Say what?" came a voice I recognized as Colfax. "I'm supposed to forget my cannon and get my ammo bag all swol?"

"You are not listening!" Now the doctor was angry. I hoped he didn't have a scalpel in his hand. "I myself conducted studies at Auschwitz and the women's high-security unit in Lexington, Kentucky."

"They closed that down in nineteen eighty-eight!" Was that the warden?

"I had nothing to do with that!" Mengele protested, getting right back on message. "What I am telling you can make all of you supermen! My work with anthropologic brain sensors reveals that the female is conditioned—in her primordial mind—to mate with the largest pair of testicles. The most *voluminous*. This is the discovery that can change the life of every man. Our species needs the pomegranate with the most seeds."

What had he done to me?

Every possibility burned like battery acid in my brain. I felt a dull thud somewhere between my legs. Had Josef Mengele numbed my privates and had his surgical way with them? Had he added or subtracted? Or had—*no, God!*—had he engineered one of his patented man-to-animal, animal-to-man transplants? Was I the before or the after?

"Mmmpphh!"

Tina clamped my mouth in warning. Why didn't she say something?

I tried to *feel* myself. *Nothing.* Out of nowhere, I remembered getting Novocain for the first time, when I was nine. How much I loved it. For hours after I got home from the dentist I stood at the mirror shooting staples into my gums, blithely spitting out blood and bone chips. Now I was elsewhere Novocained. Who knew what travesty Mengele had implanted for the amusement of his audience?

Maybe I was wrong about Zell and his prison docs. Maybe they were a cover—what he was after now was torture porn. Nazi science on parade. With me as unwilling stand-in for all the unwilling victims whose gruesome and brutal demise would have—had Harry Zell been magically on hand to film it—supplied the kind of next-level cable viewing jaded viewers were smacking their lips for now that jailhouse sodomy and medical procedurals no longer packed the impact they used to.

I worked my wrists till the skin burned in my restraints. Tried to squeeze a word past Tina's pressed-down palm. As far as I could tell she stood behind me. I rolled my eyes up to my forehead. I could just about catch the tip of her nose.

Thrilled as I was to find her up and functioning, it was disturbing in these circumstances. I could not imagine why she'd sign on for nurse duty with the doctor. But I knew her well enough to know she always had her reasons.

"At Auschwitz," Mengele remarked, "I experimented endlessly on ways to advance the master race." He chuckled like a man who practiced chuckling in front of a mirror. "Did all of the experiments achieve genetic perfection? *Nein!* But in science we have what we call the Law of Unintended Consequences. So, I confess to you, I discovered many, many secret methods for achieving cosmetic, eugenic and reproductive excellence by happy accident."

Not so happy, I thought grimly from my trussed-chicken perch, for those who accidentally found themselves in Building Number Ten. Imagine being five, lying on a pallet, full of candy after starving for weeks, listening to Mengele play Puccini while he decided if he was in the mood for inducing gangrene or extracting eyeballs. I wondered again about the man at Mengele's victim reunion in Jerusalem. Too ashamed to show his face after all those years. Not even to those—victims themselves—who would surely understand. At what depth of sadness could a human being no longer breathe? I didn't realize I was crying until Tina dabbed my eyes.

I have never been brave on purpose. There was still some back-wash of psychoactive swill sloshing around my system. Otherwise the shamefest of ending up as a naked lab monkey in the Joe Mengele show—the prospect of being his last victim—might have had me screaming like a little girl.

A piercing howl nearly blew me off the gurney. Followed by a doleful whimper and the enormous panting bulk of an Irish wolfhound being wheeled by on its flank. From my prone position, I could see that the trustee pushing the dog had traded prison blues for lime-green OR scrubs. The color nicely set off the CUT HERE tattooed on the back of his neck over a dotted line. Maybe he had the right idea.

When the dog yelped again I vomited in my mouth. Gulping back bile, I had a simple revelation: my pre–sex mutant existence was about to end. I wanted to rail and gnash my teeth. But how dare I obsess about *my* calamity and not the Mengele victims whose agonies preceded mine? The Holocaust lent their suffering dignity. Imbued it with inherent historical import and shattering profundity that spoke to all humanity. My death would have all the gravitas of a bum fight on YouTube. I was an idiot for ending up here. If my own life was any indication, it was no surprise that I would die idiotically. Ask any vulture; what's past is protein.

Apparently, every step I'd ever taken had been leading here: to the rolling display table of a celebrated Nazi sadist. What did it matter if I'd been gelded, gifted with a uterus or had the head of my penis surgically removed, sewn on and replaced with a chicken beak? I was a prop in Josef Mengele's pitch, rolled out to help him market himself as the go-to genital alteration, transplant and enhancement ace. Which, as far as I could tell, was how he intended to make a living until history decided to show up and offer him an apology.

I considered biting my tongue and spewing blood to get Tina's hand off my face. I knew Tina wouldn't let anything too extreme happen to me. But I really needed to double-check. I'd done too much reading. What wasn't documented history was fevered speculation: Mengele did not just operate on the body. To establish the mental inferiority of the lower races, he went for brains. He'd wanted at them since 1934, when the Canadian Wilder Penfield claimed to have ended epilepsy by cauterizing the nerve cluster that controlled seizures. There were side effects—ex-epileptics smelled burnt toast—but what did Mengele care? If you could stop fits then you could cause them too. Heaven.

As I thrashed in my straps, I tried to reassure myself. Tina was the toughest person I knew. There was no way the doctor could have intimidated her into collaboration. Unless, say, he'd gone into her frontal lobe and cauterized the synapse that governed free will? There were rumors of death camp zombies. Physical restraint had unchained my paranoia. What if, since the last time I'd seen her, he'd had at her cerebellum, surgically made her a slave? It was no secret that the CIA adapted Nazi techniques, along with Korean, in developing its MK-ULTRA mind-control program. If Tina had been turned into the Manchurian Nurse—

Then suddenly—*sensation*. A sleeve brushed my member. That meant I still had one—unless he'd rewired my nerves so that I just thought it was mine and not some master race science project. Had that wolfhound been . . . whole? *Fuck*. This was the kind of hell you couldn't pack for.

Mengele chose that moment to step around the gurney, give my bare foot a manly squeeze. His plastic gloves were splashed red. Besides that, the white lab coat and mike clipped under his collar made him look like a pharmacist in a TV commercial. He plucked a silver pen out of his lapel pocket with a studied flourish. He pulled it open until it was the length of a pointer. Then he poked at my exposed scrotum. When I juked, he nodded approvingly. "See how tender. Now look at this." He poked again. This time the silver pointer made a small thud. I felt a spongy pressure, but no pain.

"The discovery that women are by nature attracted to testicular girth is a welcome break for the species. Sperm production is a volume business. But look at our other option."

Again, he pointered me—but this time, for the life of me, I could not tell what he was poking. I had the wholly unique sensation of owning a body part I could not identify. I fought back nervous laughter.

"The procedure is simple." Mengele seemed almost to be singing. No doubt he was on his own chemical diet. Again, he thrust the pointer somewhere I couldn't see and felt with nervous uncertainty. He continued as though reading a cake recipe.

"Insert a small vibrating spring at the base of the prostate. Remove the two testicles and install a single, replaceable sperm tank, and it is possible to multiply the amount of vital essence twentyfold. More than ever the white race needs a bigger DNA delivery system. This was already priority number one during the Reich! Is it any different in America now, when the white race will soon be a minority in its own country?"

Sperm tank? I pictured some kind of dispenser, like liquid soap pumps in public toilets. But where was it? How big? Would it set off airport metal detectors? I imagined skulking through life as some kind of prototype, a two-legged semen warehouse. It was more grotesque than tragic. A "News of the Weird" item. Which only made it more shameful.

"When I started my research," Mengele hammered on, "the German birth rate had plummeted. It got so dire, the high command held 'sperm summits.' At the one I attended, in Munich, Himmler composed a directive requiring that whores who worked at the Kitty, the state bordello in Berlin, retrieve the used condoms from SS men and keep them on ice. Such high-grade race protein could not be wasted. At my suggestion, the condom drops were deposited into healthy Rhinemaidens, who were sent off for pampered pregnancies in *Liebensborn*—the baby factories Himmler set up to ensure that the cream of the species procreated."

By way of indicating the clot in the species' anti-cream, he clapped me on the ribs. "But of course, the last thing we want is more of this one. . . . The nation who understands the importance of genetic management is the nation that will prevail!"

"Fuck genetics—the money's in cosmetics!"

In the silence that followed I held my breath. This was the unmistakable, bullying voice of Harry Zell.

"No!" Mengele finally replied. "No, no, no! It is not either-or!" he went on forcefully, slapping the pointer down on my ribs to punctuate every word. It was like being whipped with a car antenna.

"Sure it is," said Zell, who'd apparently joined my medical practitioner at the operating table. He slapped me like a show pony under the sheet. "Look at the schlong on Rupert. Why don't you do a transplant?" I writhed harder against the straps, the burn on my skin a welcome distraction from my bigger predicament. "You get *that* bit of surgery on film, you'll put the whole penis extension racket out of business. Finally, every pinkie-dick in the country will know it's possible to go from Mini Cooper to Hummer. All they need is the cash for the operation—and they come to a prison of their choice and pick out the big boys we line up for them. Nothing a convict can do if the state decides he needs to be separated from his genitalia. All we do is invent a sex crime jacket, and we got his johnson in our pocket. Nine states still have castration on the books. Who's going to care if we take the dog and the pony?"

Mengele said nothing. I began to experience a throbbing ache that started in my perineum and radiated outward. My eyes met Tina's just as Zell asked the obvious. He stepped in front of Mengele, meeting the bottle-blond old man's perpetually entitled and indignant gaze. "You've done it before, right, Doc?"

Mengele slapped my thigh with his extendo-pen. It didn't hurt anymore.

I've tried to say this already. I know. But find the language to describe not being able to see the damage some madman has just made between your legs—to describe not knowing, for that matter, whether you were man, woman or sideshow. Tina must have seen. But she wasn't giving anything away. When I wrenched sideways I could see the shock-drunk faces of prison staff and civilians on hand. But what were they looking at? I felt like a nine-year-old Indian bride on her wedding day, eager but terrified to set eyes on the dread specter she was going to have to spend her life with.

"Come on, Doc," Zell badgered. "Spill. How many?"

"Penile transplants? No more than a hundred," Mengele replied acidly.

I could feel Zell looming. "Well *I've* never seen one, and I've seen everything. Plus," said Zell, giving my shaft a friendly pat, "we've got a doozy on our hands."

Mengele took time to work up his smarmiest sneer. "I've had a lifetime of medical experiments. Why should I share the final fruit of my research with you? Besides which, I have seen more impressive specimens."

"Where, on Woden?" Zell laughed at his own joke until he coughed. "*Huacchh!* Goddamn it, I am giving you an opportunity here. To a guy with a dinghy a speedboat's as good as a yacht."

Zell made a meal of pulling out a Cohiba and sniffing it, then slipping it back in its little cigar coffin and sliding it back in his pocket. Seeing that Mengele was on the hook, he took a big breath and blew it out slow as he spoke. "Folks have seen everything there is to see about prison. Market's saturated. Everybody's lookin' for new content. Can you imagine the money for *Lockdown, Auschwitz?* Well Harry Zell can. The networks would wet their drawers. Are you following? Prison docs are primo basic cable. Every network loves medical stuff. And Nazis are an evergreen. Harry Zell says why not marry 'em all?"

I craned my head up far enough to see him frame the words with his hands, as though picturing each one as he recited. *"Mengele: Death Camp Sex Monster or Medical Genius?* How hard would it be to find someone who wants a master race organ? Hell, I bet the warden here would like to trade up! You got two revenue streams—show business, for folks who want to want the procedure, and private party, for the guy who wants the goods."

Of all people Davey piped up, though I couldn't see where he was or if eating a prescription bottle had left any outward damage. "I'd say Major League, but not MVP. He's no Ron Jeremy."

"Howzabout you shut your ham trap? I'm tryin' to talk to swastika Joe here." Zell handled himself calmly, a man used to doing business in chaos. "What I'm saying, Doc, is we've got profit potential on two levels here: we make a bundle on the documentary of the procedure and make another bundle from the private party who wants to swing the Manny-bat. And by the way, Ron Jeremy is a Jew. If anybody wants to talk about Aryan supremacy in the schlong department."

Davey's voice quivered a little. "I was just sayin', it's not in the Hedgehog's bracket."

If the man had any concern that his son was so conversant with porn star equipment, he didn't show it. "What it is," Zell replied, "is the kind of cock a girl might want to take home to mother. Nothin' ostentatious. Not everybody's a showboat."

I wanted to scream. Now I knew the main event was intact. But for how long? And what about that sperm tank? The one silver lining was that, so far, Davey did not seem inclined to shoot me.

Mengele's pout was more reason to hate him. Could all genociders be this whiny? "There is something more than money. Is this something your people can comprehend? This is medical technology developed in the camp. On living subjects. If the public pays for it, then they are saying that they care less about the memory of those victims than they care about their own health and beauty. They are saying that I, Mengele, was justified in what I did. Because it can make them feel better."

With a flick of the wrist, Mengele freed my elevated legs and brought the tent between them down.

I saw the warden clearly, jotting something in his moleskin pad. Then Zell and Mengele both stepped in front of me, facing each other.

The doctor's stance was smug. "Think what they will give for the weight loss formulas."

Zell leaned back a little, folding his arms, so I could see the warden. He sat perfectly still, staring fixedly at whatever was going on between my thighs—which I was afraid to close for fear of hearing a clank or hitting plastic. The warden's eyes met mine, but not in a human way. He might as well have been looking at a truck tire.

The warden folded his hands and began building another church. While the old men argued, Tina worked on my wrist buckles. The Irish wolfhound—none of whose body parts, I prayed, I would have to wear home—had either succumbed or settled down for a nap. Hands loose, I could maneuver a little. But I nearly went blind when I caught a full eyeful of Zell. I'd already taken in his purple shirt. The rest of him was a revelation. Harry was decked out like he was going to the fights in 1960: that purple Banlon shirt, black and white houndstooth sports jacket, sharkskin slacks. His head and stomach were larger than I recalled. Maybe he'd heard about Dinah and ate to stuff his feelings.

I spotted Davey, holding the camera. I was still horrified about being filmed, but it was good to see he'd come into his own. Rincin was holding up the back wall, like always. I tried to get his attention. But Mengele went suddenly livid. Bellowing. "Don't shoot any of this! Stop the camera."

Davey waved his hand to calm him down. "No worries, Doc. Anything fucked now we can unfuck it later!"

"Attaboy!" Zell shot his son a thumbs-up and plopped down beside the warden. He nudged him with his elbow, chummy as a scout at a high school game. "We get a cock-swap on film, it'll be Swiss chalets for everybody."

I felt Tina's fingers undoing the leather strap that cinched my head. I stayed perfectly still.

Mengele steamed. "You do not understand! Everything I am going to demonstrate—the results are nearly instantaneous. No one but Josef Mengele can make that claim. Not like those quacks on TV. I am real. So *danke*. Thank you very much; I don't need surgery footage."

"Why not?"

"Because you could be making a case. Do you think I am stupid? I have lived with a price on my head for sixty years by trusting greedy Jews?"

"Hot damn!" said Zell, hopping out of his chair and wagging his finger. "I like you." He turned to the warden and shook his head. "Don't you like him? You hear 'Angel of Death,' you think the guy's gonna be rough around the edges. But, Doc, you got some kinda charm!"

Until then, I had not noticed how much Zell resembled Bill Clinton in his manner. Bill Clinton if he'd been shorter and older and jowlier and his name had been Clintstein. Zell held his hands up in mock surrender. "Okay, *uncle*! Harry gives! Tell me what you got."

"I told you. I've got weight loss, I've got—"

"Weight loss!" Zell grabbed the silver pointer out of Mengele's hand and broke it across his knee. "Are you mentally challenged? What's your plan? Book some cable time at three A.M. and do infomercials? That it? '*Sieg Heil, I'm Josef Mengele, you may know me from the*

Holocaust.' Talk about chutzpah!" Zell looked back at Davey. "Can you believe this mass-murdering schmuck?"

Davey just shrugged. His father swung around and faced Mengele again, hairy nostrils flaring.

"The Auschwitz Diet? Is that what I'm hearing here? *'Lose half your body weight in a week or we'll send you a full refund'*? Am I getting hot? *'Side effects may include the death of all your relatives. . . .'*"

Mengele waited patiently for him to finish. "You exaggerate. But why not? Until the National Academy of Sciences calls and offers me a prize, I have a viable commercial product. I have already applied and received patents under an alias."

Zell's voice lost some of its bluster. "Is it Alzheimer's? Is that it? I bet if you'd have cured that first, you wouldn't have ended up sounding like some demented old grifter. Well, woulda, coulda, shoulda, huh?"

"Accchh! Stop interrupting!" Mengele aimed his weirdly soft-skinned face back to the camera. If he started in on skin care, I might bite.

"Ready when you are," said Davey.

"Good!" Zell shouted. "Get this Nazi freak for posterity. I swear, it's like I'm lookin' at old man Hitler here. I mean, if the Führer, rest his soul, had lived. If he hadn't stuck cyanide up Eva's ass and made her shit in his mouth. Don't deny it—I've seen the OSS photos. What is it with you Germans? All the top Nazis—nothin' but a nest of pervs. And believe me, you, sir, do not disappoint."

"Are you through?" Mengele reconfigured his gap-toothed smile for the camera. "Faced with troublesome hip fat you cannot seem to lose? Too much stomach? Well, your worries are over! Apply Mengela-tin Fat-Burning Balm just once and see the results within one hour—or your money back! Nurse?"

And there was Tina! In her nurse's outfit. I rewound the movie of our Christian crack house visit. Vaguely remembered her stuffing something in her purse in the reverend's bedroom. She stepped on her mark and faced Davey with wholesome delight.

"I had twenty problem pounds after I had my baby. But then I discovered Mengelatin!"

Mengele held up a small brown jar with a shiny gold lid and handed it to her. Tina unscrewed the top and fingered a dollop of yellow goop. "I've watched pounds melt away in minutes. What's the secret?" Tina held the pretty jar up and tapped it. "It's all in here!"

Then, with no warning, she reached for me. She grabbed a handful of side-tire and rubbed some on. "Spread it just like butter wherever you want to lose."

Tina demonstrated. Her fingers felt wonderful—for half a second. After that the salve burned like Vicks VapoRub cut with hydrochloric acid. I let out a muffled groan.

"Just lie back," said Mengele, "and watch your love handles melt away!"

Tina rubbed in slow, lazy circles, unaffected by the chemicals that seemed to be eating through my top layer of skin.

Switching gears, Mengele gave my manhood a little pat. Tina'd spread a hand towel over it, so I still hadn't seen what I'd be wearing home. I imagined all the little heads Mengele must have patted this way. He was famously gentle with children—when he wasn't studying the effect of mercury injections in their livers or removing their spines while they were still breathing.

Tina beamed and tapped a few drops of brown fluid out of a bottle that looked like it once held soy sauce. Maybe it *was* soy sauce. Mengele broke out his best Jack Lemmon again. "Of course, there's one part of the anatomy where lots of fellas might like to put on a pound or two. For you gentlemen, there's my patented Mengelatin Mega-Men Formula. As I like to say, 'With M3, you can make normal big, big bigger—'"

"And," Tina cooed with a wink that hinted I might be playing in the Pee-Wee League, "turn a little man into a happy man."

The notion of my ex-bride as Vanna White to Mengele's Pat Sajak was not a welcome one. Before she had a chance to offer anybody the at-home game, Zell barged back up again, waving his arms. "Enough!" he shouted.

Mengele's face reddened. "Why not?" he hissed at Zell. "Have you ever seen that Jew fraud, Dr. Stein, selling MaxiDerm? 'I'm Dr. Stein, and I've spent my life investigating penile enhancement products.' The man *looks* like a penis. Unlike his sludge, mine actually works. I know. That's why I don't need the surgery. I did the experiments."

In spite of himself, Zell recoiled. "At Auschwitz? You're going to say, in a commercial, that you tested your product at Auschwitz?"

"No," said Mengele, "in an infomercial. And yes, I am only mentioning Auschwitz to you. For now. Now let me rehearse."

"You're too good for this," said Zell, trying another angle. "Set yourself apart. Go with the transplant!"

My tongue felt like a mitten.

Zell pointed at my towel. "Operate on him. After what this prick did to my son, he deserves it!"

Davey's partial face went red. "I'm fine, Dad. We were just tussling."

"Definition of FINE," Zell mocked. ' "Fucked-up, Insecure, Nervous and Emotional.' " I could see why his spawn had turned out to be such executive material. Zell leaned close. "Wanna know why my boy's got a freak show on his neck, Rupert?"

"Dad, please." Davey lowered his eyes. Even in my current predicament, I felt awful for him.

Zell jumped Davey instantly. "Oh, so now *you're* going to give me shit? How about we tell everybody your secret?"

Now it was the warden's turn to speak up. What was *he* getting out of all this? "Harry, I really think—"

"F you!" Zell screamed at him, facing away from me. I stared at the fluorescent lights, where a fat moth had either died or decided to warm its feet on one of the flickering tube lights. Sweat dribbled down my—I now realized—newly shaved chest.

"See," Zell thundered on, "his mother and I *say* he tried to commit suicide. 'Cause that sounds better. The truth is, he wanted to go around telling people he was an Iraq War vet. Thought he would meet girls. But he wanted to make it look good. So he decided to blow his ear off. *And missed*."

Zell pointed with both fingers and swept his hands toward the boy as though he were the pretty game-show spokesmodel. "Ladies and gentlemen, my boy Davey!" Then he raised his eyes to the ceiling, cursing. "Thank you, God. You *fuck*! Thank you for this one and the other genius."

This was too much. I gagged out the last of the rag in my mouth and shouted, "For Christ's sake, can I get up!"

"No!" said Mengele and Zell at once. Then the head of my penis popped out from under the towel and Zell whistled. "Reminds me of the Red Buttons gag. 'How can you can tell a Jewish dick from a gentile's? The Jew's wearin' the derby, the gentile's in a dunce cap.'"

"That's a good one," the warden called from his seat.

"I know a joke," Mengele announced. "What did the hog say to the butcher?" When there were no takers, he continued with a smile that could have poisoned wells. "You bring out the *wurst* in me!"

Crickets. In the silence that followed, I re-hated myself for not killing Mengele the moment I saw him and turned my wrath on Zell. "Why don't you just turn him in?"

"I will, goddamnit. But he ain't going anywhere. Why not make money off him first?"

Mengele smirked.

"Let him do some good for the Jews," Zell snarled, meeting Mengele's sneer with a fierce gaze of his own. "Ten years doing prison shows, a man makes contacts. I could shoot five episodes of Mengele being Mengele for more dough than he can make in twenty years hockin' jars of Lotta Cock. And FYI, Dr. Death, half goes to me, the other half to Hadassah. Yours truly buys a lot of trees in Israel. You don't believe me, ask my accountant."

"You're forgetting something," said Mengele calmly. "Either you help me out, or I go public. About everything. All the experiments. All the money you make and what you're really doing when you're pretending to make those *Lockdown* episodes."

"You don't know what you're talking about," Zell sniffed.

Mengele picked up a tape measure and slapped it in Tina's hand, snapping at her to measure my thigh, then put on the jelly. "In five minutes, he will burn off an inch. I want this documented."

Zell and Mengele glared in each other's faces. "Gonna rat me out, is that what you're saying? For *what*?"

Mengele's mustache chewing grew fevered. He sniffed in my direction. "You think junkie boy hasn't figured it out?"

"Relapse," I insisted lamely, though no one noticed.

"I am sick," Mengele railed, so angry his scalp glowed red through the peroxide buzz cut. "Sick of you getting me jobs, sick of me doing the shit work and you making the money. Sick of doing R&D for Big Pharma money. Tired of testing for epidermal burn after some VP from the Body Factory decides he wants to give sulfuric acid in acne cream a spin. Remember when the doctor from University of Pennsylvania got indicted at Holberg State Prison, for perfume tests? He was the only one as good as me. Try to find anybody else with my talent."

"Yak yak yak." Zell, I suspected, was not a well man. His outbursts were all followed by what looked like standing collapse. He slumped. Even his words sounded beat. "Your talent is torturing the incarcerated."

"Which in your country is called the War on Terror. Except it's really research and development. Just like it was in the camps." Mengele was just warming up. "The only difference is that we didn't hide the death. Or what it was worth. We knew. In your camps, well—as you might say, in your crass way, somebody's making big dough off Guantánamo. Your 'top Nazis' hide truth the same way they hide coffins."

I was about to tell Davey to film this, but Tina stepped back to me, smiling, and peeled off a pair of skin-tone lab gloves. No wonder she hadn't burned her fingers down to stumps. Facing me, she lifted the hem of her uniform, revealing nothing but leg, and dipped it in the water glass on Mengele's instrument table. Very slowly, she wiped off my love handle. "I like that you're not perfect," she whispered. "Guys with great bodies really just want to fuck themselves—or each other."

While these do-gooders debated, she discreetly freed everything that was still buckled, leaving the straps in place. I should have kept my mouth shut. There were other things to deal with—like the fact that I was wearing some kind of crinkling plastic diaper. And had no idea what had been implanted in my scrotum. I knew something happened. But even with my hands free I didn't have the nerve to look. Zell's rage had made me like him a little, so I decided to at least try to do my job.

"Hey, Doc," I said, "what are you really doing here?"

The question took him aback. "Why am I where? In this prison?"

"In this country."

"Great," said Zell, drumming his fingers on my leg. "Houdini gets loose and wants story time." He glared at Tina, who now fussed with the scalpel tray.

"We don't have all day," the warden seconded.

"Gee, Zell," I said. "I thought you wanted to ID the butcher, not bring him meat."

"Fuck you, Rupert. You're expendable."

I sat up and backhanded him. Zell rubbed his face and grinned. He seemed to appreciate it.

"See that," he sneered to Davey, "not everybody's afraid to hit an old man!"

His face-damaged son stared at his shoes. It made me want to smack Zell again. But Mengele didn't like to share the spotlight.

"Enough!" he wailed. "I was a *Hauptsturmführer.* You want to know how I got here? My skin!" He stepped to the surgical table and leaned down. "Go ahead, touch it! *Go ahead!*"

I passed. He offered a cheek to Tina, who also passed. Mengele treated us to a pout at the insult.

Side by side, the two stood out as alternate visions of seniorhood: Zell, padded and frizzy haired, a slack-jowled, loud-dressing seventy-something; Mengele, whip thin, wrinkle free and working that peroxide flattop in his nineties.

To my surprise, Zell got in Mengele's face, rehydrating it with furious sprays of spittle as he ranted. "All those experiments—the suffering, the death, the children—and you want to talk about cosmetics?"

"Six million died," Tina piped up, *"but boy, is my skin soft."* Everybody stared as if surprised that she was there. "It's fucking disgusting," she said. "You're both fucking disgusting."

Zell snorted. "Coming from you, that's funny. But I got somethin' funnier. I got a snitch tells me Dr. Eugenics here likes to look at himself naked in a full-length mirror. Likes to make little girls give him pony rides, too, if you know what I mean. You know what I could get if I had films of that?"

Mengele stiffened. He raised his chin, self-righteous, to show that he was above such concerns. "I will not address personal attacks. But I will defend my country. I have said it before: Germany did nothing your government did not advocate—we just advanced farther downfield. But I'm not a politician; I'm a scientist. I made breakthroughs! I have *notes.* And I'm tired of doing research so Lilly, Searle and Merck can get rich on my back! I discovered so-called Viagra in 'forty-three. Men were coming back from the front too shocked to copulate! We

called it *'Volks-steifer.'*[5] But where was I? Yes—look at my face! I have
the skin of a fourteen-year-old!"

"What'd you do with the rest of the body?" I asked. Mengele's
cover-girl complexion blotched with rage.

"The mockery! You know how I came to this country! I was a
pariah. But I was flown to America by a cosmetics baron. His wife
saw me sunning on the beach in São Paulo. I thought I was headed
for glamour. Instead, I get here, and next thing I know I'm testing
perfume on convicts."

Zell winked at Tina. "Who knew the Angel of Death was such a
crybaby?" Then he shouted over me to Mengele. "You don't get it. I
could sell raffle tickets for the chance to kill you. I know a dozen Israelis who'd be on the next thing smoking out of Tel Aviv. I could make
five million in ten minutes, and a hundred more than that when I sell
the DVD. Imagine being the man who captured Mengele!"

I tried to whisper to Tina. "Just tell me what's in my pants. Please!
Did he put something in there? I can't look."

But she just hushed me up. "You don't need to know," she said.
"But I'll explain later."

Meanwhile Mengele blabbered on with an old man's addled, defensive ardor. "As I was saying, I was brought over here by a very big
cosmetics man. The Jewish makeup king. One peek at the sheen
on my cheekbones and he knew I had something. But the man had
boundaries. 'Doktor Genius'—this is what he called me.

"He came all the way to Brazil. Helped me stage the drowning.
I told you, our Big Pharma, your Big Cosmetics—they had deals in
prisons all over the world. Soon they won't even need prisoners. The
Third World is wide open. There are two thousand kidney transplants
every year in Pakistan alone. And they're not going to Pakistanis. By
the way, how's that scrotum feeling?"

---

5. Roughly, "folk erection."

"I can't tell!" I blurted back in spite of myself. "What did you put in there?"

"Maybe an alarm clock. Maybe a kitten." Mengele tittered, his mirth oddly insincere, then stroked his own face. He made a show of stretching each taut, baby-smooth cheek and letting it go. "See the suppleness? The tone? You cannot fake tone."

On this note of self-satisfaction, he abruptly spun around, as if literally possessed by history. "From earliest memory," he ranted, "Bavarians have engaged in mass Jew burnings. When I was very young, every schoolbook in Bavaria had an engraving by Albrecht Dürer. *Aliquot Milia—The Several Thousand*. It showed a festival in Wurzburg, in twelve ninety-eight, where locals danced happily and set fire to Jews. There is nothing original about burning Jews. But only the rustic Germans burned them *methodically. Festively.*"

"Germany!" Zell spat. "It's not a country, it's some psychotic disease. Who puts people in ovens?"

Mengele smiled airily. "I don't remember bombing the camps."

"Enough!" The warden bulldogged between the quarreling men, using his chin as a wedge. He crooked a finger to the faithful Rincin, who still avoided my eyes. "Gentlemen," he snapped, his manner commanding. "I suggest you cease the cluster fuck. I've done good work with both of you. I say we just shoot the damn thing."

"Shoot what?" Zell locked his hands in his armpits to keep them from escaping and grabbing the warden around the neck.

"Harry, I *like* the products," said the warden. "I think there's something there." Rincin slowly broke away from the wall and drifted lazily over, like a shark with its first whiff of blood.

"Fuck that," said Zell. "We turn his ass in and make sure we got exclusive footage of the arrest, and we are *rich*. Richer than you think you're gonna get with that Christian porno you shot. And I'm not even going to bring up how you tried to cut me out and have that pimp, Reverend D, do your camera work. We'll just call that a misunderstanding."

"The reverend is a fine man," the warden said.

"For a pimp, he's a prince," Zell agreed. "So I guess the state won't mind when they find out you let him waltz in and out of your prison."

The warden reelevated his hefty chin in front of Zell, tilting his head slightly, as if calibrating the right angle to hit him with it. "Out of respect for you, Mr. Zell, I have always let your sons have . . . extra privileges."

"Yak yak. So respect me some more. Let me have Dr. Blond and we'll both be fartin' in silk." He threw his arm over the smaller man's shoulders. "You want, I could send a check to your charity of choice. I'm talking about one with a lot of zeros after it. There some kind of acromegaly club I can give to? I'm just asking, you know, with that tugboat you got for a jaw . . ."

"If anything should happen to me," Mengele informed Zell pleasantly, "the Simon Wiesenthal Center will certainly be informed about our special relationship. Warden, *I* consider you a friend—but it may look like you were keeping me here to line your pockets with money from experiments."

"To whom?" The warden didn't react, but he was man enough for proper grammar. "To whom will it look like that?"

"He's lying," said Zell. "Like he's lying about his skin care products. Probably skinned a baby to get that pretty puss. You forget who you're dealing with, Warden?"

The warden kept his gaze on Mengele, steelier than ever. "Tell me who's going to think I was lining my pockets."

"First, my near countryman, Schwarzeneggar," said Mengele, almost breezily. "What with the prison guards trying to get the governor recalled, your relationship with me may be the weapon he needs to break the union. I enjoy your Matt Drudge, your Rachel Maddow, so I would tell them. I think I would also like to tell *Newsweek,* the *New York Times* and Rupert Murdoch and maybe Steven Spielberg, the Shoah Jew. Believe me, I know how to create a Holocaust."

"I'm just a documentary filmmaker." Zell gave a self-deprecating shrug, struck suddenly modest. "Incarceration is the national pasttime. One out of a hundred Americans are in the can. That's why America loves prison shows. So ninety-nine schmucks who got bubkes can look at that one guy in a cage and feel superior."

"What about me? I feel like a piece of meat here!" I cried, surprising myself. "There are fourteen hundred other guys at Quentin. I'm not even a prisoner. Why me?"

"You signed a release," Zell said. "Remember?" To Tina, he added, "You know better than to help him, don't you, honey?"

Tina smiled sweetly. "I just work here."

Zell wanted to flirt, but I interrupted. "I thought it was a contract."

"You need to read all the shit in tiny print on the bottom."

"My judgment was cloudy. You hit me in the head with a walker."

"What I hear, that ain't what's causing the cloud." Zell rubbed a meaty hand over his face, then sniffed, as if checking for spoilage. "Here's the thing, ace: You can Q&A convicts all day. But you can't legally perform for-profit experiments on them on-screen. You, on the other hand, are not an inmate. You're an ex-cop. The same rights don't apply."

"Silence!" Mengele boasted such an authoritative yell, even Zell shut up. Mengele whirled his finger around over his head. "Cameraman, start again."

Poor Davey, the Iraq vet wannabe, sighed and hoisted his camera, a Panasonic HDX 9001. "In this vial," Mengele said, holding up a corked test tube, "I've got a custom-made stew of influenza bacillus and the common cold."

Zell deflated. "You're really going to do this?"

The doctor did not bother to answer. He bit the cork out, snatched a Q-tip from his surgery tray, stuck it in the tube and swabbed my mouth before I saw it coming.

The stuff soiled my tongue. I instantly started to sneeze. The bad kind of sneeze. The kind that explodes up from your toes and breaks stitches and shatters capillaries. The kind that ends with blood.

"Don't worry," Mengele said, back in Nazi pitchman mode. "One spritz of genetically enhanced immuno-spray, and I guarantee, you could French-kiss a leper and never catch a sniffle!"

The doctor tried to sound peppy. "Just watch how it stops the sneezing."

I sneezed again and all but shoved my quivering snout at him. He averted his head and spritzed. Seconds after a mist of antidote hit my nostrils, the sneezes ceased.

"Would you look at that!" Mengele beamed. "Would everybody look at that!"

I'd had enough. Hands and feet now free, I jackknifed forward and launched sideways off the table, knocking Zell into Tina before hitting the floor. "Well, hello!" he boomed. Tina punched him in the throat. "Aucchh. What the fuck! What the *fuck*!" Zell yammered, nursing his Adam's apple.

I jumped up, feeling ridiculous in my man diaper but more frightened about what kind of ornamental bag I had underneath. But Mengele was still pitching. "See that? Triple threat!" he declared gamely. "Lose weight! Grow bigger! Cure the common cold." But whatever lid the warden had been able to keep on the situation was about to blow off. The steel door to the conference room slammed open and banged off the wall like a gunshot. Bernstein burst in shirtless. His physique was yard perfect, his entire epidermis a celebration of Aryan supremacy in sword and thunderbolt, flaming swastika, fiery tits and Torahs. He looked ready to spontaneously combust.

"B-B-Bernie?" stammered Daddy Zell.

The max-inked Aryan Semite ignored his old man. Instead he raised an arm to salute Mengele. "Heil, A-hole! How's it feel to be yesterday's Nazi?"

The warden swung into action, shouting at Bernstein, "You best think about what you're doing, boy!"

"I'm done thinkin'," he said. "I been thinkin' my whole dumb life."

Mengele chewed his mustache frantically. But Zell, reassessing the situation, was ecstatic. "That's right, son. This is your chance to redeem yourself. Show the world Harry Zell's boy is not really some Nazi schmuck. He's a Jew."

The proud dad wiped his eyes, delirious. *Imploring.*

"Shoot him, the way we talked about. Be a Maccabee! Be the Jew who killed Mengele."

He clamped his hand over his heart, no doubt imagining future bragging rights, as hammy-sincere as Zero Mostel doing Tevye. "I can just imagine it!" he gushed. "*'That's my boy! That's my boy! He's the Jew who killed Mengele!'*"

Quickly, he swung his rye-bread-colored head my way. "And it better be Mengele."

"We're back to that?"

Zell grabbed my face and squeezed. "You know how much cash I've laid out for this?" He smiled at the warden. "In my business you need options."

Zell shoved me aside. Tina stepped next to me, transfixed. "Fathers and sons."

"Bernstein!" the warden shouted. "I am not your enemy. I am your friend. And as your friend I—"

"Shut the fuck up!" Bernstein's eyes were full of water. "You hear me? *Shut the fuck up!*"

I'd never been in a prison riot, let alone while wearing a diaper. I kept my back to the wall. Tina squeezed my arm and stared in disgusted wonder at Mengele. "If there were any justice, an army of ninety-year-old twins would pile in here with scalpels and syringes in their teeth. . . ."

Mengele eased himself away from the ALS brother. Bernstein

head-faked and Mengele stumbled backward, knocking a chair over.

"Now that's the kind of footage Harry Zell is after. That sings," said Zell as he exhorted his tattooed pride and joy. "You can do this, son. *You can do this!*"

I saw Rincin raise his shades to look at the warden, who waved a hand, palm down and flat, in response. *Easy, there . . .* But Bernstein wasn't listening. Almost lazily, he eased a homemade pig-sticker—sharpened screwdriver taped to sawed-off broom handle—out of his blues. He kept his arm straight, holding the weapon by its tip, alongside his leg.

Things went electric. I thought Zell was going to stroke out from screaming. "Kill him! Kill him! Kill him!" Over and over. And then, shifting to the son manning the camera, "You're getting this, Davey?"

Davey wasn't listening to Dad. He had the camera aimed at Bernstein. When he raised his eye from the viewfinder, I saw something pass between them.

"Do it!" Zell yelled at his son. "You putz, you schlemiel, what are you waiting for!"

Keeping his eyes on Mengele, Bernstein uncoiled fast and threw underhand.

Mengele didn't even duck. He knew. When the pig-sticker caught Zell in the throat the doctor let out a high-pitched giggle. It was the first time I'd heard him laugh.

Zell clutched his throat, trying to staunch the blood. It looked like he was trying to strangle himself. Maybe for raising such fine boys. From somewhere came the sound of a walkie-talkie. It was staticky. *"Ambulance." Crackle-crackle. "Copy that." Crackle-crackle-crackle.*

I had not even noticed the door behind us. With the private smile of the escape artist, Mengele backed toward it. Tina stuck out her foot and tripped him and he went down mustache-first, screaming, *"Scheiskopf!"*

While the doctor floundered, Davey, the warden, Rincin and Bernstein were out the front door. I didn't expect I'd be seeing them again. No doubt each man was off to an alibi.

I grabbed Mengele's ankles and dragged him to cover behind the "operating table". Zell had knocked it over when the blade hit him. If we crouched behind low enough nobody coming through the door would see us. At least not right away.

Mengele was remarkably light. But his skin, supple as it was, felt disturbingly hot and dry. Like a lizard plucked out of the sun. My need to do something did battle with the potential embarrassment of doing it diapered, packing God knows what underneath. Mengele wriggled. He freed a foot and kicked me in the head and I pinned him closer to the ground. I planted my hand over his mouth, repulsed by his wet lip-fur. I spotted the bloody screwdriver a few feet away. The thing had popped out of the sawed-off broom handle. I grabbed the raw metal and eyed the door.

Zell's body was sprawled on its back near the door. He'd tried to stagger out. His face betrayed more shame than pain. Beneath that, I thought I could decipher an expression of deep regret—now he wouldn't be able to film his own murder and sell it to the Discovery Channel.

I pressed the metal to the ancient man's taut neck. Took a deep breath, expecting to savor the moment I got to avenge my people. It should have been dramatic. Instead, all I saw were the eyes of a frail, freakishly smooth nonagenarian, gazing blankly into my own.

I raised the knife like I meant to stick him. Just to show him I could. The point was half an inch from his jugular when Tina's lips found my ear. "Kill him, you kill his secrets." She snatched Bernstein's weapon out of my hand. "You need clothes," she said, the words warm on my face.

"I know. . . . But we need to get him out of here."

From opposite sides, we peeked around the table at the scene around us. Somebody gets shanked in the joint, the incident response team is there before the paramedics. But not this time.

Shouts outside grew closer. His-and-hers paramedics rattled in with their gurney. We knew what we had to do. Mengele sensed it, too. I felt something wet on my knee, which I'd pressed on his leg to keep him pinned. I was hoping he'd be humiliated. But even pissing himself, he remained smug. No doubt it was master race pee, which made all the difference.

I grabbed the screwdriver, scooped a roll of tape from the doctor's spilled surgical tray and tossed it to Tina, who caught it one handed. We had everything we needed to tie up the paramedics and steal their uniforms. We just had to knock them out.

I dug a dozen ampoules of morphine out of the paramedics' kit. But it only took two to do the job. I wanted to knock them out, not give them an OD. The rest of the morphine I left. Let somebody else have a lucky day. I knew I'd be in throbbing pain later, when whatever he'd stuck me with to numb my nuggins wore off. Then again, if that happened, it would mean I was still alive. Life's a trade-off.

Zell's corpse farted when I rolled him over. Blood painted his hands and forearms from his doomed attempt to keep his life from gurgling out of his neck. The man didn't die pretty. But he died in battle. Kind of.

I checked his pockets, hoping for a cell phone, maybe a number on a pack of matches. Zell had to have a lot of connections. All I found was a flash-roll of hundreds and fifties. I stuffed a wad of bills in each paramedic's underwear—the one item Tina'd left on after I shot them up and she got their uniforms off. I hoped the cash would cover the cost of new ones. They looked like wholesome kids.

I dragged Zell's body off and covered him with the starched sheet I'd been staring at during my stint as Mengele's guinea pig. Done, I helped Tina pile the paramedics on top of him—girl, boy, boy—and jammed the sandwich behind the table.

Up to now we'd worked in silence, perfectly in sync, as if doping ambulance attendants and stealing their clothes was something we did recreationally.

Tina blew a bang off her forehead and looked at the stacked paramedics.

"That ought to give the staff something to talk about," she said.

"I don't know. It's a little creepy. That's twice in two days we've rearranged corpses into sex scenes."

"Sometimes you don't know you have a talent until you have to use it," she said. "It's nice to see you in pants."

"Well, I've still got that diaper thing underneath. Would you please tell me what I've got going on down there?"

"It's not important. You're still you—even if you're not, you know, symmetric." She cupped her breasts. "I'm not either, and it hasn't held me back. My life's still a dream come true."

"God, I fucking love you," I said, scrambling to arrange my outfit. I pulled the male medic's knit cap low and put on his tinted shades. We wheeled Mengele out under a sheet, so nobody would ask about the tape over his mouth.

Such was the magic of chaos. You could hide in the middle of it. Walk through like you belonged and keep on going. Just as Mengele had done, when the Americans arrested him in Czechoslovakian no-man's-land, in June 1945.

Even then his vanity saved him. SS men had their blood groups tattooed under their biceps, and all the Allies had time to do was check the prisoner's armpits for ink. But Mengele, the mama's boy, liked his own skin too much to scar it, so he'd never gotten the SS ID. Maybe he knew, even then, that eventually he would need to escape.

He gave the Americans in the internment camp his real name. And walked out a free monster, his lab notes under his arm. There is, I now understood, no better feeling than undeserved escape.

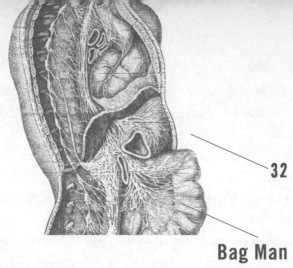

32

Bag Man

We rolled our quarry to the ambulance without being stopped. We both knew this was the easy part. When we made it to the gate, they'd no doubt want to check the cargo. If we made it that far.

Everybody we passed stared at the vehicle as if they'd never seen one before. "You think we should hit the siren?" I asked her.

"Not on the compound." Tina stared straight ahead. "Nobody'd get any sleep. Too much shit goes down at night."

"What, like guys stabbing each other in their cells?"

"No. Like heart attacks. Most guys have them between midnight and three. They hit the cherry top, but not the siren."

"How do you know that?"

"'San Quentin Emergency'—it was one of Zell's episodes."

"Of course."

"What can I say? I'm a sucker for jailhouse television. His plan was to start the APN."

"Don't tell me. The All Prison Network?"

"He was close to getting investors. The problem was he'd shot everything inside there was to shoot. He needed something nobody'd seen to get investors hot. You met the man. His big dream was 'San Quentin Nazi Sex Change.' To him, this was like dying and going to cable heaven."

"Well," I said, reaching back to make sure Mengele had a pulse, "one out of two isn't bad."

"Nice," said Tina. "All I'm saying is, along came Mengele. Dr. Peroxide opened up whole new possibilities."

"Except Zell got greedy, right?"

Tina shrugged. "It happens. Once he found out about the money the warden and Mengele were making from pharmacy companies, he wanted in. Zell was one of those guys who wants a finger in every pie—and if he can't get it he'll try to take your finger so you can't have any, either. When he saw the reverend waving a camera around, he figured the warden was gonna cut him out, start filming his own action. You think it's any accident Rev D got called to heaven early?"

"I don't know. Maybe it's no accident that Zell bought it either. And I'm still scratching my head about his wife."

I thought something flickered in Tina's eyes when I mentioned Dinah. Or not. "What's the mystery? Either he didn't care," she said, "or he'd already taken care of the situation. Zell had prison business. He wasn't about to leave Quentin and risk somebody stealing his turf. And from what I saw of the late, great Harry, he'd leave his mother's body on a slab if he thought he could make a buck selling her shoes."

"It is a loving family. You saw how he treated Davey. And I'm guessing half the reason his boy Bernstein went swasti-Hebe was to drive Daddy nuts."

"Unless Daddy wanted to open up the Aryan market and the kid was his in-house ambassador. A dime in Q and a batch of SS tats might be worth a little something on the other side."

Tina popped open the ambulance glove compartment, reached in and found a bottle of Advil. She opened it and gulped four dry and snapped the lid back on, disappointed. "Don't you hate when there's

Advil in the Advil?" She tossed the plastic bottle in the back. "Fuck! I just hope they don't find Zell's body before we get out of here."

"No!" I sat up suddenly—maybe forty yards from the gate—and it all clicked in. "We better hope they found him."

"*What?*"

"You think the warden's gonna risk taking us down if there's a chance Dr. Death here might testify? Word gets out about the money he made letting Mengele experiment on prisoners, he's going to be living in a cell instead of assigning them. Along with a few golf carts full of drug and cosmetic execs. Don't forget, thanks to the warden, the state of California's been supplying Mengele with the same thing the Nazis did."

"What's that?"

"A ready supply of expendable human beings. Only now he's not doing research for the good of the race. He's doing product testing for American business."

Up ahead of us, a lanky guard on an overhead bridge lowered a key in a blue bucket to a uniform below.

"That's your theory? The warden figures 'cause you're Jewish, you're going to take Mengele out and avenge your people?"

"Mengele's the one who wants revenge, sugar. He's had sixty years to stew about not getting the glory he deserves. If he gets a trial he's going to go Nuremberg on everybody from Coca-Cola to Gerber baby foods. He's waited all this time to name the biggest Nazi collaborator of all."

"Who's that?"

"The American government."

"Who the warden thinks sent you to kill Mengele."

"He wasn't that far off."

Tina stared as if I'd told her I was Napoleon. "Now you're scaring me. You're saying the government sent you to—"

"Not *me*. This fake Rastafarian named Jimmy. But he never got

the chance." I hadn't put it together before, but now it seemed obvious. "He said he was FBI. But I think Rasta man was on a mission of
his own."

"So why not give Mengele his day in court? Bring him to justice."

"Why give him the satisfaction? He's waited his whole life to spout
his side of reality."

"So what are you saying—we punch his ticket?"

"Fuck no! He probably thinks we were sent to kill him. I'd rather
let him live. I just need to figure a way to make him wish he was dead.
What do you give the man who kills everything?"

"I have a few ideas," said Tina.

"Me too. But it has to be something special."

"Like what?"

"I'm not sure yet. But it's going to work out."

Despite my upbeat prognostication, I stared out at the grounds
less like a tourist than a man contemplating his future home. Between
buildings, I caught a glimpse of the yard. The sight triggered the same
feeling it always did. I didn't see rapists, embezzlers or violent offenders. I saw the strolling cons and thought, *One bad move and there's me.*

I wanted to believe what I'd told Tina. That everything would
work out. But I had my doubts. Historical travesties aside, we were still
imposters in a stolen ambulance, kidnapping a prisoner taped to a gurney. We passed the old convict weeding his flowerbed, and I waved.
Now the roses looked dead.

Finally, we rolled up within three vehicles of the gate. The driver
of a DOC truck in front of us waved us by, and then it was two. Tina
slipped her hand over mine on the seat. The imminence of possible
arrest got her talking.

"Listen," she blurted, knuckles white on the wheel, "I saw how
you left a bunch of morphine back there. If we make it out of this,
maybe we can both, you know, start clean . . ."

"I always *start* clean, it's where I end up that things get messy. As you know. And I'm still wondering what that maniac stuck inside me. Whatever it was, it feels a little inflamed."

Tina held her mud.

"It was the Irish wolfhound, wasn't it? Just say it: 'Manny, you've got a dog ball.' I can handle the truth."

"Can we stop talking about you?" she said. "I'm serious here. If we make it out—"

"Don't," I said, touching her mouth. Those lips I wanted to eat. "Plans are bad luck." Mengele picked that moment to start wriggling under the sheet. I turned and smacked his head. "Stop that, goddamn it!"

Tina pulled up to the guard booth. A beefy black guard checked us out through the window. Then picked up the phone.

"I'm gonna gun it," Tina said.

"No! You do that, there's gonna be a traffic jam. And all the cars'll have cherries on top."

Tina kept her face frozen forward, staring into middle distance straight ahead. But I saw the smile she was keeping under ice. "I love when you talk like you're in a bad movie."

"Nerves," I said. "Some guys sweat, I go direct-to-video."

The longer the guard stayed on the phone, the more I squirmed. Finally I couldn't take it anymore. I told her to jump. "As soon as you're out, *I'll* fucking gun it," I said, keeping my voice low. "You disappear."

Tina gasped and put her hand on her chest. "You'd do that?"

Before I could answer, the beefy guard put down one phone and picked up another one. Then he ran out of the booth, waving his arm like a third base coach telling a runner to slide. *"Go go go!"* I shouted.

"What?"

"Just do it!" I yelled, jamming my foot down over Tina's on the gas. We plowed past the man so fast he had to jump out of the way. "Hit the siren."

Seconds later, we both remembered to breathe.

"Jesus Christ!" Tina cried. "Jesus fucking junkie Christ!"

She started laughing. Then I did. Nothing was funny. It was primal relief. Tina took the small-town curves at sixty, shouting, "I can't believe this!"

"Me neither!" I shouted back. "I feel like the hangman had his noose around my neck, then crapped his pants and fell off the scaffold."

"That's so poetic."

Without slowing down, she lurched across the seat to grab my hand. The ambulance bounced over a curb and clipped a mailbox, nearly pancaking a schnauzer and its blue-haired owner, who'd bent to scoop its droppings in a plastic bag. She saw us howling and dropped the leash.

Tina shrieked, "What just happened?"

"I think we got a message from the warden," I said, "and you almost killed a senior citizen's reason for living."

I stuck my head out the window, craning backward, to make sure puppy and Grandma were okay. Tina snaked her hand between my legs.

"'The loins,'" she sighed breathily, "'the place of the Last Judgment.'"

"Nick Cave?"

"William Blake."

"Either way."

A garbage truck pulled out of nowhere. Tina swerved, going full stunt driver. We squealed into a cul de sac of clapboard houses and scared a posse of skater kids, barely missing the nose of a speedboat poking out of a driveway. The tires screamed like they'd just seen their parents die. The ambulance spun a full 180, burning tread until the asphalt smoked. We ended up facing the wrong way down the one-way street we'd just careened off of.

The siren was still blaring. Families poured out of their houses to see who had the emergency. One workadaddy, waxing his pickup in a garage opposite, threw down the rag and ran over, Glock in hand.

"Gun!" I shouted.

Tina slammed back into drive and floored it. A woman in curlers flew out her front door with a shotgun. As she peeled out Tina pounded the wheel and shouted. "Shooting at an ambulance? What's wrong with these people?"

"Paranoid," I shouted back. "It's that 'San Quentin' on the side in big letters," I said. "They think we escaped. Neighborhood Watch probably has Stinger missiles."

She cut left through a church parking lot. "I don't want to find out. Is the old freak all right?"

I pulled back the sheet. Mengele eyed me wildly, nostrils flared over mustache and gaffer's tape.

"He's fine," I said. "Right, Herr Doktor?"

I gave his mustache a tweak. He flinched. But seeing him so helpless, I was beginning to understand. You really *could* do anything to a man if he wasn't human. I pulled the sheet back up over his head, checked on his straps, and fought back the desire to hit him with a tire iron before I clambered back up front.

"You know where you're going?"

Tina chewed her thumb. "I need cigarettes."

"Now?" I glanced back at Mengele.

"Yes. Now. There's a Seven-Eleven two blocks up. Is there a problem?"

I threw up my hands. "Problem? God no! Just because we're driving a hot ambulance with the Butcher of Auschwitz in it, that doesn't mean there's a fucking *problem*."

Tina glared and plowed through traffic.

Amazing the respect you get in an ambulance. The way cars skittered to the side, like they were afraid we were going to hit them, made me want to. "Adrenaline *is* a great drug," I shouted in Mengele's direction.

We spotted the 7-Eleven and Tina swung the ambulance past a gaggle of teens cadging beer money in the parking lot.

"Wait here," I said, scattering the boys as I jumped out and ran inside. The turbaned manager backed away from the counter when he saw me. "You call 911?" I barked at him.

"No, sir! I never—"

"Goddamn it! You think we don't have real emergencies? That's a hundred-dollar fine!"

"But, sir, I—"

"Never mind. Give me a pack of Newports. No, make it a carton."

I still had the paramedic's tinted shades on but made sure to keep my hat low and my face angled away from the surveillance camera.

I saw that the 7-Eleven gang had gathered round the ambulance. One of them, a tall boy in a sideways Raiders cap, was leaning in Tina's window. *Perfect.*

The turbaned clerk rushed back with the carton and asked if I wanted a bag.

"Just matches."

He placed the cigarettes on the counter and hesitated. "Sir, that fine . . . If you could—"

"If I could what? Take a carton of cigarettes so you won't have to pay the money? *Baksheesh?* Is that what we're talking about here?

"No! Sir, I was only asking if—"

I cut him off. "That's not how we do things in America, sahib. But just this once."

The manager looked horrified. I might as well have spit in his face and accused his mother of killing cows and fucking Gunga Din. I felt horrible. "Hey, just messin' with you," I said lamely, peeling a pair of C-notes from the wad I'd taken off Zell. Most I'd slipped to the paramedics, but a man has needs. I slapped the bills on the counter and grabbed a Slim Jim and a pack of Dentyne. "These too. Keep the change. Use it to buy a handgun and get rid of those hoodlums out front. Look at them! It's not fair to respectable people."

He took a second, but the manager smiled cautiously and I smiled back. Then we both laughed, shook hands. That was a good moment.

"Sorry for being an asshole," I said.

"Is America," he said. I knew what he meant.

"What was that about?" I asked, back in the ambulance.

"What was what about?"

"Your little confab with the local ne'er-do-wells."

"We were just chatting. Driving an ambulance looks like a pretty cool gig to a sixteen-year-old. They wanted to know how you get to be a paramedic."

"Really? So what'd you tell them?"

"Study hard and stay in school."

"Are you serious?"

Roaring through traffic had started to feel normal. Traffic parted like the proverbial Red Sea. Tina kept turning to scream at me and I kept yelling at her to keep her eyes on the wheel. She was the only woman I knew who liked car fights.

"Get off my back, Manny. You don't know what I've been through."

"What *you've* been through? I'm lucky I'm not gelded and missing my kidneys. And you still won't tell me what's in my scrotum."

"It's smaller than a bread box."

"Great. Thanks. Wait till you wake up with a joke ovary."

"Fuck you! Do you think I *liked* being there, playing nurse to that bastard? He didn't exactly have a steady hand when he was holding the scalpel. If I hadn't taken over you'd be worrying about a lot more than your left ball."

"Wait! You took over the scalpel?"

"You can thank me later," said Tina.

The ambulance swerved and a man in a wife beater dove for the curb. Tina cheered up. "The thing about you, Manny, all you ever think about is yourself."

"Not true. Since I saw your naked ass frolicking outside with your Aryan love buddy, I've spent a lot of time thinking about you. More time than I want, to tell you the truth. I mean, Bernstein, for Christ's sake!"

"You're not going to let that go, are you?"

"Oh, fuck it."

I wanted to roll down the window, let the breeze slap me across the face. But I was so pissed I grabbed the handle and ripped the window panel out of the door. Tina burst out laughing again.

"It was loose already," I said.

By now she was smacking her leg and pleading. "Stop. . . . Oh, God! I'm going to pee myself!"

I was furious. Mostly because *she* wasn't furious. But the sight of Tina laughing so hard made me start to laugh. At least it sounded like laughing.

Minutes later, siren killed, we bumped the wrong way over a speed bump marked NO ENTRY into the gravel off-street parking lot behind the Homeaway Motel. Tina nosed the ambulance into a spot in the corner under a balcony.

"I'm in two ten."

"Where's your car?"

"Right beside us."

Sure enough, there it was.

"I forgot you drive that fucking Prius! My plan was to stick Beppo in the trunk till we figured out what to do with him."

"Don't worry, it's bigger than it looks."

"Fine."

She killed the engine and I scoped out the motel. It was Motel 6 without the elegance. An Escalade took up two spots in the corner. The rest of the cars looked like their owners might have lived in them.

"Even if we can squeeze him in," I said, "I'm worried about somebody seeing an ambulance in a motel parking lot and calling the cops."

Tina grabbed her Newports. "Trust me, baby. Nobody here calls the cops."

I checked the place out again. Amazing what they can do with cinder block and rust. "Well," I said, "they're not leaving the curtains open, that's for sure. What is it, a shooting gallery?"

"Among other things. Though the fiends I've seen look pretty cranked out. Mostly, the clientele's all baby mamas and families visiting the prison, or illegals staying twenty to a room, working the pickup landscaping crews. The last thing any of 'em's gonna do is call the *policía*."

I eyed the corners. "No surveillance camera?"

"Funnily enough, when I checked in, the lady in the office told me some tweaker stole it the night before. Wonder how much crystal that buys you?"

"Maybe they just wanted the video. I'd sure want the tape of *us*. Kidnapping, driving a stolen ambulance, impersonating a paramedic . . . How many felonies can you commit in a parking lot without actually killing somebody?"

"Impersonating a paramedic's a felony?"

"I don't know. Maybe that one gets you community service. Give me a hand."

I pulled the sheet off and met Mengele's eyes, pink rimmed and hateful. Sometimes he looked old, sometimes he looked like he'd had his skin pressed. "Help me put him in the front seat."

"Why?"

"So he can get out the passenger door. Just in case. If anybody's watching, it looks a little less weird than taking his body off the gurney and throwing it in the trunk. Anything in your room have sentimental value?"

"Not really. And I registered with a fake name."

"So you won't mind if we just split?"

"Well, I would have liked the little soaps and shampoos."

Tina looked so beautiful I wanted to take a picture of her face and candy it. She raised her eyes from me to the balcony, letting one long finger slide across her parted lips. "We could hang out for a couple minutes. . . . There's something so nasty about cheap motels."

"Yeah, there is. . . ."

I let my mind drift for a second, then shook my head like a man trying to get bees out of his ears. "*No!* Why are you doing this?"

"Doing what?"

"Come on, Tina. I know how you're wired. If it's dangerous, irrational and potentially life threatening, it turns you on."

"You make me sound like Evel Knievel."

"Really? Did he enjoy pretend anonymous sex with his ex in hot-sheet motels?"

"'Evil,'" she intoned, "'is screwing strangers after cocktail parties.' Lawrence Ferlinghetti."

"I never get invited to cocktail parties. Why do you like to pretend I'm a stranger? You did that last time we were in a motel."

"Don't ask. It'll ruin the mystery. Details, details. Let's go."

———————

Once Mengele was in the front seat, Tina opened the passenger door. I eased him out gently, carrying him the way you would a fragile relative. Tina snapped the filter off a Newport, started to toss it, then put it in her pocket. The cop in me appreciated a perp who knew how to hide her tracks.

"What happens," she asked, "when they find the ambulance?"

"It doesn't matter. I guarantee the warden's got friends in local law enforcement. If he wanted to get us, we'd be got. We're more dangerous caught and talking than we are on the lam."

Curtains parted in the room across from us. A blinking ghost appeared and quickly closed them again.

"On second thought," I said, "even people who don't call the police might call the police if they see us stuffing a body in a trunk. Give 'em something to bargain with next time they get popped."

I tapped Mengele on his head, because I could. "For all we know the fucking Mossad was closing in. Or the Nakam. We're probably doing the old bastard a favor."

"What's the Nakam?"

"It means 'revenge' in Hebrew. They were vengeance squads. After the war, a bunch of death camp survivors got together to avenge the six million. They caught up with a couple thousand unpunished Nazi bigwigs. Killed them straight out. They even planned to put arsenic in the Munich water supply."

Tina stopped the flame halfway to her cigarette. "Did they do it?"

"The arsenic? No. But they did other stuff. There was an internment camp outside Nuremberg, full of SS men, and the Nakam managed to sneak in and poison the bread. A thousand Nazi POWs died."

Tina was impressed. "I had no idea Jews did that."

"Neither did the POWs. We're full of surprises," I said. The curtain parted again, then closed just as fast. "Now come on, we gotta move. The tweaker probably thinks we're coming for them next. Grab the blanket so I can wrap him up."

My ex-wife's eyes glazed over, the way they did when lust hit. She leaned over and bit my neck. "Nothing hotter than a take-charge guy."

"Just grab the fucking blanket."

"Wait—does the Nakam still exist?"

"Nobody knows."

"Wow!" Tina stood there holding the ambulance blanket. "That is *unbelievable.* . . ."

"Seems pretty believable to me."

I grabbed the blanket out of her hands and threw it over Mengele's shoulders, wrapping it high enough to hide the tape on his mouth.

I positioned Mengele more or less upright in the backseat of the Prius. Tina buckled him in, then got in back too and pulled out a nail file to press into his ear while I drove.

"Do you think the freak heard you talking about the Nakam?"

"I hope so," I said, idling at a red. By then I wasn't thinking about survivor vengeance. I was thinking about my own. But the drive to wreak frontier justice did battle with another mutant urge: to go back to San Quentin.

I checked the dashboard clock at a red light and swallowed hard. "It's twenty to one."

"So what?"

"I could still make it to class."

The red light went to green but we didn't move.

A car behind us honked. I inched forward.

"I don't understand," said Tina. "We barely made it out of there. Why the fuck would you go back?"

"I don't know," I said. "Maybe it's genetic. Some cross-generational misfiring synapse."

In the rearview, I saw the knowing crinkle form around Mengele's light-sucking obsidian eyes. I drove carefully, just under the speed limit. Tina listened the way you would to a singing dog.

"You want to explain?"

"After my great-grandfather made it out, in nineteen thirty-seven, he saved enough to bring his two sisters from Berlin to Morgantown,

West Virginia. Bessie and Essie. They were very cosmopolitan. When they saw the neighbors frying squirrel, they took the first boat back."

We made it another block before Tina spoke. "It's not so bad fried and battered. So what are you saying here?"

"I'm saying maybe I take after my great-aunts. Maybe I've got the gene that makes you go back—after you get out."

"It doesn't sound like a gene issue. It sounds like a squirrel issue."

Mengele's head had fallen to his chest. But his shoulders seemed to be riding up and down. I had the distinct feeling he was laughing at me. "That's the thing," I said, trying not to obsess about how much I was amusing the butcher next to me. "Once they went back to Berlin, the sisters wrote a letter to my great-grandfather, thanking him for everything and explaining the real reason why they went back."

"It wasn't the squirrel legs?"

"It was partly fried squirrel," I said, "partly not wanting friends and family left behind to think they didn't care."

"So what happened to them?"

"Auschwitz."

I glanced back at Mengele—considered slitting his throat—then willed my eyes back to the road and tried explaining my theory to Tina: I didn't really know if irrational, guilt-driven impulses could be passed from generation to generation. But how else to account for the soul-deep tug I felt to go back to Quentin, in spite of barely making it out, to check on my drug class guys? To show them I was *there* for them?

"You mean show them you're a fucking idiot," said Tina. "If any of those convicts found out you showed back up, after what you pulled off, they'd lose whatever faith they had in you." She reached forward and grazed a menthol-scented finger along my cheekbone. "You know this isn't about them, Mr. Guilty. It's about all the people you didn't show up for."

The finger drifted slowly down to my mouth. I could taste the sour tobacco under the minty-fresh menthol. Tina whispered in my ear. "You want to do something good for mankind? Your opportunity is riding back here."

I caught a red light, and we both swung around to steal a peek at our passenger. Mengele snored softly, a little spit-bubble wobbling on his lips.

"Look at him," said Tina. "Sleeping like a baby on Valium."

"When he's asleep he looks his age."

"Manny!" Tina snapped, loud enough to pop the old man's bubble. "Why does *he* get to sleep?"

"You're right," I said. "You are so fucking right."

The light changed. I spotted a Wal-Mart, cut across two lanes and aimed the Prius at it. It was the first time in my life I was happy to see a Wal-Mart. Tina gazed at me with real concern.

"Manny, where the hell are you going?"

"If I don't get out of this car, I might do something I regret."

"But you hate Wal-Mart."

"I need a new shirt and different shoes." I tore onto the lot and pulled into the first spot I found, beside a Winnebago. Just the sight of an RV brought back the stench of my Quentin digs. Mengele was still snoring, still spit-bubbling. My gorge started heading north. I smacked the doctor's knee. He jerked upright.

I killed the engine. A trio of largish women in leotards passed in front of us, and I saw Mengele's eyes go wide. Tina grabbed my shoulder and turned me toward her. "Now what? What's going on inside your head?"

"Don't ask me. I just work here." The truth was, I could pass on the morphine. The drug I was addicted to was Tina. And I did not want to get strung out again if the supply was going to disappear.

I had to wonder, not for the first time, if my whole marriage had been the setup for a crime: suicide by wife.

"When's the last time you ate, baby?"

"I'm not hypoglycemic," I said. "It's just, not strangling him is fucking with me."

"I feel the same," she said. For a moment we both studied our freight. "Have you seen the way he looks at fat women?"

"His mother was obese."

"Figures." She turned to Mengele and yelled in his ear. "Free mustache rides for fatties, huh, Master Racist?" She slapped him across the face. Mengele didn't flinch—but I did.

Here it fucking comes, I thought. She tipped a Newport out of the pack, cracked off the menthol filter and delivered it to her mouth.

"Go do what you have to do," she said, lighting up. "But if I'm going to be sitting here while you step into Wal-Mart, I want this *thing* in the trunk. Otherwise he'll have holes in him when you come back. Then if we change our minds, we won't be able to return him." She turned and blew smoke in Mengele's face. Despite the tape over his hands and mouth, he took this as calmly as he'd taken the slap.

Tina took another hit of menthol, working herself up. "The more I think about what he did—the babies, the twins, the dwarves, the injections, the sex torture . . ." She took one more puff and exhaled. "The surgeries, the probes, the poisoning, the sick, sadistic insanity disguised as *experiments* . . . the less I can remember why we haven't killed him already."

"The dead don't suffer," I said, popping the trunk.

"The living do," she said, lunging for him with her lit cigarette.

I grabbed her hand before she could burn him. "You don't want to do that, baby. Just wrap the blanket over his face and give me a hand."

We waited until there were no Wal-Marters in the immediate vicinity, then hauled Mengele out of the backseat and squeezed him over the spare tire in the trunk. "He really stinks," said Tina, averting her nose.

"He wet himself at Quentin."

"Who doesn't?"

Tina threw her cigarette on the asphalt and stomped it. We took a last look at this man who'd shown the world what men are capable of. Then Tina slammed the trunk.

"Thanks for stopping me just now." She kissed me on the mouth and shuddered. "I have to admit, there is *something* about treating people like they're subhuman. . . ."

"That's why people have personal assistants. Wish me luck in the menswear aisle."

Joining the other Americans on their way into Sam Walton's retail heaven, I willed myself not to look back.

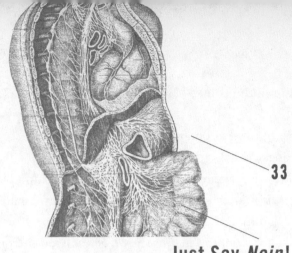

33

Just Say *Nein*!

My new flannel shirt made me feel like the Brawny paper towel man. Plus it itched. And my Husky Dog work boots squeaked. I'd thought about grabbing new jeans, but fear of dealing with whatever was throbbing inside my diaper prevented me. *Something* had happened. I just didn't want to know what. Not *yet*. I'd managed to pee without looking, so I put off the big surprise until later. My swollen scrotum was still tender but, mysteriously, not in pain. Not too much, anyway, provided I juked my leg to the right when I walked, as though semibowlegged. If there was such a thing.

I was so busy itching and juking, I didn't the see the smiling fellow in Bermudas standing in front of me when I stepped out of the Wal-Mart dressing room.

"Hey there, bunky."

I passed right by the face but recognized the voice. "Officer Rincin?"

"The very one," he said.

Without his brown corrections officer uniform, Rincin might have been any brush-mustached barbecue dad out for a bag of briquettes and extra buns. Above the screaming pink and green Bermudas, he wore one of those I'M WITH STUPID T-shirts popular twenty years ago. Below, he sported black Banlon socks with black tie shoes. I noticed the freshly waxed sheen of his calves and decided not to comment.

"Didn't recognize you without your uniform," I said instead. "So where's Stupid?"

"Left her at home," he said, "but I brought this for you."

He slid his hand under the T-shirt and I grabbed his wrist.

"Whatever you're pulling out, pull it out real slow."

"Fine instincts." Rincin nodded approvingly and let me ease his hand out by the wrist. "But technically, corrections officers cannot carry arms off duty, if that's what you're worried about."

"What I'm worried about," I said, "is why you'd follow me to Wal-Mart and stand by my dressing room."

"I guess you wouldn't believe it if I said I missed you."

"Rincin," I said, "you're a funny guy. But right now my shirt itches, I got some kind of ball situation, and you're standing between me and the outside of Wal-Mart. Just tell me what the fuck you're doing. That fucking grin of yours is starting to freak me out."

"Bell's palsy," he said. "Nobody believes me, but it's true."

What did it cost to tell a lie and make somebody happy? "I believe you," I said.

"Great. Let go and I'll show you what I got."

I did, and he did, plucking a folded-over manila envelope from the waist of his shorts. I quickly plunged the thing under my flannel shirt.

"This isn't going to explode, is it?"

"It's photos," said Rincin, the smile half-disappearing from his face for the first time. "You have to know, there are things that go on in there. . . ."

"You don't have to tell *me*," I reminded him.

"No, I do," he said, " 'cause once you showed up, there were more of them."

"What's that supposed to mean?"

"Well, Bernstein hung himself. Heard it took two belts, too. That's one AB had a neck like an elephant leg. And of course you were there when his daddy died."

Another dead Zell. Were they all my fault? My mouth was so dry, talking was like rubbing my tongue over rough concrete. "They let Davey go down to the funeral? Jews put the body in the ground the next day."

"Davey's not going anywhere," Rincin said. "He nutted up. They got him up in the dink ward, pumped full of Haldol. I don't think Davey's ever comin' back."

By now his grin had fully returned. A mother and back-to-school teen needed to get by us into a changing booth. We moved closer to the wall. Rincin scratched his shiny calf and I looked away.

"Funny thing." Rincin picked at a dried moth that somehow ended up on the shoulder of his Stupid T-shirt. "Zell brings you up there—then him and most of his whole family go dead."

"You saying I have something to do with it?"

"You? No. But the doctor. He's *dangerous*. People die. But he always lives. . . ."

I didn't need to hear the rest. I had the length of the Wal-Mart to chew on my heart for the mistake I'd made—leaving Tina alone with a bitter mass murderer who had nothing to lose. "Gotta run," I called over my shoulder. "Stay in touch!"

Passing the unopened envelope from hand to hand, I stepped gingerly from car to car. I felt a strange need to sneak up on Tina. One parking spot away, I peeked around the back of a burgundy Hummer. Then I popped out, took two steps left, and raised my eyes to the black Prius. I pressed my eye to the tinted glass. Empty.

"What did you expect?" I said, to no one in particular.

Maybe this was progress. For once in my life I'd let myself hope that nothing bad had happened. Something *bad* always happens.

Frozen between Hummer and hybrid, I mumbled to the air in front of me.

"What's behind door number three?"

"I don't know," came the reply, "but I think it's where they stick people who talk to themselves at Wal-Mart—generally the same ones who shit in the Home Depot display commodes."

I spun around and Tina held up a McDonald's bag in each hand. "I hate this crap, but I was starving. I got a couple apple pies."

I grabbed her. "You're all right? I was afraid—"

"I'm fine." She continued, "I got a Happy Meal for our little guy."

As she took my arm, I was struck by one of those thoughts you never really expect to have in life before you have them: *This would be almost like a picnic if we didn't have the Angel of Death in the trunk.*

Tina reached for the car door and I pulled out the envelope. "Wait," I said. "I ran into Rincin. He gave me this."

She just shrugged. "What is it?"

"Photographs," I said. "No doubt all the ungodly shit you did with Bernstein . . ."

She snatched the envelope and opened it before I could finish. "Fucking drama queen." She pulled out a photo, stared at it. "You're right, pretty disgusting." Then she threw it at me.

The photo showed me naked, laid out on the table as Mengele poked me with a pointer. "Oh, man," I mumbled, then checked out the second one. This time, I was lying on my side on a gurney, facing the wolfhound. The dog had its own gurney, just like I remembered. But in the photo he had a black leather muzzle over his mouth and a look of plaintive, accusatory despair in his eyes. The other photos showed my torso, grease-painted into sections like a side of beef.

"You never told me you were a medical anomaly," Tina said. "How do you get three liver transplants?"

"Pittsburgh is the liver capital, and the police had great insurance."

"Three?"

"I kept shorting them out, but I never had any problem with rejecting them."

"I think all the cock-and-balls stuff was a diversion."

I squirmed and she amended her sentiment. "Well, not all. But Mengele really loved you for your liver. He probably has people at insurance companies. Combing for freaks. The reverend's got a cousin at Folsom, said an old German dude was there a year ago, doing weird shit with a pair of dim-bulb twins from Petaluma."

"So did Zell hire me to see if Mengele was who he was—or did Mengele hire Zell to go find him a triple liver and man?"

"Probably both," said Tina. "Break it down, they're still crabs in a basket, a couple of big-league lowlifes trying to get over on each other."

By now there was no way around the looming question. I tried to sound only mildly curious, as opposed to gripped by mad-dog, pit-bull-on-hot-tar paranoia. "And why exactly were you there?"

"Manny . . . The reverend told me Mengele was looking to do a johnson relocation. He said the doctor wanted to take penis enlargement to a whole new level. I guess he heard you had a healthy specimen, 'cause he was going to make you a penis donor."

"And where would he have heard that?"

"I told you, I might have mentioned it to the reverend. When he was coming on to me. Just to let him know he wasn't all that compared to my main squeeze."

"Who wasn't technically your main squeeze."

"Manny, come on, we're getting along so well."

"Okay, okay. So he wanted to penis transplant. Why should I be bothered that none of this would have happened if maybe, you know, you'd been just a little, you know . . . discreet."

"I just told you—I got involved because of what I'd heard."

"What were you going to do about it?"

"Whatever it took to keep it from happening."

"That's a meaningful gesture, from an ex-wife."

"Just 'cause a girl gives up skiing doesn't mean she has to dynamite the Alps."

"I'm flattered. What about Bernstein?"

"Nothing happened. And even if something did—which it didn't— we wouldn't be here if we didn't go there, right?"

There was nothing to do but kiss her on the mouth or jump out of the car and bang my head on a utility pole. So I kissed her.

"Thank God!" Tina said. "I wasn't sure you'd be okay after the surgery."

"Why not? Tina—" I started, but she cut me off.

"Now listen, I found a tape recorder in the glove compartment, so I pulled the tape off his mouth, clipped on a little mike. I asked him to talk, you know, for posterity. . . ."

"How's that working out?

As soon as I opened my door I heard him. His disembodied voice ranted indignantly from behind the seat, as if he'd waited his whole life for the opportunity.

Minutes later, I held my Big Mac in front of my mouth. Untouched. Tina sat with her legs curled under her, absently twirling the straw in the strawberry shake she wasn't drinking. We could not leave the Wal-Mart lot. We were listening to Mengele. . . .

". . . was my *mutti* fat! The word does not do justice! In Gunzberg, she was some kind of . . . no, I can't say it. She was an object of scorn. Leave it at that. 'No need to pay a pfennig for a sideshow,' my friends would tease, 'we can go peek at Mengele's mother in the bathtub!' "

Tina bit her thumb, then stopped. "You know what's worse than the evil? The self-pity."

"I'm with you," I said. "Is he blaming his *mother*?"

"It's more disgusting than that." Tina kept her voice soft, which didn't diminish her contempt. "He's trying to sound human."

". . . Every day, at precisely noon, Walburga would waddle into my father's factory with his lunch. The name Mengele, I am proud to say, still graces the flank of German agriculture. Drive through farm country, and you will see that noble name showing proudly on the sides of tractors and threshers. But there was nothing noble about trailing my mother, who plowed through the ranks of sweaty men and oily machinery, her beady eyes fixed on the table ahead, where my father sat, among the men, and endured his daily visit from his three-hundred-and-fifty-pound stoat of a wife."

Tina nudged me. "Do you know what we can do with this?"

"We could erase it front of him," I said, opening the door. I re-wrapped my Big Mac and left it on the asphalt for a hungry shopper. I covered my ears, then removed my hands and let the words wash over me again. Mengele's voice was whiny, defensive, arrogant. . . .

"Have I some obsession with overlarge women? When I came to America, I could have wept at the sight of so many obese lovelies, their monster thighs and buttocks squeezed into stretch pants, children and husbands trailing them through malls like sullen, obedient dogs. Mother never knew that somewhere on this earth there waddled a race of her own kind. Not a 'master' race, perhaps. A 'massive' race. But a race that she could claim as her own.

"I am not a religious man. But I believe that heaven, for my mother, would be the Reseda Vons: food of every variety, aisles swimming with full-carted women, legs encased in suitcase-sized tumors of lard . . ."

He was still going strong a half-hour later, after we had decided to drive back to Los Angeles.

". . . Only in America would you have a 'hate crime.' America was founded on a hate crime. Is it better to kill someone you don't hate?"

Listening to him had gotten awful before we made it over the bridge. But, as if by silent commitment, neither of us suggested turning the thing off. Much as I wanted to, I didn't retape his mouth.

If so many had lived through what he had done, then we could endure what he said.

"Isn't this the fantasy of every Jew," came the voice of the erstwhile SS *Hauptsturmführer,* "to have ten minutes alone with Mengele? How much did Zell say he could get for the chance to kill me?"

We finally pulled over outside Santa Cruz. Took a random exit for gas, missed the on-ramp getting back on and ended up, as dusk blurred to dark, at the end of a two-lane blacktop that dribbled off into a dirt road through the woods and stopped by the beach.

Outside the car, there was no noise but crickets and surf. We stared up through the trees. Took a little walk to stretch our legs.

"Full moon," I said inanely.

Tina stared up in contemplation, then closed her eyes. "It looks tired."

Tina started back for the car and I followed.

"We have to feed him," I said, in no mood for lunar poetry. "Picnic with Mengele."

"Hey," she said, "I'll glue him down and leave him for the ants. Say the word."

Mengele was bent double in the trunk. I unfolded him and set him down on the ground. He was sweating, rambling into the tape with his eyes closed. But he did not sound weak. Even now his skin looked fresh—if his odor wasn't.

"You're doing the right thing," he said, "turning me in."

"Does this look like we're turning you in?"

Tina came back and kneeled beside him, chewing an egg-salad sandwich. "What do you think is going to happen? Open up."

His hands were still taped. Tina opened his mouth. She squeezed her sandwich until yellow mush oozed out the side. Then fingered a dollop and dropped it down his gullet.

He swallowed fast so he could keep talking.

"I am a part of history!"

"A lost part. You think we'd hand you over so you can tell your side of the story in a courtroom?"

"Yes, yes! That's what I want. Finally! A trial. With what I know about your prisons, your government testing, your medical and pharmaceutical corruption . . . The truth needs to be told. We did not do anything America didn't want us to do."

I wanted to throw up. "Here we go . . ."

"No, listen. I liken it to your William Pierce and—"

"William who?"

Mengele ignored the interruption.

"William Pierce, of the American Nazi Party. He wrote *The Turner Diaries*. He described how to blow up a government building. Timothy McVeigh was so inspired, he blew up a government building in Oklahoma. Very impressive, for a complete methedrine addict. After the bombing, when Pierce was interviewed, he said, 'I did not make him do it. I just wrote the book.' Well, America's laws were on the books—and Hitler read them. And yet you take no responsibility. You inspired us!"

"Triumph of the Willies." Tina laughed in his face. "Do you have any idea how pathetic you are?" She pulled a Red Bull out of the glove compartment, cracked the top, and handed it to me. I took a gulp. "Can't you do better than 'It was America's idea'?"

Mengele, who'd managed, somehow, to extricate himself from our tape job when we weren't looking, picked a mustache hair out of his teeth and examined it. If he could actually see it, his eyes were better than mine. "This narrative displeases you? Why, because your textbooks tell you Germany was your enemy? America and Germany shared the same spiritual DNA."

The thought that we ought to have tied a bow on him and mailed him to Jerusalem was like a persistent itch. "I think you're taking the twin thing a little far," I said.

"Am I? We wanted to keep the fatherland pure. Suppress the 'foreign elements' in the body of state. And what do your Minutemen want? I have seen your Lou Dobbs foam at the mouth on the subject of immigrants.

"Your president wanted to build a wall. I wanted to build a genetic wall. A barrier to keep inferior chromosomes from crossing the border and polluting our national essence. Are you going to tell me Herr Dobbs does not consider Mexicans *germs*?"

Mengele could barely wait to swallow another bite of pie before rambling on.

"Hitler understood that no border could prevent penetration by unhygienic strains of human. In stadium speeches, Himmler, the ex–chicken farmer, was fond of sharing his solution for infestation by poultry nit. It's a parasite. It survives by sucking hen ovaries. 'The war to save the race is waged on two fronts. There is the path of blood—eliminate the living vermin—and there is the bloodless method: sterilize them, ensuring that this will be the last generation of nits.'"

"All right," said Tina, "you had me till hen ovaries. Time to cover the old schnitzel hole. Come on."

"No! Please." Mengele's tone was at once commanding and abject. "Just eleven more items. Please."

"He's counted," I said.

Mengele held up a hand for silence, then began his litany. "Nazi scientists were the first to warn against asbestos, alcohol, artificial food dyes—and these are just the A's. We were the first to promote vegetarianism. First to recognize the value of fiber and condemn white bread. First to establish the link between tobacco and lung cancer. You might condemn our methods of research, but would you prefer that the nurse did not put lead over your reproductive organs during X-rays? That mercury leak out of your fillings? Did children have to die so that we could discover the value of vitamins? Would that knowledge keep you from taking vitamins?"

"The Chinese think they invented pizza," said Tina. "Is this the bedtime story you recite so you can sleep at night?"

"Jet propulsion, guided missiles, synthetic fuel, nuclear fission, computers, calculators, electron microscopes, data processing, hormone therapy . . . The first television broadcast strong enough to leave the earth, what was it? Hitler's speech at the nineteen thirty-nine Olympics."

"No wonder UFOs make themselves scarce. They probably think we're a planet of Hitlers."

"It's not exactly a stretch."

Mengele tongued chunks of egg goo off his mustache. It was so thorough, it was like he had a little animal living in his mouth. All we could do was stare at him.

"Did your sarcasm," he wanted to know, "prevent you from drinking methadone when you wanted to withdraw from opiates?"

I deflected the question. "I hear Göring had a taste for the hard stuff."

"Göring was a degenerate. But that is another subject. The softness at the heart of Western civilization prevented it from making the discoveries I just told you about. Why did medical science flourish under Hitler? Because we had no fear of pain."

"You mean no fear of other people's pain."

"Why do you treat me like an enemy? All I did was connect the dots America's best thinkers laid out at Cold Harbor, the womb from which American eugenics was sprung. Davenport at Harvard—"

"Who cares?" Tina barged in. "You're *here*. There are lots of evil assholes in the world, but I can only fit one in my trunk."

I edged her away before she lost it. Or got any closer to Mengele. I still had the image of Laurence Olivier in *Marathon Man* with his up-the-sleeve switchblade. But catch him in repose, mouth sagging, spit bubble swelling and shrinking on his lips while he snored like a one-year-old—you could forget his crimes. We'd logged enough road time that he'd morphed into a crabby bachelor uncle who needed to be driven to doctor points. Which was probably dangerous. Mengele was as cagey as they come. Maybe cagey enough to lull us into thinking he was a harmless old coot before flicking a six-inch blade out of his shirtsleeve and slitting our throats. I gave Tina a little *stay cool* squeeze on the shoulder. "Easy, baby," I said.

Mengele stewed. Whatever hardships he'd endured after a half century on the run, not getting his way appeared not to be one of them. We had passed down a sleepy lane of large California Craftsman houses and deep shady yards overhung by avocado trees and gently swaying palms. I saw the doctor watching the passing estates with something like hunger. Though, truth be told, I didn't know if he wanted to occupy one of those white-picket-fence homes or kill everybody in them. "Must be galling," I said, "just because you don't qualify as a Good Nazi, you don't get invited over here with all those other scientists."

"My enemy did not approve of me. There was a time when that was a badge of honor."

It occurred to me that his arrogance must have been an effort. He seemed to be getting smaller by the second. I could see it dawn on him: we might not be picking up the phone and dialing Interpol any time soon.

"Come on, Doc." I opened the trunk and patted the tire-well bump. "In you go."

Mengele stared into it as if it were full of faces staring back.

"Fuck this," said Tina. She ripped his mike off and pushed him into the trunk. "We have enough on microcassette. Let's tape his mouth again."

"I can't find the tape. I looked for it before we got out of the car."

"That fucking car. It's the size of an ashtray and I still lose everything in it."

"Well . . ."

"Don't say it. I don't want to hear about the army surplus store on wheels you drive around."

"Well, we need something. If he starts screaming at a stop sign, somebody's going to think we have a kidnapped Nazi in the trunk."

Mengele had been scrutinizing Tina this whole time. Finally he popped the question. "How many?"

"How many what?" She stopped pillaging the glove compartment for gaffer's tape and regarded him.

"How many have you killed?"

Things went quiet for a second. If the doctor wanted to touch a nerve Tina wasn't going to show of. "One—that I know of. But what time is it now?"

"Who was he?"

"No, who the fuck are you, to think I would even want to start swapping murder talk with you? What is that, like, porn for you? You and the other mass murderers sippin' umbrella drinks in Buenos Aires, remembering the good days when you just killed whoever the hell you wanted. No questions asked."

"You are Catholic?"

"What is this? My eHarmony application? Yes, I'm Catholic. Though I prefer to think I was held captive from birth."

Mengele stared off. "When I crossed the Brenner Pass, from Innsbruck to Genoa, Catholic priests took me in. Italian monasteries were full of escaped Nazis."

"One more reason to love the church," said Tina, digging something out of her glove compartment. "Maybe we can superglue your lips."

She waggled a tube of superglue in his face. Mengele twitched.

"For broken heels. My mother was big into pumps. It's the one bit of practical advice she ever gave me: keep glue for your shoes. That and don't give out your real phone number." She threw back her head and planted the back of her hand dramatically on her forehead, defeated. "'I gave my number to your father, and look what happened. . . .'"

Tina screwed the top off the glue. "You know about embarrassing mothers, don't you, Joe?" She bent toward Mengele. He watched her with his black, assessing eyes. "Can I call you Joe? So what's best, Joe—coating your top lip with superglue and pressing down, or coating the bottom and pushing up?"

"Wait! There's the tape," I said, spotting a roll under the jack.

"Party-poop!"

"Tape's fun, too," I said, ripping a strip and handing it to her. Then I steadied him and Tina, her eyes glinting, slapped the silver gaffer's tape over his mouth and patted his head.

"Aren't you the best little boy in the world," Tina said.

I slammed the trunk.

Life was too short to comprehend the Holocaust. Not just the deed itself—the not-quite-finite horrors, all the recorded awfulness—but the web extending from it, forward and backward: the subsurface connections, the local and international enablers and profiteers and believers before, during and after. You could go so far down trying to figure it out you'd never come back up. . . .

The word "genocide" was antiseptic. Pain wasn't sterile. But if you weren't there, even if you had relatives there, it was theoretical. Relatives who died in the Holocaust were theoretical. Until I met Mengele.

"The only thing worse than what he did," Tina said, "is enjoying doing it."

"Tell me you wouldn't have enjoyed supergluing his mouth."

"You can't arrest a girl for dreaming."

After that we didn't say much. Tina laid out the sleeping bags she'd bought from Wal-Mart to surprise me. Neither of us could get a fire going. A cold breeze came off the water and we crawled into a single Scotchgard-smelling bag with our clothes on. Then the moon went behind a cloud, leaving the world beneath it black.

I felt her hand on mine. I heard her voice from very far away, somewhere beyond fatigue. "What do you want to do with him?"

"Let's decide in the morning."

In the morning, we decided.

We let him sit in the backseat, miked and muttering into the recorder. After an hour and a half, he stopped seeming human. The thing talking in the backseat had two eyes, two legs, two arms, and bone-white hair growing out below the peroxide and out of his eerily clean ears.

All I had from my trip to Quentin was the leather jacket I'd had on when I arrived. The morning air was chilly enough to need it. When I put it on, for some reason, I stuck my hand in my lapel pocket and felt a lump. Really smushed in there. Tina watched as I tried to work my fingers down to the bottom. Then I pulled it out. A white lump of satin. Opened up, unwrinkled, it was about the same size as a Shazam pie, stitched with a baby-blue star of David. At the center of the star, right on top of the yarmulke, a button puffed up like a satin nipple.

We had the same idea at once. Tina took the top off the glue while I held Mengele's head steady. Curiously, he submitted. Too readily, he almost bowed his head. Tina narrated as she squeezed out six tiny dollops on the back of his head "Six drops," she recited. "One for each point of the Star of David." For the first time, Mengele's face betrayed fear. Tina glued the yarmulke on his head at an angle, so it looked like its owner was going for some kind of jaunty urban reggae feel. A nonagenarian Matisyahu.

"Today you are a man," I said.

"Apparently a very old Jewish man," Tina added. "The dyed hair and the satin are so working for me."

"I didn't know better, I'd say you were a real *alta kocker*."

Mengele groaned behind the tape over his lips, working his head from side to side. I ripped the tape off and waited. "What's so important?"

He eyed me with contempt. How could I not know? "I will tell them everything."

"That's it? That's the idea," I said. "Tell them who you think you are. Give a lot of details. Shrinks love details."

Tina put her hand on my arm. "That reminds me of something Bernstein told me."

"Bernstein? Now?"

"No, listen," she said. "The old warden wanted to hire COs with degrees who were also licensed therapists. But they were more shrink than cop. So it turned into a joke. 'How can you tell which guard has a degree in psychology? He's the one with the shiv in his neck.'"

"You both have problems," Mengele said. "You're both sick. You should not have children."

"Too late," I said. "My first wife was an Aryan gal. I'm a polluter."

"Me, I'm not popping one out until I know you're dead. I'm not taking any chances." Tina took a moment to step back and really take in the new yarmulke-topped Doctor Death. She nodded approvingly. "Say what you will, the man wears that yarmulke."

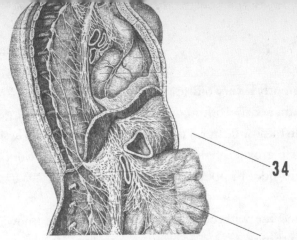

34

Love in the Time of Relapse

It's our neighbor," Tina whispered to the receptionist. "He just screams all night. And the things he says . . ."

She looked away, folded her lips into her mouth, and took a long, brave breath. The scarf was a nice touch. She'd found it in an IHOP bathroom on the way over. We might have had 2.5 kids waiting in the car. The woman could act.

"I am Josef Mengele!" Mengele shouted. "These people are kidnapping one of the most wanted men in the world."

The receptionist, a ponytailed teen volunteer with PRU on her name tag, was all open smile and helpful concern. "Who's Josef Mengele?"

Mengele slammed the counter. *Who is Josef Mengele?*

Pru stopped smiling. She took a step back from the ranting walk-in patient before her—a wiry, ready-to-foam old delusional with mustache in his teeth and dyed blond hair.

"I'm sorry," she said evenly, "were you on television?"

Mengele froze. Pru slid the clipboard forward, a battered black ballpoint dragging on a chain behind it.

"Would you sign your name, Mr. . . . Whoa! Did you direct *The English Patient*? We saw that in class."

"That's Minghella," Tina said, taking the pen. We'd realized the weak spot in our plan. We couldn't walk in with an old man in handcuffs. But if his hands were free, there was nothing to keep him from trying to strangle Pru. He wanted to be arrested. So we glued his hands in his pockets—actually one finger of each hand, so we could rip it out if we had to. "I'm afraid he has a condition. He won't take his hands out of his pockets." She lowered her eyes as if she didn't want to embarrass herself or the perky receptionist. She spoke in a stage whisper loud enough for half the waiting room to hear. "And he's not very . . . *clean*."

"We don't really know him," I said, doing my best to convey the baffled helplessness of a do-gooder who doesn't know what to do.

Mengele scanned the room frantically until he found an old man whose demeanor matched his own. A slight, goateed professorial gentleman. "Surely you know Josef Mengele."

"Mengele is dead. He died on February seven, nineteen seventy-nine, in Bertioga, Brazil. He had a stroke while he was swimming and drowned. He's buried in Embu das Artes cemetery, under the name Wolfgang Gerhardt."

I could see Mengele's ego arm wrestling his paranoia. "You seem to know quite a lot about . . . him."

"Sir, please, if you would sign?"

While Mengele was distracted by the attention he so craved, I grabbed his hand. Grinned *What are you gonna do?* to the lovely Pru. Mengele stammered out, "N-no!" I squeezed his fingers around the pen. He pulled back his hand and held it in front of him like something that needed to be bagged and burned.

"Um, Pru? All right if I just put his name down?"

"Really, sweetie, he's a nice man." Tina took the young volunteer's hand, going girl-to-girl. "Just a little, you know, n-u-t-t-y, *lonely* since the wife . . ."

"We're just the folks down the street," I said.

"Good Samaritans." Tina squeezed Pru's hand and whispered. "Last week he said he was Einstein."

"What scares me," I said to her, checking to make sure no one else was listening, "are the children."

"What?" Pru put her hand to her throat.

Tina took my arm. "Now, honey . . . We don't know for sure."

"Why would she make it up?" I looked to Pru for validation. "The girl's eight years old."

A sprinkling of harried middle-aged caretaker children and their Alzheimer-age parents looked up from their *Newsweek*s.

Pru nodded stiffly. Tina took her wrist. "We probably shouldn't even have said anything. That's how rumors get started."

We'd chosen Stanford because the psych ward had a geriatric wing. Mengele puffed himself up to full Selektor mode. He pointed at the dazed faces around the waiting room, squinting at each individually, startling them as he thrust a bony forefinger in their direction. "You! You! You—NO! You! You! You—NO! You—NO! You! You! *Schnell!*"

Pru backed away, picked up the phone. Banged a key.

The doctor arrived a few seconds later. Tall, slender, in long white coat, stethoscope around his neck. Shiny black hair and deep orange-brown skin. All topped by a lovely orange silk turban.

"I am Dr. Patel, how can I help you today, sir?"

Mengele stopped pointing and stared. He'd gone pale, a sheen of sweat on his placenta-softened skin. He studied the doctor's skull as if estimating its dimensions. I should have let him have some calipers. Mengele walked beside the doctor and studied his jawline and occiput. "Where were you born?"

"I am from Pakistan. Please, come with me."

"I want another doctor."

It got ugly fast. Tina held my arm. *Concerned*. After a brief, intense exchange, Dr. Patel left and another physician stepped forward, this one short, thick, black, bald and in no mood to have her time wasted. Her tag said DR. BROWN. "No, no, no! Another doctor!" Mengele snarled before she could open her mouth. "I want another doctor! This is the problem with America, they let your mother breed."

The doctor laughed. "Oh, we could have some fun with you. Umm-*hmmmh*."

A pair of married (or brother-and-sister) oldsters on seats facing us took each others' hands. They stared openly, the man canny and attentive and his wife in child-eyed panic.

Tina watched like it was Brecht. I waved to Pru, to get her attention. She excused herself from a sporty eightysomething with madras shorts over unabashedly varicose legs adjusting his oxygen at the sign-in desk.

"Is there, um, security we could call?"

"It's his lunch."

Dr. Patel and his successor stood with their arms crossed, conferring as Mengele lapped nervously at his mustache, searching for a word. Now the whole waiting room was on alert; even the senile were jittery.

"Another doctor?" I said to Pru. "A supervisor?"

"Is there no white man?" Mengele roared behind me. "Are there nothing but vermin? Has the world turned to *shit*?"

The third gerontologist, maintaining his equanimity, scooped the sign-in sheet off the counter and glanced at it. He was fiftyish, slightly slumped, with sad eyes and frizzy hair into which he'd clipped a knit yarmulke with a Star of David in powder blue on a white background.

"Sydney Goldstein?"

Mengele jerked as if wearing one of his own shock collars.

"Mr. Goldstein, I'm Dr. Stern. I hear you've been making a lot of noise. Why don't you come with me?"

"Goldstein? I am no Goldstein. I am Josef Mengele, Doktor Stern."

Dr. Stern froze. Mengele looked gratified. Finally, respect.

"I want a trial! I have valuable information."

"I see," said the doctor.

Dr. Stern took Mengele's left arm by the elbow. The old man shook his hand off viciously.

"Get your Jew hands off me. I am Mengele! I want a trial. I know things about your government! I have cures. I can help!"

Napkin still tucked in his collar, the security guard returned from lunch in time to take Mengele's other arm. He was as old as the doctor but Latino, with a limp and a gut. Mengele stared at the second man's club foot with professional disgust.

"They let you live," Mengele said, "with this?"

The Semitic doctor and the physically challenged Mexican-American froze. Mengele was growing more agitated. The doctor stroked his beard, sympathetic, the soul of rabbinic wisdom. "You really believe this, Mr. Goldstein?"

That was it. Mengele literally sputtered. "*I am not Goldstein!* They know," he cried, pointing directly at Tina and me. Dr. Stern gave us an inquiring glance. Every head in the waiting room turned.

I held my hands up, funny guy. "Hey, we're just the folks down the street. Have to go!"

"Good Samaritans," Tina added, sighing with befuddled affection as we backed toward the door. "Last week he said he was Einstein. . . . The week before that, who was he, hon?"

"Henry Kissinger."

Dr. Stern relaxed and stroked his beard.

"Josef Mengele," I heard him say before we were out the door. "Wait'll I tell my wife."

Dr. Stern led him, with the help of the burly security, through a pair of double doors. That's when we heard Mengele scream. "I am not Goldstein! I . . . No . . . I am not a—"

Silence.

As discreetly as possible, Tina and I turned and ambled back toward the exit. "They frown on disturbances in geriatrics," I said.

Tina threw her arm over my shoulder. "Wonder what they use to knock out a ninety-seven-year-old? It's kind of a small end for such a massive evil."

"That's why it's perfect," I said. "He wanted opera and we gave him a sitcom."

———————

Driving back to L.A., neither of us talked for the first hour. Then Tina mentioned the tapes. "Do we keep them?"

"I would have liked to burn them in his face, but now . . . I don't know."

We drove in silence another few miles. Then she spoke up again.

"The other thing, I found these notebooks, under the spare tire. I can't read German, but there are equations, sketches of organs . . . stuff that looked like locations and dates. Even some photos."

We'd gotten lost and ended up going east instead of south. When we cut back to L.A. on the 10, we passed the roadside dinosaurs at the Truckee Farm. The giant fake tyrannosaurus looked embarrassed to be standing there, along with the sullen, ratty triceratops.

"It's funny," I said, "Zell and the warden going to all that trouble to make bank off Mengele. . . . Meanwhile, now we've enough paraphernalia from hell to get rich for life."

"Wait, baby, you're not thinking . . . ?" Tina bit her thumb, genuinely offended. "There is not enough money in the world . . ."

"Or enough drugs to kill the guilt."

"Forget drugs. *Please.*" She stared out the window like there was something else she wanted to say. I knew her well enough to let it go.

"Well, I guess we have to decide whether we send the Mengele stuff to the AMA or the FBI. To tell you the truth, I don't trust either of them."

"I say nobody gets it except the Holocaust Museum. And they get it anonymously."

"Much better idea."

We drove in silence for a while. But there was too much I wanted to say.

"Tina . . . ," I began, then realized I didn't have the words. I didn't know whether to slap her, slap myself, buy us dinners, take a bite out of my own hand or ask her to remarry me on the spot.

She cast a glance in my direction, going from zero to a hundred radiant. "What?"

There was always something irrational about Tina's affection—the occasions of its arrivals and departures. I felt the same sharp desire and protective urges that overwhelmed me the first time I saw her, sitting at the kitchen table where she'd lately served her husband his fatal bowl of Lucky Charms.

Tina snuck another sideways look. "Of course, we could put some stuff in a safe. In case we wanted to get rich later."

Just when I thought I could trust her . . .

"I'm kidding, you asshole! If we made Holocaust money, what would we tell our children?"

"I don't know, what do people who own shares in Halliburton tell *their* children? It's a religious matter. Anyway, this is all abstract. Let me meet my future children, then I'll worry about what the fuck to tell them."

"You will," she said.

"Will what?"

"Meet your future children."

"What? . . . When?"

"Soon."

"Not exactly. But I'm ready."

"You're ready?"

"Listen. You know me, man, I didn't used to think I could have a normal life. Now, after all this insanity, the shit of history . . . I think I need to do this. *We* need to do this. When we fucked around in the trailer, I had a vision. Twins. Matching little Mannies."

"Twins," I repeated in spite of myself. "Mengele would be thrilled. But I still don't . . ."

"What?"

I stared straight down the highway, behind a truck full of cattle, their faces at once dumb and weirdly serene on the way to slaughter. I reached across the seat, put my hand on one of her epic cheekbones.

"If those little fuckers are born with bull necks and swastikas on their backs, you're going to have a lot of explaining."

She smacked my hand away, but not unhappily. "Trust me, they'll be yours. That's the scary part."

She was right about scary. I checked the rearview—a habit I imagined I could shake in two or three decades, when the kids I didn't know if I'd ever really have were grown up and gone. I spun the wheel and veered to a squealing stop on the shoulder.

"If we do this, it's for real," I said. "No more bullshit, no more secrets."

Tina ran her finger down my face and smiled. Our eyes found each other and had their own conversation. And yet . . . There was something tainting this romantic idyll: part of me still wondered if the woman I was ready to share my life with—again—had murdered Dinah Zell. There was still no explanation for what happened. Tina was, like myself, no stranger to insane jealousy. She might have gotten wind we were together on the plane. Might have come to the conclusion that something transpired between Harry Zell's wife and me. After that it was a simple matter of execution: find the house, drug the housekeeper, surprise Dinah in her bedroom and—all the rest.

I didn't believe it. I wanted to scour the inside of my brain with bleach and kill all these negative bacteria. But denial was a kind of relapse too. And an odd calm came with that thought. It was, I realized, the *not knowing* that would set me bolting upright at four in the morning for years to come. My true north was always the worst-case scenario within reason—or without it. But there was, here and now, one verifiable truth: I knew Tina had murdered. Once. And once upon a time I had made the conscious decision to let myself love her with that fact intact. So now I would simply live with not knowing who killed Dinah Zell. She had already mentioned, as it happened, that her first thought when she found the body was that *I* did it. Which was not all that implausible either. Even if I hadn't ground-glassed-and-Drano'd a loved one out of existence, I was hardly model-citizen material myself. We were probably made for each other in hell. And here we were.

We were probably made for each other in hell. And here we were.

But still . . . What was the point of unconditional love if it wasn't unconditional? For all we know, after creating the universe, God went into a fentanyl-and-gin blackout, saw the Holocaust when He came to and wanted to claw His eyes out. Like Oedipus. He couldn't deal with the guilt. And we are made nervous, in his image. The consequences never seem to end.

This was the history of the world. Recovery and collapse, despair and relief. The dialectic of clean and dirty. Every time is worse than the time before. The bad thing comes, days and nights and days and nights get so unbelievably fucked up, unbelievably fast, but in the end—if there is an end—everybody's best self just slogs forward, one stagger, one fall, one day, one *What the fuck just happened?* moment of oblivion and soul-broken joy at a time. All we have to do is not die.

Tina leaned across the seat and kissed me on the mouth. "Never again."

"Right," I said. "Until it happens again."

Annals of an
Abiding Liberal

BOOKS BY
JOHN KENNETH GALBRAITH

American Capitalism:
The Concept of Countervailing Power

A Theory of Price Control

Economics and the Art of Controversy

The Great Crash, 1929

The Affluent Society

The Liberal Hour

Economic Development

The Scotch

The New Industrial State

The Triumph

Indian Painting
(with Mohinder Singh Randhawa)

Ambassador's Journal

Economics, Peace and Laughter

A China Passage

Economics and the Public Purpose

Money: Whence It Came, Where It Went

The Age of Uncertainty

Almost Everyone's Guide to Economics

The Nature of Mass Poverty

Annals of an Abiding Liberal

JOHN KENNETH GALBRAITH

ANNALS
of an
ABIDING
LIBERAL

Edited by Andrea D. Williams

HOUGHTON MIFFLIN COMPANY BOSTON
1979

Library of Congress Cataloging in Publication Data

Galbraith, John Kenneth, date
  Annals of an abiding liberal.

  1. Galbraith, John Kenneth, date—Addresses,
essays, lectures. 2. Economists—United States—
Biography—Addresses, essays, lectures. 3. Economics
—Addresses, essays, lectures. I. Williams, Andrea D.
II. Title.
HB119.G33A32   330'.092'4 [B]   79-15782
ISBN 0-395-27617-9

Printed in the United States of America

V 10 9 8 7 6 5 4 3 2 1

Material from this book first appeared, often in somewhat different form, in
various publications and is here reproduced by permission:
  "The Valid Image of the Modern Economy" under the title "The Bimodal
Image of the Modern Economy: Remarks upon Receipt of the Veblen-Commons
Award" in *Journal of Economic Issues,* June 1977; "Economists and the Eco-
nomics of Professional Contentment" under the title "The Trouble with Economists" in *The New Republic,* January 4, 1978; "The Higher Economic Purpose
of Women" under the title "Women as Economic Interests" in *MS Magazine,*
May 1974; "The Conservative Majority Syndrome" under the title "The Con-
servative-Majority Fallacy" in *New York* magazine, December 22, 1975; "The
Multinational Corporation: How to Put Your Worst Foot Forward or in Your
Mouth" under the title "The Defense of the Multinational Company" in *Har-
vard Business Review,* March-April 1978; "What Comes After General Motors"
in *The New Republic,* November 2, 1974; "The Founding Faith: Adam Smith's
Wealth of Nations" under the title "Scotland's Greatest Son" in *Horizon,* Summer
1974; "Defenders of the Faith, I: William Simon" under the title "Rival Seekers
After Truth" in *The Washington Post,* May 14, 1978; "Defenders of the Faith,
II: Irving Kristol" under the title "A Hard Case" in *The New York Review of
Books,* April 20, 1978; "Defenders of the Faith, III: Wright and Slick" under the

title "The Assault on Private Enterprise" in *The New York Times*, September 15, 1974; "Who Was Thorstein Veblen?" as the introduction to *The Theory of the Leisure Class* by Thorstein Veblen (Houghton Mifflin, 1973); "A Note on the Psychopathology of the Very Affluent" under the title "Neuroses of the Rich" in *Playboy*, February 1974; "My Forty Years with the FBI" in *Esquire*, October 1977; "The North Dakota Plan" in *The Atlantic Monthly*, August 1978; "Germany: July 20, 1944" under the title "Hitler: Hard to Resist" in *The New York Review of Books*, September 15, 1977; "The Indian-Pacific Train" under the title "Across Australia by Train" in *Travel and Leisure*, September 1974; "Seven Wonders" under the title "Seven Wonders of the World" in *The New York Times*, November 27, 1977; "Circumnavigation 1978" under the title "The Thinking Man's Trip Around the World" in *Esquire*, February 27, 1979; "Evelyn Waugh" under the title *"The Diaries of Evelyn Waugh"* in *The New Republic*, November 20, 1976; "Anthony Trollope" under the title "Political Novels Past and Present" in *The New York Times*, September 12, 1976; "Writing and Typing" under the title "Writing, Typing, and Economics" in *The Atlantic Monthly*, March 1978; "John Bartlow Martin and Adlai Stevenson" under the title "Adlai Stevenson of Illinois" in *The New York Times*, March 7, 1976; "Last Word on the Hiss Case?" under the title "Alger Hiss and Liberal Anxiety" in *The Atlantic Monthly*, May 1978; "Bernard Cornfeld: Benefactor" under the title "Do You Sincerely Want to Be Rich?" in *The Washington Post*, August 15, 1971; "Robert Vesco: Swindler" under the title "Vesco and the Joy of Swindling" in *New York* magazine, November 18, 1974; "Should Stealing from the Rich Be Punished?" under the title "Crime and No Punishment" in *Esquire*, December 1977; "The Global Strategic Mind" under the title "The Strategic Mind" in *The New York Review of Books*, October 12, 1978; "John Dean, Ambition and The White House" under the title "John Dean's Total Recall of Blind Ambition" in *New York* magazine, November 8, 1976; *"RN: The Memoirs of Richard Nixon"* under the title "The Good Old Days" in *The New York Review of Books*, June 29, 1978; "Power and the Useful Economist" in *American Economic Review*, March 1973.

For Lois and Tom Eliot

Foreword

THE ESSAYS that make up this book have one major connecting link, which is that they are by the same author. Beyond that, they reflect my interests of the last eight or nine years and my feeling that some of the things that I have labored to make worth publishing once should be worth publishing again. The vanity of authors is a precious thing.

The first group of essays is on economic policy and economic affairs. All of them confront in some measure the alleged conservative trend of our time, the feeling that the less privileged and the poor will be better off if they are required to shift for themselves. Thus my title. I confess, however, that I do not think the movement to the right has been as massive or violent as is commonly proclaimed. It is hard to believe that the American people have suddenly rejected the practical compassion that has served them so well for so long. And as I argue in one of these pieces, the perception of a conservative movement is just as effective as the reality for moving the more vulnerable of legislators — or Presidents.

More specifically, this first section assembles my thoughts on economic affairs since I published *Economics and the Public Purpose* in 1973. The juxtaposition of the few vast enterprises and the many small — the basic characteristic of modern industrial structure — and its consequences are the focus of the first essay. This and the modestly more technical piece in the appendix — the latter my presidential communication to the American Economic Association — are the best summaries I can offer of my present ideas on the larger issues of economic organization, including its predilection for inconveniently rapid change. Another essay tells of what happens when economists resist change — of the results for the politicians they advise and the people for whom they prescribe when their minds remain with the past and their recommendations with the reputable applause. Not all of my discontent, however, is with the conservative stereotypes. The liberal's preoccupation with the multinational corporation has always seemed to me an intellectual blind alley. The essay here on this subject was published in the same week in the *Harvard Business Review* and the *New Statesman* in London. The sound and careful readers of the first journal remained calm; those of the second reacted with much well-reasoned abuse. In later essays I go on to other canons of the liberal faith and to contemplate those who, with various shadings of indignation, vehemence and anger, are moved to dissent.

The next section of the book is on personal history very broadly defined. (The pieces therein pave the way for a much more ambitious effort of two or three years hence). One of these essays — my history according to the FBI — was, by a wide margin, the most expensively researched enterprise with which I have ever been associated. The total cost must, with overhead, have run into hundreds of thousands of dollars. It is appropriate that I give the product of all this work to the public, for it was the taxpayers who paid. Several of the other pieces in this group tell of travel. Like many other college professors, I have frequently substituted movement for thought, although some of this has been to appease my wife. She regularly expresses regret over not yet having been to central Greenland; she has been everywhere else.

It is hard, maybe unnatural, for anyone who writes not to be interested in writers. In the section on the arts I have dealt with several of my heroes. But the concept of art is, fortunately, an infinitely elastic one. I have always been fascinated by the various forms of financial prestidigitation and its more inspired practitioners. I even regret, as I here confess, that a confidence man so accomplished that he can play successfully on the avarice and innocence of great bankers — George Moore and Walter Wriston of Citibank, for example — should be sent to jail. I am less fascinated, on the whole, by political thimblerigging of the Nixon type. But its literature, so abundant in the seventies, has also its peculiar interest.

The subject matter of all of these essays is mine; there are some things on which even the most self-effacing author can insist. But that they can be read without puzzlement as to meaning or outrage as to syntax, spelling, mistaken fact or lack of elementary good taste is entirely owing to my friend, partner and editor Andrea Williams.

JOHN KENNETH GALBRAITH

Cambridge, Massachusetts

Contents

II. PERSONAL HISTORY

III. THE ARTS AND . . .

IV. . . . THE DUBIOUS ARTS

I
Economic Affairs

1

The Valid Image of
the Modern Economy

*This article is based on my formal acceptance speech given on
receiving the Veblen-Commons Award from the Association for
Evolutionary Economics in 1976. A more technical and in some
respects more precise statement of this theme was in my presidential address to the American Economic Association in 1972.
The latter, I am not quite alone in believing, is the best short
account of my general economic position. However, it could,
here at the outset, discourage the interested but professionally
unconditioned reader, so, fearing this, I have put it into an
appendix later in this book.*[1]

I AM HERE CONCERNED to see if I can provide a comprehensive
and integrated view of the principal problems of economic
management in our time. In doing so, I shall offer an alternative picture of the structure of modern economic society. This
will compress into brief, and, I trust, sharp form without ob-
scuring detail what I have hitherto written about at much
greater length.[2] Finally, I shall attempt to apply this model to
some contemporary problems.

In considering the image of modern industrial society, one
must have clearly in mind two factors that act strongly and
persistently to distort the economist's view of that reality.

The first of these distorting factors is the very great inclina-

---

[1] "Power and the Useful Economist," p. 353.
[2] In *Economics and the Public Purpose* (Boston: Houghton Mifflin, 1973).

tion to think of the ultimate subject matter with which we deal in static terms. Physics, chemistry and geology deal with an unchanging subject matter. What is known and taught about them changes only as information is added or interpretation is revised. They are, all agree, sciences. It is the great desire of nearly all economists to see their subject as a science too. Accordingly, and without much thought, they hold that its matter is also fixed. The business firm, the market, the behavior of the consumer, like the oxygen molecule or the geologist's granite, are given. Economists are avid searchers for new information, eager in their discussion of the conclusions to be drawn. But nearly all of this information is then fitted into a fixed, unchanging view of the role of business firms, markets, labor relations, consumer behavior, and the economic role of the government. It is not an accident that economists who see their subject in evolutionary terms are a minority in the profession.

This is not a small methodological point. You will not doubt its importance if, in fact, the institutions with which economics deals are not stable, if they are subject to change. In truth, they *are,* and the first step toward a more valid perception of economic society and its problems is an appreciation of the very high rate of movement that has been occurring in basic economic institutions. The business corporation is the greatest of the forces for such change. In consequence of the movement it initiates, there has been a rapid alteration in the nature of the labor market and of trade union organization. Also in the class structure of modern economic society and in the resulting patterns of consumption. Also in the services and responses of the modern state. The ultimate effect of these changes is, in fact, to make the economic knowledge of one generation obsolete in the next. And also the prescription and policy based on that knowledge.

The second factor that distorts economic understanding is the very great social and political convenience — or so it seems —

of the wrong image of economic society. I can best give substance to this abstraction by proceeding to the structure of the modern industrial economy.

The presently accepted image of this economy is, of course, of numerous entrepreneurial firms distributed as between consumer- and producer-goods industries, all subordinate to their market and thus, ultimately, to the instruction of the consumer. Being numerous, the firms are competitive; any tendency to overprice products by one firm is corrected by the undercutting of a competitor. A similar corrective tendency operates, if less perfectly, in the purchase of materials and labor. Being entrepreneurial, the firm has a simple internal structure. Authority, power within the firm, lies with the entrepreneur, on whom, overwhelmingly, achievement depends. The entrepreneur being the owner, the partial owner or the direct instrument of the owner, the motivation is also simple and straightforward. It is to maximize return.

To say that the firm is subordinate to the market is to say that it submits to prices that it does not control and that it submits, ultimately, to the will of the consumer. Decision originates with the consumer, and this decision, expressed through the market, is sovereign. If the consumer has sovereign power, the firm cannot have any important power at all in the market; there cannot be two possessors of sovereign power. The business firm is also, by assumption rather than by evidence, without organic power in the state.

In one exception, the firm has influence over prices and output; that is the case of monopoly or oligopoly, or their counterparts, in the purchase of materials and components, products for resale or labor. But monopoly — the control of prices and production in an industry by one firm — and oligopoly — control by a few firms — are never the rule in this image; they are always the exception. They are imperfections in the system. The use of the word imperfection, which is the standard reference to monopoly and oligopoly, affirms that these are departures from the general competitive rule.

To any economist the broad image of economic society that I have just sketched will not seem replete with novelty. It is also admirable proof of the resistance of the subject to change. In the last hundred years the notion of oligopoly has been added to that of monopoly, and the notion of monopoly has been widened to include partial monopoly in brands, services or the like — monopolistic competition. On occasion, there is now in basic economic instruction some bow to the managerial as distinct from the entrepreneurial character of the modern great corporation. Otherwise the basic structure — competitive entrepreneurial firms, the supremacy of the market, the flawing exception of monopoly — is not very different in the modern textbook from that described in Alfred Marshall's *Principles of Economics,* which was first published in the year 1890. Anyone not deeply conditioned by conventional economic instruction must wonder, as he or she reflects on the extent of economic change in our time, if so static a theory of basic economic arrangements can be valid. It is right to do so.

The image is not valid. But it does contribute both to the tranquillity of the economist's existence and to the social and political convenience of modern corporate enterprise.

The service of the accepted image of economic life to the political needs of the business firm — the large corporation in particular — is, in fact, breathtaking. Broadly speaking, it removes from the corporation all power to do wrong and leaves with it only the power to do right.

Are its prices too high? The corporation is blameless. Prices are set by the market. Are profits unseemly? They too are determined by the market. Are products deficient in safety, durability, design, usefulness? They only reflect the will of the sovereign consumer. The function of the firm is not to interpose its judgment, only to accept that of the consumer. Is there adverse effect on the environment? If so, it reflects (with some minor effect from external diseconomies) the higher preference of people for the goods being produced as opposed to the protection of air, water or landscape. Is there criticism of the influence of corporations on the state — of the devastating foreign policy of Lockheed in Italy, Japan, Holland? These are aberrations, for an organic relationship between the business firm and the state does not exist.

One sees how great are the political and social advantages of this image of economic life. It is not easy to think of the accepted economics as the handmaiden of politics. Most economists suppress the thought. None should.

However, self-delusion also has its cost — and this is great. Specifically, this image conceals from us the workings of the modern economic system, the reasons for its successes and its failures and the nature of the needed remedial action. Among the victims of this concealment are those most intimately involved — those with the greatest need to understand the correct image — and they are businessmen themselves. And there is a damaging public effect. People cannot accept as valid an image of modern society that makes the great corporation the helpless, passive instrument of market forces and itself a force of minimal influence in the state. This is too deeply at odds with common sense. So they come to believe that there is something intrinsically deceptive about the modern corporation, and perhaps also about the economics that projects the conventional image. Better and safer the truth.

The valid image of the economic system is not, in fact, of a single competitive and entrepreneurial system. It is of a double or bimodal system. The two parts are very different in structure but roughly equal in aggregate product. In the United States, reflecting the force of the corporation for change in the last century, around 1000 to 2000[3] firms contribute about half of all private economic product. In 1967, for example, 200 manu-

---

[3] The statistical difference between 1000 and 2000 is not, in fact, great, for the contribution of the second thousand is small as compared with that of the first.

facturing corporations (out of 200,000) shipped 42 percent of all manufactured goods by value. Later figures suggest further concentration. Of 13,687 commercial banks in 1971, 50 had 48 percent of all assets; of 1805 life insurance companies, the 50 largest had 82 percent of all assets.[4] Set against this half of the economy is the dispersed sector; depending on what is called a firm, this consists, in the United States, of between 10 and 12 million small businesses — farms, service and professional enterprises, construction firms, artistic enterprises, small traders. They contribute the other half of product. The division in other advanced industrial countries is roughly similar. Thus the valid image of modern economic society is the division of the productive task between a few large firms that are infinitely large and many small firms that are infinitely numerous.

The large corporation differs organically from the small; the burden of proof cannot seem excessive for the individual who asserts that there is a fundamental difference in organization and structure between General Motors, Shell or Volkswagen and the small farm, neighborhood restaurant, cafe or retail flower shop. The coexistence of these two very different structures and the resulting economic behavior are themselves features of the greatest importance. But first a further word on the corporate sector — what I have elsewhere called the planning system.[5]

The most obvious characteristic of the corporate half of the economy is the great size of the participating units. In the

4 Jonathan R. T. Hughes, *The Governmental Habit: Economic Controls from Colonial Times to the Present* (New York: Basic Books, 1977), p. 203. William Leonard, adjusting for some underreporting — the tendency to assign some manufacturing activities to mining for tax reasons — puts the share of manufacturing employment of the largest 200 corporations at 60 percent in 1974. "Mergers, Industrial Concentration, and Antitrust Policy," *Journal of Economic Issues*, vol. X, no. 2 (June 1976), pp. 354–381.

5 In *The New Industrial State*, 3rd ed. (Boston: Houghton Mifflin, 1978) and *Economics and the Public Purpose*.

United States a handful of industrial corporations — General Motors, Exxon, Ford, a couple of others at most — have sales equal to all agriculture. Size in turn contributes to the two features of the modern large firm that differentiate it from the entrepreneurial and competitive enterprise and explain its impact on the society. The first of these is its deployment of market and political power. The second — one that is less noticed — is its diffusion of personal power.

The deployment of market and political power is diverse and, except as described in economic instruction, also commonplace. The modern large corporation has extensive influence over its prices and over its costs. It supplies much of its capital from its own earnings. It strongly influences the tastes and behavior of its consumers; even professional economists when looking at television have difficulty concealing from themselves the impact of modern advertising, although many succeed. And it exists in the closest relationship with the modern state.

The government gives the corporation legal existence; establishes the environmental and other parameters within which it functions; monitors the quality and safety of its products and certain of the advertising claims it makes for them; supplies, in the manner of highways to the automobile industry, the services on which sale of its products depends. Also — an increasingly important function — the government is the safety net into which the firm falls in the event of failure. Above a certain size — as the recent history of some large American banks, the eastern railroads in the United States, the Lockheed Corporation, Rolls-Royce, British Leyland, British Chrysler, Krupp and the vast agglomerations of IRI in Italy all show — a very large corporation is no longer allowed to go out of business. The social damage is too great. Modern socialism is extensively the adoption by reluctant governments, socialist and otherwise, of the abandoned offspring of modern capitalism. Being thus so dependent, the corporation must seek power in the state. This power, like that in the market, is not plenary. But its

existence can be denied only by those who are trained extensively to ignore it.

As earlier noted, the role of the modern great corporation
in diffusing personal power is less celebrated than its deployment of market and public power, but it is not, I believe, less
important. In its fully developed form, the corporation, as
others have emphasized, removes power from the ownership
interest, the traditional locus of capitalist authority. In doing
so, it removes it from the representatives of the stockholders —
the board of directors. No director of General Motors, Exxon
or IBM who is not a member of management — I speak carefully here — has any continuing effective influence on company
operations. The ceremony which proclaims that power —
usually of aged, occasionally senile men meeting for a couple
of hours on complex matters six times a year — is almost
wholly implausible except to the participants. Directors do not
make decisions; they ratify them. But to remove power from
the owners and their alleged representatives — from the capitalists — is only a part of a larger process. That larger process
involves extensive diffusion of such power. As power passes
from capitalist to management in the large firm, this diffusion
occurs in three ways.

First, decisions being numerous and complex, they must be
delegated and redelegated, and the decision-making process
passes down into the firm. This all recognize to be necessary.
Nothing so criticizes an executive as the statement, "He cannot
delegate responsibility."

Second, decisions being technically and socially complex,
they become the shared responsibility of specialists — engineers, scientists, production men, marketing experts, lawyers,
accountants, tax specialists. Power, in other words, passes from
individuals to groups — to what I have called the technostructure of the modern corporation.

Finally, where there is no participation in decision, organization takes form to influence it. Thus the trade union. Union

power is the natural answer to the power of the corporation. Only in the rarest cases in the developed industrial world is there a large corporation where labor is not organized.

The diffusion of power extends beyond the boundaries of the corporation, for the corporation brings into existence a vast array of supporting professions and services — law firms to advise on, or sometimes bend, the law; accountants to record, and sometimes create, its earnings; universities, colleges and business schools to train its executives and specialists or those who will so pass; dealers to sell its products; repairmen to service the products or advise that they are beyond repair. Marx held that, in its final stages of development, the capitalist firm devoured the small entrepreneur. This may well be true as regards small competitors. But the modern corporation also nurtures and sustains a large penumbra of independent firms. These peripheral groups and firms also assert their right to power. Lawyers and accountants have their special claims on decisions. So do consulting firms and custodians of expert knowledge from the universities. Dealer relations departments exist to consider the rights of those who sell and service the products. All have a claim on power.

We should not test our image of the economic system by its political convenience, or we should not if we are interested in analytically serviceable truths. We should see, instead, whether our image accords with observed circumstance, observed need.

The first test of the system I have just been describing has to do with the foremost problem of our time, the disagreeable and persistent tendency for severe unemployment in the modern industrial society to be combined with severe inflation.

If one accepts the competitive and entrepreneurial image of economic society, this combination does not and cannot occur. There can be inflation. But by conventional macroeconomic monetary and fiscal policy — restricting bank lending and tightening the public budget — the aggregate demand for goods and services in the economy can be reduced. Since, in this image, no firm controls prices, production is affected only as prices fall — that is what brings to the firm the message of declining demand. So, as the first effect, prices will cease to rise, which is to say the inflation will come to an end. Later, as prices and earnings fall, production may be curtailed and there may be unemployment. But unemployment and inflation do not and cannot coexist. One is cured before the other is caused.

Similarly, if there is unemployment, aggregate demand in the economy can be expanded by monetary and fiscal action — more public expenditure, reduced taxes, easier lending and thus more spending from borrowed funds. The initial effect will be more sales, more jobs. Prices may then rise. But, once again, that is because unemployment has been cured or, at a minimum, is by way of being cured.

In the bimodal image of the economy, a combination of inflation and unemployment must be expected at least for so long as fiscal and monetary policy are the sole instruments of economic management. Trade unions, as we have seen, have power over their wages in the corporate sector of the economy. Corporations, having power in their markets, have the ability to offset concessions to trade unions with higher prices. Modern collective bargaining has lost much of its old-fashioned acerbity for a very simple reason: as an alternative to confrontation, unions and management can reach agreement and pass the resulting cost on to the public. Complaints over the cost of wage settlements now rarely come from employers. Almost invariably they come from the government, which is concerned over the inflationary effect, or from the public, which has to pay the higher price.

When this wage-price inflation is attacked by the traditional methods — monetary and budget restraint to reduce demand — prices do not automatically fall. The firm has the power to maintain its prices. The first industrial effect is, instead, on sales, output and employment. And if unions continue to press for higher wages, prices will continue to increase. Only when unemployment is very severe — so severe as to deter the unions from pressing for wage increases and the corporations from exercising their power to raise prices — do the traditional monetary and fiscal measures begin to bite. Meanwhile unemployment and inflation, as in the world today, do coexist.

Before monetary and fiscal policy act on the corporate sector, however, they work on the competitive and entrepreneurial sector of the economy. Here, as before, prices do respond to monetary and fiscal measures to restrain demand. Also in this half of the economy are industries — housing and construction being the notable cases — that exist on borrowed funds, which makes them uniquely vulnerable to monetary action, to restrictions on bank lending. (This vulnerability is in contrast with the position of the large corporation, which has resort to retained earnings for capital and which, in the event of outside need, is a priority customer at the banks.) So, while inflation continues in the corporate half of the economy, there can be falling farm prices and a painful recession in the entrepreneurial and competitive sector. That too accords fully with recent or present circumstances. Beginning in 1974, monetary restriction was brought sharply to bear on the then serious inflation. There followed a serious recession, the worst, in fact, since the Great Depression. Farm prices fell. Housing, where output fell by more than a third, was seriously depressed. Unemployment rose to around 10 percent of the labor force. And industrial prices — those of the corporate sector — kept right on rising.

The practical conclusion is that inflation cannot now be arrested by fiscal and monetary policy alone unless there is willingness to accept a very large amount of unemployment. There remains only one alternative; that is to restrain incomes and prices not by unemployment but by direct intervention — by an incomes and prices policy. Such action is not a substitute for orthodox monetary and fiscal management of demand but an essential supplement to it.

There is a further test here of the validity of the revised

image, for the policies appropriate to it reflect the direction
in which most of the industrial countries of the nonsocialist
world are moving — against the advice of all the more clamor-
ous voices of conventional economics. In Germany, Austria,
Switzerland and Scandinavia wage negotiation is in accordance
with an implicit incomes policy that considers the effect of wage
concessions on both domestic inflation rates and external competitive position. Britain, a peculiarly resistant case, has, at this
writing, a comprehensive incomes and prices policy. France has
a more limited one. And the United States government in its
guidelines has conceded the need for such a policy and is reluctant only to bring it to effective reality.

The bimodal view also explains the increasingly unequal
development of the modern economy and the measures that
governments find themselves taking to deal with it. The corporate half of the economy combines advanced organization,
high technical skills and relatively ample capital with the
ability to persuade the consumer and the state as to their need
for its products. In consequence, in all industrial countries,
automobiles, lethal weapons, household appliances, pharmaceuticals, alcohol, tobacco and cosmetics are amply supplied.
The very notion of shortage, inadequacy, in these commodities
would strike all as distinctly odd. The contemporary experience
with oil shortages is deeply traumatic. But in the competitive
entrepreneurial sector, where organization, technology, capital
and persuasion are less available or absent, inadequacy is assumed. Housing, health care, numerous consumer services and,
on occasion, the food supply are a source of complaint or anxiety
in all of the developed countries. All governments find themselves seeking ways to compensate for the inadequacies of private enterprise in this half of the bimodal economy. The conventional economics has only one explanation for this unequal
development: it reflects consumer choice, which is to say that
the consumer is unaware of his — or her — needs. Where

housing, health care and food are concerned, this is hard to believe.

The bimodal image of the economy serves also our understanding of inequality of opportunity and reward in the modern economy and its consequences. In the conventional image of the economy, inequality is the result of differences in talent, luck or choice of ancestors. But between occupations it is constantly being remedied by movement from lower- to higher-income jobs. If this remedy is to work, people must, of course, be able to move.

The corporate sector of the economy deserves more approval than it receives for the income it provides. In the United States it is doubtful if any union member with full-time employment in this sector falls below the poverty line. But there are grave barriers to movement into this area. In particular, so long as inflation is the chief problem and monetary and fiscal policy are the remedies, there will be unemployment in this sector — either chronic or recurrent. If there is unemployment, there obviously cannot be easy movement of new workers into its higher paid employment. The old unemployed have first chance.

In the entrepreneurial part of the economy, by contrast, employment can often be found either by taking a lower self-employment return or possibly low pay in an industry that has no union. There is, accordingly, a continuing source of inequality between the two parts of the economy derived from the occluded movement between them. We have here another reason for forgoing exclusive reliance on monetary and fiscal policy for controlling inflation. The resulting unemployment is also a source of occluded movement and thus of further inequality as between the different sectors of the economy.

If fiscal and monetary policy alone are used to control inflation in the modern economy, it will be controlled only by creating unemployment. There must, as noted, be enough unemployment to require unions to forgo added wage claims and to cause consumers (and corporations) to resist price increases. Or there must be an incomes and prices policy. No two countries are likely to resolve this problem with the same choice of measures. In recent years Switzerland, Austria and the German Federal Republic have had low rates of inflation. Something must be attributed to economic wisdom. But more must be attributed to governments that have a history of concern for inflation and trade unions that are cautious about pressing inflationary wage claims. And something must also be attributed to the policy of balancing out the labor force with imported labor. It eases social tension if some of the unemployed, when not needed, are in Italy, Spain, Turkey or Yugoslavia. In Britain and the United States the reserve unemployed are within the country itself.

For the above and yet other reasons different countries solve the unemployment-inflation problem in different ways and with differing degrees of success. The result is widely differing degrees of inflation in the several industrial countries. With different inflation rates there will be, it is certain, compensating movements in exchange rates, and there is no formula for international currency stabilization that will produce stability in the international exchanges in face of these widely varying rates of internal inflation. This is something to remember whenever one hears that central bankers and other monetary experts are meeting on international currency reform. In the absence of broadly coordinate policies to control domestic inflation, there can be no international exchange stabilization that has any hope of being permanent. Promises to the contrary are a fraud.

There are further tests of the image of the economy I am here describing. Let me conclude by combining several into one. In removing power from owners, diffusing it through the technostructure and accepting and even nurturing the organized response of workers, the modern corporation does more than diffuse power. It takes a long step, if not toward a classless society, at least toward one in which class lines are extensively blurred. This, in turn, has a major effect on consumption patterns. Specifically, there is no longer in the corporate sector of the economy full acceptance by any group that it was meant by the nature of its occupation to consume less. And this acceptance will continue to erode. The pressure so exerted both for private goods and services and the requisite wages is one source of inflation. Pressure for such public services as education, health care and public transportation is another source. The thrusts for more private income and consumption and for more public goods and services have, we see, the same sources and can be equally strong. They are associated with the power — the power diffused by the corporation — to make the claim effective. In consequence, to cut consumption of private goods through taxes or for that matter through an incomes policy or to cut the consumption of public goods through reduced public outlays is very difficult. The bimodal image of economic society helps explain the new budget pressures with their inflationary effect as well as the new sources of inflation in the wage-price spiral. And it tells us also why control is politically and socially so difficult.

The business units in the corporate sector of the economy, becoming large, become international. The modern corporation internationalizes its income and wage standards as entrepreneurial industry never did. It also creates an international civil service — men who, like the servants of the Holy Church, are at home in all lands, who differ only in owing their ultimate allegiance not to Rome but to IBM. The international corporation defends relative freedom from tariff barriers and other constraints on trade. That is because competition is rarely cutthroat between large firms; they are restrained by oligopolistic convention. And international competition is never serious if you own the international competitor. It was the growth of the corporate sector of the modern economy that made possible the Common Market — made it necessary, perhaps, because intra-European trade barriers had become only a nuisance for the large corporation. Agriculture and other entrepreneurial enterprises have not changed their attitude on international trade. Their instinct is still protective. Farmers and other small producers would never have brought the EEC into existence. They are the source of at least 90 percent of its problems. Again the bimodal image fits the history.[6]

Finally, the image of the economy here offered explains the new tensions in the relationship between economic institutions and the state. The competitive and entrepreneurial firm seeks services from the state; seeks protection from competition, as just noted; is subject to regulation; pays taxes. This is a familiar and limited relationship. This firm never, by itself, competes with the state in the exercise of power. The modern large corporation, on the other hand, has a far wider range of requirements from the state. It also brings its power directly to bear on the instrumentalities of the state — both the bureaucracy and the legislature. Its needs, since they are put forward by the technostructure — an influential and articulate sector of the population — have a way of becoming public policy. Americans have recently had a substantial education in the way the financial resources of the corporation have been deployed for the purchase of politicians and political influence. And in numerous matters the corporation exercises power of a purely public nature. In recent years the aircraft companies have had more success, of a sort, in the making and unmaking of foreign politicians and governments than has the CIA. No one doubts that the oil companies conduct a policy in the Middle East that sometimes supersedes that of the Department of State. A

[6] I return to this theme in the later essay, "The Multinational Corporation: How to Put Your Worst Foot Forward or in Your Mouth."

good many people believe that General Motors has had considerably more to do with setting policy on mass transportation in recent times than has the United States government.

These tensions are a great and important fact of life. As with inflation and unemployment, unequal development and inequality, we presently deal with them in the industrial countries by resort to an image of industrial society which holds that they do not exist. Or which holds that they are aberrations *sui generis*. This is unconvincing to the average citizen who, unlike the more acquiescent economist, is untrained in illusion. It precludes effective diagnosis and effective remedial action. It is safer and wiser as well as intellectually more rewarding to accept the reality.

Economists and the Economics
of Professional Contentment

By the time of the Great Depression of the nineteen-thirties economics had become a subject of respected instruction, research and public guidance in the United States and was an academic discipline of no slight prestige. Harvard, Columbia, Yale, Chicago, Princeton, California and Wisconsin were major centers of such effort. F. W. Taussig, the noted Harvard teacher, tariff-maker and wartime price-fixer; Joseph Schumpeter, who came to Harvard in these years from Germany; Wesley C. Mitchell at Columbia University; Fred R. Fairchild at Yale, whose textbook with Furniss and Buck instructed and depressed many undergraduate generations; all had reputations of national reach. In universities and colleges around the country there were others of only slightly less esteem. In other countries, especially in Britain and Germany, economists enjoyed similar fame.

The Great Depression, beginning in the autumn of 1929 and continuing for ten years until washed out by military expenditures in 1940–41, was, rivaled only by the Civil War, the most traumatic event in the American experience. It lingers more strongly than any other in the social memory of Americans. When the economic prospect is uncertain, men and women still ask in fear, "Will there be another depression?" In those years output — Gross National Product — fell by a third. Farmers, still numerous and vocal, went bankrupt and were dispossessed by the tens of thousands. By the mid-thirties the farm debt exceeded the assets, at current values, of all farms. American agriculture was, literally, insolvent. Unemployment rose to around a quarter of the labor force. There was no unemployment insurance. Until 1933, there was no effort to enhance job opportunity and until then no organized assistance to the impoverished. As now in relation to the urban crisis, men of high reputation took their stand on deprivation on principle; far better suffering and despair than any impairment of the rule of local responsibility for local problems.

Nor was the misfortune only that of the poor. By the end of March 1933, 9000 banks had failed and around 100,000 other commercial and industrial enterprises. By the mid-thirties bankruptcy was no longer the misfortune of the weak and the small; numerous of the large banks, utilities and railroads were in receivership or in peril. The president of the New York Federal Reserve Bank had observed that while "[the effects of the failure of] the small banks in the community could be isolated," danger to the big New York banks had to be taken seriously.

The great economists, with a few exceptions, reacted to these misfortunes with professional detachment and calm. Called on for advice, as they were, most warned of the dangers of "untried experiment," experiment usually being of such character. Or they stressed the danger of inflation. The United States had had a serious inflation in World War I and following; prices had approximately doubled. In Germany and Austria and elsewhere in Central Europe, the purchasing power of currencies had totally collapsed, with maximum impact on a generation of scholars, many of whom later migrated to the United States. In the manner made famous by generals, the great economists showed a marked affinity for fighting their past wars and did so through a deflation that, between 1929 and 1933, brought the wholesale price index down by more than a third.

There was also, in these years, notable stress on the importance of patience as a therapy — a treatment that is believed to be easier with academic tenure on a regular income. Especially powerful were the warnings from Joseph Schumpeter of Harvard and Lionel Robbins of the London School of Economics. They affirmed that depressions ended only when they have corrected the maladjustments and extruded the poisons by which they were caused.

On occasion there was organized effort to resist action or support inaction. In the autumn of 1933, many of the more prestigious members of the profession banded together under Edwin W. Kemmerer of Princeton to oppose monetary and fiscal experiment. A year or so later several Harvard economists collaborated in an astringent attack on the economic experimentalism of the New Deal. This was especially notable, for the effort involved not only the older professors but also younger members of the faculty who were still actively pursuing tenure. The most common mood, however, was one of judicious scholarly contentment. Professors remained concerned with accustomed teaching, research and writing in economic theory, money and banking, statistics and economic history. At the great universities there were few tense seminars on the causes of the Depression or its cure. Little such discussion was reflected in the professional journals. Sometime in 1934 or 1935, Roosevelt returned to Harvard to dine with his sons and their friends at their undergraduate club. As he passed along the street, he was greeted by students with shouts of "Fire Tugwell!" This reflected the dominant lesson of their practical economic instruction; among the economists in the administration, Rexford Guy Tugwell was the most notable activist and thus the most widely criticized.

There were exceptions to this mood — the professional eccentrics and deviants. Many university campuses had one or two — men or the occasional woman who kept asking what might be done nationally, locally or on specific matters to alleviate the suffering. Agricultural and labor economists, living close to their clientele, had a special tendency to be involved, and at considerable cost to their scholarly reputations. Academically speaking, they were always second-class citizens. At the University of Wisconsin, under John R. Commons, there was a widely remarked concern with such issues as unemployment insurance, utility rate regulation and taxation. Wisconsin was thought by many a peculiar place.

Elsewhere two men were outspoken in advocacy of their preferred remedies for the Depression. One of these was Irving Fisher of Yale; the other, of Cambridge and various London preoccupations, was John Maynard Keynes. Fisher urged deliberate expansion of the money supply through reduction of the gold content of the dollar. Keynes urged energetic expenditure by governments from borrowed funds. Both men were regarded with deep distaste by the economists of established reputation. The *New York Times* in 1933 thought it "should hardly be necessary to say" that the ideas of Fisher and Keynes "have been long before the public, and that both have been rejected by the large consensus of economic and financial judgment." Keynes and Fisher, with Commons, are among the few economists from the time who are not forgotten. And the veil is kind, for, with the passing years, those who continued to sit stolidly on their prestige paid heavily for their contentment. Their comfortable negativism, so far as it is remembered, is treated with amused contempt in the intellectual history of these years.

I recur to this history because detachment and contentment are again the tendency of economists in our time. Politicians and the public, and not least economists, should know that it is a normal cyclical phenomenon in our profession. What is understood may not be more easily forgiven, but there is a chance that it will be more promptly remedied.

The contentment of the early Depression years was followed in the late thirties, in the war years and thereafter, including through the Eisenhower years, by a period of excitement and active innovation in economic policy. This was overwhelmingly

in reaction to the increasingly visible acquiescence and inepti-
tude of the great men of the past. The polar figure was, of
course, Keynes; the unifying idea was the belief that something
could be done and had to be done by government to lift and
sustain the level of output and employment in the modern
capitalist economy. There was much here to be discussed. And
the discussion was further sustained by the myriad of new
economic tasks occasioned by the war and by the development
and use during these years of the National Accounts — the
incorporation into professional thought of National Income,
Gross National Product and aggregates of consumer and business spending and saving. Almost simultaneously there was a
breakthrough in the ideas as to what should be done to overcome unemployment and depression and in the measurement
thereof. Again, however, the very great men of the profession,
with such rare exceptions as the late Alvin Hansen of Harvard,
continued aloof. Men of lesser reputation with less reputation
to lose made the Keynesian Revolution.

The tactically careful and self-regarding had reason for caution. Those actively associated with the new policies in government were, like Tugwell, subject to severe rebuke. The most
general complaint was from businessmen; it was that economists were impairing or destroying confidence. Some reactions
were very specific; when the Employment Act of 1946 was
under consideration, the National Association of Manufacturers, through Donaldson Brown, a General Motors executive,
filed a brief holding that it would enhance government control,
destroy private enterprise, unduly increase the powers of the
Federal Executive, legalize federal spending and pump-priming,
bring socialism, be unworkable, impractical and promise too
much. There were also other defects. No prudent scholar would
wish to be associated with such destructive activity.

But the heaviest charge was the more general effect on confidence. The American business psyche is an acutely vulnerable
thing; it associates all change with perverse ideological intent.
No large group of similar size and fortune in history has ever

been so insecure as the American business executives. The only form of reassurance that serves them is either lower taxes or inaction, and these are required and expected no matter who wins elections. However, in the thirties and forties and continuing in the fifties and into the sixties, the results of inaction seemed intolerable, and not least for business itself. So the onslaught was faced. Economists accepted their controversial role. And, in time, the more secure and mentally accessible executives came to accept the Keynesian rescue.

With the innovative and combative mood of economists went nearly a quarter century of economic success. At the end of 1968, the President's Council of Economic Advisers congratulated itself on its accomplishments. The language, which then did not seem remarkable, is now rather wonderful to recall:

> The Nation is now in its 95th month of continuous economic advance. Both in strength and length, this prosperity is without parallel in our history. We have steered clear of the business-cycle recessions which for generations derailed us repeatedly from the path of growth and progress... No longer do we view our economic life as a relentless tide of ups and downs. No longer do we fear that automation and technical progress will rob workers of jobs rather than help us to achieve greater abundance. No longer do we consider poverty and unemployment permanent landmarks on our economic scene...
>
> Ever since the historic passage of the Employment Act in 1946, economic policies have responded to the fire alarm of recession and boom. In the 1960's, we have adopted a new strategy aimed at fire prevention — sustaining prosperity and heading off recession or serious inflation before they could take hold...
>
> Meanwhile, a solid foundation has been built for continued growth in the years ahead.[1]

These words will suggest what all should have feared — that economics had once again settled into a mood of self-congratu-

---

[1] *Economic Report of the President, 1969*, pp. 4–5.

lation with its associated contentment. And this was happening just as the Keynesian measures, once so wonderful, were showing by the clearest of all possible evidence that they produced not inflation, not unemployment, but an unyielding combination of the two. The evidence was in the plain history of the next ten years. The only relief from this combination would be for a brief period preceding the presidential election in 1972, a breathing spell which reputable economists have dismissed as the purchase of an election at the price of far worse troubles to come. Not again would economists speak of strategies for "sustaining prosperity and heading off recession or serious inflation before they could take hold." Or say that poverty and unemployment were not "permanent landmarks on our economic scene."

In 1977, when he assumed office, President Jimmy Carter accorded effective Cabinet rank to five economists of the highest professional qualification. A Ph.D. in economics replaced a law degree as the basic license for practicing the science and art of public administration. In the next two years unemployment receded somewhat, but for the disadvantaged it remained very high. Inflation got much worse. Plainly these talented men and women came to office at a dismal moment in the history of economics.

They were, in fact, caught in another of the great downswings which, as in the Great Depression, render the profession innocuous or worse. In the universities and research institutes the mood was not totally bland. There was an active academic discussion of tax incentives and penalties for holding the line on prices and wages, a policy that would require the government to proclaim and, in effect, enforce standards for permissible increases. This discussion led on, inevitably, to a consideration of alternatives, including guidelines and controls. Numerous younger economists and some older ones were not in doubt as to the futility of the accepted approach to inflation and unemployment. But the more general response was passive. The small tasks of more pleasant times and their refinement continued to command major attention. Perhaps the accepted design for monetary and fiscal policy did not work. But it could still be taught and also avowed in Washington, for, after all, it once had served. It is essential that economists and noneconomists alike understand the reasons for this recurrent mood. They are deeply ingrained in the sociology of the profession.

The sociology begins with the instinct of economists for applause, an instinct by no means exceptional to our profession. And with the companion wish to avoid rude controversy. These attitudes must then be set against the deeply inconvenient fact that whatever is good for economic performance will always be deeply controversial. And what is most acclaimed for sustaining business confidence — here I speak with caution — will almost always be bad for economic performance. All have heard of contradictions in modern capitalism; all should know that the major immediate contradiction is here. In its great moments economics has understood this contradiction. At the low points in its cycle, as of late, it has not.

In the great creative years during and following World War II, it was taken for granted in Washington that to be effective was to arouse business hostility. Likewise in the universities. Robert M. Hutchins once noted that economics appointments were the most perilous with which, as president of the University of Chicago, he had to deal, and, it may be added, he and his successors in office made selections that were well designed to minimize the risk. When economists avoid controversy and reach for applause, their advice becomes worse than worthless; it becomes affirmatively damaging. It follows that, unless this is clearly understood by economists in responsible positions, their service will also be affirmatively damaging.

These truths — laws I am prepared to call them — must, some will say, be motivated by a deeply antipathetic business sentiment on my part. It is not so. In contrast with many of my liberal friends, I long ago came to terms with the American business system. Liberals, many of them, would break up the large corporations that now, in the number of a thousand or two, account for more than half of all private product in the United States. I would not. Conservative economists would move similarly against the unions. These, like the large corporations, I accept as part of the broad irreversible current of history. I not only wish to see the system survive, but so deep is my effectively conservative commitment that I want it to have the first essential for survival, which is that it work. I am only persuaded that, as experience so well shows, economists have a remarkably plain choice: they can be popular and applauded in the short run and be failures in the long run. Or they can be controversial in the short run and a success in the long run. I pass over a third possibility, which is to be innocuous in both the short run and the long run. That requires no special instruction.

Controversy is inevitable both as regards effective policy to expand the economy and effective action to restrain inflation. All policy to expand the economy will be more successful the more successfully it provides income to those who need it most. The expenditure of that income is then prompt and complete. Such policy also usefully reduces social tension, for, although much effort has been devoted to showing the opposite, income is a remarkably useful antidote to poverty and its associated discomfort. But the policy that professional business spokesmen and the affluent in general will always most approve, the policy that is best for business confidence, will always be that which gives these more fortunate groups the most after-tax income.

The situation is similar where inflation is involved. Any policy that restricts or restrains the freedom to set prices and incomes will be heavily attacked and will be held bad for business confidence. But in a world of large corporations and strong unions no policy that contends successfully with inflation can avoid some restraint on the freedom of business action — on prices charged and incomes paid or received. So a successful anti-inflation policy must also be sharply controversial — and again bad for confidence or what is so described. And the capacity to articulate alarm and to be heard is strongly correlated with business position and income. These voices are wonderfully audible; those of the poor are not. No tendency in modern political economy, as I shall argue elsewhere in these essays, is so powerful as for the voice of the affluent, and that of the business spokesmen in particular, to be mistaken for the voice of the masses.

A commonplace example will illustrate my point. Nothing is more regularly advocated as a support to business confidence than a large horizontal cut in the personal income tax accompanied by an equally substantial reduction in the corporate income tax and a compensatory slash in welfare expenditures. Such action is reliably praised by professional business spokesmen for its motivating effect. In 1978, a tax cut then, as usual, being under discussion, the *Wall Street Journal* put the prospective business response with admirable clarity:

> A general tax cut is well worth trying ... provided it is not shaped by perverse theories. The key is to let producers keep more of what they produce, and the biggest effect will come from cutting rates where they are the highest. If the tax cuts reduce rather than improve rewards for the economy's most gifted, talented and skilled producers, they will be worse than nothing at all.

Mr. Alan Greenspan, with Mr. William Simon the principal source of President Gerald Ford's economic advice and thus, alas, of his ultimate defeat, went further. He held that a tax cut wholly confined to corporate income would be the very best for business confidence. We are a friendly people. We listen respectfully even to established architects of political disaster.

However, the applause apart, such tax cuts have little positive business effect. They have little motivating effect on the modern organization man — the significant business figure in our time. That is because he is already required by all the weight of the organization ethic to give his best to the business, and he does. Such tax reduction has little immediate effect on either consumer spending or business investment. If profit prospects are good, a corporate tax cut is not needed to encourage investment. If they are bad, no tax cut will make them good. As practical experience with past tax reduction has shown (and as was duly reported by the Council of Economic Advisers), the initial effect of a cut in personal taxes is overwhelmingly to increase savings. Income so saved does not buy goods, and modern business investment, some special pleading to the contrary, proceeds independently of the supply of savings. Only good economic performance — good employment and demand — will encourage borrowing of these funds. The reduced welfare spending that would be so much applauded would, of course, reduce demand.

In contrast, an energetic jobs program to train and employ the poor, black and young or, in the absence of jobs, provide the income that, with whatever damage to the soul, does do something for the body, would have a deeply adverse effect on business confidence. So likewise expenditures to help make life in the large cities, if not pleasant, at least safe and tolerable. So federal spending to reduce the dependence of cities on regressive property taxes, a point affirmed since this was first written by the California backlash on property taxation reflected in Proposition 13. So, in particular, building and rehabilitation work in the central slums. And the expansive effect of action along these lines is optimal; money so distributed is put immediately into circulation by people whose marginal propensity to spend is one. The effect on the performance of a lagging economy is total — almost nothing is lost to savings.

There is another advantage in such action. As noted, modern unemployment is highly structured. Shortages of labor in numerous areas and occupations are combined with disastrous surpluses among the minorities, those without work experience, among women and those in the urban ghettos away from job opportunities. The measures just described are by far the best for reaching those most in need of jobs. Tax reductions, even if widely distributed among various income groups, add to pressure on labor markets that are already strong. Measures that are directed specifically at the unemployed — targeted, in the offensive current jargon — have their initial effect on labor markets that are weak. They are, in consequence, much less inflationary than action that rewards the affluent.

There is a further inverse correlation between what serves business confidence and what best serves the future of capitalism. None surely can doubt that the long-run future of capitalism will be more secure if the poor, the black and the young have the stake in the system that a steady income provides. There is much talk these days of a taxpayers' revolt. It will not, in the higher-income brackets, be the kind of revolution that involves much raw violence. The revolutionary impulses of David Rockefeller, Walter Wriston and Gabriel Hauge can be contained. One cannot be so sanguine about anger in the slums.

So both control of inflation and the prevention of unemployment involve controversy and are held to impair business confidence. But it is not easy to be overtly in favor of either misfortune. Inflation suggests loose public management; there is ample evidence that people both so regard it and much dislike it. Unemployment has a few more open supporters. The defense of a "natural level" of joblessness unites technical economists who eschew all concern for political consequences with the editors of *Fortune*. And as Robert Lekachman of Lehman College in New York has pointed out, there are many who have noticed that a little fear makes a labor force more productive or acquiescent or both. But no economist in untenured public office can be in favor of unemployment. So, given the need to be against inflation and unemployment and also the need to avoid the controversy and adverse business reaction inherent in all effective remedial action, economists have only one choice. That is some talented form of evasion. This means, in practice, the simulation of action as a substitute for action.

*

In the universities such evasion is relatively easy. As in the thirties, one can remain with accustomed preoccupations and ignore inflation or the now associated unemployment as irrelevant to one's particular specialization. A posture of scientific preoccupation is then adduced to support such retreat. The scientist, all agree, is an unworldly figure undiverted by practical concerns. So an economist can, in good conscience, reject the world and be proud of his emancipation from useful matters. In public life the simulation of activity as a substitute for action involves more varied techniques. These range from banality to sophisticated fraud.

The most engaging such effort in modern times was President Gerald Ford's invention and distribution of the WIN — Whip Inflation Now — buttons. It was attractive because it was transparently honest in intent — in seeking to suggest action without risking any of the pain or controversy that action requires. Economists in or sometimes out of official office usually prefer more sophisticated designs.

The first and most popular of these designs is to avow that some as yet uninvoked form of monetary magic will reconcile stable prices with low unemployment. If Professor Milton Friedman or anyone else could indeed achieve such a result, it can hardly be believed that his revelation would have remained so long unused.

A second evasion involves government regulation. When economists were assembled by President Ford in 1974 to attack inflation, the nearest agreement was on eliminating "unnecessary regulation" as a contribution to price stability. President Carter's economists were subsequently so inspired. The merits of regulation may be debated. But the removal of all debatable business regulation would not alter the consumer price index by more than half a percent in half a century. And this most economists know.

The third evasion is to promise to restore competition to the economy — in effect to re-establish the structure of the economy in which the established fiscal and monetary remedies can work. Liberal economists, when all else fails, call for enforcement of the antitrust laws as an inflation remedy. It is the last wavering gasp of the bankrupt mind.

Bringing representatives of capital and labor together for agreement on price and wage policies in a smoke-filled Washington room is a more recent design for simulating action. As an isolated, unstructured effort, unbacked by serious government purpose, such consultations exploit only the constitutional right to free assembly.

The most elaborate evasion involves bringing moral pressure to bear on trade unions and corporations to moderate their wage claims and price increases. As this goes to press, this evasion is the one being favored. Under President Ford the Council on Wage and Price Stability was established to simulate action. It was denied all power except that of free speech. Under the ensuing Democratic administration the illusion of action was extended by appealing first to the political competence of Mr. Robert Strauss and then to the administrative enthusiasm of Dr. Alfred E. Kahn. Limits were set on permissible wage and price increases with no penalties against those that were deemed impermissible. That would have involved controversy. It was, perhaps, a mark of the improving public perception of such efforts that, except by those immediately involved, nothing was expected of them. Those involved were assumed to be serving not for the results but, more legitimately perhaps, for the pay.

Finally, there is a continuing use of prediction as a substitute for action. It is announced each month, as the inflation and unemployment figures are released, that everything will be better in the third quarter hence. The press does remain very tolerant of this evasion and duly reports it as though true.

One sees the glum position in which economists of comfortable inclination now find themselves. The stark, blunt fact is that orthodox monetary and fiscal policy give us not a choice between an unacceptable rate of inflation and an unacceptable level of unemployment but an unacceptable combination of the two.[2] Only the uniquely brave or reckless, whether liberal or conservative, can say that the combination of inflation and unemployment is something the system can suffer and survive. All must promise improvement. And, it will be seen, the techniques of evasion, though still much practiced, are running out. There remains only the ability of all in our profession, when in office, to believe that because the fates have been so wise as to place them there, they will, even in the absence of effort, rescue and provide. Conservative economists, if sufficiently archaic, have some justification for this theology; the full employment equilibrium is basic to the conservative creed, and inaction is the way to realize that equilibrium. Liberal economists must believe that they are of the chosen — that, as I've said often, God is a Keynesian Democrat.

All modern industrial countries are subject to the same tyrannical circumstance. In all, the large corporations, unions and numerous individuals have escaped the discipline of the market and gained power over their incomes. The exercise of this power drives up prices. When orthodox monetary and fiscal policy are used to arrest this upward thrust, it is production, not price, that is curbed. And with the curtailment of production goes curtailment of employment. Until unemployment is very great, perhaps up in the recession range of 10 percent or more of the labor force, unemployment and inflation coexist. Germany, Switzerland and Austria have gained substantial control over incomes through nationwide collective bargaining that limits increases to what can be afforded from stable prices. Britain has been working to the same end. The United States has still to master this disagreeable task. It's an ungrateful world.

---

[2] It is, perhaps, proof either of progress or of the detachment to which the academic community can rise that the Ford Foundation has announced a series of grants for the study of this problem. (Ford Foundation *Letter,* April 1, 1977.) One of the studies is expected to last for five years.

Just as economists come into public office in unprecedented numbers, we discover that the economist's life was not meant to be a happy one. Anciently it has been said that ours is a subject that deals with choice. Now we discover that this is true even of public careers. They can be peaceful, fraudulent and fear-ridden. Or they can be innovative, successful and very controversial.

Certainly no President should be in doubt. If his economists are winning applause, inspiring confidence, avoiding acrimony, he should be deeply alarmed. The effects will spill over on him with politically fatal results. I am not reaching for paradox or exaggeration; the historical affirmation is complete. Three Presidents in the last fifty years have enjoyed supreme business confidence — Herbert Hoover, Richard Nixon and Gerald Ford. Mr. Nixon didn't finish his term. Mr. Hoover and Mr. Ford were the only two Presidents in this century who failed in their bids for a second term.

But more is at stake than presidential careers. Unless economists understand that our subject is intrinsically contentious — that what is good for the poorest of our people is best for economic performance but worst for gaining applause — economic policy will be a failure. We will have more tax cuts with heavy incidence on the always articulate affluent, tax cuts that bypass the terrible needs of our cities; that lodge themselves heavily into savings; that, when spent, affect most those markets where labor is already tight; and that thus make the greatest possible contribution to inflation. Unless the same economists proceed with the greatly contentious task of working out a system of income and price restraint over those who have gained some control of their prices and incomes — a task that must combine patient consultation with use of the powers of the state — inflation will either be uncontrolled or, as now, partially controlled by unemployment. And people, especially the poor, will come to wonder if having economists in office instead of lawyers is all that good.

[3]

The Higher Economic Purpose
of Women

IN THE NINETEEN-FIFTIES, for reasons that were never revealed to me, for my relations with academic administrators have often been somewhat painful, I was made a trustee of Radcliffe College. It was not a highly demanding position. Then, as now, the college had no faculty of its own, no curriculum of its own and, apart from the dormitories, a gymnasium and a library, no academic plant of its own. We were a committee for raising money for scholarships and a new graduate center. The meetings or nonmeetings of the trustees did, however, encourage a certain amount of reflection on the higher education of women, there being no appreciable distraction. This reflection was encouraged by the mood of the time at Harvard. As conversation and numerous formal and informal surveys reliably revealed, all but a small minority of the women students felt that they were a failure unless they were firmly set for marriage by the time they got their degree. I soon learned that my fellow trustees of both sexes thought this highly meritorious. Often at our meetings there was impressively solemn mention of our responsibility, which was to help women prepare themselves for their life's work. Their life's work, it was held, was care of home, husband and children. In inspired moments one or another of my colleagues would ask, "Is there anything else so important?"

Once, and rather mildly, for it was more to relieve tedium than to express conviction, I asked if the education we provided wasn't rather expensive and possibly also ill-adapted for these tasks, even assuming that they were combined with ultimate service to the New Rochelle Library and the League of Women Voters. The response was so chilly that I subsided. I've never minded being in a minority, but I dislike being thought eccentric.

It was, indeed, mentioned that a woman should be prepared for what was called a *second* career. After her children were raised and educated, she should be able to essay a re-entry into intellectual life — become a teacher, writer, researcher or some such. All agreed that this was a worthy, even imaginative design which did not conflict with *basic* responsibilities. I remember contemplating but censoring the suggestion that this fitted in well with the common desire of husbands at about this stage in life to take on new, younger and sexually more inspiring wives.

In those years I was working on the book that eventually became *The Affluent Society*. The task was a constant reminder that much information solemnly advanced as social wisdom is, in fact, in the service of economic convenience — the convenience of some influential economic interest. I concluded that this was so of the education of women and resolved that I would one day explore the matter more fully. This I have been doing in these last few years, and I've decided that while the rhetorical commitment of women to home and husband as a career has been weakened in the interim, the economic ideas by which they are kept persuaded to serve economic interests are still almost completely intact. Indeed, these ideas are so generally assumed that they are very little discussed.

Women are kept in the service of economic interests by ideas that they do not examine and that even women who are professionally involved as economists continue to propagate, often with some professional pride. The husband, home and family that were celebrated in those ghastly Radcliffe meetings are no longer part of the litany. But the effect of our economic education is still the same.

Understanding of this begins with a look at the decisive but little-perceived role of women in modern economic development and at the economic instruction by which this perception is further dulled.

The decisive economic contribution of women in the developed industrial society is rather simple — or at least it so becomes once the disguising myth is dissolved. It is, overwhelmingly, to make possible a continuing and more or less unlimited increase in the sale and use of consumer goods.

The test of success in modern economic society, as all know, is the annual rate of increase in Gross National Product. At least until recent times this test was unquestioned; a successful society was one with a large annual increase in output, and the most successful society was the one with the largest increase. Even when the social validity of this measure is challenged, as on occasion it now is, those who do so are only thought to be raising an interesting question. They are not imagined to be practical.

Increasing production, in turn, strongly reflects the needs of the dominant economic interest, which in modern economic society, as few will doubt, is the large corporation. The large corporation seeks relentlessly to get larger. The power, prestige, pay, promotions and perquisites of those who command or who participate in the leadership of the great corporation are all strongly served by its expansion. That expansion, if it is to be general, requires an expanding or growing economy. As the corporation became a polar influence in modern economic life, economic growth became the accepted test of social performance. This was not an accident. It was the predictable acceptance of the dominant economic value system.

Economic growth requires manpower, capital and materials for increased production. It also, no less obviously, requires increased consumption, and if population is relatively stable, as in our case, this must be increased per-capita consumption. But there is a further and equally unimpeachable truth which, in economics at least, has been celebrated scarcely at all: just as the production of goods and services requires management or administration, so does their consumption. The one is no less essential than the other. Management is required for providing automobiles, houses, clothing, food, alcohol and recreation. And management is no less required for their possession and use.

The higher the standard of living, that is to say the greater the consumption, the more demanding is this management. The larger the house, the more numerous the automobiles, the more elaborate the attire, the more competitive and costly the social rites involving food and intoxicants, the more complex the resulting administration.

In earlier times this administration was the function of a menial servant class. To its great credit, industrialization everywhere liquidates this class. People never remain in appreciable numbers in personal service if they have alternative employment. Industry supplies this employment, so the servant class, the erstwhile managers of consumption, disappears. If consumption is to continue and expand, it is an absolute imperative that a substitute administrative force be found. This, in modern industrial societies, is the function that wives perform. The higher the family income and the greater the complexity of the consumption, the more nearly indispensable this role. Within broad limits the richer the family, the more indispensably menial must be the role of the wife.

It is, to repeat, a vital function for economic success as it is now measured. Were women not available for managing consumption, an upper limit would be set thereon by the administrative task involved. At some point it would become too time-consuming, too burdensome. We accept, without thought, that a bachelor of either sex will lead a comparatively simple existence. (We refer to it as the bachelor life.) That is because the administrative burden of a higher level of consumption, since it must be assumed by the individual who consumes, is a limiting factor. When a husband's income passes a certain level, it is expected that his wife will be needed "to look after the house" or simply "to manage things." So, if she has been employed, she quits her job. The consumption of the couple has reached the point where it requires full-time attention.

Although without women appropriately conditioned to the task there would be an effective ceiling on consumption and thus on production and economic expansion, this would not apply uniformly. The ceiling would be especially serious for high-value products for the most affluent consumers. The latter, reflecting their larger share of total income — the upper 20 percent of income recipients received just under 42 percent of all income in 1977 — account for a disproportionate share of total purchases of goods. So women are particularly important for lifting the ceiling on this kind of consumption. And, by a curious quirk, their doing so opens the way for a whole new range of consumer products — washing machines, dryers, dishwashers, vacuum cleaners, automatic furnaces, sophisticated detergents, cleaning compounds, tranquilizers, pain-relievers — designed to ease the previously created task of managing a high level of consumption.

Popular sociology and much associated fiction depict the extent and complexity of the administrative tasks of the modern diversely responsible, high-bracket, suburban woman. But it seems likely that her managerial effectiveness, derived from her superior education, her accumulating experience as well as her expanding array of facilitating gadgetry and services, keeps her more or less abreast of her increasingly large and complex task. Thus the danger of a ceiling on consumption, and therefore on economic expansion, caused by the exhaustion of her administrative capacities does not seem imminent. One sees here, more than incidentally, the economic rationale, even if it was unsuspected for a long time by those involved, of the need for a superior education for the upper-bracket housewife. Radcliffe prepared wives for the higher-income family. The instinct that this required superior intelligence and training was economically sound.

The family of higher income, in turn, sets the consumption patterns to which others aspire. That such families be supplied with intelligent, well-educated women of exceptional managerial competence is thus of further importance. It allows not only for the continued high-level consumption of these families, but it is important for its demonstration effect for families of lesser income.

That many women are coming to sense that they are instruments of the economic system is not in doubt. But their feeling finds no support in economic writing and teaching. On the contrary, it is concealed, and on the whole with great success, by modern neoclassical economics — the everyday economics of the textbook and classroom. This concealment is neither conspiratorial nor deliberate. It reflects the natural and very strong instinct of economics for what is convenient to influential economic interest — for what I have called the convenient social virtue. It is sufficiently successful that it allows many hundreds of thousands of women to study economics each year without their developing any serious suspicion as to how they will be used.

The general design for concealment has four major elements:

First, there is the orthodox identification of an increasing consumption of goods and services with increasing happiness. The greater the consumption, the greater the happiness. This proposition is not defended; it is again assumed that only the philosophically minded will cavil. They are allowed their dissent, but, it is held, no one should take it seriously.

Second, the tasks associated with the consumption of goods are, for all practical purposes, ignored. Consumption being a source of happiness, one cannot get involved with the problems in managing happiness. The consumer must exercise choice; happiness is maximized when the enjoyment from an increment of expenditure for one object of consumption equals that from the same expenditure for any other object or service. As all who have ever been exposed, however inadequately, to economic instruction must remember, satisfactions are maximized when they are equalized at the margin.

Such calculation does require some knowledge of the quality and technical performance of goods as well as thought in general. From it comes the subdivision of economics called consumer economics; this is a moderately reputable field that, not surprisingly, is thought especially appropriate for women. But this decision-making is not a burdensome matter. And once the decision between objects of expenditure is made, the interest of economics is at an end. No attention whatever is given to the effort involved in the care and management of the resulting goods.[1]

The third requisite for the concealment of women's economic role is the avoidance of any accounting for the value of household work. This greatly helps it to avoid notice. To include in the Gross National Product the labor of housewives in managing consumption, where it would be a very large item which would increase as consumption increases, would be to invite thought on the nature of the service so measured. And some women would wonder if the service was one they wished

---

[1] There is a branch of learning — home economics or home science — that does concern itself with such matters. This field is a nearly exclusive preserve of women. It has never been accorded any serious recognition by economists or scholars generally; like physical education or poultry science, it is part of an academic underworld. And home economists or home scientists, in their natural professional enthusiasm for their subject matter and their natural resentment of their poor academic status, have sought to elevate their subject, homemaking, into a thing of unique dignity, profound spiritual reward, infinite social value as well as great nutritional significance. Rarely have they asked whether it cons women into a role that is exceedingly important for economic interest and also highly convenient for the men and institutions they are trained to serve. Some of the best home economists were once students of mine. I thought them superbly competent in their commitment to furthering a housewifely role for women.

to render. To keep these matters out of the realm of statistics is also to help keep them innocuously within the sacred domain of the family and the soul. It helps sustain the pretense that, since they are associated with consumption, the toil involved is one of its joys.

The fourth and final element in the concealment is more complex and concerns the concept of the household. The intellectual obscurantism that is here involved is accepted by all economists, mostly without thought. It would, however, be defended by very few.

The avowed focus of economics is the individual. It is the individual who distributes her or his expenditures so as to maximize satisfactions. From this distribution comes the instruction to the market and ultimately to the producing firm that makes the individual the paramount power in economic society. (There are grave difficulties with this design, including the way in which it reduces General Motors to the role of a mere puppet of market forces, but these anomalies are not part of the present story.)

Were this preoccupation with the individual pursued to the limit, namely to the individual, there would be grave danger that the role of women would attract attention. There would have to be inquiry as to whether, within the family, it is the husband's enjoyments that are equalized and thus maximized at the margin. Or, in his gallant way, does he defer to the preference system of his wife? Or does marriage unite only men and women whose preference schedules are identical? Or does marriage make them identical?

Investigation would turn up a yet more troublesome thing. It would be seen that, in the usual case, the place and style of living accord with the preferences and needs of the member of the family who makes the money — in short, the husband. Thus, at least partly, his titles: "head of the household," "head of the family." And he would be seen to have a substantial role in decisions on the individual objects of expenditure. But the management of the resulting house, automobile, yard, shopping and social life would be by the wife. It would be seen that this arrangement gives the major decisions concerning consumption extensively to one person and the toil associated with that consumption to another. There would be further question as to whether consumption decisions reflect with any precision or fairness the preferences of the person who has the resulting toil. Would the style of life and consumption be the same if the administration involved were equally shared?

None of these questions gets asked, for at precisely the point they obtrude, the accepted economics abruptly sheds its preoccupation with the individual. The separate identities of men and women are merged into the concept of the household. The inner conflicts and compromises of the household are not explored; by nearly universal consent, they are not the province of economics. The household, by a distinctly heroic simplification, is assumed to be the same as an individual. It thinks, acts and arranges its expenditures as would an individual; it is so treated for all purposes of economic analysis.

That, within the household, the administration of consumption requires major and often tedious effort, that decisions on consumption are heavily influenced by the member of the household least committed to such tasks, that these arrangements are extremely important if consumption is to expand, are all things that are thus kept out of academic view. Those who study and those who teach are insulated from such adverse thoughts. The concept of the household is an outrageous assault on personality. People are not people; they are parts of a composite or collective that is deemed somehow to reflect the different or conflicting preferences of those who make it up. This is both analytically and ethically indefensible. But for concealing the economic function of women even from women it works.

One notices, at this point, an interesting convergence of economics with politics. It has long been recognized that women are kept on political leash primarily by urging their higher commitment to the family. Their economic role is also concealed and protected by submerging them in the family or household. There is much, no doubt, to be said for the institution of the family. And it is not surprising that conservatives say so much.

In modern society power rests extensively on persuasion. Such reverse incentives as flogging, though there are law-and-order circles that seek their revival, are in limbo. So, with increasing affluence, is the threat of starvation. And even affirmative pecuniary reward is impaired. For some, at least, enough is enough — the hope for more ceases to drive. In consequence, those who have need for a particular behavior in others resort to persuasion — to instilling the belief that the action they need is reputable, moral, virtuous, socially beneficent or otherwise good. It follows that what women are persuaded to believe about their social role and, more important, what they are taught to overlook are of prime importance in winning the requisite behavior. They must believe that consumption is happiness and that, however onerous its associated toil, it all adds up to greater happiness for themselves and their families.

If women were to see and understand how they are used, the consequence might be a considerable change in the pattern of their lives, especially in those income brackets where the volume of consumption is large. Thus, suburban life sustains an especially large consumption of goods, and, in consequence, is especially demanding in the administration required. The claims of roofs, furniture, plumbing, crabgrass, vehicles, recreational equipment and juvenile management are all very great. This explains why unmarried people, regardless of income, favor urban living over the suburbs. If women understood that they are the facilitating instrument of this consumption and were led to reject its administration as a career, there would, one judges, be a general return to a less demanding urban life.

More certainly there would be a marked change in the character of social life. Since they are being used to administer consumption, women are naturally encouraged to do it well. In consequence, much social activity is, in primary substance, a competitive display of managerial excellence. The cocktail party or dinner party is, essentially, a fair, more refined and complex than those at which embroidery or livestock are entered in competition but for the same ultimate purpose of displaying and improving the craftsmanship or breed. The cleanliness of the house, the excellence of the garden, the taste, quality and condition of the furnishings and the taste, quality and imagination of the food and intoxicants and the deftness of their service are put on display before the critical eye of those invited to appraise them. Comparisons are made with other exhibitors. Ribbons are not awarded, but the competent administrator is duly proclaimed a good housekeeper, a gracious hostess, a clever manager or, more simply, a really good wife. These competitive social rites and the accompanying titles encourage and confirm women in their role as administrators and thus facilitators of the high levels of consumption on which the high-production economy rests. It would add measurably to economic understanding were they so recognized. But perhaps for some it would detract from their appeal.

However, the more immediate reward to women from an understanding of their economic role is in liberalizing the opportunity for choice. What is now seen as a moral compulsion — the diligent and informed administration of the family consumption — emerges as a service to economic interests. When so seen, the moral compulsion disappears. Once women see that they serve purposes which are *not* their own, they will see that they can serve purposes which *are* their own.

[4]

The Conservative Majority
Syndrome

In 1978, following the adoption of the Jarvis-Gann tax limitation amendment (Proposition 13) in California, a giant wave of conservative enthusiasm and evangelism was held to be sweeping the country. This article was written two years earlier, before the 1976 election. A conservative mood was *then* held to be enveloping the Republic.

MY THOUGHT in this essay is to explain in a scientific way the powerful and wonderfully persistent forces that, recurrently, seek to persuade us that conservatism is the wave of the American future. These instruments of persuasion are brought to bear at all times and with much success on the Congress. And before all elections they are directed with great energy at the Democratic Party and the nation at large.

The purpose does not vary. It is to persuade all susceptible citizens, but legislators and candidates in particular, that the country has, at long last, moved sharply to the right. Politically speaking, there are no poor, no aged, no sick, no black, no other minorities, no people seriously squeezed by inflation, not many for whom unemployment is a major issue, no one whatever whose health, education, food, shelter, protection from economic abuse or exploitation, or even whose survival itself depends on the services of government. Instead there are in this Republic only indignant taxpayers deeply angry about the willful idleness of public servants and the unemployed. The only sophisticated policy is their appeasement. The prime enemy of the people is the government, save as it involves itself in the exigent and increasing needs of national defense and those of bankrupt but still meritorious corporations. The ultimate tendency (and hope) of our politics is toward two equally conservative parties competing for the votes of the great conservative electorate.

We should have a name for this phenomenon; I propose that it be called "The Conservative Majority Syndrome." In an earlier time it would have been called "The Dayton Housewife Discovery." That excellent woman, the invention of Messrs. Scammon and Wattenberg in the political campaign of 1972, was also unblack, unpoor, definitely uninterested in anything as unrefined as women's rights and, you can be sure, deeply concerned about taxes. She was the typical American. Americans and Dayton were greatly libeled.

The success of the conservative majority syndrome depends on four motivating factors, all powerful in our time. The first is the susceptibility of much of our political comment and many of our political commentators and columnists, most notably the great men of television, to the rediscovery of the wheel. Its special manifestation is the recurrent analysis, offered each time as a breathtaking revelation of only slightly less than scriptural impact, that people of means would rather not pay taxes. This is never combined, most regrettably, with the companion revelation that people of means are infinitely more articulate than anyone else. So it is not noticed that, by its sheer volume, the voice of relative affluence in our land gets mistaken for the voice of the masses. Anyone in doubt on this point should try to recall how many welfare recipients were heard on the question of the profligacy of New York City in its troubled days as compared with the volume of expression that emanated from the Chase Manhattan Bank, the investment banking house of

Lazard Freres and then Secretary of the Treasury William Simon. The Westchester County budget, it was announced in the autumn of 1975, would rise by 22 percent in 1976. In those mostly pleasant and affluent precincts this was held to be the result of changing population structure, inflation and recession. In New York City the same increase would have been attributed entirely to the people on welfare and to the unions.

The second support to the conservative majority syndrome lies in the deep desire of politicians, Democrats in particular, for respectability — their need to show that they are individuals of sound, confidence-inspiring judgment. And what is the test of respectability? It is, broadly, whether speech and action are consistent with the comfort and well-being of people of property and position. A radical is anyone who causes discomfort or otherwise offends such interests. Thus, in our politics, we test even liberals by their conservatism. Nothing, in fact, should be so damaging to a liberal as an approving editorial in the *Wall Street Journal*. Were it only so!

There is a self-reinforcing aspect to this particular conservative thrust that works with special effect in Washington. There some conservative legislator to whom the economics of Andrew Mellon would have seemed advanced examines a probable action and concludes that it will cause pain to the privileged. This sorrow he then identifies with popular outrage, and he relays his views to either Mr. Evans or Mr. Novak. These scholars tell of the intended action and cite as general the belief that it will be a source of much indignation, if not of mass anguish. The progenitor reads their story and is affirmed in his fears. So are others. It is, I once concluded, the only completely successful closed-circuit system for recycling garbage that has yet been devised.

The third strength of the conservative majority syndrome lies in the superb tactical position of conservatives when they are in power. They can attack the government for indifference, callousness or incompetence and then justify the attack by making it so. This was uniquely the achievement of Richard Nixon. Government, we might recall, was not thought callous, indifferent or incompetent in the days of Roosevelt or Truman or of Kennedy or Lyndon Johnson.

We must never minimize the importance of good public management and administration, a dull but important business. It has not had the attention from liberals that it deserves. But let us not join in the currently fashionable tendency to defame either government or those who work for government. The civil service of the United States is as honest, effective and certainly as innovative as that of any other country. It was stubbornly honest people in the Department of Justice, the FBI, the IRS and elsewhere who frustrated the tax evasion, obstruction of justice, subornation of perjury and constitutional subversion of Richard Nixon and the unimaginative felonies of Spiro Agnew. Had our public servants not been honest, our case would have been hopeless.

The final buttress to the conservative majority syndrome is, oddly, many of the economists of the liberal establishment. Here I must proceed tactfully; I am speaking of conscientious people, excellent citizens, good parents, kind friends. But time, alas, in its ineluctable march, has made them pillars of the conservative edifice. This is partly because some of them yearn, as always, for Establishment applause and test their performance by its volume.

Also many of these scholars serve within an institutional framework; and some are sustained visibly and directly by the banks and corporations they assist, advise or, on occasion, operate. Out of institutional identification comes a largely innocent and natural desire to avoid embarrassing one's colleagues and employers by urging policies that are at odds with the respectable view. And out of corporate service comes the less innocent desire to protect one's income. Much of what was once called liberal economics has become very conservative in our time.

One manifestation of this conservatism in contemporary economics is the unwillingness to proceed with the painful actions that are required to control inflation and reduce unemployment.[1] Better, especially when in power, to sit quietly and hope. Or, when pressed, say that the real need is for more expansion, jobs and economic growth for which the required policies — easier money and tax reduction — are pleasant to prescribe. So far as this guidance is accepted, our political life is then divided between conservatives who prefer unemployment to inflation but do not say so and conservatives who prefer inflation to unemployment but do not say so.

There is no future for liberals in such a debate. Unemployment hurts a smaller number of people a lot; inflation hurts a larger number of people a little. We cannot defend either. It is not possible to persuade people — as some liberals would — that inflation is an overrated evil. For the person wondering how to stretch limited income or savings over urgent needs, inflation is real. And people's dislikes are as they are. It is not the liberals' business to try to say they are wrong.

A further support to conservatism in established economics — and this is a very important matter — is in its favored formula for expanding the economy. In recent years its remedy has always been the reduction of federal income taxes. This prescription is offered all but automatically whenever the economy is operating at less than full capacity, which, of course, has been frequently. Nothing has so effectively played into the hands of conservatives.

There was always the danger that tax reduction would be

[1] See the earlier essay, "Economists and the Economics of Professional Contentment."

part of a disguised effort to limit public expenditures — excluding, of course, defense and those in which the modern large corporation has a prime interest. Gerald Ford, to his credit, removed the disguise. He asked for tax reduction and made it conditional on expenditure reduction. Those who had feared this result should be grateful to him for clarifying a difficult point.

We should be grateful as well to Professor Milton Friedman, a man of inconvenient honesty, who also made the conservative position wonderfully clear. He has reported himself in favor of a federal tax cut at all times as the only way to exert effective pressure on Congress to keep down federal spending.

Public expenditures are progressive in their incidence — they have their greatest effect on those who are least able to provide income, schools, health services, housing or police protection for themselves. So tax reductions that pave the way for expenditure reductions — outlays for defense services and corporate spending always being exempted — have a special impact on the poor.

It is federal income taxes that are reduced. These, in substantial though not exclusive part, are on middle- and upper-income brackets of the personal income tax and on corporations. This reduction in recent years has been at a time when states and cities, in consequence of the recession a tax reduction was to cure, were being forced to raise *their* taxes. Local taxes, invariably, are more regressive. In 1975, while the House Ways and Means Committee was discussing the extension of a cut in federal income taxes, Secretary of the Treasury Simon, in a typically compassionate mood, proposed that New York City raise its sales tax to 10 percent. State and city taxes were raised instead. And the services of a city already deep in public squalor were curtailed.

In the same week that the Ways and Means Committee reported out that tax cut bill, the Commonwealth of Massachusetts agreed on a tax increase of $364 million, all of it in relatively regressive taxes, for no others were available. (Two hundred and eighteen million dollars would come from taxes on sales and meals.) The *Boston Globe,* noting the juxtaposition of these events, said it made no sense. They were right. There was, needless to say, no economic stimulation in a shift from progressive federal to regressive state and local taxes. The only joy was for the affluent. Such is the service of the established economics to conservatism.

5

The Multinational Corporation: How to Put Your Worst Foot Forward or in Your Mouth

IN THE LAST THIRTY YEARS no institution has so intruded itself on the economic landscape as the multinational corporation. None has provoked so much discussion or been the subject of such obsessive concern,[1] and almost every reference has had in it a note of anxiety or even hostility.

Such hostility, the existence of which no corporate executive will deny, rests, most executives will plead, on public misunderstanding. They look at themselves, their colleagues, their hours of work, their service to customers and tax collectors, and at their families, churches, charities and largely innocent recreations, and ask if they are really wicked men. Their answer, quite rightly in the main, is no. But the executive of the multinational corporation should be in no doubt as to who is responsible for the misunderstanding. He is misunderstood because, usually after some deliberation and often with some passion, he insists on misunderstanding himself. He puts forward an

---

[1] The literature of the multinational enterprise must have the largest proportion of spoil to ore of any field of economic writing, theoretical and mathematical model-building possibly apart. I've cited it sparsely in this essay, but I would like to make special mention of the recent book by my colleague Raymond Vernon, *Storm over the Multinationals: The Real Issues* (Cambridge: Harvard University Press, 1977), which provides admirable background for the matters here examined.

explanation of himself and his company that is based on out-worn economic theory with a strong aspect of theology. It is, in consequence, almost wholly implausible. No man, to para-phrase Keynes, is so much a slave of such defunct economists.

There are difficulties with a defense of the multinational corporation that is based on reality. They arise because such a defense must concede what for so long was so indignantly denied. Nonetheless the time has come when a realistic ap-proach is not only wiser but even, I would judge, unavoidable.

I've lived most of my life in close professional association with the large modern corporation. I have come to accept that it is inevitable. Among other things, it combines energies, ex-perience, engineering and scientific and other specialties for results far beyond the abilities or, on occasion perhaps, even the conceptual reach of any individual. The deeply collectivist character of this effort is in the sharpest contrast with the individualist economic, social and political case that it makes for itself. I would like in this essay to look first at the circum-stances that explain the rise of the multinational corporation; then at the exceptionally primitive ideas that now guide its defense; then at the case as it might be made; and, finally, at the management behavior that this defense requires.

The multinational corporation — the company that extends its business operations under one guiding direction to two or more countries — gained major public attention in the thirty years following World War II. During these years it moved heavily into industrial operations — into the manufac-turing or processing of goods, their marketing and sales. In its multinationality it had, however, three antecedents in non-manufacturing fields, all of them exceedingly ancient. These had something, in fact much, to do with the reputation of, and the reaction to, the industrial corporation when it became the dominant corporate form operating across national frontiers.

First: Since the rise of the modern national state, banking

operations have been carried on across national borders, partly to finance international trade, more significantly for present purposes to take capital from countries of relative abundance to those of relative scarcity and consequent higher return. Second: The resource industries, mining in particular, have long been multinational. These industries have gone, as a matter of course, to develop operations where the ore, natural products or, latterly, the oil were available. Third: Multinational trading corporations have traditionally brought the products of the industrial countries to the economically more backward lands.

In each of these antecedent forms there was a major element of adverse reputation that became part of the legacy of the modern multinational. The international banker had a notably sinister reputation: his concern for his capital transcended national interest and caused him on occasion to consort with the enemies of his sovereign. He was invariably richer than the borrower; and he was thought to exploit the profligacy or unwisdom of the latter or, in any case, was celebrated for so doing. In the absence of other available ill fame, anti-Semitism could often be evoked.

Resource industries, inevitably, were held to be robbing the countries where they operated of their patrimony — their natural wealth. They were thought to exploit local labor, though partly because it had an even lower local opportunity cost. And they did bend weak local governments to their purposes.

In India, Indonesia and Indochina the trading corporations were intimately linked with colonialism and in China with foreign penetration and domination. Socialists still celebrate them as the *compradors*.

Thus, like so many children, the multinational industrial corporation was unwise in the choice of its parents and is visited with their sins.

The case for the modern multinational begins with its considerable differences from its three antecedents, something that has been but rarely noticed. The older multinational operations mostly traded between the rich countries and the poor. They bridged the gap between those countries with more capital than they needed and those with less, those with manufacturing industries and those countries that could supply only raw materials and agricultural products, those with finished products to sell and those that, being devoid of modern industry, could only buy.

These antecedent forms have themselves changed. International banking continues, but operations between the rich countries and the poor are not what now evokes the modern image of the multinational banking corporation. Most of its operations — and to a singular degree its better recent fortune, as the experience of the big New York banks affirms — have been between the industrial countries. Raw materials, including oil, and some tropical food products still come from the poor countries to the rich. But the greatest suppliers of wheat, feed grains, coal, wood and wood pulp and cotton fiber are the two North American countries, the United States and Canada. (If to be part of the Third World is to be a hewer of wood and a supplier of food and natural products, the United States and Canada are, by a wide margin, the first of the Third World countries and should vote accordingly in the United Nations.) And the trading corporation, has, of course, receded greatly in relative importance.

Thus even the older forms of multinational operations are now mainly, though of course not exclusively, between the developed countries. This, however, is most strongly the case in the new and burgeoning area of multinational operations — manufacturing. And this is for a very special and much neglected reason. The multinational corporation is the nearly inescapable accommodation to international trade in modern capital and consumer goods. One must emphasize this central point.

The products principally traded in past times — foodstuffs,

cotton, cotton textiles, wool, coal, steel rails — required no connection or communication between producer and consumer. They could be and were shipped and sold through intermediaries, exporters and importers; the producer never saw the user. Products were also sold in the market, and, very often, the market price and sometimes the destination were unknown when the goods were shipped. Before 1914, grain ships approaching Land's End from North America regularly received a signal as to where they should proceed in Europe for the best price. For this trade, and similarly for simple unbranded manufactures such as cotton greige goods, there was no role for a multinational enterprise, and we need scarcely remind ourselves that the original producers were, in the vast majority of cases, very small.

To a greater extent than one likes to think, this view of international trade still rules in the economics courses and textbooks. It is one of the several reasons why formal economics has had difficulty in coming to terms with the multinational firm.

The modern industrial enterprise, on the other hand, has products that must be marketed. Only in the textbooks is the consumer left to his or her sovereign decision. There also must be control over final prices; it is elementary that General Motors and Volkswagen do not ship their vehicles for sale, in the manner of wheat, for what the market will bring. Both the merchandising and the market regulation require a well-controlled sales organization, as do the instruction, repair and service that many modern products need and often receive.

The modern industrial enterprise has, as well, numerous needs from the government of the country in which its products are sold — far more things than the mindless litany of private enterprise admits. The government is an important customer. It is also the source of the airports, airways, highways, television channels, telephone communications, weapons orders and financial aid without which many, perhaps most, modern industrial products cannot be produced or sold. And it is the source, as well, of a wide and increasing range of permissions and restrictions governing the sale and use of these products.

So the modern manufacturing corporation must have an intimate relationship — dependent, symbiotic, sometimes suborning — with the modern government. It must, in short, have influence and power in its own markets — over its prices, costs and means of consumer persuasion. And similarly it is impelled to seek influence and power in the modern state.

Power is a word that, in deference to conventional economics and its more general public effect, every business executive seeks to avoid. There is something exceptionally improper about its possession. But power is indispensable to the operations of the modern large corporation. It must have power over its prices; its planning operations could not possibly survive the kind of price instability that characterizes most small entrepreneurial industry. It must have a measure of control over its earnings; these are a vital source of capital, as all accept. It has a long production period involving heavy investment; it must, accordingly, have power to persuade the consumer to want the product that eventually emerges. It lives with the consent of and by the support of the state; so living, it seeks to influence the decisions of the government.

This exercise of power is not a matter of choice but of necessity. It is true of the national corporation. And it is wholly and equally true of the large multinational corporation.

Along with the omnipresent impulse to growth, the need to exercise extra-market power is the prime impulse to multinationality. A corporation in New York or Pittsburgh that is confined in its operations to the United States cannot bring power to bear in France to protect its prices in French markets, develop its dealer organization, defend or advance its position with the French consumer and protect or advance its position with the French government. Yet if the corporation is to do business in France, it will have to bring such power to bear, unconventional economic liturgy and official corporate rhetoric notwithstanding. It must have a base or presence there for the exercise of the market power and the public power needed to develop and protect its market position and its public position. The extent of the influence and power that can be so exercised will be in very rough proportion to the scale of this national presence.

Such facts explain the corporate tendency to go on from international sales representatives to a sales and marketing organization to a more fully integrated international development. This is the dynamic of modern international trade. This dynamic is reinforced by several further factors.

Where advanced technology is involved, only multinational operations realize the full economies of scale — the returns on one development cost are realized in several or numerous national markets.[2] And multinational intrusion by the corporations of one country also forces reciprocal action by those intruded upon. If there is no such response, markets are lost with no chance of compensatory gain. Such riposte may be necessary as well to preserve what economists call the "oligopolistic equilibrium" — meaning that the intruding corporation will not cut prices, for, if it does so, it will be vulnerable to the same action in reciprocal form in its own home country.

The forces just adumbrated are not transitory or casual. They will continue, and so, accordingly, will the development of multinational enterprise. This development would invite less anxiety if those involved were to learn to defend the multinational corporation with some semblance of plausibility and if they were to avoid behavior that cannot be defended. Before they can do this, they should examine the present defense.

Not seeing that the multinational corporation is the necessary manifestation of international trade in manufactured prod-

---

[2] As Peter J. Buckley and Mark Casson have shown in *The Future of the Multinational Enterprise* (London: Macmillan, 1976), there is a rough correlation between the research intensity of an industry and the extent of multinational operations.

ucts, its spokesmen rarely make this point. Failing also to see that power is an essential aspect of corporate development, they urge with great implausibility that none is exercised. Instead they argue that the foreign corporation — a guest in the house — must be most cautious about influencing the habits, tastes, markets or public opinion of the host country, and especially so the actions of its government.

The denial that the corporation has power derives from its acolyte economists, the neoclassical scholars who provide the accepted economic and business theology. This holds that markets are made by numerous entrepreneurs, and all are ruled by the market. All accept and should accept the instruction of the sovereign consumer. Anything else is monopoly or oligopoly or monopolistic competition — a market imperfection — and thus an aberration. And as market power is absent, so also is public power. The classic corporation, like the citizen, can petition the state; any further exercise of power is irregular and improper. Its association is "with words like free trade and free enterprise and laissez-faire, [which] holds that business is politically neutral, existing only to satisfy the economic desires of the world's people."[3] To concede that a corporation has market or public power in the neoclassical economic tradition is to confess to impropriety or antisocial behavior.

Having taken the position that they have no power, the executives of the multinational enterprise then go on to exercise power in the most visible possible fashion. An increasingly attentive public observes, and it sees, therewith, the mendacious or ridiculous character of the corporate defense. Having denied that he exercises power, having conceded that his possession of such power is improper and having conceded its especial inappropriateness for a foreign-based enterprise, the executive of the multinational corporation proceeds with the

[3] "People, Politics and Productivity: The World Corporation in the 1980's." Address by Walter B. Wriston in London on September 15, 1976. Mr. Wriston, the head of Citicorp and Citibank, here makes another common and deeply damaging error. That is to assume that being the leader of a large corporation somehow compels belief for wholly implausible assertions.

utmost reliability to convict himself by his own actions. The day after he disavows market power, explains that his corporation is wholly subordinate to the market and denies any thought of interfering with the government, his company announces a price increase, launches a major advertising campaign to alter consumer preference and is revealed to have brought public pressure in some world capital in favor of or against some regulation, or on behalf of some new weapon, or to have contributed substantially to some domestic or foreign politician not as an act of philanthropy.

The only reasonable defense of the multinational corporation is now the truth. That the corporation has power must be conceded. The only durable defense then is to hold that such exercise of power is inevitable and, if subject to proper guidance and restraint, can be socially useful.

A related line of defense of the multinational has been to seek to conceal or deny its foreign base and origin. The literature of multinational operations stresses this point *ad nauseam;* so, one judges, do the internal manuals, handbooks and lectures. The corporation operating in a foreign country should always keep what executives with a less than original gift for language unite in calling "a low profile." It should also make maximum use of local technical and managerial personnel; the number of people from the country of origin should be kept to a minimum. The corporation must always be a good local citizen.

This defense is also implausible, and self-defeating as well. No one worth persuading will ever believe that General Motors in its origins is anything but American, BP anything but British, Fiat other than Italian. Persuasion is possible but not against elementary common sense.

And there is also question as to why, in an adult industrial world, there should be apology for this kind of international development. International trade had always to be defended against those who saw only its costs, never its advantages; who saw only the intrusion of foreign competitors, never the resulting efficiency in supply or products or the reciprocal gains from greater exports. The multinational corporation comes into existence when international trade consists of modern technical, specialized or uniquely styled manufactured products. Accordingly, it should be defended, as international trade was defended, for its contribution to efficiency in production and marketing, to living standards and to reciprocal opportunities in other lands for the enterprises of the host country. This affirmative defense is excluded if a negative defense concedes, in effect, that there is something wrong with being a foreign corporation. And this is precisely what talk about "a low profile" or minimizing the foreign presence concedes. It would be a poor defense of foreign trade to pretend that French wines in the United States or American cotton in Britain were really domestic products or somehow not foreign. This tactic would concede that there was something wrong with international trade in these commodities. The "low profile" strategy of the multinational corporation is the equivalent.

A third defense of the multinational corporation, more often implicit than explicit, has been that it reflects special aptitude in the development of management skills. The multinational reflects, merely, the extension of this supposedly American skill to the other industrial countries of the world.

This defense lurks strongly in the consciousness of many American executives, but it also owes something to the flattery, genuine or contrived, of their foreign colleagues in the business world. In the prose of one British leader, the "track record of the United States — in business as well as government — makes legitimate your leadership of the rest of us in tackling the world's economic problems."[4] The multinational corporation,

---

[4] Sir Reay Geddes (Chairman, Dunlop Holdings, Ltd.), "A Multinationalist's View," *The Future Role of Business in Society* (New York: The Conference Board, 1977), p. 17.

so viewed, is the natural result of American economic leadership, the natural expression of a basic American skill, the
natural flowering of the American economic system.

The recent history of multinational development solidly
refutes this case. It is possible that American companies give
more prestige to business managers than do other countries,
Japan apart. No other country is so deferentially frightened of
anything that is thought to be damaging to business confidence.
We can certainly take credit for pioneering in the field of
business education and the theory and practice of management.
But it is nonsense to suppose that there is an American business or managerial genius, that there is anything known to
anyone from Illinois or California that cannot equally be
learned by anyone from England, Switzerland or Sweden. In
some aspects of multinational operations, in fact, there is an
American inferiority complex based, as with the Japanese, on
a congenital inadequacy in languages.

However rewarding to national or corporate vanity, the
notion that the multinational corporation reflects American
achievement or leadership is uniquely poisonous. Those who
take credit for it as an American achievement must then defend
it against the counterpart charge that it is an instrument of
American economic, cultural or military imperialism.

Let me now turn to the affirmative arguments — the case
that, with candor and a modest exercise of practical intelligence, could be made.

This requires, first of all, that the power of the multinational
corporation, like that of the national corporation, be conceded.
The point to be stressed is that this power is deployed, on
balance, for socially useful ends; where it is not, it must expect
to be restrained by the state.

The social and practical achievements of the international
corporation should then be mentioned. Thus, governments
spend notable energy seeking to improve the performance of

national industries — agriculture, housing, health services. Success is far from complete. The supply of automobiles, chemicals, computers, television sets, tobacco, alcohol and other products of multinational origin is rarely a source of complaint as to quantity or cost. Other achievements of the multinational corporation are the protection of international trade, the reduction of international friction, the creation of an international civil service, the fostering of local managerial autonomy and the more rapid dissemination of technology around the world.

Business firms, large and small, have never been indifferent to government policy on international trade. They have not hesitated to use their power to influence such policy. It has rarely been noticed or urged that, as the multinational manufacturing corporation has grown in influence, the importance of tariff barriers has receded. The barriers are not needed by the multinational firm; for integrating and rationalizing operations as between plants in different countries, they are a nuisance. Foreign competition also diminishes greatly in terror when you own the relevant competitor. So power that was once deployed on behalf of tariffs is no longer exercised. On balance, it is deployed against them. The European Economic Community did not come into existence because of a sudden access of economic enlightenment after World War II; it came into existence because modern corporate and multinational organizations had made the old boundaries and barriers obsolete. European farmers, with their different, earlier and essentially classical economic structure, would never have created the Common Market. They are now the source of most of its disputes and nearly all of its crises.

The great reduction of the importance of tariffs, except in agriculture and a few other national industries, has, in turn, removed or reduced an important source of international friction. This reduction is one substantial accomplishment of the multinational corporation, and it has made a yet more profound contribution to international amity. The absence of economic conflict, like peace in general, is so unobtrusive that we often do not notice it. It is almost never a part of the multinationals' defense.

In the last century national industries, notably in steel, coal, ship- and machine-building, were the natural allies of national governments in the development of armaments. They had an economic interest in fostering international tension, as Marxists rightly emphasized — even if they may have overemphasized it in relation to ordinary public and political chauvinism and professional military ambition and insanity. That there is still an economic interest in arms and their development no minimally perceptive person will deny. But no multinational corporation can be suspected of promoting tension between the governments of countries in which it operates. IBM cannot be associated with any suspicion of stirring up trouble between France and Germany in order to sell computers, or ICI in order to sell chemicals. And it is persuasive that such suspicion in a suspicious world does not even arise. We should wish that there were more multinational operations between the Soviet Union and the West.

The multinational corporation also brings into existence the world's first truly effective international civil service — men and women who have a nominal loyalty to their country of origin, a rhetorical commitment to the country in which they serve and a primary loyalty to Shell, Du Pont, Philips, Nestlé or whatever company employs them. In a world that has suffered so much from national chauvinism, and especially in this century, this development is a small pacifying influence, a civilized step on from narrow, militant nationalism. But in the corporate rhetoric this dividend also goes completely unmentioned.

A wholly reliable tendency in the modern very large corporation, national or multinational, is for authority to pass from the stockholders or owners to the management. This means that it matters less and less, and eventually not at all, who ultimately owns the corporation or where it is owned, for the owners are without power. And as power passes to the management of the multinational company, it passes in part to the management of its various national entities. They have and, as a matter of course, must have a voice in the operations in which they are directly involved. While ownership of a multinational can be concentrated in the originating country, management, by its nature, must always be partly local.

This defense is also very rarely used. Failure of imagination may again be a factor. But many managements are unwilling to abandon the ridiculous fiction that their stockholders have power. All know that in the great multinational they are dispersed and passive, vote their proxies automatically for the management slate and are never otherwise heard from. But one must sustain the myth that the owners are still somehow important. The principal corporate folk rites, the stockholders' and directors' meetings, must be so scripted and staged as to give the impression that the owners are somehow a force in the affairs of the corporation.

In consequence, Canadians are not allowed to notice that the Canadian management of a U.S. company has, and must have, an extensive say in its Canadian operations. They are allowed to see only that the corporate shares are held mostly in the United States and to believe that this is the fact of importance. They are never persuaded to the view that, since those stockholders are totally without power, it makes little practical difference whether the shares are held by Canadians, Americans or Saudi Arabians.

Once again the approved mythology is damaging to multinational corporations; the truth is favorable. Nor would this truth have cost. Most stockholders know they are without power. To say and keep saying that the real power lies with management, that ownership is irrelevant and that extensive managerial autonomy must be granted to national entities as a matter of simple necessity would combine truth and plausibility with the calming of national fears.

Finally, critics allege that the multinational corporation exports jobs, capital and technology. This is one of the few matters on which the multinational enterprise has developed a partial defense. It holds that, in one way or another, it cares most about its home country and labor force — these are its primary interests. It should hold more often than it does that, as it goes abroad, others from abroad come in. The aggregate result is a more rapid spread of technology, a better international division of labor, greater productivity, greater aggregate employment. This is the old case for international trade.

It is an indication of the poverty of thought brought to these matters that even this traditional defense is so imperfectly made.

No one should assume from the foregoing that the multinational enterprise is without capacity for antisocial action. And its opportunities for such action are important, for they mark out the zones of danger that the leadership of any sensibly run enterprise would avoid.

The first of these zones of danger lies in the peculiar advantage held by the multinational enterprise in its relationship to the national state. The large corporation, national or multinational in its nature, has power in the state — a point I again emphasize. As a general rule, the foreign-based company brings its power to bear more tactfully than the domestically based multinational. Volkswagen could not risk the kind of lobbying in Washington on emission standards that is usual for General Motors. General Motors in Canada would not dream of instructing Ottawa as to company needs with the wonderful arrogance that Canadian Pacific once considered appropriate to its corporate dignity.

Though the multinational by its corporate nature must speak and work for its public needs, some things it must not do: in the face of unwanted regulation, environmental constraints or unpleasant labor relations, it must not threaten to move operations to another country. This threat exploits a particular advantage of multinationality; it will always, and reasonably, be considered an unfair exercise of such advantage.

The multinational must eschew bribery, even though this is an accepted source of political revenue or personal income in the country in question. There is, in all countries, something peculiarly pejorative about being in foreign pay. Bribery is especially unwise for an American multinational, for to be paid by Americans, who are thought to be rich and powerful and therefore ill-intentioned, is especially indiscreet. And only the hopelessly obtuse can now be unaware of the first truth concerning the United States, which is that there is no such thing as a secret in the American Republic, only varying lengths of time until it is revealed.

The multinational company must be extremely cautious about moving large funds in anticipation of the fall in a national currency or its appreciation. Such action also exploits an advantage peculiar to multinationality; and it helps precipitate the depreciation or appreciation against which the speculative action is taken. In an age of currency instability such action by large multinationals is certain to provoke attack.

Perhaps eventually, since injunctions to virtue are not often compelling in such matters, large international movements of funds by the multinationals will bring some kind of international registration and regulation. This I would welcome, as should all multinational executives whose primary concern is with less damaging ways of making money.

The multinational must also be cautious in matters concerning the environment. There is no reason to suppose that the foreign intruder is likely to be more damaging to ambient air, water, landscape or the tranquillity of life than the native enterprises. Industrial progress has, with rare exceptions, involved a movement from dirty processes to cleaner ones — from coal to oil and gas and from the filthy steam engine to the internal combustion engine and the electric motor. The modern problem of pollution arises not from the fact that processes have become dirtier but from the fact that, though cleaner, so much more is produced and consumed. Local industries, being generally older, will often be dirtier than the newer arrival from abroad with the newer process or product.

But no one should doubt that foreign dirt is worse than domestic dirt and also that a little new dirt (or noise or damage to the landscape) is worse than old dirt (or noise or damage) to which the senses have become adjusted. The multinational corporation must be acutely sensitive to community feelings on environmental issues. It should rarely if ever seek to override them. It should be scrupulous in conforming to existing laws and regulations and be the last to object to valid or seemingly valid new constraints. It should lose no opportunity to improve voluntarily on present practice. None of this is to get its executives a reward in heaven. It is to maximize their hope for peace on earth.

The most important precaution has to do with weapons and the arms trade. It cannot have escaped anyone's notice that, over the last several years, weapons producers, along with the oil multinationals, have attracted an overwhelming share of the criticism that has been directed at the international operations of corporations. All multinational firms have suffered for the errors and absurdities of Lockheed and Northrop.

The weapons business will always be regarded with unease, as well it should. No sensitive person can look with equanimity on investment in the instruments of mass death; in recent times much of this business has been with countries that have other and more pressing needs for their resources. Arms have absorbed money that could and should have gone to other and better purposes. And the fact that this business (like much oil business) is with governments and politicians adds appreciably to the likelihood of scandal. Payments to politicians are bribes; the same payments, when made to businessmen, are a finder's fee or commission.

So if a multinational enterprise wishes to steer clear of attack, it should steer clear of the arms trade (though one cannot have much hope of this advice being taken if the company is already in it). But most multinationals are not in this trade. And it might be stressed that Lockheed and Northrop and the weapons firms generally are not, in the strict sense, multinational corporations. Exceptionally for organizations of their size, they do not have a substantial overseas presence. (Much of their trouble came from the operations of footloose and irresponsible agents and operators.) In the recent scandals civilian manufacturing multinationals have not been much involved. An habitual but misguided clubbiness among businessmen has kept the civilian companies from emphasizing this fact. One way to avoid guilt by association would be to make clear that there is no association.

There are other matters on which the multinational enterprise, because it is in conflict with never completely latent national suspicion, must be cautious. But let me conclude with a word of summary. The literature of multinational enterprise is vast, and volume has been notably a substitute for good sense. Quite a bit has been written with a view to telling the multinationals what they would like to hear — or what they might like to pay to hear. Regularly it denies or elides the power that is evident to all seeing eyes. The conclusion from such a defense is that the multinational enterprise should not exist. And a large further part of the literature, the critical as distinct from the sycophantic half, accepts that it should not. This literature then omits to say what should take its place. The attack from the left on the multinationals is a curiously dead-end exercise.

My case is that the multinational should affirm the possession and exercise of power, accept that it must be responsibly employed, and then urge, as it is entitled to do, that there have been substantial advantages from such employment of power in the past. But it must also concede that there is opportunity for the exercise of power that is socially damaging. So, subject to negotiation, prohibition of abuses must be accepted if not always welcomed.

All this will require thought — a scarce and ill-regarded commodity in this area. I urge it nonetheless, not out of compassion, not out of fear for the future of the multinational enterprise, not even from any especial warmth of friendship but rather out of a sense of offended art. Great organizations which pride themselves on their performance in so many other matters should not be so outrageously obtuse in the case they make for themselves.

6

What Comes After General Motors

FOR MOST THINGS that are used, enjoyed or are otherwise in the service of man, the possibility of improvement is assumed. In technology and science a quest for something better is required. So, certainly, in the production of goods. So also, in principle at least, in government. To be sure, we are less confident than we once were that what is new is better. It may only be different and a handle for the salesman. And, as with DDT or the SST, there is a heightened suspicion that long-run damage may outweigh short-run miracles. But on one thing agreement remains. Man must keep trying. To say that anything artificed by humans — machine, consumer product, service, organization — is perfect and thus beyond further change is intolerable, a declaration of intellectual and possibly even moral bankruptcy.

There is, however, one exception. That is the modern large corporation. It is the ultimate work of God and man. In the United States belief in its final excellence is nearly absolute. There is a continuing discussion in economics departments and law schools as to whether it is too big and should be broken up. But all but the most pathologically optimistic or intransigently imperceptive recognize that this discussion is wholly liturgical. Nothing, it is known, will happen in practice. And there is, further, no discussion of how the corporation might be altered as to ownership or restructured as to management and public control.

In Europe matters are only marginally different. In Britain there are recurrent proposals from the left wing of the Labour Party for the nationalization of selected large corporations. These suggestions are accompanied by energetic, on occasion rather desperate, assurances from avowedly more responsible leaders that nothing in the way of practical action is really meant. In recent elections in France the left coalition offered a platform of nationalization for a considerable list of large corporations. This was widely regarded as reflecting an effort by the Communists to embarrass their socialist colleagues by insisting on impractical as well as unpopular action. There is active discussion in Europe and some affirmative steps to place representatives of workers on boards of directors. This, for reasons that will be noted presently, does not portend great change.

So General Motors is, indeed, thought to be the final work of God and man. That this is so is more than slightly strange, for GM and its corporate counterparts are known to displease a great many people. Their products invite less than universal acclaim. They are thought unresponsive to public need and convenience. Legally through their executives or illegally by various laundries, numerous corporations have been shown to have bought heavily into the recent Republican administration in the United States and to have invested, if less heavily, in some Democrats as well. Politicians and parties in foreign countries have been even more generously subsidized. This generosity has been much criticized, even though it is thought more wicked to receive than to give. In its pricing, procurement of materials, persuasion of consumers and distribution of the resulting income, the modern large corporation, numerous scholars now concede, functions increasingly as an independent force — as an instrument for the exercise of power in which there is responsibility primarily to itself. And this power is independent of, perhaps even above, the modern state.

Thus that the corporation should be exempt from the general and required instinct for change and improvement is surprising. One is led to wonder if one of the more subtle, but also one of the more vital, instruments of its power is the way in which it makes unfashionable, even vaguely eccentric or irresponsible, all discussion of how its basic constitution might, over time, be changed or reformed. I've often urged that this is one of the prime services of contemporary economic instruction. It presents the modern business firm as the powerless puppet of the market. So emasculated, why should it be the cause of any worry?

This, however, is an argument I need not again pursue. My purpose here is rather to raise the forbidden question: Were the modern large corporation not exempt from the general quest for improvement, along what lines would this proceed? I have, I must confess, little hope of progress. But, just possibly, we might get the discussion under way.

The central tendency of the modern large corporation — and the source of the problems which increasingly provoke discussion — can be quickly summarized: with time, increasing size and the increasing technical and social complexity of its task, it loses its legitimacy as an entrepreneurial and capitalist institution. It becomes instead an instrument of its own organization. There is even considerable technical agreement among students of the corporation as to what occurs. In the large, fully developed modern corporation the stockholder or owner is the functionless and powerless recipient of income and capital gains or, on occasion, of capital losses. He is represented nominally by a board of directors which is selected by the management and which, in one of the most predictable of political rites, then appoints the managers that appointed it. Token ownership of stock by the directors is required. But no member of the board of General Motors, the world's largest industrial firm, owes his position to the votes he commands. The last man of whom this could be said was Mr. Charles Stewart Mott, who died in February 1973. His entrepreneurial drive in pursuit of his property interest had by then receded a bit. He was ninety-seven.

Until a few years ago all directors of the Standard Oil Company of New Jersey, now Exxon — in 1977 the second largest in earnings and assets among industrial corporations in the world — were members of the top management hierarchy itself. They elected themselves to the board, which appointed them to their management posts. Such elections are hard to lose and such appointments hard to miss. More recently, this arrangement being so candid as to seem a trifle obscene, some outside directors have been selected. The selection, of course, was by the management.

Although the euthanasia of stockholder power has long been recognized as a basic tendency in the development of the great corporation — in the United States ever since the path-breaking work of Adolf A. Berle and Gardiner C. Means in the nineteen-thirties[1] — the reality is still thought embarrassing. So the board of directors is accorded ratification rights where expenditure of money is concerned; this is because action involving money, however symbolic, always conveys the impression of power. Members of the board are usually of mature years. This ensures that they will be given the respect that civilized men rightly accord to age or incipient senility. These gestures, together with the impressive solemnity that surrounds directorial proceedings, help suggest stockholder power. And important interests are served by this charade. The corporate management achieves an aspect of capitalist legitimacy. The comfort-seeking economist can continue to speak of "the owning and profit-maximizing entrepreneur" who is the pivot of his system and, in a more practical way, of the textbook market. The radical can keep the capitalist as an enemy, for the latter far more readily inspires antipathy than the faceless industrial

[1] Adolf A. Berle and Gardiner C. Means, *The Modern Corporation and Private Property* (New York: Macmillan, 1933).

bureaucrat. But it is a charade that should mislead no one — and, in fact, it misleads no one save the innocent and those with a vested interest in the myth. The modern large corporation is a powerful thing. And it is a creature in the service of its own bureaucracy — of the massive organization that I have elsewhere called its technostructure.

Having independent power and being the creature of its own organization, the modern corporation, not surprisingly, serves the purposes of its own management. These purposes are frequently different from those of the public or substantial parts of it, and the latter are less than pleased. Specifically, the corporate bureaucracy, like all organization, seeks its own expansion. On such growth and aggrandizement, promotion and the resulting salary, prestige and perquisites of the management depend. Increasingly the persuasion of the customer and the power of the state are brought to the support of this expansion. Those who are not persuaded or who do not concur in this use of the power of the state — who do not respond to the need for more weapons, space exploration or highways and the supporting outlays that these require — deplore the result.

Also the expansion that rewards the industrial bureaucracy proceeds at different rates in different industries — in automobiles more rapidly on occasion than in refining capacity, in air conditioning more rapidly than in power supply, in advertising more rapidly than in newsprint. Nothing reliably relates growth in one industry to growth in related and dependent industries; thus we have fuel crises, power crises, newsprint crises. And we find governments creating planning authorities to do what the market no longer accomplishes. This has been true even of Republican administrations in the United States, although Republicans prefer to speak of czars rather than planners. The word *czar* has an indubitably conservative ring, and no one has told these worthy gentlemen what comes after a czar.

Economic expansion has also come to be thought indifferent to environmental considerations; either industries or their products are thought negligent in their treatment of air, water, the countryside or our ears. That a bureaucracy empowered to pursue its own interest in growth should be hostile to such environmental effects accords also with expectations. So does the frequent claim of the auto industry that inflation could easily be cured by allowing a little more air pollution. In the modern large corporation truth tends to be what best serves economic interest.

We have also, in highly visible form, the effect on the distribution of income. There is first the distribution within the corporate hierarchy itself. As an individual rises in this hierarchy, his bureaucratic power increases — and among the things so increased is the power to set his own compensation. Thus compensation in the large corporation has become very generous. No one can seriously pretend (although some do) that it depends on the scarcity, and thus the market price, of the talent involved. It is the nature of organization that it takes men of average ability but diverse knowledge and combines their efforts for a result that is far better than any individual could achieve. To a marked extent organization provides a substitute for exceptional talent — something that is wholly recognized by the total indifference of the stock market to the changes in command in the great corporation and by the Stygian obscurity into which the greatest executive disappears on the day on which he retires. The name of no past president of General Motors, General Electric, General Dynamics or General Mills can be recalled by anyone except near neighbors, relatives and his wife.

Not only is compensation in the modern corporation unrelated to function, it can, on occasion, be inversely related to performance. The letters ITT are now a code reference to ill-considered and improper exercise of political influence. Political matters are peculiarly the responsibility of top management; on nothing, one would expect, could the man in charge be held more sternly to account. And this is especially so if the effect of such administration on earnings and securities values is adverse. For many recent years the manifold securities of ITT were among the least well regarded of portfolio assets. Mr. Harold Geneen, the head of the enterprise, was, all during this time, one of the three or four most highly paid executives in the United States. In 1973, the Chairman and chief executive of General Motors, Mr. R. C. Gerstenberg, received $923,000, and President Edward N. Cole, $833,000. This for both was an increase. The year is important, for it was the one in which these men failed to foresee the first fuel shortage and a shift to smaller cars. For the year ending January 1976, one of the highest paid executives in the United States was Meshulam Riklis. His conglomerate, Rapid-American, was one of the less profitable of its kind.

The salary of the chief executive of the large corporation is not a market reward for achievement. It is frequently in the nature of a warm personal gesture by the individual to himself. This no one likes to say. In all economic discussion we praise pecuniary motivation and consider it a legitimate as well as socially serviceable thing. But we are reluctant to suggest that the chief executives of the modern large corporation, when setting their own pay, are motivated to go after all the traffic will bear.

The compensation of the stockholder in the modern firm is no less anomalous. In the large corporation he is only rarely called upon for equity capital. Capital is all but exclusively provided out of earnings or by borrowing. The stockholder, we've seen, has no power and hence no role in the running of the firm. What then is the case for the private participating interest? None that wouldn't be as well served by converting his property right to a fixed return.

Associated with the position of the stockholder is the increasingly asymmetrical role of profits and losses in the modern large corporation. Profits may still be made. Their function is still much celebrated. So are the virtues of private enterprise. And so are its immunities — its right to be free from government interference. All this changes dramatically when the great corporation sustains a loss. Then it becomes too large and too important to be allowed to fail and go out of business. So long as they were making profits, the Penn Central, Lockheed and the Franklin National Bank were flagships of the private enterprise system. Once their profits turned into losses, they became the highly deserving wards of the state. A few years back Consolidated Edison, which prudently calls itself an "investor-owned utility," entered upon a particularly dark period in a generally dark life. The *New York Times* ran a question-and-answer series on its probable fate. Would it go bankrupt? "No, the ramifications of such action are too severe." Would it be taken over by the public? "Yes, for investors this might be the better way." This, it was agreed, would invite "a major ideological change." It was implied that, as an alternative to bankruptcy, this ideological change could be accomplished with relative ease.

As in the United States, so in other countries. In Britain, there is strong objection to public ownership except as in the case of Rolls-Royce, British Leyland, the shipyards or the earlier instance of the coal pits, where private mismanagement or miscalculation brought disaster. Then it is favored. The Italians have built a large public sector of the economy from the failures of private enterprise and the French a slightly smaller one. The tendency is the same elsewhere. When considering what comes after General Motors, we cannot exclude some considerable role for the government. The public and private embrace is already great.

The first change in the modern large corporation should involve, plausibly, the two bodies that have lost function — the stockholders and the board of directors.

The case for private ownership diminishes drastically when the stockholder ceases to have power — when he or she or it becomes a purely passive recipient of income. Then, since the management is a self-governing, self-perpetuating bureaucracy, no claim can be made to the traditional immunity associated with property ownership. A logical course will be for the state to replace the helpless stockholder with an effective supervisory and policy-setting body. One forthright way to accomplish this would be to have a public holding company take over the common stock. There is, of course, no case for singling out one class of property for sequestration. The common stock would be valued, perhaps by reference to past stock market prices or perhaps by more specific appraisal of assets, and the stockholder paid off with fixed, interest-bearing securities. Whether these should be guaranteed by the state is an interesting question. It is possible that they should be; this would accept as fact the public rescue of creditors that is now normal. It should be noted that no public expenditure would be involved in this transaction, only an exchange of assets.

Were the criterion for this action that the firm be a full, self-governing bureaucracy — that the power of the management be plenary and that of the stockholder nil — some hundred or more of the largest industrial firms in the United States would be eligible, together with a fair number of the larger utility, transportation, financial and merchandising corporations. In practice, as a man of recognized caution, I would be content to start with three obvious categories. The first would be the big weapons firms — Lockheed, General Dynamics, Thiokol — which are now, except in name, public enterprises. The government is overwhelmingly their most important customer; it supplies them with most of their working and much of their fixed capital, covers their cost overruns and otherwise stands by to rescue them when they are in trouble. What is called private enterprise is here a disguise for costly and unexamined access to the public trough. Then there are the oil majors. These have a strong environmental impact, a large influence on foreign policy and a stranglehold on the public pocketbook. Public ownership in this field has worked well elsewhere, notably in Britain, Austria and numerous other countries. It would, no one should doubt and least of all the oil men, be widely popular. And the earnings would offset the losses from the third and inescapable category, which, of course, is the losers — the railroads and the other yet undisclosed candidates for public assistance as they come on hard times. It is now taken for granted that the state will inherit the turkeys. And this is necessary; we can't get along without railroads, banks or perhaps even the Chrysler Corporation, which has already required rescue in its British manifestation. But, this being so, it is surely proper that the public should also inherit some profit-makers. There is a case for symmetry of a sort here.

As equity passes to the public, so would capital gains. Thus would be eliminated a wholly adventitious source of public enrichment derived extensively from the accident of parentage or grandparentage. The blight that was always over the careers of men like Nelson Rockefeller would thus, in time, be removed.

However, it is important that liberals not have false hopes of the effect of the change on operational detail. One reason the private stockholder was excluded from management was that his intrusion, since it was uninformed, was damaging. So it is with any outsider; a public owner cannot and should not participate in the routine of management. This has come to be well understood in many countries, with the consequence that public ownership has been reconciled with extensive managerial autonomy and marked commercial success. The example of automobile manufacturers — Renault, Alfa-Romeo, Volkswagen — is especially impressive.

Where the private stockholder disappears, the board of directors should be replaced with what might variously be called a board of public auditors or a board of public inspectors. I propose to use the first name; it is important only that the designation carry no connotation of operational authority. This board should be of moderate size — perhaps eight members. A minority of the members, perhaps three, should be selected, as now, by the management. This minority would include the senior executives of the firm. The remaining five would be designated as public members by the state. Like judges, they should be men and women of quality and strong public instinct. They should not be of excessive age; they should be of persistent, informed and disciplined curiosity. They would be expected to take their jobs seriously, meet at least monthly, and they would be paid. Since the board of public auditors would have no operational duties, I do not see it as a useful place for the exercise of trade union or other specific participant interest. Nor do I think that participation on present boards of directors, which are operationally powerless bodies, much serves trade union ends. Here also the defense of the worker interest is more effectively served by traditional union means. That the board of public auditors would reflect the consumer interest is inherent in its public character. The consumer *is* the public and vice versa.

The board would ratify the selection and promotion of top management and, in the event of self-perpetuating mediocrity, replace it. And, in addition to the conventional financial audit, it would maintain continuing surveillance to ensure honest conformity with legally established public goals on bribery, safety of products, pollution, political neutrality and the rest. To this end, it should, of course, have full access to the information available in the firm — to prices, costs, investment planning, product design, advertising and merchandising methods and plans, and much more. On important or continuing matters it would function by committee and could request staff assistance.

The board of auditors would also generally be the place for informed discussion of the public impact of the major policies of the firm. Some public benefit would come from this discussion and the resulting response. Policy directives on public matters would, of course, be binding on management. It would be important, however, that this power be used sparingly. Management must retain the major powers of decision and therewith the capacity to perform. And it must be held responsible for effective performance. It is a sound rule that matters of public urgency — those pertaining to the environment, product design, advertising — should be controlled by general law, not by individual company decision.

Both the findings and deliberations of the board of public auditors should be known. Any notion that the great corporation is a private entity is obsolete. From the reaction to what is made available by the board of public auditors would come some of the knowledge that would guide its discussions and findings. From this information and discussion would also come the raw material for legislation setting and refining the rules on what can be done to air, water, the tranquillity of life, the safety of consumers and by way of public bamboozlement — in short, for establishing the parameters within which corporate growth and profit-making should proceed. These parameters, all conservatives should recognize, are increasingly their protection against assault on the idea of growth itself.

Plenary power should, obviously, be accorded to the board of public auditors for setting the range of top executive compensation. That power is now exercised by the people who receive the compensation themselves or by their appointees. This is far too convenient. While to reduce executive compensation in the new public corporations to civil service levels might be too radical a step, there is no excuse for the present munificence, and there is no relation to incentives. That is because no executive can possibly have it suggested that he adjusts his effort or the exercise of his intelligence to his compensation.

If large tasks are to be performed, large corporations are necessary. In considering what comes after General Motors the task is to bring the large organization into line with the modern reality. As it develops, stockholder power becomes irrelevant, the stockholder representation by the board of directors a farce. The corporation becomes a self-governing and self-perpetuating instrument of its management, and this the myth no longer conceals. By ridding it of the obsolete features, substituting a public surveillance and at the same time safeguarding its operational autonomy, the chances for the orderly survival of the great corporation could well be strengthened. What I here suggest, modified no doubt by further discussion, could well be a goal of all enlightened executives. Of this, however, I have no great hope. The most one can ask is that a few rational professionals here and there will be repelled by the myth of stockholder power and directorial omniscience that they are now required to perpetrate and perpetuate and will accept that the corporation is unfinished business, that there might be room for further change.

7

The Founding Faith:
Adam Smith's *Wealth of Nations*[1]

> It is not from the benevolence of the butcher, the brewer, or
> the baker, that we expect our dinner but from their regard to
> their own interest. We address ourselves, not to their humanity
> but to their self-love, and never talk to them of our own neces-
> sities but of their advantages.
>
> *Wealth of Nations*

ADAM SMITH, not to put too fine an edge on matters, was Scotland's greatest son. *Wealth of Nations* is his greatest and almost
his only book. As Karl Marx is much too valuable a source of
social insight to be left as the exclusive property of the Communists, so Adam Smith is far too wise and amusing to be
relegated to conservatives, few of whom have ever read him.

Smith was born in 1723 in what was then the small port town
of Kirkcaldy on the Firth of Forth across from Edinburgh. The
enduring exponent of the freedom of trade was the son of the
local collector of customs. After study at the evidently excellent
local school, he went on to the University of Glasgow and then
to Oxford (Balliol College) for six years. Returning to Scotland, he became, first, professor of logic and then, in 1752, pro-

---

1 This is a revision of a paper given in Kirkcaldy, Scotland, Adam Smith's birthplace, in June of 1973, at a gathering to celebrate the 250th anniversary of his
birth. In *The Age of Uncertainty* (Boston: Houghton Mifflin, 1977) I have dealt
at more length (and with some overlapping) with the events of Smith's life.

fessor of moral philosophy at the University of Glasgow. This chair he resigned in 1763 to travel on the Continent as the well-paid tutor of the young Duke of Buccleuch, a family possessed to this day of a vast acreage of dubious land on the Border. In Europe Smith made the acquaintance of the Physiocratic philosophers and economists Quesnay and Turgot, as well as Voltaire and other notable contemporaries, and used his time and mind well. He then returned to Kirkcaldy where, for the next ten years, subject to lengthy sojourns in London and to the despair of some of his friends who feared he would never finish, he engaged himself in the writing of *Wealth of Nations.*

This book was published in 1776, a few weeks before the Declaration of Independence, and there was some relationship between the two events. Unlike his friend David Hume (who died that August) and consistently with his economic views, Smith deplored the separation. He had wanted instead full union, full and equal representation of the erstwhile colonies in Parliament, free trade within the union, equal taxation along with equal representation and the prospect that, as the American part developed in wealth and population, the capital would be removed from London to some new Constantinople in the West.

Wealth of Nations, at least among the knowledgeable, was an immediate success. Gibbon wrote: "What an excellent work is that with which our common friend Mr. Adam Smith has enriched the public...most profound ideas expressed in the most perspicuous language."[2] Hume, in a much quoted letter, was exuberant:

> Euge! Belle! Dear Mr. Smith. — I am much pleased with your performance, and the perusal of it has taken me from a state of great anxiety. It was a work of so much expectation, by yourself, by

2 Edward Gibbon, quoted in John Rae, *Life of Adam Smith* (New York: Augustus M. Kelley, 1965), p. 287.

your friends, and by the public, that I trembled for its appearance, but am now much relieved . . . it has depth and solidity and acuteness, and is so much illustrated by curious facts that it must at last attract the public attention.[3]

The public response — to two volumes costing £1 16s., the equivalent of perhaps forty dollars today — was also good. The first edition was soon sold out, although this intelligence would be more valuable were the size of the edition known. Smith spent the next couple of years in London, being, one gathers, much feted by his contemporaries for his accomplishment, and then, having been appointed Commissioner of Customs in Edinburgh, an admirable sinecure, he returned to Scotland. He died there in 1790.

By this time, *Wealth of Nations,* though at first ignored by politicians, was having an influence on men of affairs. A year and a half after Smith's death, Pitt, introducing his budget, said of Smith that his "extensive knowledge of detail and depth of philosophical research will, I believe, furnish the best solution of every question connected with the history of commerce and with the system of political economy."[4] Not since, in the non-socialist world at least, has a politician committed himself so courageously to an economist.

Smith has not been a popular subject for biographers. He was a bachelor. His best-remembered personal trait was his absent-mindedness. Once, according to legend, he fell into deep thought and walked fifteen miles in his dressing gown before regaining consciousness. His manuscripts, by his instruction, were destroyed at his death. He disliked writing letters, and few of these have survived. The papers of those with whom he did correspond or which reflected his influence were destroyed, mostly because of lack of interest, and some, it appears, as late as 1941 or 1942. Adam Smith's only other major published

3 David Hume, quoted in Rae, p. 286.
4 William Pitt, before the House of Commons on February 17, 1792, quoted in Rae, pp. 290–291.

work, *The Theory of Moral Sentiments,* reflects interests that were antecedent to his concern with political economy. No biography of Adam Smith has superseded that by John Rae, first published nearly eighty years ago.

Though Smith's life has attracted little attention, much has centered on *Inquiry into the Nature and Causes of the Wealth of Nations,* to give the title of his masterpiece its full resonance. With *Das Kapital* and the Bible, *Wealth of Nations* enjoys the distinction of being one of the three books that people may refer to at will without feeling they should have read them. Scholarly dispute over what is Smith's principal contribution has continued ever since publication. This is partly because there is so much in the book that every reader has full opportunity to exercise his own preference.

Exercising that preference, I have always thought that two of Smith's achievements have been neglected. One, mentioned by Gibbon, is his gift for language. Few writers ever, and certainly no economist since, have been as amusing, lucid or resourceful — or on occasion as devastating. Many people rightly remember his conclusion that "People of the same trade seldom meet together, even for merriment and diversion, but the conversation ends in a conspiracy against the public, or in some contrivance to raise prices."[5] There are many more such gems. He noted that "The late resolution of the Quakers in Pennsylvania, to set at liberty all their negro slaves, may satisfy us that their number cannot be very great."[6] And, anticipating Thorstein Veblen, he observed that "With the greater part of rich people, the chief enjoyment of riches consists in the parade of riches . . ."[7] On the function or nonfunction of stockholders, no one in the next two centuries was more penetrating in however many words: "[Stockholders] seldom pretend to understand

---

[5] Adam Smith, *Wealth of Nations* (Edinburgh: Adam and Charles Black, 1863), p. 59.

[6] Smith, p. 172.

[7] Smith, p. 79.

any thing of the business of the company; and when the spirit of faction happens not to prevail among them, give themselves no trouble about it, but receive contentedly such half-yearly or yearly dividend as the directors think proper to make to them."[8] One of Smith's most useful observations, which should always be kept in mind when alarm substitutes for thought, is not in *Wealth of Nations*. On hearing from Sir John Sinclair in October 1777 that Burgoyne had surrendered at Saratoga and of his friend's fear that the nation was ruined, Smith said, "There is a great deal of ruin in a nation."[9]

Also neglected now are the "curious facts" that enchanted Hume and of which *Wealth of Nations* is a treasure house. Their intrusion has, in fact, been deplored. As a writer Smith was a superb carpenter but a poor architect. The facts appear in lengthy digressions which have been criticized as such. But for any discriminating reader it is worth the interruption to learn that the expenses of the civil government of the Massachusetts Bay Colony "before the commencement of the present disturbances," meaning the Revolution, were only £18,000 a year and that this was a rather sizeable sum compared with the expenses of New York and Pennsylvania at £4500 each and of New Jersey at £1200. (These and numerous other details on the colonies reflect an interest which John Rae believes was stimulated by Benjamin Franklin.)

Also, were it not for Smith, we might not know that after a bad storm, or "inundation," the citizens of the Swiss canton of Underwald (Unterwalden) came together in an assembly where each publicly confessed his wealth to the multitude and was then assessed, *pro rata*, for the repair of the damage. Or that, at least by Smith's exceptionally precise calculation, Isocrates earned £3333 6s, 8d. (upward of 60,000 of today's dollars) for "what we would call one course of lectures, a number which will not appear extraordinary, from so great a city to

8 Smith, p. 333.
9 Adam Smith, quoted in Rae, p. 343.

so famous a teacher, who taught too what was at that time the most fashionable of all sciences, rhetoric."[10] Or that Plutarch was paid the same. Or, continuing with professors, that those who are subject to reward unrelated to their capacity to attract students will perform their duty in "as careless and slovenly a manner as that authority will permit" and that in "the university of Oxford, the greater part of the public professors [those with endowed or salaried chairs] have, for these many years, given up altogether even the pretence of teaching."[11]

So no one should neglect Smith's contribution to expository prose and "curious facts." Now as to economic thought and policy. Here a sharp and obvious distinction must be made between what was important in 1776 and what is important now. The first is very great; the second, save in the imagination of those who misuse Smith as a prophet of reaction, is much less so. The business corporation which Smith deplored and the wealth that accumulated in consequence of his advice combined to reduce the later relevance of that advice. But first we must consider his meaning in 1776.

Smith's economic contribution to his own time can be thought of as falling into three categories — method, system and advice. The second, overflowing onto the third, is by far the most important.

As to method, Smith gave to political economy, later to become economics, the basic structure that was to survive almost intact at least for the next hundred and fifty years. This structure begins with the problem of value — how prices are set. Then comes the question of how the proceeds are shared — how the participants in production are rewarded. These latter are the great trinity of labor, capital and land. Along the way is the role of money. Thereafter come banking, international trade, taxation, public works, defense and the other functions of the

10 Smith, p. 61.
11 Smith, p. 342.

state. Other writers, notably the Physiocrats, had previously given political economy a fairly systematic frame, although, as Alexander Gray, a later Glasgow professor, observed, they had "embellished it with strange frills." But it was Smith who, for the English-speaking world, provided the enduring structure.

The framework, in turn, was more important than what it enclosed. Although Smith's treatment of value, wages, profits and rents suggested what was to follow, it was, in all respects, a beginning and not an end. Thus, as one example, Smith held that the supply of workers would increase, *pari passu,* with an increase in the sustenance available for their support. David Ricardo translated this thought into the iron law of wages — the rule that wages would tend always to fall to the bare minimum necessary to sustain life. And Thomas Robert Malthus, going a step further, adduced his immortal conclusion that people everywhere would proliferate to the point of starvation. Subsequent scholars — the marginal utility theorists, Alfred Marshall, others — added further modifications to the theory of prices, wages, interest, profits and rent, and yet further transmutations were, of course, to follow. Smith was left far behind.

But the structure he gave to economics and the explanation of economic behavior that it contained were, for Smith, only steps in the creation of his larger system — his complete view of how economic life should be arranged and governed. This was his central achievement. It provided a set of guiding rules for economic policy that were comprehensive and consistent without being arbitrary or dogmatic.

In the Smithian system the individual, suitably educated, is left free to pursue his own interest. In doing so, he serves not perfectly but better than by any alternative arrangement the common public purpose. Self-interest or selfishness guides men, as though by the influence of "an invisible hand," to the exercise of the diligence and intelligence that maximize productive effort and thus the public good. Private vice becomes a public virtue, which has been considered ever since a most convenient thing.

In pursuit of private interest, producers exploit the opportunities inherent in the division of labor — in, broadly speaking, the specialized development of skill for the performance of each small part of a total task of production. Combined with the division of labor is the natural propensity of man "to truck, barter or exchange." The freedom of the individual to do his best both in production and in exchange is inhibited by regulation and taxation. Thus the hand of the state should weigh on him as lightly as possible. The limiting factor on the division of labor — roughly, the scale of specialized productive activity — is the size of the market. Obviously this should be as wide as possible. Thus Smith's case against internal monopolistic or international restrictions on trade.

Smith's precursors, the mercantilists, held that national well-being and national strength derived from and required the accumulation by the country of precious metal. Smith held — as one would now say and as he in effect did say — that they derived instead from the productivity of the labor force. Given an industrious and productive labor force, in the most majestic of Smith's arguments, there would be no need to worry about the stock of gold. The gold would always come.

Such, in greatest compression, is the Smithian system — the one that Pitt proclaimed as "the best solution of every question connected . . . with the system of political economy."

Smith's third contribution was in the field of practical policy. His advice — on banking, education, colonies, support of the sovereign (including his famous canons of taxation and extending even to recommendations for the reform of taxation in France), public works, joint-stock companies and agriculture — was infinitely abundant. No economist since has offered more. With many exceptions and frequent modifications to fit the circumstances, this advice is in keeping with Smith's system. The bias in favor of freeing or unburdening the individual to pursue his own interest is omnipresent, and so is Smith's belief that men will toil effectively only in the pursuit of pecuniary self-interest. There will be occasion for a further word on this advice; now we must see what of Smith survives.

Needless to say, the mordant language and the curious facts remain; it is too bad they are not more read and enjoyed. Also Smith's concept of the economic problem and the division of the subject between value and distribution are still to be found in that part of the textbooks that economists call microeconomics. His particular conclusions as to how prices, wages, rents and return to capital are determined and his views on gold, paper currency, banks and the like are now mostly of antiquarian interest.

Nor does all of the abundant advice just mentioned have modern meaning. It better illuminates life in the eighteenth century than it does any current problems. Until recently the textbooks on taxation included reverent mention of Smith's four great canons. But no one now coming to them without knowledge of their author would think them very remarkable. That taxes should be certain or predictable and arbitrary in their bite; that they should be so levied and collected as to fit the reasonable convenience of the taxpayer; and that the cost of collection should be a modest part of the total take were all important in 1776. They still are, but these things are fairly well accepted now.

Smith's fourth canon, that the "subjects of every state ought to contribute towards the support of the government, as nearly as possible, in proportion to their respective abilities; that is, in proportion to the revenue which they respectively enjoy under the protection of the state,"[12] could be taken as a prescription for a proportional (i.e., fixed percentage) as distinct

12 Smith, p. 371.

from a progressive income tax. Some beleaguered rich have so argued. In fact, Smith was speaking only of what seemed possible and sensible in his own day. He would, almost certainly, have moved with the times. It might be added that his modest prescription gives no place to tax shelters, special treatment of state and municipal bonds or the oil depletion allowance and no comfort to those who otherwise believe that they were intended by nature to be untroubled by the IRS. Numerous of the great rich in the United States would find even Adam Smith's proportional prescription rather costly as compared with what they now pay.

The next and more interesting question concerns Smith's system — his rules for guiding economic life. What of that survives? Is economic life still directed in appreciable measure by the invisible hand — in modern language, by the market? What has happened to the notion of the minimal state, and is it forever dead? And what of Smith's plea for the widest possible market both within and between nations?

Nothing so rejoices the conservative soul as the thought that it all survives. It doesn't. Smith was the victim of one major miscalculation. And, as earlier noted, he was damaged by the institution that he deplored, the business corporation. His system was also gravely impaired by the very success of the prescription that he offered.

Smith's miscalculation was of man's capacity, perhaps with some social conditioning, for cooperation. He thought it negligible. Men would work assiduously for their own pecuniary advantage; on shared tasks, even for shared reward, they would continue to do as little as authority allowed. Only in defeating or circumventing that authority — in minimizing physical and intellectual toil and maximizing indolence and sloth — would they bring real effort and ingenuity to bear. But not otherwise. People work only if working for themselves; there is no more persistent theme in *Wealth of Nations*. It is why government tasks are poorly performed. It is why civil servants are an uncivil and feckless crew. It is his case against the British bureaucracy in India. It is why the Oxford professors on a secure salary lapsed into idleness. And especially it is why, in Smith's view, joint-stock companies, except for routine tasks, had little to commend them. Their best chance for survival, one to which the minds of the directors almost invariably turned, was to obtain a monopoly of their industry or trade, a tendency to which Smith devoted some of his finest scorn. Otherwise their officers concerned themselves not with enriching the company but with enriching themselves or not enriching anyone.

In fact, experience since Smith has shown that man's capacity for cooperative effort is very great. Perhaps this was the product of education and social conditioning, something that no one writing in the eighteenth century could have foreseen. Conceivably Smith, handicapped by his environment, judged all races by the Scotch (as we are correctly called) and their much celebrated tendency to self-seeking recalcitrance. Most likely he failed to see the pride people could have in their organization, their desire for the good opinion or esteem of their co-workers and their satisfaction in what Thorstein Veblen would call "the instinct of workmanship."

In any case, governments in the performance of public tasks, some of great technical and military complexity, corporations in pursuit of growth, profit and power, and advanced socialist states in pursuit of national development and power have been able to enlist a great intensity of cooperative effort.

The most spectacular example of this cooperative effort — or perhaps, to speak more precisely, of a successful marriage of cooperative and self-serving endeavor — has been the corporation. The way in which the corporation has come to dominate economic life since 1776 need hardly be emphasized. This development Smith did not foresee, an understandable flaw. But he also thought both the form or structure and the cooperative or organized effort inherent in corporate development flatly impossible.

The corporation that Smith did not think possible was then extensively destructive of the minimal state that he prescribed. This destruction it accomplished in several ways. The corporation had needs — franchises, rights-of-way, capital, qualified manpower, support for expensive technological development, highways for its motor cars, airways for its airplanes — which only the state could supply. A state that served its corporations as they required quickly ceased, except in the minds of more romantic conservatives, to be minimal.

Also, a less evident point, the economy of which the great corporation was so prominent a part along with the unions was no longer stable. The corporation retained earnings for investment, as did the individuals it enriched. There was no certainty that all of such savings would be invested. The resulting shortage of demand could be cumulative. And in the reverse circumstances wages and prices might force each other up to produce an enduring and cumulative inflation. The state would be called upon to offset the tendency to recession by offsetting excess savings and stabilizing the demand for goods. This was the message of Keynes. And the state would need to intervene to stabilize prices and wages if inflation were to be kept within tolerable limits. Both actions, traceable directly to corporate and counterpart union development, were blows at the Smithian state.

The corporation, as it became very large, also ceased to be subordinate to the market. It fixed prices, sought out supplies, influenced consumers and otherwise exercised power not different in kind from the power of the state itself. As Smith would have foreseen, this power was exercised in the interest of its possessors, and on numerous matters — the use of air, water and land — the corporate interest diverged from the public interest. It also diverged where, as in the case of the weapons firms, the corporation was able to persuade the state to be its customer. Corporate interest did not coincide with public interest as the Smithian system assumed. So there were appeals by the public to the government for redress and further enhancement of the state. All this was not as Smith would have thought.

Finally, Smith's system was destroyed by its own success. In the nineteenth century and with a rather deliberate recognition of their source, Britain was governed by Smith's ideas. So, though more by instinct than by deliberate philosophical commitment, was the United States. And directly or through such great disciples as the French economist J. B. Say, Smith's influence extended to Western Europe. In the context of time and place, the Smithian system worked; there was a vast release of productive energy, a great increase in wealth, a large though highly uneven improvement in living standards. Then came the corporation with its superior access to capital (including that reserved from its own earnings), its great ability to adapt science and technology to its purposes and its strong commitment to its own growth through expanding sales and output. This, and by a new order of magnitude, added to the increase in output, income and consumption.

This increase in well-being was also damaging to the Smithian system. It was not possible to combine a highly productive economy and the resulting affluence with a minimal state. Public regulation had to develop in step with private consumption; public services must bear some reasonable relationship to the supply of private services and goods. Both points are accepted in practice, if not in principle. A country cannot have a high consumption of automobiles, alcohol, transportation, communications or even cosmetics without public rules governing their use and public facilities to rescue people from accidents and exploitation. The greater the wealth, the more men need to protect it, and the more that is required to pick up the discarded containers in which so much of it comes. Also in rough accord with increased private consumption goes an increased demand for public services — for education, health care, parks and public recreation, postal services and the infinity of other things that must be provided or are best provided by the state.

Among numerous conservatives there is still a conviction that the minimal state was deliberately destroyed by socialists, planners, *étatists* and other wicked men who did not know what they were about, or knew all too well. Far more of the responsibility lies with Smith himself. Along with the corporation, his system created the wealth that made his state impossible.

In one last area, it will be insisted, Adam Smith does survive. Men still respect his inspired and inspiring call for the widest possible market, one that will facilitate in the greatest degree the division of labor. After two centuries the dominant body of opinion in industrial nations resists tariffs and quotas. And in Europe the nation-states have created the ultimate monument to Adam Smith, the European Economic Community. In even more specific tribute to Smith, it is usually called the Common Market.

Even here, however, there is less of Smith than meets the eye. Since the eighteenth century, and especially in the last fifty years, domestic markets have grown enormously. That of insular Britain today is far greater than that of Imperial Britain at the height of empire. The technical opportunities in large-scale production have developed significantly since 1776. But national markets have developed much, much more. Proof lies in the fact that General Motors, IBM, Shell and Nestlé do not produce in ever larger plants as would be the case if they needed to realize the full opportunities inherent in the division of labor. Rather, they regularly produce the same items in many relatively small plants all over the world. Except perhaps in the very small industrial countries — Holland, Belgium, Luxembourg — domestic markets have long been large enough so that even were producers confined to the home market, they would realize the full economies of scale and the full technical advantages of the division of labor.

The Common Market and the modern enlightenment on international trade owe much more to the nontechnical needs of the modern multinational corporation than they do to Adam Smith. The multinational corporation stands astride national boundaries.[13] Instead of seeking tariff support from the state against countries that have a comparative advantage, it can move into the advantaged countries to produce what it needs. At the same time modern marketing techniques require that it be able to follow its products into other countries to persuade consumers and governments and, in concert with other producers, to avoid the price competition that would be disastrous for all. So, for the multinational corporation, tariffs, to speak loosely and generally, are both unnecessary and a nuisance. It would not have escaped the attention of Adam Smith, although it has escaped the attention of many in these last few years, that where there are no corporations, as in agriculture, the Common Market is more contentious and less than popular. The tariff enlightenment following World War II has resulted not from a belated reading of *Wealth of Nations* but from the much more powerful tendency for what serves the needs of large enterprises to become sound public policy.

But if time and the revolution that he helped set in motion have overtaken Smith's system and Smith's advice, there is one further respect in which he remains wonderfully relevant. That is in the example he sets for professional economists — for what, at the moment, is a troubled, rather saddened discipline. Smith is not a prophet for our time, but, as we have seen, he was magnificently in touch with his own time. He broke with the mercantilist orthodoxy to bring economic ideas abreast of the industrial and agricultural changes that were only then

13 See the earlier essay, "The Multinational Corporation: How to Put Your Worst Foot Forward or in Your Mouth."

just visible on the horizon. His writing in relation to the Industrial Revolution involved both prophecy and self-fulfilling prophecy. He sensed, even if he did not fully see, what was about to come, and he greatly helped to make it come.

The instinct of the economist, now as never before, is to remain with the past. On that, there is a doctrine, a theory — one that is now elaborately refined. And there are practical advantages. An economist's capital, as I've elsewhere observed, lies in what he knows. To stay with what is accepted is also consistent with the good life — with the fur-lined comfort of the daily routine between suburb, classroom and office.[14] To such blandishments, economists are no more immune than other people. The tragedy lies in their own resulting obsolescence. As the economic world changes, that proceeds relentlessly, and it is a painful thing.

Remarkably, the same institution, the corporation, which helped to take the economic world away from Adam Smith, has taken it away from the mature generation of present-day economists. As even economists in their nonprofessional life concede, the modern corporation controls prices and costs, organizes suppliers, persuades consumers, guides the Pentagon, shapes public opinion, buys politicians and is otherwise a dominant influence in the state. In its contemporary and comprehensively powerful form it also, alas, figures only marginally in the accepted economic theory. That theory still holds the business firm to be solely subordinate to the market, solely subject to the authority of the state and ultimately the passive servant of the sovereign citizen. None of this being so, scholars have lost touch with reality. Older economists and some younger ones are left only with the hope that they can somehow consolidate their forces and live out the threat. It is a fate that calls less for criticism than for compassion.

It is not a fate that Adam Smith would have suffered. Given

14 See the earlier essay, "Economists and the Economics of Professional Contentment."

his avid empiricism, his deep commitment to reality and his profound concern for practical reform, he would have made the modern corporation and its power and the related power of the unions and the state an integral part of his theoretical system. His problem would have been different. With his contempt for theoretical pretense and his intense interest in practical questions, he might have had trouble getting tenure in a first-rate modern university.

[8]

Defenders of the Faith, I:
William Simon

WHILE I AM NOT ACQUAINTED WITH Mr. William Simon, I don't believe that I would be his first choice to review his defense of the free enterprise system, *A Time for Truth*.[1] The former energy "czar" and Secretary of the Treasury here urges business-men to give their money to people and institutions of which he approves. He told a group of college administrators a while back that I was more or less precisely the kind of person he did not have in mind. It is obvious that I must lean over backwards to be judicious and fair. But happily that is, in any case, my tendency.

In this spirit I would like at the outset to say that Mr. Simon has a strong point; this, like all other occasions, *is* a good time for truth. In economics, unfortunately, one person's truth is another's fallacy (although with this Mr. Simon does not agree), so, to ensure fairness on the subject, I propose to leave eco-nomic questions aside, at least for the time being.

I must also leave aside the question of whether Mr. Simon is as secure in his views as he asserts. A truly secure author doesn't usually get someone else to write a preface as a crutch. I find it disturbing that Mr. Simon uses two such prostheses,

[1] Preface by Milton Friedman. Foreword by F. A. Hayek. (New York: Reader's Digest Press, McGraw-Hill, 1978.)

one from Milton Friedman, another from F. A. Hayek. One thinks of a man negotiating a personal loan who gets an endorsement from both Walter Wriston and David Rockefeller. I do note that Professor Friedman calls this case for capitalism "brilliant and passionate ... by a brilliant and passionate man ... a profound analysis of the suicidal course on which our beloved country is proceeding ...." Perhaps Mr. Simon found that this sort of praise is hard to reject, although it could also jeopardize Professor Friedman's reputation for careful, restrained, scientific statement. However, he may have thought that overstatement would not be much noticed in this volume.

I must leave aside as well a yet more objective conflict with truth, which is whether Mr. Simon is truthful when he says he wrote this document. Others have held that it was written by Ms. Edith Efron, who here gets credit only for assistance from "conception to execution [sic]." But this will be a matter for later attention. With some others I am planning a new organization to require all statesmen, orators and Washington malefactors and their publishers to reveal the true source of their prose. This force for truth will be called SAD — Society for Authorship Disclosure.

Finally, all devotees of the truth will wish Mr. Simon had been less discriminating in its use. He is commendably frank in his political likes and dislikes. He despises all Democrats, most Republicans, all congressmen, almost all newspapermen, many businessmen and bankers, and especially he despises bureaucrats. (Apart from Professors Friedman and Hayek and Mr. William Buckley, there aren't too many people he does not despise.) But he tells here of going to Moscow in April 1975 for a worthy but modest public relations exercise on behalf of Soviet-American trade. What he calls "a staff group from the departments of State and Commerce; and others" went along. It was a relief, he tells, to be on the way home, and as they soared out of the Soviet capital on Air Force Two, "seventy-eight dignified representatives of the United States of America shouted and applauded like youngsters in sheer relief . . ." A more candid man would condemn taking seventy-eight people all that distance for such a job. That, in all truth, Mr. Simon, was bureaucracy run wild.

There has also been complaint that the author is a trifle disingenuous (truth again) in the treatment of his relationship to the great New York City financial disasters of the mid-seventies. His indignation over the hocus-pocus and concealment in New York financial management is unlimited. But he is himself a certified and experienced municipal bond expert, and during the worst of the thimblerigging and prestidigitation he was a member of Comptroller Abe Beame's Technical Debt Advisory Committee. His job was to advise on New York's financial transactions. An *expert* should have been more alert to funny stuff. A member of such a committee should have got his back into things and made it his business to find out what was going on. On this a truly truthful man would have confessed to negligence.

But Mr. Simon, if not always rigorous in the pursuit of truth, is adequately uncompromising in the pursuit of principle. He takes full credit for preventing "election-eve political compromises" to ease and improve economic performance in the autumn of 1974, and speaks with near satisfaction of the ensuing loss of forty-three House and three Senate seats by the Republicans. It was in a good cause. Again, in 1976, he has warm praise for the way Gerald Ford followed his advice and that of Alan Greenspan to resist concessions to the electorate right down to election day, although he is more reserved in taking credit for Ford's defeat. He does emerge as a devout follower of Lenin in his belief that a small disciplined body of true believers is far to be preferred to a large, amorphous, compromising majority. There could, one supposes, be a different view by those, such as Mr. Ford, who got sacrificed to such principle.

Mr. Simon extends this commitment to principle to his old friends in Wall Street, and they take a terrible beating. Felix

Rohatyn becomes "Felix-the-Fixer"; David Rockefeller of Chase Manhattan, Robert Swinarton of Dean Witter and William Grant of Smith Barney are all "gutless financiers"; and the worst fate of all befalls Walter Wriston of Citibank and Citicorp. On one page he is recognized "not only as a superb banker but, also more important, as a financial statesman." Alas, the short life of the modern financial statesman; a page later Wriston has "caved in and . . . joined the others," those others being the gutless crew that wanted a bail-out on New York.

Mr. Simon could, however, be right in arguing that a New York default would have been less catastrophic than the bankers made it out to be and that people who lend money must expect on occasion to lose it. Also, a point he does not make, default might have been less serious than some of the cuts in services and increases in interest charges that were necessary to avoid it.

He is also right in assigning political power and importance to the New Class — to the teacher, preacher, writer, scientist, technocrat and like intellectual. It does, indeed, exercise great influence. I'm forced to agree here, for Mr. Simon, perhaps unwittingly, is my disciple. I developed the case in *The Affluent Society* (in a chapter called "Labor, Leisure and the New Class") in 1958, having myself taken the phrase from a somewhat different usage by Milovan Djilas. Mr. Simon appears to believe that the concept comes from Irving Kristol, but Kristol is a much later convert. I tell all this not out of any abnormal desire for self-enhancement but to let Mr. Simon know that he can follow an ex-closet socialist (as he classifies me) and a uniquely rigorous kind of Communist (as was Djilas) and be right. Doubtless he will want to try it more often.

Mr. Simon's economic case, to which finally I come, is that the market has been rejected in favor of bureaucratic planning and regulation. He attributes this to stupidity, cupidity, weakness of character and bad education by the New Class. He does not spare his friends in the business world. Here is what he says of them:

> During my tenure at Treasury I watched with incredulity as businessmen ran to the government in every crisis, whining for handouts or protection from the very competition that has made this system so productive. I saw Texas ranchers, hit by drought, demanding government-guaranteed loans; giant milk cooperatives lobbying for higher price supports; major airlines fighting deregulation to preserve their monopoly status; giant companies like Lockheed seeking federal assistance to rescue them from sheer inefficiency; bankers, like David Rockefeller, demanding government bailouts to protect them from their ill-conceived investments; network executives, like William Paley of CBS, fighting to preserve regulatory restrictions and to block the emergence of competitive cable and pay TV. And always, such gentlemen proclaimed their devotion to free enterprise and their opposition to the arbitrary intervention into our economic life by the state. Except, of course, for their own case, which was always unique and which was justified by their immense concern for the public interest.

I find myself in agreement with this; my economic complaint, an objection to some rather overheated writing apart, concerns instead Mr. Simon's further cause and his cure. There is, in fact, a general retreat from the market in our time. The modern large corporation is the outstanding manifestation. So are unions, farmers and their support prices, recipients of the minimum wage, the OPEC countries, the airlines, railroads and truckers. All are part of the escape. This leads, in turn, to various kinds of planned adjustment of supply to demand and a lessening of the sovereignty of the market. It was the rise of OPEC, as Mr. Simon himself agrees, that made him energy czar.

However, Mr. Simon attributes the fall of the market not to this great historical thrust but, as I've noted, to stupidity and related mental or moral aberration or incapacity. Accordingly, he believes that it can be reversed, and the market can be restored by education. Putting his beliefs into practice, he tells proudly in this book that, while in office, he "logged tens of thousands of miles speaking from Miami to Portland, spelling out the danger." For Simon that was pleasant, a source of much agreeable applause, an escape from official drudgery. But it was a terrible waste of time and public money. That applause, as always, came from the already persuaded. As an experienced educator and diligent evangelist, I have learned that economic education is not that powerful, history not that easily reversed. Liberal or conservative, one must come to terms with it. The Secretary should have stayed in Washington and tried his best to make things work. That, not popular spellbinding, is also what Secretaries of the Treasury, Republican or Democratic, are paid for. As this is written, the Democrats are in power. Mr. Simon surely wouldn't want Michael Blumenthal neglecting his work, going up and down the country singing the praises of the mixed economy, the welfare state or, God forbid, anything that could be called closet socialism!

9

Defenders of the Faith, II:
Irving Kristol

I'VE OFTEN THOUGHT how pleasant, easy and also remunerative it would be, were one so motivated, to make the case for modern business organization. One would avoid, above all, the cataleptic and self-refuting litany of the neoclassical market. No one of sound mind, unless extensively conditioned by economic instruction, can any longer be persuaded that the great business firms that constitute the characteristic sector of the modern economy conform to the market-controlled and politically passive model of the neoclassical creed. They have, a dreary and oft-repeated point, that highly visible ability to raise prices. Since watching television is still common, the effort to cross the market and manage the consumer is also widely seen. And papers speak of corporate pressures on the Congress, as does Jimmy Carter, a man who seems safely above any suspicion of being anti-business. The unique foreign policies of the oil companies, ITT and Lockheed have also been well celebrated. So also corporate demands on the United States government. In 1977, the steel companies converted in a matter of weeks from warnings about excessive regulation and big government to demands for more of both to protect them from Japanese competition. The close and symbiotic relationship between the Pentagon and the weapons firms was highlighted nearly twenty years ago by Dwight D. Eisenhower. And, with all else, General Motors, Exxon and IBM simply do not look like the textbook microcosms. So the defense would begin by no longer trying to get people to believe the patently unbelievable about the subordination of the modern large firm to the market and the state, an effort that principally persuades people that there must be something vaguely illegitimate or fraudulent about the large corporation since it tries so elaborately to misrepresent itself.

Having accepted that the corporation transcends its market and has power in the state, then an effective and adequately insouciant defender would say, "What a good thing!" By controlling its prices and managing its customers, it can plan. If hundreds of millions of dollars and several years are to be spent on producing a new automobile model, there must be some assurance as to the eventual price of — and consumer response to — the particular compromise between novelty and banality that is so expensively contrived. If billions are to be put into an oil pipeline across Alaska or a gas pipeline across Canada, there must also be a tight grip on its eventual price. It would be insane to leave that to the unpredictable gyrations of the competitive market. The big corporation eliminates or subdues market forces and substitutes planning. In the modern economy planning is essential.

It would also be held that only a big corporation can deal effectively with big government; the small competitive entrepreneur doesn't have much access even to Michael Blumenthal, James Schlesinger and the other Carter populists, and it is not concern for the small man's state of confidence that has made modern economic administration a minor branch of psychiatry.

Further, as the corporation develops, it takes power away from owners or capitalists and lodges it firmly and irrevocably with the management — the corporate bureaucracy. Capitalists, no one needs to be reminded, were a socially indigestible force

— individualistic, uncompromising, power-hungry, often rapacious, always ready for a fight. Modern corporate bureaucrats, in contrast, are faceless, cautious, courteous, predictable and given to compromise. As a consequence, and because of their power over prices, which they can raise to offset cost increases, we have had in the big-business sector of the economy an unprecedented period of labor peace, though, to be sure, at the price of persistent inflation.

For the same reasons, references to the class struggle, the prelude to the final conflict, have come to have a slightly archaic sound, and among full-time union employees of the thousand largest corporations in the United States there aren't many, perhaps not any, who fall below the poverty line. Nor are there any complaints of shortages of automobiles, depilatories, weapons and other mass products of the corporate sector. This sector extends its technology to agriculture, and the government there follows the corporate practice of giving producers reasonably firm prices against which they can invest and plan. Housing and health care please almost no one, but this could be because they do not lend themselves to large-scale organization and planning.

Large corporations do pursue their own goals and not those of the public in general. And there is the problem of inflation. But the small numbers involved make solution of these problems administratively feasible. In the defense we are now outlining, it would be readily conceded that much must be worked out with the government. And more in the future. Prices and incomes must be restrained if inflation is to be within tolerable limits. And, as the market is replaced by planning, there is no way by which supply is surely adjusted to demand. Energy, where the need for such planning is now accepted in principle if not in actual legislation, is a portent. It is agreed that, with the passage of time, there will have to be an increasing number of planned adjustments of demand to supply. Corporate and public bureaucracy will become increasingly intermingled, as already is the case with oil, atomic energy and space adventure. The corporation, it would be said, paves the way for the requisite national planning and, by removing power from the owners, even goes far toward socializing itself.

Finally, it would be part of this defense that while in the manner of all disciplined organizations the corporation denies liberty of expression to quite a few people, those so oppressed do not in the least seem to mind. The repression operates against the important participants in the management. In all public utterances they are well advised to reflect an institutionally acceptable viewpoint, what is often called, even in non-Communist countries, the party line. Very often they are required to say what the guardians of the official truth, the public relations executives, have written out for them — a derogatory thing. And the sanctions for speaking in conflict with the corporate perception of truth, if subtle, are severe: those so disposed may be praised for their character, but they are not promoted. That, over time, becomes expensive.

There is also, in the upper ranks of the corporation, an equally subtle discouragement of other forms of expression. Here is an exceptionally privileged and compensated group of men which produces almost no poets, essayists, novelists, painters, philosophers or composers and, as compared with the law and the universities, very few politicians. The understanding, never explicit, is that such expression is to be avoided. A man whose interests and energies are partly so engaged may again be praised, but he is also thought a trifle eccentric and unreliable. So it is part of the corporate discipline that he set such matters aside. The repression appears almost innocently in the dictum: "We expect a man around here to give his full time to his job."

But it can be held on behalf of modern enterprise that this repression, however real, is loved. The pecuniary rewards are large enough to compensate for the surrender of individual views to corporate thought and expression. The pecuniary and social costs of contracting out are high but less painful than in the formally planned economies. And there is even, as John Steinbeck once said I would find of the State Department, a measure of contentment and comfort in knowing that thought is available, along with all else, from the organization.

Meanwhile thought and expression by people outside the corporation are not controlled or condemned. They may be considered inconvenient or annoying, but the modern corporate man, in contrast with the old-fashioned capitalist entrepreneur, does nothing about it. A generation ago every reputable university board had a few vintage entrepreneurs who were stoutly in search of heresy in the economics department. The modern corporate man would not dream of intervening, even though, as I shall note presently, there is some thought that, financially speaking, he should.

All in all, it's quite a good case, and it only becomes possible when one has dispensed with the conventionally implausible authority of the market. Much is missing, including such matters as distribution of income, distribution of power, the position of minorities, social values and purposes, the tendency of the well-articulated desires of corporate executives and the generally privileged to be mistaken for the needs of the masses, and the risks that are taken of nuclear extinction. But I have been concocting a sample brief, not offering a balanced view.

Were I asking for someone to make this case, I've long thought it would be Irving Kristol. He is Henry Robinson Luce Professor of Urban Values at New York University, and his academic auspices[1] are exactly right. Harry Luce, in a groping, erratic, charming way, spent much of his adult life

---

[1] A powerful influence, this. For much of my life I was Paul M. Warburg Professor of Economics at Harvard. The donor of the chair, the late James Warburg, was, by most calculations, a socialist. Mr. Kristol in his writings is almost tearfully distressed that I am not more generally recognized to be such.

looking for a rationale for the kind of big businessman that, to his unending astonishment, he had become. Mr. Kristol is also far too sophisticated to buy the primitive neoclassical and free enterprise model in its Simple or William Simon form. He has even the good judgment to put himself at some distance from Milton Friedman. A further qualification, which honesty requires me to record, is the breadth of his reading, which, as *Two Cheers for Capitalism*[2] makes abundantly, even repetitively clear, extends to all of my books, and with nearly total recall. Only a greater measure of agreement might be wished.

Alas, although Kristol tried, this recent book falls short of making the case, as I trust even less partisan judges will find to be so. Mr. Kristol accepts the decline of the market and agrees that the modern corporation has political power. And he is intensely critical of the way both power over prices and power in political matters are used or not used. Thus he thinks the oil companies, after the Arab boycott and the OPEC price hike, were insane to rake in the money while explaining that profits were not as high as they once were or should be. It is, obviously, their decision he is attacking, not the impersonal award of the market. He also believes corporate executives are more interested in excluding their stockholders from power in the corporation than in mobilizing them as a constituency for political ends, and he sees much other misused or unused political power. He concedes that the managerial revolution is real and that the corporate technostructure *is* the decisive political force. One could not ask for more on these matters.

But having gone all this distance, he then retreats, I would say abandons his real defenses, and makes the neoclassical market the bulwark of his defense of capitalism. He notes that "Americans who defend the capitalist system, i.e., an economy and a way of life organized primarily around the free market, are called 'conservative,' " and he leaves no doubt that, subject

[2] (New York: Basic Books, 1978.)

to some "neo-conservative" concessions to government intervention, this is how he classifies himself. It is the peculiar national sin of American liberals, he asserts, that they do not see that the market is on their side. And even more powerfully he avows that "One of the *keystones* [my emphasis] of modern economic thought is that it is impossible to have an *a priori* knowledge of what constitutes happiness for other people; that such knowledge is incorporated in an individual's 'utility schedules'; and this knowledge, in turn, is revealed by the choices the individual makes in a free market."

This particular defense is truly unwise. For if, as Mr. Kristol concedes, the corporation can influence prices, those absolutely indispensable "utility schedules" operate not against the free market that he so specifically requires but, in practice, against a rigged price schedule, one that reflects the economic power of the corporation. In consequence, the corporation deeply influences consumer choice through the relative prices it charges. (This result is wholly conceded even in neoconservative, neoclassical economic thought and is readily verified if one thinks of the effect that decisions on oil prices, for example, have on consumer choice.) And if, as Mr. Kristol partly agrees — and would have difficulty wholly denying — the modern firm spends hugely to influence consumer taste, that sacrosanct utility schedule, already destroyed by corporate price-fixing, is itself partly the creation of the corporation.

So Mr. Kristol is a truly devastating force against his own keystones. He could have argued that, in a relatively rich society, many of the prices and tastes so influenced by the corporation have no very profound effect on well-being — that the consumer is malleable because, being well supplied, his or her needs are not so urgent as to command deep thought. But this he does not stress, and there are limits beyond which, even in the most gracious of moods, one can go in making another author's case.

In Mr. Kristol's case for capitalism the corporation is the

enemy of the market by which he then defends the corporation. But this curious result, not surprisingly, he does not wish to concede, perhaps even to himself. So, since he cannot rescue the corporation by restoring the market, he uncovers another inimical force from which it needs to be saved. This is professors, journalists, scientists and assorted pundits — a community which, accepting my earlier lead,[3] for which I am duly grateful, he groups together as the New Class. The New Class reacts adversely to the corporation partly out of a sense of inferiority, partly out of envy of executive pay and expense accounts and partly out of a defensive reaction to the economic achievements of the corporation and specifically to its service to the consumer economy. This last, in contrast with the concerns of the mind or soul, the New Class holds to be vulgar. Derived from these attitudes are an excessively costly concern for the environment (which Mr. Kristol, after conceding the adverse effect, would leave entirely to his imperfectly functioning market), a prodigal attitude toward public services and the welfare state and a generally feckless commitment to closing tax loopholes and redistributing income. The need, he believes, is for a strenuous effort by business and its friends to educate the New Class, although he has only contempt for past business efforts to promote a better understanding of free enterprise, and, characteristically, he thinks advertisements and other such efforts do as much harm as good.

The nature of the desirable remedial education, which one imagines will be a fairly challenging task, Mr. Kristol does not make completely clear. He does say that corporations should distinguish between their friends and their critics in distributing corporate largesse. And, as to both this and the remedial education, he urges that they be guided by their friends within the New Class, a convocation that almost certainly would include Mr. Kristol.

---

[3] See the earlier essay, "Defenders of the Faith, I: William Simon."

One wonders, however, if such discrimination would not stir a certain amount of adverse comment and even antagonism in the New Class, although I do agree with Mr. Kristol that a fair number of our Classmates are open to purchase if the price is sufficiently high. I would be more troubled by his diagnosis. Over the years, as a certified member, I have not noticed the envy or sense of inferiority of which he speaks. My impression, rather, is of people who tend, if at all, to a definite self-regard and self-assurance. Maybe Mr. Kristol, during the course of his researches, should have made a brief field trip to the Harvard Faculty Club in Cambridge. I would judge that our Classmates manifest a concern for corporate behavior, as for government, not out of envy but because they sense rightly that this is where the power lies. Were trade unions, the Baptist Church or *The Public Interest* (edited by Mr. Kristol) equally powerful, they would be equally the object of attention.

But the ultimate question in educating the New Class gets back to what case can be sold. Here Mr. Kristol has his greatest reason to worry. He is too sophisticated and open to the evidence to accept the case for the market. But being a conservative in mood as well as in politics, he cannot bring himself to sell anything else. So, having destroyed the case for the market, he goes back to it.

This is generally thought to be a cold season for liberals. Mr. Kristol, in a literate and learned way, has shown that it is also a hard time for conservatives.

10

Defenders of the Faith, III:
Wright and Slick

SOME TIME AGO a small volume — nine pages in all — came to me in the mail. Its author was Mr. M. A. Wright, then Chairman of Exxon, U.S.A. The title, arresting and even alarming, was *The Assault on Private Enterprise.* My first thought was that another business executive was trying to communicate. On the first page was the telltale sentence: "Business has failed to do an effective job in communicating its point of view to the general public." All disasters in executive prose begin with these words. Then came the compulsive cry: "Let there be no mistake: an attack is being mounted on the private enterprise system in the U.S. *The life of that system is at stake.*" (The emphasis on the overstatement is mine.) These are the trademarks, invariable, utterly reliable, of executive communication.

Politicians have a curious contempt for the art of conveying thought. A surprising number give speeches over a lifetime without ever learning to make, write or even read a speech. Lecture-circuit impresarios are worse; all feel that nothing so moves an audience (and justifies their fee) as a suffocating recital of the commonplace, combined with a deeply condescending manner. Social scientists, although perhaps improving, have their own special instinct for fraternal obscurity. But there is no doubt that business executives are the worst of all. Theirs is the egregiously optimistic belief that people will believe anything, however improbable, if it is said with emphasis and solemnity by the head of a really big company. With the ultimate corporate promotion comes the right to proclaim truth.

Mr. Wright, I concluded, was a man of orthodox and hence profound, even perverse, inadequacy in communication. But the pamphlet, and the circumstances of its circulation, led me to wonder if something more than normal executive incoherence might be involved. I was sent the document by Mr. W. T. Slick, Jr., a senior vice president of Exxon, U.S.A. He sent it with a transmittal note summarizing Mr. Wright's main point: all business, not just the oil companies, is being bombed by its enemies, and a great closing of ranks is called for. Then, significantly, Mr. Slick went on to hope that readers would find the document "highly thought-provoking." This, perhaps even more than Mr. Slick's name, seemed the clue. No friend of free enterprise could conceivably want to provoke thought on Mr. Wright's dialectics. One could only conclude that the enemies of free enterprise do abound and that one of them, Mr. Slick, was right inside Exxon. The evidence was and remains circumstantial but, nonetheless, overwhelming.

Mr. Wright began by stressing the climate of "suspicion and, it must be said, hostility" in which the business firm now operates. Then he went on to offer the first proposition on which the sinister Mr. Slick was out to provoke thought. It was that in the sixties there was the war in Vietnam, the riots in the cities, then inflation, then pollution or, in Mr. Wright's more awesome words, "a belated recognition of the burden placed on the quality of air and water by our highly industrialized society." All this got people in a foul mood which extended to their attitudes toward business. Then came an outburst of dissatisfaction with consumer products — Americans got discouraged with the quality, design, safety, reliability and dealer-servicing of the things they bought, and, being in this state of mind, they fell prey to consumerism. Finally came Watergate which crystallized public distrust of almost everything and everybody. While all this was happening, according to Mr. Wright, most business executives were innocently going their own way — "too busy," he said, "competing in the private enterprise system to concern themselves with communicating its virtues."

Mr. Slick, I concluded, could not possibly be unaware of the consequences of provoking or otherwise stimulating thought on these propositions. He was a senior vice president, after all. No, he knew that Mr. Wright's plea would surely remind people of those old arguments over who makes money out of wars. More often a corporation than a slogging foot soldier. And it would make them wonder why Exxon didn't consider cities and their people part of the system. And it would get people's minds strongly on the effect of oil prices on inflation. And, where pollution is concerned, on gasoline fumes and oil on the beaches and those big, high oil-company signs on the roadsides. And what guileless oil man would urge thought on that really big one about the tycoons being too busy competing to notice even their own prices?

Slick was being yet more obviously subversive of Wright when he invited reflection on the consumer movement and the ungreening of the consumer. Stupidity is still a problem in this Republic. But neither he nor anyone in his position could expect people to believe that manufacturers are without responsibility for the quality, durability, design and safety of their products, however busy they are competing in the free enterprise system.

Slick came even closer to blowing his cover on Watergate. What kind of vice president would want thought on where the money came from for the burglars? (Most from oil, the rest from soybean oil.) And on who helped to launder it through Mexico? (Oil men again.) And where the biggest single bundle of cash came from for the cover-up? (Northrop this time.) And why would he want to put people's minds on those secret contributions by corporate executives and the illegal political contributions by the corporations themselves?

Mr. Slick got in some other, less transparent blows. Thus, Mr. Wright was indignant about suggestions that the depletion allowance be abolished. No well-intentioned vice president would invite reflection on the free ride thus being given to the oil companies. Mr. Wright was dismayed by suggestions that the foreign tax credits on income earned overseas be disallowed. This provoked an especially dangerous new line of thought, for what the oil companies call a tax credit and subtract from their tax bill is really a royalty payment that should come off their costs. And Mr. Wright cited James Buckley of New York and Paul Fannin of Arizona as the two statesmen who still defended the oil company position at the time. That these were the available advocates is a small but damaging detail on which to have people pondering.

Mr. Wright then went on to warn that government is steadily moving in on private enterprise. In urging thought on that, Mr. Slick must have known that the most retarded or reluctant mind would turn to Lockheed, Penn Central, the eastern railroads and the Franklin National Bank, all, in fact, examples of private enterprise moving strongly in on the government. Mr. Wright inquired if there wouldn't some day be a U.S. Automobile Corporation or a Federal Steel Company. People who reflect will conclude that sure as hell there will be. It will happen on precisely the day when a big enough automobile company or a big enough steel company loses a big enough sum of money so that a rescue operation is demanded of the good old federal government.

Finally came Mr. Slick's real coup — a small miracle, among other things, of timing. Mr. Wright argued that the public has a ridiculously exaggerated view of the earnings of companies such as his, and being economically illiterate (my phrase), they "do not understand the role of profit or the function of the free market." A few days after these words were circulated, Exxon's second-quarter earnings report was published in the paper, and no one can say that Mr. Slick didn't know it was coming. It told that profits (these were for the company as a whole) were up 59 percent over the previous year and that for the first six months they were up 52.8 percent, for the second quarter 66.7 percent, in each case also as compared with the year before. All records had been broken.

With a supporter like Slick, one wonders if either Wright or free enterprise needs enemies.

There is further possible proof of the point, although something, no doubt, can be attributed to natural causes. Not long after the above was written, Wright was superseded. So was Slick.

11

Who Was Thorstein Veblen?

> There is always an aura of playfulness about his attitude to-
> ward his own work in marked contrast to the deadly serious-
> ness of most economists.
>
> Wesley C. Mitchell

THE NEAREST THING in the United States to an academic legend
— the equivalent of that of Scott Fitzgerald in fiction or of
the Barrymores in the theater — is the legend of Thorstein
Veblen. A legend is reality so enlarged by imagination that,
eventually, the image has an existence of its own. This happened to Veblen. He was a man of great and fertile mind and
a marvelously resourceful exponent of its product. His life,
beginning on the frontier of the upper Middle West in 1857
and continuing, mostly at one university or another, until 1929,
was not without romance of a kind. Certainly by the standards
of academic life at the time it was nonconformist. There was
ample material both in his work and in his life on which to
build the legend, and the builders have not failed. There is
also a considerable debt to imagination.

What is believed about Veblen's grim, dark boyhood in a
poor, immigrant Norwegian family in Wisconsin and Minnesota, his reaction to those oppressive surroundings, his harried
life in the American academic world in the closing decades
of the last century and the first three of this, the fatal way he

attracted women and vice versa and its consequences in his tightly corseted surroundings, the indifference of all right-thinking men to his work, has only a limited foundation in fact.

Economics is a dull enough business, and sociology is sometimes worse. So, on occasion, are those who teach these subjects. One reason they are dull is the belief that everything associated with human personality should be made as mechanical as possible. That is science. Perhaps one should, instead, perpetuate any available myth. When, as with Veblen, the man is enlarged by a nimbus, the latter should be brightened, not dissolved.

Still, there is a certain case for truth, and the facts in Veblen's case are also far from tedious. He is not, as some have suggested, a universal source of insight on American society. Like Smith and Marx, he did not see what had not yet happened. Also, on some things, he was wrong, and faced with a choice between strict accuracy and what would outrage his audience, he rarely hesitated. But no man of his time, or since, looked with such a cool and penetrating eye at pecuniary gain and the way its pursuit makes men and women behave.

This cool and penetrating view is the substance behind the Veblen legend. It is a view that still astonishes the reader with what it reveals. While there may be other deserving candidates, only two books by American economists of the nineteenth century are still read. One of these is Henry George's *Progress and Poverty*; the other is Veblen's *The Theory of the Leisure Class*. Neither of these books, it is interesting to note, came from the sophisticated and derivative world of the eastern seaboard. Both were the candid, clear-headed, untimid reactions of the frontiersman — in the case of Henry George to speculative alienation of land, in the case of Veblen to the pompous social ordinances of the affluent. But the comparison cannot be carried too far. Henry George was the exponent of a notably compelling idea; his book remains important for that idea — for the notion of the high price that society pays for private ownership and the pursuit of capital gains from land. Veblen's great work is a wide-ranging and timeless comment on the behavior of people who possess or are in pursuit of wealth and who, looking beyond their possessions, want the eminence that, or so they believe, wealth was meant to buy. No one has really read very much social science if he hasn't read *The Theory of the Leisure Class* at least once. Not many of more than minimal education and pretense get through life without adverting at some time or other to "conspicuous consumption," "pecuniary emulation" or "conspicuous waste," even though they may not know whence these phrases came.

Veblen's parents, Thomas Anderson and Kari Bunde Veblen, emigrated from Norway to a farm in rural Wisconsin in 1847, ten years before Thorstein's birth. There were the usual problems in raising the money for the passage, the quite terrible hardships on the voyage. In all, the Veblens had twelve children, of whom Thorstein was the sixth. The first farm in Wisconsin was inferior to what later and better information revealed to be available farther west. They moved, and, in 1865, they moved a second time. The new and final holding was on the prairie, now about an hour's drive south from Minneapolis. It is to this farm that the legend of Veblen's dark and deprived boyhood belongs. No one who visits this countryside will believe it. There can be no farming country in the world with a more generous aspect of opulence. The prairie is gently rolling. The soil is black and deep, the barns are huge, the silos numerous and the houses big, square and comfortable, without architectural ambition. The Veblen house, with a long view of the surrounding farmland, is an ample, pleasant, white frame structure bespeaking not merely comfort but prosperity.[1]

---

[1] In recent decades it had fallen on difficult times. Partly as the result of a television program based on this essay, and my plea to then Governor Wendell Anderson — "only Scandinavians are so negligent of their heroes" — it was acquired as a national historic site, and rehabilitation is in prospect.

Families in the modern suburban tract are not housed as well.

Since this countryside was originally open, well-vegetated prairie, it must have looked very promising to the settler a hundred years ago. Thomas Veblen acquired 290 acres of this wealth; it is hard to imagine that he, his wife or, by their instruction, any of their children could have thought of themselves as poor. Not a thousand, perhaps not even a hundred farmers working their own land were so handsomely provided in the Norway they had left. Nor, in fact, did the Veblens think themselves poor. Later, in letters, Thorstein's brothers and sisters were to comment, sometimes with amusement, on occasion with anger, on the myth of their poverty-stricken origins.[2]

If this part of the Veblen story is unremarkable and commonplace — the tearing up of roots, departure, hardship, miscalculation, eventual reward — there were other things that separated the Veblens from the general run of Scandinavian settlers and that help to explain Thorstein. Thomas Veblen, who had been a skilled carpenter and cabinetmaker, soon proved himself a much more than normally intelligent and progressive farmer. And, however he viewed the farm for himself, he almost certainly regarded it as a steppingstone for his children. Even more exceptional was Kari, his wife. She was an alert, imaginative, self-confident and intelligent woman, lovely in appearance, who, from an early age, identified, protected and encouraged the family genius. In later years, in a family and community where more hands were always needed and virtue was associated, accordingly, with efficient toil — effectiveness as a worker was what distinguished a *good* boy or girl from the rest — Thorstein Veblen was treated with tolerance. Under the cover of a weak constitution he was given leisure for reading. This released time could only have been provided by remarkably perceptive parents. One of Veblen's brothers

[2] The letters are in the archives of the Minnesota Historical Society in St. Paul, to which I am grateful.

later wrote that it was from his mother that "Thorstein got his personality and brains," although others thought them decidedly his own property.

Thorstein, like his brothers and sisters, went to the local schools, and, on finishing these, to Carleton College (then styled Carleton College Academy) in the nearby town of Northfield. His sister Emily was in attendance at the same time; other members of the family also went to Carleton. In an engaging and characteristic move their father acted to keep down college expenses. He bought a plot of land on the edge of town for the nominal amount charged for such real estate in that time and put up a house to shelter his offspring while they were being educated. The Veblen legend further holds that the winning of an education involved Thorstein in major and even heroic hardship. This can be laid decisively to rest. A letter in the archives of the Minnesota Historical Society from Andrew Veblen, Thorstein's brother, notes that money was available, if not abundant: "Father gave him the strictly necessary assistance through his schooling. Thorstein, like the rest of the family, kept his expenses down to the minimum. . . all in line with the close economy that the whole family practiced."[3] A sister-in-law, Florence (Mrs. Orson) Veblen, wrote more indignantly and with a characteristic view of what was virtue in those times: "There is not the slightest ground for depriving my father-in-law of the credit of having paid for the education of his children — *all* of them — he was well able to do so; he had two good farms in the richest farming district in America."[3]

It was, nevertheless, an exception to the general community practice that the Veblen children should be sent to college rather than be put to useful work, as Norwegian farmers would

---

[3] These letters were written in 1926 to Joseph Dorfman, Veblen's distinguished biographer. Dorfman, alas, does something to perpetuate the legend of deprivation.

then have called it, on the farm. Exceptionally too they were sent to an Anglo-Saxon denominational college — Carleton was Congregationalist — rather than to one of the Lutheran institutions which responded to the language, culture and religion of the Scandinavians. The Veblen myth (as the family has insisted) has also exaggerated somewhat the alienation of the Norwegians in general and the Veblens in particular in an English-speaking society. It is part of the legend that Thorstein's father spoke no English and that his son had difficulty with the language. This is nonsense. But in the local class structure the Anglo-Saxons were the dominant town and merchant class, the Scandinavians the hard-working peasantry. The Veblen children were not intended for their class.

Carleton was one of the denominational colleges which were established as the frontier moved westward and by which it was shown that along with economic and civic achievement in America went also culture and religion. Like the others of its age, it was unquestionably fairly bad. But, like so many small liberal arts colleges of the time, it was the haven for a few learned men and devoted teachers — the saving remnant that seemed always to show up when one was established. Such a teacher at Carleton in Veblen's time was John Bates Clark, later, when at Columbia University, to be recognized as the dean of American economists of his time. (He was one of the originators of the concept of marginality — the notion that decisions concerning consumption are made not in consequence of the total stock of goods possessed but in consequence of the satisfactions to be derived from the possession or use of another unit added to the stock already possessed.) Veblen became a student of Clark's; Clark thought well of Veblen.

This must have required both imagination and tolerance, for in various of his class exercises Veblen was already giving indication of his later style and method. He prepared a solemn and ostentatiously sincere classification of men according to their noses; one of his exercises in public rhetoric defended the drunkard's view of his own likely death; another argued the case for cannibalism. Clark, who was presiding when Veblen appeared to favor intoxication, felt obliged to demur. In a denominational college in the Midwest at the time, cannibalism had a somewhat higher canonical sanction than intoxication. Veblen resorted to the defense that he was to employ with the utmost consistency for the rest of his life. No value judgment was involved; he was not being partial to the drunk; his argument was purely scientific.

Veblen finished his last two years at the college in one and graduated brilliantly. His graduation oration was entitled "Mill's Examination of Hamilton's Philosophy of the Conditioned." It was described by contemporaries as a triumph, but it does not survive. While at Carleton Veblen had formed a close friendship with Ellen Rolfe; she was the daughter of a prominent and prosperous Midwestern family and, like Veblen, was independent and introspective, very much apart from the crowd and also highly intelligent. They were not married for another eleven years, although this absence of haste did not mean that either had any less reason to regret it in later leisure. The legend holds Veblen to have been an indifferent and unfaithful husband who was singularly incapable of resisting the advances of the women whom, however improbably, he attracted. The Veblen family seems to have considered the fault to be at least partly Ellen's. She had a nervous breakdown following an effort at teaching; in a far from reticent and, one supposes, deeply partisan letter in the St. Paul archives,[4] a sister-in-law concludes: "There is not the least doubt that she

4 From Florence Veblen, 1926. In an earlier account of the Veblen family (Orson Veblen, "Thorstein Veblen: Reminiscences of His Brother Orson," *Social Forces*, vol. X, no. 2 [December 1931], pp. 187–195), Florence Veblen also dealt harshly with Ellen. However, an unpublished comment (again in the St. Paul archives) by Andrew Veblen dissents at least in part, noting also that the two women had never met.

is insane." Only one thing is certain: it was an unsuccessful and unhappy marriage.

After teaching for a year at a local academy following his graduation from Carleton, Veblen departed for Johns Hopkins University in Baltimore to study philosophy. At this time, 1881, Johns Hopkins was being advertised as the first American university with a specialized postgraduate school following the earlier European design. The billing, as Veblen was later to point out, was considerably in advance of the fact. Money and hence professors were very scarce; the Baltimore context was that of a conservative southern town. Veblen was unhappy and did not complete the term. He began what — with one major interruption — was to be a lifetime of wandering over the American academic landscape.

His next stop was Yale. It was an interesting time in New Haven — what scholars inclined to metaphors from the brewing industry call a period of intellectual ferment. One focus of contention was between Noah Porter, a seemingly pretentious divine then believed to be an outstanding philosopher and metaphysician, and William Graham Sumner, the American exponent of Herbert Spencer. The practical thrust of Noah Porter's effort was to prevent Sumner from assigning Spencer's *Principles of Sociology* to his classes. In this he prevailed; Spencer was righteously suppressed. Porter's success, one imagines, proceeded less from the force of his argument against Spencer's acceptance of the Darwinian thesis — natural selection, survival of the fittest — as a social and economic axiom than from the unfortunate fact that he was also the president of the university. In Veblen's later writing there is a strong suggestion of Spencer and Sumner. Natural selection is not the foundation of Veblen's system, but it serves him as an infinitely handy explanation of how some survive and prosper and others do not.

There has been much solemn discussion of the effect on Veblen's later writing of the philosophical discussion at Yale and of his own dissertation on Kant. My instinct is to think it was not too great. This is affirmed in a general way by the other Veblens. In later years his brother Andrew (a physicist and mathematician) responded repeatedly and stubbornly, though, no doubt with some exaggeration, to efforts to identify the sources of Thorstein Veblen's thought: "I do not think that any person much influenced the formation of his views or opinions."[5]

After two and a half years at Yale — underwritten by a brother and the Minnesota family and farm — Veblen emerged with a Ph.D. He wanted to teach; he also had rather favorable recommendations. But he could not find a job and so he went back to the Minnesota homestead. There, endlessly reading and doing occasional writing, he remained for seven years. As in his childhood, he again professed ill health. Andrew Veblen, later letters show, thought the illness genuine; other members of his family diagnosed his ailment as an allergy to manual toil. He married, and Ellen brought with her a little money. From time to time he was asked to apply for teaching positions; tentative offers were righteously withdrawn when it was discovered that he was not a subscribing Christian. In 1891, he resumed his academic wandering by registering as a graduate student at Cornell.

The senior professor of economics at Cornell at the time was J. Laurence Laughlin, a stalwart exponent of the English classical school, who, until then, had declined to become a member of the American Economic Association in the belief that it had socialist inclinations. (There has been no such suspicion in recent times.) Joseph Dorfman of Columbia University, an eminent student of American economic thought and the preeminent authority on Veblen, tells of Laughlin's meeting with Veblen in *Thorstein Veblen and His America,* a massive book

---

[5] Letter in the St. Paul archives.

to which everyone who speaks or writes on Veblen is indebted.[6,7] Laughlin "was sitting in his study in Ithaca when an anemic-looking person, wearing a coonskin cap and corduroy trousers, entered and in the mildest possible tone announced: 'I am Thorstein Veblen.' He told Laughlin of his academic history, his enforced idleness, and his desire to go on with his studies. The fellowships had all been filled, but Laughlin was so impressed with the quality of the man that he went to the president and other powers of the university and secured a special grant."[8]

Apart from the impression that Veblen's manner and dress so conveyed, the account is important for another reason. Always in Veblen's life there were individuals — a small but vital few — who strongly sensed his talents. Often, as in the case of Laughlin, they were conservatives — men who, in ideas and habits of life, were a world apart from Veblen. Repeatedly these good men rescued or protected their prodigious but always inconvenient friend.

Veblen was at Cornell rather less than two years, although long enough to begin advancing his career with uncharacteristic orthodoxy by getting articles into the scholarly journals. Then Laughlin was invited to be head of the Department of Economics at the new University of Chicago. He took Veblen with him; Veblen was awarded a fellowship of $520 a year for which he was to prepare a course on the history of socialism and assist in editing the newly founded *Journal of Political*

6 Although members of the family have disputed Dorfman on numerous details. In the library of the Minnesota Historical Society there is a heavily annotated copy of Dorfman's book giving Emily Veblen's corrections and dissents. Numerous minor points of family history are challenged; like other members of the family, she protested all suggestions that the family was poor or that it was alienated from the rest of the community. And she thought that Dorfman's picture of Thorstein as a lonely, shabby, excessively introverted boy and student was much overdrawn.

7 Joseph Dorfman, *Thorstein Veblen and His America* (New York: Viking, 1934).
8 Dorfman, pp. 79–80.

Economy. He was now thirty-five years old. In the next several years he advanced to the rank of tutor and instructor, continued to teach and to edit the *Journal* (known to economists as the J.P.E.), wrote a great many reviews and, among other articles, one on the theory of women's dress, another on the barbarian status of women and a third on the instinct of workmanship and the irksomeness of labor. All these foreshadowed later books.

In these years he also developed his teaching style, if such it could be called. He sat at a table and spoke in a low monotone to the handful of students who were interested and who could get close enough to hear. He also discovered, if he had not previously learned, that something — mind, manner, dress, his sardonic and challenging indifference to approval or disapproval — made him extremely attractive to women. His wife now found that she had more and more competition for his attention. It was something to which neither she nor the academic communities in which Veblen resided ever reconciled themselves.

In 1899, while still at Chicago and while Laughlin was still having trouble getting him small increases in pay or even, on occasion, getting his appointment renewed, he published his first and greatest book. It was *The Theory of the Leisure Class.*

There is little that anyone can be told about *The Theory of the Leisure Class* that he or she cannot learn better by reading the book himself or herself. It is a marvelous thing and, in its particular way, a masterpiece of English prose. But the qualification is important. Veblen's writing cannot be read like that of any other author. Wesley C. Mitchell, regarded, though not with entire accuracy, as Veblen's leading intellectual legatee, once said that "One must be highly sophisticated to enjoy his [Veblen's] books." [9] Those who cherish Veblen would like, I

9 Wesley C. Mitchell, *What Veblen Taught* (New York: Viking, 1936), p. xx.

am sure, to believe this. The truth is of a simpler sort. One needs only to realize that, if Veblen is to be enjoyed, he must be read very carefully and very slowly. He enlightens, amuses and delights but only if he is given a good deal of time.

That is because one cannot divorce Veblen's ideas from the language in which they are conveyed. The ideas are pungent, incisive and insulting. But the writing is a weapon as well. Veblen, as Mitchell also noted, writes "with one eye on the scientific merits of his analysis, and his other eye fixed on the squirming reader."[10] And he startles his reader with an exceedingly perverse use of meaning. This never varies from that sanctioned by the most precise and demanding usage, but in the context it is often unexpected. His usage Veblen then attributes to scientific necessity. Thus, in his immortal discussion of conspicuous consumption, he notes that expenditure, if it is to contribute efficiently to the individual's "good fame," must generally be on "superfluities." "In order to be reputable it [the expenditure] must be wasteful."[11] All of this is quite exact. The rich do want fame; reputable expenditure is what adds to their repute or fame; the dress, housing, equipage, that serve this purpose and are not essential for existence are superfluous. Nonessential expenditure is wasteful. But only Veblen would have used the words "fame," "reputable" and "waste" in such a way. In the case of "waste," he does decide that some explanation is necessary. This is characteristically airy and matter-of-fact. In everyday speech, "the word carries an undertone of deprecation. It is here used for want of a better term . . . and it is not to be taken in an odious sense . . ."[12]

And in a similar vein: The wives of the rich forswear useful employment because "Abstention from labor is not only an honorific or meritorious act, but it presently comes to be a

10 Mitchell, p. xviii.

11 Thorstein Veblen, *The Theory of the Leisure Class* (Boston: Houghton Mifflin, 1973), p. 77.

12 Thorstein Veblen, p. 78.

requisite of decency."[13] "Honor," "merit" and "decency" are all used with exactness, but they are not often associated with idleness. A robber baron, Veblen says, has a better chance of escaping the law than a small crook because "A well-bred expenditure of his booty especially appeals ... to persons of a cultivated sense of the proprieties, and goes far to mitigate the sense of moral turpitude with which his dereliction is viewed by them."[14] Scholars do not ordinarily associate the disposal of ill-gotten wealth with good breeding.

One sees also from this sentence why Veblen must be read slowly and carefully. If one goes rapidly, words will be given their usual contextual meaning — not the precise and perverse sense that Veblen intended. Waste will be wicked and not a source of esteem; the association of idleness with merit, honor and decency will somehow be missed, as well as that of the social position of the crook with the public attitude toward his expenditure. *The Theory of the Leisure Class* yields its meaning, and therewith its full enjoyment, only to those who also have leisure.

When Veblen had finished his manuscript, he sent it to the publisher, and it came back several times for revision. Eventually, it appears, publication required a guarantee from the author. The book could not have been badly written in any technical or grammatical sense. Veblen by then was an experienced editor. Nor was he any novice as a writer. One imagines that the perverse and startling use of words, combined no doubt with the irony and the attack on the icons, was more than the publisher could readily manage. But, on the other side, some very good reader or editor must have seen how much was there.

The Theory of the Leisure Class is a tract, the most comprehensive ever written, on snobbery and social pretense. Some

13 Thorstein Veblen, p. 44.
14 Thorstein Veblen, p. 89.

of it has application only to American society at the end of the last century — at the height of the gilded age of American capitalism. More is wonderfully relevant to modern affluence.

The rich have often been attacked by the less rich because they have a superior social position that is based on assets and not on moral or intellectual worth. And they have also been accused of using their wealth and position to sustain a profligate consumption of resources of which others are in greater need, and of defending the social structure that accords them their privileged status. And they have been attacked for the base, wicked or immoral behavior that wealth sustains and their social position sanctions. These attacks the rich can endure. That is because the assailants concede them their superior power and position; they only deny their right to that position or to behave as they do therein. The denial involves a good deal of righteous anger and indignation. The rich are only reminded that they are thought worth such anger and indignation.

Here is Veblen's supreme literary and polemical achievement. He concedes the rich and the well-to-do nothing; and he would not dream of suggesting that his personal attitudes or passion are in any way involved. The rich are anthropological specimens; the possession of money and property has made their behavior interesting and visibly ridiculous. The effort to establish one's importance and precedence and the yearning for the resulting esteem and applause are matters only of sociological and anthropological interest and are common to all humans. Nothing in the basic tendency differentiates a Whitney, Vanderbilt or Astor from a Papuan chieftain or "for instance, the tribes of the Andamans." The dress, festivals or rituals and artifacts of the Vanderbilts are more complex; the motivation is in no way different from or superior to that of their barbarian counterparts.

That is why the rich are not viewed with indignation. The scientist does not become angry with the primitive tribesman because of the extravagance of his sexual orgies or the vengeance of his self-mutilation. So with the social observances of the rich. Their banquets and other entertainments are equated in commonplace fashion with the orgies; the self-mutilation of the savage is the equivalent of the painfully constricting dress in which, at that time, the women of the well-to-do were corseted.

One must remember that Veblen wrote in the last years of the last century — before the established order suffered the disintegrating onslaught of World War I, V. I. Lenin and the leveling oratory of modern democratic politics. It was a time when gentlemen still believed they were gentlemen and that it was mostly wealth that made the difference. Veblen calmly identified the manners and behavior of these so-called gentlemen with the manners and behavior of the people of the bush. Speaking of the utility of different observances for the purpose of affirming or enhancing the individual's repute, Veblen notes that "Presents and feasts had probably another origin than that of naive ostentation, but they acquired their utility for this purpose very early, and they have retained that character to the present . . . Costly entertainments, such as *the potlatch or the ball,* are peculiarly adapted to serve this end."[15] The italics equating the potlatch and the ball are mine; Veblen would never have dreamed of emphasizing so obvious a point.

While *The Theory of the Leisure Class* is a devastating put-down of the rich, it is also more than that. It brilliantly and truthfully illuminates the effect of wealth on behavior. No one who has read this book ever again sees the consumption of goods in the same light. Above a certain level of affluence the enjoyment of goods — of dress, houses, automobiles, entertainment — can never again be thought intrinsic as, in a naive way, the established or neoclassical economics still holds it to be. Possession and consumption are the banner that advertises achievement, that proclaims, by the accepted standards of the

15 Thorstein Veblen, p. 65.

community, that the possessor is a success. In this sense — in revealing what had not hitherto been seen — *The Theory of the Leisure Class* is a major scientific achievement.

Alas, also, much of the process by which this truth is revealed — by which Veblen's insights are vouchsafed — is not science but contrivance. Before writing *The Leisure Class,* Veblen had, it is certain, read widely in anthropology. Thus he had a great many primitive communities and customs at his fingertips. And he refers to these with a casual insouciance which suggests — and was meant to suggest — that he had much more such knowledge in reserve. But the book is devoid of sources; no footnote or reference tells on what Veblen relied for information. On an early page he explains that the book is based on everyday observation and not pedantically on the scholarship of others. This is adequate as far as Fifth Avenue and Newport are concerned. There accurate secondhand knowledge could be assumed. But Veblen had no similar access to everyday knowledge about the Papuans.

In fact, Veblen's anthropology and sociology are weapon and armor which he contrives for his purpose. He needs them to illuminate (and to make ridiculous) the behavior of the most powerful — the all-powerful — class of his time. By doing this in the name of science and with the weapons of science — and with no overt trace of animus or anger — he could act with considerable personal safety. The butterfly does not attack the zoologist for saying it is more decorative than useful. That Marx was an enemy whose venom was to be returned in kind, capitalists did not doubt. But not Veblen. The American rich never quite understood what he was doing to them. The scientific pretense, the irony and the careful explanations that the most pejorative words were being used in a strictly nonpejorative sense put him well beyond their comprehension.

The protection was necessary at the time. And there is a wealth of evidence that Veblen was conscious of its need. During the years when he was working on *The Leisure Class,* liberal professors at the University of Chicago were under frequent attack from the neighboring plutocracy. The latter expected economics and the other social sciences to provide the doctrine that graced its privileges. In the mid-nineties Chauncey Depew told the Chicago students (in an address quoted by Joseph Dorfman) that "This institution, which owes its existence to the beneficence of Rockefeller, is in itself a monument of the proper use of wealth accumulated by a man of genius. So is Cornell, so is Vanderbilt, and so are the older colleges, as they have received the benefactions of generous, appreciative, and patriotic wealth."[16] In 1895, Edward W. Bemis, an associate professor of political economy in the extension, i.e., outpatient, department of the university, attacked the traction monopoly in Chicago which, assisted by wholesale bribery, had fastened itself on the backs of Chicago streetcar patrons. There was a great uproar, and his appointment was not renewed.

The university authorities, like many godly and scholarly men in academic positions, took for granted that their devotion to truth accorded them a special license to lie. So they compounded their crime in dismissing Bemis by denying that their action was to appease the traction monopoly or that it reflected any abridgment of academic freedom. The local press was not misled; it applauded the action as a concession to sound business interest. In a fine sentence on scholarly responsibility, *The Chicago Journal* said: "The duty of a professor who accepts the money of a university for his work is to teach the established truth, not to engage in the 'pursuit of truth.' "[17] A forthright sentiment.[18]

16 Chauncey Depew, quoted in Dorfman, p. 122.
17 *The Chicago Journal*, quoted in Dorfman, p. 123.
18 The history of Bemis's discharge is the subject of a recent study by Harold E. Bergquist, Jr., "The Edward W. Bemis Controversy at the University of Chicago," *AAUP Bulletin*, vol. 58, no. 4 (December 1972), pp. 384–393, which appeared after this article originally went to press. While suggesting more complex circumstances than here implied and also a less than innocent role for J. Laurence Laughlin, Mr. Bergquist's conclusions as to the dismissal of Bemis are much as above.

Veblen did not miss this lesson. The last chapter of *The Leisure Class* is on "The Higher Learning as an Expression of the Pecuniary Culture." It anticipates a later, much longer and much more pungent disquisition by Veblen on the influence of the pecuniary civilization on the university (*The Higher Learning in America; A Memorandum on the Conduct of Universities by Business men,* published in 1918.) In this chapter Veblen stresses the conservative and protective role of the universities in relation to the pecuniary culture. "New views, new departures in scientific theory, especially new departures which touch the theory of human relations at any point, have found a place in the scheme of the university tardily and by a reluctant tolerance, rather than by a cordial welcome; and the men who have occupied themselves with such efforts to widen the scope of human knowledge have not commonly been well received by their learned contemporaries."[19] No one will be in doubt as to whom, in the last clause, Veblen had in mind. Elsewhere, contemplating university administration, he notes that "As further evidence of the close relation between the educational system and the cultural standards of the community, it may be remarked that there is some tendency latterly to substitute the captain of industry in place of the priest, as head of seminaries of the higher learning."[20]

Given such an environment and given also his subject, it will be evident that Veblen needed the protection of his art. On the whole, it served him well. In the course of his academic career he was often in trouble with university administrators — it was they, not the great men of industry and commerce, who kept him moving. His more orthodox and pedestrian, though more fashionable, academic colleagues also disliked him. A man like Veblen creates great problems for such people. They cherish the established view and rejoice in the favor of the Establishment. Anyone who does not share their values is a threat to

19 Thorstein Veblen, pp. 245–246.
20 Thorstein Veblen, p. 242.

their position, and, worse still, to their self-esteem, for he makes them seem sycophantic and routine, which, of course, they are. Veblen, throughout his life, was such a threat. But the rich, to whom ultimately he addressed himself, rarely penetrated his defenses.

Veblen also enjoyed a measure of political immunity in a hostile world because he was not a reformer. His heart did not beat for the proletariat or otherwise for the downtrodden and poor. He was a man of animus but not of revolution.

The source of Veblen's animus has regularly been related to his origins. As the son of immigrant parents, he had experienced the harsh life of the frontier. This was at a time when Scandinavians were, by any social standard, second-class citizens. They were saved only because they could not readily be distinguished by their color. What was more natural than that someone from such a background should turn on his oppressors? *The Theory of the Leisure Class* was Veblen's revenge for the abuse to which he and his parents were subject.

This misunderstands Veblen. The Veblens, we have seen, were not of the downtrodden. And as one from a similar background perhaps can know, there is danger of mistaking contempt or derision for resentment. Some years ago, to fill in the idle moments of an often undemanding occupation — that of the modern ambassador — I wrote a small book about the clansmen among whom I was reared on the north shore of Lake Erie in Canada. The Scotch, like the Scandinavians, inhabited the farms. The people of the towns were English. They were the favored race. In Upper Canada in earlier times, Englishmen, in conjunction with the Church of England as a kind of holding company for political and economic interest, dominated the economic, political, religious and social life to their own unquestioned pecuniary advantage.

Our mood, really that of the more prestigious class, was not, I think, different from that of the Veblens. We felt ourselves superior to the storekeepers, implement salesmen, grain dealers and other entrepreneurs of the adjacent towns. We worked harder, spent less, but usually had more. The leaders among the Scotch took education seriously and, as a matter of course, monopolized the political life of the community. Yet the people of the towns were invariably under the impression that social position resided with them. Being English and Anglican, they were identified, however vicariously, with the old ruling class. Their work did not soil the hands. We were taught to think that claims to social prestige based on such vacuous criteria were silly. We regarded the people of the towns not with envy but with amiable contempt. On the whole, we enjoyed letting them know.

When I published the book, I received a quite unexpected flow of letters from people who had grown up in the German and Scandinavian towns and small cities of the Midwest. They told me that it was their community that I had described. "That was how we felt. You could have been writing about our community." The Veblens regarded themselves, not without reason, as the representatives of a superior culture. The posturing of the local Anglo-Saxon elite they also regarded with contempt. *The Theory of the Leisure Class* is an elongation of what Veblen observed and felt as a youth.

The Theory of the Leisure Class, when it appeared, admirably divided the men of reputable academic position from those who were responsive to ideas or capable of thought. One great man said that it was such books by dilettantes that brought sociology into disrepute among "careful and scientific thinkers." Science, as ever in economics and sociology, was being used to disguise orthodoxy. He went on to say that it was illegitimate to classify within the leisure class such unrelated groups as the barbarians and the modern rich. Another predictable scholar avowed that the rich were rich because they earned the money; the gargantuan reward of the captain of industry and the miserly one of the man with a spade were the proper valuation of their contribution to society as measured by their economic efficiency. The names of these critics are now lost to fame.

Other and more imaginative men were delighted. Lester Ward, one of the first American sociologists of major repute, said that "the book abounds in terse expressions, sharp antitheses, and quaint, but happy phrases. Some of these have been interpreted as irony and satire, but . . . The language is plain and unmistakable . . . the style is the farthest removed possible from either advocacy or vituperation."[21] Ward was admiring but a bit too trusting. William Dean Howells, then at the peak of his reputation, was equally enthusiastic. And he too was taken in by Veblen. "In the passionless calm with which the author pursues his investigation, there is apparently no animus for or against a leisure class. It is his affair simply to find out how and why and what it is."[22] (For these reactions, I am again indebted to Dorfman.) The sales of *The Leisure Class* were modest, although few could have guessed for how long they would continue. Veblen was promoted in 1900 to the rank of assistant professor. His pay remained negligible.

In the years following the publication of *The Theory of the Leisure Class* Veblen turned to an examination of the business enterprise in its social context — an interest that is foreshadowed in *The Leisure Class* in the distinction between "exploit," which is that part of business enterprise that is devoted to making money, and "industry," which is that part that makes things. (In a characteristically matter-of-fact assertion of the shocking, Veblen notes that "employments which are to be classed as exploit are worthy, honorable, noble"; those involving a useful contribution to product being often "unworthy, debasing, ignoble.")[23] In 1904, Veblen developed this point (and much else) in *The Theory of Business Enterprise*. Out of

21 Lester F. Ward, quoted in Dorfman, p. 194.
22 William Dean Howells, quoted in Dorfman, p. 196.
23 Thorstein Veblen, p. 29.

his meager income, he was still required to pay a good part of the publishing cost himself.

In introducing a recent (and handsomely selling) French edition of *The Theory of the Leisure Class,* Raymond Aron argues that Veblen was better in his social than in his economic perception. With this I agree. The basic idea of *The Theory of Business Enterprise* is a plausible one — I can still remember my excitement when I first read the book in the thirties while a student at Berkeley, where the Veblen influence was strong. There is a conflict between the ordered rationality of the machine process as developed by engineers and technicians and the moneymaking context in which it operates. The moneymakers through competition and interfirm aggression, and the resolution of the latter by consolidation and monopoly, sabotage the rich possibilities inherent in the machine process. But — though some will still object — the idea has been a blind alley. Organization and management are greater tasks than Veblen implies; so is the problem of accommodating production to social need. And so is that of motivation and incentive. All of this has become evident in the socialist economies, where far more difficulties have been encountered in translating the rationality of the machine process into effective economic performance than Veblen would have supposed. In the thirties, after Veblen's death, the political movement (perhaps more properly the cult) "technocracy" was founded on these ideas by Howard Scott. For a while it flourished. Had the technocrats been given a chance, they would have faced the same problems of management, organization and incentives as have the socialist states. Though much read in the first half of the century, *The Theory of Business Enterprise,* unlike *The Theory of the Leisure Class,* has not similarly survived.

Veblen's writing continued, and so, in 1906, did his academic peregrinations. His classes were small, his reputable academic colleagues adverse and his married life perilous — he was increasingly disinclined to resist the aggressions of admiring women. But in a minor way he was famous and thus a possible academic adornment. Harvard, urged by Frank W. Taussig, who had a recurring instinct for dissent, considered inviting him to join its department of economics but soon had second thoughts. David Starr Jordan, then creating a new university south of San Francisco, was not so cautious. He invited Veblen to Leland Stanford as an associate professor. Veblen survived there for three years. But his domestic arrangements — sometimes Ellen, sometimes others — were now, for the times, a scandal. Once he responded wearily to a complaint with a query: "What is one to do if the woman moves in on you?" Jordan concluded that there were adornments that Stanford could not afford. Veblen was invited to move on. By the students, at least, he was not greatly missed. Though dozens were attracted to his classes by his reputation, only a handful — once only three — ever survived to the end of the term.

After he left Stanford, another established scholar with an instinct for the dissenter came to his rescue. H. J. Davenport, then one of the major figures in the American economic pantheon, took him to the University of Missouri. There he encountered some of the students on whom he had the most lasting effect. One, Isador Lubin, was later to be a close aide of Franklin D. Roosevelt and a protector of Veblen in the latter's many moments of need. Veblen divorced Ellen and in 1914 married Anne Fessenden Bradley, a gentle, admiring woman who did not long survive. In 1918, she suffered severe mental illness, and in 1920 she died. From Missouri Veblen went to Washington during World War I as one of the less likely participants in the wartime administration. From Washington he went on to New York to experiment with life as an editor and then to teach at the New School for Social Research. His writings continued; as were the early ones, they are sardonic, laconic and filled with brilliant insights.[24] As with

24 *The Instinct of Workmanship and the State of the Industrial Arts* (1914); *Imperial Germany and the Industrial Revolution* (1915); *An Inquiry into the Nature of Peace and the Terms of its Perpetuation* (1917); *The Higher Learning*

The Theory of Business Enterprise, many develop points of which there is a hint or more in *The Leisure Class.* The men of established reputation continued to be appalled. Reviewing *The Higher Learning in America* in the *New York Times Review of Books* in 1919, one Brander Matthews said of Veblen, "His vocabulary is limited and he indulges in a fatiguing repetition of a dozen or a score of adjectives. His grammar is woefully defective . . ."[25] The book is, in fact, one of Veblen's most effective tracts. Other reviewers were wiser. Gradually, step by step, it came to be realized that Veblen was a genius — the most penetrating, original and uninhibited source of social thought in his time.

This did not mean that he was much honored or rewarded. Veblen's students and disciples frequently had to come to his support. Employment became harder to find than ever. In the mid-twenties, aging, silent, impecunious and tired, he returned reluctantly to California, and there, in 1929, he died.

The Nation, following his death, spoke of Veblen's "mordant wit, his extraordinary gift of . . . discovering wholly new meanings in old facts,"[26] saying in one sentence what I have said in many. Wesley C. Mitchell wrote an obituary note for *The Economic Journal,* the journal of The Royal Economic Society, then the most prestigious economic publication in the world. Saying sadly that "We shall have no more of these investigations, with their curious erudition, their irony, their dazzling phrases, their bewildering reversals of problems and values,"[27]

---

in America; A Memorandum on the Conduct of Universities by Business men (1918); *The Vested Interests and the Common Man* (1919); *The Place of Science in Modern Civilisation and Other Essays* (1919); *The Engineers and the Price System* (1921); *Absentee Ownership and Business Enterprise in Recent Times; The Case of America* (1923). At the end of his life Veblen resumed an early interest in his Norseland origins and studied the Icelandic sagas. His last publication was *The Laxdaela Saga* (1925).

25 Brander Matthews, The *New York Times Review of Books,* March 16, 1919, p. 125.

26 *The Nation,* vol. 129, no. 3345, p. 157.

27 Wesley C. Mitchell, "Thorstein Veblen: 1857–1929," *The Economic Journal,* vol. 39 (1929), p. 649.

he also observed that *The Economic Journal* had reviewed but one of Veblen's books. In 1925, it had taken notice of the ninth reprinting of *The Theory of the Leisure Class*. This was twenty-six years after its original publication.

12

A Note on the Psychopathology
of the Very Affluent

A SERIOUS LAG exists between the avowed political concerns of our time and the kinds of studies that are being done in universities and other places of solemn thought. For many decades, beginning at least with the thirties, the official concern of the country has been with the poor. In consequence, they have been much studied. Their education, ethnic composition, marital and sexual tendencies, psychiatric afflictions, unemployment and shortage of income have all been subjects of exhaustive academic attention. They still are, and therein lies the lag.

For the official concern of the government, we all know, has now changed. President Nixon made it perfectly clear, to use his words, that those who have asked what they could do for themselves and have found a profitable answer are now the proper object of public concern — along with those whose ancestors asked and answered for them and, additionally, it now appears, quite a few who simply helped themselves. Concern especially for the taxes of the affluent has especially increased. Yet the academic preoccupation remains unchanged. The poor are still being studied. The Ford Foundation is funding practically no work on the rich. It is this situation that the present essay is designed, in some small part, to correct.

I've been studying the problems of the rich under exceptionally favorable circumstances in the village of Gstaad in Switzerland. Partly this is the result of an accident; I started going there to write some twenty-five years ago, and the rich moved in on me. Of necessity, though, my observation has been somewhat at second hand. A scholar who is working on Watts, Bedford-Stuyvesant or the Appalachian plateau can get out with his people. If you are a serious writer, that is impossible with the rich. It is the nature of the wealthy existence that it involves the most elaborate possible waste of time, not that wasting time is unknown in university circles. Some of my colleagues have identified it with academic freedom and raised it to the level of a scholarly rite. However, hearing of my interest, a couple of exceedingly handsome women — one the wife of a motion-picture producer, the other of an Italian automobile magnate — volunteered to help. Both were in a position to waste a great deal of time.

The last great tract on the problems of the rich was *The Theory of the Leisure Class,* published just before the turn of the century.[1] Much, we have discovered, has changed since then. In 1899, wealth, by itself, was a source of distinction. It was necessary only that people knew one had it. Accordingly, Thorstein Veblen wrote of the ways by which the wealthy advertised their wealth — of the methodology of conspicuous consumption, conspicuous waste and conspicuous leisure. Mansions, carriages, clothes and social festivity were the most suitably conspicuous forms of consumption. If carried beyond a certain point of excess, all involved a satisfactory manifestation of waste. Leisure, in a world where nearly everyone had to work to survive, was sufficiently conspicuous in itself. But the point could be driven home by clothing — corsets, hoop skirts, high silk hats — that was palpably inconsistent with any form of toil.

The modern problem of the rich is both simpler and more difficult: wealth is no longer exceptional and therefore no

---

1 See the preceding essay, "Who Was Thorstein Veblen?"

longer a source of distinction. Yet the rich still yearn for distinction. The problem is exacerbated by their strong tribal tendencies. They flock and hunt together, and if everyone around is loaded, money and conspicuous expenditure do even less for an individual. (In addition to the usual inducements — the seasons, tradition and the tax authorities — whim appears to play a role in the migratory tendencies of the rich. My researchers told me that on a certain day last winter Gstaad suddenly became unfashionable, and the rich all went to Rio for the carnival. An aging fellow traveler of the affluent who was without funds but could not afford to be separated from the mob took himself, according to legend, to the neighboring town of Bulle during carnival time and asked a trusted ally to mail prearranged postcards home from Brazil.) In any case, last winter a man who lost $100,000 at backgammon in one evening got almost no notoriety from his outlay and very few invitations as a result. In an even sadder case, a woman who combines great wealth with repellent appearance and advanced nymphomania paid $300,000 for a lover — the technique is to deposit the money in the local bank and ensure reliability and durability by limiting the amount that can be withdrawn in any one month — and got no mileage from it at all, only the lover. One of my assistants, the wife of the motorcar man, says she was once propositioned by a twenty-year-old Italian who simply wanted an automobile. She offered to put him in touch with the wife of a good used-car dealer.

There is a further problem with the classical forms of conspicuous consumption: they are often positively inconsistent with the quest for distinction. Thus extra weight and a boozy appearance, once an index of rank, are now damaging for a woman and no longer do much even for an Englishman of noble birth. The average proletarian, after having dined with the rich, would need to stop on the way home for a hamburger. Similarly, houses without people to manage them reduce the owners to work, which is an undistinguished thing. Broadly speaking, no one in the United States or Europe ever serves anyone else except as a matter of stark necessity. Additionally, houses that are merely expensive are said to lack taste — because they usually do. Something can be done to neutralize the latter charge by hiring a decorator. A local aspirant gets some mileage from having the only house decorated by Valerian Rybar. (It was for a reputed hundred grand.) But with most other decorators there is the problem that one must live with the result. Sometimes, although not often, even the rich are sensitive.

Finally, although it is tough to work, idleness no longer has any affirmative value. On the contrary, it has come to be believed that an idle man is unimportant. If a woman is sufficiently beautiful and has a good figure, she can survive idleness, for it is taken for granted that she has ways of occupying at least part of her time. But this role also now invites criticism.

So a person must be both rich *and* distinguished, and distinction is something that money will no longer buy. To be rich and commonplace is to live on the edge of despair. There are the tribal dinners, cocktail parties, gay informal luncheons, receptions for visiting movie producers, stars or directors, and the undistinguished remain at home. They essay festivities on their own, but except for a few characters of deficient wit who are said to be getting by *on* their wits, no one shows up.

Meanwhile an effort to cultivate an aspect of importance encounters grave natural handicaps. The local sample of the rich includes a number of individuals whose families, former husbands or business firms consider it highly advantageous that they live at the greatest possible distance. That is usually because they lack intelligence, charm, emotional stability or any other known attainment, including the ability to read without undue movement of the lips. And, quite generally, the merely rich lack the ability to command the favorable attention they crave, and the ability to do so disintegrates further with age. One of my researchers says firmly that the average rich man has only one chance to excel these days: "He's got to be a real clown." To fend off age, a fair number even resort to a local clinic, where they are injected with cells said to be superior to their own that are supposed to keep them young and virile. However, my other researcher is bearish, or certainly not bullish, about this: "The most it's ever done for any man I've known is to give him a sore ass." In addition to the cells, there are fraudulent pills to prevent aging supplied to a major concentration of customers who want them by the two drugstores in Gstaad.

From the foregoing, it will seem that the affluent are now not nearly as happy as the conspicuous and uncomplicated rich of earlier times. The past year, however, may have altered things a bit. Some of the rich, oddly enough, have had their neuroses subsumed by old-fashioned worry about money. In Gstaad a distinction is made between the rich and "the only two-house rich." The latter, who may also be refugees from alimony or the IRS, spend pretty much all of the money they get. For many, income comes in dollars. The several devaluations and slumps have had a marked effect on people's personal economy. Quite a few of the afflicted have stopped me in the village to ask my views on the monetary situation; and twice couples have crept into our apartment to inquire. One man, with a look of woe I haven't seen since our troops overran Dachau, said he might even have to go to work.

I endeavored to help by telling my patients, if they were Americans, that they should count on the dollar's going to zero or perhaps a trifle below. As I developed this thesis, I could see a different look — that of anxiety — spreading over the leisure-ravaged faces. I knew I had rescued fellow humans from the deeper anxieties of the rich and returned them to the simple, old-fashioned, manageable worries about money that everyone else has.

II
Personal History

13

My Forty Years with the FBI

The graduate students with whom I associated in the thirties were uniformly radical and the most distinguished were Communists. I listened to them eagerly and would liked to have joined both the conversation and the Party but here my agricultural background was a real handicap. It meant that, as a matter of formal Marxian doctrine, I was politically immature. Among the merits of capitalism to Marx was the fact that it rescued men from the idiocy of rural life. I had only very recently been retrieved. I sensed this bar and I knew also that my pride would be deeply hurt by rejection. So I kept outside. There was possibly one other factor. Although I recognized that the system could not and should not survive, I was enjoying it so much that, secretly, I was a little sorry.

I WROTE THE ABOVE nine or ten years ago for a volume celebrating the centenary of the University of California, to which I had proceeded for graduate study in 1931 after taking a degree in animal husbandry at the Ontario Agricultural College. I am able to reproduce the item without going back to the manuscript, for it appears in my FBI file under date of September 17, 1971, just forty years after my original temptation. Government employment was not involved; on the undesirability of that at the time Mr. Nixon and I were in an unnatural agreement. Rather, I was about to be elected President of the American Economic Association, an honor often associated with longevity, and a member of the association had written to J. Edgar Hoover, enclosing the foregoing confession and saying that while he did not expect any action, he did want Mr. Hoover to know that "the trend is of concern to many in the profession." The Director, who had much such help, replied six days later with a three-line letter of thanks, beginning "Dear Dr." and carrying a total of, possibly, ten different initials according clearance.

This mild item is included in my FBI file, the most interesting set of government documents that has ever come my way. This file, good for several days' reading, cultivates a sense of deep paranoia, less one's own than that of the large number of one's fellow citizens who live in fear of Communists and Communism and the even larger number who once desperately feared they would be thought soft on Communism and in consequence be heaved out of their jobs. It tells, also, how difficult it was to decide what qualified an individual as a Communist or a dangerous radical or as being otherwise inimical to the system. Dubious personal traits, even a badly exaggerated ego, might serve. The file is unparalleled in my experience as a mine of misinformation. Also it proves conclusively that on the matter of being a security risk — perilous one day, safe the next — the age of miracles is not over.

While the impression of other people's paranoia is great, my own was diminished by the fact that while the documents are full of deeply damaging intentions, virtually nothing unpleasant ever happened as a consequence. (But one can see how the only slightly more vulnerable must have suffered. It is good to be on even the raffish fringe of the Establishment.)

The file also proves, and here beyond the most pallid shadow of a doubt, that the government of the United States has, in these matters, a colossal capacity for wasting money. Some tens of thousands of old-fashioned real dollars were spent in 1950 investigating my fitness to continue in a job in which I had rendered no service and of which I was unaware until the investigation culminated one day in a demand that I tell all details of my association with Mr. Corliss Lamont. Mr. Lamont, a neighbor, friend, radical, civil libertarian and son of a Morgan partner, was considered an especially dangerous companion for anyone employed without his knowledge in a nonexistent job. On this, as on other matters, there is much that is very funny. There is also much that evokes one's sympathy, even admiration, for the rank-and-file member and down-the-line agent of the FBI struggling with these pathetic tasks. But let me begin at the beginning.

My first jobs with the United States government involved only the most benign of relationships with the FBI, and at the outset none at all. In June of 1934, on the way from Berkeley to Harvard, I stopped over in Washington and was promptly put on the payroll for the summer by a former professor as an associate economist in the Agricultural Adjustment Administration. Economists were in short supply. The AAA had, during this period or just before, enrolled a number of radicals of later fame, including Alger Hiss, Lee Pressman, John Abt, Nathan Witt, Nathaniel Weyl as well as Jerome Frank, George Ball and Adlai Stevenson. As with the Berkeley radicals, I never at the time achieved the distinction that allowed me to know any of them.

In those days one went on the payroll without FBI clearance, the FBI being generally regarded as a law enforcement agency, and I don't remember that I was even asked if I was a citizen, which I was not. Clearance was, however, required from James A. Farley, custodian and dispenser of Democratic patronage. His representative had an office on the top floor of the South Building of the Department of Agriculture, and he called me up and made me affirm that I was a Democrat. This I did with good conscience. In southern Ontario everyone adored Roosevelt, and certainly no one at Berkeley had been for Hoover.

I worked further on various public tasks in the next few years without being aware of the Bureau or vice versa. This changed in the summer of 1940, when I was employed by the

Advisory Commission to the Council of National Defense. Elementary investigations were ordered to exclude spies from such posts. The resulting reports can be read with nearly undiluted admiration of both one's self and of the investigators. At Berkeley, Cambridge, Princeton and the American Farm Bureau Federation in Chicago, all places of my previous study or employment, the agents were told, and faithfully reported, that I was "brilliant," an "excellent writer," possessed of "a keen sense of sportsmanship" (something of which I was not then or thereafter aware), of a "good personality," "not obnoxious," a "good conversationalist" and with no adverse credit record, in fact none at all. It was said, no one being perfect, that the subject "was impressed with his own knowledge and importance" and "was too deep a thinker for undergraduates." Also, "a poor public speaker."

From those very earliest days one detects a tendency, highly developed in all later investigations, for one's friends to sense with precision what statement would be the most damaging to one's public career and then to volunteer, with great emphasis and some talent for invention, the precise opposite. Eventually there were to be numerous (by FBI standards) derogatory items in the file, to which I will come, and while the good things disappear, the bad live on. Gresham's Law operated relentlessly here. But more than half of the file by volume consists of extravagant attestations to whatever quality would most allay suspicion. Thus, during the 1940 investigation, the longtime Chairman of the Harvard Department of Economics — a deeply conservative scholar of modest attainments named Harold Hitchings Burbank (he is easily identified from the context) — was forced to concede, as a matter of simple intellectual honesty, that "the subject leaned as far to the left as President ROOSEVELT," who was then in office. But then he moved quickly to retrieve. I was extremely loyal. I also had a fine military aspect — "commanding appearance due to his height of 5'6" [I am 6' 8½"] and his dignified bearing." Another

Harvard professor went further to urge that I "was a conservative thinker and talker," and a Berkeley academician went all out and described me as "reactionary" and therefore "entirely desirable from every angle." One agent did pick up word that I was currently in Cuba having a nervous breakdown. My nerves at the time were fine; Cuba, although then a thoroughly respectable place for a holiday, I had never seen. The misinformation begins at the beginning.

Needless to say, I was cleared, and in the next few years I had even more reason to love the FBI and J. Edgar Hoover, for there was the small matter of a murder rap. One day in late 1941 or early 1942, I arrived at the OPA offices (I had been put in charge of all prices in the United States without any evident investigation) to find two staff members waiting for me, their faces gray with anxiety. A few weeks before, the Navy, a major consumer of sponges for some arcane shipboard reason, had complained about the prices it was having to pay. The two men had gone to Tarpon Springs, Florida, an acknowledged center of the industry, to hold hearings prior to setting a ceiling. The first hearing came to a violent end, the violence having been provoked by the local leader of the sponge fishermen, a man of Greek antecedents and forthright reputation, named — on this, invention replaces history — Nikolas Bolenkus. Further hearings were called and attended by no one because Nick's men were patrolling in a menacing way outside. Eventually Nick called in at the hotel to suggest, helpfully, that our chaps might just as well go back to Washington; they were accomplishing nothing in Florida. In the presence of numerous witnesses, one of my men told Nick that he was about to meet with a major misfortune at the hands of another individual who was bigger and just as tough as he. This man, he said — combining emphasis with imagination — was his boss, J. K. Galbraith. It was legal disaster that he had in mind, but that was not made clear. The threat delivered, the two price-fixers left for Tampa and the plane to Washington. The evening before our meeting in the office, someone had called them from Florida. Earlier that day Nick had stepped on the starter of his automobile to which someone had wired a very large charge of dynamite. Both the car and Nick were totaled. My men then remembered their threat.

I recall thinking at the time that my alibi was better than my worried friends imagined. But I put in a call to one of Hoover's acolytes at the FBI and told him the situation. Toward noon Edgar, as, believe it or not, we called him in those days, phoned back. A cursory inquiry had revealed that I was twenty-ninth in plausibility (that is my recollection of my rank) as suspected murderer among those who had been heard threatening to knock off the late Bolenkus. My men were relieved, and I had achieved a story which I've since told a hundred times. Not every Harvard professor has been involved, however remotely, in a gangland killing.

Over the next nine years my relations with the FBI remained pleasant and also fragmentary. In the closing days of the war and for some time thereafter I was myself involved in investigatory activities. In 1944, President Roosevelt, having, as I've often said, mastered the first principle of modern warfare, which is that the claims of air generals as to what they are accomplishing have no natural relationship to truth, asked that a special study group — the U.S. Strategic Bombing Survey — be constituted to establish the facts. Others, including George Ball, were urging the same need. I became a director the following year, but this involved no new investigation of my background. However, I did become knowledgeable on economic conditions in Germany and Japan, and this led to my being given charge of economic affairs in these countries (as well as Korea and Austria) in the State Department in early 1946.

My years as a price-fixer had been richly controversial. I was thought to enjoy severity for its own sake, which may have been true, and "radical theorist" was the term of opprobrium on which all of my critics eventually converged. My resignation from the OPA in 1943 had provoked more conservative applause than I have achieved since. In consequence, the Civil Service Commission and the special security investigators of the State Department were moved to investigate at the time of my new appointment. The State Department was not, in those days, a nest of radical theorists.

The job was not one I enjoyed. General Lucius Clay in Germany was not impressed with my guidance on economic affairs, and General Douglas MacArthur in Japan may not have been aware of it. The investigation as to my suitability for the task was not completed until after I had concluded, in the autumn of 1946, that I wasn't being very useful and had left.

These investigators turned up the usual and numerous encomiums on my loyalty and conversational tendencies, and on my loyalty these were as eloquent as before. However, now there was some bad-mouthing from people whose prices I had fixed or those who disapproved of fixing on principle. Congressman John Taber, an articulate fossil from upstate New York with whom I had often clashed, told a Civil Service investigator that Galbraith "was fired by the President and the Board of Trustees from his job as Professor at Princeton University because he was a Communist. He is a member of many Communist front organizations . . . a Totalitarian . . . would be a whole lot more effective using a pick and shovel . . . [in the State Department] would absolutely be a menace." And someone I judge to have been an aged Princeton professor of economics advised the investigator that I was pretty doctrinaire in my views, "in favor of anything Russia was in favor of." The reference to Russia did not survive, but his description of me as doctrinaire was a near-catastrophe, for it was heard as "Doctorware" by the investigator and was held to imply that I was a follower of an otherwise unidentified sub-

versive called Doctorware, later promoted, academically, to
"Dr. Ware." For the next twenty years, whenever my file was
examined, the superb testimony on my personality, garrulity
and loyalty was never reproduced. Only the references to radical theory, to Dr. Ware and to the action of the Princeton
President and Trustees. In time, the FBI, having come into
possession of the Civil Service files, sent an agent back to interview Taber, and he then denied all knowledge of my discharge
from Princeton. (As the university frequently advised the
Bureau, I had been an assistant professor, and my three-year
term had expired while I was on leave with the OPA.) He also
denied all other firsthand knowledge of my life and loyalty.
He passed the FBI on to his own source, an "investigator" for
the Republican National Committee, and *he* denied all knowledge of any kind. Still, the impression remained permanently
in the file that there was something very funny about my
departure from Princeton. Perhaps it was thought that the
Communists had somehow got to those who said it was routine,
although here I am just guessing.

Another durable piece of information from these years came
from a newspaper clipping. During the war it was charged that
my controls on newsprint prices were drying up the supply.
This a congressman had publicized as proof that I was a member "of a group that participated in 'an effort to curtail drastically the amount of newsprint available to [the] free press.'"
This charge also survived and, indeed, was never disproved.

In consequence of the foregoing information, or such as was
by then available, and the controversy over my price-fixing, the
Security Screening Committee of the Security Office of the
Department of State on January 25, 1946, formally disapproved
my appointment as a security risk. It also concluded that my
being on the payroll would "draw sharp criticism of the Department . . . and . . . jeopardize as a result . . . certain programs and
appropriations." It concluded that "It cannot be conceived that
this applicant possesses qualifications which will in anyway [sic]

offset or compensate for the resulting damages to the Department's prestige." After this finding, I was promptly and routinely appointed and did not know of the interdict until I got the file. The investigatory routine had already become silly. During the war I had worked closely with James F. Byrnes, who was now Secretary of State, and W. L. Clayton, his Assistant Secretary for economic matters. They knew me well, and it was natural that they would ignore investigators who did not.

It was in 1950 that my relations with the Bureau became really intimate and detailed. Of this I was also unaware. In 1948, I left *Fortune* magazine where I had been an editor — *Fortune* had only a moderately more subversive reputation then than now — and returned to Harvard. During the summer of 1950, I was in Europe on vacation with my wife and son, and in Switzerland one day I received an urgent telephone call from the Economic Cooperation Administration in Washington — the back-up organization of the Marshall Plan — asking if I would go to Frankfurt and Bonn and work out arrangements involving a joint German-American commission to examine the refugee problem, a matter on which I was deemed to have some special competence. It was several days before travel clearance arrived, and later, when I was back in Washington, I asked the man who had called me why, after all the urgency, all the delay. He told me that it was a time-consuming task to read my security file and that the man who had started on it had been transferred to another job before he finished. During those summer days the file was, in fact, growing at a spectacular rate.

Earlier that year — on the 24th of February to be exact — I had attended for a few hours a meeting at the Department of Commerce in Washington to consider the effect of the agricultural subsidy programs on the economy. I had filed various forms to claim travel and compensation, matters I have never been inclined to neglect. Unknown to me, one of these had put me on the rolls of the Department of Commerce as a consultant when, as and if employed — which, since I was not again employed, was not at all. This, in turn, made me subject to the deepening concerns over the LOYALTY OF GOVERNMENT EMPLOYEES, as the investigative forms were headed — a concern then gathering force in response to the trials of Alger Hiss and the fear of Senator Joseph R. McCarthy. A preliminary check by the FBI turned up the alarming references to radical theory, Dr. Ware (still called Doctorware), the righteous if imagined action of the Princeton President and Trustees, the conspiracy against the free press and a couple of items of real if less than subversive substance. In 1941, at a congressional hearing, I had come to the support of a onetime Berkeley professor of mine, Robert A. Brady, who was under heavy fire for having had a book distributed in England by the Left Book Club. I had assured the committee that the Left Book Club, which specialized exclusively in works from well left of center, was the English equivalent, more or less, of the Book-of-the-Month Club. There was a large element of fantasy here; there is always a temptation in such hearings to say whatever will tranquilize an aroused committee and then get out of the room. You never should. Further, in 1944, I had been active in the National Citizens Political Action Committee, a body organized by Sidney Hillman to work for the reelection of President Roosevelt. It unquestionably enrolled some very active Communists, an association which I'm glad to say I did not then, and have not since, believed destructive. And we had all been for the reelection of Roosevelt. Although the NCPAC was not one of the proscribed organizations of the Attorney General or even of the House Un-American Activities Committee, it had fallen under the ban of the relatively much less discriminating California Committee on Un-American Activities. Their list of subversives and subversive organizations had a kind of cadet standing and was regularly reviewed by Washington. All this was enough to cause the Department of Commerce to ask the

Civil Service Commission to request the FBI on March 28, 1950, to convert the superficial check into what the FBI calls an FFI — a Full Field Investigation. Frightened officials in Commerce and not the FBI, it should be noted, were responsible.

It was a very full investigation indeed, and it was this that must have run into the real money. Men were deployed, according to a later memorandum, in Washington, New York, Boston, Chicago, Newark (meaning Princeton), Newark again, Detroit, San Francisco (meaning Berkeley), Chicago, Richmond (meaning suburban Washington), Richmond again, Birmingham, Albany, Boston again and St. Louis. A request went to the State Department for research, via the consular offices, into my Canadian background and my activities while a student thirteen years before in England. "Should substantive information be developed [in these countries] reflecting disloyalty on the part of the Appointee, it would be appreciated if signed statements are obtained from persons furnishing such disloyal information." No disloyal information, so attested, seems to have been forthcoming. My book reviews were also read by a scholarly agent at the New York FBI office and were found not to "reflect any information that may be pertinent to this investigation." The single exception was a review of Merle Miller's *The Sure Thing*, a novel having to do with the current witch-hunting, and this was sent as an enclosure with the New York agent's report.

The same agent noted that "The Biographical Morgue file of the 'New York Times' newspaper on the appointee was reviewed by the writer. The file did not reflect any information reflecting on the loyalty of the appointee to the United States."

Such precise language is a passion of the FBI. Summers during the war years we took a house in suburban Virginia on the grounds of an Episcopalian seminary there. The agent reporting on this residence advised the Bureau that "Other efforts to locate persons residing in the vicinity of the appointee's former address on Seminary Hill, Alexandria, Virginia, who were residing there during the appointee's residence, were met with negative results."

In each of the several cities, Communists of known reliability who were operating in the Party on behalf of the FBI were visited.

Confidential Informants New York City T-2, T-3, T-4, T-5 and T-6, who are reliable and are familiar with general Communist activities in the New York City area, advised that they were not acquainted with the appointee.

Also a helping hand right at Harvard:

Boston Confidential Informant T-1, of known reliability, closely associated with activities at the school of Public Administration, Harvard University, advised having been acquainted with Appointee... T-1 expressed the firm belief that GALBRAITH was without question a loyal American citizen.

To such of these subversives as survive, my warm thanks.

As before, the FBI agents were overwhelmed with testimony on my loyalty. The speeches were even more extravagant than in 1946 but now with a difference. Before, the agents had heard how affirmatively loyal I was; now they heard how negatively anti-Communist I was. Before, the testimonials had led me to wonder how I escaped high office in the American Legion; now they conveyed the clear impression that I was in hard training for service on or with the HUAC.

There were, however, some nasty notes. A Detroit advertising man named Lou Maxon with whom I had clashed in OPA, after first stressing his personal dislike in a very decent way, "described Appointee as a 'Fly-by-night' economist who seemed determined to inject a Socialist trend in policies and directives of the Office of Price Administration." A Washington agent reported that Mr. J. B. Mathews, research director of the House Un-American Activities Committee and a formidable opponent of Communism and syntax, had testified that "J. KENNETH GALBRAITH has had a connection with one of the Com-

munist books, magazines and other literature but it is not indicated as to exactly [with] which publication GALBRAITH
was affiliated." That book, magazine or other literary affiliation
could only have been with *Fortune*. Other informants who had
suffered under my management of wartime price control or
didn't like it on general principles also got in their licks:
"Screwball in economics" was one of the milder phrases from
a witness, who added that he wouldn't say I was a Communist
"but more of a fellow traveller." Here, however, and with no
nonsense, I must again put in a good word for the Bureau.
On August 21, 1950, as the FFI was getting under way, a
memorandum was sent from Washington to all relevant offices,
advising that my administration of price control during the
war had been viewed with distaste by "many people in this
country, principally members of Congress and business and
industrial leaders" and that I had become a "very controversial
figure." It then went on to say:

> This is being brought to the attention of all offices conducting
> this investigation because it is entirely possible that some witnesses
> may be inclined to give adverse information concerning GAL-
> BRAITH because they were not in agreement with his economic
> theories and policies and such testimony may be given intention-
> ally or otherwise in such a manner to bear adversely upon his
> loyalty. It is therefore suggested that all offices be alert in securing
> testimony in this investigation because of GALBRAITH's back-
> ground.

That was handsome, and I am led to remind the reader once
more that this particular act of investigatory nonsense was in-
stigated not by the FBI but ultimately by the President of the
United States and immediately by the Civil Service Commission
and the Personnel Operations Division of the Department of
Commerce on behalf of the Commodities Division, Office of the
Director, Office of Industry and Commerce, U.S. Department of
Commerce. These are to be blamed. To any of these who also
survive, a vulgar gesture.

The investigation ground on. On October 19, there was a

chilling note. James M. McInerney, an Assistant Attorney General now lost to fame, sent to the Civil Service Commission for the whole file "in connection with this Department's consideration of the above entitled case from the standpoint of possible criminal prosecution under Title 18, Section 1001, U.S.C." This provision of the Code punishes people who lie to federal officials. Leavenworth did not beckon. The request seems only to have been a form letter used to keep the Justice Department in touch with investigations and prepared to act in case those investigated did a snow job on the agents. I was safe; having been asked nothing, I had not lied.

Eventually in late December I did become witting, as the CIA puts it. I received a letter in Cambridge from the Loyalty Review Board of the Department of Commerce, asking, in slightly peremptory fashion, that, as an employee, I disclose my relationship with three men, one of whom I did not know; one of whom, E. Johnston Coil, was my closest friend; one of whom, inevitably, was Corliss Lamont. They wanted also to know about any membership in "subversive" organizations. I answered — friends were friends, of dangerous organizations none. (That parsimony was a restraining factor I did not admit.) Then I asked how come? I wasn't employed. My statement that I didn't hold the job was promptly accepted as a resignation from the job I didn't hold. The investigation, though incredibly still incomplete, was brought to an end. Not quite, in fact. In ensuing years the files kept turning up the fact that I had resigned before my loyalty was established. That was slightly bad.

During the Eisenhower years the risk of even unwitting non-employment by the government was minimal, but this did not keep me out of the files. The Republic could be threatened in other ways, and my best effort involved a plot to collapse the stock market. This was accomplished one day in March 1955, when I testified before the Senate Committee on Banking and Currency on current conditions in Wall Street and a mini-boom that was then in blossom. During my testimony the market slumped — a total of some $7 billions in values was lost or, as some would have preferred, confiscated. There was a memorable headline, EGGHEAD SCRAMBLES MARKET, and Walter Winchell went on the air to warn Senator Fulbright, then the Chairman of the Banking Committee, that I had been a member of the National Citizens Political Action Committee. "This outfit, Senator, is listed by the House Un-American Activities Committee as a 'Red' front." (Winchell had the wrong committee, but he was not given to precision on such details.) Fulbright was deeply unimpressed, but the message from Winchell did get through to Homer Capehart, Republican of Indiana, then ranking minority member of the committee. He hadn't been around the day I testified; now, on television, he demanded that I come back and explain the plot. He cited a pamphlet on postwar reconstruction issued by the National Planning Association (an upright organization of businessmen, farmers, trade unionists and professors that still functions) in which I was alleged to have said something agreeable about Communism. It was not unrestrained praise; it couldn't have been, for my thoughts had been endorsed by Allen Dulles, by then head of the CIA, and by Milton Eisenhower, a friend from my agricultural days and the brother of the President. I had heard that Capehart was going to unleash and had warned him that a reading of the document would show that it did not serve his purpose. However, though a generally pleasant man, he was not unduly literate and was further handicapped by being deeply obtuse.

When Capehart's attack came, I was prepared. I shouted back with some vigor, and a day or two later, while attending a meeting at Purdue University, I questioned whether anyone so uninformed as to my views should be allowed to represent the people of the state of Indiana. I noted, also, that the contents of the pamphlet had first been given as a lecture at Notre

Dame. This made the Senator guilty by association of an attack on the leading Catholic university in the country and a monument to culture and football in his own state.

I sensed at the time that Capehart was struggling. I was right. The files show a desperate appeal for help. The CIA refused to assist, but Sinclair Weeks of Massachusetts, the Secretary of Commerce, rallied to the Senator's side and asked the FBI for help. A grudge was involved here. Weeks, known to his friends as Sinnie, had taken strong exception to my earlier economic views, and, in reply, I had publicly noted his resistance even to the Renaissance. J. Edgar Hoover, who may, perhaps, have anticipated the Senator's need and Weeks's request — the timing here is difficult to establish — sent a *Washington Post* clipping to his men with the question, "What do our files show on Galbraith?" There followed a frantic scramble for adverse information. "At approximately 4:30 P.M. today . . . I talked to XXXXXX [the X's mean the name is deleted in the file] . . . At 5:50 P.M. I called XXXXXX. Special Memo Section complete a review of all references to Galbraith during the evening of 3-9-55 . . . at 8:50 A.M. . . . I contacted XXXXXX." The contact was with Capehart or Capehart's contact, and the information he or it passed must have been a sore disappointment to Homer. The pamphlet that had seemed to him subversive could not be found in the Bureau's files. It was noted that I had twice been investigated by the FBI. Of the first effort it was said "Investigation favorable except conceited, egotistical and snobbish." This was not favorable, but it was also not the kind of thing that would surprise a United States senator. The second investigation — the FFI — had yielded principally the fact that I had resigned from that nonemployment at Commerce before my loyalty was fully established.

Weeks's request and Hoover's help were highly improper, but once again the FBI was more misused than misbehaving — misused this time not by frightened bureaucrats such as those in Commerce but by a Cabinet member and its own Director. They were the ones to blame. Blame attaches also to President Truman, who tried to protect himself from right-wing criticism with these insane investigations — no other democracy needed them — and later to Presidents Kennedy and Johnson, who should have retired J. Edgar long before God came to the assistance of the Republic.

The files in these years show a more important Hoover aberration that has not, I believe, been celebrated previously. As in the campaign four years before, I served on the speech-writing staff of Adlai Stevenson in 1956. In October of that year, this came to the attention of one of Hoover's ever-vigilant volunteer informants; he wrote urging and very nearly demanding that ghostwriters for candidates be subject to a proper measure of surveillance. ". . . for some time it has been the custom to assign Secret Service men to protect the person of both the principal Presidential candidates in presidential election years. I believe that this procedure should be broadened so as to protect not only the bodies of the candidates, but their minds as well . . . if a president [sic] has not the wish, nor the ability, to put his thoughts into his own words, the 'ghost writer' becomes someone of enormous power . . . It is of the utmost importance to the nation that the 'ghosts' be 'above reproach' like Caesar's wife . . ." I was one of the Stevenson ghosts who did not, in this patriot's view, come even close in purity to the late Mrs. Caesar and was, in fact, one who sent "chills down the spine of any American with a knowledge of the left wing conspiracy to take over our Republic."

There was, of course, some comparative logic in this concern. Were one out to get the free enterprise system and had a choice, one would write speeches for a presidential candidate rather than be an unwitting and nonemployed employee of the Commodities Division, Office of the Director, etc., etc., of the U.S. Department of Commerce. However, on these larger matters, Hoover moved more cautiously. He wrote to the Attorney

General: "I am transmitting herewith a copy of a communication I have received from XXXXXX who suggests that steps be taken to make available to XXXX [Adlai Stevenson] any information pertaining to the background of his alleged 'ghost-writers' . . ." He went on to say that he had acknowledged the letter, "pointing out that this was not a matter within the purview of our responsibility, and I have advised him that I am calling his letter to your attention."

By 1960, however, Hoover had enlarged perceptibly his purview of his responsibility. In that year I was working (though not particularly as an alleged ghostwriter) for John F. Kennedy. On July 5, taking note of this association, Hoover called for a full survey of the files. With the commendable promptness that the Director's wishes produced, five pages of inspired misinformation were on his desk the very next day. The dishonorable discharge from Princeton was there, although by now it was subject to the aforementioned doubts. The Commerce Department was now reported as saying that, in my nonemployment there, I had been viewed as one of 51 "poor security risks," and my departure had been upgraded to a precautionary act — a "voluntary resignation" had been obtained.

Hoover was also told that I was associated, as a Kennedy helper, with Arthur Schlesinger, Jr. There was mention again of Dr. Ware, and it was noted that in 1959, at the suggestion of Adlai Stevenson "with whom he was associated during 1952 and 1956 Presidential campaigns," I had "contacted" the Soviet Embassy. I *had* been associated with Schlesinger even more closely than with Dr. Ware; the approach to the Embassy (unless for a visa) was news.

One learned also what fine distinctions the Director could handle when it came to political views. He was told that mine were " 'left of center,' but not 'left wing,' 'pink' or 'leftist.' " And from the ever-present and decent civil servant came the redeeming note: "Many who disagreed with his economic theories were insistent that while Galbraith's views were 'left of center,' Communism or Socialism could and should not be imputed to Galbraith." The FBI and Hoover had no business so concerning themselves with politics.

While my file does not show that my subversion ever, in the end, kept me off a public payroll, there was some modest pecuniary damage in these years. On one or two occasions people in the CIA asked that I be invited to lecture to the "intelligence community." This was denied by higher authority on the grounds that I was a grave security risk, made worse by the danger that my instruction might provoke criticism from those on the Hill who disliked my views. I was also disapproved for a covert operation, this being a glorious convocation of liberal intellectuals in Milan in 1955 — Hugh Gaitskell, Roy Jenkins, Anthony Crosland, Arthur Schlesinger, George Kennan, many others — which the CIA was secretly funding. (We were told it was funded by a foundation.) But something went wrong here, for, in fact, I attended. After I published *The Affluent Society* in 1958, lower echelons of the United States Information Agency asked regularly for my services as a lecturer and for the book for their libraries. These requests too were firmly refused by more responsible authority. The risk to security and of political criticism was intolerable, although again there was a slip, for I remember giving a lecture under such auspices in Rome.

In this prosaic and excessively intellectual age, there are men and women who do not believe in miracles. Let all be clear: miracles of biblical magnitude still occur. At one point in time, as it is now said, you cannot give a lecture to the CIA or for the United States Information Agency; you are too grave a security risk. At the next point in time, twelve months later, you can be responsible in a vast country for what those agencies do. No ceremony of purification or trial of epuration is involved. Only the continuing marvel of democracy. All this the history now proves.

The earlier investigations were prelude to the biggest investigation of all — that of a putative ambassador. I knew, of course, that this was in progress. It occurred after I had moved into the White House in January of 1961, a fairly strategic location, one would think, where security matters are concerned but one that required no investigation of any kind. Indeed, so far as the files show, the FBI seems never to have discovered that I was there. One day, while my appointment to India was pending, I ran into Adlai Stevenson, who told me he had just been quizzed at length about my loyalty. That impressed me, for earlier on the very same day I had been asked about his. I had told the agent, who was very pleasant, that were Stevenson a subversive, it would rank as one of the more dangerously delayed discoveries of all time.

This investigation revealed another striking fact about the loyalty of government officials. If you are a member of the administration and about to become an ambassador, things go better. Adverse information disappears or even becomes favorable. Thus the Princeton discharge disappeared. So, at long last, did Dr. Ware. My relations with Commerce were reexamined, my letter explaining that I had never been employed was unearthed, and my candor in admitting to my questionable friendships became, I would judge, a plus. All mention of the voluntary/involuntary separation from Commerce before loyalty adjudication vanished. Instead it was noted with emphasis that President Truman had bestowed on me the Medal of Freedom for "exceptionally meritorious achievement" during the war, although, I discovered for the first time, "without palm." I had never missed the palm. My wife's family was now discovered and cited as "of fine character, conduct and reputation and loyal Americans." One or two critics complained that I was "inexperienced in business," and there was, of course, the customary misinformation. My birthplace was given as Ottawa (it appears elsewhere as Toronto and a town on the Detroit River called Sandwich where I have never been and which has since disappeared). I was described as deeply anti-Communist, which I am not; it was alleged that I sometimes said "no" in a tactless fashion when, in fact, I have difficulty saying it at all. But the errors, like the slurs, were lost in the massive wave of applause. After noting, among other things, that I had been described as "a great national figure of unquestioned ability," the FBI became sated and concluded its report with the truly breathtaking statistic that "ninety-eight other persons were interviewed and commented favorably concerning the character, reputation and loyalty of Mr. Galbraith. They also highly recommended him for a position of trust and responsibility with the Government." The investigatory language, however, was as careful and stately as ever. A Boston report, dated February 15, 1961, advised that ". . . personnel, Reference Libraries, Boston Herald-Traveler and Boston Daily Globe Corporations, both firms which publish newspapers on a daily basis at Boston, Massachusetts, made available information in the name of appointee, which has been utilized during this investigation."

The final report was made on March 6, 1961. A week or two earlier I had heard in the Washington rumor underground that my appointment was in deep trouble on Capitol Hill — on security grounds. Bourke B. Hickenlooper, a Republican senator from Iowa and a devout, articulate and loquacious but not especially malicious defender of the system, was standing firm against me. He had learned that the State Department had once denied me a passport. An ambassador without a passport could never get on intimate terms with the leaders of the country to which he was accredited and could well be a nuisance around Washington. Hickenlooper wanted yet another FFI. President Kennedy told me he thought the whole business degrading. Then suddenly the clouds cleared. Hick, as he was called by numerous colleagues and constituents, had been appeased. I was puzzled about the original charge, for I had never been denied a passport. This, at long last, my file explained;

it was only a slight problem in nomenclature, which anyone should have understood.

On February 23, 1961, an FBI agent, checking into things at the State Department, reported back that the files there "disclosed that JOHN KENNETH GALBRAITH was refused an American Passport on 2/20/53 because he was a member of subversive organizations, based on a communication from FBI dated 12/19/51." The same report showed that shortly thereafter I was issued a passport. The first but not the second fact had been sent by some helpful soul to Hickenlooper. A few days later an agent went back to check again. "It was determined by SA [special agent] that this refusal notice does not signify or imply that passport was refused, it is a misnomer, and merely serves as an administrative lookout notice for proper routing of mail within the Passport Office." Anyone should have known this. I went off to India.

There I found that *The Affluent Society* and my other books were still on the Index. They could be risked in libraries only with the special permission of Washington. Few acts of my life ever gave me such a feeling of righteously exercised power as the step I now took to declare my own writing safe for general use.

My association with the FBI had now passed its peak, but it was a long while (in the cost of Xeroxing the file, another ten or fifteen dollars) in decline. While back from India in 1961, I appeared on "Meet the Press" and was asked by one exceptionally handicapped reporter if I thought (as did Nehru) that India should deal with the Russians and Americans on the same moral plane. I said no and observed that an affirmative answer would endanger my security clearance. One of Hoover's volunteer helpers wrote the President in distress — "any loyal American would answer with an unqualified no," and he sent the transcript to J. Edgar for action. Hoover passed. However, in these months another unidentified but more persistent patriot in Birmingham, Alabama, went to the local office of the FBI to tell them that I was in India to encourage the Communist takeover of the country, that I had already encouraged the Indians to take over Goa, that I had once "praised the Russian education [sic] system" in *The Saturday Evening Post,* and that I had been responsible for a visit to India by Mrs. John F. Kennedy. A broad spectrum view of subversion. He identified me as Kenneth D. Galbreath. This intervention was taken rather seriously; the Birmingham man, who claimed to have met me during the war, was accepted as an expert on my past. Thereafter, when any question arose, the FBI went back to see him.

In 1963, I returned from India and spent another few weeks in the White House. Again no one alerted the FBI, although this time there might have been reason. I had been asked by the President to represent the United States in working out the basic arrangements for a new agreement on air flights between Canada and the United States. Until then, not having anything to give in return, the Canadians had been severely restricted in their flights to Florida, California and other American centers of sunshine and rest. In a highly irregular but extremely efficient gesture, Mike Pearson, then the Canadian Prime Minister and an old friend, told Kennedy that for these very preliminary findings and recommendations, since I had often praised myself as a onetime Canadian, I could be considered as representing Canada too. So I did — a clear case of divided loyalty. Negotiating with myself, I readily reached agreement. The arrangement showed that loyalty, like being a security risk, can be an on-and-off thing.

The next burst of concern, considerable but hardly approaching that of 1961, came in the autumn of 1964. Lyndon Johnson appointed me that year to a board that was to oversee the poverty program, something which I had had a small hand in developing. Though I had been an ambassador, no risk could be run; association with the poor, far more than with diplomacy, has always brought out the strongest in left-wing tendencies. The files were searched and the field offices put to work once more, although now with a certain delicacy and restraint: "assign to experienced personnel and conduct no neighborhood investigation unless some reason for doing so arises, at which time Bureau approval should be secured." The principal new discoveries were that I had served as ambassador and also as a consultant on the "President's Commission on Heart Diseases, Cancer and Stroke (no dates indicated)." Of my onetime Commerce nonemployment I had eventually been apprised; of my unservice on heart, cancer and stroke I had never heard until I got the file. The FBI also learned that "the appointee appeared to take pleasure in criticising the Department of State and its policies, while serving the Department as our Ambassador in India," and the man in Birmingham was visited by an agent in what the files call a Special Inquiry. He now conceded, rather handsomely, that "he had no specific information that GALBRAITH was a Communist or enemy agent." He did think it significant that in a photograph taken at the time of Nikita Khrushchev's first visit to the United States I was shown standing next to him and he "suggested KHRUSHCHEV may have requested GALBRAITH's presence." Once again my appointment went through. However, I was detached in an administrative shuffle when I began making speeches against the Vietnam war.

The Vietnam war produced my last important encounter with the FBI, although there were a few minor brushes unrelated to that conflict. In 1968, an internal memorandum had reviewed my novel, *The Triumph*. "The book primarily is a 'spoof' and satire against the State Department, Dean Rusk and American policy to uphold dictators in power for the reason of overthrowing communism ... Several miscellaneous references are made to the FBI, but nothing of any pertinence. The references are not derogatory." The following year two commencement addresses were given in New England which the Boston SAC (Special Agent in Charge) thought worthy of mention. One speaker attacked me, praised Hoover and said in a further letter to the *Boston Globe* that "No student of Hoover's ever burned his country's flag, beat up his instructors, or screeched obscenities at school the day he graduated." The other speech was mine, criticizing Hoover. The agent thought Hoover might want to send a letter of thanks to the first speaker and have a transcript of my speech, which the agent promised to get.

Sometime in the mid-sixties President Johnson summoned me to Washington to work on some plans having to do with food for India. I met him at the plane at Kennedy Airport — with J. Edgar Hoover he had been in New York to attend the funeral of the wife of Emanuel Celler, long the head of the House Judiciary Committee. I hadn't seen Edgar for many years; I thought he lacked affability and conveyed, in fact, a certain aspect of disapproval and mistrust. This must have deepened as the Vietnam war became a major issue.

On July 10, 1967, and again on December 6 of the same year, the White House asked the FBI for information on me and was wonderfully candid as to kind and purpose. The first asked for a name check on Galbraith (and three other individuals) "who allegedly are endeavoring to raise money for the re-election, during the coming election year, of a number of 'Dove' U.S. Senators." I had been so engaged, with much success. People who couldn't do anything else about Vietnam positively liked to give money. This highly improper request was filled, and as to the impropriety the FBI was not itself in doubt. Hoover carefully advised the White House that "A copy of this communication has not been sent to the Attorney General."

The later request in December from the White House was more specific as to what was wanted, for, in responding, the FBI said: "The following is being furnished in reply to your

request for the results of any investigation conducted concerning the above individual [this being Galbraith] *wherein information of a subversive nature was developed.*" My italics.

Once again nothing happened; as always in the government
of the United States, evil intention is only marginally related
to evil action, a fact of which all who are in any way susceptible to paranoia should be aware. The memoranda submitted
were, apparently, the previous crap. But no one at the White
House had any business asking such questions for such a purpose; whoever did is morally if not legally on a par with the
Nixon men who went to the minimum security slammers. Nor
had Hoover any business responding.

However, the Nixon men also came to offend in the same
way. On October 6, 1969, around eight months after Mr. Nixon
came to office, his counsel asked for information about me,
none of which could have been for the purpose of offering employment. He was sent material that had gone over under the
previous administration.

This White House intervention leads me to my concluding
thought. Once many years ago my wife worked with the FBI
as a language expert through a long trial of alleged Nazis in
Newark. She was struck with the extreme decency of the individual agents and especially with their effort to establish the
bias of anyone who was providing information adverse to a
suspect. "We want to know their angle — what axe they have
to grind." The decency is generally manifest in my file — in
the faithful reporting of favorable comment and the warnings
that I have noted against those with an angle. What was wrong
with the FBI was the archaic, angry and, in the end, senile
old despot who headed it and the people who were too frightened to retire him. Also the people, as at the White House,
who used it for their own political ends. Also all who acquiesced
in the scrutiny of subjective beliefs and attitudes — including
those of us who responded tolerantly, as though they were

needed, to questions about the loyalty of men such as Adlai Stevenson. Also, and perhaps most important, those who saw Hoover, his anti-Communism and the FBI as instruments against liberals, and the officeholders, including the liberals, who went along out of fear. It is impossible not to have fun at the expense of the FBI. But there is need to distinguish between the members of the FBI rank and file and the people who so egregiously misused them.

14

The North Dakota Plan[1]

IN TIMES PAST, I have found a certain amusement in maintaining a watching brief on international affairs and then enlarging on its inherently comic tendencies. The Dulles brothers, as an example, were a fine opportunity to this end. With very little effort one could picture John Foster, with his capacity for losing friends and making enemies, and Allen, with his talent for truly spectacular misjudgment, as agents of the Communist conspiracy which each so feared and featured. Any issue of *Foreign Affairs* provided inspiration for a dozen imagined articles, all equally unreadable and each with a slightly more ludicrous title than the last. One that came almost automatically to mind, ghostwritten for the Panamanian foreign minister, was "Panama Looks North and South." Another, an original work by one of my very reputable Harvard colleagues, would be called "Germany Divided." A third by the Finnish foreign minister would be "Finland Looks East and West."

Of late, however, I've been stopped by the Buchwald Syndrome, something I've mentioned on other occasions. This is the problem that Art Buchwald faced during the days when

---

1 In 1978, a Paris-based organization called APHIA (Association for the Promotion of Humor in International Affairs) made its annual award to a presumptively innovative figure in the field. In accordance with its rules, the recipient was required to make a significantly imaginative contribution to the art of foreign policy. This, as the recipient, I tried to do; thus the North Dakota Plan.

Ron Ziegler was promoting Richard Nixon as a model of rectitude and public grace. Nothing Buchwald could invent, he said, was as funny as the original; there was no room for improvement. And so it is now with international affairs.

Thus I do not believe that anyone can improve for amusement on the thought that Ethiopia is now a workers' paradise. Or that Somalia, which was last year's workers' paradise, is now a bastion of liberty and free enterprise and that soldiers fighting well inside what used to be Ethiopia were recently the victims of Ethiopian and also Soviet and Cuban imperialism.

Nor could any humorist surpass the recent efforts of my one-time Canadian compatriots to explain to an Eskimo named, I believe, John Smokehouse, that he shouldn't pick up radioactive fragments of a space satellite. John, it was explained by the distinguished engineers and scientists involved, had never heard of radiation or satellites. Nor had he ever heard of space.

The last great generation of Frenchmen and Englishmen defended their empires as the cutting edge of Western civilization. Now the adequately motivated sons and daughters of the empire-builders are defending their homelands from the people who were so civilized. Only one generation separates the two sets of heroes. God, I believe, so arranged things. He wanted some relief from the terrible solemnity of His new companions, Larry Flynt and Chuck Colson.

Only where American foreign policy is concerned can one be more lighthearted than the reality. That is because Barbara Walters and Walter Cronkite, who are taking it over, are terribly sober and responsible people, as all can see on television. So, of course, is Cyrus Vance as he looks on.

Since foreign policy offers no opportunity for noninherent humor, one is forced to be serious and constructive. In consequence, I've worked out a grave plan that will relieve the tensions of present-day international relations. No one will be in doubt as to what any such plan should do:

Great power rivalry must be eliminated; it is dangerous.
Ideological conflict must be turned into peaceful indifference.
There must be no cause for quarrels over international boundaries.
Armies and navies must be curtailed.
Political ambition must be reduced.
To the greatest extent possible, all countries must have a good ethnic mix. As President Carter once said, or greatly wished he had, there is no case for ethnic purity.

The plan I have developed accomplishes all of these things. It invites, as world government does not, the support of those who affirm that small is beautiful. The plan is associated with one of the deathless names in the field of innovative international action, a name especially evocative here in Paris, that of Bismarck — Bismarck, the capital of North Dakota, To coin an old phrase (as Samuel Goldwyn once said), I believe the hour has struck. The time has come for the North Dakota Plan.

In the North Dakota Plan the map is the message. Every needed reform in international relations can be achieved if national boundaries are simply redrawn so that all countries, without exception, are the shape and size of North Dakota.

All boundaries would then follow the lines of latitude and longitude. These are well known or can be discovered without difficulty; accordingly, there could no longer be any boundary disputes.

One exception to the strict rectangular form would be permitted. That is where, as in the case of the eastern boundary of North Dakota, the new national territory impinges on water. Then it would accept the natural boundary and stop rigidly at the high-water mark. This is vital, for it keeps the Plan from being a device by which countries can own any ocean.

Also, the eastern boundary of North Dakota is the Red River. This makes the North Dakota Plan attractive to the Soviets and also, and especially, to the Chinese.

Under the North Dakota Plan great power rivalry disappears. This, as competent logicians will agree, is the plausible consequence of there no longer being any great powers.

The arms problem is partly solved. Few countries will have a seacoast; none will have an ocean. That eliminates navies. In any case, one does not readily think of North Dakota as a naval power.

Other armaments involve more serious difficulties. But they are taken care of by what the cognoscenti call the Eugene V. Rostow Doctrine. Working with the Pentagon and the Rand Corporation and therefore getting wholly reliable advice, Rostow's Committee on the Present Danger has calculated that seven Minuteman missiles and ten Cruise missiles in each of the new states will keep every one of them completely safe from nuclear attack.

In the interests of an equal start, it will be necessary to dismantle the antiballistic missiles now installed in the actual state of North Dakota. But they were to be phased out anyway as an economy measure. Indeed, a few weeks ago legislators from North Dakota proposed, as a compromise, that the sites be manned only during working hours. This reflected the belief that the Soviet Union, the workers' fatherland, is no less firmly committed than the United States to the eight-hour day and the forty-hour week.

In many if not most of the new countries ideological differences will be irrelevant. Not many will worry over whether the several Dakotas that occupy northern Siberia, the central Sahara, most of Australia, Greenland or the Gobi Desert are capitalist or Communist, although I have to admit that a certain number of Americans may. Dean Rusk and maybe Henry Kissinger will also question the reference to the Red River.

The North Dakota Plan will reduce political ambition and associated tension. This it will accomplish in the only possible way, which is by satisfying such ambition. Any person who wishes to become a president, a prime minister or, reflecting a more affluent modern goal, a shah, an emir or a sheik, can move to one of the completely unpopulated Dakotas of the world and set himself up there as a chief of state. It is well known that many of the more enterprising breed of modern politician

can overcome the apathy they arouse in no other way. The plan
will be especially attractive to Senator Howard Baker.

The man whose ambition has been so satisfied can then go
on state visits to the heads of the populated nations, and here,
drawing on my own observations in India where there was a
state visit nearly every week, I wish to make a truly serious
point, if a slight digression. It concerns the reason state visits
are made. They are not to discuss business. That can almost
never be risked, for serious conversation between great men
can easily lead to uninformed agreement. State visits are made
because the visitor is greeted with a combination of pageantry,
food, alcohol and affection that he knows he will never receive
or deserve at home.

The boundaries established by the North Dakota Plan will,
unite French and Germans, Arabs and Jews, Indians and Pakistanis, and keep the Scotch from trading the high road to
England, which Dr. Johnson rightly identified as one of the
noblest prospects ever seen by one of my race, for a mess of
North Sea oil. In all cases international tension will be turned
into harmless local hatred. But internal tensions will also be
reduced. In the separate successor nations of the former United
States there will be fewer conservatives to hate liberals, fewer
whites to fear blacks and fewer Georgians to arouse sympathy
and sustain condescension.

The key to reduced tensions, national and international, is
the borders — borders that cut straight through every animos-
ity, however cherished. These borders give us the slogan, the
letters that, inscribed on our banners, mark the end to international relations and thus to all resulting sorrow. The
letters are reminiscent, lovable and different — KIA, "Keep It
Arbitrary."

I come to one final point. The question has been asked in
the United States in these last weeks if the North Dakota Plan
will not impair national sovereignty. On this we have the assur-

ance of Ronald Reagan, former and future presidential candidate and one of my colleagues as a founding pillar of Americans for Democratic Action. Sovereignty, Governor Reagan has pointed out, is a good thing. The Panama Canal treaties which he opposed were a bad thing, for they diminished the most fragile form of sovereignty — sovereignty we never had. But the North Dakota Plan, in contrast, enormously enhances the number of sovereign states. There will, by my calculations, be twenty-seven in Western Europe, one hundred and twenty in North America, one hundred and twenty-three in the USSR and eighty-five in Antarctica alone. Thus will the sum total of sovereignty in the world be increased. No one can be against that.

15

Berlin

MY FIRST VISIT to Berlin was in the summer of 1938. Although I was a liberal, a New Dealer, a confirmed anti-Nazi and otherwise possessed of all the reputable views of the time, there seemed nothing inappropriate about spending a relaxed summer in Hitler's Germany. Partly this was because there was much curiosity about German economic policy at the time, and this seemed to justify my presence. By one school of economists, Hjalmar Horace Greeley Schacht, who was assumed to be Hitler's economic *éminence grise,* was thought to have worked miracles with the German economy. By another school, he was thought to have resisted unsuccessfully the measures that would soon bring its total collapse. Both schools, it later developed, were wrong. He had done almost nothing. Hitler used Schacht to provide a veneer of respectability for economic policies — deficit spending for employment, control of incomes and prices — that were then thought insane and which other countries eventually adopted. When the war came, he was retired. Some associates of mine in military intelligence matters interviewed him in 1945. They discovered that he was very angry but deeply uninformed. This became evident at Nuremberg, and, his reputation as Hitler's banker notwithstanding, he was acquitted.

More important than the need to study the German economy was the feeling in 1938 that to be an American was to be detached from responsibility. One could study wickedness and oppression without being in any way related to it. Earlier that summer my wife and I had been in Vienna; this was in the days immediately following the *Anschluss.* Then we went on to Prague. Outwardly both cities were calm. If there was an underlying current of fear, it was something to be noted carefully and, of course, with sympathy, and reported on when one got home. Late one night we crossed by automobile from Czechoslovakia into Germany north of Karlovy Vary or, as was then preferred, Carlsbad. On the Czech side parties of soldiers were moving along the road, and we were stopped at checkpoints for inspection. We had debated earlier that day whether it might not be a good idea to buy an American flag to fly on the front of our Ford. It would be, we thought, a badge of innocence.

Ever since that summer, Berlin has seemed to me one of the most interesting cities in the world. I have a simple test: it is whether, no matter how many times I've been there, I still feel a glow of excitement on the moment of arrival. That glow has always been present on going into San Francisco, strangely on landing at Dum Dum Airport in Calcutta and on arriving in Paris. In May of 1974 — my most recent visit — a friend with an unremitting interest in good works asked me to come with him to Berlin for a few days; with the support of equally well-meaning Germans and Americans he is organizing a discussion center somewhat along the lines of the Aspen Institute in Colorado in a villa on the Schwanenwerder peninsula in the Havel. Here, he hopes, scholars, politicians, officials and businessmen or plant managers from Eastern and Western Europe, the United States and the rest of the world will meet to consider matters of common interest. It was thirty-six years since my first visit to Berlin, and I had been back often in the interim. But on going into Tempelhof Airport there was, once again, the glow.

*

During the summer of 1938, we lived for a while on Potsdamerstrasse and then moved to a pension on the Kürfürstendamm. We were only recently married, and my wife, who had studied in Germany, had many friends there. All were discreetly anti-Hitler, and it was something of a shock to find that the aged husband of our landlady was a passionate Nazi. He was, I believe, the only avowed Nazi we met that summer; even the guide later provided by the German agricultural ministry to take us on a visit to the estates of the Junkers in East Prussia — I was then interested in agriculture, and the Germans had rather overestimated my importance in the field — assured us at the end of the tour that his party membership was purely a matter of necessity. Once a classmate of my wife's, who was doing his military service with a cavalry outfit north of Berlin, came down to join us and, contrary to regulations, shed his uniform for the visit. Whenever a party of soldiers came in view, he turned and studied the nearest shop window, once giving detailed attention to a display of bathroom fixtures. He had chosen the cavalry because he liked to ride and thought it would be useless if Hitler went to war. Later he served on the Eastern Front, was taken prisoner in the last hours of the war and survived five years in Russia, getting over one difficult spell by volunteering for work on a dairy farm where he had unlimited access to milk. On his return he joined the German diplomatic service. We last saw him at the christening of one of his children by Richard Cardinal Cushing. He was then serving as Consul General in Boston and, like most others in the vicinity, had become very fond of the Cardinal.

Life in Berlin in 1938 was not very expensive, and we had enough money to make the rounds of museums, galleries, palaces and restaurants and, in the evenings, the music halls and cabarets. Some of this was because such activity seemed compulsory in Berlin. To go home in the evening was somehow to concede defeat; Dorothy Thompson and Sinclair Lewis in their day would not have done so. One of the principal tourist centers at the time was the Haus Vaterland on Potsdamer Platz, a kind of Disneyland of regional restaurants, cafés and cabarets. It still stands today, a dismal, blackened hulk, one of the few buildings in Berlin that has been neither rebuilt nor removed. I was being sustained in Europe for educational purposes by the Social Science Research Council and, ultimately, the Rockefeller Foundation and was recurrently assailed by the feeling that I should justify their outlay. So I went to visit economists, some working (sometimes apologetically) for the government, some at the once notable Institute for Business Cycle Research (*Institut für Konjunkturforschung*), a few who had been rendered idle by the Nazis. One of the latter was Professor Max Sering, in his day a notable authority on agricultural economics. He had disapproved of National Socialist economic policy from the outset, mostly on conservative grounds, and soon after the advent of Hitler had published a pamphlet adumbrating his objections. It was promptly suppressed. I visited him one day in a large house on a tree-lined street in Dahlem. He reiterated his objections to Hitler in a voice that could have been heard through the open study windows for half a block. Since no one was there to listen, I judged that the Nazis didn't much care. Years later in Cambridge I had a visit from another scholar whose acquaintance I made that summer. Not long after we were in Berlin, he had been sent to Dachau by the Nazis as politically unreliable. Then during the war he was released and rehabilitated and made a regional commissar for food and agriculture. He had tried hard to prove his patriotism and after the fall of the Reich he was put back in Dachau as a war criminal. When he came to see me, he had just been rehabilitated for the second time. He was, like Schacht, a bitter man.

National Socialism was not obtrusive that summer. Uniforms were few; we never saw Hitler, Goering, Goebbels or any of the other high Nazis. Possibly we lacked curiosity. Earlier, in Munich, my wife had lived in a student hostel with Unity Mitford, Hitler's admired and admiring English friend. Miss Mitford, always after much preparation, departed at intervals for appointments with Hitler and returned to tell of them. As a result, Hitler's name was rather a household word around the *Studentenheim*. He was taken for granted by the students and by us.

Our only noteworthy encounter with the Nazis occurred one day when we had to go to the neighborhood of the Wilhelm-strasse to get the papers required for taking an automobile across the Polish Corridor to Danzig and East Prussia. The Nazis were, that day, welcoming a more-than-routine function-ary of the Italian Fascist Party — its Secretary-General or some such, as I recall. The Brown Shirts (the SA) had been assigned to line the streets from the Kaiserhof Hotel to Templehof, a considerable show. Evidently they had been ordered out several hours too early, for, by the time we arrived in the neighbor-hood, they were visibly bored, and many were fairly drunk on beer passed out from the bars. Traffic was much disrupted, and somehow we took a wrong turn and found ourselves going the wrong way down the Wilhelmstrasse between the two disor-derly lines of Storm Troopers. The top of the car was down. Seeing something to break the tedium, an American Ford at that, the officers called their men to attention, and they quickly deployed across the cross streets to keep us from turning off. Hands, some still holding beer mugs, came up in the forearm salute. The shouts of "Heil Hitler" were, if not deafening, at least uproarious. We faced the prospect of going all the way to the airport before we were released. However, after a few blocks, we came upon a streetcar which was cautiously making its way across the street. We turned in behind it and followed it off. A picture of the occasion featuring the salute, had it sur-faced three or four years later in Washington, would have at-tracted attention. I was by then running wartime price control and was widely charged with employing authoritarian tech-niques.

I was next in Berlin in the summer of 1945. This was as one of the directors of a considerable organization, the United States Strategic Bombing Survey, which was assessing the effects of the air attacks on the German economy. The members of our group were clad in indifferently fitting uniforms without insignia and were regarded with suspicion by legitimate officers whose brisk style we tried, unsuccessfully, to imitate. The American forces had then just moved in, and although the city had fallen several weeks earlier, streets were still blocked by tanks and self-propelled guns, and the rubble still smelled of decaying bodies.

By this time we were no strangers to bombed-out buildings and devastated cities. But Berlin seemed the ultimate waste-land. The Tiergarten was the worst. It was filled with the detritus of battle; the distant skyline was made by the jagged, formless edges of the ruins. It was evening when I first crossed the park, and the setting sun had an orange brickish color from, so it was said, the dust of bricks and stones still being carried in the air. I remember thinking, rather imprecisely, that on the day the world ended it would look like this. The more common reference was to the landscape of the moon, but that also was imprecise. We have now seen the moon landscape, and, though austere, it is less alarming.

Russian troops were still passing through the city — dirty wagons, small shaggy horses, ragged harness, dusty men. In appearance they must have been closer to the formations of Genghis Khan than to the American motorized battalions that were also moving in. In front of the new Reich Chancellery a Russian guard was doing a stirring business in unissued medals that had been found inside. For my wife and several friends, I bought copies of the special Honor Cross that Hitler had issued to exceptionally fertile mothers and an Iron Cross for Harry Luce, from whose employ I was then on leave.

The vast Chancellery, the work of Albert Speer, was a partial but by no means complete ruin. Many of the great cere-monial rooms were nearly intact. The furniture was still in place but stripped of its leather by Russian soldiers much in need of it, I believe, for footwear. A few weeks earlier, under examination in Flensburg, Speer had told us at length of the climactic hours in the bunker below the adjacent garden — a story that has been retold a hundred times since and, as compared with the first telling, with astonishingly little variation or improvement. A Russian sentry, when we went to see it, was prohibiting all entry to the bunker. This whole side of the Wilhelmstrasse — which also included the Presidential Residence — is now a waste of irregular grass stretching away to the Wall.

Then, as ever since, the meeting place of East and West was a few yards away at the Brandenburg Gate. Here in the evenings American and Russian soldiers met, almost exclusively to do business. Watches were, of course, the main item of commerce. One night I went there with Paul Baran, later to become, with Paul Sweezy, one of the two most respected Marxian economists in the United States — and as a professor at Stanford almost the only Marxist to hold a senior academic post. Baran was then my immediate assistant and possibly the most remarkable technical sergeant in the United States Army. His father, before the revolution, had been in exile in Switzerland. While there, his interest had shifted from politics to medicine, and he had emerged, after World War I, as one of Europe's leading specialists in lung pathology. After teaching for a period in Berlin, he returned in the mid-twenties to the Soviet Union. There, some time after Stalin came to power, he received word from an old friend that if his son was not over the border within a day or two, he would face a long period of corrective detention, presumably in Siberia. Though a persuaded Marxist, Paul Baran had always been a man of inconvenient independence who expressed his views with a terrible combination of clarity, humor and derision. Using a Polish passport, he got away to Finland and made his way on to Berlin, where he joined the university and made his living partly writing advertising copy, partly writing theses for less qualified doctoral aspirants. One piece of his advertising copy became famous. It was for a condom, the name of which I vaguely and perhaps incorrectly remember as Nims. The ad showed a tombstone; on it were

engraved the words: HERE LIES NO ONE. HIS FATHER USED NIMS.
Later in 1945, Paul and I went to lunch one day outside Tokyo
with a Japanese businessman. While representing one of the
big Japanese combines in Berlin before the war, he had gone
to the university, and Paul had written his Ph.D. thesis for him,
a distinguished piece of work on Japan's future in the world
economy. It had later been published in Japan, and Baran asserted that it had won the nonauthor an honorary professorship
in a major Japanese university.

Although he would dearly have loved to become an officer,
Baran never made it. This was partly owing to his appearance;
his stomach bulged over his web belt, a tendency that was only
slightly disguised by his shirt, which was often outside his
trousers. Once at our headquarters in Bad Nauheim he showed
up on parade in carpet slippers. He couldn't remember to salute
except when it took officers by surprise. They often assumed
from Baran's face that he was laughing at them, an impression
that was accurate. Some weeks after the surrender he uncovered, living in Wiesbaden, Franz Halder, former Chief of the
German Army General Staff, who was fired by Hitler in 1942.
Halder had expected to be flown to see Eisenhower on the day
the Americans arrived. Instead he had been left in solitary
neglect. For reasons that had little to do with our task but much
to do with Baran's curiosity concerning matters which had
earlier been his responsibility at OSS, he interviewed Halder at
great length. When he was finished, the general asked if the
American Army had many intelligence officers of like quality.
"If it has," I remember the transcript reading, "it explains
much about this war. I may tell you that your knowledge of
the problems facing the Wehrmacht on the Eastern Front is
markedly greater than was that of the Führer."

At the Brandenburg Gate the night of our visit Paul questioned a Russian officer on the allegations, already common
from the German population, that the Russian soldiers were
being very rough with women and given to rape. "We have
walked all the way from Stalingrad," the officer replied, ges-

turing toward a group of German girls who were loitering ostentatiously nearby (and who, it should be added in compassion, were probably hungry), "and we are not inclined to take unnecessary exercise." A day or so later Paul told me that, again for reasons of his own, he had been to interview the head of the largest construction firm in Berlin. He had found him in a large office on top of one of the few undamaged office buildings in the city. The windows looked out on limitless acres of devastation. The builder, a man of advanced years, gazed contentedly on this wasteland and told Baran that he thought the building industry faced a *Hochkonjunktur*.

With George Ball, later Under Secretary of State and Ambassador to the United Nations and then my colleague in the investigation of the effects of the air war, I attended, as an uninvited volunteer, the Potsdam Conference. Truman, Stalin, Churchill and later Clement Attlee. I've previously told the story[1] and will spare myself the pleasure of repetition. Despite our presence, Potsdam seemed an inordinately amateurish effort. Certainly it lacked the grandeur one had always associated with Versailles. Also, while affirming the division of Berlin into sectors and Germany into zones, it left largely undefined the relation between the sectors and the zones, the occupying powers and the Germans. The authority of the Allied Control Council was vague, and the relation of Berlin to the rest of Germany was susceptible to differing interpretations. The question of reparations, including amounts and whether they were to be from existing capital equipment or renewed production, though discussed at length, remained obscure.

Here were the sources of much future conflict. Instead the Potsdam Conference was the prelude to a third of a century of peace (as this goes to press), with the prospect of more. There also ensued the greatest prosperity that Germany and Europe

---

[1] In *The Age of Uncertainty* (Boston: Houghton Mifflin, 1977), p. 229.

ever experienced. Maybe the sheer fragility of the agreement caused all concerned to treat it with more caution than would otherwise have been the case.

Berlin was much on my mind the rest of the summer. When it had fallen, nearly all of the high Nazis escaped to the West, in accordance with the sound estimate that the Americans and the British would run more agreeable jails than the Soviets. One exception was a man we much wanted to see — the chief statistician of the Speer ministry, whose name was Rolf Wagenfuehr. In the closing days of the siege of Berlin he had expressed interest in what the Soviets would be like; some of his colleagues whom we had earlier arrested said that maybe he had been a roast-beef Nazi — brown outside, red inside. Wagenfuehr was needed for interpreting and advising on the reliability of the mountain of statistical information which, by this time, was in our hands. Speer, among others, had stressed his importance. Presently we heard that he was living in West Berlin, and I sent Paul Baran there to bring him to Bad Nauheim.

In those days, like other intelligence agencies, we had the right of summary arrest. However, except in the case of military men and the most senior and criminal of the Nazis, the power seemed unnatural, as indeed it was, and I had instructed that we use it with restraint. Lesser civilians were to be given a day or two of notice. Given such warning, Wagenfuehr removed himself and his wife to East Berlin, where he had already found employment putting the statistical services of the Reich back together for the Soviets. Baran recruited a soldier or two, went to East Berlin, found him in bed and brought him out of the city. The Soviet occupation authorities, not surprisingly, were outraged, and not long after Wagenfuehr arrived in our small detention center, word came, I'm not sure how, that a severe protest was making its way from Marshal Zhukov to Eisenhower. In those days Ike was thought to have a bad temper. Superiors were held responsible for the actions of their subordinates, and I was the superior. Baran was also having second thoughts about his own exploit. His association with the action had become known; Stalin was then alive; and Baran's father and mother were still living in Moscow.

Another onetime Berliner came to our rescue. This was Jurgen Kuczynski, a devout Communist who was working for me on the problem of manpower supply in the wartime Reich. Kuczynski had been petitioning at weekly intervals to go to Berlin where, among other things, he wanted to see what had happened to his library. He now assured me that such was his reputation with the Soviets that he could take Wagenfuehr back, reinstall him in the *Statistisches Amt* and otherwise calm Soviet tempers if only I would authorize his trip. He was as good as his word. A Boston lawyer, James Barr Ames, then a colonel with the Survey, went along at my request to supervise what amounted to the unkidnapping of Wagenfuehr. Jim accompanied Kuczynski and Wagenfuehr to the Soviet sector where Kuczynski was very warmly received by his comrades. They did not press their complaint.

During the week or two he was in custody, Wagenfuehr worked diligently to advise us on the scope and reliability of the statistics with which he had been concerned. Later he moved west to assume a research position with the German trade unions and once asked me to come back to speak at a big trade union conference. I was unable to go. In the latter part of 1945, Kuczynski returned to Germany and to East Berlin to occupy various senior political and (later) academic positions in the GDR. A few years ago I had a letter from him asking me to ask the State Department to reverse a decision that had denied him a visa to lecture in the United States. He didn't mention having saved me from the Eisenhower wrath. I tried but failed. The grounds for refusing the visa — for not waiving the bar against Communists — were, as usual, unworthy.

During 1946, I was again in Berlin. Earlier that year William L. Clayton, then Assistant Secretary of State, asked me to take charge, in a manner of speaking, of economic affairs in the occupied countries — Germany, Japan, Austria and Korea. We were both impressed by the knowledge of these countries I had accumulated while investigating the effects of the bombing. As I've told elsewhere in these essays, it was a highly unsatisfactory job. Neither General Clay in Germany nor General MacArthur in Tokyo considered himself in my line of command. Occasionally, in those months, we amused ourselves in the Department by imagining that MacArthur might declare total independence from the United States — UDI as it came to be known with Ian Smith and Rhodesia. What would we do? There was similar uncertainty at all levels at the time as to what our policy in Germany was or should be. Some thought we should foster recovery and encourage rehabilitation of the German industrial plant. Otherwise the Germans would be a heavy burden on our backs. I leaned in this direction. And an economist could not look at a demoralized and prostrate economy without contemplating the steps that might revive it. But the Morgenthau Plan for reducing Germany to a pastoral and petty bourgeois state still had vigorous adherents. They warned with no little vehemence of the dangers of a resurgent Reich. To restore Germany was also to risk arousing the Russians. One who felt this danger keenly, and I thought properly, was my close associate, Walt W. Rostow.

By the summer of 1946, Americans, officers and civilians, had settled in nicely in Berlin — many thought too nicely. They occupied great shaded mansions in Dahlem, Zehlendorf or out in Wannsee. House servants, gardeners as well as drivers had become an accepted part of the American way of life. Cooks were compared; the eccentricities of the German servant class were the subject of much animated conversation. The second in command in the State Department mission under Robert Murphy, an old friend from my agricultural days, concerned himself exclusively with his housekeeping. But in other houses more of the conversation, which was long and intense, was about the occupation, that is to say what to do about the Germans and the Russians. The Nuremberg trials were then in progress, and denazification was a question of continuing, although receding, interest. More attention was being given to affirmative programs, as they were called, notably re-education. Hitler, it was being observed, was not an accident; he was the natural product of an authoritarian family and social tradition and an even more authoritarian educational system. Intelligent remedial action required that these be democratized, the previous damage undone. How this was to be accomplished was not clear. It was not yet realized that although the Germans were the captives of their educational tradition, Americans were the captives of their social science.

A more practical discussion was on coal and food, two matters that were closely related. Coal was desperately scarce and remained so, partly because the men who mined it didn't have enough to eat. The British, who had fought the war on the principle of equal rations for all, canteen feeding apart, were reluctant to give the miners extra food for their heavy work. Coal output lagged, and, in consequence, so did everything else. The problem was partly solved by giving the miners a substantial on-shift serving of thick soup or stew in addition to their ration. Since they couldn't bring containers into the pits, they couldn't take this semiliquid food home to their wives and children. To this day I can't think of this solution, which I favored, without pain.

We were, that summer, scraping the very bottom of the bins of food. The shortage was far more severe than at any time during the war. On occasion we had to ship corn to Germany to stretch out the supply of bread grain. A few months later the German Director of Economics for the British and American Zones, Johannes Semler, made a speech in Erlangen in which he voiced a number of complaints about occupation policy. In passing, he referred to the *Hühnerfutter* that we were sending to Germany. *Hühnerfutter* meant feed grain, but in military government translation it came out more literally as chicken feed. "What the Americans are sending us is chicken feed." General Clay was furious. He fired Semler and ordered a search for a more tractable, amiable and cooperative man with no Nazi taint to take his place. One was found and thus began the career of Ludwig Erhard.

Most of all, the discussion during the summer of 1946 was of the Russians. Relations with the Soviet occupation authorities were still ostentatiously amiable, and a conscious effort was made to draw them into any important social activities. I remember a large dinner party one night in a huge house on the Schwanenwerder that had belonged (I believe) to Joseph Goebbels. My partner was the handsome and, considering the time, exceptionally well-dressed wife of a senior Soviet official. She was stunned to discover that I had a passing familiarity with the writings of Marx and Lenin; she had not supposed they were much read in the American occupation establishment, and she was right. In resourceful and idiomatic English she proceeded to give me her view of the application of Marxist-Leninist principles to Soviet occupation policy. I thought it exceedingly interesting, revealing and rather logical, given the premises, and it told something of Soviet policy in Germany. Included was expression of the most profound abhorrence of anything that might risk more war. However, when I repeated it to State Department colleagues the next morning, I found it dismissed as dinner-table talk. It was a lesson I was to rediscover in later years. Professional diplomats set great store by entertainment and justify it for the important information so obtained. But then, often no doubt rightly, they discount, more or less totally, the value of all such information as gossip.

It was fourteen years before I was back in Berlin. In 1948 and 1949, the Allied Control Council broke down, and the pretense of four-power administration came to an end. The Soviets then blocked the roads, and the airlift followed. This episode, to me at least, remains something of a puzzle; I've always felt that there was substance to General Clay's contention that had a truck convoy pressed its way to the barriers, it would have been allowed through. The Soviets would not have wanted to fight. As on other occasions, having airplanes, we rejoiced in showing what they could do. It is basic to all American military doctrine that because we have air power, air power is decisive. But I do not know — and one is well advised to avoid the commonest of all errors where foreign policy is concerned, which is to compensate for inherent uncertainty with excessive certainty of statement.

Following the lifting of the Berlin blockade in 1949, I was in Germany again as a member of a joint German-American commission which was to settle the question of the German refugees from the East — those from Eastern Germany, Poland, the Sudetenland and from the ethnic German communities, many of long standing, that had been scattered elsewhere over Eastern Europe. But Berlin had no major refugee problem, and we didn't go there. Our commission had barely finished its work before another migrant wave — refugees from the poor farm villages of Italy, Spain, Turkey and, most notably, Communist Yugoslavia — was set deliberately in motion by the Federal Republic. These were the *Gastarbeiter,* the foreign workers, about which I will say more later.

In economics, timing is often everything. In the fourteen years between 1946 and 1960, there occurred the West German economic miracle. This, by June of 1960, was evident in West Berlin, as throughout the Federal Republic. Most, although not quite all, of the broken buildings had been repaired. The streets were full of cars, the shops with merchandise, and the sidewalks, day and night, were crowded with pedestrians. Kempinski's, once the most famous restaurant in Berlin and one which I particularly remembered from the days when one's consumption of Rhine wine and Moselle was restricted only by money, was now a hotel on the Kürfürstendamm. Not far distant was a new Hilton hotel which Arthur Schlesinger, who was with me on this visit, heard someone refer to as the Adolf Hilton.

My 1960 trip was to attend a week-long conference under the auspices of the Congress for Cultural Freedom, which the *New York Times,* in its dispatches on the sessions, described as "an independent [sic] worldwide organization established . . . to defend intellectual liberties." About 200 attended from some fifty countries, including George Kennan, Julian Huxley, Ignazio Silone, Stephen Spender and Constantine Fitz Gibbon. The meetings were held in the sparkling and spacious new American-built Kongresshalle between the Tiergarten and the Spree, which one entered through banks of flowers, but, in contrast with the surroundings, the world outlook was deemed, almost universally, to be dark. The tone was set by Robert Oppenheimer in the opening address; he thought war probable and, in a much quoted phrase, warned that "none of us can count on having enough living to bury our dead." The only hope he saw was in the resulting "grim and ironic community of interest, not only among friends but among friends and enemies." Others were even less optimistic. Nothing, to be sure, has yet happened to prove them wrong.

However, I was almost as troubled by the length and vehemence of the speeches as by their tone of despair. So were others. One morning I deserted and, in a nostalgic mood, visited the animals in the zoo. Returning to the hotel at noon, I encountered Huxley and asked him how things had gone. "Ah, yes," he said, as only an Englishman can, "Carlos was the speaker," mentioning a prominent South German professor and politician. "He spoke for an hour and then, poor chap, he realized he hadn't said anything. So he went on for another hour in what I would say was an unsuccessful effort to retrieve."

Another day, also outside the hotel, I encountered Charles Wyzanski, the noted Federal District Court Judge and a Cambridge neighbor. He said: "Do you know who is paying for all this?" I said I supposed some foundation, and he said, "You should know it's the CIA." I got hold of the controller of the Congress, whom I had met skiing, and questioned him about where the money came from. He somewhat confirmed my suspicions because he didn't know. A controller, I thought, would surely know the source of honest money.

While my suspicions were aroused, my indignation remained at a very moderate level. I thought I wouldn't attend any more conferences without knowing who was paying. But I had decided not to attend any more conferences anyway. Later when it developed that the Congress for Cultural Freedom had, indeed, been financed by the CIA, I thought it best to moderate my outrage and help to put the Congress under the aegis of the Ford Foundation. There was a happier consequence. A year later in India I encountered more CIA cultural and political activities, all foolish. Supported by the President and Robert Kennedy and taking advantage of the weakened condition of the Agency after the Bay of Pigs, I abolished them all. I was less impressed by the duplicity than by the ease with which, as in Berlin, one could find out about them.

In 1960, in contrast with West Berlin, East Berlin was a desert. Cars were few, clothes were shabby, as were the shops. There were still ruins, and what had been rebuilt was in some respects worse, the pretentious buildings along the then Stalin Allee being the leading example. Unter den Linden, once so fine, was a very barren passage.

Since World War II, numerous countries have achieved a very high production of goods in face of seemingly unfavoring circumstances. Hong Kong and Singapore, city states with no natural resources of any kind, have had a major success. Austria, written off as a hopeless case between the wars, has been far more prosperous than under Franz Josef. Israel, Formosa, Korea and Spain have similarly made much out of unpromising prospects. Yet economic success continues to occasion surprise. Its occurrence is taken without question to suggest social, cultural and even moral superiority. That is how it was interpreted in Berlin in 1960, and not alone by the West Berliners. The people of East Berlin and East Germany enthusiastically agreed and were removing themselves to the higher culture in droves. In August of 1960, an estimated 16,000 moved into West Berlin, which they could do at the time by walking over or catching the subway. The year following came yet another Berlin crisis and the Wall. I was in New Delhi by this time, and at the peak of the crisis Prime Minister Nehru expressed doubt one day about the right of the Western powers to be in Berlin. I guessed that the result of his statement would be a mighty explosion in Washington. I took the evidence on Berlin over to Nehru who, in the kind of gesture that must have worried his officials no end, told me to go out and issue an appropriate correction to the press. This, with much pleasure, I did. The episode caused him to recall a conversation he had had with Khrushchev about East Germany and Berlin: "I told him that I didn't think much of the Ulbricht government," Nehru had said. "We don't either," said Khrushchev, who went on to tell of another problem. "One morning in that country they find that the plant manager has left for West Berlin. That wouldn't be so bad if his deputy hadn't left the day before, along with the chief engineer. Then," Khrushchev concluded, "they put a new man in and a week later he leaves too."

I didn't see the Wall myself until the late sixties when I was back in Berlin for a day to give a lecture for money to an international congress of advertising men. The vice president for social responsibility of a big New York agency presided at my session. He introduced me, explaining proudly to the assembled craftsmen from many lands that it was typically American that all kinds of views, even mine, were being heard. Afterward I took a taxi to Potsdamer Platz and climbed a platform that allowed one to look over the Wall to East Berlin. An East German guard examined me without interest. Like others, I was principally impressed by how badly the Wall was built. The concrete blocks were ugly to begin with; that they had been piled one on the other in great haste was evident.

The Wall is, indeed, an insulting thing. But it is also, like the Potsdam Agreement, a monument to the errors of experts in foreign policy. All thought it the prelude to a deeper, sharper, more dangerous conflict in and over Berlin than ever before. There has been no further crisis since.

My 1974 journey was fourteen years after the Congress of Cultural Freedom/CIA convocation. In 1960, after leaving Berlin, I went to Hamburg to give a lecture at the request of a friend, Professor Karl Schiller, then of the University of Hamburg. In 1974, I caught the plane to Berlin from Hamburg after a visit with Schiller who, in the intervening years, had risen to heights in German and European economic affairs and was now seeking to resume his academic and business career. Hamburg always had an aspect of solid wealth; it was now a place of unparalleled affluence. This was evident in the miles of streets around and back from the Aussen-Alster, all lined with huge villas and beautifully tended lawns, and also in the working-class districts where the blocks of flats had an exceedingly spacious, airy, even elegant appearance. It was also evident in the Vier Jahreszeiten, which those who are knowledgeable in such matters praise as Europe's best hotel, and even slightly in the red-light district of St. Pauli, through which we detoured on the way to catch the plane at Berlin. One of the puzzling things about prostitution and pornography is the blight they bring where they flourish. Were they as financially enticing as they are presumed to be, they should promote investment, increase real estate values and improve the physical tone of the community. St. Pauli suffers from the blight but much less than Times Square.

As before, one came into Tempelhof over a big cemetery. The terminal building was large and ugly and featured a great protruding roof that sheltered the planes or some of them. Forty years ago when the terminal was much smaller, it had a nice restaurant on the roof where one could sit in the evening and watch the Lufthansa flights taking off for every major city in the Reich. It must have been one of the first airports in the world where this was possible, and novelists made much use of it. Now there was no restaurant, and very soon there would be no Tempelhof either. It is no longer possible to have so large an airport in the middle of a city.

Still adjacent to the airport were the buildings where we were billeted in 1945. Then the Russians had just moved out, and they were indescribably filthy. I remember asking a laconic American soldier, a premature Cold Warrior, if the Soviets had stabled their horses there. "No," he said, "their infantry."

Like Hamburg, Berlin in 1974 had an air of urban opulence and cleanliness that was especially striking to anyone accustomed to New York. Except for a small area around Potsdamer Platz and in the adjacent onetime embassy section, the scars were all gone. The trees were thick and at that season freshly green, and they were now half-grown again over Unter den Linden. East Berlin was still not as obviously affluent as West Berlin, but there was no longer any very sharp contrast between the two. Checkpoint Charlie had been greatly reinforced to prevent anyone from crashing through with a car or truck (or for that matter a tank), but the guard who surveyed our Embassy station wagon and glanced at our passports was middle-aged, amiable and appreciably overweight. The streets in East Berlin were full of cars amidst which ours attracted no attention. Somewhere near Alexanderplatz there was a huge supermarket — it must occupy most of a city block. An acquaintance from the State Department, who was an authority on East German affairs, cautioned me that it was a display item, pretty much the only one of its kind. Still, he admitted that it was impressive. One is reassured to be reminded how closely we and the Communists now agree on our indices of achievement. The young in East Berlin were indistinguishable from the young across the Wall.

Both sexes wore the same abused jeans, had hair of the same length. In one pack of adolescents near Alexanderplatz were two who had "Dartmouth" on their T-shirts.

At various gatherings in West Berlin — a reception at the City Hall, a dinner one evening, a luncheon at the house of the American Minister — I encountered a small but not negligible cross-section of the Berlin political, academic and business establishments. Their preoccupations had become wonderfully commonplace. Ernst Reuter and Willy Brandt, in their days as mayor, were the defenders of West Berlin from the East. During a pleasant chat with Mayor Klaus Schutz and two of his immediate associates, problems of East-West relations came up only as one of them offered to arrange for me to visit Jurgen Kuczynski (for which, in the end, there was not enough time). Instead inflation, municipal administration, education, student discipline in the Free University, problems of the Turkish minority, the redevelopment of Potsdamer Platz, the best and most economical way of subsidizing the opera and some recently expressed views of Mayor Kevin White of Boston on urban planning were the matters discussed.

The migration from Turkey was now much more on the minds of Berlin officials than any movement past or in prospect from the GDR or East Berlin. There were at the time some 500,000 Turks in West Berlin, some thought more, out of a total population of 2.2 million. They lived frugal lives in closely knit communities, saving their money against the time when they could return to Anatolia and either buy land or go into business. But some were settling down in the city, and the city government was actively recruiting Turkish-language teachers and arranging instruction for Turkish children.

In all industrial countries there is now a new subproletariat that does the menial, dirty or repetitive work that other economically more advanced toilers no longer wish or are available to do. Blacks, Mexicans and Puerto Ricans in the United States; Algerians in France; Southern Italians in Switzerland; Indians,

Pakistanis and West Indians in Britain; and Turks and Yugo-
slavs in Germany all so serve. Yet no one quite wishes to accept
this pattern as normal and certainly not as permanent. A sub-
class of hewers of wood and haulers of water — one which is
racially or ethnically distinct — is repugnant to almost everyone's democratic sense. Thus the German euphemism *Gastarbeiter* or guest worker. When I suggested one day that honesty
required that we accept this new class structure as permanent
and face up to its implications, I had the feeling that some of
those present thought I was carrying honesty too far.

As I've indicated, one luncheon during my visit was at the
residence of the American Minister, i.e., the resident State Department official, in Berlin. This was, once again, one of the big
villas on a tree-shaded street in Dahlem. One of the guests was
a senior member of the Soviet Mission. We walked out together,
and he said he always found American hospitality pleasant; the
talk was so often about practical matters. It seemed a very nice
observation. Earlier I chatted with the commanding general of
the American forces in Berlin, who was about to depart with no
great enthusiasm for a tour of duty in the Pentagon. A mild-
mannered officer, he told me that his various army duties had
kept him from spending a great deal of time on my books, although he had been attracted by one title. I asked him which.
He said it was *How to Control the Military*. The Soviets or East
Germans were not on his mind either. He very soon turned the
conversation to the problem of race relations within the American forces and to the devastation worked by the Vietnam war
on morale and organization. In earlier years, much in the manner of the East German factory described by Khrushchev, no
sooner was a unit at reasonable efficiency than its officers and
noncommissioned officers disappeared to Saigon. Things had
since become better, and on race relations he thought the corner had been turned. It was not a problem, he observed, for
which growing up in Texas naturally prepared a man.

One morning I was collected in a car by an exceedingly handsome German woman whom I had met some years earlier when she was a Pan Am stewardess. Because of her intelligence and good looks she had been assigned to a flight that was bringing Mrs. John F. Kennedy and her offspring back from a holiday in Switzerland and on which my wife and I were also returning. We drove out through Zehlendorf to the Havel to see her new place of work and passed the zone of low buildings inherited from the Luftwaffe that once had been occupied by General Clay, Robert Murphy, Joseph Dodge, William Draper and the other archons of the American occupation. Buses make the rounds of the American installations, and waiting for one were two wives, both very pregnant. "They don't have a great deal to do," my companion said.

From Berlin I went down to the Rhineland to give a lecture at the great Benedictine Monastery of Maria Laach. (It was there that Konrad Adenauer took refuge from the Nazis.) My speech was not to the monks but to a group of German business-men who, over the Feast of the Ascension, go into retreat at the monastery to talk about economics and management. I was, however, the guest of the Abbot for dinner, in whose quarters silence is maintained except for a reading by one of the members from the Bible and a Palestinian history. I then stayed over-night in the Bishop's apartment. Though many members are old, the monastery is still at full strength. I learned, however, that for running the adjacent hotel and other auxiliary enter-prises, German nuns are no longer available. Nuns must be re-cruited from Yugoslavia. Guest workers again.

16

Germany: July 20, 1944

ON JULY 20, 1944, with the Russians fewer than a hundred miles to the east and the Western Allies known by the Wehrmacht to be on the verge of a breakthrough in Normandy, a professional German Army officer of great courage and determination, Colonel Claus Schenk Graf von Stauffenberg, left his briefcase in the hut at the East Prussian headquarters (Wolfschanze) where Hitler and his generals were assembling for the noonday briefing and went out, ostensibly to make a telephone call. Minutes later a captured British-made explosive in the briefcase went off with a terrific bang, killing four officers but leaving Hitler physically more or less undamaged. It was Stauffenberg's third try.

In Berlin, meanwhile, Stauffenberg's fellow conspirators at the headquarters of the German Replacement (i.e., Reserve) Army on the Bendlerstrasse, Lieutenant-General Fritz Thiele and General Friedrich Olbricht, were waiting to set in motion the troops, seize the installations, make the arrests and dispatch the messages calling for similar action throughout the shrinking German empire which would oust the Nazis and establish military rule by the Wehrmacht. But the news they now got from East Prussia seemed confusing so they went out to lunch and did not get back until 3 P.M.

Count von Stauffenberg, not without luck and difficulty, got by the perimeter guards around Hitler's headquarters and back to Berlin in a special plane which he had standing by. On arriving in the city, he had some trouble getting a car, a defective bit of planning, but in late afternoon he arrived at the Bendler-strasse, since renamed the Stauffenbergstrasse. Here, as chief of staff of the Replacement Army, he managed for a while to make things move. Two of the major Berlin radio stations were occupied, although, unfortunately, by men who didn't know how to run them. An officer was sent to arrest Goebbels, the highest Nazi currently in town, but was talked out of the action. Telexes were dispatched to the headquarters of the *Wehrkreise* (regional defense districts) into which Germany and Austria were divided and to Brussels, Paris and Prague. These alerted the scratch forces there available to the regional military commanders and ordered the arrest of Gauleiters, top SS officers, Gestapo officials and other inimical types. Unfortunately it seemed only proper that orders overthrowing a government should go out Top Secret, although it was hardly something that could be kept quiet for very long, and this meant major coding and decoding delays and, at the points of receipt, the need to find officers of sufficient rank to read them.

It was early evening before the messages were in hand, and by then most of the headquarters had shut up shop for the day and the responsible officers were variously attending receptions, shooting dice, having a drink or en route home and unavailable. The Gauleiters had similarly bunged off. One was celebrating his tenth and manifestly last anniversary in office, another was at a funeral and Frank, the Nazi minister in Prague, was at a ceremony opening an SS training school, as was the general ordered to arrest him. German efficiency and attention to duty were everywhere at full flood. So, except in Paris, where Gestapo, SS and Party officials were taken into custody, nothing much happened.

Meanwhile Hitler's people in East Prussia, proceeding in only slightly less confusion, had come to realize that something more than an assassination attempt was involved and were getting out word that orders from Berlin should be ignored. Finally Hitler himself went on the air to prove that he was still alive, and it was all over. On the Bendlerstrasse Colonel-General Friedrich Fromm, the commander of the Replacement Army, though he had previously shown sympathy for the conspirators, had thought it wise to sit out the afternoon under detention in his office. Now with the first display of determination of the day he resumed command, convened a court martial, had the conspirators (including, of course, Stauffenberg) convicted, one gathers in a matter of minutes, and taken down to the courtyard and shot. (Colonel-General Ludwig Beck, who was scheduled to be interim head of the new government, first tried, without success, to shoot himself.) Management was still sloppy. The insurgents were buried in their uniforms with their medals. To preserve proper indignity, they had to be dug up again next day and burned.

There followed, in the ensuing weeks, a ferocious massacre of those of the conspirators who did not anticipate their own executions. Among the casualties was General Fromm who was bumped off for cowardice. Nazi justice was not always imprecise. Justice of another sort was even visited on Dr. Roland Freisler, the unspeakable Nazi judge (so-called) who dispatched the top participants. While he was engaged in handing out automatic death sentences — usually by hanging on a rope over a hook — the courthouse was brought down on his head by a bomb. The executions continued at an informal level quite literally up to the week of the surrender in 1945.

While the action of July 20 was largely confined to the Army, the conspiracy extended to a group of conservative and aristocratic civilians and on to a number of moderate (and a few romantic) socialists. There were overtures to the Communists, who had their own operation, but this association was limited by the extreme distaste of the conspirators for such people and the very great hope of many, although it dwindled as the war continued, that with Hitler out of the way the Western Allies would happily join in a march against the USSR.

*

The story just recounted was of the supreme and, in some respects, the only moment of the German resistance to Hitler. It
has been told before, and another ordinary account would
hardly be needed. But Professor Peter Hoffmann — he is a German by birth and early education who has studied and taught
in the United States and is now a professor of German history
at McGill — has made it impossible for anyone ever to deal
with the subject again, although no doubt some will try.[1] He
has researched the July 20 events in Berlin, East Prussia, the
provinces and in Prague, Brussels, Vienna and Paris down to
the last minute and sergeant. And he has gone into all of the
antecedent efforts and conversations going back to 1933. *The
Times Literary Supplement,* reviewing the German original,
said that it was "the essential and surely final handbook" on the
subject, and the words "essential," "final," "handbook," are all
well chosen.

In recent times an offensively imaginative revisionism has
come to suggest that Hitler was a political and military genius
who, in his lofty and statesmanlike way, was only marginally
aware of the butchery of the Jews and the Poles. Much of this
book consists of the case which German civilians and generals
made to each other for deleting Hitler. They were not in the
slightest doubt as to what his brainless military megalomania
was doing to Germany or what he personally was doing to the
Eastern peoples and the Jews. Indeed, the details in Professor
Hoffmann's book accumulate into one of the most horrifying
pictures of Hitler yet. One shudders as always that such a mad
criminal with such a pack of followers could get loose in a
civilized country in this century.

At a less ominous level, Professor Hoffmann's account shows
the extraordinary autonomy of the German Army in managing
its own affairs and in keeping its own secrets. Scores, perhaps
hundreds, of high officers, including a brace of field marshals,

---

[1] *The History of the German Resistance 1933–1945,* translated from the German
by Richard Barry (Cambridge: The MIT Press, 1977).

knew of the contract being put out on the Führer. Individuals were assigned and reassigned to facilitate the operation. The reaction was slow at Wolfschanze because Hitler's people there had no hint of the subversion. All who examined German wartime management, without, I believe, any qualified exception, were struck by its unimaginative incompetence.[2] Professor Hoffmann shows that this extended even to the field where the greatest expertise was imagined, namely political repression.

At an even less ominous level, Professor Hoffmann gives a superb, often grimly funny picture of the folk habits of the German officer class as it then was and of their aristocratic civilian counterparts. One forthright thought for giving Hitler the business in 1943 was to pull a gun on him while he was lunching with officers during a visit to the Eastern Front. Field Marshal Gunther von Kluge had to be warned so that he would keep out of the line of fire. (Kluge was passively sympathetic and after July 20 committed suicide to keep off the meat hooks.) He vetoed the method, saying, "It was not seemly to shoot a man at lunch," and adding that there might be casualties among "senior officers [including himself] who would have to be there and could not be spared if the front was to be held." Partly because there was nothing else they could do, the civilian members of the conspiracy spent their time drawing up lists of future cabinet officers which later were a great gift to the Gestapo, and getting into line the less pressing details of post-Nazi government. At one session they considered policies on the multinational corporation, and, on June 21, 1943, Julius Leber, a regular socialist leader, "met Lukaschek, Husen and Yorck of the 'Kreisau Circle' in Yorck's house; they discussed the important question of church or state schools and Leber [a tolerant proletarian] accepted the right of parents to choose."

2 This has been dealt with in Burton Klein's *Germany's Economic Preparations for War* (Cambridge: Harvard University Press, 1959). Further documentation is in the several reports of the U.S. Strategic Bombing Survey 1945–1946, of which I was a director. On returning from Germany in 1945, I wrote a piece entitled "Germany Was Badly Run," which appeared in *Fortune* in December 1945.

The military discussion, almost continuous after 1933, of ways and means of eliminating Hitler was also, I would judge, mostly a substitute for action. Any excuse, ranging from an officer becoming unavailable because of a new posting, to Neville Chamberlain flying to Berchtesgaden, to the unconditional surrender demanded by the Allies, would cause a contemplated move to be postponed. Some like Fromm were caught between the pressure to do right and the equal or deeper impulse to save their own skins. But more, it is plain, were caught up in the conflict that besets all organization men — the same conflict that is faced by a Gulf Oil executive considering a political slush fund or a General Motors man seeing a clandestine engine switch or that was the private trauma of numerous State Department and Pentagon officials contending with the war in Vietnam. The difference in degree in Nazi Germany, however, was enormous. Hitler and the Nazis were a throwback to Attila (whose Stauffenberg was the equally unsuccessful Vigilas), and with no real disguising social or moral purpose. But for the officers the ancient Prussian mystique of the state combined with the powerful tradition of disciplined military service to make dissent uniquely difficult. Americans, Englishmen or Frenchmen would not more easily have resolved such a conflict. The Latin American military *golpe* is entered upon without such difficulty, for the underlying conditions are almost exactly the reverse. The state has no similar prestige; the Latin American army is not a disciplined organization but a loose association of more or less ambitious individuals. There is no personal crisis of loyalty or discipline in acting to throw out a government. It also helps, no doubt, that failure can usually be survived.

Withal, as Professor Hoffmann shows more clearly than anyone before, the July 20 effort was a near thing. Among the high Nazis the handwriting of defeat was being read. As nearly as one can ever be certain on such matters, there was no one besides Hitler who was capable of gathering authority in his hands, taking even the feeble action that would have been required to put down the revolt and showing the much greater strength that, in face of certain defeat, would have been required to carry on. In Berlin, when threatened with arrest, even Goebbels fingered his cyanide pills. In Paris, where the military end was most clearly in view, the SS leaders and Party officials surrendered readily to the Army and cooperated as far as possible afterward in keeping word of what had happened from Berlin.

Count von Stauffenberg, as the result of wounds received in North Africa, was without one hand and a couple of fingers on the other. While getting the explosive organized in his briefcase a few minutes before the explosion, he was interrupted and had to sacrifice half the charge. (He managed to throw the unused explosive out of the car on the way to the plane.) Had the explosion been twice as strong, it is not credible that even Hitler would have expected to survive, and without his frenetic desperation, National Socialism would have come to an end that day. There would have been a different set of German leaders to reckon with in the years following, and the relations between the West and the Soviet Union would also have been interesting. Assuming, as I would, that the British and Americans rejected the overtures that would surely have come, the Western Front would hardly have been held by the Germans with the same determination as that in the east. Certainly there would have been no winter offensive in the Ardennes if the war had lasted that long. But this is not a line of speculation that is usefully pursued. No one can now tell how things would have been changed and by how much.

I first heard of the July 20 affair, newspaper accounts and speculation around military headquarters apart, from Albert Speer in May 1945. He was then a minister in the government of Admiral Doenitz, which, in a manner of speaking, was still functioning in Flensburg on the Danish border, and we were interrogating him on the effect of the air attacks on arms production and related matters having to do with the German war economy. He spoke of the participants in the plot — my memory is not completely firm on the point — as conservative, parochial and without much mass appeal. I remember more clearly his criticism of their penchant for lists, for his name had appeared on one, and for some weeks, in consequence, he had been regarded in a thoughtful way by the Gestapo. On one of the lists in Professor Hoffmann's book Speer continues in charge of armaments, although it is noted that his agreement has yet to be obtained. That anyone so close to Hitler, both personally and officially, would be thought an acceptable figure in a post-Hitler government is a further indication of the ambiguity of the enterprise.

During the course of that summer it became a joke among Allied personnel in Germany that July 20 must have been the largest conspiracy in history, for it embraced the entire German population. Scarcely a general came into our hands who had not, by his voluble account, been deeply involved. However, Professor Hoffmann shows that, at the level of conversation, a great many had been — we were right only in our guess that the operational importance of most people's participation increased greatly after the surrender.

There was also in those days a parallel desire to detach from the ensuing slaughter. In June or early July we were interrogating Goering, Ribbentrop, Funk, Ley and the top Nazi generals at the special high-level jail called Ashcan which had been established in Luxembourg. Because the war crimes investigators — the Donovan Committee — had no similar personnel and access, we had been asked to get several of the people we were questioning on the record as to their more odious achievements. Field Marshal Keitel had presided over the Wehrmacht honor court that turned the conspiring generals over to Freisler for execution. He was asked how many had been so consigned. A man of comfortably obtuse manner, somewhat resembling a terminal career case as vice president of Chase Manhattan, he replied that there had been none. He was then reminded of the condign punishment, possibly enhanced for the occasion, that, according to regulations, awaited those who supplied false information to the occupation forces. He asked for a chance to think, for him a time-consuming exercise, and came up with a revised estimate of a dozen or two. Someone on our team expressed astonishment at the humanity and restraint that he had shown, and later that evening he approached us on our way from another interrogation, fingering a piece of paper. There had been a further upward revision, this time to several score. The Field Marshal too had been caught in a conflict — this between the consequences of lying and the consequences of truth. Hoffmann puts the number of executions resulting directly from the July 20 events at around 200.

My final memory of these matters in that electric summer was of returning to our headquarters at Bad Nauheim near Frankfurt from a trip (as I recall) to Hamburg. It was a few days before the British election which was to choose between Attlee and Churchill, and, on my arrival, George Ball, one of my fellow directors of the U.S. Strategic Bombing Survey, told me with much delight that an unresolvable choice between military responsibility and political faith awaited me.

Earlier that day, Nicholas Kaldor, the noted economist, now Lord Kaldor and then a civilian recruit to our staff, together with Kurt Martin, another distinguished political economist who shared Kaldor's strong social democratic views, had interrogated Colonel-General Franz Halder. Halder had told them in rich and unduly firm detail of the plans of the Army to take over the Reich in September 1938 to forestall war over the Sudetenland. All the generals were set for the action when, on September 15, news came that Neville Chamberlain was flying to Berchtesgaden. This meant that the British were caving in. Kaldor and Martin wanted orders allowing them to fly to London by military courier plane — the only transportation available — to give the facts to Clement Attlee for an election speech.

Tory appeasement had been the cause of a wholly unnecessary war. With that news Attlee would be sure to win. I went to face Nicky; our meeting lasted for two or three hours.

I too wanted to see Attlee win. But if I allowed American Army transport to be used for so flagrant a political purpose, the blame and punishment would fall on me and not Kaldor. I also doubted that Attlee would use the information. Churchill had been anything but an appeaser; mention of the plot would have brought from him a terrifying rebuttal. "And to whom are my opponents now turning for support? They are turning to the defeated Naaa-zzi generals."

But my real commitment, also, was to the organization ethic. When I confessed this to Kaldor, he was distraught and deeply disappointed by my lack of character. However, a lifetime of enmity and recrimination was avoided when, a few days later, Attlee won anyway. Kaldor and I have been close friends ever since. Professor Hoffmann's conclusions make it clear that my supine course was really an act of democratic virtue. For if Kaldor had gone and if Attlee had used the information, it would have been a terrible fraud on the British electorate. Halder and Field Marshal Walther von Brauchitsch, the Army Commander-in-Chief whose participation in the takeover was also needed, were, as Professor Hoffmann shows, the ultimate in ambiguity and reluctance. Had it not been the trip to Berchtesgaden, they would, it is reasonably certain, have found some other excuse for bugging out.

The Indian-Pacific Train

THE MOST BEAUTIFUL railway terminal in Sydney, Australia, perhaps anywhere, is a Gothic-arched sandstone monument called the Old Mortuary Station. In civilized times the dead and the mourners came together here after the funeral, were loaded on a funeral train and, in decent dignity, were conveyed to the Rockwood Receiving House at the suburban Rockwood Cemetery. It made an interesting day; for the railway it was also, the *Sydney Telegraph* said some time ago in a nostalgic article, a lucrative run. Motor hearses eventually did it in. The final moment of the old Mortuary Station came in World War II when, somewhat tactlessly, it was used for the dispatch of troops on their way to combat in the South Pacific.

To go across Australia from Sydney to Perth, one of the few long and luxurious railway voyages in the world, one leaves from the more conventional main station which rather resembles a library and has, as its most serious pretense to grandeur, a very decent imitation of Big Ben. All American railway stations now have the empty and archaic aspect of the Baths of Caracalla. The Sydney station, especially as the 3:15 P.M. departure hour of the Indian-Pacific train approaches, has a rewarding bustle of passengers, porters, train crews and people speeding their parting guests, spouses or offspring on their way. The train itself, immensely long, is no Amtrak makeshift but a thing of gleaming silver. However, the everyday coaches and sleeping cars on the adjacent tracks remain a dull and shabby red with every indication of squalor within. The Australians have done great things for their transcontinental travelers, but one senses adherence to the accepted view that those going short distances should be subject to normal abuse.

Travel on the Indian-Pacific train — named, of course, for the two oceans it joins — is greatly approved by Australians. Just prior to its departure, my wife and I were entertained to lunch at one of the big banks by a fair cross-section of the Australian Establishment. All present were enthusiastic about our good judgment in taking the time to see their vast country by train. Our host then asked around the table as to how many had taken the trip. None had.

All should have done so. The two and a half days and three nights so spent are excellent, even memorable. The beds are long and comfortable and better perhaps than the roadbed. Each cabin, as it is called, has closets, toilet, basin and shower. Meals are by successive sittings, efficiently served and highly palatable with no false claim to elegance. The lounge cars feature comfort, the beer by which the whole Australian nation is irrigated and a piano which, on our train, was the center of an enduring amateur hour.

At exactly 3:15 P.M., the stationmaster (who, along with the head conductor, our car conductor Mr. King and the dining-car steward, had dropped by to welcome us aboard) unrolled first a white flag, then a green flag, and we were on our way. Ahead of us lay the endless stretches of the Australian outback and desert and the almost equally endless stretches of the Sydney suburbs. An hour later we were still passing square bungalows of wood or brick veneer with red tile or red-painted metal roofs, each house surrounded by a pleasant garden. The Australians were wise to choose such a large country, for of all the people in the world they clearly require the most space. Because they need so much and all wish to live within reach of Sydney or Melbourne, prices of building lots are heroic. Demand for land has somehow outrun an inexhaustible supply.

Eventually the city dwindles away, and the train runs into the mountains — the Great Dividing Range. The mountains are not very great, as even Australians concede; they lack, comparatively speaking, the wild grandeur of the Poconos or the lower foothills of the Berkshires. At precisely eighty-six miles from Sydney, the train reaches the summit and begins its descent. This also is not a moment of major excitement; the maximum elevation is around 3500 feet. We supped and then slept.

Next morning at our request Mr. King brought us breakfast in our cabin and told us in a concerned tone that, when the train changed management after Port Pirie, this grace might require renegotiation. Australia has had an interesting experience with its railways. They were built and are still mostly operated by the states. Other subordinate communities within national states have expressed their individuality in their language, music, dress or orgiastic sexual rites; the Australians expressed theirs in the width of their railway gauges. Each state had a preference; the state of South Australia had three. This is a matter where small, even marginal differences are exceptionally significant, so, when changing states, one once had to change trains. Only in 1958 did a commission — the Wentworth Committee — devise a scheme for partial standardization, and only in 1970 did through passenger service from Sydney on the East Coast to Perth on the West become possible. The Indian-Pacific train is the joint enterprise of New South Wales, South Australia, Western Australia and the Commonwealth of Australia, functioning through a joint agency called the Railways of Australia. Lindbergh, on being felicitated for crossing the Atlantic all alone, is held to have said it would have been more remarkable had he done it with a committee. Our movement is, clearly, the supreme accomplishment of a committee.

The first morning finds one still much closer to Sydney than even to the center of the continent. The country is green to grey-green at this spring season with high grass, low fibrous vegetation and scattered trees — a parklike aspect. Here and there are stretches of brilliant red or blue flowers. At wide intervals are grazing sheep or, more occasionally, cattle. There are also emus — vast birds on the general scale of an ostrich — and, in something less than abundance, kangaroos. Of these one has only a glimpse, for, as the train moves to the west, they, for reasons that are unclear, move rapidly east.

The kangaroo strikes one as an exceptional achievement in animal design. It has two main back legs, all that are required for efficient movement. But two supplementary front legs remain available for resting and for holding food. The pouch is a major added convenience, and even the tail has some inexplicable balancing function. With everything else, kangaroos are said to be moderately intelligent, with a slightly mean personality that earns them respect.

Returning to the countryside, it is pleasant, even beautiful, though with a hint of more parched regions to come. One begins also to develop the feeling that there may be more of it than is really necessary. A rewarding aspect is that one can sleep any time for an hour, certain in the knowledge that nothing will be missed. The farms are mercifully sparse and so are the villages — mercifully because the domestic architecture of the rural Australians is untidy, and the landscape features an abundance of abandoned automobiles.

At around nine o'clock in the morning extreme air pollution signals an approach to civilization. It is the great mining town of Broken Hill. As the train stopped, I was called to the signal office for a telephone call and was reminded how wonderfully a train insulates you from the world. A Melbourne newspaper wanted a comment from a visiting sage on the Australian stock market which had crashed ignominiously the day before — the worst slump in eight years. I was able to say quite honestly that I hadn't heard.

The promise of aridity is postponed. Suddenly well to the west of Broken Hill the train climbs to a high plain and emerges on a land of emerald green — green pastures, green wheat fields, green oats, all running away to low, rounded, greenish hills. The farmsteads, though still sparse, are larger and range from habitable to mildly grand. The towns show pride, and grain elevators on the scale of those in North Dakota or Saskatchewan tower over all. The sheep are now dense on the pasture and, it being the season, are freshly shorn. Everywhere there is a brilliant blue flower which inquiry identifies as Salvation Jane, a most noxious weed which sheep will eat only as a last resort. At an improbable siding, our train meets the one that will reach Sydney tomorrow. In a matter of three or four minutes our crew is replaced by the men from the eastbound who are to take us to Port Pirie an hour or two ahead. A tiny town we pass has a pleasant park kept neat by a large flock of sheep; nearby is a sizable racecourse.

Port Pirie of 17,000 in population is near the head of a long, narrow bay jutting north from Adelaide. (The train runs well inland from the southern coast of the continent.) Here we paused for an hour or two. The mayor, as he occasionally does, came down to welcome the train and took us on a brief tour of the town — docks, adjacent lead smelter, parks, playgrounds, schools, new sewers, a Boy Scout camp. Port Pirie is an industrial opportunity that in this day could be unique. It warmly welcomes industry, especially American industry, wants badly to grow, is wholly unworried about air pollution and has free land for new enterprise. There is no danger that any of these attitudes will change with a leftward swing in government. Labour, which is as far left as you can go, is already solidly in. Any firm worthy of Port Pirie should get there before the rush.

At Port Pirie, or rather its neighbor Port Augusta to the north, the serious business of crossing the continent begins — the railroad puts itself on a straight course and keeps it. On one notable stretch of 297 miles the tracks do not turn whatever or at all. The train begins on the Longest Straight at dawn of the second morning. The first turn in the track comes at 12:35 P.M.

This is the Nullarbor (meaning no trees) Plain. It is utterly flat, utterly empty and astonishingly beautiful. This year there has been rain, so, most exceptionally, it is covered with green grass and shrubs to a depth of ten inches or a foot, the shrubs moving like waves in the constant wind. And interspersed throughout are the flowers — white, yellow and startling red, the last being wild hops. Along with the grass and shrubs are patches of bright red earth, and in less favored years and seasons the voyager would see a lot more of it. On arising the second morning, we were told by our car conductor to have an eye out for kangaroos, foxes and dingoes (wild dogs), all of which are present and even abundant. However abundant, they were also invisible. So now, because of the scarcity of water, were the sheep. At Cook, a railway operating center of some importance with a population of (by rough estimate) 200, there is an ambiguous sign in front of the hospital, "Hospital needs your help. Please get sick." West of Cook the hamlets — inhabited mostly by railroad workers — immortalize Australian politicians. No town is so insignificant that it does not rate a prime minister or vice versa. Also celebrated are Field Marshal Lord Kitchener of Khartoum and Field Marshal Sir Douglas Haig. Their settlements appear to be especially insignificant, reflecting, one imagines, the unquestioned distinction of the two gentlemen as the most disastrous generals in British imperial history and the special authors in World War I of the slaughter of some tens of thousands of young Australians.

At mid-morning, privilege raised its lovely head, and we were invited to ride for the next hundred miles or so on the locomotive. The track stretches ahead of the diesel to the horizon, giving, quite erroneously, the impression of a downslope beyond. The telegraph poles on their equally endless march are more honest. They curve gently, reflecting the tendency of the earth. In all normal experience the men who run trains are old. This train was competently managed by an assistant driver (i.e., assistant engineer) in his late twenties and his companion a few years older. I asked Mr. Fraser, the engineer, if his run over the Longest Straight didn't cost him practice in steering. He said the problem was not as serious as the layman might imagine. Boredom is a greater threat. Incidentally, the old dead man's grip or foot pedal which, unless grasped or pressed, will stop the train has gone. Instead there is a clock which, if not punched every ninety seconds, first blows a whistle and then, if unattended, brakes the train to a halt. As Mr. Fraser and I talked, it occasionally whistled.

The assistant driver expressed a compassionate concern over the way the train blew young birds under its wheels. We passed a work crew, young and robust, standing by the track. The nearest towns to them were Port Pirie 700 miles east, Kalgoorlie 400 west. "They have," the assistant driver said, "a very quiet life." In the days of steam a third or more of all the cargo carried on the trains was coal and water to propel them. Diesels were a major breakthrough. But tank cars still go down the line two or three times a week to water the way stations. Our sojourn on the locomotive ended when the train stopped to oblige a wayside dweller who needed a prescription filled.

It must have been a fairly esoteric drug. Beside each of the tiny towns an airfield is marked out for the use of Australia's famous flying doctors. And the hamlets and remote farms or stations are stocked with drugs, each bearing a number, which the doctor prescribes by radio or land line. "One of number 16 after each meal and at bedtime. Report on bowel movements in the morning." Later in Perth a woman who had lived on one of the distant stations told me of her pleasure, even excitement, in listening in on these sessions each day. "It isn't the thing, really, but everyone does it." There was also, she said, a legitimate gossip hour when everyone within a radius of forty or fifty miles got together on the radio to exchange personal news and beliefs.

Eventually the Longest Straight gives way to some gentle

curves which then usher in another straight stretch of only forty-odd miles.

We had, by now, discovered our fellow passengers. They filled the train to capacity, and all were traveling for pleasure. Thirty or forty were members of a women's lodge in Sydney, the Sisters of Gomorrah or some such. "We are like your Benevolent and Protective Order of the Bison in America," one explained. Numerous of the Sisters had brought their husbands, and most of the women had prodigious appetites. One adjacent to us had for breakfast orange juice, corn flakes, eggs, bacon, lamb chops, toast and coffee. Another in a black silk pant suit I met in the train corridor. She backed hard against the wall. I tried to squeeze by. Eventually I made it, but there was a terrible rending sound. She said, "It's nothing." I thought her wrong; mastectomy is no slight matter.

By late afternoon of the third day one is deep in Western Australia. Now fences and sheep reappear and so do trees — really, low-growing scrub. For once, a kangaroo went in our direction at a distance of a hundred yards or so, racing the train but falling gradually behind. The dining-car steward, whose voice, like that of the head conductor, is piped into all cabins, announced early hours for dinner because the dining-car abandons the train in Kalgoorlie. The conductor then came on to advise that a government inspector would come aboard in Parkeston to "confiscate" all fruit, this being to quarantine against the spread of disease. At dinner our table companion, a gentle, recently retired teacher of music from England stated firmly that the community singing in the lounge car was the worst she had ever heard. My wife, whose judgment I trust in these matters, listened and thought it fine.

At Kalgoorlie, capital of the goldfields, there is a three-quarter-hour pause while the train undergoes yet another change of management — this time to the Western Australia railways. Kalgoorlie expanded from nothing to a temporary peak of 15,000 souls (or the mining-town equivalent) in the six years after gold was discovered in 1892. It then had three daily papers, three breweries, two stock exchanges and a great deal of more sedentary vice. The main street, consisting of one-story, verandahed stores of white-painted wood, is still out of more routine Republic movies. At a classic saloon across from the station, into which we peered, a fair number of local citizens were whooping it up, though in a relatively circumspect way. From Kalgoorlie to Perth on the Indian Ocean it is dark.

On the approach to Perth the conductor called with a cup of tea at six. I had then to contend with an engineering problem no one will have solved even when moon travel is at excursion rates. That is the stuck zipper. When it was released, the suburbs of Perth were at hand. It is a sparkling city, as yet only slightly betrayed by freeways, facing a wide estuary and surrounding a lovely park.

Later that morning the mayor — the Lord Mayor, to be exact — told me he still farmed land rather to the north of the terrain we had traversed. He has a million acres, this being the maximum permitted under legislation enacted some years ago by a leftist government to ensure against excessive holdings. As Malcolm Muggeridge once said, socialism is a trivial thing. However, the mayor's land can sustain a flock of only 40,000 sheep, which means that an animal needs to cover some twenty-five acres to stay alive. This cannot but involve a lot of walking. The train traveler's impression of the distances in Australia must be shared by the average merino ewe.

18

Seven Wonders[1]

I MUST BEGIN this piece with more than the usual number of disclaimers. The most important is that I have never been to Egypt, the Cairo airport apart. My list also excludes natural flora, fauna and waterfalls, the economics of Milton Friedman and the last rites of Elvis Presley. It is confined, in other words, to architectural wonders. And it occurred to me as an economist that my choices might be combined, which can easily be done, thus saving on travel costs. Finally, I am excluding the things that nowadays one sees anyway.

Thus I love to look at the Manhattan skyline at the best hours of the day at the proper levels of pollution. There is, I'm totally persuaded, nothing so wonderful in the whole world as the Ile de la Cité with Notre Dame, the Conciergerie and Sainte Chapelle, and only a step over to the Louvre. But no one can get credit for imagination by committing himself to such available treasures. I travel, as do so many others, partly to arouse the envy of my friends and neighbors who have to stay at home, a feat that is increasingly difficult to accomplish these days.

My first pair of permitted wonders, beginning in the East and coming west, would be the Great Wall and the Forbidden City.

1 A year or so ago *The Sunday Times* of London asked a few pathologically peripapetic individuals to specify the several sights which, were they so empowered, they would now establish as the seven wonders of the world. And to give their reasons. Here are my wonders; a truly astonishing number of letters disputed nearly all of my choices.

The Great Wall, I've been told, is the only man-made structure on earth that is visible from the moon. For the life of me, I can't see why anyone would go to the moon to look at it when, with almost the same difficulty, it can be viewed from China. Everyone has seen pictures of its angled passage up hill and down across the Chinese landscape for its unimaginable 1684 miles. (This figure is from Guinness; there is little agreement on the exact length.) The Wall was not completely successful as to purpose. The Maginot instinct has always been powerful but militarily defective; had more Frenchmen visited the Great Wall, they would have saved themselves much expense and eventual grave disappointment. There is a further detail which should be known to all aspiring tourists. By visible evidence, everyone visiting the Wall has felt an overpowering urge to carve his name on it; Richard Nixon seems to have been the only exception. All who struggle for this perhaps questionable access to immortality should take along some tool for making the requisite inscription. Ample writing space is still available.

I had an excellent mental picture of the Great Wall before visiting it. Of the Forbidden City I had no prior sense. Perhaps some decayed and moth-eaten buildings with roofs that were low in the clichéd Chinese manner. I had assumed also that there would be somewhere close by a stretch of deep sand. This would be where exponents of the kind of discipline that, one gathers, the British National Front now favors, buried criminals up to their necks. A stream of honey then guided ants across this landscape and into the felonious mouth. The ants were expected to finish off the malefactor, though not before he had had time to reflect on his misdeeds, and they performed fully to expectation.

In fact, no such place of punishment was evident, and the Forbidden City itself is a vast congeries of the most fastidious and elegant buildings ever seen. The effect is of great rectangular interiors of wonderful symmetry and perfectly aged and polished wood. So complete is law and order in China that treasures of inestimable value are displayed in these halls with a minimum of protection. Perhaps like that in Britain of the trenches of World War I, there is a lingering social memory of those ants. My further experience of the Forbidden City is of the most courteous, gracious and informed guides I have ever encountered, along with the impression that, whatever the merits or demerits of the Chinese Communists, they did a marvelous job of cleaning up this treasure. It was, I gather, in rather tacky condition when Mao Tse-tung took over. My guide said that several inches of bird dung had to be removed, along with several tons of less nutritious refuse. Other maintenance had been similarly deferred.

The next two wonders, only twenty-odd miles apart, are Fatehpur Sikri and the Taj Mahal. Fatehpur Sikri is, as indeed it has been called, the world's most perfectly preserved ghost town. The houses of the masses were, no doubt, cheap and nasty, and they have disappeared. But the walls, palaces and public buildings are still as when Akbar the Great abandoned them after fifteen years' use in about 1586. They are made of the most elegant building material, a salmon-red sandstone quarried on the ridge nearby. The proportions are perfect and the architectural embellishment superb. When more than a couple of tourists have assembled, a group of exhibitionists hurl themselves off the top of the Gate of Victory into a water tank below. They seem to enjoy the work, and the last time I was there — it was with Mrs. John F. Kennedy, as she then was, when she was visiting India — they excelled themselves in the extravagance of their gestures in the course of their descent. Why Akbar abandoned Fatehpur Sikri is unknown. All of the thoughtful explanations are highly implausible; it is quite likely that the great Moghuls, always restless and of nomadic stock, simply decided to move on.

Agra, close by, was another of the Moghul capitals; it was inhabited for an appreciable period by Shah Jahan, Akbar's grandson. It is an incredible and depressing thought that many people visit Agra and the Taj without being aware of the lesser symmetry but greater grandeur of Fatehpur Sikri close by. I don't suppose there is anything to be added about the Taj Mahal; more than of any other building in the world, it has all been said. Never, especially in architecture, was there a similar tribute by a man of his love for a woman. The literal and physical aspect of that affection is generally affirmed by the fact that Mumtaz Mahal died while giving birth to her fourteenth child. In pictures the Taj Mahal seems rather fine, almost precious; in actual presence it is vast. It also needs to be viewed from early morning until starlight or moonlight, for it is a building of many colors and many moods.

Nothing is more remarkable about the Taj than that it has survived. It is now nearly as perfect in all aspects as when it was completed in its various stages from 1632 to 1650. There was a long time, up to seventy-five years ago, when it was threatened. Some of the semiprecious stones which embellish and enhance the structure were being dug out and removed. Other vandalism was rife. To Lord Curzon, imperialist of imperialists, goes the credit for its preservation, as it does for that of many other monuments in India, including the Ajanta and Ellora Caves, which I would also list as wonders were I in need of more. Curzon is remembered in the history books for his climactic row with Kitchener and the lurking elitism which led to his surprise, perhaps apocryphal, when he visited the Western Front and saw some Tommies bathing; he had not previously realized, he said (or was said to have said), that "the lower classes had such white skin." Perhaps his most enduring monument is, literally, the Taj Mahal.

My next two wonders were, in more peaceful days, within easy range of Beirut. One of them, of course, is Baalbek in the Bal Valley in Lebanon. Perhaps there are more wonderful Roman ruins elsewhere in the world — the Colosseum, for example, or the Pont du Gard. But I doubt that anything exceeds

Baalbek in its combination of grandeur, proportion and beauty. Or better persuades you what truly prodigious people the Romans were. That the eighty-four tall stone columns came from Aswan up the Nile and were rolled or hauled over the mountain from the Mediterranean adds powerfully to the latter point. So does the thought that work continued on the Temple of Jupiter for around two centuries. Not many buildings have been under way in London since the ministry of Lord North or in New York since George Washington. However, both New York and Washington do have cathedrals that are unlikely to be finished for another century or so, money and the building trades being as they are.

Baalbek is magnificent and strong. It is not, however, romantic, and for that one must go north and into Syria to Krak des Chevaliers, which, without any cavil or question (as Julian Huxley averred), is the world's most wonderful castle. It covers the carved-off top of a whole barren mountain, and, in more recent times, a couple of villages have been built out of its walls. The looted stones are hardly missed. However, Krak owes much of its excellent condition to the French, who spent a good deal of time and money putting it back into shape during the years of their Syrian mandate.

Krak des Chevaliers was garrisoned by the Knights of the Order of the Hospital of St. John. These were the armed monks who began as the protectors and healers of pilgrims going through the Islamic wasteland to the Holy City and then became the sword arm of the Crusades. Then, after being driven from the Holy Land and expelled from Cyprus, they combined pious works with diligent piracy from the island of Rhodes. Eventually they went on to Malta. Through the great angled gate of Krak des Chevaliers, a whole company of the mounted monks could gallop in or out at full speed. A majestic curtain wall surrounds the castle proper; in the keep is a lovely chapel and a fine vaulted chamber which housed the local head of the order. We visited Krak one cold rainy spring day in 1955 and were at the time the only tourists within miles and, I would judge, days. We were shown around by an aged Arab who made up in hospitality what he lacked in personal hygiene. At the end of our tour he took us to his quarters and a warm fire. There he told us that he had learned his English in Montreal where he had worked for the Canadian Pacific Railway. I was at that time a consultant for the CPR, which had recently sought the guidance of a group of Harvard economists in, among other things, using its new Univac computer for a study of its more egregious costs. I was able to bring him up to date on life at the railroad. He told us how he yearned to see Windsor Station in Montreal once more. There is no accounting for tastes.

I have many candidates for my final and odd-numbered wonder. The dead cities in Ceylon are interesting but do not succeed in competition with Fatehpur Sikri. There is the Black Pagoda at Konarak on the Bay of Bengal just north of Puri in India. It is a great stone chariot mounted on beautifully executed wheels and drawn by a team of gorgeous horses. It is covered with exquisite carvings showing the kind of sexual recourse that my generation once associated exclusively with the Place Pigalle. I first visited Konarak in 1956 with the late John Strachey. John looked at one couple who had sustained a highly calisthenic embrace since the mid-thirteenth century (maybe longer), drew a deep breath and said, "Jolly good! *Jolly good!*" I hadn't previously realized that British M.P.s and former cabinet ministers could express such depth of feeling with such eloquence. Had Cambodia been left in the obscurity and peace it deserves and for which its people unquestionably yearn, I might have managed to get to Angkor Wat. That never happened. Nor did I ever get to Petra. Once when I was in India, the new Jordanian ambassador, a most agreeable and jovial man, asked me to stop over in Amman and promised he would take me there. Unfortunately a day or two later he fell afoul of the Indian currency exchange regulations. As he was entering the country, he had included, in a thoughtless way, a trunk or mattress full of gold with his household possessions, this being marketable at a premium in India. Whatever it was broke open in Palam Airport, and the gold made an impressive sight on the floor. In consequence, he was held *persona non grata,* and I thought it a little uncouth to ask him to keep his promise.

I am left, since I wish to be suitably esoteric, with Machu Picchu. The actual ruins themselves are impressive. So is the thought of the primitive stone tools by which they were accomplished. So, above all, is the site. The city stands on top of a high Andean mountain which is shaped like a greatly attenuated beehive. One looks across the endless green of the jungle and down to the fast waters of the Urubamba River far below, and one reflects that this city, with its temples, walls and houses, remained undiscovered until 1911. In that year Hiram Bingham, believing more or less in the legend of the lost city of the Incas, came upon it and had all doubt dispelled. Bingham, I should say, was a Yale professor of Latin American history and later a United States senator from Connecticut. He shares with Joseph R. McCarthy the distinction of being one of the few senators in our history who was ever formally censured by that body. Bingham's crime, which in modern times would be considered a commendable exercise in legislative diligence, consisted in bringing a business lobbyist from his state into the Senate Chamber to advise on an impending tariff bill. His son, Jonathan Bingham, is a former ambassador and now a senior and highly distinguished member of the House of Representatives from New York. This has nothing to do with Machu Picchu, but no one going to South America should miss it. And indeed not many will. South America is singularly barren of architectural wonders. If these are one's interests, one should go there after the tenth visit to Europe, Asia or the Middle East, the fourth (if one is a European) to the United States and just before going to Australia.

19

Circumnavigation 1978

September 10 — Sunday

We are traveling around the world. The direction reverses Sir Francis Drake, but the purpose remains the same — exploration, adventure and pillage, the last directed not at Spanish galleons but at lecture audiences in both Europe and Asia. Mark Twain had the same view of lecturing I do: "A man can start out alone and rob the public, but it's dreary work and a cold blooded thing to do." I have also in mind observing some of the current generation of statesmen in action, revisiting old scenes in India and seeing friends in Thailand. Also doing a great many things in Japan. There is no alternative to doing a great many things when in Japan.

My publisher in Tokyo, IBM and Management Centre Europe are paying our way, with some overlapping revenue to the IRS. In consequence, we are traveling first class. At the TWA counter at Kennedy, where the turmoil was barely supportable, the line at the first class counter was the longest of all. Maybe the income pyramid is at last inverted. Wider at the top; better to be poor. This I doubt.

Once we were on the plane, an engine required repair, and the TWA 747 scheduled for 9 P.M. was two hours late out of New York. The pilot has now twice told us the flying time will be around seven hours to Milan. This is very troubling, for we are supposed to be going to Rome.

September 11 — Monday

Leonardo da Vinci Airport was as congested as Kennedy but at a lower level of decorum. In my liberal youth I thought how good it would be if everyone could have a vacation in Europe. Now all do. Two lone immigration officials examined passports and checked names against a list of known terrorists. Surely any sensible known terrorist would carry false identification.

The Hotel Hassler on top of the Spanish Steps remains, to a limited extent, a haven of rest. This could be because our room, of modest size, costs $110 a day — to my publisher, fortunately. I detect another interesting economic tendency. The affluent in these days of mass travel seek seclusion. This the best hotels ensure by setting exorbitant rates. The more they raise their rates, the more seclusion they claim to offer and hence, no doubt, the more customers they have.

At dinner there was mention of the peace that has descended on Rome. The Red Brigades are thought to have gone on vacation. Gore Vidal and I exchanged thoughts on publishing in the Soviet Union. He is currently the most popular American fiction writer there; my books are not seriously competitive. We both find the Soviet editors meticulous. They make few changes and are careful to ask about all alterations. Luigi Barzini and I discussed work. We agreed that what we do, namely write, should not be confused with physical toil; that all societies invest great effort and emotion in propagating the myth that good solid physical labor is ennobling, something that every normal upright person seeks, glories in and enjoys. There is no ethic like the work ethic. Then all who can, make their escape to physically less taxing occupations and carefully pretend that these are work too. Vidal said he writes two hours a day. I write about four.

September 12 — Tuesday

Today I had a long discussion on television about the Italian economy with leaders or near-leaders of the Christian Democratic, Socialist and Communist Parties. Like the British economy, that of Italy, which seemed hopeless a few months ago, now seems quite promising again. The inflation rate has fallen sharply. Incredibly, and at least momentarily, the balance of payments is in surplus — tourist revenues, overseas remittances and small business exports are all high. Some capital that took flight when it seemed that the Communists might come to power is thought to be returning.

I was asked repeatedly if I would approve of the Communists being part of the government. I replied that my approval is not necessary. However, I would approve. Modern industrial development disperses power to many claimant groups. Where once capitalists confronted workers, there are now managers, intellectuals, trade unions, organized farmers, civil servants and many others, all demanding a voice in public affairs. So the monopoly of power by capitalists or workers as envisaged by Marx is no longer possible. A legislature becomes the only way of arbitrating as between the different claimants when none can be denied. I was pressed as to how general was this view in the United States. I said that no one should assume that the basic Cold War mind is the best we have; it is merely the most fixed.

In the early evening I visited Gianni Agnelli at his flat; various members of the Italian Establishment dropped in. Agnelli is the most intelligent businessman I know. Exceptionally among executives he does not believe that he runs his business by divine right, and he refuses to express any indignation as the scope for entrepreneurial decision narrows around him. Rather, he always seems a little surprised that Fiat has survived so successfully for so long. The talk was of economics, and someone suggested that Italy was turning the corner because it was being discovered that hard decisions, especially on the budget, could be popular. Greatly needed is better management of the publicly owned industries, of which those in Italy are extensive.

On politics, I was asked if Edward Kennedy saw himself as an alternative to Carter and if he wasn't deterred by the fate of his brothers. Agnelli intervened to suggest that danger could be interesting. I noted that the Kennedys didn't tell their friends their secrets, for they had learned that their friends didn't keep them.

September 13 — Wednesday

I had to cancel a meeting with Enrico Berlinguer, the head of the Italian Communist Party, in order to be sure of getting my plane to Nice to speak to a gathering of IBM executives. The inevitable triumph of capitalism.

Anyone leaving Rome should allow half a day for doing so. Long lines at the ticket counters, longer ones at passport control, a terrible jam before the baggage-viewing machines. Though I cleared the ticket counter with forty-five minutes to spare, I barely made the plane.

The Nice airport was much better, and the Riviera was covered with a soft, hazy autumn sunlight mixed with smog. I had dinner with an eclectic gathering of the heads of IBM in various countries, their presence here being a reward for exceptional achievement in computerization. During the meal my dinner companion, a woman of agreeable aspect, told me that she had once worked for IBM but had quit the business when she married Ralph A. Pfeiffer, Jr., our host and the head of one of the international divisions, who was present in an overpowering pair of pea-green pants. Since retiring to her family, she had interested herself in theater and communications. I listened in a condescending way and am glad I did, for there were toasts later in the evening celebrating the day's announcement in the *Wall Street Journal* that she had just been named Chairman of NBC.

September 14 — Thursday

A lovely day on the Riviera — warm sun, locally still some soft smog. The IBM seniors listened with attention to my lecture and avoided the questions that normally turn such occasions into disaster, "Professor, wouldn't any restraint on prices and incomes be the end of free enterprise as we know it?"

After lunch I went with a friend to see a huge Giacometti exhibition at the Maeght Foundation at Saint-Paul de Vence. The gnarled, enormously attenuated sculptures are so expressive that it is possible to survive their profusion. This is not so of the drawings and paintings. Some day some heroic museum will have an exhibition at which only the ten best things of an artist are shown. More than fifty involve not a diminishing but a negative return.

The Maeght is on a hillside looking distantly toward Nice and the Mediterranean. It's an intricate combination of garden space for sculpture and small glass-sided galleries, these on several levels — the work of my Cambridge neighbor José Luis Sert. It is lovely, and so are the Miró ceramics, which it features. A museum official identified me and thought it "nice that someone came from Cambridge to see Sert." I'm staying overnight in Auribeau in a tiny house of great delicacy of taste and line, Auribeau being a small village of medieval provenance on top of a high hill between Grasse and Cannes. Cars must be left outside; within, steps replace streets or even footpaths. Sublime.

September 15 — Friday

In the morning a walk of several miles along the Siagne in perfect weather. Then by car to Cannes and along the Mediterranean shore road to Nice. The waterfront is now indistinguishable from Long Beach, California, but rather more hideous. Women of good appearance approach the sea in a general way without bathing-suit tops, which is sensible, cool, attractive and, I would judge, economical. Air Inter flies beautiful big planes

of an undisclosed type from Nice to Paris. The color scheme
is pleasant; there is plenty of leg room; an excellently simple
meal is served with efficiency and dispatch. The French airports
are busy, but the crowds move with well-synchronized discipline.
I'm reminded once again of Nancy Mitford's comment that the
French manage well everything the British are supposed to
manage well.

September 16 — Saturday

I have two books being published almost simultaneously in
Paris so I spent nearly all the day in literary self-praise. The
method is to combine unconvincing modesty with an underlying commitment to extreme worth. I also did an interview
with Walt Whitman Rostow with whom during the Vietnam
years I had deep disagreements. But I judge him, unlike others,
to have put much of his past behind him. He has not joined the
Committee on the Present Danger, in which the erstwhile warriors preserve their hopes for the new war that will retrieve
their reputations for foresight and alarm. Anyhow, there are
better things than stroking old wounds. We spoke of the Carter
administration, the need to cut oil imports and get incomes and
prices under control and the tendency of administration economists to remain balanced between the fear of action and the
fear of the consequences of inaction.

In the afternoon I had a long interview with *Paris Match*.
When my answer pleased my inquisitor, he wrote it down.
When it didn't, he ignored my response. A man of character.

In Paris I avoid the memorable restaurants. That's because
while talking, I rarely notice what I'm eating so I spare the
expense. But Nicole Salinger, whose long interview with me
had made one of the books I am here to celebrate, persuaded
me to go to Maxim's. A wandering violinist came by and asked
me for my favorite song. Alan Jay Lerner was at the next table
so I suggested that the musician play extensively from *My Fair
Lady*.

September 17 — Sunday

Sunday and more self-praise — this for French radio. My interlocutor asked me not to mention economics. "That," he said, "causes people to turn off their sets." Since the purpose was to interview me — and Nicole — on a book on economics, the restriction seemed a trifle confining.

At noon I had lunch with Maria Teresa de Borbón Parma, a woman of striking, dark-haired, dark-eyed beauty and a direct, if slightly distant, descendant of Louis XIV. Her brother is (or was) the Carlist claimant to the Spanish throne; like her brother and sister, she is a convinced democrat and socialist. After one hundred and fifty years, more or less, of intense hostility, the Carlists are now on speaking terms with the legitimate or, anyhow, more successful line. She is rather admiring of Juan Carlos's skill in guiding her country back to democracy, although she worries about lurking intransigence in the army and on the extreme left and right. With her brother and sister, Maria Teresa is standing for parliament in the next election, always assuming that she (and they) get their citizenship back first.

This evening I walked with a friend along the Seine. At one of the booksellers a man was reading Henry Miller. His companion, quite lovely, was reading Raymond Vernon (of Harvard) on multinational corporations.

September 18 — Monday

This morning's duty was a three-hour meeting with Japanese businessmen who are touring Europe as the "Study Group on World Economic Forecast." About thirty were involved; with translation and questions, it took a full three hours. With travelers of any other nation I would assume that the education was a disguise for tax deduction. Not my students. All took extensive notes to supplement personal tape recordings and an overall transcript. Questions were intensely practical and frequently flattered my competence. There was much discussion of the point on which Barzini and I had touched — is it inevitable that as industrial countries mature, people will work less hard and increasingly reject tedious, repetitive work? I so held and noted that the tendency had been partly concealed in the United States by drawing on new drafts of labor eager to escape the worse life and greater toil of Appalachia, the Old South and the Puerto Rican cane fields. And in Europe it has been disguised by the heavy use of foreign labor. Japan, a young industrial country, has not faced this problem. Some day it will.

Lunch was with Claude Gallimard, my exceptionally talented and attractive French publisher and his equally agreeable staff.

In late afternoon my taxi tackled the traffic to Charles de Gaulle. Quite unexpectedly we broke out of what seemed to be the ultimate tangle and arrived.

September 19 — Tuesday

Copenhagen is cool and sparkling clean. My housing in the local Sheraton is low-level plastic. Since I was last here two or three years ago, pornography seems greatly to have declined. I've long been persuaded that sex is commercially successful only when illegal or immoral; otherwise it lacks cachet and attracts too much everyday talent.

I spent the day lecturing businessmen on behalf of Management Centre Europe, an organization devoted to the greater enlightenment of entrepreneurs. I was the keynote speaker, although the other speakers did not respond audibly to the note I struck, if any. The most urgent question by the business audience: "Should a well-run European firm have a foothold, i.e., should it own a business, in the United States?" The answer from all my European fellow sages was an unequivocal "Yes." There was a definite impression that while all European countries are in varying measure socialist, the United States remains devoutly capitalist. I pointed out that social legislation in Europe is enacted to advance socialism, while the same measures in the United States are put into effect to safeguard the free enterprise system.

September 20 — Wednesday

I had lunch today with Warren Manshel, the newly arrived American ambassador. A financial man of sorts, he was a stalwart opponent of the Vietnam war, and it was then we became friends. It's hard to see how anyone with such a past qualifies for a high diplomatic position. We usually prefer men who are willing to show, even at the expense of being wrong, that they are capable of taking a hard line with people of peace-loving tendencies. Several newspapermen joined the lunch, which, rejecting all precedent, was not at the Embassy Residence but at an excellent downtown restaurant. They asked, as usual, about Jimmy Carter and why his economists were doing so badly. I explained that under our system of upward failure the economists who do worst, get the most publicity and thus personally do best. Alan Greenspan and William Simon first inspired and then guided Gerald Ford to the economic policies that lost him the election. Both went on from this disaster to careers of great distinction as a result.

In the evening to Brussels.

September 21 — Thursday

Another long day of lectures to business executives, again for Management Centre Europe. Much of the interest was in the proposed monetary union for the Common Market. French francs, Deutsche marks, lire, Belgian francs, will remain and all will have a stable relationship with each other. This association is called "the snake," reflecting the general incapacity of financial men for metaphor. Supported by an articulate Swiss banker, I held that it had not the slightest chance of surviving with any binding relation between the parts as long as different countries have different wage, price, fiscal and monetary policies and thus different rates of inflation. An alignment of internal policies must come first; until this is done, currencies will fluctuate — or, at a minimum, the snake will periodically come apart. The audience mostly disagreed. Businessmen, even more than politicians or the simpler kind of economist, want to believe that there is some as yet undiscovered magic in the management of money.

September 22 — Friday

A very quiet day in Brussels. Its Sheraton is less reprehensible than that in Copenhagen. Lunch was with Léon Lambert, who lives with lovely paintings (and more Giacomettis) on top of his own bank. Attending were senior Belgian politicians and businessmen, the Establishment. An aide to the King rebuked me gently for neglecting to call on His Majesty. I promised improved manners henceforth. The talk was of the future. I have reached the age where I comment on this with confidence, for I won't be around to hear about it if I am wrong. What will be the major anxieties ten years hence? Some kind of rapport will have been established on incomes and prices and the regulation of public and private expenditure so that inflation will not be the primary problem. In Europe there will be much concern over regularizing the role of the mass of foreign workers. No one should imagine that they can be kept forever as a special subproletariat. All the older countries will be reconciled to the departure of the simple, tedious industries to the more competent countries of the Third World. Steel, heavy chemicals, tires, ordinary textiles, shipbuilding, will be gone. (Steel is already in deep trouble in the United States, France, Britain and the old districts of Belgium.) The older industrial countries will still have computers, aircraft, missiles and other advanced weapons of mass destruction. And if they survive their excellence in the latter, they will have the industries which require good or original art and design.

September 23 — Saturday

I left early this morning and was warned before departure of various airline strikes. All went normally to Frankfurt, and

Pan Am 2 to Tehran and Delhi was late only in the normal way. The Pan Am people were greatly surprised to see me boarding, all reservations having been accidentally erased. I became intensely disagreeable, which, when righteously inspired, is true joy. I remembered and reminded the local official that they only flew into various Indian airports because I had got them landing rights. Later it occurred to me it was TWA I had helped.

September 24 — Sunday

Anarchy, if sufficiently unrelieved, can become a mild form of business genius. Pan Am started the movie so late it was only half finished when we reached Tehran. Thus all disembarking there will have to take the same plane back in order to see the ending. They then ran it right through the forty-five-minute stopover, thereby keeping the through passengers from contemplating the revolution outside.

This is my first significant return to New Delhi since I served here fifteen years ago. (I came once to represent L.B.J. at a funeral, and I passed through once when raising money for the Bangladesh refugees.) Nothing is more inconvenient for an ambassador than to have a predecessor on the premises, so we had arranged to billet ourselves at the Indian International Centre. But the Goheens, being absent, had us moved to the Roosevelt House, the majestic Edward Durell Stone creation of my years and the official Embassy Residence. I named it for F.D.R. and, to be sure all knew it was for him, got Averell Harriman to donate a Jo Davidson bust for the entrance. The Republicans, when they came, dug up a bust of T.R., I would judge from a Long Island antique shop. I never heard that T.R. had much to do with Indian independence.

Tonight we dined with the head of the Foreign (External Affairs) Office, an old friend. We have still to go, with Richard Roth (the movie producer), to a celebration on behalf of lions, tigers and other wildlife. In a country where so many people have so little to live on, one must be cautious about expressing too much concern for animals. I remember a woman in Calcutta straight out of Evelyn Waugh who told me that it couldn't be good for the cows to be loose on the streets with so many people.

September 25 — Monday

This morning I called in at the Embassy Chancery, still perhaps the most beautiful building ever accomplished by the government of the United States — an elegant rectangular shell surrounding a beautiful water garden. I was reminded of taking Lyndon Johnson into it in the spring of 1961. He said with indignation, "What did this cost?" But I knew L.B.J. of old. He was a master of intimidation, and the remedy was homeopathic. I said sternly that it had, indeed, cost a great deal and was worth every cent of it. He agreed.

At noon I met with numerous Indian editors and publishers, and we discussed the relative decline of the superpowers since my years in Delhi. At that time, the two giants towered over all others; Indian foreign policy was that of the nervous embrace. It wanted the considerable rewards that came from attempted seduction by one or the other without the seduction.

Now much has changed. China challenges Russia in the Communist world. The vision of a unified Communist conspiracy has been abandoned, it is said, even by James Angleton.[1] On the other side, the industrial eminence of the United States is powerfully challenged by Germany and Japan. As the perfectibility of socialism has given way to worry over the problems of management and especially of agriculture, so the wonders of free enterprise in the age of Keynes have given way to worry over inflation and unemployment. Only Walter Wriston has yet to hear that capitalism has problems. Meanwhile Vietnam showed us the limits of our power in countries geographically distant and culturally different from our own. In China, Algeria, Ghana, Egypt and Somalia the Russians have

[1] See page 336.

been taught, and one hopes have learned, the same lesson. I emerged without damaging challenge. Some of my audience, I sensed, still prefer a world in which foreign policy involves only a choice between two superpowers.

I had a long talk with Aisha Jaipur, in my time the elegant Maharani of Jaipur, who in recent years has had a major stay in the stony lonesome. Government mine detectors, as I recall, uncovered a major deposit of metal in the environs of one of the Jaipur princely palaces. It turned out, disastrously, to be undeclared gold. Possibly it had been buried there in past times and forgotten. Aisha didn't care much for the experience. She also regretted some errors in her autobiography (written with Santha Rama Rau), which was published while she was in the clink. The proofs, she said, had to be smuggled in and out and read surreptitiously. That was bad for accuracy.

September 26 — Tuesday

The Indian Airlines plane to Kashmir operates with a 90 percent load factor in summertime, has a forty-five minute turn-around time in Srinagar, and, I'm told by the local manager, makes a great deal of money. Kashmir is one of the few disputed territories in the world that is worth the trouble and expense. The others are places that civilization reached last, and for good reason.

Here we are staying with L. K. Jha, once a fellow economics student in England; later, as Secretary of the Ministry of Finance in New Delhi, my constant companion when we were extensively the underwriters of the Indian balance of payments; then an exceedingly popular ambassador in Washington. Now he is Governor of the state of Jammu and Kashmir. The Raj Bhavan or Government House is on a hill overlooking Dal Lake, the famous floating islands, the near and distant mountains and the Srinagar television tower. A pleasant, rambling wooden structure, it was built by the last Maharajah before independence, when he was advised by competent astrologers, who must have been closet democrats, that he could only have a son if he married a woman of low birth. This he did, but since dignity, as distinct from democracy, did not allow him to go to a low house for the wedding, one had to be built in decent grandeur especially for the bride and the ceremony. The original palace is a few hundred yards away and is now an excellent hotel. At this season in Kashmir flowers are everywhere.

The state of Jammu and Kashmir lies on the two sides of Banihal Pass. Kashmir is high in the mountains; Jammu is on the hot plains. Snow comes to Kashmir in the winter; Jammu is pleasantly warm. Accordingly, as autumn recedes, the state government, down to the lowest clerk and the most neglected file, moves to Jammu. This takes about a week as compared with the weekend required in British times to take the entire government of India from Delhi up to Simla.

September 27 — Wednesday.

A day in the Vale of Kashmir and lovely beyond easy description. Rice harvest was in progress. The grain is cut by hand; women and teenagers carried away prodigious loads of straw on their heads. A team of two cows — not oxen — was plowing the stubble with a wooden plow unchanged, I would judge, in the last five hundred years. Unchanged also are the Shalimar Gardens, going back to the Mughals, and a major riot of red, yellow and purple. We had lunch at a game sanctuary, once the private hunting preserve of the Maharajah. There is some tension among the animals in the enclosure. The snow leopard recently bit the leg of a rare and valuable species of deer. The leopard died, and the deer survived. On Dal Lake, as we returned, the *shikaras* (gondola-like boats) were out, and people were pulling up the reeds and other water debris that make the floating islands that grow vegetables. On the way to Srinagar we paused to visit Claremont Houseboats, G. M. Butt proprietor, who has numbered among his clients everyone of official importance who has come to Kashmir in the last forty

years. Pictures of all remain. Mine is next to Nelson Rockefeller's; Nelson's, however, is in color. Then we took a long
shikara ride down the Jhelum, the main river of the valley
passing through the city of Srinagar, which rises densely on
either side for two or three miles. Then we drove back through
the city. In most places handicrafts are something that people
who combine nostalgia, artistic sensitivity and a certain excess
of funds seek, unsuccessfully, to encourage. In Srinagar every
kind of hand manufacture — carpets, carving, papier-mâché,
copper jewelry, furniture, footstools and more, ad infinitum —
has an explosive life of its own. Thousands of shops proclaim
the resulting wares. One advertises "thrilling" shawls.

A large sign in the center of Srinagar would have usefully
warned Richard Nixon and Spiro Agnew:

INCOME TAX EVASION IS A DISGRACE

IT IS ALSO ILLEGAL

September 28 — Thursday

The day was spent in bed with a sinus attack. Dinner tonight
was with Sheikh Abdullah, the Chief Minister, and a small
party including the Vice-Chancellor of the University. (There
are two state universities, one here and one at Jammu.) Sheikh
Abdullah, the Lion of Kashmir, is a most impressive figure,
very tall and solid in proportion. He was for long the advocate
of independence for Kashmir. In consequence, he lived for
many years under one form of restraint or another. Now he has
become the voice of moderation against the irreconcilables who
still want to be part of Pakistan.

We talked mostly of economics; the growing population of
Kashmir, up by 50 percent since independence; the booming
tourist trade and the need to build more hotels; the need to
keep houseboats from disfiguring Dal Lake; the boom in handicrafts, in which Srinagar leads the world in extent and variety;
the need for more money to finance further development.
Withal, the people of the valley, or most of them, remain dis-

mally poor and must also, unlike the people of the plains, contend with a cold winter. At the lower levels of poverty they don't heat their houses; instead, as of old, they carry a small firebox of live coals around under their clothes. It is an acute carcinogen. Skiing is a growing industry.

Sheikh Abdullah told of having to go to the university to tell the students to take an examination to which they were objecting. Their protest was on the usual political grounds — the test was too hard and thus discriminated adversely against those who were not by nature bright. Most of the universities in northwestern India are in poor shape; some ran as few as fifty days last year and were closed the rest of the time by one form of agitation or another. The agitation is not without purpose; a student who combines ambition with a deep allergic reaction to books becomes an agitator. This then marks him out as a political leader and a potential legislative candidate when he graduates. It is a kind of natural selection of the worst. The resources for running India's huge university system come out of a very poor community. I was always angered that the students, a highly privileged group studying at the public expense, were allowed to make such bad use of such scarce resources.

Kashmir has two disputed borders. One is with Pakistan, where, in the main and as regards the best land — the valley — the Indians are in possession. The other is in Ladakh, where the Chinese hold the actively disputed territory. Time is gradually resolving both disputes in favor of the tenants-in-being.

September 29 — Friday

On this golden morning we went shopping in Srinagar, a joyous exercise, for at this time of year in any one of the thousand shops you are the only customer, perhaps the only one of the day, and welcomed accordingly. I called in on the famous emporium of Suffering Moses, and the owner told me he wasn't selling anything; he was taking stock to see what, if anything, had recently been stolen. A tailor, Mr. Kahn, from whom I bought a jacket sixteen years ago, recognized me on the street, asked how the garment was wearing and as to my need for a replacement. At noon we caught the plane back to Delhi.

There we went to make a courtesy call on the President, Sanjiva Reddy, whom I knew years ago as Chief Minister of Andhra Pradesh. There is a style about such ceremonies in India that is sadly lacking in Washington. For one thing, the Rashtrapati Bhavan, in its red-sandstone, Mughal-garden magnificence, dwarfs the White House approximately as the Empire State Building dwarfs Altman's. For another, the aides who greet, salute and guide you into the labyrinth are to the White House policemen as the Rockettes to Radcliffe freshmen. No wonder Richard Nixon wanted something more Mikado. Our conversation was extensively reminiscent.

Then I went to the Indian International Centre, a handsome collection of buildings adjacent to the Ford Foundation and the World Bank in the Lodi Gardens. There I gave a lecture, and the hall was crowded, including all standing room. The tribute is to the affection with which I am regarded in India and which I find so pleasant that I greatly wish I had cultivated it in the United States. The lecture was on the economic problems of the developed countries. Most economists visiting India feel obliged to speak on the problems of the poor countries and what should be done about them. This is deeply insulting. Also the advice is usually either wrong or politically or administratively inapplicable, and, in any case, it is disregarded.

From the lecture we went to dinner with a small cross section of the New Delhi Establishment — old friends, lovely wives. The evening's discussion turned to the stability of Indian democracy. There was a variously expressed feeling that Indians, influential and less so, have a strong sense of participatory power in their government and are determined not to lose it. Thus the surprise at the defeat of Mrs. Gandhi is readily explained: some millions took the thoughtful precaution of expressing themselves in her favor before going to the polls to vote against. I long have had the further feeling that, in a country not exactly replete with recreational opportunity, politics is a source of much enjoyment. Speeches, promises, acrimony, scandal, victory, defeat, change. This no one or not many wanted to lose.

All contemplating a trip to India should think of late September. Warm days, cool nights, all green after the monsoon. None of Kipling's pile of sand under a burning glass.

September 30 — Saturday

This morning we went to visit Prime Minister Morarji Desai. We were shown to corner seats in the large living room of his residence so that pictures could be taken with a maximum of convenience. He came in looking a couple of decades younger than his eighty-two years, certainly no older than when he was Finance Minister under Nehru and I used to see him every week.

Our talk ran first to his recent visit to Moscow and the desire of the Soviets for a SALT II agreement. He then expressed his warm approval of Cyrus Vance and Jimmy Carter and asked me how I now saw Indian relations with China, in which I was once (at the time of the 1962–63 war) considerably involved. I urged the need for letting the boundary dispute in Ladakh (beyond the Himalayas) lie fallow. The real estate involved is uniquely barren; what could not be settled sixteen years ago could be more easily settled now, and in another ten years passions would further cool. He demurred, adverting to political pressure for getting the Chinese off Indian soil, however distant and inexpensive. We agreed in our distaste for any inclination to make capital from the tensions between China and Russia. He said that he had pressed the point on Jimmy Carter, who also agreed. He asked me if there was some tendency to the contrary in Washington. I pointed out that we had always to contend with those who, having read the books, saw themselves in the mantle of Machiavelli, Talleyrand or J. Foster Dulles.

He said that he had little trouble in identifying the person or persons so motivated. Altogether it was a pleasant time.

We had lunch with a large group of journalists and civil servants, and the discussion was on North-South relations, as all intercourse between rich and poor countries is now described. This is an area of great surprise. The rich countries strongly encouraged the industrialization of the poor countries as an unexceptionable good — who could be against economic development? Now the question of buying the resulting textiles, steel, steel products and other industrial goods has come up. That, naturally, no one expected; these things were all supposed to be consumed at home. It is the weakest industries in the advanced countries and those with the highest labor content and cost that feel the competition. So protectionist sentiment is reinforced by compassion. It will be an interesting cause of tension in times to come.

Then came an interview with the *Hindustan Times* by a sensationally good-looking woman, who began by asking me my I.Q. I told her truthfully that I had never had it measured. She left me wondering. She asked how we raised our children and why we had remained married so long. I enlarged on the need to devote as little time as possible to one's offspring lest they acquire one's bad habits; to one's virtuous tendencies, if any, they are naturally immune. I held also that marriage being a perilous and improbable association, it is safe only if the principals don't see too much of each other. She wasn't altogether persuaded but copied it down.

Then I did a long interview on All-India Radio — interesting, fast-paced questions which I much enjoyed — and this was followed by a dinner by the Government of India. The latter, of much style, was at Hyderabad House, a place for official entertainment which is on the same scale as the Metropolitan Museum and is the onetime Delhi headquarters of the Nizam of Hyderabad. Journalists, senior civil servants and a few politicians were there. The speeches and conversation were mostly of a lighthearted sort. I was queried on the tendency of the Asian subcontinent to what I once called the North American solution. The doctrine in question holds that North Americans are no less belligerent than normal and could be more so, but peace prevails because the British and Spanish left behind one big country with a rim of smaller ones. The big country is morally restrained from attacking the small ones; and no American politician can make much capital by assailing Canadians, Mexicans or Guatemalans. Cuba proves the point; Cubans became bad only when they came to seem dangerous. The Canadians and Mexicans in turn have become accomplished in living beside a big country and getting out of their situation as much independence as they can.

The same solution should have emerged on the Indian subcontinent — India and a fringe of much smaller states. It was delayed by the perverse genius of the American global strategists led by Dulles who sought to build up Pakistan as a military ally. That made attacks on Pakistan a profitable occupation for Indian politicians and led on to three wars. Now, with the independence of Bangladesh, the shrinkage of the relative position of Pakistan and the decline of the global warriors in Washington, the subcontinent has settled into the North American equilibrium. The theme served for an hour or so without encountering serious objection, save for some words of caution as to what the Pakistanis might one day yet do.

October 1 — Sunday

Nothing of importance transpired at lunch or later at a picnic of incredible charm on the edge of Delhi. An estimated eight cities, some say seven, have occupied the approximate site of the present capital. Where we went is a once densely inhabited, vast archeological area called Mehrauli near Qutb Minar. Our picnic was on the top of the house and tomb of an early sixteenth-century poet named Jamali and his brother Kamali. Ruins, all unexplored, stretch endlessly around. We watched the sunset from the flat balustraded roof.

In the evening we had dinner with Rajeshwar Dayal, who was for many years a senior figure in the Indian foreign service and who, in the days immediately after the independence of the Congo, was sent by the UN to rescue it from civil war and the even more dangerous attentions of our cold warriors. I was Dayal's conduit to President Kennedy, who was highly sympathetic. I talked at length with S. Mulgaokar, the editor of the *Indian Express.* I held that the Indian newspapers, although contentious and lively, devote far too much attention to political speeches and political news in general. If a politician speaks but says nothing, only this fact should be mentioned. Mulgaokar partly agreed but insisted that Indians have an inordinate appetite for political news. Speeches are also cheap to report, and politicians have something to do with the supply of newsprint and advertising. (This morning's *Hindustan Times,* generally thought the best in Delhi, had a three-column headline announcing that GANDHI COMBINED IDEALISM AND PRAGMATISM. Prime Minister Desai was speaking on the eve of Gandhi's birthday.)

We went to bed at 11:30 P.M. and got up at 4 A.M. to catch a Lufthansa flight to Bangkok.

October 2 — Monday

This is my first visit to Bangkok in seventeen years — almost to the month. President Kennedy sent me out to Saigon in 1961 to make a report after I had expressed myself against the Maxwell Taylor/Walt Rostow paper urging greater military intervention in Vietnam. Troops were to go in disguised as flood control workers. I stopped in Bangkok afterward to send on my views. That was because the Saigon embassy and ambassador were pressing strongly for troops, and it seemed a little crude to file from there saying they were full of it.

Bangkok, with a population of over four million, is now enormously larger, and the resemblance is not to the old city of the canals but, generally speaking, to Atlanta. As always, the people look infinitely more prosperous than those in India, as indeed they are. A former Harvard student of much charm met us at the airport after arranging for the elision of all entrance formality. We are housed in a fine suite on top of the Hotel President, which her husband owns.

The most talented man in Southeast Asia is Kukrit Pramoj. With some royal connections, he is also a newspaper publisher, journalist, a student of Thai dancing, music, art, antiquities and architecture, and a former prime minister. He lives in an assembly of ancient Thai houses — long, with steeply curving roofs like those of the Forbidden City. Within, there is a glistening vista of polished teak. All is a museum of Thai art and culture. We went there for dinner. Beside the dining room is a small theater, and back of that for the evening was a small orchestra. With dinner we had Thai music and a succession of classical Thai dances by students and friends of Kukrit. It was a major evening. There was only passing mention of Thai politics. Kukrit did say of one cabinet officer, a man of some education, that he threw cultured pearls before real swine.

October 3 — Tuesday

This morning I gave my inevitable speech, this to a combined assembly of all the various professional economic organizations of the city. The questions were sensible and thus unnotable. Then we went to a superb small museum in the house of Princess Chumbhot, a woman of charm and power in the land. She greeted us, as did a huge pelican which accompanies all visitors around the grounds. We saw a smallish temple of much elegance, replete with shrines and artifacts and some exceptionally durable pottery dating to 4000 B.C., which is thought by many to establish Siam's priority in this branch of art and manufacture. The point seems well taken. Also some excellent old boats of strictly ceremonial aspect.

October 4 — Wednesday

This morning we toured the adjacent city and countryside by boat. We went down the Chao Phraya River heavily in flood and then circled through canals in what was once the great orchard area of Siam, to return to the river considerably upstream from our starting point. All life — houses, shops, shopping centers of a modest aquatic sort, temples and schools — is related to the water, and everywhere children were swimming in it without apparent damage. Some strength must be needed to shove through. Mark Twain said that old Mississippi river hands, when taking a drink, stirred up the sediment in the river water in order to be sure of getting the nourishment. Here it would not be necessary.

At lunch we did get around to politics. A constitution is being drafted; it is believed to promise that half the parliamentarians will be elected, half appointed by the government. Some younger people present saw in it a chance for a civilian front to win power from the army. Kukrit was not attracted by the idea. The present government is corrupt; the new arrangement would merely share the booty.

In the Buddhist lands, it should be noted, graft is not quite the same as in the West. One may steal for the purposes of enhancing comfort but not for gaining wealth. And the official who takes graft must give value to the source. Pure graft, meaning without *quid pro quo,* is against national custom.

I have been impressed in these last days with the confidence of the Thais in relation to Laos, Cambodia and Vietnam. The latter are learning the great truth — Marxian, oddly enough — that socialism, with its enormous demands upon administrative talent, belongs to a later stage of economic development. So, for now, in these countries, there is deprivation and despair. In Thailand, in contrast, there is great and attractive vitality. This leads to a quite wonderful paradox: the strategic theorists who gave us the domino doctrine were, in fact, the captives of the Communist vision. They took for granted that the Communist example would be persuasive. With a little military push, the dominoes would fall. Instead the dominoes are leaning slightly in. The Thai (and Malayan and Singaporean) examples are a threat to Indochina.

At lunch Kukrit spoke at length of his visit to China in 1975. Mao, by then, was unable to speak. An interpreter, half Chinese and half American, read his lips and then checked the meaning with him in Chinese before rendering him into English. Mao nonetheless was exceptionally amusing and jovial withal and told Kukrit that China would not follow the Russian example of imposing its system and influence on reluctant neighbors. This would be not so much out of kindness as because it was impractical.

October 5 — Thursday

Two hours before required check-in time and three hours before the flight was scheduled to go, we left for the airport, a half hour's driving time away. The traffic requires such a margin. It took us half an hour. Kukrit accompanied us out, arranged our passage through the various airport functions, and we then had a couple of hours to review our respective achievements of recent years in a suitably self-laudatory way. A unique companion.

Yesterday I was reminded of the ceremony in ancient times governing the royal succession in Siam. All male claimants seated themselves, lotus position facing inward, around an area spread evenly with honey. Each then drew back his member, as it is decently called; the one who, on release, killed the most flies won the succession to the throne. This, incidentally, was how the capital got its name.

October 7 — Saturday

A day lost from this chronicle. We arrived a bit late, night before last, at Narita Airport, to a ceremony comparable with anything since Admiral M. Calbraith Perry. Television cameras, a dozen news photographers, publishing company executives, television men, a press conference and then champagne and a small banquet, all at the airport. More than Houghton Mifflin would do for John Milton. It was toward midnight before we left for Tokyo. There being little traffic, it took only an hour and a half.

"Why is Narita so far from town?"

"Everyone is asking."

Yesterday began with a visit with the executives of TBS — Tokyo Broadcasting System — who, with the assistance of the exceptionally enlightened Kirin Beer Company, broadcast my series *The Age of Uncertainty* to the Japanese viewing public. Then there was a radio interview — questions in English repeated by the interrogator in Japanese, answers and translation. It was both faster and funnier than one could have expected. Then I had some lunch with book and television executives and an hour-long television discussion with Masayoshi Ohira, former Foreign Minister, now Secretary General of the Liberal Democrats and a candidate for Prime Minister. [This office he has since achieved.] Ohira, an acquaintance from past times, masks a very sharp mind with a deceptively bland manner. Our discussion was of industrial development. I asked if the days of aggressive, single-minded economic growth might not now be in the past in Japan. He thought so; in the future more attention will be given to the quality and tranquillity of life.

After Ohira came a long interview with *Mainichi Shimbun*, one of the three biggest newspapers in Japan, an interview which covered the world and several pages this morning and is to be continued tomorrow. Then at the end came a dinner with TBS executives, Ambassador Mike Mansfield and his wife Maureen and the Shigeto Tsurus. Tsuru is the most distinguished of Japanese economists — a Harvard graduate and Ph.D. and a friend of mine for some forty years. Mike looked rested and relaxed, which he attributed to being away from Washington. We discussed the Japanese penchant for pessimism and insecurity. All questions half assume the inevitability of disaster. Someone explained that it is ethnic: Americans expect to prosper; Japanese regard good fortune as highly unnatural. There was discussion as to why when the Swiss franc gains and the Swiss balance of payments booms, all is attributed to the virtue of the Swiss — solid, reliable folk. When the same happens to the yen and the Japanese balance of payments, as now, all agree that the Japanese are at fault. The point was not resolved.

At any given time Washington economists have a fantasy that gains substance from each telling the others of its depth of truth. The current one is that Germany and Japan should stimulate their economies more aggressively. They would then have more inflation, and the dollar would be stronger because the mark and the yen would be weaker. By this formula we would remedy our errors by getting other countries to imitate them. The point came up often during the day, for a huge U.S. trade mission is in town with carefully coordinated explanations of the inadequacy of American economic policy. I commented with unnatural grace and restraint.

This morning we caught the "bullet train" to Atami on the Izu Peninsula and the peace of Hotel Torikyo, meaning Land of Peach and Pear. The comfort is perfect. Chaste rooms; beds prepared on the floor; our own garden; the sea below and beyond. Dinner was with the Tsurus and former Prime Minister Takeo Miki and his wife. Miki became Prime Minister to give the Liberal Democrats a new image of honesty, and he is still regarded as dangerously upright. The subject of discussion: all know the dark prospect of life, that being nuclear catastrophe. What are the bright prospects? Probably the tendency for the socialist and nonsocialist worlds to converge, to the dismay of the professional ideologues in both. The underlying and less agreeable tendency is that public and private activity in both becomes increasingly organized and bureaucratic. The organization man is much the same everywhere. All countries denounce bureaucrats but have no substitute.

The most intractable problem, my friends urged, is the great and growing difference in wealth between the rich countries and the poor. A transfer of capital from the rich to the poor has value but is not a cure. Tsuru, one of the world's leading philosophical Marxists, shares my doubts about socialism for the poor lands and its tendency to load the greatest administrative burden on the countries least able to bear it.

Population pressure is also intractable. One discusses all possibilities without optimism.

October 8 — Sunday

After a parboiling in the local hot spring — there is a small pool in our own bathroom — I worked through the morning on my lectures. I had arrived with good drafts, but quite a bit of cross-cultural and last-minute information has always to be added. Eight thousand people have applied for around nine hundred seats. Admission is by lottery; cassettes will be sold. Harvard undergraduates were never so discriminating. At lunch Tsuru gave me the results of a poll recently conducted by *Mainichi*. What Japanese and what non-Japanese would you prefer for prime minister of Japan? Living or dead could be chosen. I nosed out Einstein in the external competition, an indication of the power of economics and television as compared with mere theoretical physics. Ronald Reagan was nowhere.

This afternoon we toured the local fishing villages and seacoast — a landscape of breathtaking views.

October 10 — Tuesday

The bullet train back to Tokyo yesterday rolled into Atami station on the precise minute and, I would judge, the precise second. A large crowd waited, but there was room in the spacious blue-gray rooms for all. A most pleasant way to travel that other countries should adopt.

In Tokyo I went to the Press Club for a lively luncheon, a couple of hundred attending. My thesis for the day: in the last century and early on in this one, nations sacrificed internal stability and accepted heavy unemployment in order to maintain stable international exchanges. Now the reverse: internal stability and external instability. However, some countries, including the United States, are having some success in getting instability in both areas. The circumstances and the absence of alternatives dictate the action — restraints on corporate, trade union and other organized power. The questions were sharp and to the point. One man did ask if I thought Japan was in a recession. I told him this was hard to perceive.

After lunch we went to TBS-Britannica, my publisher, we being a caravan of three cars, one of which carries photographers and one assistants and logistical support. At TBS-Britannica, the whole staff, to the number of a hundred or so, was down on the street to cheer us in. Then, after visiting the president, all hands assembled in the main offices for speeches, toasts and the presentation of a stunningly beautiful *No* statuette, which filled me with pleasure.

Toward evening prizes were given in a downtown hall in an essay contest on the subject "Japan in the Age of Uncertainty." The winner had dealt with the uncertainties of health from firsthand knowledge. He was a paraplegic in a wheelchair. The second prize went to a woman well into her seventies. She didn't seem disturbed when referred to as "this old woman." In Japan age is still good. I followed with my lecture to the happy few. It was unduly complicated, and I outpaced my interpreters. A very poor performance.

October 11 — Wednesday

I continue a day behind. Yesterday morning we visited two bookstores of enormous size, one of them Yaesu Book Center, said to be the largest in the world. Each is of several stories, each floor two or three times Doubleday Fifth Avenue and packed not only with books but also with customers. A juvenile section at Kinokuniya, the first store, was filled shoulder to shoulder with youngsters aged eight to ten, all diligently reading free. The owner, aging, articulate, highly amusing and a local political mogul, Moichi Tanabe, led our procession through the store. Pointing to the numerous signs of welcome overhead, he assured me that my honor was fleeting. All would be taken down tomorrow. We then went to the handsome headquarters of Soka Gakkai, the large Buddhist religious group (some 13 million members), to meet Daisaku Ikeda, its leader. With his followers he is a force of considerable power in the East. A hundred or so attractive women were outside and in the halls to welcome us. Our meeting was in the footsteps of such diverse visitors and visited as Chou En-lai, Kissinger, Kosygin, Kurt Waldheim and Arnold Toynbee, not in order of importance. First we had questions and answers over sherry and smoked salmon and then over an elegant Japanese luncheon featuring large and small shrimp cooked in the hollow square of a large rectangular table, a variety of fish and vegetables, beer, saki and Moselle and much else that I failed to notice. The first question was whether I believed in a life after life. I thought I might paraphrase Mencken's answer and say: "No, but if I am wrong, I will walk up to God in a manly way and say, 'Sir, I made an honest mistake.' " Instead I fell back on a more general commitment to continuity and added that I would soon have an opportunity for firsthand investigation. The next question was easier.

"What is happiness?"

"The respect of good men and the affection of lovely women."

We then passed on to practical matters — China, Russia, control of atomic weapons, help to the poor lands, Japan's special responsibilities there. When asked, I asked back; there was little on which to disagree. Ikeda was especially concerned about U.S. relations with China. I urged, as usual, that history would see the hostility between us in the twenty-five years following the Chinese Revolution as an aberration and that even our more compulsive anti-Communists — Henry Jackson, the Committee on the Present Danger — have now made the Chinese Communists honorary non-Bolshevists. The greater danger was from our excessively self-instructed foreign policy wizards — the Milli-Metternichs — who wish to play games as between the Soviets and the Chinese. Useless and dangerous. Ikeda agreed. We also agreed that Nixon and Kissinger deserved a bow for breaking through the crust of opposition on relations with the Soviets and the Chinese. Ikeda then urged me to a deeper Buddhist commitment to life's never-ending stream, to its guidance into a calm and pacific course. This I promised.

In the evening there was a seminar with fifty or sixty Japanese economists and business leaders — "The Theatre of Ideas." A current of anxiety about Japan's future ran, as usual, through the questions. Growth cannot continue at recent rates; what happens when it slows down; what, in effect, are the social tensions when a fixed, not an increasing product must be shared? And what — a familiar note — of the intruding presence and the higher costs of government? One or two speakers cited the inefficiency of Japanese government services, the railroads being an example. In any other country the Japanese railroad system would seem a thing of unbelievable efficiency.

I was pressed on the tax revolt in the United States. I returned the thought that it is a revolt of the affluent, who pay the larger share of the taxes, against the poor, who, in education, police, urban and health services, recreation and welfare, are the most dependent on public services and support. And there is the magic belief of some that taxes and expenditures can be cut and services kept the same. This, I ventured, might not be so.

October 12 — Thursday

Yesterday we called on Mike Mansfield in the new — since my last visit — sparse skyscraper that maintains the American presence. Mike was as agreeable and lovable as ever. We talked of economics. He thinks we will have to come to wage and price controls, as does Jim Rowe, who is visiting Tokyo and the Mansfields. Rowe, a major Washington lawyer, was one of the early, anonymous assistants to F.D.R.

From the Embassy I went to address the International Press Club, an audience of Japanese and overseas correspondents presided over by the local CBS man. There being no problem of translation, it was considerably easier than appearances before Japanese groups, where, because of the interpreter, all humor, all obliquity and especially all irony are a risk.

Then we boarded the subway to the main Tokyo railroad station, guides, photographers, *et al.* accompanying. By car in Tokyo traffic, (as in Bangkok) you either allow an excessive margin of time — an hour or so a mile — or miss the train. Our particular subway was fast, clean and uncrowded. At the station we waited while a crew, five or six to a car, cleaned the train. Departure for Osaka was four or five minutes behind time; we couldn't leave until everything was spotless.

October 13 — Friday

Yesterday morning we drove through the urban jungle of Osaka for several miles, arriving eventually at the headquarters of Matsushita Electric, the largest maker of color television sets in Japan. We then had an hour or so of discussion with Konosuke Matsushita, the eighty-three-year-old founder of the company and of a school of politics and government he is establishing near Tokyo. I was pressed on the experience of the Kennedy School of Government in Cambridge and told him we found politicians quite educable — new congressmen go to the school after election and now also new mayors. It is important to have an admixture of young students with senior and experienced civil servants. Our host thought it possible and important to inculcate an improved level of ethics and a stronger sense of the philosophy of public service. From conversation we advanced to an excellent lunch; I am full of admiration for the chefs employed by Japanese corporations. Then we went on a tour of the plant. Machines stamped some components into the sets; some hundreds of exceptionally tidy, blue-uniformed girls stamped more. Gray-clad young men ran the heavier machines. A five-minute break came, and all did calisthenics. Large overhead signs exhorted everyone to an extra 10 percent. Because of the appreciation of the yen and our restrictions on imports, some production is being shifted to a plant near Chicago. Productivity there is lower "but improving." The American work force does not lend itself to calisthenics.

At around 6:30 P.M., I gave a lecture in a vast hall where the exceptionally diligent had been waiting since three, and it was much better than in Tokyo. If something must be translated into Japanese, the pace must be very slow and the ideas in straightforward form. After dinner with numerous booksellers and book wholesalers we went on by car to Kyoto. We are installed in the Japanese-style pavilion of the Miyako Hotel with four or five rooms, two baths and a bottle of Glenfiddich. Somehow the news spread that I like malt Scotch, which I do much better than it likes me. So a bottle is always waiting. My wife thinks Fitzgerald, Hemingway and Faulkner all went wrong from visiting Japan.

October 14 — Saturday

Yesterday our convoy went to Nara, the ancient eighth-century capital of feudal Japan, or such part as could then be considered subject to central rule. We surveyed a Buddha of giant proportions, which, like one in Hangchow, China, and a third which reclines in Bangkok, is described as the largest in the world. An unseemly competition. The temples were interesting, some of the gardens lovely and the visiting tourists most interesting of all. The latter were uniformed schoolchildren of identical age groupings, all brought thither by bus. They were eager, noisy, disciplined and clean. Discipline suffered severely when I was recognized. Television as ever.

We lunched grandly at a local hotel and made our way back to Kyoto, the journey, as seems always so in Japan, through an endless industrial and residential wasteland. Traffic was just below total stasis. Our guide for the day was an attractive former executive at my publisher's, whom I judge to be as reliable as she is charming. We agreed that Japan combines a commitment to Japanese manners with an obsession with American style. She held that discipline among the young is still fairly strong. In elementary and high schools the desire to get into university remains a major incentive. (In Nara there is a fence where, after writing out one's prayers, one twists them onto the wire. A very large number ask success on examinations and consequent passage into university.) However, sex has been discovered in the high schools; teenage pregnancy is increasing; the pill is not a sufficient antidote; and while drugs are not a problem, the sniffing of paint-thinning fluid is popular. In the universities idleness is fashionable and, as in the United States and especially Europe, extensively identified with reform.

We eventually arrived back in Kyoto and went to an ancient and beautiful house, a several-hundred-year-old place of aristocratic rest and relaxation and a literal dream of flower arrangements, wall paintings and gardens. The tea ceremony was by a *taiyu,* a woman socially several steps above a *geisha.* In past times a *taiyu* might have been the mistress of some major feudatory but with the culture and personal dignity that allowed her to reject a lover of any rank whom she found inadequate in manners or intellect. I liked ours very much. She was magnificently dressed, and two small girls, equally well accoutered, assisted her in the ceremony.

Then we had dinner at Kitcho, described as the best restaurant in Japan. There was no evidence to the contrary. *Geishas* sat at our elbows, anticipated our choice of victuals and then played and danced for us as the meal came to an end.

This morning I had a discussion of various publication matters. At lunch a cook doing the beef in front of us whipped out a book to be autographed. We were fifteen minutes early at the Kyoto station. Before our train arrived — precisely on time — three other express trains arrived and departed on the same track in the same direction. Several locals moved on more distant tracks.

The entire distance from Kyoto to Tokyo, 310 miles by rail, is now urbanized, the hills above the railroad tunnels and a few odd stretches partially apart. Rice lands (and vegetables and some tea) are interspersed, lot by lot, with single family houses, industrial plants, storage yards, junk yards and parking lots. On not everything are the Japanese careful; in a land-scarce country there is a prodigal waste of land.

October 15 — Sunday

After we arrived in Tokyo last night, Tsuru and I had a long recorded conversation of much interest to me and perhaps also to the audience. He thinks the overvaluation of the yen (meaning that it buys more when converted into dollars or other currencies than it does in Japan) will soon bring a shrinkage in Japanese exports, a reduction in the present surplus of exports over imports and some decline in the rate of growth. This means that Japan will not reach the 7 percent expansion in Gross National Product "agreed on" [sic] at a recent meeting of chiefs of state in Bonn. He thinks further that the Japanese economy is maturing rapidly and encountering, in consequence, competition from lower-wage countries. Steel production is beginning to move from Japan to Korea, shipbuilding more so. We agreed that setting growth targets by international conference agreement is a sublime absurdity. It implies far more capacity for economic management than exists. Economic advisers persuade politicians (as they earlier have persuaded themselves) that such goals have meaning. Negotiation then proceeds which is without content or common sense. Neither the public nor the politicians know enough to expose the fraud.

After dinner we went to a small nightclub in the Ginza, the first such resort I've visited in some decades. It is a wholesome place given to music and alcohol "where you can bring your wife." We were joined by some articulate and very wholesome-looking young women in conservative western dress. One singled me out and pressed me on my books. I asked her the source of her excellent and idiomatic English.

"Mostly in bed, but I also studied it in school."

This morning — my birthday — we went to the top of the Okura Hotel for a massive party combining intricate and graceful Japanese ceremony with the singing of "Happy Birthday" and "Auld Lang Syne" and a cake that I cut with a Samurai sword. Then came the long drive out to Narita. Various security procedures preceded another large party. We are now taking off in heavy rainfall, and the pilot has promised rough weather ahead.

October 15 — Sunday (again)

Today, because of the time zones, was also and again October 15. Two birthdays at an age when having one is clinically depressing. After Tokyo, San Francisco looked spacious, leisurely and very dirty.

October 16 — Monday

We slept last night at the Stanford Court, a worthy hotel on Nob Hill, far from inexpensive. This morning the Boston plane is filled with doctors returning from a convention of the American College of Surgeons in San Francisco. Until a short time ago all in adjacent seats and across the aisles thought themselves in a convivial mood. In point of fact, they were obscenely noisy as they shouted greetings and insults to one another across the plane. Eventually I told them with great authority that they were to be quiet. They obeyed. All are now silent, even glum. The chief flight attendant, a tall, personable, slender young woman, just sat down beside me to render warm thanks.

Little more is expected to happen on this journey.

III

The Arts and...

20

Evelyn Waugh

"WE WERE JOINED at lunch by an ungainly and deeply garrulous American who called himself an economist and spoke admiringly of my books and piously of the prospect for socialism and similar depravities in the United States. Eventually I was forced to tell him it was a subject in which I had no interest whatever."

I never met Evelyn Waugh so this entry cannot be found in his diaries.[1] Everything else was calculated to repel me. Except for Randolph Churchill, a couple of the Mitford sisters, a writer or two and one economist, the late Sir Roy Harrod of Oxford, I know or knew none of the people mentioned. Nor did I feel deprived. I learned some years ago that alcohol and barbituates, either separately or in modest combination, interfere with writing and, increasingly as you grow older, make you sick. Accordingly, there was no surprise in Waugh's endless chronicle of inebriation, drugs and their consequences. As an American liberal with impeccable credentials in the faith, I don't like slighting references to Jews, "Negroes" and manual workers, and I don't believe that ever in my life I have actually heard anyone refer to working people as "the lower classes." In the diaries such references abound. My early religious education, if such it can be called, was extensively concerned with the li-

1 *The Diaries of Evelyn Waugh*, edited by Michael Davie (London: Weidenfeld and Nicolson, 1976).

turgical excrescences of the Catholic Church, as we were required to regard them. The virtue of these, at least in their traditional form, was one of the few things in life which Waugh held in unwavering reverence, and they get much attention in his diaries, although considerably less than liquor does.

Yet I read compulsively and from the beginning of the diaries to the end. So, I think, will thousands of others whose knowledge of the people and scene is no greater than mine.

On two matters, his travels and his World War II experiences, Waugh is a serious diarist. He writes well and vividly and gets perceptively into his subject. In consequence, although it is hard to believe that this was his intention, he makes a genuine contribution to the understanding of modern warfare. All who have had even the most marginal association with martial enterprise know the sheer awfulness of having to deal with drunks and incompetents suddenly released from the penalties and constraints of civilian existence and endowed with military swagger and some power. All know the damage they do, the foul-ups they perpetrate and how this behavior and its consequences are diminished in both the histories and the unwritten (as distinct from the American Legion) recollections. This is especially so on the side that won. Waugh's postwar trilogy — *Men at Arms, Officers and Gentlemen, The End of the Battle* — tells this history, but, as with *Catch-22,* one attributes some or much to invention. The diaries, telling of training in Britain, the expedition to Dakar, staging in Egypt, fighting in Greece and his mission with Randolph Churchill to Tito and the partisans, must be the most sustained account of military fecklessness, incoherence, cowardice and intoxication of World War II and maybe any war. There was, no doubt, a more responsible side; Waugh was not one to struggle for even-handed judgment. But anyone with military experience will know how great was the balance to be redressed.

Social purpose, however, is not Waugh's claim to accomplishment — the thought alone is slightly bizarre. His claim, even when telling of aristocratic nonentities, drugs or drunkenness, is in the way he tells it. Many have said it before: there was not in our time, perhaps in our century, such a master of the craft. As a test, one need only open the diaries at random. There is, for example, the name of Ruth Blezard. I have never heard of her, but I learn with immediate delight that she "is a fat woman with ugly hair and a puzzled expression in her eyes" and that her father "is paralysed through evil living" and "her mother [is] a fool." So much for Ruth and her parents. Next day some boys visiting in the Waugh household were "allowed to listen to a concert on the wireless because [the father of one] . . . was singing. It confirmed me in the detestation of the invention." Two days later comes one of the best entries of all: "I think nothing happened." Even the schoolboy passages show signs of the quick, flashing stroke that disposes of everything and everyone.

Somewhere at Harvard, and perhaps also at Cambridge and Oxford, young scholars are dissecting Waugh's sentences, ascertaining, probably with the aid of a computer, the nature of their magic. I await the result without interest. Waugh's art is safely beyond the reach of research.

It leads me to a harsh word in conclusion for the editor of the diaries. Though, I'm sure, a scholar and a gentleman, Mr. Davie, either on his own motion or (more rarely) at the behest of the Waugh estate, felt obliged to delete "libellous" and "offensive" passages as well as other entries that might have caused unnecessary distress. In justification, he cites Waugh's "taste for exaggeration and fantasy" and the resulting danger of misrepresentation. This is trite, blithering nonsense! Is British justice dead? Would any British judge award damages to a plaintiff, otherwise only a titled nullity, who had achieved the supreme distinction of being misrepresented by Evelyn Waugh? The judge, if he has any right to be on the bench, would hold that the plaintiff should pay for being so singled out, so honored. And as to the exaggeration, fantasy and misrepresentation leading to "unnecessary distress," no decently literate person in the English-speaking world can surely believe that because Waugh said something it was true.

One cannot read these diaries without sensing that Waugh's firmest intention was to be nasty, even vicious. No one, I assert, had the right to frustrate so clear a purpose, and certainly not after the author is dead.

21

Anthony Trollope

IN THE MID-NINETEEN-SEVENTIES, the novel came into its own as a medium for highly topical political and behavioral comment, Spiro Agnew, John Lindsay, John Ehrlichman and Ms. Elizabeth Ray, the nontyping friend of former Congressman Wayne Hays, being the principal protagonists. John Ehrlichman, perhaps as an exercise in some obscure form of retributive justice, suffered here from guilt by association. As a writer, he had an excellent sense of scene, could sustain suspense and seemed capable of a substantial exercise of imagination. But his own character, personality and service to Richard Nixon rather than his writing got reviewed by some critics. That for Ehrlichman was not good. One may also be a little unfair to Ms. Ray in associating her with Mr. Agnew. Her book was five times as good as his, for it was only one-fifth as long. Reviewing Mr. Agnew's book, I said that it had "one hell of a plot." I meant it as one would say, "he had one hell of a cold." The publisher seized, nonetheless, on the ambiguity and used the quotation in his advertising for many weeks. I thought of sending a letter of explanation to the Federal Trade Commission.

However, my purpose here is not to discuss the work of these former and soon-to-be-forgotten public servants, if one may speak loosely of some, but to recommend as an alternative the novels of another and earlier public figure, the British postal official Anthony Trollope. I turned to him between Agnew and

Ehrlichman, and not at all by accident. I turn to him constantly when I need some improvement over the present. That time it was to *The Last Chronicle of Barset,* which I consider the best of Trollope's works, as earlier, after rereading *Barchester Towers, Doctor Thorne, The Eustace Diamonds, Orley Farm* and *Phineas Finn,* I had considered each of *them* the best. There is, however, a higher recommendation for *The Last Chronicle.* Of it Trollope said: "Taking it as a whole, I regard this as the best novel I have written."

The Last Chronicle resembles the work of the more modern officials and acolytes in two significant respects. It was written, like everything Trollope did, with an eye to the money. It earned £3000, which, assuming a three-fold deterioration of the pound in relation to the dollar since 1867 and a roughly four-fold deterioration of the dollar, would round out at about $35,000. (Trollope estimated his lifetime earnings from writing at £70,000 or, by the same calculation, around $850,000. The income tax was nominal.) Then as now, though possibly with less reason, obsession with cash was thought inconsistent with the artistic spirit, and Trollope's detailed accounting of his revenues in his *Autobiography* has always been thought one of the things that put him under a cloud for fifty years or so after his death. It's likely that his work habits had more to do with it. "While I was in Egypt, I finished *Doctor Thorne,* and on the following day began *The Bertrams.*" All writers want it thought that a long respite is required between their orgies of effort. Trollope was also merciless in arguing that alcohol is as inimical to writing as to shoemaking. This few wish to believe. Finally, he reminded his colleagues, as I have urged elsewhere, that waiting for inspiration by a writer, the most common of all excuses for indolence, is as absurd as by a "tallow-chandler for the divine moment of melting." All of these beliefs were in conflict with the union rules.

Along with money, Trollope, like the more recent novelists, greatly loved politics. This affection was most strongly manifested in the parliamentary novels, which tell, along with much else, of Plantagenet Palliser's crusade, almost exactly a century ahead of success, to provide the English with a decimal currency. *The Last Chronicle*, however, is also a political novel, it being about clerical politics, and no one should suppose that the most subtle and ruthless practice of this art is to be found in legislatures or bureaucracies. In the early days of his presidency Gerald Ford had no fewer than three Harvard professors — Henry Kissinger, Daniel Patrick Moynihan and John Dunlop — in his Cabinet and, for good measure, another former faculty member, James Schlesinger. Even Mr. Ford must have sensed the unique subtlety, skill and malignity with which these scholars, drawing on their Harvard faculty experience, operated in Washington. And let all recall the exquisite grace with which Kissinger disposed of both Moynihan and Schlesinger.

The opposing clerical factions in Barset were equally accomplished. One was headed by Archdeacon Grantly, the son of the old Bishop, and a very tenacious man with a grudge. The other was captained by Mrs. Proudie, the wife of the present Bishop, an antagonist before whom Bella Abzug would have quailed and surrendered. A seeming curiosity of the political struggle in Barset was that no one quite knew what it was about. The distribution of power was accepted by everyone but Mrs. Proudie. There was patronage, but its dispensation was so crass and flagrant, and also so completely regulated by custom, that there was almost nothing to quarrel over. The Grantly faction was High Church, Mrs. Proudie relentlessly Low, but this conflict never went deeper than approval or disapproval of foxes as distinct from fox-hunting. At Harvard, in years past, I used to think that the major political issue had to do not with appointments, research funds or ideas but with prestige. Did it belong, as a matter of right, to the president of the university, in my time a dutiful, mannered, well-scrubbed gentleman of no scholarly pretense, and those of equally fine bearing who upheld his hand and occupied the offices of presumed distinction in University Hall? Or was prestige properly the possession of the pushy, raucous, less couth figures who found their distinction in their science or subject matter or the world at large? The political struggle in Barset was the same. Maybe it was the genius of Trollope that he saw that politics does not need issues, only competition for esteem.

On one feature, however, no contrivance can produce a parallel between Trollope and the recent political novelists. His characters are unforgettable where those of the modern writers may be as forgettable as any in history. There are three superb people in *The Last Chronicle*. One is the Reverend Septimus Harding, who, in the remunerative sinecure of Warden of Hiram's Hospital, had, years earlier, launched Trollope in Barchester in *The Warden*. The brief chapters on his decline and death in this novel are wonderfully affecting. Then there is Mrs. Proudie, whom Trollope later described as "a tyrant, a bully, a would-be priestess, a very vulgar woman, and one who would send headlong to the nethermost pit all who disagreed with her; but ... conscientious, by no means a hypocrite, really believing in the brimstone which she threatened, and anxious to save the souls around her from its horrors." She too dies in *The Last Chronicle*, suddenly of a heart attack after subjecting the Bishop to terrible humiliation in pursuit of justice and virtue as she sees them. One is at first relieved to see her go but then discovers with sorrow how empty the world has become. That is because Trollope felt the same way. While working on the novel one day in the Atheneum Club in London, he overheard two clerygmen discussing it. (In keeping with contemporary practice, the novel was being serialized as written.) They were giving Mrs. Proudie the business and in very severe terms. Trollope rose, advanced on them and said that, in light of their disapproval, he would promptly kill her off. He delighted in their shock and embarrassment and then almost immediately regretted his promise. This regret he makes the reader share.

But his supreme achievement, perhaps his greatest ever, is the Reverend Josiah Crawley, the perpetual curate (meaning the pathetically underpaid minister) of the poor parish of Hogglestock. Crawley, a most learned man, is a masterwork of psychological conflict. He believes himself to be both greatly superior and deeply inferior to other men. He loves his family and insists on their deprivation and abuse. He demands kindness and sympathy from others and profoundly resents it when they are displayed. On a scale of personal rectitude which would put the Nixon men around zero, the average honest citizen around seventy, Crawley would come in at maybe a hundred and fifty. That is because he is not only relentless and unbending as regards himself, but he is impelled to make everyone else the same. The plot concerns a check which, *in extremis,* he passes on and for the possession of which he cannot account. He comes to believe, because he is too honest to deny the possibility, that in desperation he must have stolen it. So there is a final climactic conflict between Josiah Crawley's view of himself as a paragon of integrity and the seeming fact that he is a thief. With all else, Crawley is given to psychotically depressive episodes and extreme absentmindedness.

As with other of Trollope's characters, Crawley is also incapable of conversation, only of speeches. At the end of the novel, cleared of the charge of theft, he is offered a much more remunerative living.

"And you will accept it — of course?" his lovely daughter asks.

"I know not that, my dear. The acceptance of a cure of souls is a thing not to be decided on in a moment — as is the colour of a garment or the shape of a toy. Nor would I condescend to take this thing from the archdeacon's hands . . ." The speech continues.

The recent political novelists are also great on speeches as a substitute for conversation. Still, Trollope's ending is a document on man's moral progress in the last century. The ending is happy because Crawley proves to be corruptible. He leaves the poor people of Hogglestock and Hoggle End who are devoted to him and where, clearly, his clerical obligation lies, and goes to the higher remuneration and much easier life of suburban St. Ewold. Everyone of importance in Barset is overjoyed. Honesty and duty have yielded to reason and moderation. No recent author has had such a thought.

22

Writing and Typing

NINE OR TEN YEARS AGO, when I was spending a couple of terms at Trinity College, Cambridge, I received a proposal of more than usual interest from the University of California. It was that I take a leave from Harvard and accept a visiting chair in rhetoric at Berkeley. They assured me that rhetoric was a traditional and not, as one would naturally suppose, a pejorative title. My task would be to hold seminars with the young on what I had learned about writing in general and on technical matters in particular.

I was attracted by the idea. I had spent decades attempting to teach the young about economics, and the practical consequences were not reassuring. When I entered the field in the early nineteen-thirties, it was generally known that the modern economy could suffer a serious depression and that it could have a serious inflation. In the ensuing forty years my teaching had principally advanced to the point of telling that it was possible to have both at the same time. This was soon to be associated with the belief of William Simon and Alan Greenspan, the guiding hands of Richard Nixon and Gerald Ford, that progress in this field is measured by the speed of the return to the ideas of the eighteenth century. A subject in which it can be believed that you go ahead by going back has many problems for a teacher. Things are better now. Mr. Carter's economists do not believe in going back. But, as I've elsewhere urged, they are caught in a delicate balance between their fear of inflation and unemployment and their fear of doing anything about them. It is hard to conclude that economics is a productive intellectual and pedagogical investment.

Then I began to consider what I could tell about writing. My experience was certainly ample. I had been initiated by two inspired professors in Canada, O. J. Stevenson and E. C. McLean. They were men who deeply loved their craft and who were willing to spend endless hours with a student, however obscure his talent. I had been an editor of *Fortune*, which in my day meant mostly being a writer. Editor was thought a more distinguished title, and it justified more pay. Both as an editor proper and as a writer, I had had the close attention of Henry Robinson Luce. Harry Luce is in danger of being remembered only for his political judgment, which left much to be desired; he found unblemished merit in John Foster Dulles, Robert A. Taft and Chiang Kai-shek. But more important, he was an acute businessman and a truly brilliant editor. One proof is that while Time, Inc. publications have become politically more predictable since he departed, they have become infinitely less amusing.

Finally, as I reflected on my qualifications, there was the amount of my life that I have spent at a typewriter. Nominally I have been a teacher. In practice I have been a writer — as generations of Harvard students have suspected. Faced with the choice of spending time on the unpublished scholarship of a graduate student or the unpublished work of Galbraith, I have rarely hesitated. Superficially at least, I was well qualified for that California chair.

There was, however, a major difficulty. It was that I could tell everything I knew about writing in approximately half an hour. For the rest of the term I would have nothing to say except as I could invite discussion, this being the last resort of the distraught academic mind. I could use up a few hours telling how a writer should deal with publishers. This is a field of study in which I especially rejoice. All authors should seek to establish a relationship of warmth, affection and mutual mistrust with their publishers in the hope that the uncertainty will add, however marginally, to compensation. But instruction on how to deal with publishers and how to bear up under the inevitable defeat would be for a very advanced course. It is not the sort of thing that the average beginning writer at Berkeley would find immediately practical.

So I returned to the few things that I could teach. The first lesson would have had to do with the all-important issue of inspiration. All writers know that on some golden mornings they are touched by the wand; they are on intimate terms with poetry and cosmic truth. I have experienced those moments myself. Their lesson is simple; they are a total illusion. And the danger in the illusion is that you will wait for them. Such is the horror of having to face the typewriter that you will spend all your time waiting. I am persuaded that, hangovers apart, most writers, like most other artisans, are about as good one day as the next (a point that Trollope made). The seeming difference is the result of euphoria, alcohol or imagination. All this means that one had better go to his or her typewriter every morning and stay there regardless of the result. It will be much the same.

All professions have their own way of justifying laziness. Harvard professors are deeply impressed by the jeweled fragility of their minds. Like the thinnest metal, these are subject terribly to fatigue. More than six hours of teaching a week is fatal — and an impairment of academic freedom. So, at any given moment, the average professor is resting his mind in preparation for the next orgiastic act of insight or revelation. Writers, by the same token, do nothing because they are waiting for inspiration.

In my own case there are days when the result is so bad that no fewer than five revisions are required. However, when I'm greatly inspired, only four are needed before, as I've often said, I put in that note of spontaneity which even my meanest critics concede. My advice to those eager students in California would have been, "Don't wait for the golden moment. Things may well be worse."

I would also have warned against the flocking tendency of writers and its use as a cover for idleness. It helps greatly in the avoidance of work to be in the company of others who are also waiting for the golden moment. The best place to write is by yourself because writing then becomes an escape from the terrible boredom of your own personality. It's the reason that for years I've favored Switzerland, where I look at the telephone and yearn to hear it ring.

The question of revision is closely allied with that of inspiration. There may be inspired writers for whom the first draft is just right. But anyone who is not certifiably a Milton had better assume that the first draft is a very primitive thing. The reason is simple: writing is difficult work. Ralph D. Paine, who managed *Fortune* in my time, used to say that anyone who said writing was easy was either a bad writer or an unregenerate liar. Thinking, as Voltaire avowed, is also a very tedious process which men or women will do anything to avoid. So all first drafts are deeply flawed by the need to combine composition with thought. Each later one is less demanding in this regard; hence the writing can be better. There does come a time when revision is for the sake of change — when one has become so bored with the words that anything that is different looks better. But even then it may *be* better.

For months when I was working on *The Affluent Society,* my title was "The Opulent Society." Eventually I could stand it no longer; the word opulent had a nasty, greasy sound. One day, before starting work, I looked up the synonyms in the dictionary. First to meet my eye was the word "affluent." I had only one worry; that was whether I could possibly sell it to my publisher. All publishers wish to have books called *The Crisis in American Democracy*. The title, to my surprise, was acceptable. Mark Twain once said that the difference between the right word and almost the right word is the difference between lightning and a lightning bug.

Next, I would have stressed a rather old-fashioned idea — brevity — to those students. It was, above all, the lesson of Harry Luce. No one who worked for him ever again escaped the feeling that he was there looking over one's shoulder. In his hand was a pencil; down on each page one could expect, at any moment, a long swishing wiggle accompanied by the comment: "This can go." Invariably it could. It was written to please the author and not the reader. Or to fill in the space. The gains from brevity are obvious; in most efforts to achieve it, the worst and the dullest go. And it is the worst and the dullest that spoil the rest.

I know that brevity is now out of favor. The *New York Review of Books* prides itself on giving its authors as much space as they want and sometimes twice as much as they need. Writing for television, on the other hand, as I've learned in the last few years, is an exercise in relentless condensation. It has left me with the feeling that even brevity can be carried to extremes. But the danger, as I look at some of the newer fashions in writing, is not great.

The next of my injunctions, which I would have imparted with even less hope of success, would have concerned alcohol. Nothing is so pleasant. Nothing is so important for giving the writer a sense of confidence in himself. And nothing so impairs the product. Again there are exceptions: I remember a brilliant writer at *Fortune* for whom I was responsible who could work only with his hat on and after consuming a bottle of Scotch. There were major crises for him in the years immediately after World War II when Scotch was difficult to find. But it is, quite literally, very sobering to reflect on how many good American writers have been destroyed by this solace — by the sauce. Scott

Fitzgerald, Sinclair Lewis, Thomas Wolfe, Ernest Hemingway, William Faulkner — the list goes on and on. Hamish Hamilton, once my English publisher, put the question to James Thurber: "Jim, why is it so many of your great writers have ruined themselves with drink?" Thurber thought long and carefully and finally replied, "It's this way, Jamie. They wrote those novels, which sold very well. They made a lot of money and so they could buy whisky by the case."

Their reputation was universal. A few years before his death, John Steinbeck, an appreciative but not a compulsive drinker, went to Moscow. It was a triumphal tour, and in a letter that he sent me about his hosts, he said: "I found I enjoyed the Soviet hustlers pretty much. There was a kind of youthful honesty about their illicit intentions that was not without charm." I later heard that one night, after a particularly effusive celebration, he decided to return to the hotel on foot. On the way he was overcome by fatigue and the hospitality he had received and sat down on a bench in a small park to rest. A policeman, called a militiaman in Moscow, came along and informed John, who was now asleep, and his companion, who spoke Russian, that the benches could not be occupied at that hour. His companion explained, rightly, that John was a very great American writer and that an exception should be made. The militiaman insisted. The companion explained again and insisted more strongly. Presently a transcendental light came over the policeman's face. He looked at Steinbeck asleep on the bench, inspected his condition more closely, recoiled slightly from the fumes and said, "Oh, oh, Gemingway." Then he took off his cap and tiptoed carefully away.

We are all desperately afraid of sounding like Carrie Nation. I must take the risk. Any writer who wants to do his best against a deadline should stick to Coca-Cola.

Next, I would have wanted to tell my students of a point strongly pressed, if my memory serves, by George Bernard Shaw.

He once said that as he grew older, he became less and less interested in theory, more and more interested in information. The temptation in writing is just the reverse. Nothing is so hard to come by as a new and interesting fact. Nothing is so easy on the feet as a generalization. I now pick up magazines and leaf through them looking for articles that are rich with facts; I don't much care what they are. Evocative and deeply percipient theory I avoid. It leaves me cold unless I am the author of it myself. My advice to all young writers would be to stick to research and reporting with only a minimum of interpretation. And even more this would be my advice to all older writers, particularly to columnists. As one's feet give out, one seeks to have the mind take their place.

Reluctantly, but from a long and terrible experience, I would have urged my class to recognize the grave risks in a resort to humor. It does greatly lighten one's task. I've often wondered who made it impolite to laugh at one's own jokes, for it is one of the major enjoyments in life. And that is the point. Humor is an intensely personal, largely internal thing. What pleases some, including the source, does not please others. One laughs; another says, "Well, I certainly see nothing funny about that." And the second opinion has just as much validity as the first, maybe more. Where humor is concerned, there are no standards — no one can say what is good or bad, although you can be sure that everyone will. Only a very foolish man will use a form of language that is wholly uncertain in its effect. And that is the nature of humor.

There are other reasons for avoiding humor. In our society the solemn person inspires far more trust than the one who laughs. The politician allows himself one joke at the beginning of his speech. A ritual. Then he changes his expression and affects an aspect of morbid solemnity signaling that, after all, he is a totally serious man. Nothing so undermines a point as its association with a wisecrack; the very word is pejorative.

Also, as Art Buchwald has pointed out, we live in an age when it is hard to invent anything that is as funny as everyday life; how could one improve, for example, on the efforts of the great men of television to attribute cosmic significance to the offhand and hilarious way Bert Lance combined professed fiscal conservatism with an unparalleled personal commitment to the deficit financing of John Maynard Keynes? And because the real world is so funny, there is almost nothing you can do, short of labeling a joke a joke, to keep people from taking it seriously. A number of years ago in *Harper's* I invented the theory that socialism in our time was the result of our dangerous addiction to team sports. The ethic of the team is all wrong for free enterprise. Its basic themes are cooperation; team spirit; acceptance of leadership; the belief that the coach is always right. Authoritarianism is sanctified; the individualist is a poor team player, a menace. All this our vulnerable adolescents learn. I announced the formation of an organization to combat this deadly trend and to promote boxing and track instead. I called it the CAI — Crusade for Athletic Individualism. Scores wrote in to *Harper's* asking to join. Or demanding that baseball be exempted. A batter is, after all, on his own. I presented the letters to the Kennedy Library.

Finally, I would have come to a matter of much personal interest, one that is intensely self-serving. It concerns the peculiar pitfalls for the writer who is dealing with presumptively difficult or technical matters. Economics is an example, and within the field of economics the subject of money, with the history of which I have been much concerned, is an especially good case. Any specialist who ventures to write on money with a view to making himself intelligible works under a grave moral hazard. He will be accused of oversimplification. The charge will be made by his fellow professionals, however obtuse or incompetent, and it will have a sympathetic hearing from the layman. That is because no layman really expects to understand about money, inflation or the International Monetary Fund. If he does, he suspects that he is being fooled. Only someone who is decently confusing can be respected.

In the case of economics there are no important propositions that cannot, in fact, be stated in plain language. Qualifications and refinements are numerous and of great technical complexity. These are important for separating the good students from the dolts. But in economics the refinements rarely, if ever, modify the essential and practical point. The writer who seeks to be intelligible needs to be right; he must be challenged if his argument leads to an erroneous conclusion and especially if it leads to the wrong action. But he can safely dismiss the charge that he has made the subject too easy. The truth is not difficult.

Complexity and obscurity, on the other hand, have professional value; they are the academic equivalents of apprenticeship rules in the building trades. They exclude the outsiders, keep down the competition, preserve the image of a privileged or priestly class. The man who makes things clear is a scab. He is criticized less for his clarity than for his treachery.

Additionally, and especially in the social sciences, much unclear writing is based on unclear or incomplete thought. It is possible with safety to be technically obscure about something you haven't thought out. It is impossible to be wholly clear on something you don't understand; clarity exposes flaws in the thought. The person who undertakes to make difficult matters clear is infringing on the sovereign right of numerous economists, sociologists and political scientists to make bad writing the disguise for sloppy, imprecise or incomplete thought. One can understand the resulting anger. Adam Smith, John Stuart Mill and John Maynard Keynes were writers of crystalline clarity most of the time. Marx had great moments, as in *The Communist Manifesto*. Economics owes very little, if anything, to the practitioners of scholarly obscurity. However, if any of my California students had come to me from the learned professions, I would have counseled them that if they wanted to keep the confidence of their colleagues, they should do so by always being complex, obscure and even a trifle vague.

You might say that all this constitutes a meager yield for a lifetime of writing. Or perhaps, as someone once said of Jack Kerouac's prose, not writing but typing.

23

John Bartlow Martin
and Adlai Stevenson

IN THE SUMMER OF 1952, not long after the Democratic Convention in Chicago had nominated Adlai Stevenson, a young *Saturday Evening Post* writer with a reputation for detailed, meticulous and far from abbreviated reporting showed up at the Stevenson campaign headquarters in Springfield, Illinois. He was John Bartlow Martin. Presently he moved from the press office to a literary ghetto that had been established on top of the Springfield Elks Club. Here he became one of Stevenson's best speech writers and certainly his most reliable. His specialty was the short five- or ten-minute airport or whistle-stop address; no one then, and I think no one since, could make a point more succinctly, support it more sharply with evidence and then, surprisingly for him, stop. Martin repeated the performance in 1956, and, as late as 1972, while intense younger colleagues at campaign headquarters were resolving the difficult questions of personnel and policy to be faced by their new president following the election, he was doing the same thing for George McGovern.

During the Kennedy-Johnson years Martin was ambassador to the Dominican Republic, an exceptionally awkward assignment in the aftermath of Trujillo. By then he was already writing a biography of Adlai Stevenson.[1] In this work, now published, he retains the view (which we shared during Stevenson's life) that Stevenson was a greatly misunderstood figure mostly because he relentlessly and imaginatively cultivated such misunderstanding. Martin's biography is really a discovery of Adlai Stevenson. He also brings to his work an encyclopedic and horrifying knowledge of Chicago and Illinois politics and a firsthand knowledge of the people and the scene. He is without malice or meanness, but friendship is never allowed to do down a fact. And he has a nearly uncontrollable delight in detail. He has given it full rein on Stevenson's parents, family, friends, women friends, political allies and foes, and has organized it all into a far more coherent and interesting story than anyone would have thought possible. Some writers take many words to say little; John Bartlow Martin takes many words, but fewer than would be supposed, to say everything.

One learns that Stevenson's father was interested in getting the Zeppelin franchise for the United States; that Adlai's exact salary in law practice was $1450 in 1927 and rose countercyclically to $4847 in 1932; that in the Agricultural Adjustment Administration, before deductions, it was $6500 (more than twice mine as an economist in the same agency at almost the same time); and that, unsullied by prior love, he was married at 4 P.M. on December 1, 1928, in a Presbyterian chapel on the Chicago Gold Coast with a seating capacity of thirty people, the walls of which were covered with greenery. Those who know Martin know that most likely he spent several days trying to track down the particular kind of plant or tree that made the green and was desolate when he failed.

But this essay is not about Martin's history but the man it discovers, for Adlai Stevenson was a compulsive role-player. He presented himself to the world and equally to his friends as he

[1] *Adlai Stevenson of Illinois* (New York: Doubleday, 1976) and *Adlai Stevenson and the World* (New York: Doubleday, 1977).

liked to believe he was. There was a public and a private Stevenson. The real service of Martin's relentless accumulation of fact is in penetrating this extraordinary screen.

Thus, for millions of his admirers, Stevenson was a lonesome, brooding intellectual — a man who made up his mind only after long struggle and then remained uncertain in his view. He loved the image — there all by himself, buffeted by the conflicting evidence and argument. What could he do?

But none of this was so. Stevenson was greatly gregarious. He rejoiced in company, admiration and an audience and hated to be alone. Night or day he rarely was. John F. Kennedy was thought to be much in the arms of his mistresses. He was, I'm persuaded, a Gandhian ascetic as compared with Adlai Stevenson. There were other odd contrasts. Stevenson the brooding intellectual hardly ever read a book. Kennedy, with no similar reputation, was a voracious reader; he accomplished at least twenty books to Stevenson's one.

Stevenson's reputation for indecision was also carefully cultivated. He gave his finest demonstrations of searching self-doubt when he had already made up his mind — as all with a different view eventually discovered. On small matters, such as whether to go out to dinner or a party, he could be endlessly troubled, although in the end he almost always went. On important matters, though he was responsive to opposing views, it was only rarely and very gradually to the point of changing his own.

The thespian Stevenson was at his best on the American political and campaign scene. There he presented himself as a harried and driven figure made to do things that were unnatural to his character or disastrous to his career, of which the most notable case, of course, was his draft by the Democrats in 1952. Later from his campaign plane came a stream of letters to friends, most of them to Alicia Patterson (whom he called Elisha), telling of the indignities to which he was subject, his doubts as to whether it would ever be over. As Martin tells (and as those who were with him knew), Stevenson, after protesting the political show, always acquiesced, and beneath all he greatly liked coming into town to the music of the high school band. There is more than a hint in Martin that, for at least a year before the Chicago convention, he had his thoughts on the nomination. Maybe he saw or sensed that reluctance was precisely the thing that would set him apart from the other contenders. No reluctance in later years kept him from being other than extremely available for the United Nations delegation, State Department employment or the Illinois senatorial nomination.

A greater mystery surrounds Stevenson's economic and political views. Here there is a genuine question as to his beliefs, whether he was a liberal or a conservative. He did have a stalwart commitment to civil liberties in a difficult time. But he had an equally solid commitment to the American class structure — specifically to a privileged and affluent elite of which he was happily a member. In 1952, he had grave doubts about unions. And he regarded Keynesian economics, to the extent that he understood it, as a transparently spurious alibi for a sloppy management of public finances. He had given no attention to any matter seriously related to economic policy since his undergraduate days at Princeton. There he had been exposed to a rigorously primitive version of classical economic theory.

Martin tells of Willard Wirtz, later Secretary of Labor under Kennedy, and Carl McGowan, now a judge of the Circuit Court of Appeals, struggling with the text of Stevenson's Labor Day speech in Detroit in 1952. So, for some troubled days, did I. Our problem was that Stevenson was basically in sympathy with the Taft-Hartley Act, then for the unions the symbol of all capitalist repression. There was no chance that he would urge repeal; the question was how far he would go in criticizing it. In what we regarded as a triumph, he came to Cadillac Square and advocated not the repeal but the *replacement* of the act. Our triumph pleased almost no one.

This willingness to yield, however reluctantly, to persuasion leads Martin (as it much earlier led McGowan) to argue that Stevenson's conservatism was also a pose. He was a liberal, but he did not wish to seem, even to himself, a man of catatonic response. He had to be persuaded, but he could be persuaded. After the 1952 campaign a series of seminars were held, with Adlai as the student, in Thomas Finletter's apartment in New York. These modernized his views even on economics.

I'm less sure than Martin as to the extent of this persuasion. I continue to think that the conservative vein was rather strong and that it was disguised by Stevenson's talent for insisting on his case with skill, charm and great good humor. Martin tells of Stevenson's return to Springfield after his first swing through the West in 1952. At a meeting that evening he warned those of us there that he was being pressed too far to the left by his staff; the time had come to get back — his words — squarely to the middle of the road. Incredibly, for nothing else is omitted, Martin fails to tell the rest of the story. David Bell, a liberal Truman aide, the Director of the Budget under Kennedy and now a high official of the Ford Foundation, was acting as chief of Stevenson's research and speech-writing staff. He protested, "You had a great response to your speech in Los Angeles, Governor."

Stevenson surveyed Bell sternly for a moment. (The speech had been to a large political rally.) "That crowd, David, would have applauded if I had advocated pissing on the floor." Then sensing that he might have bruised the man's feelings, he quickly added, "But that's something we should be for. Let's get it into future speeches."

One part of Stevenson's personality was always rightly read. He was a man of kindness, sensitivity and fun. And this, in turn, disposes of another misconception. Stevenson's marriage failed; he tried twice for the presidency and failed; he ended his life serving at the United Nations under a Secretary of State who was infinitely his inferior in stature and wisdom. It has been said that his was a disappointing life — indeed, a tragedy. That is far from the truth. Adlai Stevenson enjoyed both the campaigns. His personal life was rich in friendship. There was never a day without mirth — when something ridiculous didn't catch his eye and give him joy. There was no Stevenson tragedy. If there is to be sorrow, it must be for the country that didn't use him more wisely.

IV

...the Dubious Arts

24

Last Word on the Hiss Case?

FOR ANYONE born after 1940, the Alger Hiss case must be a major puzzle. There is the question of how he could have been considered guilty. Both the prosecution and the associated persecution were led by Richard Nixon. With such an enemy it's hard to suppose that Hiss could have done much that was wrong.

And there is even deeper wonder about why so much was made of the case, something contemporaries of Hiss and Chambers must themselves ask. Alger Hiss was a middle-level figure in the New Deal pantheon. He did not remotely rank with Haldeman, Ehrlichman, Mitchell, Kleindienst or Helms, the truly powerful malefactors in the later Nixon era, and perhaps not much above Chuck Colson. In the Roosevelt years a sharp distinction was made between routine functionaries and those called the Real New Dealers. At least by the war years Hiss was no longer a Real New Dealer. By many of his contemporaries he was thought polite, diligent but cautious, and somewhat of a stuffed shirt.

There was proof in his employment. When first hit by the House Un-American Activities Committee, he had just become president of the Carnegie Endowment for International Peace. The practical services of this organization to peace over the years have been one of the best-kept secrets of American life. The chairman of its board of trustees was then John Foster Dulles, and no one will now believe this meant a major commitment to

reducing great power tensions, avoiding dangerous brinkman-
ship or otherwise promoting international comity and tranquillity. The Endowment has, for long, in fact, been a highly reputable refuge for admirably respectable people lacking gainful
employment in the field of foreign policy. (There is never any
noticeable leadership, let alone any passion, for limiting arms
sales, the SALTs or countering the propaganda of the compulsive warriors.) Hiss had been at Yalta in a routine capacity, at
San Francisco in a more responsible administrative role, and he
had a moment of singular glory when he was pictured carrying
the United Nations Charter back to Washington or wherever.
But he was principally important because of his friends, a point
to which I will return.

If Alger Hiss was an accidental choice for historical eminence,
Jay Vivian (called by himself Whittaker) Chambers was an incredible one. In an age when Allen Dulles could accomplish
the Gary Powers U-2 disaster and the Bay of Pigs fiasco within
a year of one another, and E. Howard Hunt could, in one lifetime, mastermind both the Bay of Pigs and the Watergate operation (as well as the work on Dr. Fielding's office), we have
learned not to expect much of secret operatives.[1] But even by
such relaxed standards the selection of Whittaker Chambers by
the Soviets for that kind of work was luminously insane. His
past relation to the American Communist Party (where he had
shown sympathy for the Lovestone heresy) was one of demonstrated unreliability. He was dangerously romantic and even
more dangerously given to self-glorification. After he went underground, he surfaced at frequent intervals to let his non-
Communist friends, most of them of compulsive literary habit,
know of his exciting way of life. And he was otherwise incapable
of accepting discipline.

I knew Alger Hiss slightly in the late war and postwar years.
I don't remember meeting Chambers, but I heard much of him,

[1] See a later essay, "The Global Strategic Mind."

for he was an editor at *Time* when I was, more briefly, one at *Fortune*. After Harry Luce, Whittaker Chambers was one of the major subjects of conversation in the community. People spoke of his literary ability and learning with awe, and his politics, then far to the right and paranoiacally anti-Communist, with dismay. He was often described as a little crazy.

Alger Hiss was charged not with espionage nor with being a Communist but with perjury for denying such matters. In the second of two major trials he was found guilty. While not everyone will ever be satisfied, Allen Weinstein, in his long-awaited book,[2] has gone as far as any historian could to establish the formal validity of the verdict. He has pursued witnesses to Hungary and Israel, information to estates, libraries and lawyers and into the files of the FBI. His treatment of the resulting material strikes one as both judicious and properly skeptical; he writes of it with clarity and restraint.

For many, the best Hiss defense was the suggestion that Chambers and the FBI had forged the typed documents by which he was convicted. This was accomplished, the defense suggested, by getting access to the Hiss typewriter or, when this seemed too improbable, by building another machine with the same idiosyncrasies of type. Weinstein tells that a major effort was indeed mounted by Hiss's lawyers to duplicate the typewriter to show that it could be done. The effort failed.

For what it may be worth, I years ago concluded (as, I expect, did numerous other liberals) that to believe Hiss truthful was to strain the liberal faith too far. Only a conclusion that he had lied under oath would fit the vast and incredibly diverse and interlocking array of evidence. Weinstein has added greatly to the facts, and they force one to the same conclusion.

He has also caught without emphasis or false drama the mood of the time, of the trials that were so tensely watched, and also

2 *Perjury: The Hiss-Chambers Case* (New York: Knopf, 1978).

of the hyperbole and the red-baiting by the Hiss defense. Lloyd Paul Stryker, who led it, said of his client, "Though I would go into the valley of the shadow of death I will fear no evil, because there is no blot or blemish on him." And of Chambers he said that he was for "twelve long years . . . a voluntary conspirator against the land that I love and you love. He got his bread from the band of criminals with whom he confederated and conspired."

Professor Weinstein's contribution, then, is major, and I would say definitive. When one has lived with people and events and then later reads accounts of them, one almost invariably notices slips in the handling of initials, names, geography and minor happenings. It's a measure of Weinstein's competence that those who were around at the time will find few such errors in his book. There has been complaint that he misreported conversations with some of his sources. Perhaps he did, although people can alter their memory as to what they said. But, in any case, this complaint does not speak to the substance of his case.

So he has resolved one of the problems of the early middle-aged and young. To have Nixon as an accuser does not make one whole. Because it was not part of his task, Weinstein does not answer the other question: why did the case cause such an enormous fuss?

Communists were not remarkable in the nineteen-thirties. To be immune to doubts as to the excellence and success of capitalism in that dismal decade was to be unusually insensitive to the world around. For those who thought they responded to an uncluttered, unfearful, forthright mind, Communism was the obvious answer. Yet their numbers were always insignificant. By the time of the Hiss trials, it required a certain susceptibility to paranoia to believe that Communism was a serious force in the United States, its position in a few unions possibly apart.

Espionage would seem a more serious matter. But dozens of spies have since been arrested without achieving any similar distinction. Klaus Fuchs, the physicist and atom spy, was obviously a far more serious operator than Hiss, and, by comparison, he is now nearly forgotten. And it's a genuinely important as well as a much neglected point that Hiss spied at a time when there were almost no secrets. Few things can be so bad for espionage as a government in which everything is known. Much of what he passed on to Chambers for the Russians could have been had for the asking; more of it could have been had by listening to any one of the evening discussions that were compulsive in those days with those who were saving the country. I knew Washington well in the thirties and from within the government, and I can't remember ever having seen a paper stamped secret or hearing of materials so described.

In 1941, with the war at a critical point in Europe and our own participation imminent, my wife and I were visited in Washington by an Oxford-trained German friend named Jochem Carton, in later years the respected head of an important Montreal shipping company. He went one day to eat and drink with Rhodes Scholar friends and on the way back to our house felt urgent need for a men's room. He turned from Pennsylvania Avenue into the State, War and Navy Departments (now the Executive Office Building) and, inside, seeing an unlocked slatted door — a singular feature of the interior architecture of that aristocratic pile at the time — took it to be a toilet. It was, instead, an office, empty and with papers strewn over the desk. He tried the next door with the same result. Eventually he came to a door, this of solid wood, which did protect a toilet. That night he held forth on his experience with some vehemence; though an anti-Nazi who had recently become a British subject, he observed with emphasis that, with war in the offing, he was also about to become an ex-enemy alien. Such casualness, he thought, was incredible.

The wife of a onetime Soviet operative in the United States said of Washington during that period that one could have worn a placard proclaiming oneself a spy and not aroused the police.

What Hiss and Chambers were up to, Josephine Herbst, the novelist, thought, was "busy work," invented to engage the energies of the New Deal converts to Communism in a seemingly useful way. In fact, until well along in the thirties, the Russians in charge of covert operations in the United States did not think that Hiss or others similarly situated had any secrets that were worth the trouble. So the question remains: why the fuss?

It was partly, as many have said, that Hiss was a way of flogging F.D.R., the New Deal and the liberal Democrats. Numerous right-wingers had believed all of them subversive; the exposure of Hiss as a Communist and as a spy usefully affirmed the point. His exposure and conviction were also seen as a way of forcing a harder line on domestic radicals and toward Russia. But F.D.R. wasn't really in the line of fire. Nor were the New Dealers, many of whom were still in office. Nor, in any real sense, was the Democratic Party. At the most, the trials only stimulated the anti-Communist hysteria and witch hunts.

A further and better explanation concerns my fellow liberals and their anxieties. Allen Weinstein believes that Alger Hiss had divided his life into two compartments: on the one hand, he was the activist radical committed to world revolution as then perceived; on the other, he was the disciplined, motivated careerist, eager to be socially acceptable and a figure in what was soon to be called the Establishment. (Whittaker Chambers, it could be imagined, had a similar double existence: he was, at once, the romantic underground revolutionary and the learned, highly independent, compulsively articulate intellectual.) For what it may be worth, I have always imagined that there was an easier explanation of Alger Hiss: he was strongly subject to the fashions of his time, and, when disaster struck, he was in transition from the fashionable radicalism of the thirties to the prestigious foreign-policy establishment views of the postwar years, the Marshall Plan and the Cold War.

In either case, when Hiss came before the HUAC and to trial, he felt it necessary to deny his past. And the war and the post-war tensions with Stalin had given that past a seemingly new and greatly ominous dimension. Communism was now categorically wicked. Secrets, as the result of the war and the bomb, had become secrets indeed, and their security was now a ruling passion in Washington. Espionage had come in from the cold and was now called treason.

In the post-Watergate years, numerous politicians and corporation executives complained that once commonplace actions were now being judged by the post-Watergate morality. It was a defense for which Alger Hiss could have wished. And had he used it, it is interesting to reflect, he would have escaped. If, when he was first before Committee Chairman J. Parnell Thomas (soon himself to go to jail), Richard Nixon (eventually to be rescued by pardon) and the other exponents of the new Cold War morality, he had acknowledged that he knew Chambers and told of his strong Communist sympathies in the dark days of the thirties, of his fear of Hitler and fascism, of his consequent if deeply questionable help to the Soviets in pursuit of these beliefs, there would have been a major four-day furor. But when it subsided, he would probably still have been resting innocuously at the Carnegie Endowment.

But, instead, he agreed that the behavior of which he was accused was terrible, even unforgivable. This Lloyd Paul Stryker loudly proclaimed. Thus he denied his past. Since anyone, and especially a public official, leaves large tracks through life, such a denial can only be sustained by further improvisation. And this must be sustained by yet further lies. The task is of exponential difficulty, and the end, if pursued, is inevitable. Both Alger Hiss and Richard Nixon, his self-proclaimed nemesis, succumbed to the ruthless geometry of covering up the cover-up of a cover-up.

It was his condemnation of the actions of which he was accused and the denial that have given the Hiss case its impact. There weren't many liberals in the late forties who had been

Communists, and in the absence of secrets there were few Communists who would have been useful sources of information for the Soviets. But most liberals had *something* in their past — friends, suspect organizations, support for Loyalist Spain, sympathy for the Soviet experiment or a strong commitment to the wartime alliance with Russia and the hope that it would last. When Alger Hiss agreed that any such association was treasonable and otherwise totally reprehensible, he spoke for their past life as well. A whole generation of liberals was made to feel vulnerable. What most had to admit or deny, in the light of the new morality, was not very much. But, unlike Hiss, they would not have Justices Felix Frankfurter and Stanley Reed, Dean Acheson, William Marbury (for many years of the Harvard Corporation), Stryker and a half-dozen other great and famous lawyers as supporters, counsel or friends. If one so supported was threatened, who, however less his aberration, could be safe? And as the loyalty probes and investigations got under way and the blacklists proliferated, there was ample evidence that quite a few weren't safe. Additionally, by this time, a further few had, like Hiss, asserted, often with some indignation, that they, of all people, had never had a remotely pro-Communist thought, had never done anything even vaguely inimical to the sacred principles of free enterprise. They had also accepted a standard of past behavior by which they could themselves be impeached.

Here was the source of the interest, more precisely the anxiety, that made the Hiss case endure. It lived because thousands of intellectuals, reflecting on their past sympathies, actions or organizations, found themselves personally involved with it. And quite a few, by their disavowals, had set themselves up for similar assault, similarly provided themselves with glass jaws and, in consequence, were spending uncomfortable days praying, in most cases successfully, that they wouldn't be hit.

25

Bernard Cornfeld: Benefactor

PEOPLE ONCE BELIEVED that, given the lessons of the Great Crash and the Great Depression and the ministrations of the SEC, the days of truly fine financial levitation — on the scale of Ivar Kreuger as distinct from Bobby Baker — were over. Dull morality had set in. I had half thought so myself. It isn't so. Fools and their money can still be parted on as magnificent a scale as ever before. And with a certain artistry, as the story of Bernie Cornfeld proves.

Investors Overseas Services, IOS for short, was his command ship for a convoy of mutual funds, firms to manage mutual funds, firms to sell mutual funds, banks and insurance companies (including some shadowy financial figments that were so designated) and other more ethereal entities, all the brainwork of a Harvard-trained lawyer named Edward Cowett. Old Harvard men can take him as proof that we haven't been turning out only radicals; we still produce a very imaginative class of free enterpriser. The IOS mutual funds, which included the Fund of Funds which invested in other funds (although the other funds turned out, incestuously, to be mostly IOS funds), were sold by a sales staff that was orchestrated by another big operator named Allen Cantor. Statesmen of no slight distinction — James Roosevelt, once an excellent congressman; Sir Eric Wyndham White, a distinguished international civil servant and the longtime head of GATT; Erich Mende, once Vice

Chancellor of the German Federal Republic — graced the board, to their intense subsequent regret. It is said in their defense, and I think with truth, that they had no very accurate view of what was going on upstairs. Conducting was Bernard Cornfeld himself. The birth, rise and fall of IOS extended almost exactly over the decade of the sixties. Billions of dollars were extracted from the aspiring citizens of a dozen or more countries, with particular emphasis on Germany. (IOS resolved, in a manner of speaking, the old question of whether the Germans should pay World War II reparations.) One's sorrow for those who lost is tempered by the thought that so many suffered for their own cupidity.

For the rise of IOS was a testament to the continuing power of greed when reinforced by massive gullibility and a certain amount of spare cash. The warning signs were ample. It is elementary that no one should be trusted with money who does not convey, on all public occasions, an aspect of extreme solemnity. In behavior and general appearance, Bernie Cornfeld inspired somewhat less confidence than John Lennon, although more than Abbie Hoffman. Edward Cowett brought to the presidency of IOS a background of proven financial misadventure that would have seemed alarming to the late Samuel Insull. IOS was not allowed to do business in the United States, and eventually the SEC went so far as to extract from it a promise not to sell securities to any American citizen anywhere in the world. This far-reaching act of financial paternalism was well known. In 1966, Brazil, usually a fiscally tolerant jurisdiction, took numerous IOS salesmen off to the slammer for questioning. This completed, IOS was kicked out of the country. The organization was recurrently in trouble with the Swiss, who are also tolerant, and eventually it had to move its office operations from Geneva to a dismal village just across the border in France. Among other things, the Swiss took exception to an effort by IOS to pass a good part of its office staff off as students at the University of Geneva in order to get them work permits.

Yet IOS salesmen promised to make people rich, and people believed it and they bought and bought and bought. It was characteristic of the sixties, no doubt, that IOS professed some very elevated motives, such as bringing capitalism (the capital, not the exploitation) to the masses. And while it served extensively as a device for squirreling money out of the less developed countries and into some of the least promising of American enterprises, it pictured itself as a powerful instrument of enlightened economic development. People who did not lose money will be relieved to know that capitalism still functions according to the old rules. If Cornfeld and Cowett had, indeed, been the instruments of spiritual and moral regeneration, a great many other assumptions about capitalism, capitalists and their motivation would require revision, and Gideon Bibles would be enclosed with annual statements.

In fact, IOS was a gigantic sales organization operating at very high pressure. And that was about all. Its salesmen not only sold the funds (or more precisely, undertakings to buy into the funds over a period of years), but they also sold other salesmen on the idea of selling funds. So, in time, a salesman graduated from collecting commissions on his own sales to collecting on the sales of those whom he had sold on selling. And then with more expansion he would collect on the sales of those who were collecting on the sales of those who had sold yet others on selling. (By the end, this pyramid was around six stories high in Germany.) The salesmen and the various hierarchs who were called sales managers were also rewarded with the right to buy shares in IOS. Many, believing devoutly in their own sales spiel, borrowed money to do so. When the shares of IOS became more or less worthless after its crash, they suffered a fate somewhat worse than that of their victims. Their shares became wholly worthless. It is a fixed feature of all such disasters that many of those involved expropriate themselves.

The surviving worth of the underlying funds was not excessive, for the large cost of selling was deducted before the cash was invested. So were other charges. With the passage of time also, IOS tried to improve the value of its funds by investing heavily for performance, and it hired and rewarded investment managers in accordance with their ability to get capital gains. This is approximately the same as saying that it rewarded them for finding insane investments, for that is where the chance of capital appreciation (at least for as long as a particular stock was attracting the attention of other gunslingers) seemed to be. No similar magic could be expected from AT&T or Shell. In the latter days of IOS, investment even took the form of heavy loans to its own executives. Sales had to increase to cover the steadily increasing costs of the sales operation and also the high living costs of the IOS management. The stock market slump in 1969 put the handwriting on the wall, and the crash brought down the wall. Robert Vesco, as the next essay tells, then came in, and the real looting began.

It would be fun to go on telling the story. One John King of Denver, Colorado, made a fine appearance in the play, and the collaboration of King and Cowett in writing up the value of exploration rights on a vast stretch of Arctic oil lands (and ice) was a little masterpiece of its kind. A small acreage was sold at a very high price; this was then taken as justification for the revaluation of exploration rights over a huge water- and landscape. IOS then collected a performance fee on the increase. It deserved it, for the original sale was a sweetheart deal arranged between insiders to inflate the value of this indubitably and literally frozen asset. Toward the end, IOS was an enormous buyer of its own securities. That, for those who sold, was a very charitable action. It is also the common and costly act of desperation of promoters for whom the end is in sight but no more visible to them than to their victims.

The history of Cornfeld and the IOS has been written with competence and restraint by three talented British reporters, Charles Raw, Godfrey Hodgson and Bruce Page.[1] They bring Bernie Cornfeld's girls, castles and planes into the story mostly as these contributed to expense. They refrain from throwing up their hands or gasping with indignation. A great deal of time and patience is given to unraveling the more intricate of Cowett's deals. I have only one small personal quibble.

In the early summer of 1967, Cornfeld provided the funds for Pacem in Terris II. (It now seems that he didn't pay but instead put the bite on his brokers.) This was a gathering in Geneva of scholars, journalists, divines and professional men and women of goodwill to urge the case for peace in general and in Vietnam in particular. Justice William O. Douglas, Martin Luther King, Jr., Senator Joe Clark, were among those who attended. The authors think those present, of whom I was one, were a bit innocent and must have been embarrassed when they knew more of the auspices.

I don't think that's so. Although they are not breathlessly interesting, such convocations are useful, for they remind people, the press and the politicians that peace also has a constituency. There is more than NATO, Lockheed and Rockwell International. However, I specifically raised the question of the auspices with Robert Maynard Hutchins, who was running things. He replied that those who beg on behalf of good causes can't look a gift horse in the mouth. The metaphor aside, I think he was right. I did take the precaution of paying my own way, but that was more out of prudence than principle. So we were not all uninformed.

One reason I tended to be suspicious was that I had previously written about the 1929 crash, and IOS looked impressively like a replay of the work of Goldman Sachs and the other public benefactors of the period. Also, I go frequently to Switzerland to write (and to Geneva where I am a largely honorary professor), and I had heard the Swiss bankers on IOS. They ranged from denunciatory to malevolent. Most un-Swiss. And finally Jimmy Roosevelt had once journeyed to Cambridge to

---

1 *Do You Sincerely Want To Be Rich?* (New York: Viking Press, 1971).

sound me out on joining the Board of IOS. I handle financial matters with care, better on the whole than does the average professional investment man. But my effect on the nerves of people with money to invest is often adverse. Any financial concern proposing to make me a director, and for window-dressing at that, was surely suspect.

26

Robert Vesco: Swindler

No SPECIES of literature has given me so much pleasure over the years as that celebrating high-level fraud. I never miss a book on the subject; the occupationally most obtuse publishers have learned this and send me proofs of work that is often barely literate. I read it all and praise it all, for I enjoy all of it.

My pleasure comes partly from working out how the fraud is done. This is a simple, undemanding form of puzzle, for there are only a very few basic forms of financial graft, on which, in turn, there are a variety of engaging themes. By far the largest family are the pyramids which can exist in time, space or both. All collect from many, pay something out as bait and concentrate the rest on the swindler. All pyramids involve nice judgment as to when to get out, something that is beyond the power or discrimination of almost every crook. So, with rare exceptions, swindlers are open themselves to the deception they are employing. They end up swindling not only the public but themselves.[1]

The pyramid in time is the Ponzi operation.[2] Earlier investors are paid off with the money invested by later ones. The later take must grow exponentially if it is to cover the increasing pay-off required by the earlier gulls. Thus the pyramid. The trick is to get to Brazil before the pay-off is too big in re-

1 As indicated in the preceding essay.
2 See p. 325.

lation to what is retained by the swindler. The most recent example of the Ponzi pyramid was Home-Stake, an operation in nearly nonexistent oil; its variation was in using men of extreme financial sophistication, up to and including high officers of Citibank, as unknowing shills for people, mostly from show business, who laid claim to no financial sense whatever, only to more money than they could use. The first in were paid off by those who came later until not enough came. There was a delightful aftermath to the Home-Stake story. A *Fortune* writer, reporting on the enterprise, denounced a new and exceptionally depraved tendency in public regulation; that was for regulatory agencies to concentrate on protecting only the poor. The Home-Stake saga, he said, with indignation, showed that the SEC "was interested in the small investor, not the rich." SEC officials denied there was "any such discrimination." I take up Home-Stake in the next essay.[3]

The franchise operation is a pyramid in space. A salesman recruits other salesmen and gets an override — a share in what they receive as down payments. And then the salesmen so recruited recruit yet other salesmen and take a similar cut before passing the residue back to the individual who recruited them. As long as the operation is expanding, the salesmen are greatly inspired to sell other salesmen on selling. And revenues pile up back on the originator. The trick is to go public and unload the stock in the ultimate company while the expansion is still going on. For when recruitment and sales fall off, revenues are absorbed along the way. Not much or nothing gets on up to the ultimate company.

The holding company or investment trust pyramids are a pyramid in both time and space. Debentures or preferred stock are issued, along with common stock, to buy into yet other firms, which buy into yet others. In the late nineteen-twenties, before the law intruded, this was repeated through half a

[3] "Should Stealing from the Rich Be Punished?"

dozen or more layers. As long as the earnings or capital value of the ultimate company go up, these accrue not to the pre-ferred-stock- or debenture-holders, whose returns are fixed; they concentrate upstream on the holder of the ultimate common stock. This is leverage, and in every boom the wonders of lev-erage are rediscovered. The thing here, of course, is to get out while earnings and values are going up, for when they go down, all values and more are absorbed as collateral by the senior securities along the way. Nothing is left for the common stock and certainly none for the ultimate common stock.

Again almost no one involved in this kind of swindle gets out in time. All see in the rising stock and the way the pyra-miding is accomplished a reflection of their own intelligence in stock selection and corporate design. Financial genius, it cannot be said too often (although I have tried), is a rising market.

As I've described in the preceding essay, Bernard Cornfeld's achievement in IOS, his girls with the tired eyes apart, was a multiple pyramid, an admittedly complex metaphor. He com-bined the pyramiding in sales operations earlier noted with the financial pyramiding just described. IOS rewarded itself according to the performance of its funds. The principal fund, the Fund of Funds, got performance by investing in other mutual funds that featured performance, which invested, then, in firms that featured rising values. This greatly rewarded IOS as long as there was performance. Thereafter there was nothing.

There are swindles other than the pyramids, but they are not very interesting — peddling of worthless securities, em-bezzlement and corporate looting. Equity Funding, the great California insurance swindle, although at first glance it seemed new, was really a Ponzi operation. The insurance companies were being gulled into buying insurance contracts on non-existent souls out of Gogol. They were paid off from the initial proceeds of the sales of yet more policies on equally nonexistent souls. The fraud was partly concealed by computer operations which the state regulatory agencies did not understand, by a good deal of creative accounting and by hiring people to fake the contracts who mostly didn't know what they were doing.

Along with the simple pleasure of identifying and classifying the type of crime, there are the very distinguished people that one encounters in this kind of work. I first became aware of this reward some twenty years ago while searching out the details of the great Goldman Sachs expropriation of the late twenties; the most prominent name associated with this rape of the innocent, an association I have celebrated elsewhere,[4] was none other than the God-fearing, or anyhow God-invoking, John Foster Dulles. By the time of my study, nonvirtue had reaped its frequent reward. Dulles was Secretary of State.

Other and equally gamy operations of the late twenties enlisted some of the more saintly economics professors of the time. In later years the New Dealers, with some exceptions, steered clear of such involvement, perhaps partly because of lack of opportunity. But in the boom of the sixties there was a dismaying migration from the New Frontier into the more egregious of the offshore funds. Many of those so moving were believed to be inspired by a strong sense of public duty. Having done good in Washington, they wanted to help the poor and abused of the world become rich through sage, imaginative use of their savings.

In the age of Nixon there was a new crop of swindles and a new crop of names, although the Nixon men, to their credit, had unmixed motives; they were not under the impression that they were doing the poor any good. The most depraved faces from this period were those surrounding Robert Vesco.

The story of Vesco has been told by Robert A. Hutchison, a careful man who writes well, with just the right note of contempt for all concerned.[5] Vesco moved in on Cornfeld when IOS seemed to be on the verge of collapse in 1970, and he pro-

---

[4] In *The Age of Uncertainty* (Boston: Houghton Mifflin, 1977), pp. 208–209.
[5] *Vesco* (New York: Praeger Publishers, 1974).

ceeded to ensure that collapse. The financial pages of the newspapers, from incompetence and gullibility the nearly invariable
allies of the crooks, described him in terms that he had largely
invented for himself — a dynamic New Jersey financier and
industrialist who, one would assume, was in daily touch with
David Rockefeller. A single candid column would have alerted
the SEC, maybe the IOS board of directors and possibly even
the local police, for Vesco was, in fact, a ragged-ass operator
whose assets were as exiguous as his commitment to truth. IOS,
however, was his opportunity. By 1970, the investment pyramid
and the sales pyramid had both collapsed and therewith its
revenues and the value of its stock. Fixed charges continued.
Those involved reacted not like accomplished criminals but
like frightened juveniles. Vesco showed up and agreed to pour
in new money in return for effective control. Bernard Cornfeld
seems to have been one of the few who recognized that however
bad he himself might be, Vesco would be a hundred times
worse. Over his objections Vesco got control for virtually nothing, and certainly nothing of his own. The rest was inevitable.

For Vesco was not a pyramid artist but a simple, dull looter.
Before he arrived, not too much had happened to the vast pools
of money that had been assembled for investment by the funds
that were mismanaged by IOS. Values had shrunk; a fair
amount had been dissipated in lunatic efforts to achieve or
simulate performance. Some of the wealth, as noted in the last
essay, was from writing up the value of a vast acreage of Arctic
oil land, terrain which suffered from, among other handicaps,
not being land at all but ice or very cold water. The collapse
took even less time than the write-up. Yet substantial assets
remained. Vesco proceeded to get these out of their previous
custody and reinvested in corporate shells, in which, not surprisingly, the primary ownership interest was with Vesco. His
larceny was not especially deft or artistic. It was remarkable
only for the sheer bulk of the assets so transferred and seques-
tered. A really accomplished crook with any pride in his work

would not, I think, have wished to associate with him.

Those who did get involved were low types, including John Mitchell, Maurice Stans and numerous Nixons. Vesco's plan was to loot two or three hundred million and fend off the SEC by buying up the Nixon family and the Republican Party. So he invested in both of the President's brothers, Edward and Donald, as well as the son of Donald Nixon, also called Donald. This last Donald, Vesco carried around with him as a combined talisman, hostage and souvenir. Then he put $250,000 into CREEP — the 1972 Committee to Re-Elect the President.

For a while it all seemed to work. Maurice Stans served him as impartial ombudsman for a citizen with a problem; so did John Mitchell and John Dean. As Attorney General, John Mitchell got Vesco sprung after the Swiss, far more perceptive than we, tossed him in the lonesome when one day, through an error in judgment, he showed up in Geneva. In the end these men found themselves in more trouble than Vesco, for he moved on to Costa Rica and they were forced to stay.

Part of my delight in this whole subject matter is the occasional encounter with a truly splendid rascal — someone in the tradition of Jim Fisk, Jay Gould and Ivar Kreuger. Vesco wasn't. But he had one quality that commands admiration. Most of those who kicked in the big money for Nixon and the Republicans, when required to explain, said it was because of their deep commitment to American democracy or their desire to save the country from George McGovern and socialism. That they should want anything for themselves — well, perish such acquisitive thoughts. Vesco, on the other hand, when he handed over the $250,000, made himself, as Richard Nixon often said before obscuring an issue, perfectly clear. He only wanted protection from the SEC. No nonsense about saving democracy or even free enterprise.

27

Should Stealing from the Rich Be Punished?

ALTHOUGH I DON'T KNOW HIM personally, I have for several years been an admirer of Mr. Walter B. Wriston. Partly, of course, it is for the huge amount of money over which he presides as the head of Citicorp, operator of the nation's second largest bank. Partly it is for the impeccable information that he often conveys to the public. At a meeting in London not long ago he began by reminding his audience that "Much has been said about the future fate of all of us who live on this planet." (It does seem wise to omit reference to the excessive volume of writing on man's past fate and also to the highly unreliable literature on life on other planets.) He went on to say, also truthfully, that "Today, as always, there is good news and bad news." But no man is perfect. Instead of stopping while ahead, Mr. Wriston proceeded to assail critics of business for saying that it is "what 20th century mathematicians call 'a zero sum game,' " which is to say that a profit for one chap always means a loss for someone else. Perhaps only momentarily and because only two hundred-odd grand was involved, Mr. Wriston had forgotten that he personally had sat in on one of the greatest zero sum games of recent times, the great Home-Stake swindle, and that historians being what they are, he might be even better remembered for this than for his thoughts on good and bad news, although I hope this won't be so.

I want to get away from Mr. Wriston and on to the swindle, but I have to add that he showed in this whole episode not only that the head of the second largest bank in the country can have the common touch, be as competently gulled as anyone else, but also that, for a charitably minded man, the zero sum game can, like poker, have a floating version. Mr. Wriston gave part of his participation in his excessively nonproductive, sometimes nonexistent, oil wells to the Fletcher School of Law and Diplomacy at Tufts University. According to university sources, the Tufts gift was valued for income tax purposes at around $38,000. The ultimate return to the university was not quite zero; Tufts realized $100. That episode and associated deductions may well confirm another of Mr. Wriston's truths, one that was quoted in the *New York Times* on August 2, 1977. "People with equal incomes," he declared, "pay unequal taxes."

The details of the ride on which the great banker was taken (and which he so thoughtfully shared with universities and the sick) are from David McClintick's *Stealing from the Rich: The Home-Stake Oil Swindle.*[1] McClintick has done well; the only conceivable fault with his book lies in the title and possibly in its approach to punishment, to which I will come later. The title, as the author admirably establishes, should have been *How the Rich Swindled Each Other and Themselves.* More passive victims were the United States Treasury, which got hit by a large number of dubious tax deductions, and numerous charitable and educational institutions (including the Library of Congress), which were given highly valued but worthless investments, mostly, it would appear, after their generally ethereal nature had been perceived by the various angels of mercy who bestowed them.[2]

*

[1] (New York: M. Evans and Co., 1977).

[2] In 1971 and 1972, the Library of Congress received gifts of Home-Stake participations valued for charitable purposes at $485,750. By the end of 1974, these should have yielded the Library between $59,500 and $119,000. Actual returns were $1660.87.

The enterprise that Mr. McClintick so elegantly describes got under way in the mid-nineteen-fifties, the work of a lawyer-entrepreneur named Robert Simons Trippet of Tulsa, Oklahoma. Mr. Trippet combined a major instinct for piracy with, most exceptionally, a careful, rather conservative intelligence. It was his belief or discovery that the financially highly solvent get most of their investment information from each other, do not investigate, do not or cannot read, are otherwise deeply retarded on financial matters and would rather lose a large sum of money than pay a smaller amount to the government. On all points he was proven right. In pursuit of these principles he learned that to swindle the rich, you don't need to do very much, you only need to do it very well. You must, in particular, never forget that it is style, not substance, that counts.

As I've argued in an earlier essay, there are no new forms of financial fraud; in the last several hundred years there have been only small variations on a few classic designs. Trippet's fraud is that associated with Charles Ponzi, an energetic Boston operative who, in the early twenties, took hundreds of affluent fellow Bostonians to the cleaners. But the same design was present in the operations by which John Law bilked an even larger number of Parisians between 1716 and 1720, and there are many indications of its far earlier use. It consists, simply, of paying off earlier investors with the proceeds of the sales to the later ones. The earlier ones, because they are getting a handsome return, bring in the later ones, sometimes with an incontrollable rush. Trippet's variation made use of the tax laws. He sold participation rights in the drilling of sometimes hypothetical oil wells which, had they all been real and had the costs actually been incurred, would have allowed the investor a legal, although quite possibly unjustified, tax deduction for the whole amount in the year of the expenditure. Trippet carefully and selectively rewarded the earlier investors from the later investment flow and, on occasion, returned the original investment. His special concern was for those who were most likely to advertise either their good fortune or their loss.

He here raised to the level of high art another classic financial technique, namely the conscientious greasing of the squeaking wheel. He also drilled some wells so there was something that any abnormally curious investor could see, although at the Santa Maria Field in California some were shown imaginatively painted irrigation pipes which they were told involved oil. Most important of all, Mr. Trippet knew the value of name-dropping. He pyramided both money and names.

His method, which may have worked better than even he could have foreseen, was to get two or three gulls with a reputation for great financial wisdom in each of a half dozen intellectually and socially incestuous banking, business, social or professional circles — the close-in convocations in which people regularly convey highly unreliable information to each other, often in the strictest confidence. While these gulls were telling each other that they were on to a good thing, Mr. Trippet and his small coterie would help the process by dropping in the names of their leading shills. This was a service that the Wriston name rendered when dropped in the New York financial community, although there was much sincere help from George S. Moore, Wriston's predecessor at Citibank, Hoyt Ammidon, head of the United States Trust Company, Thomas S. Gates, former Chairman of Morgan Guaranty, and Reese H. Harris, Jr., executive vice president of Manufacturers Hanover Trust Company. Such names fall among bankers with an infinitely reassuring clang. Hoyt Ammidon, a pleasant man whom I know, was an especially poignant name for me, for not only did he get taken for $218,500, but his company has looked after my wife's and my small financial affairs for around a third of a century. This they have done with intelligence, integrity and a pleasant freedom from loss. Our only serious difference of opinion came a few years ago when they proposed that we interest ourselves in oil, cattle or other tax shelters. I rebuked them, not because I knew anything about Home-Stake or other shelters but because it occurred to me that if the risk weren't excessive or there weren't some other flaw, no one would be paying any taxes at all. It was also my deepest conviction that no New York banker could possibly know anything whatever about cattle and not much about oil.

What Moore and Wriston did as pilotfish for the bankers, Fred J. Borch, former Chairman of General Electric, did for industrialists, and he was terrific. When he swam in, so did a whole school of GE men. In an appendix to his book, Mr. McClintick lists the principal victims by industrial, legal or other occupational groupings. There were so many GE vice presidents and vice chairmen, along with a treasurer and a couple of chairmen — thirty-five in all — that they make up a special class by themselves. Other heavy and light industry is well, though less munificently, represented. Present also are two former Secretaries of Defense.

A third community was the great New York and Washington lawyers — members of the big firms that specialize in keeping the big corporations solvent as well as honest. The Washington lawyers seem to have suffered from the guidance of an old friend of mine and fellow economist, Dr. Redvers Opie, a onetime member of the Harvard faculty and later a fellow of Magdalen, one of the most cherished of Oxford colleges. Redvers spread word of the wonders of Home-Stake around Washington and received a modest commission whenever, in consequence, some affluent legal sucker hit the bait. He seems, by the best possible evidence, to have been wholly innocent of any larcenous intent. He, in fact, put his own money into Home-Stake and appears on Mr. McClintick's list of losers.

There was also a Los Angeles community of business and financial fleecees, and there and in New York was the most alluring, romantic and enchanting group of all, the great entertainers and artists. Among these lambs the slaughter was simply appalling. Jack Benny, Candice Bergen, Faye Dunaway, Bob Dylan, Mia Farrow, Liza Minnelli, Mike Nichols — the list goes on and on, and for many the amount was up in the Ammidon range. For any first-rank performer to be off this list is to arouse real suspicion; unless terrific alimony is the explanation, the individual was working way below rates and faking his or her salary to the press. Barbra Streisand's name appears so impressively in the book that when the author mentions Santa Barbara, the printer spells it Barbra too.

Of the established forms of graft, none has been so common in Hollywood for so long as the looting of motion picture innocents by their business managers or sometimes their lawyers and brokers. I've known many Hollywood folk over the years, partly out of interest in what they do, partly in our common pursuit of Democratic politics and contributions. They have a tendency to pour out their personal financial history to an economist; this, for almost all, includes memory of some massive exploitation by a hitherto deeply trusted, deeply larcenous business adviser, manager, agent or friend. Home-Stake was in a great artistic tradition.

Three things protect the simple-minded investor from thievery under our system. These are the watchful eye of the independent auditor, the menace of the law and the courts and the supervision of the Securities and Exchange Commission. Over the nearly twenty years that he survived in fraud, Trippet was only mildly bothered by these impediments. Auditors repeatedly uncovered or suspected thimblerigging and theft; if they persisted in their suspicious way, Trippet simply got others of more agreeable disposition, denser mind or greater need for the pay. Once or twice his highly creative annual accounting was issued without benefit of an auditor's attestation. No one much noticed. As the years passed, he was sued by investors who had come, however gradually, to realize that they were being scammed. The lawsuits attracted virtually no attention outside of Tulsa. And, in a nice gesture to his friends and neighbors and perhaps also because they were insufficiently innocent, he largely refrained from stealing at home. The SEC was a risk; it requires, as all know, that future investors be advised through a prospectus of the risks they are running. Trippet, in his prospectuses, never got around to telling the whole truth, but he did tell quite a bit. Thus the 1970 admonition, more explicit than those that preceded it, said:

> THESE SECURITIES INVOLVE A HIGH DEGREE OF RISK AND THE EXISTENCE OF THE POSSIBILITY OF SUBSTANTIAL COMPENSATION TO THE OPERATOR [Home-Stake]. To date, none of the investors in any of the prior programs which Home-Stake and its subsidiary operators have offered to investors have recovered their entire investment.

Trippet's guess, however, was that a fool who really wanted to be parted from his money would not read or would not understand such warnings. He was right.

At long last, in 1973, in close step with the Watergate uncover-up, the Home-Stake fraud did unravel, and in the following year it came to pieces. The general press, over the years, had shown itself, as always, to be worthless for searching out financial hocus, even when this was massive and practically overt. The head of any great news-gathering organization who was promised a return of several hundred percent on his investment should immediately have alerted editors, reporters and researchers to find out what was going on. Such intervention with the editorial side by the corporate brass is never criticized. Alas. James R. Shepley, the President of Time, Inc., got such a promise of improbable wealth, ordered no investigation, but invested himself. It remained for the *Wall Street Journal,* with its subversive instinct for assembling dull facts, to reveal the true nature of the Trippet expression of the free enterprise system. That was a worthy act; it had the further great advantage of bringing McClintick into the play, for he is a *Journal* reporter and, in consequence, wrote this book.

Brought to the bar of justice, as it is often called, Trippet pleaded no contest to charges that he had performed a total of some ten felonious acts at the expense of the trusting. U.S. District Judge Allen E. Barrow, who presided over the trial, which featured a generally inept prosecution, distinguished himself for both his sympathy for the wrongdoers and the deeply tortured character of his prose — "... certain aspects of the so-called Home-Stake trial have become clear to me as the trial judge. Not the least of these is that the whole thing is not what was pictured by some Eastern newspapers and magazines in their colorful or sensational reporting, however you want to call it, as the century's greatest swindle. . . . I have seen evidence that there was a grandiose promotional scheme that went sour . . . These men admit having done wrong, having violated the trust that the individuals reposed in them. One must accept these confessions of fault and abide by the judgments upon themselves thereby pronounced." To this possibly bearable personal judgment, the judge added a maximum fine, ordered a contribution of $100,000 to a fund for any stray widows, orphans and children who had been rendered destitute by Trippet's operations (they had not been a rewarding target; they didn't have enough money and, in contrast with the New York bankers, may have been too prudent in handling what they had), but confined more sanguinary punishment to the jail time already served. That had been one night in the local cooler. Trippet wrote a note of warm thanks to the judge.

David McClintick is critical of Barrow. However, his awful prose apart, there is something to be said for him. The people of the United States were cheated by the high value given to valueless gifts and the consequent tax deductions. As a participant citizen and resulting victim, I want to see every effort at recovery and I hope the IRS will be held closely to account on this. But the judge was only marginally involved with this aspect of the case. He was more concerned with the original swindle, and it may be that people who don't treat their money with intelligence and respect, who have so much that they don't need to do so and who are willing to entrust it to any scoundrel as an alternative to paying part of it to the government are beyond the protection of the law. Had Trippet not taken them, it would have been someone else. Maybe Judge Barrow was right to go easy on the man; he merely managed to get in on the top floor first.

28

The Global Strategic Mind

IN THE SUMMER of 1978, there was a small but interesting explosion in Washington over the effort by an old Harvard colleague of mine, Samuel P. Huntington, then on assignment to the White House, to get Senator Daniel Patrick Moynihan, also recently of Harvard, to make a public assault on a presidential decision involving trade with the Russians. I was sorry to read about this. I had repeatedly urged my Harvard colleagues, when they go to Washington, not to practice the kind of politics which is commonplace in Cambridge. Washington is not ready for it. But I was much more alarmed by an earlier communication from Sam Huntington in which he defended a briefing on strategic balance that he had given to the Chinese. It involved, he said, no secrets; it was one of many such briefings he had been giving. This was an indication that global strategic thought, sometimes called relentless strategic thought, was again rampant in Washington. There is nothing about which the country should be more concerned. President Carter can shrug off the odd professorial attack. But all recent experience shows that Presidents cannot survive the strategic mind. If life on this planet dissolves one day in an intense sheet of flame with great overpressure, the guidance to our demise will have been given by a relentless strategic mind, a particularly tough exponent of global balance.

*

The strategic mind is readily identified and, on the whole, rather simple as well as straightforward. It is drawn uncontrollably to any map of the world, and this it immediately divides into spheres of present or potential influence. The nature of the influence is never specified. Nor are the consequences of its exercise, if any, except as there may be vague references to essential raw materials, naval bases or the control of adjacent waters by local aircraft — threats that, in the end, do not materialize, perhaps because they only rarely have anything to do with modern military need or technology.

A hostile sphere of influence always requires a prompt and lethal reaction. That is partly because nothing else will be understood by our opponents and partly because it must be shown that we are capable of such a reaction. Those who question the need and ask consideration of the consequences show by their insistence on thought that they are indecisive. The man of relentless strategic mind substitutes bravery for thought and action for reflection.

Above all, it is an essential of strategic thinking that it ignore experience. That is an intensely practical matter. Once the strategic mind starts reflecting on experience, as I will presently urge, it is down the drain. Experience is the one thing by which it cannot, under any circumstances, be guided.

The strategic mind manifests itself among the scholarly classroom warriors at Harvard; rather harmlessly in onetime summer soldiers and diplomats in the New York corporations and law firms who meet nostalgically at the Council on Foreign Relations to recall their days of glory; in the Pentagon, the CIA and, though more fugitively, in the State Department; in the National Security Council, alas; and it flourishes among the housecarls of Senator Henry Jackson. It is disastrously represented in other countries, the disaster being, as usual, for the governments it guides. But let me recur to the experience that, professionally, it is required to ignore.

*

The most vital recent experience was, of course, in Vietnam. For a little while after the war, it must be said, the strategists were a trifle subdued. Hundreds of thousands of ethnically diverse lives and many billions of dollars had been spent to keep Saigon out of the Chinese sphere of influence. There had also been concern about the Russians, but the Chinese were the nearer and more dominant force. It had been said that in the absence of our effort, the dominoes would fall. Chinese Communist influence would extend across Thailand to Malaysia, Singapore and beyond. Now, however, the Vietnamese and the Chinese have fallen out. Chinese assistance to Hanoi has been stopped. Chinese long resident in Saigon are being expelled, and there has even been fighting on the border. As for the Russians, they face a bitterly hostile China, which increasingly we befriend. The men of strategic mind concede that there is a lesson from Vietnam: we must not allow it to weaken our will to intervene the next time.

These global strategists also complain that Vietnam still dominates our thoughts to an excessive degree, and in this I concur. There should be much more thought about Africa, for that has long been a positive addiction of the strategic mind. It is there, above all, that we need to reflect on past experience.

Thus, in the nineteen-sixties, there was a deep strategic concern over Tanganyika *cum* Tanzania, where the Chinese were building a railroad; there was even greater worry over Guinea, which had been all but written off to the Communists; and in the early days of the Kennedy administration there was a near frenzy over the Congo, now Zaire. The latter, we were all told, we simply could not afford to lose. In time, strategic intervention having been resisted or kept ineffective, the Tanganyikan railroad was forgotten; the Soviet ambassador got kicked out of Guinea, where we are now mining the bauxite; and Zaire lapsed into a system of eclectic, universal but not especially innovative corruption. As a footnote proving that the strategic mind is ever resourceful: In 1961, when as ambassador to India

I first called on Nehru, he expressed concern about one Clare Hayes Timberlake, then our ambassador in the Congo. He thought him to have an unduly sanguinary strategic mind. Timberlake had served previously in India where so great was his strategic commitment that he had endeavored to keep Nehru out of the hands of the Communists. Nehru had not thought it necessary.

All of this was overture. In the next years the strategic minds became alarmed over Algeria, a major bridgehead into Africa, where Ahmed Ben Bella was being advised and supplied by the Soviets. Then one day in 1965, Colonel Houari Boumedienne took Soviet tanks into Algiers and arrested Ben Bella, who, having spent the Algerian war in jail, was now put permanently back in confinement. A very restricted life. A member of the Soviet Embassy in Washington whom I asked about this development said, "At least they didn't use our advisers."

In these years the exponents of global balance also expressed great concern over Soviet influence on Kwame Nkrumah in Ghana. The Soviets were training his praetorian guard, were influencing his economic policy and were thus a threat, although this was not stressed, to our chocolate supply. In 1966, Nkrumah was thrown out; the worry had been to no purpose.

Concern then shifted to Egypt, where earlier John Foster Dulles, the modern prophet of all strategic minds, had paved the way for the Russians by trying to accommodate Gamal Abdel Nasser to our sphere of influence in the matter of the Aswan Dam. Soviet aircraft, anti-aircraftmen, advisers, some thought even pilots, had thereafter swarmed in. The strategic minds were at the point of paranoia; at a minimum we should encourage the Israelis to put an end to it all. Then the Russians were all sent home by the Egyptians.

Of late, in that general part of Africa, attention has been on Ethiopia. This was once a bastion of the free world; now Ethiopian military men whom we trained have come dangerously under Soviet influence as they fight against Somalia, once a

Soviet enclave but now itself a bastion of the free world. In one powerful strategic view, Somalia must not be defeated because Ethiopia, and thus Russia, would then dominate the oil routes into the Red Sea. This is where long-range guns come in, one gathers.

To the south and west in Angola, the strategists, earlier on, had translated their alarm into actual intervention. The former Portuguese colony was by way of becoming a Cuban and Soviet colony — to the strategic mind a quite plausible exchange. And it would dominate the supertanker routes to Europe — more of those long-range guns. However, our goal was not to keep the Cubans and Soviets out but to make that imperial effort as costly as possible and to prove that, after Vietnam, we were still capable of response, however insane. This story has been told in impressive and convincing detail by John Stockwell,[1] a former field-grade officer of the CIA. It should not be missed. Since strategic thought survives by ignoring experience, it has a highly professional interest in avoiding accounts such as this. By the same token, all who are alarmed about the tendency toward such strategic thinking should welcome Mr. Stockwell's book, which is both well-written and interesting.

The usual final word is now emerging on strategic thought in Angola. Evidently that country wasn't lost either. Its government and economy are being sustained all but exclusively by money from Gulf Oil. That sort of thing takes the edge off a Communist victory. And we are moving to establish friendly relations. One sees again why the global strategists must ignore experience. We have won only when we have resisted the impulse to intervene.

In the old witch-hunting days it was a routine precaution, on uncovering American overseas aberrations, to come up with some counterpart Soviet mischief or misbehavior. That is no

---

[1] *In Search of Enemies: A CIA Story* (New York: W. W. Norton, 1978).

longer essential, but there is no escaping the fact that the relentless strategic mind, pervasive and omnipotent, functions in the Soviet Union as the mirror image of American error. And then vice versa again.

Thus it was once central to Soviet strategic thinking that China was part of a wonderfully expansive sphere of Soviet influence. To this end technicians and money were dispatched in quantity. And our strategists saw eye to eye with the Russians. Dean Rusk called China a "Soviet Manchukuo," lacking in even the barest essentials of sovereignty. From this position he retreated to argue that any division between the Soviets and the Chinese was only over the tactics for destroying the free world. For many years James Angleton presided with what seems to have been clinically acute paranoia over counterintelligence activities. William Colby, former head of the CIA, in another book which, sometimes unwittingly, illuminates the workings of the strategic mind,[2] says that Angleton never accepted the Sino-Soviet split as genuine, "at least until a few years ago." It was, Angleton avowed, an artful Communist way of misleading the nonstrategic minds.

Returning to the Soviet strategists, were it professionally permissible for them to reflect on their experience, they would have to concede that Indonesia and Sukarno were an investment gone sour. And likewise, of course, Ben Bella. And similarly Nkrumah. And in an especially costly way also Egypt. And similarly Somalia. And now possibly Angola. Nor is this all. India under Indira Gandhi was held by the best American strategists to be moving dangerously into the Soviet orbit. The Soviet strategists must have been as pleased as ours were worried. Now, as this is written, India is back again in the free world.

The Russian strategists have also, over the years, witnessed the defection of Albania (which has again defected, this time *from*

2 *Honorable Men: My Life in the CIA* (New York: Simon and Schuster, 1978).

China) and, of course, of Yugoslavia and to some extent of Rumania. Only Poland, Bulgaria and East Germany are imagined to be absolutely firm, and, in the case of the Poles, it is hard to suppose that only Zbig Brzezinski is ethnically at odds with the old Russian rulers. A friend of mine holds that our best strategic minds are merely generous men. Seeing the Russian failures in the Third World, they seek to intervene in a kindly way to forestall error and save the Soviets from further trouble. This I doubt.

All joking aside, though it is hard not to have fun, the interventionist records of the United States and the USSR in the former colonial world have been, literally, an unmitigated disaster.

It is one of the prime tenets of the strategic mind that ideological affiliation overrides nationalist sentiment or passion. We can be certain that it does not. And the poorer the country, the greater can be that certainty. That is because nationalist feeling does not diminish with income, but ideological passion does diminish in the absence of capitalism and thus in the absence of anything to socialize or anything much to protect from socialism. Though the point does not figure in modern strategic thought in the East or West, it was basic for Karl Marx.

Also where there is no effective industrial and governmental structure, influence is over a vacuum, which is another thought that seems largely to have escaped the exponents of global strategy and balance. Instead, influence is, at most, over individual politicians who can change their affiliation from one day to the next or be changed from one day to the next. Also, to control only one politician can be to alienate the alternatives and the relevant public, as our Vietnam experience so well revealed. It follows that seeking influence can be a superb design for ensuring that one's influence will come abruptly to an end when the favored politician comes to his end, as later, or more often sooner, he does.

William Colby, though he mentions it as an easily rectified difficulty, is also impressed by the trouble American strategic operatives in Saigon had in communicating with the Vietnamese, with the resulting conflict and misunderstanding. But far more serious is the kind of people who get selected and select themselves for this line of work. Colby, Stockwell and another CIA-affiliated author, Frank Snepp,[3] are all, intentionally or otherwise, emphatic on this point.

In the last century, colonial influence and power were expressed through pedestrian civil servants — in the British case, hard-working, disciplined, unspectacular men who lived within a fairly firm legal frame. In contrast, the sword arm of relentless global strategy is a romantic egoist in whom bravery or bravado — Colby calls it *macho* — takes the place of good sense. The most vivid characterization is in Snepp's book. The CIA station chief in Saigon was not merely lacking in common sense; he had lost touch with reality and lived in a world manufactured out of, and peopled by, his own illusions. Snepp's portrait of the men who had been guiding the Vietnamese to democracy drinking their turn to the helicopters is also unpleasant. However, the older orthodox colonial ventures, virtually without exception, were equally notable for their messy end.

Stockwell is also vivid on the American operatives and even more on the local talent with whom they worked. The station chief in Zaire who directed the Angola intervention in 1975 and 1976 was an ego-hedonist of startling inadequacy. The money that the CIA sent over to hire mercenaries or win support in Zaire went into a series of larcenous rat holes, which, perhaps, was the one thing better than having it used to sustain combat. In the past I've known quite a few CIA people; most of them were sensible, restrained and undramatic men and women engaged in routine reporting and research. I would like to think that the serious and careful public servant is still the

3 *Decent Interval: An Insider's Account of Saigon's Indecent End* (New York: Random House, 1977).

norm. But this, it is terribly clear, isn't the kind of person who is attracted to the strategic and mostly covert enterprises.

It could be supposed that Stockwell and Snepp, since both published their books without official authorization, were inclined to give an unduly unfavorable picture of these CIA troops. Otherwise they would have gone through channels. Unfortunately for this theory, the worst view of all is given by William Colby. He shows, without quite intending it, that irrationality and dementia in covert and strategic operations also occurred at the top. Were the men of strategic mind as effectively self-protective in suppressing books as in ignoring experience, they would have buried William Colby's and let the others go.

Colby's case for irrationality is made partly by exclusion. He never asks why we are competing with the Chinese or the Soviets in Vietnam or elsewhere. Or what we accomplish. The competition itself is the only and sufficient thing. Find a Communist and automatically you react. He also powerfully reinforces my earlier point about national leaders. No matter how unpopular these may be, Colby is unswerving in their support. At the same time (since, to his credit, he would rather be inconsistent than dishonest), in talking of Vietnam he concedes the unpopularity of the ghastly Nhus and affirms his strong belief that the war had to be won with the people. This isn't the only inconsistency that he refuses to paper over. We lost, in his view, because we didn't take "into account the determination of the Vietnamese, Southern as well as Northern, to make their own decisions and fight each other to decide what sort of life Vietnam should lead." But, according to Colby, we were winning almost up to the day of the helicopters. Then Congress cut back on military aid.

Colby is, however, most devastating on the kind of people who carry out the policy. The illicit authors tell of romantic incompetence at the bottom; Colby shows that irresponsibility went right to the top and that misjudgment and the resulting proven capacity for disaster nowise detracted from reputation.

Few men ever so admirably proved themselves incapable of prudent thought as Allen Dulles. In less than a year he was responsible both for the Gary Powers flight over the Paris Summit and the fiasco at the Bay of Pigs. He was then sacked for his errors but wrote a book on the craft of intelligence for which, it appears, he recruited E. Howard Hunt as the expert ghost. Colby remembers Dulles as a "superlative spymaster" and ends his book with a biblical tribute to his insight. Similarly Richard Bissell, who was immediately in charge of the Bay of Pigs (and was in earlier times a very competent economist), emerges from that disaster in Colby's view as a "brilliant, intense" man. All with experience of the CIA knew the late Desmond FitzGerald. He was charming, uncontrollably activist and given dangerously to self-dramatization. When he came to India, I was deeply uneasy and, out of considerable bureaucratic experience, made sure that I knew everything he was doing. Here is Colby on FitzGerald: "I urged that Des FitzGerald be chosen [to be responsible, for God's sake, for all covert activities], but I cautioned Helms that he would have to maintain tight control over him to keep him from charging off into some new Bay of Pigs. Helms did choose FitzGerald . . ." Colby, the source of this remarkable personnel judgment — the selection of the man who would have the single most alarming job in the United States government — went on, himself, to be head of the whole works.

It was the men of relentless strategic mind who guided Lyndon Johnson on Indochina and sent him back to Texas. It was their operatives who went in to bug the Democratic National Committee and sent Richard Nixon back to San Clemente. (Colby disavows Howard Hunt, although he couldn't possibly have been more dangerous than FitzGerald.) I don't especially believe in the rule of three. But I would urge Jimmy Carter to watch those relentless strategic minds. I, personally, would feel far, far safer with Bert Lance.

29

John Dean, Ambition
and the White House

ONE DAY during the 1976 political campaign I flew down from
Boston to New York to get a literary award of pleasant intent
but negligible intrinsic value. A big crowd was waiting to get
on the shuttle, and at the luncheon I told a small fable of how
I made it aboard: just ahead of me in line was John Dean, and
when he got on, four ex-Nixon hands of depraved appearance
hastily got off. No one laughed at my small fantasy, and had I
then read Dean's book,[1] I wouldn't have thought it funny either.

John Dean, as all now know, is a man of total recall, and this
is combined with a superb instinct for whatever is most damaging to his fellow malefactors. At the time he wrote his book, it
was hard to imagine that anyone could come up with anything
that would be newly detrimental to Richard Nixon. But Dean
has Nixon talking about typewriters and remembering to Chuck
Colson that "We built one in the Hiss case," which, of course,
is what the Hiss partisans have always most wanted to believe.
If true, which I doubt, it robs Dick of the accomplishment on
which his whole reprehensible career was founded. (I imagine
that, in fact, he mumbled something about building the legal
case on the typewriter.) John Connally is also a hard man to

1 *Blind Ambition: The White House Years* (New York: Simon and Schuster,
1976).

hurt, but Dean has Richard Kleindienst (as Attorney General) exclaiming, "For Christ's sake, John Connally was over here not long ago trying to get me to handle a problem for him. And when I refused, the President started climbing all over my back." What was that one, John?

Then, almost without effort, he ropes in Kleindienst, a law officer who seems not to have supposed that he was meant to report crime, only to complain that, as Attorney General, guilty knowledge of wrongdoing was embarrassing to him. After his departure from the Department of Justice, in a slightly tense ceremony in the favoring presence of one of his successors, Edward Levi, Kleindienst's portrait was unveiled to shine forth there with those of his predecessors. There is enough in Dean's book on the Kleindienst view of the law to require lawyers in the DOJ or elsewhere, if they have any professional pride at all, to get it moved into some reasonably roomy broom closet.

Henry Petersen becomes an excessively reliable conduit to Nixon; Howard Baker, as Sam Dash has also told, is shown to have brought the cover-up into the Ervin Committee while looking like a novitiate scoutmaster on television; a federal judge, Charles Richey, is "a Nixon appointee, who was sending encouraging signals through our contacts."

Even the Christian credentials of Charles Colson take a beating, and it will be a relief to Jesus to have it publicly known that their association is not nearly so intimate as Chuck has been claiming. Here is Colson on Jeb Magruder, long after being born again: "Magruder's full of shit. That bastard tests my Christian patience to the breaking point." Not the language you would expect to hear along the Stations of the Cross.

I greatly enjoyed John Dean's book despite my guilty knowledge as to the reason: the attraction of the Watergate literature lies in your ability to believe that you are reading history while, in fact, you are getting a mean and unworthy pleasure from the disasters of people you don't know but know you don't like.

(Though I've been moderately around, I have never met any of the Watergate delinquents.)

However, in the Dean story there is some redeeming social content, and it could be considerable. He (or more likely a retarded editor) came up with the title *Blind Ambition*; in fact, Dean saw quite clearly that ambition had brought him into the most lethal single location in the United States. The lesson is here.

Although it was on the way before, the White House personnel underwent a huge expansion in the Eisenhower years. In the military tradition, Ike was a man for staff. Perhaps in consequence, though there had been minor misfortunes before, the first major White House casualty was his chief assistant, Sherman Adams. Since then the toll has been great. The Kennedy-Johnson foreign-policy people were deeply damaged. The Nixon domestic-policy people were devastated. The reason lies in the most aberrant act of administrative insanity known to modern government: every four or eight years a large band of men, mostly without previous experience of government, often young, all dangerously euphoric because of recent and sometimes accidental political success, all billed initially as geniuses by the Washington press corps and believing their own notices, all persuaded that they were meant by the stars to reinvent the wheel, are given great ostensible and even actual power in the White House.

Added to the insanity of this action is the absence of any need for congressional clearance, any need to answer to congressional inquiry, an "in" atmosphere that limits conversation to those who are also in and the knowledge that people elsewhere in the government will snap to attention by the phone when word comes that the White House is on the line, even if it is only to ask for the youth unemployment figures. It is also part of the ghastly mystique that the President — variously the leader of the free world, occupant of the world's most powerful post or "the man in the Oval Office" — is entitled to unquestioning fealty even when unquestionably wrong and that, above all, he must be protected, including from those who might usefully tell him that he *is* wrong.

A new Cabinet officer is subject to the formidable discipline of the civil service, which is a rich and often overpowering source of information on the perils of the kind of brilliant innovation which so many before have found fatal. The White House staff is not subject to this restraint. And there is the seductive effect of the royal standard of presidential living — the planes, limousines, special telephones, air-to-ground communications, the offices, mess, doctors and the wonderful ethic of command and obedience — all of which become available in greater or less measure to the denizens. George Reedy was eloquent on all this a few years back. Dean has many words to add, including a small but revealing comment to his lawyer about those who leave the White House: "No matter what they say, it always rips them up. They come back begging for mess privileges and invitations and stuff like that."

For Nixon, we now know, the presidency was overwhelmingly important as compensation for the economic deprivation for which his family had seemed by nature to be intended. Thus the presidential palaces in the sun, the new and more extravagant airplanes of which Dean tells admiringly, the King Carol uniforms and the inauguration extravaganza which Nixon once said is what the presidency is all about. His staff, in consequent imitation, was more than normally concerned with perquisites; Dean tells, with surprise, how Haldeman used an automobile to commute from his quarters to San Clemente, when going by car, helicopter and then car again took only a little longer. I spent the early weeks of the Kennedy Administration in the White House; neither the President nor his entourage was that fascinated by apparatus. But it was a heady experience. We all felt that the country had been forced to wait too long for our attention. And in later years several of my friends (and President Johnson as well) succumbed to their surroundings and the feeling not that they were above the law but that they were above military and associated political error.

As I write this, Governor Carter is preparing to bring a new bunch into the White House. I hope they and he are aware of the terrible risk on which they are entering and that the country is duly alarmed. Mr. Carter does promise a reorganization of the government. On the basis of all recent experience, it should begin with the creation of a nonpolitical White House secretariat, a small group of bureaucrats, no less, who know the perils of the post. He should then ask for legislation limiting to a couple of dozen at most the number of new professional appointments a President can make to the White House staff. Tasks that these men cannot perform should be passed down to the departments and agencies. Perhaps he should ask that the most senior of his staff be subject to Senate confirmation. The Senate will normally be compliant; the faceless men will not thereafter be quite so faceless, and they will have an indication from the beginning that the people and the Congress, not the President, are the ultimate authority.

30

RN:
The Memoirs of Richard Nixon[1]

THE AUTHOR will surely think it appropriate, perhaps inevitable, that I review his book, for he tells, at around his average level of truth, that I both started him on his public career and helped, however marginally, to bring that career to an end.

The beginning was in January of 1942 when he was brought into the Office of Price Administration to work on rubber and tire rationing, tasks then under my direction. (The management of price control and that of rationing were shortly afterward separated, to the benefit of both.) He tells in his book that he had earlier tried for the FBI but was turned down, not on grounds of character but because of an appropriations cut. So once, under Hoover, the FBI had its appropriations cut. However, in line with a notable Nixon tradition, I must plead that I didn't know what was going on. I didn't meet Mr. Nixon either then or later.

My contribution to ending his career was in the mid-sixties when the Kennedy Library asked me for my papers. On leaving OPA, the State and War Departments and on ceasing to be an ambassador, I didn't think to take my official papers, which I supposed belonged to the government and, in any case, were

---

[1] (New York: Grosset & Dunlap, 1978.)

rather bulky. (I've since had to go to the National Archives on occasion to look things up.) I did send to the Kennedy Library manuscripts of *The Affluent Society, The Great Crash,* other folk classics, a mass of personal correspondence and, by accident, our canceled checks, bank statements, marriage license, my naturalization certificate and our old income tax returns. Taking a tax deduction on old tax returns would have been a major breakthrough in sophisticated tax avoidance. However, David Powers, the Kennedy friend and librarian, sent these, the checks and the other detritus back.

On the manuscripts and correspondence, including that with J.F.K., his wife, Adlai Stevenson, Averell Harriman, Arthur Schlesinger, numerous editors, economists and literary types, Nathan Marsh Pusey and various government loyalty boards, the Internal Revenue Service allowed me a stunning (as it then seemed) $4500. This, Mr. Nixon here says, later encouraged him to take a deduction of $576,000 on his more official papers, with endlessly damaging results, made worse because that kind of deduction had ceased to be legal and the gift was backdated without his knowledge. He also blames Lyndon Johnson, George Wallace, Hubert Humphrey and others for putting him on this downward path.

I tell the foregoing partly for my own pleasure but also because it reflects a central theme of this book. Mr. Nixon never did anything wrong unless someone else had done it first. And all evil disappears if it has a precedent.

As committee work goes, his book is not badly written. And, as in the matter just cited, it bears the undoubted imprint, for better or worse, of Mr. Nixon's personality, which is certainly not without interest. He is imaginative and resourceful, and, if one is to believe in democracy, one must find some qualities to explain and justify his twice serving as Vice-President, twice being elected President. It isn't as though he weren't known. I think it was this resourcefulness and imagination that allowed him to see, along with Henry Kissinger, the opportunity that the frozen Cold War diplomacy of his predecessors had given him. Thus the ensuing and important improvement in relations with China and the Soviet Union. This resourcefulness also explains his almost incredible ability (until Watergate) to battle his way out of an endless series of personal and political disasters — misfortunes, it is even more interesting to reflect, which were invariably invited by his own bad judgment.

In turn, the source of this bad judgment, one gathers, was his inability to think, or anyhow believe, that he himself could do anything wrong. That Nixon was a rascal is now generally accepted. But, as his political career revealed and this book superbly affirms, he was and remains a rascal who either considers himself a deeply moral man or, more precisely, believes that he can so persuade any known audience.

This belief bears heavily on the reader of this book. Were it a candid account of the author's lifetime of political and personal tergiversation, it would be wonderful reading. But the compulsive search for precedent, the innumerable explanations of the ineffable and the belief that all his accusers are ill-motivated except when they say something on his side (as even Archibald Cox once did) get to be a bore.

Not entirely, however, for one gets caught up in the game — in looking for the flaw in his explanation. Thus, as he sees it, one of the typically egregious misunderstandings to which he was subject concerned that $100,000 that Bebe Rebozo got in 1970 from Howard Hughes. Bebe, "one of the kindest and most generous men I have ever known," intended to hold it for the 1972 campaign. But then various feuds within the Hughes empire and the danger of exposure and embarrassment caused him to sock it away in a safe deposit box and not even tell Nixon about it for a long while. Later, when the risk of exposure was still acute, it was returned. There couldn't have been anything funny about the transaction, according to Nixon, for an inspection of the bills showed that they had been issued by the Treasury well before the date when Rebozo said he got the money. No switch.

One's mind dwells, inevitably, on why the payment was in cash, why 1972 campaign contributions were being collected so early, what would have happened to the bills had there been no danger of exposure. Here is the real interest. Nixon's explanations almost always invite such thoughts, and they don't greatly tax the mind. I'm persuaded that most of his disasters came from his conviction that if he could persuade himself that something was virtuous or legitimate, he could persuade almost everybody else.

There are other aspects of the Nixon personality that command attention. Sometimes it is less the resourcefulness than the convolution:

> I was concerned that Haldeman handle the matter deftly. I did not want him to strong-arm Helms and Walters, nor did I want him to lie and say there was no involvement. I wanted him to set out the situation in such a way that Helms and Walters would take the initiative and go to the FBI on their own. I told Haldeman to say that I believed this thing would open up the whole Bay of Pigs matter — to say that the whole thing was a sort of comedy of errors and that they should call the FBI in and say that for the sake of the country they should go no further into this case.

This passage makes one weep even for Haldeman. Lompoc or whatever must have been a blessed relief.

Nixon is not only a master of convoluted thought, but he appreciates it in others. Here is his account of his briefing by Dean Rusk on Vietnam during the 1968 campaign:

> Rusk, one of the ablest and most honorable men ever to serve as Secretary of State, made the point that the rest of Asia would be in a "panic" if the United States were to withdraw from Vietnam without an honorable peace settlement. He said that he held this view completely apart from the domino theory, which he considered simplistic. He believed that American withdrawal from Vietnam would leave the Chinese Communists as the only major power on the Asian mainland, thus creating the panic.

The ability to distinguish between the simplistic domino theory and the sophisticated panic theory is the kind of thing Mr. Nixon cherishes. He also responds well to a really complex metaphor. He remembers and quotes Bryce Harlow as telling him on April 23, 1973, that "If Haldeman, Dean and Ehrlichman have undertaken actions which will not float in the public domain, they must leave quickly — they are like a big barnacle on the ship of state, and there is too much at stake to hang on for personal reasons."

Perhaps because of professional pecuniary interest, I'm against people boycotting books. And quite a few will find the reading and associated unraveling, if not a pleasure, at least a challenge. I'm also against a too violent reaction to Mr. Nixon's belief, here affirmed, that the misuse of the FBI, the IRS and other federal agencies is one of the accepted rights of incumbency. He tells with sorrow that Patrick Gray and the FBI were out of his control in their misguided pursuit of wrongdoing and that the IRS was not adequately motivated in the investigation he ordered of Larry O'Brien and the McGovern supporters during the 1972 campaign. These efforts *were* indefensible, but the book is a testament to the number in the federal government who would not go along with any such wrongdoing.

Indeed, next only to the self-justification and the convolution, the book comes across as Mr. Nixon's bill of complaint against civil servants, members of Congress, Kennedy types, newspapers and television people who were out to sabotage his intentions. These intentions were bad, but Nixon was far from effecting them. Our liberties were not curtailed. On the contrary, there never was a time when more Americans were expressing themselves more stridently and diversely with so little fear as in the Nixon years. I'm firm in the belief, a minority view of long standing, that anyone who spoke out under Richard Nixon had little to fear, anyone who was shut up by Richard Nixon had nothing to say.

Appendix
Index

Power and the Useful Economist[1]

WITHIN THE LAST DOZEN YEARS what before was simply known as economics in the nonsocialist world has come to be called neoclassical economics. Sometimes, in tribute to Keynes's design for government intervention to sustain purchasing power and employment, the reference is to Keynesian or neo-Keynesian economics. From being a general and accepted theory of economic behavior, this has become a special and debatable interpretation of such behavior. For a new and notably articulate generation of economists a reference to neoclassical economics has become markedly pejorative. In the world at large the reputation of economists of more mature years is sadly in decline.

However, the established economics has reserves of strength. It sustains much minor refinement which does not raise the question of overall validity or usefulness and which is agreeable employment. It survives especially in the textbooks, although even in this stronghold one senses anxiety among the more progressive or commercially sensitive authors. Perhaps, they are asking, there are limits to what the young will accept.

The arrangements by which orthodoxy is conserved in the modern academy are also still formidable. Economic instruction in the United States is about a hundred years old. In its first half century economists were subject to censorship by outsiders.

1 This was my presidential address at the Eighty-fifth Annual Meeting of the American Economic Association in Toronto, Canada, in December 1972.

Businessmen and their political and ideological acolytes kept watch on departments of economics and reacted promptly to heresy, the latter being anything that seemed to threaten the sanctity of property, profits, a proper tariff policy and a balanced budget, or that suggested sympathy for unions, public ownership, public regulation or, in any organized way, for the poor. The growing power and self-confidence of the educational estate, the formidable and growing complexity of the subject matter of economics and, no doubt, the increasing acceptability of our ideas to conservatives have largely relieved us of this intervention. In leading centers of instruction faculty government is either secure or increasingly so. But in place of the old censorship has come a new despotism. This consists in defining scientific excellence in economics not as what is true but as whatever is closest in belief and method to the scholarly tendency of the people who already have tenure in the subject. This is a pervasive test, not the less oppressive for being, in the frequent case, both self-righteous and unconscious. It helps ensure, needless to say, the perpetuation of the neoclassical orthodoxy.

There are, however, problems even with this control. Neoclassical and neo-Keynesian economics, though providing unlimited opportunity for the demanding niceties of refinement, has a decisive flaw. It offers no useful handle for grasping the economic problems that now beset the modern society. And these problems are obtrusive; they will not lie down and disappear as a favor to our profession. No arrangement for the perpetuation of ideas is secure if the ideas do not make useful contact with the problems they are presumed to illuminate or resolve.

I propose in this essay to mention the failures of neoclassical economics. But I want also to urge the means by which we can reassociate ourselves with reality. Some of this will summarize arguments I have made at greater length on other occasions. Here even conservatives will be reassured. To adumbrate and praise one's own work is in the oldest and most reputable tradition of our profession.

The most damaging feature of neoclassical and neo-Keynesian economics is the arrangement by which power — the ability of persons or institutions to bend others to their purposes — is removed from the subject. The business firm is said to be wholly subordinate to the instruction of the market and thereby to the individual or household. The state is similarly subordinate to the instruction of the citizen. There are exceptions, but they are to the general and controlling rules, and it is firmly on these rules that neoclassical theory is positioned. If the business firm is subordinate to the market — if that is its master — then it does not have power to deploy in the economy, save as this is in the service of the market and the consumer. And it cannot bring power to bear on the state, for there the citizen is fully in charge.

The decisive weakness is not in the assumptions by which neoclassical and neo-Keynesian economics elides the problem of power. The capacity even (perhaps especially) of scholars for sophisticated but erroneous belief based on conventionally selected assumptions is very great, particularly where this coincides with convenience. Rather, in eliding power — in making economics a nonpolitical subject — neoclassical theory destroys the relation of economics to the real world. In that world, power is decisive in what happens. And the problems of that world are increasing both in number and in the depth of their social affliction. In consequence, neoclassical and neo-Keynesian economics relegates its players to the social sidelines. They either call no plays or urge the wrong ones. To change the metaphor, they manipulate levers to which no machinery is attached.

Specifically, the exclusion of power and the resulting political content from economics causes it to identify only two intrinsic and important faults in the modern economy. One of these is the problem of market imperfection — more specifically, of monopoly or oligopoly, control of a market by one firm or jointly by a few. This fault leads, in turn, to insufficient investment and output and to unnecessarily high prices. The other fault is a tendency to unemployment or inflation — to a deficiency or excess in the aggregate demand for goods and services in the economic system as a whole. The remedies to which the accepted economics then proceeds are either ridiculous, wrong or partly irrelevant. Neither its microeconomic nor its macroeconomic policy really works.[2] Meanwhile it leaves other urgent economic issues untouched and mostly unmentioned. Let me specify.

Beginning with monopoly and oligopoly, it is now the considered sense of the community, even of economists when unhampered by professional doctrine, that the most prominent areas of market concentration — automobiles, rubber, chemicals, plastics, alcohol, tobacco, detergents, cosmetics, computers, bogus and other health remedies, space adventure — are areas not of low but of high development, not of inadequate but, more likely, of excessive resource use. And there is a powerful instinct that in some areas of monopoly or oligopoly, most notably in the production of weapons and weapons systems, resource use is dangerously vast.

In further contradiction of the established conclusions, there is much complaint about the performance of those industries where market concentration is the least — the industries which, in number and size of firms, most closely approach the neoclassical market ideal. Housing, health services and, potentially, food supply are the leading cases. The deprivation and social distress

---

[2] Neoclassical economics, in modern times, has divided itself into two broad areas of specialization, research and instruction. There is microeconomics, which concerns itself with firms, industries and their response to the market. And there is macroeconomics, which involves itself with aggregative movements in the economy — with Gross National Product and National Income and with employment and general price movements.

that follow from the poor performance of these industries nearly all economists, when not in the classroom, take for granted.

The well-blinkered defender of established doctrine argues that the ample resource use in the monopolistic industries and the deprivation in the dispersed small-scale industries reflect the overriding fact of consumer preference and choice. And in the areas of deprivation he insists that the fault lies with firms that, though small, are local monopolies or reflect the monopoly power of unions. These explanations beg two remarkably obvious questions. Why does the modern consumer increasingly insist on self-abuse and increasingly complain of the discomforts from that self-assault? And why do the little monopolies perform so badly and the big ones so well?

In fact, neoclassical economics has no explanation of the most important microeconomic problem of our time. That is why we have a highly unequal development as between industries of great market power and industries of slight market power, with the development, in defiance of all doctrine, greatly favoring the first.

The failure in respect to unemployment and inflation has been, if anything, more embarrassing. Save in its strictly mystical manifestation in one branch of monetary theory, the accepted policy on these matters depends for its vitality and workability on the existence of the neoclassical market. That market, whether competitive, monopolistic or oligopolistic, must be the ultimate and authoritative instruction to the profit-maximizing firm. When output and accompanying employment are deficient, the accepted policy requires that aggregate demand be increased; this increases market demand, and to this firms, in turn, respond. They increase output, add to their labor force and reduce unemployment.

When output in the economy is at or near the effective capacity of plant and labor force, prices rise and inflation becomes the relevant social discomfort. The remedy is then reversed. Demand is curtailed, and the result is either an initial effect on prices or a delayed one as surplus labor seeks employment, interest rates fall and lower wage and material costs bring stable or lower prices.

Such is the accepted basis of the policy. It follows fully from the neoclassical faith in the market. The market renders its instruction to the producing firm. The latter cannot, because of competition, much raise its prices while there is idle capacity and unemployment. When these disappear, restraints on demand through monetary or fiscal policy or some combination of the two can prevent it from doing so. The practical consequences from pursuing this policy need no elucidation. It has been tried in recent years in every developed country. The result has been either politically unacceptable unemployment or persistent and socially damaging inflation or, normally, a combination of the two. That combination the neoclassical system does not and cannot contemplate. Modern medicine would not be more out of touch with its world if it could not embrace the existence of the common cold.

We should not deny ourselves either the instruction or the amusement that comes from the recent history of the United States in this matter. In 1969, Mr. Nixon came to office with a firm commitment to neoclassical orthodoxy. Any direct interference with wages or prices was explicitly condemned. In this position he was supported by some of the most distinguished and devout exponents of neoclassical economics in all the land. His later announcement that he was a Keynesian involved no precipitate or radical departure from this faith; the discovery came nearly thirty-five years after *The General Theory*.[3] But in 1971, facing reelection, Mr. Nixon found that his economists' commitment to neoclassical and neo-Keynesian orthodoxy, however admirable in the abstract, was a luxury he could no longer afford. He apostatized to wage and price control; so, with exemplary flexibility of mind, did his economists.

[3] John Maynard Keynes, *The General Theory of Employment Interest and Money* (New York: Harcourt Brace, 1936).

There was an effort to reconcile the need for controls with the neoclassical market. This involved an unrewarding combination of economics and archeology with wishful thinking. It held that an inflationary momentum developed during the late nineteen-sixties in connection with the financing — or under-financing — of the Vietnam war. And inflationary expectation became part of business and trade union calculation. The momentum and expectation survived. The controls would be necessary until the inflationary momentum was dissipated. Then the neoclassical and neo-Keynesian world would return, along with the appropriate policies in all their quiet comfort: no inflation; no serious unemployment. We may be sure that will not happen. Nor will we expect it to happen if we see the role of power and political decision in modern economic behavior.[4]

The assumptions that sustain the neoclassical and neo-Keynesian orthodoxy can no longer themselves be sustained. The growth of the modern great corporation has destroyed their validity. Instead of the widely dispersed, essentially powerless firms of neoclassical orthodoxy, we must now come to terms with the world of the modern large corporation. Laymen will be astonished that we have not already done so.

Specifically, we must accept that for around half of all economic output there is no longer a market system but a power or planning system. (Power is used to control what was previously external to the firm and thus unplanned. To stress not the instrument, power, but the process, planning, seems to be more descriptive as well as, possibly, less pejorative.) The plan-

---

[4] As I've said, this was written in the autumn of 1972 for the Christmas holiday meetings of the American Economic Association. Early in 1973, in accordance with the doctrine just adumbrated, Mr. Nixon's economists urged and obtained the abandonment of controls. They promised price stability; there followed the worst peacetime inflation so far in our history. This was eventually arrested, though not completely, by the most serious recession and the most severe unemployment since the Great Depression. There is danger in praising one's foresight, for the gods are not always kind. But the risk on these matters is less than usual.

ning system in the United States consists of, at the most, 2000 large corporations. They do not simply accept the instruction of the market. Instead they have extensive power over prices and also over consumer behavior. They rival, where they do not borrow from, the power of the state. My conclusions on these matters will be somewhat familiar, and I shall spare myself the pleasure of extensive repetition. The power that these ideas ascribe to the modern corporation in relation to both the market and the state, the purposes for which it is used and the associated power of the modern union would not seem implausible or even very novel were they not in conflict with the vested doctrine.

Thus we agree that the modern corporation, either by itself or in conjunction with others, has extensive influence over its prices and often over its major costs. And, accepting the evidence of our eyes and ears, we know that it goes beyond its prices and the market to persuade its customers. We know also that it goes back of its costs to organize supply. And it is commonplace that from its earnings or the possession of financial affiliates it seeks to ensure and control its sources of capital. And likewise that its persuasion of the consumer, joined with the similar effort of other firms — and with the more than incidental blessing of neoclassical pedagogy — helps establish the values of the community, notably the association between well-being and the continuously increased consumption of the products of this part of the economy.

As citizens if not as scholars, we further agree that the modern corporation has a compelling position in the modern state. What it needs in research and development, technically qualified people, public works, emergency financial support when troubles loom, socialism when profit ceases to be probable, becomes public policy. So does the military procurement that sustains the demand for numerous of its products. So, perhaps, does the foreign policy that justifies the military procurement. And the means by which this power is brought to bear on the state is widely accepted. It requires an organization to deal with an organization, and between public and private bureaucracies — between General Dynamics and the Pentagon, General Motors and the Department of Transportation — there is a deeply symbiotic relationship. Each of these organizations can do much for the other. There has been between them a large and continuous interchange of executive personnel.

Finally, over this exercise of power and much enhancing it is the rich gloss of reputability. The men who guide the modern corporation and the outlying financial, legal, legislative, technical, advertising and other sacerdotal services of corporate function are the most respectable, affluent and prestigious members of the national community. They are the Establishment. Their interest tends to become the public interest. It is an interest that numerous economists find it comfortable and rewarding to avow, while denying in instruction and thought the power that produces that reward.

The corporate interest is profoundly concerned with power — with winning the acceptance by others of the collective or corporate purpose. This interest includes the profits of the firm. These are a measure of success. They also ensure the freedom of the management — what I have called the technostructure — from stockholder interference. The stockholders in the large corporation are aroused, if at all, only by inadequate earnings. And profits are important because they bring the supply of capital within the control of the firm. But of greater importance is the more directly political goal of growth. Growth carries a specific economic reward; it enhances the pay, perquisites and opportunities for promotion of the members of the technostructure, and it rewards most those whose product or service is growing most. But growth also consolidates and enhances authority. It does this for the individual — for the man who now heads a larger organization or a larger part of an organization than before. And it increases the influence of the corporation as a whole.

The unmanaged sovereignty of the consumer, the ultimate sovereignty of the voter and the maximization of profits with the resulting subordination of the firm to the market are the three legs of a tripod on which the accepted neoclassical system stands. These are what exclude the role of power in the system. All three propositions, it will be seen, tax the capacity for belief. That the modern consumer is the object of a massive management effort by the producer is not readily denied. The methods of such management, as noted, are embarrassingly visible. Modern elections are fought extensively on the issue of the subordination of the state to corporate interest. As voters, economists accept the validity of that issue. Only their teaching denies it. But the commitment of the modern corporate bureaucracy to its expansion is, perhaps, the clearest of all. That the modern conglomerate pursues profit over aggrandizement is believed by none. It is a commonplace of these last years, strongly reflected in the price of securities, that agglomeration has been good for growth, bad for earnings.

There does remain in the modern economy — and this I stress — a world of small firms where the instruction of the market is still paramount, where costs are given, where the state is remote and subject through the legislature to the traditional pressures of economic interest groups and where profit maximization alone is consistent with survival. We should not think of this as the classically competitive part of the system, in contrast with the monopolistic or oligopolistic sector from which the planning system has evolved. Rather, in its admixture of competitive and monopolistic structures, it approaches the neoclassical model. The corporation did not take over part of the neoclassical system. It moved in beside what the textbooks teach. In consequence, we have the two systems. In one, the power of the firm is still, as ever, contained by the market. In the second and still evolving system, this power extends incompletely but comprehensively over markets, over the people who patronize them, over the state and thus, ultimately, over resource use. The coexistence of these two systems becomes, in turn, a major clue to economic performance.

Power being so comprehensively deployed in a very large part of the total economy, there can no longer, except for reasons of game-playing, busy work or more deliberate intellectual evasion, be any separation between economics and politics. When the modern corporation acquires power over markets, power in the community, power over the state and power over belief, it is a political instrument, different in form and degree but not in kind from the state itself. To hold otherwise — to deny the political character of the modern corporation — is not merely to avoid the reality. It is to disguise the reality. The victims of that disguise are the students we instruct in error. The beneficiaries are the institutions whose power we so disguise. Let there be no question: economics, so long as it is thus taught, becomes, however unconsciously, a part of the arrangement by which the citizen or student is kept from seeing how he is, or will be, governed.

This does not mean that economics now becomes a branch of political science. Political science is the captive of the same stereotype — the stereotype that the citizen is in effective control of the state. Political science too must come to terms with corporate enterprise. Also, while economics often cherishes thought, at least in principle, political science regularly accords reverence to the man who knows only what has been done before. Economics does not become a part of political science. But politics does become a part of economics.

There will be fear that once we abandon the present theory with its intellectually demanding refinement and its increasing instinct for measurement, we shall lose the filter by which scholars are separated from charlatans and windbags. The latter are a danger, but there is more danger in remaining with a world that is not real. And we shall be surprised, I think, at the new clarity and intellectual consistency with which we see our world once power is made a part of our system. To such a view let me now turn.

In the neoclassical view of the economy a general identity of interest between the goals of the business firm and those of the community could be assumed. The firm was subject to the instruction of the community through either the market or the ballot box. People could not be fundamentally in conflict with themselves. However, once the firm in the planning system is seen to have comprehensive power to pursue its own interest, this assumption becomes untenable. Perhaps by accident its interests are those of the public, but there is no organic reason why this must be so. In the absence of proof to the contrary, divergence of interest between individual and corporation, not identity of interest, must be assumed.

The nature of the conflict also becomes predictable. Growth being a principal goal of the planning system, it will be the greatest where power is greatest. In the market sector of the economy, growth will, at least by comparison, be deficient. This will not be, as neoclassical doctrine holds, because people have a congenital tendency to misunderstand their needs. It will be because the system is so constructed as to serve their needs badly and then to win greater or less acquiescence in the result. That the present system should lead to an excessive output of automobiles, an improbable effort to cover the economically developed sections of the planet with asphalt and a fantastically expensive and potentially suicidal investment in missiles, submarines, bombers and aircraft carriers is as one would expect. These are the industries with power to persuade and to command resources for growth. Thus does the introduction of power as a comprehensive aspect of economic thought correct present error. These, however, are exactly the industries in which the neoclassical view of monopoly and oligopoly (and of associated price enhancement and profit maximization at the expense of resource use and production) would, of all things, suggest a controlled inadequacy of output. How wrong are we allowed to be!

The counterpart of relatively too great a share of manpower, materials and investment in the planning system, where power is comprehensively deployed, is a relatively deficient use of such resources where power is absent. Such will be the flaw in the part of the economy where competition and entrepreneurial monopoly, as distinct from great corporate organization, are the rule. And if the product or service so penalized is closely related to comfort or survival, the resulting discontent will be considerable. That housing, health services and local transportation are now areas of grave inadequacy is agreed. It is in such industries that all modern governments seek to expand resource use. Here, in desperation, even devout free-enterprisers accept the need for social action, even socialism.

Economics serves badly this remedial action. Its instruction not only disguises corporate power but makes remedial action in housing, health care and transportation abnormal — the consequence of *sui generis* error that is never explained. What should be seen as a necessary and legitimate function of government appears, instead, as some kind of accident. This is not the mood that conduces to the imagination, pride and determination which should characterize such important public action.

When power is admitted to our calculus, our professional embarrassment over the coexistence of unemployment with inflation also disappears. Economics makes plausible what governments are forced, in practice, to do. Corporations have power in their markets. So, and partly in protective response, do unions. The competitive claims of unions can most conveniently be resolved by passing the cost of settlement along to the public. Measures to arrest this exercise of power by limiting the aggregate demand for goods must be severe. Only if there is much unemployment, much idle capacity, is the ability to raise prices impaired. Until then, unemployment and inflation coexist. Not surprisingly, the power of the planning system has also been used to favor those restraints on demand that have least effect on its operations. Thus monetary policy is greatly favored. This policy operates by restricting bank lending. Its primary effect, in consequence, is on the neoclassical enterpreneur — the construction firm, for example — which does business on borrowed money. It has little impact on the large established corporation which, as an elementary exercise of power, has ensured itself a supply of capital from earnings or financial affiliates. The power of the planning system in the community has also won immunity for public expenditures important to itself — highways, industrial research, rescue loans, national defense. These have the sanction of a higher public purpose. If demand must be curtailed, these are excepted. There has been similar success with corporate and personal taxes. They are what you now reduce to stimulate employment, support the incentive to invest and ensure against capital shortages. In such fashion, fiscal policy has been accommodated to the interests of the planning system. This has been done with the support of economists in whose defense it must be said that they are not usually aware of the forces by which they are moved.

In this view of the economy we see also the role of controls. The interaction of corporate and trade union power can be made to yield only to the strongest fiscal and monetary restraints. Those restraints that are available have a comparatively benign effect on those with power, but they weigh adversely on people who vote. When no election is in prospect, such a policy is possible. It will earn applause for its respectability. But it cannot be tolerated by anyone who weighs wisely its popular effect.

As with the need for social action and organization in the market sector, there are many reasons why it would be well were economists to accept the inevitability of wage and price controls. It would help keep politicians, when responding to the resonance of their own past instruction, from supposing controls to be wicked, unnatural and hence temporary and to be abandoned whenever they seem to be working.[5] This is a poor mood in which to develop sound administration. And it would cause economists themselves to consider how controls can be made workable, how the effect on income distribution can be made equitable. With controls this last becomes a serious matter. The market is no longer a device for legitimizing inequality, however egregious, in income distribution. Much inequality is then seen to be, as it is, the result of relative power.

There are differences in development, in performance, as between the planning and market sectors of the economy. With them goes a difference in income between the two great sectors of the economy. In the neoclassical system it is assumed that labor and capital will move between industries — from lower to higher — to equalize interindustry return. If there is inequality, it is the result of barriers to such movement. Now we see that, given its comprehensive market power, the planning system can protect itself, as a matter of course, from adverse movements affecting its income. The same power allows it to accept unions, for it need not absorb, even temporarily, their demands. In the market system, limited areas of monopoly or union power apart, there is no similar control. And in this sector of the economy, because of the absence of market power, there can be no similar yielding on wage costs, for there is no similar certainty that they can be passed on. It is because of the market character of the industry he sought to organize, not his original power, that Cesar Chavez was for so many for so long the new Lenin. In chemicals or heavy equipment he would not have been noticed. In the market system the self-employed have

5 When Secretary of the Treasury George Schultz announced the abandonment of the Nixon controls a few months after this was written, he said, in effect, that it was because they were working.

the option of reducing their own wages (and sometimes those of families or immediate employees) in order to survive. That possibility does not exist in the highly organized planning system. This is the source of further inequality.

Thus there is a built-in inequality in income between the two systems. And thus also the case in the market sector for minimum wage legislation, support to trade unions in agriculture, price support legislation and, most important perhaps, a floor under family income as antidotes to inequality. All of these measures have their primary impact on the market sector. And again this view of matters fits our present concerns. Minimum wage legislation, price support legislation and support to collective bargaining are questions of continuing political moment as they apply to small business and agriculture. They are not issues in highly organized industry — in the planning system. And the question of a floor under family income, a further matter of political interest, has shown some indication of dividing workers in the planning system, who would not be beneficiaries, from those in the market system, who would be. There is surely some reassurance in a view of the economy that prepares us for the political questions of our time.

The inclusion of power in our economic calculus also brings into focus the debate over the environment. It is the claim of neoclassical economics that it foresaw possible environmental consequences from economic development. It early embraced the notion of external diseconomies of production and, by inference, of consumption. The price of the product did not include the cost of washing out the soot that descended from the factory chimney on the people of the surrounding city. The owner of the automobile or cigarette did not pay for the damage to other people's air and lungs. Alas, this is a modest claim. The noninclusion of external diseconomies was long viewed as a minor defect of the price system — an afterthought, obtaining at most a paragraph in the textbooks or a comment in classroom discussion. And the notion of external diseconomies does not offer a useful remedy. No one can suppose, or does suppose, that more than a fraction of the damage — especially that to the beauty and tranquillity of our surroundings — could be compensated for in any useful way by including in the cost of the product a provision for remedying the damage from its production or use.

If growth is the central and rewarding purpose of the firm and if power is comprehensively available to impose this goal on the society, conflict between the private interest in that growth and the public interest in the environment is inherent. And also inherent, since this power depends extensively not on force but on persuasion, is the effort to make pollution seem palatable or worth the cost, including the effort to make the advertising of remedial action a substitute for action. And so is the remedy to which all industrial countries are being forced. This is not to internalize external diseconomies, add them to the price. It is to specify the legal parameters within which growth may proceed. Or, as in the case of automobile use in central cities, airplane use over urban areas, the SST or industrial, commercial and residential appropriation of countryside and roadside, to prohibit development that is inconsistent with the public interest. We would have saved ourselves much corruption of our surroundings if our economics had held such result to be the predictable consequence of the pursuit of present economic gals and not the exceptional result of a peculiar aberration of the price systems. We see again how the accepted economics supports not the public but the special interest.

Finally, when power becomes part of our system, so does Ralph Nader. If the consumer is the ultimate source of authority, his abuse is an occasional fault. He cannot be fundamentally at odds with an economic system that he commands. But if the producing firm has comprehensive power and purposes of its own, there is every likelihood of conflict. Technology is then subordinate to the strategy of consumer persuasion. Products are changed not to make them better but to take advantage of the belief that what is different is better. There is a high failure rate in engineering because its preoccupation is not with what is good but with what can be sold. So the unpersuaded or disenchanted consumer rebels. This is not a rebellion against minor matters of fraud or misinformation. It is a major reaction against a whole deployment of power by which the consumer is made the instrument of purposes that are not his own.

There are two conclusions to which this exercise — the incorporation of power into our system — compels us. The first is encouraging. It is that economists' work is not yet done. On the contrary, it is just beginning. If we accept the reality of power as part of our system, we have years of useful professional work ahead of us. And since we will be in touch with real issues, and since issues that are real inspire passion, our life will again be pleasantly contentious, perhaps even usefully dangerous. Members of the profession will be saved from the paltry suburban slumber that is the fate of the passive, irrelevant or harmless scholar.

The other conclusion concerns the state. For when we make power and therewith politics a part of our system, we can no longer escape or disguise the contradictory character of the modern state. The state is the prime target in the exercise of economic power. In greater or less measure it is captured by the planning system. Yet on all the matters I have mentioned — organization to offset inadequate performance in such areas as housing and health care, wage and price controls, action to correct systemic inequality, protection of the environment, protection of the consumer — remedial action lies with the state.

Thus perhaps the greatest question of social policy in our time: is the emancipation of the state from the control of the planning system possible?

I would be presumptuous to say yes, even more so to suggest that it will be easy. But there is a gleam of encouragement. Elections are now being fought extensively over issues where the purposes of the planning system diverge from those of the public. The question of defense expenditures is such an issue. That of tax reform is another. The deprivation in housing, mass transportation and health services is yet another — one that reflects the relative inability of these industries to organize and command resources. The question of a guaranteed income, though momentarily quiescent, is another. The environment is such an issue — with its conflict between the technostructure's goal of growth and the public's concern for its surroundings. So is wage and price control. Our politics, forced by circumstance, are coming to accept and deal with this great contradiction between the needs of the planning system and the needs of the public.

It would not be wrong, I believe, to ask that in this effort, economists identify themselves with the public interest, not that of the corporations and the planning system. But if that is too much, I would happily settle for neutrality. Economics now tells the young and susceptible (and also the old and vulnerable) that economic life has no content of power and politics because the firm is safely subordinate to the market and the state and for this reason it is safely at the command of the consumer and citizen. Such an economics is not neutral. It is the influential and invaluable ally of those whose exercise of power depends on an acquiescent public. If the state is the executive committee of the great corporation and the planning system, it is partly because neoclassical economics is its instrument for neutralizing the suspicion that this is so.

*

Index